The Casitians Universe Omnibus:

The Casitians Return
The Story of New Earth
Humans Untied

Maxwell Pearl

Published by Ursa Minor Publishing

Introduction to the Omnibus Edition

I wrote these novels starting 15 years ago. I was a different person and a different writer then. The timeframe of these novels is such that most of the years they are set in have passed or are present now. I thought about re-writing these, because there is so much I would change about the characters, and about my image of the Casitians, but I didn't really have time – I am too busy with new work and new ideas. I removed them from sale when I changed my name and gender, because I didn't want novels with my old name still being sold. But I didn't want these novels to just die on my hard drive.

So here is the compendium of the first three novels. There are two prequels, and one seqel. These three have been slightly edited: mostly copy edits and better language and such. Nothing substantive has been changed, for better and for worse.

The Casitians Return

Chapter 1:
Emergence

Palo Alto, California, Earth, April 20, 2011
Joel rocked back and forth in his squeaky chair and looked at the three flat-screen monitors mounted above a desk strewn with papers. He felt sleepy, even though it was only late morning; he had stayed up far too late writing a paper for the next SETI conference, which got smaller every year. He squinted at colorful graphs of data from the aging radio telescope at Arecibo, which was slated to go offline in a few months. As he scrolled through graph after graph, he got more and more bored, so he almost missed it. There it was, a real signal: clear, focused, and no doubt, artificial. It was suspiciously strong.

As the excitement of this new signal built inside him, the old sadness that he was the last scientist left working full-time on SETI came back to him. Since the big scandal three years ago, all the others had either left the field, or were doing work in small snippets of time they could spare between other projects. All the graduate students had left to do other sorts of projects. He was utterly committed to SETI, so he kept on, and refused to think about a future without SETI science. He was convinced that somehow, someday, he would find the thing that would finally validate all of his efforts.

He brought his attention back to the signal, realizing its possible importance. The first task was to look at where it was coming from. Checking the direction of the antenna at the time of the signal, he brought up a star chart on his screen, and cross-checked it with the directional information from the antenna. He cursed. Mars. Mars? Who set the telescope to be looking at Mars at this time, when everyone knew the orbiter was operating? Damn, he thought.

He flagged it, just in case, and kept going, looking at the rest of the runs, feeling more bored and more dispirited than before. His stomach started to grumble, and he thought fondly of his favorite pizza place. Pepperoni and anchovy pizza sounded like a good antidote to his current mood.

Marianne walked down the busy street, and she could see the sky darken between buildings as she looked toward the ocean. This evening she needed time to relax, and think, and her favorite watering hole seemed the best place to go. As she approached the bar, the neon lights that advertised Budweiser and Coors hanging in the glass window blinked a little, the latter lights sporting strange rainbow-colored mountains. What would they think of next? "Felicia's," the name of the bar, shone in neon above the window, with the 'l' and 'c' having small blank spots in them.

She found the door and swung it open, and familiar scents wafted to her nose. Preoccupied, she almost tripped walking in. As she made her way to a bar stool, and her eyes adapted to the dim light, she looked at the new bartender. Her spiky blond hair and tattoos, and a particularly painful looking piercing at the bridge of her nose, were all somewhat intriguing. But in the end, Marianne decided, not all that attractive.

"What would you like?" Her smile was cute, though.

Marianne debated. MUNI was her ticket home, so there was little need for care. Besides, her day had been one that she wouldn't mind forgetting.

"Whisky sour, please." She rarely drank mixed drinks or hard liquor, but today had started out badly, and ended up even worse. She watched the bartender prepare her drink. It always interested Marianne how bartenders worked; some were very utilitarian, others showing a kind of flair that she enjoyed. This one looked like she noticed Marianne watching, and wanted to show off.

After all the flourish, the bartender finally placed the drink in front of Marianne, smiled, and moved on to other customers. Marianne swirled the thin straw, fingered the stem of the cherry, and thought back to her day. She had awoken to her phone ringing at 5:00 a.m. with the slurred voice of her most recent ex, Suzanne. She wanted to see her, and Marianne had to firmly refuse, even though she felt a little guilty.

Once she got to the office, it had been one of those days full of glitches and bugs and unexpected problems. She was a stickler for good code, which sometimes ran afoul of the goals of the company she worked for, whose only current source of revenue was contracts from NASA/JPL. Her late afternoon meeting with Chuck, the project manager, who knew too much management, and not enough project, had been a complete disaster. She'd been called into his office at 4 PM, and she walked in to see a grim look on his small, pasty, pudgy face.

"Marianne, we need to have a talk about the amount of time you've been spending on this project. We're running too close to the line on this budget."

"Chuck, you should recall that we talked about how we would have to front-load most of the development in these new missions to Mars and Saturn, but that work would allow us to mostly sail through the work we need to do for the second mission to Mars, and the Venus lander."

"We can't afford to do that any longer. We have no choice. I heard from the resource manager that we're running out of cash, and our investors aren't going to give us any more money. You need to trim the development budget. I can see a few shortcuts here you can use."

He pulled out some sheets of paper, diagrams that she had worked up for the project several months ago. She could see some parts were circled in red. In the end, she had to cave into his demands for shortcuts for two new missions to Mars and Saturn. She had been livid and had said some things to him that would have cost her job, had she not been one of the most important assets to the project.

As she was finishing the last of her drink, looking deeply into the melting ice, she could feel someone watching her. She turned to look down the bar and saw a woman with the most striking green eyes she had ever seen. Her face was almost a perfect oval, with light brown complexion, and gorgeous eyes that were almond shaped. She had close-cropped dark brown hair, and she was wearing a tank-top, so it was easy to see that she was well-muscled. She was smiling directly at Marianne, who was instantly intrigued, and attracted. She hesitated, and then got up and went to sit next to her.

"Hi. You look pretty new around here—I don't think we've met before." Marianne felt completely weak with that beginning.

"Hello. No, we haven't met before." The woman's voice was melodious, her accent unfamiliar, and Marianne was enchanted. "I am new. I just moved to the city a little time ago. My name is Ja'el."

"That's a beautiful name. My name is Marianne." She extended her hand. Ja'el took it, almost too gently, and shook.

"What brought you here, a job?"

She nodded. "Yes, you could say that." That was all she said.

"I've lived here for five years now. I'm a programmer. I work on algorithms for space vehicles." Ja'el nodded. People usually looked at Marianne with surprise when she told them of her work, but Ja'el almost seemed as if she'd known.

Ja'el looked toward the pool tables. "Want to play?"

Marianne agreed immediately. She liked to play pool, it was a nice icebreaker, and she was quite good at it, beating almost everyone she played. She offered to rack, and to have Ja'el break. As Ja'el lined up her shots, Marianne watched her move her body. There was something unfamiliar, something strange about the way she held the pool cue and made the shot. But several balls made it into pockets anyway. It was quickly clear that Ja'el was much better at pool than Marianne. She won handily, several times.

"OK, I give up! You are a great pool player."

Ja'el looked almost embarrassed—like she'd made a mistake. "I've just had a lot of practice lately, that's all."

Marianne smiled. "That's OK, really. I don't mind." They made their way back to the stools, and Marianne offered to buy Ja'el a drink.

"Thanks. I'll have... what you're having."

"A whisky sour?"

"Sure. I'll have that."

As the bartender was preparing their drinks, Ja'el asked in her unfamiliar accent, "I'm new to the city—is there a place you can recommend that I see?"

"Well, there is the new museum in Golden Gate Park. It has a lot of great art from all over the world. Also, they have a new photography exhibit by my favorite photographer."

Marianne could tell Ja'el looked a little confused for a minute. "Will you take me there?"

Marianne was taken aback. "Um, sure, I was thinking of going on Saturday, anyway." It would give her the perfect excuse not to work that day. "Where do you live? I'll come pick you up."

Ja'el said quickly, almost too quickly, "No, I'll come by your place."

"OK, if you want." Marianne was surprised by Ja'el, but she was far to intrigued by her to protest. She took her wallet out of her pocket, grabbed one of her cards, and wrote on the back her home address and cell number, handing it to Ja'el. "Why don't you come by around 10:00? There is a great brunch place we can go to on the way."

Ja'el nodded. "See you then." She slipped off the bar stool and walked toward the door. She paused, turned to look at Marianne and smile, then completed her trip to the door, and out of the bar. Marianne's eyes followed her, and when Ja'el had left, she finished the last of her second whisky sour, resisted ordering a third, and walked out herself, making her way more slowly than usual to MUNI. On the trip home, she couldn't help obsessing a bit about Ja'el, and the mystery that she was.

Palo Alto, California, Earth, April 20, 2011

Joel was daydreaming again, while he continued to sift through the Arecibo data. He was startled out of his daydream by a loud beeping sound. He looked at the small window that had popped up on the screen to his right. It was an instant message from Dwight, his old college friend from Nevada.

Words appeared in the window: "Did you hear about the sighting last week? The publicity on it is building." Joel only barely tolerated Dwight's obsession with being a "UFOlogist" as he called it, but Dwight thought of both of them as brothers in the same obsession. "No, I haven't heard anything." Joel was already bored.

"It was Tuesday. About a hundred people in four different locations saw them. They were different than any kind of UFOs seen before. Completely convincing."

Joel was far from convinced. "Any pictures?"

"Quite a few, and some of the news outlets are beginning taking this seriously. I'm surprised you haven't heard."

Joel didn't pay much attention to the news, and less to UFOs. But something stirred in Joel's memory. "Did you say *Tuesday*? What time?"

"Between 19:40 and 19:50 GMT."

"Are you absolutely positive about that?"

"Yes, dude, totally. Everyone's timing agrees—it all happened during those ten minutes. What's up?"

He typed, keys quickly tapping, "Email me everything you've got, as soon as possible!"

"Why? What's going on?"

"Just do it. I'll be in touch, I promise."

Joel closed the instant messenger window without waiting for a reply and brought up the signal he'd flagged earlier that day. His stomach began to do flip flops, and it wasn't because he was hungry. That strong, clear signal appeared again on his screen, the one that was supposed to be from Mars. It had come precisely at 19:44 on Tuesday. This couldn't be a coincidence. He needed some sort of corroboration this wasn't from the Mars orbiter.

He did a search on the NASA/JPL website for the Mars orbiter mission, and according to the data there, the orbiter had been on the other side of Mars at the exact time of the signal. Further, the site said that the orbiter had stopped sending signals, because it had been in internal calibration mode for at least six hours during that day, easily encompassing all of the time during the signal.

He had to tell somebody about this—it just was too important to ignore.

San Francisco, California, Earth, April 21, 2011

The office was buzzing when Marianne walked in the door the next day. She felt a bit sleepy and fuzzy because of the drinks last night—two drinks on a weeknight were more than she could handle. As she was walking to her cubicle, David, Marianne's best friend, as well as her coworker, intercepted her. To Marianne, he looked an odd mix of haggard and excited—he had dark circles around his eyes, as if he hadn't slept for a while. But there was also a bit of a sparkle in his blue eyes.

"Did you hear about the UFO sightings?" Ah, that was what the buzz was all about. Marianne always thought that her co-workers' obsession with UFOs and aliens was a bit over the top.

"Obviously not. What UFO sightings?"

"Like one hundred people in Nevada and Utah saw these UFOs last week. And they even got pictures! It made the news last night." David was showing his excitement—hands waving in the air, smile on his face. She was surprised at how excited David was.

"OK, send me the links, I'll have a look." He smiled and looked like he wanted to jump up and down like a little boy. Marianne put her hand on his arm.

"And... I have a date. Well, I think it's a date."

"A date? Who is she? What does she do?"

"Her name is Ja'el. I don't know what she does, she wouldn't tell me. She creamed me at pool. She's, well... she's interesting."

"*She* creamed *you* at pool? And she didn't tell you what she does? Be careful—you have terrible taste in women." David smiled.

"No, I think she's different, I really do."

"I'll believe it when I see it. When's the date?"

"Saturday. I'll fill you in on the details, I promise."

Marianne finally made it to her cubicle, after being interrupted in her travels three more times by co-workers who wanted to tell her about the UFO sightings. She sat down to start reading her email and saw, in one of the first, that Jonathan, the programmer they had hired a few weeks ago, was having problems with vector algorithms. She got up to talk with him, and before she knew it, the day passed in a blur. Although there were moments of daydreaming of what it would be like to be with Ja'el, she never got back to David's email.

Palo Alto, California, Earth, April 21, 2011

Joel paced nervously in the waiting room of his boss Katherine's office. She always made him cool his heels and wait to see her. He stared at her office door, a dark wood paneled affair, with a silver placard announcing in bold letters, "Katherine Robinson, Ph.D. Chief of Research."

"Joel, come in." He heard her muffled voice from behind the door. He opened the door and walked into the office. It always seemed smaller to him than he remembered. This time, he almost felt the walls closing in on him.

"Thanks for agreeing to see me, Katherine."

"Joel, you know that your job here as SETI researcher is quite tenuous. Last year the board almost voted to eliminate the program. The only reason why they didn't was because I convinced them that there was still at least some value left in SETI research, and that you in particular had made very valuable contributions to the SETI program."

"Thank you, Katherine, I know..."

"Joel, I may not be able to pull a rabbit out of the hat again next year. You need to start thinking about your future."

"I know. People tell me I'm crazy to keep concentrating on SETI. But I am convinced that it's the right thing to do. And I have something that might prove it."

She looked up at him, her long, thin face forming into a severe expression.

"I doubt that is possible."

"Please hear me out. Last Tuesday, Arecibo picked up an especially strong signal."

He swiveled his laptop around and showed her the graph.

"That's quite interesting. Where was this coming from?"

He swiveled the laptop back around, clicked a few keys and brought up two new windows, and swiveled it back.

"At the time, Arecibo was looking at Mars. However..."

"Mars! Joel..."

"However, from NASA/JPL data, the Mars orbiter was on the far side of Mars at the time and was also in radio silence most of that day, doing internal calibration routines."

"Joel, mistakes happen. This signal must be from the Mars orbiter. There is no other reasonable explanation!"

He swiveled the laptop again, to open up windows with the pictures of UFOs to show her.

"At the exact same time as the signal, I mean within a strict 10-minute timeframe, there were several credible sightings of UFOs in Nevada and Utah."

She sat back in her chair, and Joel could see the red starting to suffuse her face.

"Joel, how *dare* you come to me with this crap?" Spittle started to escape the corners of her mouth, as her face became completely red, and her eyes were wide open.

"Katherine…"

"Joel, get the hell out of this office right now! If you bother me again with any more shit like this, you are going to be out on your ass faster than you can count to one. Am I completely clear?"

Joel sighed, closed the laptop, and looked at his boss.

"I'm sorry Katherine, I won't bother you again."

He could hear her banging things around in her office as he walked down the hall from her office. He knew, deep in his bones, that something strange was happening. He needed help in figuring it out—there must be *someone* who could help him.

San Francisco, California, Earth, April 23, 2011

She tossed and turned most of the night. Between stress at work and her date with the mysterious Ja'el, she could hardly sleep. She finally got out of bed and went to the shower, and let the hot, steamy water wake her up. She realized she needed some good, strong coffee, so started a pot brewing, while she finished getting dressed. As she sat at her kitchen table, looking out of the window at the fog still covering the hills, she wondered idly what her day with Ja'el would be like. How would it end?

Ja'el rang the bell exactly on time, and Marianne walked down the stairs to meet her at the front. It was still quite cool out, with the fog hanging in the air, cool droplets of water coalescing on her clothing. Ja'el was wearing only a tank top and a light pair of pants.

"Aren't you cold? Do you need something warmer?"

Ja'el shook her head, and said in her strange accent, "Thanks, no, I'm fine; it feels pretty warm out to me." Her accent was smooth and light, almost like the accents she'd heard from people from South Asia, or perhaps the Middle East. Yet it wasn't like that at all.

"Are you used to a colder climate?"

She nodded. It was the kind of nod that was not followed by any explanation, nor did it invite further questions, so Marianne pointed the way toward the MUNI station, and they started walking. At the station, Marianne noticed Ja'el hang back as Marianne was adding money to her card. On a whim, or perhaps out of habit, Marianne bought Ja'el a card, and handed it to her.

Ja'el smiled. "Thank you."

They went through the station and managed to just catch a train as it was about to leave. As they sat down, Marianne noticed Ja'el's unease.

"Have you been on MUNI before?"

"I've never been on a... this kind of vehicle before."

"Really?" Marianne was incredulous. "How do you get around town?"

"I mostly take... taxis." The word "taxis" was said slowly, with a slight rise of pitch, as if it were a question.

Marianne was silent, as the train moved on. As she looked at Ja'el, she mused, where could she be from? A cold climate with that accent and complexion? Never having been on a train? And getting around San Francisco in taxis? She began to spin out a strange tale in her head, of rich diplomats from strange countries and their sheltered daughter finally leaving the nest and finding herself in a new unfamiliar city. Marianne felt a protective impulse.

"So where were you born?" Marianne decided to start a series of questions that she hoped would get her closer to the truth of Ja'el.

"Nowhere you would know."

"Try me, really. I know a lot of places."

"It's... well, it's very complicated. I'd like to tell you, but ... well, I hardly know you."

Marianne realized that all the hints were there. She should have known that she'd hit a brick wall. She had a hard time with reticence like this, but Ja'el was compelling, so Marianne decided on a different tack, to try and walk around the wall.

"Alright, how about if I tell you some things about me?"

She started to weave her tale on the train and continued as they found their way to the small restaurant that was Marianne's favorite brunch place. There was a brief interruption as she answered Ja'el's many questions about the menu.

Ja'el did seem intrigued and genuinely interested as Marianne told her the story of her life. She was born in New York City, and lived there until her junior year in high school, when her father got a job managing a large industrial plant in rural Missouri. She hated rural Missouri—hated the closed-minded people and the small-town mentality. She left as soon as she could, moving far away, and getting her bachelor's and master's degrees in Computer Science at MIT. Marianne's younger sister, Yolanda, had stayed in Jefferson City, getting married to a local company man, and now had two daughters Marianne seldom saw. Marianne moved to San Francisco a couple of years after she finished school.

Ja'el listened intently, almost seeming to hang on every word. She looked empathetic and touched Marianne's arm at moments when she spoke of things that were difficult—like her time in Missouri. When the check came, Marianne took it, and said, "My treat," even though she still was nursing the illusion that Ja'el was a rich diplomat's daughter. They left the restaurant, and walked leisurely down to the museum, still chatting about Marianne's life.

When they got into the first exhibit hall, Marianne saw an immediate change in Ja'el. This was the new museum's exhibit of abstract expressionists, with a huge Jackson Pollack on one wall, splashes of color riotously challenging each other for attention on the canvas. On another wall was a serene and simple Rothko, layers of subtly different shades of blue in rectangles sitting vertically on top of one another. In front of each, Ja'el stood for minutes, gazing at them as if she'd never seen art before.

"It's so beautiful. Where I come from... we have art all around, outside, in public spaces. We live with art constantly."

Marianne was silent, listening to the first words Ja'el had really said about her life. As she watched Ja'el move from painting to painting, and from photograph to photograph in the Annie Leibowitz exhibit, a big alarm bell was going off in her head. This was someone for whom this art, all of the art in the museum, was completely new: the sculptures from all over the world, the impressionists, the abstract expressionists, the fabric art of South America, the photorealists, and the photographers. Marianne realized that Ja'el had never experienced any of it in her life. Yet, she had just said she had lived with art all around her. This combination, Marianne decided, was simply impossible.

They finally left the museum, after being kicked out because it was closing. The guards had been eyeing them suspiciously for quite a while. Marianne could tell that Ja'el would have stayed in there for hours more if she had been able to.

"That art is so beautiful. I can't understand why it's hidden away in that building, instead of out in the streets." Marianne didn't have an answer for Ja'el because it seemed a question born out of a stunning naïveté. Marianne suggested a stroll around the neighborhood, and they came to one of Marianne's favorite churches, St. Julian's, which was only a couple of years old. It had beautiful, rounded walls, with long stained-glass strips, mostly of blues, going from the bottom of the building to the top.

As they passed, Ja'el asked, "What is this—it's such a beautiful building?"

"It's a church."

"Can we go in?"

Marianne knew that it was often open to the public, so they went around to the front, and tried the door. It was open. As they went in, they could see the high ceiling, and the last of the sun shining through the large stained-glass mural in the back. It was not visible from the street, because it faced a courtyard.

They sat down in a pew near the mural. Ja'el looked at it intently.

Marianne said, "That mural is a depiction of the life of Julian of Norwich, a 14th century mystic in England. She was what was called an 'anchoress' - she lived in a church and spent most of her day in prayer and meditation, but she also would see lay people. She would give them advice, and pray with them, and the like. She wrote an amazing mystical work."

Ja'el looked around the inside of the church, as if examining every little candle and chalice.

"Is it unusual to name a church after a mystic?"

"Yes, quite unusual. Christianity has had a... somewhat troubled relationship with mysticism."

"Most churches don't look like this, do they?"

Marianne nodded. "This church has very unusual architecture."

"The inside?"

"Well, the contents of the inside, these pews, the altar, the cross, that stuff, that's pretty standard."

"Are these kinds of things also in the church you go to?"

"Mine is a little different. I'm not an Episcopalian. The stuff in my church is a bit more, well, muted, less elaborate." Marianne didn't want to get into a conversation about the differences between Protestant denominations. In fact, she didn't really want to get into any more conversations with Ja'el about anything at all until she knew more. She could no longer ignore the alarms going off in her head. She took a deep breath and turned toward Ja'el.

"Ja'el, I've had a really nice day with you, and I think I've told you almost everything in my life there is to tell."

Ja'el smiled, and chuckled, "Well, I'm sure there is a lot more. Like you haven't told me anything about ..."

Marianne gave Ja'el a look that made it clear she was serious. "Ja'el, please. I still haven't heard a word about you. You know a lot about me now, and we've spent some time together. I'm not going to bite, or give away some secret that you have. But I need to know more about you—I mean how else..."

Ja'el put her hand on Marianne's cheek, which was wonderfully warm, and sent shivers down her body, threatening to melt her. "I understand, and I apologize. I know I have been withholding, but what I have to say is very, well, sensitive, and I needed to get a better feeling for who you are."

"Better feeling? Sensitive? I don't..."

"Marianne, I will tell you everything, but not now. Can we meet again next week? I'll come to your place in the afternoon?"

"Um, next week? Saturday? OK." Marianne was disappointed to have to wait that long.

Ja'el got up, and Marianne followed, and they walked back to the street. Marianne started to walk toward MUNI and noticed Ja'el wasn't next to her. She stopped and turned around and saw Ja'el several feet behind her.

"Actually, my home is... that way." She was pointing in the other direction. Strangely, she pointed directly toward the park. Marianne was puzzled but decided to leave it until next week.

"Oh, OK. Well, then I'll see you next Saturday."

Marianne waved, and turned back, and started to walk, getting lost in thought about Ja'el, and what she might learn next week. She heard a whooshing sound behind her. She turned around, and Ja'el had completely vanished.

Chapter 2:
Exposure

San Francisco, California, Earth, April 25, 2011

The office was quiet as she walked in. People were hunched over their work in deep concentration. The Mars orbiter mission was doing some especially careful mapping of the poles of Mars, and her company was deeply involved in the processing of that data.

She wore a heavy jacket this morning, the fog having prevented the sun from warming things up. She hung it up on the rack nearest her cubicle, and was about to sit down at her desk, when David swooped over and stood in front of her.

"I need your help."

"Anything, you know that, David."

"I have this friend, an old friend, who is a SETI scientist."

"There are still some of those?"

"Yeah, just one. Anyway, he found a signal from Tuesday the 14th—remember that day? It was the same day as the UFO sightings."

"OK, and?"

"He says it came from the direction of Mars, and he needs official corroboration that it wasn't a signal from the Mars orbiter."

"When on Tuesday?"

"19:40 GMT."

"It couldn't be – the orbiter was in radio silence."

"You sure?"

"David, I coded those diagnostic routines, I'm damn sure."

"Well, he needs corroboration." "Alright, have him send me the signal, and I'll have a look."

"Thanks!" David looked again like he wanted to jump up and down like an excited little boy. "This could be it, Marianne! Finally proof that UFOs are real and we are being watched." He turned serious.

"So how was your date Saturday?"

Marianne thought back briefly on the day, the mystery, and the shivers Ja'el gave her when she looked at her. "It went ... it went fine. She's really interesting, and different."

"That's what you said about Suzanne after your first date."

"No, no, not interesting and different in that way, David!"

"Well, interesting and different how?"

Marianne relayed the whole story to David from the beginning. She told of Ja'el's not having ever been on a train, not telling her much of where she was from, her many questions at brunch, her strange accent and mannerisms, her behavior at the art gallery, and what she'd told Marianne about art "where she was from."

"It doesn't add up, Marianne."

"I know, I know."

"I hate to say it, but... could she be psychotic?"

"David!"

"No, I'm serious. Really, this simply doesn't add up."

"David, she's not psychotic. Her behavior and everything she has told me has its own true, consistent logic. But the problem is that I don't know the rules."

"Well, my dear, you have only one other option."

"And that is?"

"She's an alien." David laughed, and walked back to his desk. Marianne sat down at her desk and pondered. It was a really strange thought, but she let her mind run away with it. What if she were an alien, somehow? Grew up on a totally different planet, with a different climate, no trains, and art everywhere. Earth was completely foreign.

But she was undoubtedly human. Ja'el had touched Marianne's arm and face, and Marianne had seen her up close and face to face for hours. It would have to be an amazing costume or technology in order for her to have truly been an alien species.

She shook her head vigorously and went to work. In a few minutes, the email from Joel was highlighted in her inbox, and she downloaded the huge raw signal file. After doing a Fast Fourier transform on the signal, she whistled. There was absolutely no way that this signal came from the Mars orbiter, or any human-made object in space. The frequencies and combinations were far outside the range of any equipment she knew of.

She wrote up an email, with charts of the FFT, the specifications and schedule of the Mars orbiter, and, of course, lots of caveats about not having any way of knowing where the signal was coming from. David said, "official corroboration," so she copied her boss, Chuck, and clicked "send."

Even as that email was making its way back to Joel, and eventually to many, many other people in ways that would later create what her mother liked to call a "shitstorm," Marianne was weighing what David had said, and came to her own conclusion. She looked forward to Saturday when she could find out whether she was right. She figured that if she was, today's email and Ja'el's identity would come together in some very interesting ways.

Hol'venif, Casiti 90 Hevl, 780

Hetl'zef kept feeling mixed emotions as he remembered his time with Silandra while they were preparing to leave to go to the spaceport. He was saying his final farewell since Silandra was to be away from Casiti so long. They had spent a long evening together, eating a dinner of Hetl'zef's mid-summer harvest, some fittls from the tank, baked in the oven, and some fermented yutzi drink. And they had spent hours in languid lovemaking, moving again and again between touching and not-touching. The invisible threads coursed between them, creating currents and circuits of pleasure and joy. Finally, they slept, and just a few hours later, when the small orange sun rose in the purple sky, Silandra dressed, picked up her already packed bag, and followed Hetl'zef into his small vehicle.

After setting the destination for the spaceport, they had two more hours together. They talked about the culture of the humans on Reit'al, or "Earth," as those humans called their planet. They speculated about how it would be for Silandra to see Ja'el again. And they marveled at Gwet'po's huge sculptures along the travel-way, and the new art pieces which had recently been added to the landscape, providing a dynamic three-dimensional display as they drove. It was very inventive, and Hetl'zef made a mental note to look up the artist later.

When they finally arrived, Silandra hurried off to meet her ship, and Hetl'zef busied himself with joinings with folks who lived in the spaceport village. He didn't go to the spaceport often, so there were a lot of people to see. It wasn't until the solitary trip home that he thought about how much he would miss Silandra. He had no plans ever to leave Casiti, his home, and he didn't know if or when he would see her again. Yet, at the same time, his heart was filled with the joy of knowing she would be happy and in her element, facilitating the contact between Casitians and Terrans. As he passed the majestic sculptures again, he realized that it might be time for him to think about a new companion. He thought of Torf'ki, with whom he'd had a very pleasant and productive joining, discussing his new ideas about greenhouse design. He thought, to himself, "Torf'ki might actually make a very nice winter companion."

Palo Alto, California, Earth, April 29, 2011

The two security guards that Joel saw standing inside the front entrance to the building were ominous signs. Usually there weren't any security guards around. One of them was scrawny, and the other tall and burly, with muscles bulging inside his uniform jacket.

The scrawny one said, "We are here to escort you to Dr. Robinson's office."

The burly one nodded behind him, looking as if he could break Joel in two with ease. Joel decided to do exactly what they said. He followed them to Katherine's office, where the door was ajar.

As he walked in, he could see that Katherine was furious. She was standing behind her desk, her face red, her hands balled up into fists. Her eyes scrutinized him savagely. Joel couldn't remember ever having seen her so angry, not even when he'd first talked to her about the signals. Her normally controlled demeanor had completely cracked, and she started screaming at him, loud enough to make him want to cover his ears.

"How *dare* you go outside of this organization, and outside of my jurisdiction?" Her face was so red that Joel was worried that she might drop dead right in front of him.

Despite her behavior, Joel tried to keep his voice steady, even though he knew it was futile to try and save his job.

"Honestly," he lied, "I thought the result would be that you were right—that it was just a stray radio signal from the Mars orbiter. But I figured it was my job to confirm that, because the result was just so irregular. I wanted to avoid any possible embarrassment for the program. And I had no idea that Marianne would copy other people besides me on that message. I should have told her how classified this is. I'm sorry my actions caused problems for you. I'll do my best to follow proper channels in the future."

"You've made it quite clear what your priorities are," Katherine said, with quite a bit less volume than before, but her face still very red. "Promising to 'follow proper channels in the future' means nothing when you've already violated them so flagrantly. You've dragged us into what is clearly SETI scandal number two, and this will completely invalidate any SETI research forever. To top it off, this situation has gotten the attention of the National Science Foundation, and they're re-evaluating our level of funding for *all* of our programs for next year. You've put us in a very precarious situation, just so you could advance your own stupid, harebrained, unprovable theories. You're fired, Joel— effective immediately."

Joel took a deep breath. He'd known there was a good chance that his job, and quite possibly even his career, would end over this. He'd taken the precaution of cleaning his desk earlier, and he'd taken home a lot of data as well.

"Thank you for your support, Katherine," he said, with all the irony he could muster. "There is nothing to gather. I'm happy to let your 'assistants' escort me directly to the door." Katherine nodded stiffly. At the front door, the guards took Joel's badge and key card from him and closed the door with a decisive click. He walked to his car with both determination and anger competing for his attention.

San Francisco, California, Earth April 30, 2011
By Saturday, there had been a veritable explosion of news, blog, and Twitter reports on the UFO sightings and the SETI connection. Marianne's boss Chuck had apparently decided it was good publicity for the company to send a reporter the story. To her dismay, Marianne had

become a minor celebrity. There had been a mountain of emails and phone calls, and she'd turned down more requests for interviews than she could count. When she heard the buzzer of her apartment ring, for an instant she feared it was another reporter. She pushed the intercom button and said "hello" into it a couple of times. After a few moments of silence, she was relieved to hear Ja'el's familiar, melodic voice.

Marianne opened the door, and felt a warm feeling seeing Ja'el walk up the last few steps of the stairs to her apartment. Marianne opened the door wide to let Ja'el in. She went to sit down on Marianne's couch. Marianne closed the door and joined her. Ja'el looked very serious and had a very different demeanor from the previous week.

"The first thing I need you to promise me is that until I give you permission, you cannot tell anyone else what I am about to tell you. Not David, not Diana, not your mother, sister or father. No one must know right now. You are in the spotlight at the moment, which makes this all the more precarious."

Marianne was only mildly surprised. It made perfect sense that Ja'el knew facts about Marianne that she hadn't told her. She had told Ja'el all about her family, and she probably had mentioned David, but she knew for sure she hadn't mentioned her friend and ex-lover Diana.

She nodded. "I won't tell anyone."

Ja'el continued, "If you don't believe me, you will never see me again, and there will be no evidence of my existence. Do you understand?"

Once Ja'el had walked into Marianne's apartment, and had spoken with such clarity and certainty, Marianne had known, finally, that Ja'el was completely sane, as well as being completely alien.

Marianne nodded. "Yes, I completely understand. Please explain."

Ja'el took a deep breath, shifted on the couch, and started to tell the story. "It all started about five thousand years ago. I know about two of my very remote ancestors. Arak, my many-times great grandmother, came from an ancient land you call Sumer. Chan, my many-times great grandfather, came from what is now China, a small settlement that would become Beijing. Of course, under normal conditions, they would never have met each other.

But along with about ten thousand other people from all over Earth, Arak and Chan were kidnapped by an alien species we call the

Tud'scla. The Tud'scla brought my ancestors to a number of planets, where they worked, and their populations grew. Over time, there were several revolts, and the Galactic Community learned of our slavery under the Tud'scla. After about two thousand years, and Galactic Community intervention, humans were finally freed. The Galactic community gave them an uninhabited planet to colonize. My ancestors named that planet Casiti. That is where I was born."

"Wow. Why didn't they come back here?"

"By then there were many of them, and it was felt that they had become too advanced, and too... different. They would have an influence on Earth that would be unpredictable. I know this must be difficult for you to believe."

Marianne smiled. "No, it's not. I figured out you were an alien last week. What I feel is mostly relief that you are human, too."

Ja'el laughed. "I should have known you'd figure it out. It was so hard to not tell you last week."

Marianne said, "So tell me more. What is this Galactic Community?"

"There is a lot to tell you... I'll take this a step at a time. The Galactic Community is a very old civilization made up of 32 species. There are some species that have no representation and are being restricted to their home planetary systems—including the Tud'scla.

"The galactic community watches many planets for the emergence of intelligent life—200 species are being watched for potential inclusion in the Community. Most of those are relatively primitive in development, like humans on Earth. Most of those species will not end up being members—they will either exterminate themselves, or never become civilized, and be restricted."

"Humans on Earth are not what I'd call primitive—we're civilized."

Ja'el shook her head, and Marianne detected something in that motion that was both adamant and mysterious. "Earth Humans are not civilized as defined by the Galactic community. This has nothing to do with what kinds of machines you can invent, or what you can build. Of course, there is an intelligence threshold, but the most important factor is having the ability to form enduring, peaceful, and sustainable communities that benefit all members of a society. In fact, there is just one species on Earth ready for membership in the Galactic Community at the present time."

Marianne had to admit that she could see why the humans on Earth didn't meet that definition of "civilized," so she was confused by Ja'el's last statement. "What species is that?"

"Bottlenose dolphins," Ja'el answered, giving Marianne a moment to let that sink in.

Marianne was now trying to figure out why Ja'el was here in the first place. "So why are you here?"

Ja'el uncrossed her legs and took a sip of the orange juice Marianne had brought her.

"Basically, I'm here because the Sejo, the Casitian word for the Galactic Council, determined that it was time for the dolphins to become full citizens of the Galactic Community, and also for the branches of the human species to be reunited. My role is to facilitate the latter goal—bringing these two branches of humanity back together—in a way that also serves the former goal, Galactic enfranchisement for the dolphins."

Marianne asked, "So, did you have anything to do with those ships that were sighted by the UFO folks two weeks ago?"

"Yes, those were ours. It was not intentional, but the fact that they were sighted—and the role you have already played—may end up being helpful to our cause in the long run."

Marianne's was starting to feel dizzy as her brain started to put all the puzzle pieces together. There seemed to be some missing pieces, some things that Ja'el was not telling her, but most of it was making sense, now.

"So, why me?"

"Our research found you to be an ideal candidate," Ja'el answered matter-of-factly. "We realized that you were likely to believe our story, and that you would be able to explain all of this to others in a manner that could help them to believe and understand it, too."

And even as these thoughts swirled through her mind, Marianne was grappling with the realization that her life would never be the same. That chance meeting at the bar—which, of course, she now knew had been no chance at all—would change everything, not only for Marianne, but for all human beings on Earth.

Chapter 3:
Contact

Moon Station, 103 Hevl, 780/April 30, 2011

Erit'ala emerged from her meditative state feeling relaxed and alert. Walking to the window, she spoke into the air, "Please determine location of Ja'el z Kadarin."

A soft melodic voice of her AI replied, "In the presence of Relation One." Erit'ala thought: Ja'el must be telling Marianne the story. She wondered how Marianne would react, and whether Ja'el could bring her to their aid.

Erit'ala was one of a team of ten Casitians who had spent the entire year on the planet Reit'al, or Earth. She recalled the many hours of joinings and discussions regarding which human should be their first contact relation. Many teachers thought that it was a mistake to choose someone from the United States, since that country's culture was so dominant. But Erit'ala and Ja'el had argued, not for the United States, but for Marianne. They had spent several weeks observing Marianne, and felt she was the best candidate for contact, despite her culture of origin. She was highly sensitive, smart, open to new things, and was able to evaluate new concepts based on their merits. She didn't have a lot of intertwined family relationships, which would have made things more difficult. And she was connected to a variety of communities that would be important to the success of the mission. Interestingly, Erit'ala thought, Marianne was more Casitian than Terran in her personal qualities and orientation. She was eager to hear Ja'el's report.

Interstellar Vessel, 103 Hevl, 780/April 30, 2011

Silandra liked to look at the stars during the slow passage to the wormhole. Even though she intellectually understood why, it had always struck her as strange that it took days to get to the wormhole, and then just seconds to get to another system—even though that system might be tens, hundreds, or even thousands of light years away.

As she sat in the observation deck, looking at the constellations she'd learned over the years, she realized she wasn't likely to see them again for a while. By now, she knew, Ja'el would have told Marianne, their chosen "Relation One," the whole story. She wondered what steps Marianne would suggest they take. They had worked out various tentative scenarios, each with apparent advantages and disadvantages. And despite their extensive observation of Earth, there was a great deal they still didn't understand.

Silandra's primary talent was in seeing large patterns, and her role was to help shape how to proceed based on those patterns. After the last report from Earth, she was concerned. The patterns which had emerged following the sightings of the ships were not encouraging. There seemed to be an effort on the part of some to discredit those who had seen the ships and those who had become aware of their signals. The SETI scientist who had first realized the significance of the signal had gotten fired, and most news stations had seized on this as evidence that SETI was futile, fraudulent, or both. It was hard for Silandra to understand the arrogance of these responses. The Earth humans—at least those who were in charge—seemed so certain of how the universe worked. Silandra suspected that the coming changes were going to be very difficult for such people.

Silandra was also troubled by some Earth humans' ways of assimilating new information. It wasn't just that they lacked knowledge; they seemed actively to resist it, to feel threatened by it. This cultural difference would make it challenging to integrate Earth and Galactic humans. And since there were so many more Earth humans, the Caraj had become concerned that the Earth humans' ways of perceiving and responding could overwhelm those of the Galactic humans. It was going to be the Caraj's role, as the governing body of the human members of the Galactic Community, to make sure that all humans could peaceably coexist, and remain represented in the Galactic Council. The Sejo had made it completely clear that Earth human culture would not be allowed to be represented in the Galactic Community. If Earth human culture overwhelmed—or even unduly influenced—the culture of the Casitian humans, it was probable that the entire human species would be placed on a long probation period, or perhaps even face restriction. Silandra sighed. She would have to work very hard indeed to ensure that this possibility was averted.

Silandra thought about the provisional species, which Earth humans called "dolphins." Their culture was so different from that of the humans on Earth, even though they shared the same planet. It was such a shame that humans hadn't learned from Dolphins—in fact, the great majority didn't seem to care in the slightest about the Dolphin's welfare.

The midday meal chime rang, and Silandra got up and left the dome, still musing. As she walked along the corridors to the dining hall, she couldn't help admiring the murals displayed along the walls. She knew they were early works of the revered painter, Ghe're z H'hult. It was amazing to see how much her work had changed over the years.

Interstellar Vessel, 103 Hevl, 780/April 30, 2011

Jal'end'a stopped dictating, because of the sound of the midday meal chime. Her stomach grumbled, as if to remind her that she'd missed the early meal. She got up and made her way step by step to the common meal room. It had been a challenge to adapt to taking meals with others, having taken meals alone for so many years.

"Jal'end'a! Blessings on you." She turned and saw Silandra approaching her in the corridor.

"Ah, hello Silandra, I'm glad to see you. I wanted to have a conversation with you sometime soon. I have some questions about Earth religions that you might be able to answer."

Silandra laughed. "I would adore having a conversation with you, but I can't imagine that I can give you any information about Earth religions that you don't already know!"

Last summer, Jal'end'a had been asked by the Caraj to meet with spiritual teachers on Earth. She had done her homework but was still mystified by the request. Jal'end'a was looking forward to talking with some of the religious teachers on Earth, such as Buddhists, Sufis, and those who studied the set of teachings called the Kabbalah. She thought that she could share some insights with those who called themselves Benedictines, perhaps the Jesuits as well. But she felt that she would have little to share with most religious teachers on Earth.

Jal'end'a was a contemplative—content to spend her life in solitude, supported by the community. Although she had questioned the wisdom of the Caraj teachers, she obeyed them, having lived under the support of the community for so many years.

Jal'end'a looked at Silandra. "Silandra, you are a seer of patterns, and I don't understand why people who are called 'fundamentalists' are so common in some places. I need to understand this better."

Silandra stood for a moment, thinking. "Give me a few days, and I'll do some more research, and we'll have a joining about it then. I have given some thought to it, and I would love to share what I learn with you. Perhaps together we can solve the riddle."

Jal'end'a smiled. She was grateful. Perhaps with different perspectives and approaches, she might be able to understand some of Earth's troubled religious landscape.

Jal'end'a hadn't started out studying religions. Ever since she was a teenager, Jal'end'a had been on a search to understand the universe's origins. She had originally decided to study physics and had been trained by some of the best teachers on Casiti. She had remained unsatisfied by the process of translation of texts written by the ancients, and the theoretical and experimental approaches to understanding what many thought of as the earliest moments of the universe.

The deeper Casitian physicists delved into the origins of the universe, the more they found the face of the divine. Some physicists were working to use their methodologies to understand the divine, as Jal'end'a's major teacher did. She had even begun to work with a number of other teachers in crafting theories that unified various fields of knowledge: from origins of the universe, lyre'es'gkin, theories of the mind and brain, and other phenomena.

In the end, Jal'end'a felt the call to go within herself, to sit, to contemplate, to connect deeply with the divine wisdom inside of her in order to understand the divine wisdom of creation. She withdrew from science, requested permission to be supported by the community, and lived alone, in a small dwelling far from the city.

About two Casitian years later, she started to tell others what she was learning. She wrote several articles, and slowly, but surely, the demand for more and more writing came from many corners of the galaxy. She remembered the time that she got an official request to translate her work into the language of the Kwalloo, one of the oldest species in the Galactic Community. It wasn't the first time she'd gotten a request for permission to translate—but she was astonished that a species that was considered so wise wanted to read what she had to say. Slowly she got used to it, but it was sometimes still a surprise. She hoped that her wisdom would be of use here.

San Francisco, California, Earth, April 30, 2011
Marianne needed food. It seemed funny to want to eat after having a conversation that had shifted her entire perspective and world view, but on the other hand, cooking calmed her down, and helped her figure things out.

"Would you like to eat? Is there anything in particular that you like, or don't like? I remember that you're basically a vegetarian."

Ja'el nodded. "Yes, we have something on Casiti that is a lot like your fish, but otherwise, we don't eat any animals. I've tried a lot of Earth food, and like it a lot. Just go ahead and cook anything that comes to mind. I'm sure it will be fine."

Marianne decided to make lasagna. She rooted around in her cabinets and refrigerator, and found, to her delight, that she had all the ingredients. She placed the noodles and tomato sauce on the counter. She would sauté onions, garlic and peppers to add to it, and blend ricotta, mozzarella and parmesan cheeses for the filling. She discovered that she even had some asiago cheese and fresh basil to add to it. That made her happy.

Ja'el got up. "Is there anything I can do?"

Marianne wondered about this. "Do you Casitians cook?"

Ja'el laughed. "Yes, we cook all the time. We don't have what you call 'restaurants.' So cooking is a necessity, but also, for many, it is an art. I am not one of those, but I am pretty good at it. Why don't I start with the chopping?"

Marianne nodded, and showed Ja'el where the cutting board and knives were, and she pointed out what parts of the vegetables to cut, and what parts to take out. As Ja'el was chopping, she asked, "Why is it that so many Earth humans don't cook? Why do people like to go out and have strangers cook for them? For us, when we're not in the mood to cook, we call a friend, or if it's winter, we might switch off with our companion."

Marianne looked at Ja'el. "What do you mean by 'companion'? Is that a spouse, or partner? Or something else, like a lover?"

Marianne could see Ja'el consider what she was about to say. "The Casitian way is very different than what I've learned is common on Earth. We do not have categories like 'spouse' or 'partner.' All we have are people we call our companions. And companions may remain together for different lengths of time, but often, especially when people are young, a companionship will generally last just one winter, or perhaps two in a row. Most people spend at least one half of a Casitian year without a companion.

"A few people do choose to have permanent companions. This is not at all frowned upon, especially as one gets older. But it is still quite different from the Earth system. It seems as if on Earth, people are expected to choose permanent companions very young. And in most cases, those permanent companions are of the opposite sex. To us, this seems very odd."

Marianne said, "I'm sure you know that we have a lot of divorces and 'breakups' in those allegedly 'permanent' companionships of ours. But are you saying that most people on Casiti are not heterosexual?"

Marianne saw Ja'el hesitate. "Most Casitians are what you would call pansexual. Some prefer companions of one sex or the other, but most of us have had companions of both sexes at some point in our lives."

"So what about children?" Marianne asked. "I mean, where do they live if their parents are moving around from companion to companion? Isn't that unstable for them?"

"For one thing, most people have two or three children relatively early in their life. Some choose never to have children, like me. But those who do, choose someone who they feel would be best suited to serve as a parent with them. Most often, that person has never been their companion. We have learned not to confuse these two roles, that of companions and of parents. We think that makes things much more difficult for children.

"Generally, the two parents live in communal houses of seven to ten families, all of whom are having children at the same time, so children really have many parents. These communities give us what you would call our 'last names.' All of the children are raised together, and when children reach puberty, they move out of the communal house and into youth communities. Two years later they are considered adults, and can begin to have children themselves, if they wish. Most adults are finished with childbearing and rearing at around age eight or what would around age 32, here."

Marianne spent some time taking this in, as she took the chopped vegetables from Ja'el and started the sauté for the sauce. "Well, you're right that it's very different from our conventions. I have to admit I like it though. But it worries me."

Ja'el looked up. "Why?"

Marianne felt pensive. "Well, I don't know if you know how polarized our society is around issues of 'morality.' People take very strong stands on things like sexuality and parenting here. Huge political battles are fought over these kinds of issues."

Ja'el nodded. "Yes, we have observed that, and it is one of the things we found puzzling. Why would someone care so much about how another person wants to live, if they are happy? What is this 'morality' that makes people feel they can make choices not just for themselves, but also for others?"

Marianne laughed. "Well, I couldn't agree more! And fortunately, there are quite a few people who think as you and I do. Many people, especially in this country and in Europe, have an attitude of tolerance toward what they call 'lifestyle choices.' But there are also many religious people, both in the United States and in many other countries, who will react very strongly against the kinds of practices you have described. Tell me, what do you have in mind for the 'reintegration' of Casitian and Earth humans? Does it mean that Earth humans would have to adopt the Casitian ways of living?"

"Oh, no," Ja'el answered quickly. "Casitians understand that there are many different cultures, and we respect people's freedom to choose the ways they want to live—as long as those ways are not violent or harmful to others, of course. We expect that perhaps there will be some Earth humans who are drawn to our ways of life."

Marianne pinched some herbs into her sauté pan along with the vegetables, then added the tomato sauce and stirred. "Well, it's good that you won't be imposing anything on Earth humans, as you call us. We're a pretty stubborn species."

Ja'el nodded. "I know. But in fact, there are certain changes that *will* be imposed on the Earth. They don't have anything to do with sexuality or parenting, though. They have more to do with the environment, and its impact on the dolphins, as you call them. We will need your advice about how to introduce these changes in ways that do not generate so much resistance."

Marianne placed the lasagna noodles into the pot of boiling water. "How much time do we have? I mean, when is it that we absolutely have to tell people about all this?"

Ja'el thought a moment. "It depends a little bit on how contact goes with the dolphins. I'd say that we have at least six months, but probably no more than nine months. Our activities with the dolphins will become more observable by Earth humans as time goes on. In addition, there are specific dangers to the dolphins' environment now, and the sooner those can be reversed, the better."

Marianne heard something that disturbed her in Ja'el's voice, but she decided to let it go for now. The noodles were bubbling, so she turned the flame down under them.

"Okay. Here's what I'm thinking so far. I'm going to need a lot of help—a lot of advice and expertise from other people, who have information and knowledge that I don't have. I think we should gather a small group of people who can keep a secret—kind of a preliminary team. Then that group can decide how to let the world know about your existence and help implement whatever needs to happen after that. I hate to think of what our government would do with this information. The United Nations might be a better place to start, but I'm not sure. That's not really what I'm good at."

Ja'el said matter-of-factly, "We know what you are good at, and we know that you will be able to help us. We have access to a great deal of technology that is currently unfamiliar to Earth humans. So, one way or another, we will make this work. Our concern is simply to minimize the chaos and disruption, and we know that it will take several generations before full integration can be achieved."

Marianne felt like an abyss had opened up under her feet. She was slowly realizing that she was not only going to witness the end of her civilization as she'd known it – she was actually going to facilitate its demise. That was a good thing, in a way. It certainly was a civilization in need of change. But she was surprised by how sad she felt. And it was also quite daunting to imagine the political uproar and battles that would likely come about. She felt suddenly scared.

Ja'el reached out her hand and gently touched Marianne's forehead. Immediately, Marianne felt a deep sense of calm come over her. She looked at Ja'el in surprise.

Ja'el smiled. "Is there anything else I can do? I'm not familiar with what you are preparing."

Marianne shook herself. "Yes, you can help me assemble the lasagna. Basically, this is a dish made up of layers of noodles, sauce, and cheese. We put it together and then bake it in the oven." They worked together in companionable silence for a little while.

San Francisco, California, Earth, April 30, 2011

David was working on Saturday again. He did have a big project deadline, but that wasn't really why he was working. He was working because he and Gerard were fighting.

David had been in love with Gerard since he interned at his office when he was in college, fifteen years before. At the time, Gerard had been a city supervisor, and David had found his passion and ambition inspiring, even though they disagreed bitterly on the issues. But that same ambition had turned out to be a disaster for their relationship as Gerard inched his way higher and higher on the political ladder. Gerard had been the only conservative supervisor and had only gotten more conservative the higher up he got. He moved out of the city, officially, so that he could represent a more conservative district. He was in Congress now, and he was planning to run for president.

Of course, this meant that Gerard had to remain deeply in the closet. He actually lived with David much of the time, but his official address was an elegant McMansion in the outer suburbs that he shared with his wife—a woman who had agreed to marry him for her own reasons. David liked Juliana, but the farce was too much for him to bear. Gerard had made it very clear that he would never come out of the closet—his political ambition was the most important thing in his life. Yet he wanted David to stick around anyway.

David had finally come to the painful realization that he couldn't do it. He knew he would always love Gerard, but he simply couldn't remain in this kind of relationship. Their latest fight had been about Gerard's suspicion that David was seeing someone else on the side. Gerard had screamed obscenities at David, and had even struck him, something Gerard hadn't done in a long time. He hadn't even apologized for it yet.

Of course, it was a completely absurd accusation; David was completely devoted to Gerard, and Gerard knew that David would never cheat. But perhaps the real issue was Gerard's dawning awareness that David was going to leave. David hadn't said anything about it yet, but he knew he needed to soon, especially with this escalating anger from Gerard. His stomach knotted up at the thought.

He thought about calling Marianne. She was such a good listener, it usually made him feel better to talk to her. But talking to her would also force him to move forward, in a way he wasn't quite sure he was ready to do. So, for the moment, it was easier just to distract himself with work.

New York, New York, Earth, April 30, 2011

Diana groaned, and pulled the covers off of her body. It was four o'clock in the afternoon, and she was just waking up. The late-night negotiation sessions were really starting to take their toll. Of course, it was the best time to do virtual conferences with the Far East. But she wished they could compromise, occasionally, and adapt their schedule to her time zone instead.

She thought about the most recent session, which had started at midnight and ended just after 7:00 a.m. They had been discussing the international treaties regarding the use of purse seine fishing nets. Through the effort of a great many people, most of the world's fishing industries had signed voluntary agreements to stop using those nets many years before. But recently, overfishing and global climate change had resulted in a decreased tuna harvest, causing many fishermen to revert to using the nets in an effort to boost their catch. This meant that large numbers of dolphins were again being killed by the tuna fishing industry.

As chair of the World Trade Organization Fisheries Subcommittee, Diana had been trying to cajole countries with the largest numbers of dolphin deaths to return to the safe methods. They had started with Japan and Taiwan. But Diana was not optimistic. The WTO lacked clout. They had no significant financial incentives to offer, and no fines to mete out on the other end. No carrots and no sticks. Consequently, even fishing fleets in the United States were starting to return to using the purse seine nets. Meanwhile, U.S. congress people were putting pressure on the WTO about their failure to enforce the signed agreements.

Diana felt demoralized. She had dedicated her entire adult working life to trying to create systems for sustainable fishing. She loved the international work, and she felt passionate about the cause. But lately it seemed as if all of her efforts were for naught.

Sighing, Diana got up. She had a few things to do this evening, and she knew she needed a shower to help her wake up. As she stepped into the hot, steamy water, she resolved to try to let it wash her discouragement away. Despair was an indulgence she simply couldn't afford.

San Francisco, California, Earth, April 30, 2011

The smell of baking lasagna filled Marianne's apartment as Ja'el and Marianne came back from their walk through Marianne's neighborhood. "Wow!" Ja'el said. "What wonderful smells!"

Marianne laughed. "Thank you. That's very sweet." They set the table together and sat down. "Do you say a blessing?" Ja'el asked.

"Sometimes. Usually only when I'm with other people who do."

"Will you let me say a blessing?" Ja'el asked. "It might be a bit different than you expect—and the translations are not going to be exact."

Marianne agreed. "Oh, yes. Please do."

Ja'el paused, closed her eyes, and started. "We thank Creation for the nourishment here on the table, the efforts of Marianne's giftors, who grew it, and Marianne's effort in preparing it. May we remember where it, and where we, came from."

"That was lovely," Marianne said, as they started to eat. "But who are my 'giftors'? I didn't understand that part."

"On Casiti, each person either grows their own food, or, if they can't, they have food gifted to them by someone they know. All people go through time in adulthood when they cannot grow their own food -- pregnancy, sickness, old age. A few people never grow their own food because of infirmity, or other specific reasons. We understand this as normal. Everyone who grows food grows enough for the people who live with them, like their companion or children, and also some to be given as a gift to someone in need."

"That's a very direct system, and it seems very thoughtful," Marianne mused. "But isn't it also, well, inefficient? Here, one farmer can grow food for hundreds or even thousands of people. That leaves those people free to spend time doing other things."

Ja'el shrugged. "Yes, your farming methods are in some ways more efficient, but efficiency is not everything—and that which is efficient in the short run is not always sustainable. We love growing food, having that connection to the land, and being fed by it. A lot of people here have gardens, right? We hope to encourage more people, even people who live in cities, to grow their own food."

"Well, there may be a lot of resistance to that," Marianne said. "For one thing, there are so many corporations that make money from the current agricultural system. There is a very big farmers' lobby in the government." She thought for a minute. "Yes, I think the United Nations and other international organizations are the best place for us to start, rather than with the U.S. government. I actually know someone who will be able to help us here."

"Diana?" Ja'el guessed. "We have actually been observing her, because she is an important person in terms of our work with the provisional species."

Marianne was confused. "What do you mean? Diana's work involves international treaties within the fishing industry."

"Yes, and many of those treaties are designed to protect dolphins," said Ja'el. "Of course, Diana has been fighting—how do you call it? A losing battle."

Marianne nodded. "Of course, you're right." It had been a while since she had spoken with Diana. The time difference made it difficult, and Diana was so busy. But when they did talk, they got into such long conversations that it felt as if no time had passed. And Diana was always the person Marianne went to when things got difficult.

"Okay," said Marianne, getting up and going to her desk. "I think it's time to make a list of all the people we can ask to join our initial team." Even as she spoke, she realized she was thinking of the team as "ours" - hers and Ja'el's.

"I guess you already know all the people I'm close to, right?"

Ja'el nodded.

"Well, then you can tell me if I'm leaving anyone out. We want Diana, of course. I think we should also invite David, because I trust him, and he knows a lot about the political system. Also, David's friend Joel, the SETI scientist who got fired. He knows the scientific community, and his background may give him some extra credibility." She thought a moment. "I also have an old friend named Laura Hernandez. She's the executive director of a large human rights organization—I think she could offer some good feedback about how people will react, and which nonprofit or nongovernmental organizations should be involved."

"That sounds like a good start. Then maybe the preliminary group can figure who to bring in next."

Marianne nodded. "I guess the next step is to invite all of them to meet with you. But how can we prove your story to them? They trust me, but..."

Ja'el smiled. "Would a ride on a ship to the moon help? That's where we are all based."

Marianne's eyes widened. "You're kidding, right?"

Ja'el shook her head. "No, I am not 'kidding' at all."

Washington, DC, Earth, April 30, 2011

The remnants of her boss' reedy voice remained in Rita's ear as she put down the phone. But that did not stop her jubilation. It had taken some wrangling, but she'd finally persuaded her boss at National Public Radio to assign her to interview Marianne Michelson. No reporter had yet succeeded in interviewing Marianne, who'd achieved instant fame through her involvement in the latest SETI scandal. Rita had been Marianne's roommate during their freshman year at MIT, so she hoped that would give her an in.

Like most of the press, Rita was convinced that the "case of the strange signal," as it had come to be called, was merely a well-designed hoax. What she didn't know was whether Marianne herself was in on the hoax or had actually been duped. She found it difficult to believe Marianne had been duped—she was intelligent enough to see through any but the most elaborate hoax. But Marianne was an honest person—in fact, Rita grimaced, she had been entirely *too* honest. Their brief friendship had ended late one evening, after a few rounds of Kahlua and cream in their dorm room, when Marianne had confided that she was a lesbian. That had made Rita so uncomfortable that she had put in for a room transfer the next morning. Except for a few awkward run-ins around campus, they hadn't seen each other since.

She was still hopeful that their old connection would make Marianne more likely to talk to her. If she succeeded, it would be her ticket to a bigger role, perhaps as an international correspondent. She had been working for years at this business, watching the profession go down the tubes in favor of independent bloggers and rogue news sources, while conventional journalists vied for fewer and fewer positions at fewer and fewer mainstream news organizations. She was ready for a leg up.

Rita immediately got online and arranged a flight to San Francisco, leaving the following day. On the Metro, heading home to Virginia, she wondered what Henry would have to say about this. He wasn't so keen on her building her career. He himself was interested in an anchor position on Fox News, and if he got it, he'd have to move to New York. He'd made it clear that he expected her to move with him, despite her career ambitions. She felt torn about this. On the one hand, his career was more important than hers on many counts. He was the man, he made more money, and he ultimately had more prospects for advancement. If they had children, she'd have to interrupt her own career anyway. She believed this was the right thing to do, yet she felt conflicted about it at the same time. The truth was, she loved being a journalist, and she wasn't eager to give it up.

Luckily, she hadn't gotten pregnant yet. But they had stopped using birth control, so she figured it was just a matter of time. And when it happened, that might be the end of her life as a journalist—at least for a while. Rita sighed. She hoped she could make a name for herself before then.

San Francisco, California, Earth, April 30, 2011

Ja'el and Marianne had talked until well after midnight. Finally, Marianne could no longer stifle a yawn. "It's late, Ja'el—would you like to stay? This couch folds out into a bed."

Ja'el shook her head. "Thank you, Marianne. But it's actually very easy for me to get back home to the moon."

Marianne raised her eyebrows. "Easy?"

Ja'el smiled. "Yes, easy. I come back and forth on a small shuttle. K'flef, my co-worker, hangs out down here, and can come to pick me up wherever I am. It's a quick trip. It takes less than one of your hours."

Marianne said, wonderingly, "I can't believe you actually commute from the moon! I mean, I do believe you, but..."

"Yes, I can see why that sounds funny. The technology of Earth humans is still so cumbersome for space travel," Ja'el agreed. "Casitians have the advantage of being able to access technology from the entire Galactic community, so our space travel is very easy and quick. You'll come up to the moon station sometime soon. It's quite nice."

Marianne put her hand on Ja'el's arm. "Well, I don't know quite what to say. This has been the most amazing day of my life, I think. It will take some time to get used to all this, but it's been wonderful at the same time. When will I see you next?"

Ja'el gave Marianne a questioning look. "Well, it seems that your next task is to assemble this preliminary team and arrange a meeting with them. Tell me when you've scheduled the meeting, and I'll be there."

Marianne felt a little disappointed. She hoped it didn't show. "But don't we have a lot to talk about? Won't I see you before then?"

Ja'el shook her head. "I don't think that is really necessary. Do you?"

Marianne grew quiet. "No, it isn't. I guess I just ... oh, never mind. How should I contact you when I've set the meeting up?"

Ja'el reached into her shirt pocket and removed a small, slim box that was gunmetal gray. It had what looked like a tiny LCD display that was dark. Handing the box to Marianne, she pointed to a small, slightly recessed red circle under the display. "Run your finger over it," she instructed. Marianne expected the display to light up, but instead, after a pause, a three-dimensional person of about 1/10 size showed up above her palm, speaking in a very heavy accent.

"Hi, I'm K'flef. Later, when use this, Ja'el will answer."

"Hello, K'flef. I'm Marianne. Can you see and hear me?"

"Yes, yust fine," K'flef answered, and then disappeared.

"Well, if I still needed any proof, I guess you've just given it to me! That was amazing." Marianne looked at Ja'el. "I see what you mean about the Galactic technology. I can't wait to see what else you're able to do."

Ja'el got up. "Thank you for... dinner. It was delicious."

Marianne walked Ja'el to the door. She had a question on her mind but didn't know if she should ask it. She decided it wasn't the right time.

Ja'el placed her hand briefly on Marianne's arm, and again, a feeling of calm and ease entered Marianne. Then Ja'el opened the door. "Good night, Marianne."

"Good night, Ja'el," Marianne echoed softly, closing the door. She wondered whether there would ever be a right time.

Sol Station 106 Hevl, 780

Silandra was in a reclined position on her bunk in the small cabin she had been assigned to on the transport ship. She had been in this ship for several days and was getting used to living in such a small space. She was flicking through the most recent reports from the moon station looking at the AI's initial analyses of the current status of the contact with humans.

She felt a slight change in the ambient sounds in the ship, and a dulcet voice announced from somewhere above her head that they had arrived at Sol Station. She rose, quickly gathered her things into her travel bag, and entered the hallway. She walked toward the docking ring, where the transport ship joined the station. There were a few others also walking through the corridor with her. She greeted several that she knew.

She lined up with the others in the main corridor of the transport ship, taking a last appreciative look at the murals on the walls as she did so. They were so beautiful—they reminded her of home.

"Are you ready to meet some Earth humans?" A voice stirred her out of her reverie. She turned to find Re'il standing next to her. Re'il was a mining specialist who was on his way to the moon for a different project. He had been given the task of overseeing mining operations on the moon, to provide the moon station with the raw materials it needed to be self-sustaining. She hadn't seen much of him during their passage to the station.

Silandra said, "Yes, Re'il, I am. It should be quite interesting. I'm looking forward to it."

Re'il frowned. "I'm not sure you'll like what you find. I've been watching reports from their television, and..."

Silandra knew what was coming. She'd heard quite a few similar sentiments expressed on Casiti.

"Re'il, as a culture, they do have problems. But we have had many advantages from our association with the Galactic community, and it's time for us to share those with them and help them advance. We're all the same species, after all."

Re'il frowned again. "Well, I wish you the best. Better you than me, if you don't mind my saying so." As the dock doors opened, he turned away from Silandra, and joined the line of people who had begun to filter out of the corridor, through to the station.

Silandra was troubled. People like Re'il didn't seem to realize that by being intolerant, they were displaying the same qualities they disparaged in Earth humans.

As she walked through the docking ring and into the central corridor of the station, she enjoyed the paintings and sculptures she saw along the way. She remembered that there had been a controversy when a group of Casitian artists had proposed that half of the walls and spaces in the Human parts station be reserved for Earth artists' work. The station staff hadn't wanted to have to live with walls without any art. So they had reached a compromise, concentrating the empty corridors in areas that were not going to be used much until the station was in full operation.

The station had a huge capacity, but only a very few ships were docked now. If everything went as planned, though, this station was projected to become a major way station for Galactic commerce. Most space stations were bustling places, with dozens of ships, hundreds of staff and thousands of visitors from many species. Fully half of the station was designed for dolphin habitation. It had corridors and open spaces almost filled with sea water. It was strange how deserted Sol Station was, but, Silandra thought, it was quite peaceful, too.

Silandra noticed a tall, lanky man looking at her. She guessed he must be her escort to the moon. "W'ren?" The man moved toward her, nodding.

"Hello, Silandra." He held out his arm to her, and they exchanged the clasped arm embrace. "It's wonderful to meet you. I've heard so much about your work," Silandra told him. W'ren was a pilot, who was also becoming known as a talented planetary specialist. He had written what many Casitians considered a brilliant plan to make Mars more habitable for human beings. He had made it his personal project to learn as much as possible about other, similar planets that had been made habitable by Galactic civilizations, a process that Earth humans would call "terraforming."

"Likewise." W'ren grinned back at her.

"Are we ready to go to the moon? How long will it take?"

"It's about a four-day trip" W'ren answered. "We just finished refueling and restocking the stores. Once we gather up all the passengers, we'll be ready to go."

Chapter 4:
Plans

Marianne had intended to go straight to bed when Ja'el left, but she quickly realized she was far too excited to sleep. So instead, she sat on her couch, laptop on her lap, and started to write a series of emails. Quick notes, really—four of them, to David, Diana, Joel, and Laura Hernandez. The ones to David and Joel were easy; she knew they'd agree to come to a meeting about the "ramifications of the SETI signal and UFO sightings," even if they weren't sure why Marianne was setting it up. It would be harder to get Diana to come, especially given her schedule, and the fact that it would involve a cross-country flight. But Marianne knew that if she said it was urgent, Diana would come no matter what. Marianne also stressed in the email that even though she couldn't provide details right now, the meeting was highly relevant to Diana's work.

The email to Laura Hernandez was the most difficult. Marianne had known Laura since high school, where they had bonded because they were two of the only non-white students in the class. She knew Laura trusted her, but they hadn't been much in contact in the last few years. And it was hard to explain to Laura why she should come to a meeting to talk about SETI and UFOs. Marianne crafted the message carefully, implying that the meeting was far more important than she could safely say in an email. She expected that Laura would call her before committing to flying to California.

San Francisco, California, Earth, May 2, 2011

Uncharacteristically, Marianne hadn't checked her email all day on Sunday. After the late night with Ja'el on Saturday, she'd given herself a break, knowing she needed time to rest and prepare herself. She'd spent Sunday walking along her favorite trail on a cliff high above the Pacific Ocean. By Monday morning when she arrived at work, she was looking forward to reading responses from Laura, Diana and Joel.

She was surprised on most counts. Laura and Diana both agreed to fly out for the meeting and had surprisingly few questions for her. Joel, on the other hand, was suspicious. He'd written back that he believed Marianne was "overstepping her bounds" and moving into his territory, and that he felt it would not be "worth his while" to attend the meeting she had called.

Marianne was pondering how to respond to this email when David poked his head into her cubicle and said, "Yes, totally, count me in. Sounds fascinating."

"Oh, it's so great to see you, David!" Marianne actually hadn't realized until that moment just how wonderful it would feel to see her old friend. She felt like at least a year had passed since the previous Friday. "I knew I could count on you. But can you talk to Joel? His feathers are ruffled and he's refusing to join us. I'd really like him to be in on this, and once he knows what's happening, he'll be glad to be included. I wish I could tell you more, but I have to wait until we're all together."

"Well, aren't you the mysterious one," David teased. "Well, I'll tell Joel that I've got no idea what's going on, but that you must have some good reason up your sleeve. And better he should hear it from you than read about it later in the tabloids, no?"

"Thanks, David," Marianne said gratefully. "I can't tell you how glad I am that you're going to be part of this."

"No problem, glad to oblige."

Marianne looked at David. She noticed, finally, his haggard face and worried look.

"Are you OK? You look tired. What's happening?"

David hesitated before saying anything.

"I'm OK, Marianne. Gerard and I..."

She frowned, but then immediately regretted it, and said, "What's going on between you? I know how much you love him."

"He's getting paranoid and angry. He's afraid that I'm seeing someone else. The truth is, I don't think I can live with him anymore."

"Have you told him?"

"No, not yet, but I know I need to soon. I've started to look for places to live."

"You know you can always stay with me if you need to!"

David nodded. "I know. Thanks. I need to get back to work."

As he walked away from her cube, Marianne could see the effect this was having on him, and worried.

Sol Station, 110 Hevl, 780

Silandra heard the light bell of the door chime ring, and she got up from her desk and opened the door, to see Jal'end'a standing before it.

"Please, come in, Jal'end'a. I have been looking forward to this joining."

Jal'end'a smiled. "Thank you so much for helping me understand this. The religious landscape of Earth has been somewhat of a mystery to me."

"Well, Jal'end'a, my hope is that you'll be able to meet with people from Earth. I expect that the religious communities of Earth are the ones that might have the most trouble with the existence of other species."

Jal'end'a nodded. "Yes, I think that is so. What have you learned about the United States?"

Silandra frowned. "It's a very strange place. Yes, it is one of the countries where science is the most advanced—but as you know, its science of a somewhat different sort—it sees itself as an opposition to the religions of the country."

"Well, I imagine that makes sense, given the almost enforced ignorance of many of the religions. How could anyone actually suggest that the Earth is only a few thousand years old?"

Silandra looked at Jal'end'a. "Well, I understand, actually. I did find some very interesting writings about very religious people in that country. And I read some of what they'd written, and I've read a wide variety of other things. I've also had my AI do a bit of research, and I have an interesting conclusion—one that makes a lot of sense. These very religious people are responding to some of the same things that we find problematic about Earth culture—they are looking for a sense of meaning—and the culture is not providing it for them, so they are defining it for themselves."

"But the way they are responding..."

"Yes, yes, it's far from appropriate. But given historical trends, and the cultural environment in part of the United States, it makes sense."

Silandra said, "Have a look at some of these interaction charts that my AI has developed, based on our research."

Jal'end'a and Silandra spent the next few hours talking about patterns in religions on Earth, until it seemed to Silandra that Jal'end'a understood better what was happening. Jal'end'a finally said, "Ah, Silandra, I think I've taken in all that I can—but I feel much more comfortable with what I understand about Earth, and religion, and more about their science, too. I'm really looking forward to talking with some of their religious teachers. Blessings for the time you've spent helping me with this."

Silandra smiled, "I am happy to help, and so glad that you are here. I'm looking forward to hearing what happens when you meet with teachers."

Jal'end'a got up, looking a bit tired, and they shared a hug. Jal'end'a left, and Silandra decided that it might be a good time to sit in meditation, before the next meal.

San Francisco, California, Earth, May 25, 2011
Marianne woke early, as the first rays of sunshine came through her window. She was happy the day was starting out sunny, not the foggy usual. She could hear the city morning beginning outside, people chattering in the street, trucks honking. She had a lot to do, but the truth was, she couldn't stop thinking about Ja'el. She kept remembering Ja'el's touch on her forehead, or the time that Ja'el had touched her hand briefly at dinner. She had felt such calm and peace from Ja'el's touch, yet there was also a tingle or spark at the same time. She sighed. Now more than ever, it seemed so unlikely that anything would be possible between then. This time she hadn't found someone with borderline personality disorder, just someone from a different solar system! David was going to laugh when she finally told him.

It was no use lying in bed anymore, she realized. She was fully awake. She gave in, sat up in bed, and opened up her laptop to start in on the day's planning. The meeting would be held at her place. She planned to start right in by introducing Ja'el and having Ja'el tell her story. She thought about each member of the group, and how they might react. Joel had finally agreed to meet with them, but Marianne felt wary. She was worried that he would try to take over. It was true that he was the only scientist on the team, and the person who'd identified the initial signal. But he also stood to gain more than the rest of them, since there was a good chance that the information at the meeting would save his career from ruin. She hoped that David could help keep him in line long enough for Joel to make a considered response, at least.

Marianne's best guess at this point was that the initial team she had called together—David, Diana, Laura, Joel and herself—would continue to meet until they could assemble a bigger team, with perhaps as many as twenty people working on multiple committees. Then that larger team would create the plan for introducing the Galactic humans to the Earth human world. It was going to be quite an intricate process. She hoped that everyone would be able to commit substantial time and energy to the endeavor, but she wasn't sure quite how that might happen. After all, she knew there was still rent to pay, and food to buy. But perhaps Ja'el could offer some assistance. She seemed to have substantial resources at her disposal, though they weren't Earth resources. Anyway, Marianne thought that developing and implementing a detailed plan would be key for averting chaos—the kind of chaos that could ensue if the news broke too early, and they lost control of the process.

Marianne had no idea what would happen to her after the news broke. There would no longer be any need for a space program, obviously, so she assumed she'd be out of a job. Maybe the Casitians needed software developers? Marianne doubted it. She would have to find some other line of work, eventually. David would be in the same boat, as would a lot of other people. Once again, Marianne was sobered by the ramifications of what was going to take place. But she knew she couldn't let herself go too far down that road. She needed to maintain her focus on the immediate future.

San Jose, California, Earth, May 27, 2011

"Current temperature in San Jose, 82 degrees. Watch that 101 going north. Expect twenty to thirty minute delays due to construction." The clock radio blared in Joel's ears, and he lunged for the snooze button, then turned over and groaned. Waking up was always the worst part. When he woke up, he remembered he didn't have a job to go to, or a career to care about. He could sleep as long as he wanted, and it wouldn't matter. But he couldn't give in to that. He needed to figure out a way to get back into some kind of research, even if it was as a technician. He'd work his way back up in another field. He'd leave SETI behind, and never touch it again.

Then he remembered the meeting he was supposed to go to the next day. He had been livid when he got the email from Marianne. For one thing, he hadn't forgiven her for copying other people on that email about the signal, instead of just sending it to him. Her careless move had cost him his job. And then on top of that she had the temerity to call a meeting about the UFOs, when he was the one who'd identified the signal, and his friend Dwight was the one who knew the most about the UFO sightings. Who did she think she was? But David seemed to think it was important and had intimated that maybe there'd even be a way to save his career. Joel had no such hopes. At this point he believed the signal and sightings were real, but it didn't matter. It was going to be impossible to prove that to the people who mattered, who held the SETI research purse strings. So why bother? But he figured he'd go to the damned meeting, explain to them how wrong they all were, excuse himself, and then keep trying to find a job. He rolled out of bed and made his way toward the shower, hoping the hot water would help improve his mood.

After the shower, he decided to see if Dwight was around. He figured if Marianne knew something, Dwight probably knew more. He sat down, clicked on "Available" on his IM client, and saw Dwight was awake.

"Hey Dwight, I have a question for you."

There was a pause, then a beep. "What?"

"Has there been any more activity or chatter around those sightings, or the SETI signal?"

Dwight replied, "Well, I've heard some reports about other sightings, but they're pretty spotty and unreliable. Otherwise, no chatter. Why? What's up?"

Joel typed, "Just checking. Marianne Michaelson invited me to some mysterious meeting about all this, so I wondered what you knew about it."

Dwight's words appeared after a short pause. "Hmm, I don't know. Write me about it afterward, okay? I think there are a lot of people who are interested."

"No problem," Joel typed. "I'll keep you posted. The meeting is tomorrow."

San Francisco, California, Earth, May 27, 2011—7:10 a.m.

Rita got out of her rental car and stood in front of Marianne's building, deciding if it were too early to try and ring the bell. Suddenly, a tall woman with a short afro that Rita recognized as Marianne walked out of the door. Rita intercepted her.

"Hi Marianne."

"Yes. Who are you?"

"I'm Rita, from MIT. Remember me?"

Marianne's lips thinned. "Rita," she said in a polite, but strained manner, "What are you doing here?"

"I've been assigned to interview you. I just need a few minutes of your time."

Marianne looked surprised. "What? You're a journalist?"

Rita nodded. "I work for NPR, primarily for 'All Things Considered.' I'd really appreciate it if you could help me out."

"Excuse me?" Marianne's tone was no longer polite. "And just why would I want to do that?"

"We were friends," Rita said. "An interview with you would really help my career. And it's no skin off your back. I just need a few minutes."

Marianne shook her head. "First of all, I'm in a hurry. Second of all, I haven't granted a single interview, nor do I intend to—at least not for the foreseeable future. And third of all, yes, we were friends—until you dumped me after I came out to you. What kind of friendship is that?"

"You're right," Rita said, somewhat insincerely. "I was young, I was naïve. I'm sorry. So can you just give me a few minutes?"

"I already told you, I'm not giving interviews—to anyone. And if and when I do, you'll be last in line. Now, if you'll excuse me, I have to get to work." Marianne pushed past Rita and walked toward the BART station.

Something in Marianne's manner had alerted Rita. Yes, Marianne was angry at her, and clearly didn't want to talk to the press. Rita had gotten the definite impression that there was also something she was hiding. She decided that a stakeout would be a good idea. She had always wanted to do one, and she got a little thrill at the idea of a real *investigation*. She resigned herself to the fact that she probably wouldn't get an interview, but she might get something else instead—something she could use in a report.

She decided to return in the early evening. Arriving early, she parked her car directly across the street from Marianne's lobby and took out her binoculars. Yes, she could see which buttons people pushed on the door. She got out her laptop and camera and started her wait.

San Francisco, California, Earth, May 27, 2011—5:50 p.m.
Marianne inched the Zipcar slowly up until she was right next to the Jet Blue sign outside the airport terminal. She spotted Diana's short gray hair and conservative suit, and honked, then opened her door and stepped out, smiling.

"Diana! It's so good to see you." Marianne felt the familiar feel of Diana's body as it folded into hers for a hug.

"Oh, Marianne, it's great to see you too. I just wish I wasn't so exhausted." They pulled apart, and Marianne lifted Diana's bags into the trunk, then started the slow drive back to her apartment.

"So what's going on?" Marianne asked, as soon as they were back on the freeway. "Pulling all-nighters again?"

"Yep," Diana admitted. "It's been a hell of a few weeks. We're in a crisis over tuna."

"Tuna?"

"Well, purse seine fishing, to be exact. Do you remember the whole dolphin-safe tuna issue?"

Marianne nodded.

"Well, it's back. These days, because of global warming, the tuna are scarce. So to try to up their yields the fleets are going back to old techniques—which net them more tuna, but also kill dolphins in the process."

"Oh, no! They're killing dolphins?" Marianne was horrified.

Diana looked puzzled. "Yes, it's terrible. But I never knew you cared so much about that."

Marianne caught herself. "Well, a lot has changed. I can't explain it now, but you'll understand after tomorrow's meeting."

Diana shrugged. "I'll wait with bated breath, mystery woman. I know you wouldn't drag me out here for nothing, after all."

San Francisco, California, Earth, May 28, 2011

Everything was ready. Marianne had set out some snacks, juice and coffee on the table. She figured everyone would bring their laptops, but she even had some pens and paper available, just in case. Diana was awake but resting in the bedroom. The buzzer rang.

"Hello, it's Ja'el." Marianne felt a thrill when she heard Ja'el's melodic voice. "Great, come on up," she said, pushing the button. She was glad Ja'el had arrived first.

"Marianne, it's so good to see you," Ja'el said warmly as she reached the doorway, holding her arms open for a hug. Marianne moved into her embrace but felt herself stiffen at the same time. She'd waited so long to hug Ja'el again, and now she'd ruined it by being self-conscious. She saw Ja'el's puzzled look, and said quickly, "Diana's here, but she's in the bedroom. Apart from her, you're the first to arrive."

"Good, I'd hoped so. I wanted to tell you a few things before everyone else gets here." Marianne nodded, and they sat down on the couch.

Ja'el began, "Our team is in place now, and ready to work. Silandra, a specialist in pattern recognition, arrived at the moon station last week, as did Jal'end'a, a contemplative, and specialist in religious and spiritual issues. They will be part of the group that will have joinings with your group, to help move the process along."

"Joinings?" Marianne asked.

"Hmmm, it might be an odd translation. It means a gathering of people for a specific purpose, to listen to each other, and come to consensus."

"Oh, you mean a meeting. Although for us, a meeting doesn't necessarily mean consensus. It could mean the boss decides what to do anyway." Marianne grinned, but Ja'el looked very serious.

"Well, by consensus I mean that everyone agrees on the outcome, or at least agrees to go along with it."

"It's very rare that people work by consensus on Earth," Marianne explained. "In the old activist days people used to do that sort of thing, but it took forever. No one does it now."

"It is imperative that your group work by consensus," Ja'el said firmly. "We take that very seriously. Your team must operate in the same way a Casitian team would operate."

The bedroom door opened, and Diana emerged, looking a bit more rested. "Good morning, sleeping beauty," Marianne greeted her. "Diana, I'd like you to meet our guest of honor this evening. Her name is Ja'el. Ja'el, this is Diana Westinghouse." Diana reached out her hand, and Ja'el shook it, looking a little uncomfortable.

"It's nice to meet you, Diana."

"It's nice to meet you, too, Ja'el..?" Diana hesitated. "And what is your last name?"

Ja'el said, "I don't really have a last name, but my full name is Ja'el z Kadarin. Kadarin is the name my family group chose for themselves."

Diana looked puzzled. "That's all part of what we'll be talking about," Marianne reassured her, just as the bell rang again. "I'll bet that's David."

Everyone arrived quickly after that. Soon David, Joel, Laura, Diana, Ja'el and Marianne had settled into Marianne's living room, munching on food and sipping drinks. Finally, Marianne decided it was time to start things going.

"Hello everyone and thank you for coming. Without further ado, I'd like to have you hear from Ja'el. She's the real reason I've invited you here."

Joel's face clouded with suspicion. "What do you mean? I thought this was about SETI and the UFO sightings?"

"It is, Joel. Please be patient. It will all make much more sense in a little while."

Ja'el got up from her seat.

"The story I am going to tell you will be hard for you to believe. I can also say that it will go much better for everyone if you can keep this a secret until you are ready to release it to the rest of the world in a planned manner. It all began about 5,000 years ago..." Ja'el repeated the story she'd told Marianne, with a little more detail. At the end she explained the source of the SETI signal, and the UFO sightings. She also explained how Marianne had been chosen to serve as first contact.

Laura was the first to speak. "Wow. This all helps me make sense of some of the strange incident reports I'd been getting."

Joel was shaking his head. "What is this, a practical joke?" He looked impatiently around the room. "Do the rest of you really believe this crock? There's no such thing as interstellar flight. Most of what this woman is saying is completely impossible. You science fiction nuts can sit around and entertain each other, but I don't have time for this." He stood up and reached for his laptop.

David stood up, too, using the calming tone Marianne knew so well. "Hold on a minute, Joel. I know this all sounds a little farfetched, but it does fit a lot of pieces together."

Joel sat back down, looking fiercely at Ja'el. "Okay, then. If you want me on your team, I need proof. Unequivocal proof."

Ja'el nodded. "I expected that some of you would want that. I have a plan. Would you be willing to take a short trip?"

"A trip?"

"Yes, a trip to the moon station," Ja'el said matter-of-factly. "Would that provide the proof you need?"

Marianne could see Joel gulp. She wondered if he hated flying.

"How long will it take?"

Ja'el smiled. "We'll be back before midnight."

David's eyebrows went up. Laura said "Um, I think I'll wait here, if you don't mind. I mean, I believe you, and I'm sure it would be very interesting, but I don't want to get sick. I get seasick, air sick, car sick..."

"I guarantee you won't get sick," Ja'el reassured her. "Will you come with us, please?"

Laura looked doubtful, but said "Okay, I'll come." Marianne looked questioningly toward Diana, who nodded.

"Let's go, then," Ja'el said briskly. She walked toward the door, opened it, and walked out. Everyone else followed her as she left the apartment building and crossed the street, heading into the park. "This way, just follow me." As Ja'el walked forward, a rounded entryway suddenly appeared. "Just come this way," Ja'el repeated, entering it. Marianne went last, and as soon as she walked through the doorway, it closed behind her.

San Francisco, California, Earth, May 28, 2011

Watching from her car, Rita had seen Marianne and Diana arrive in the evening the night before. She had stayed for several hours more, finally going back to her hotel to sleep. Rising early the next morning, she stationed herself in the same spot once again. She figured she had hit pay dirt when she watched four people, two men and two women, arrive one by one. Using her binoculars, she confirmed that each of them rang bell number 5—Marianne's bell—and were then admitted. She snapped photos of each of them, hoping she'd be able to find out who they were. One of the women was particularly interesting-looking, and one of the men looked familiar to her—she thought she recalled having seen him at a fundraiser for the conservative rising star politician, Gerard Hopkinson.

Over two hours went by without further activity, and she was beginning to consider a break for lunch. After all, maybe all those people would remain in Marianne's apartment all day, and even the finest stake-out reporters had to eat. She almost missed the moment that would forever ensure her fame. Suddenly, one by one, the entire group emerged from Marianne's apartment building, with the strange-looking multiracial woman—Rita was most curious to find out who she was—in the lead. Rita snapped more photos of them as they crossed the street. They were oddly silent, almost as if they were on some sort of mission, she thought. She watched as they entered the park, curious about what would come next.

Suddenly, out of nowhere, a dark oblong narrow door appeared. Rita blinked. She'd seen that same spot between the trees before, and there had been nothing there. What she was seeing made no sense to her. The strange-looking woman went first, opening the door of the oblong and walking directly in. Each of the others followed, with Marianne last. On auto-pilot now, Rita snapped photo after photo. Then, as strangely and silently as it had appeared, the dark oblong and all of its passengers were gone, leaving only a brief, strong wind which ruffled the leaves and let her know she hadn't imagined the whole thing.

Rita's adrenaline surged. It was the finest moment of her career. She crossed herself, and then, to her own surprise, she actually kissed her camera. She had no idea what she had just seen, yet she knew she had captured it for the eyes of the world. She couldn't wait to get back to Washington and show her treasures to the NPR science advisor.

Moon station, 137 Hevl, 780/May 28, 2011

They found themselves in a small corridor, lit dimly by some light from above. There were murals on both sides of the corridor. They were filled with pictures of snow and ice, mountains, and multiracial people. Marianne wondered if these were images of Casiti. Ja'el kept walking forward until another door opened, and, as each one followed her, they found themselves in a larger area, with comfortable-looking seats and rows of windows. They were still in the park—they could see it through the glass.

"How did you do this? How did you hide this ship?" David asked.

"It's a mirroring device," Ja'el answered. "I don't really understand exactly how it works, since I'm not an engineer. From what I understand, the coating of the ship is actually a display - mirroring the environment around it. But we try not to stay in any one place for too long, because the ship is solid, so people could bump into the ship. Please, everyone, sit down." Ja'el took the seat next to a woman who had similar coloring to her own but was shorter and stockier.

"This is Rew'l, our pilot today. Rew'l, this is Marianne, David, Joel, Laura and Diana."

"Welcome," said Rew'l. "We have no—what is it you said, Ja'el? We have no carbonated beverages or peanuts to offer you. But please make yourselves comfortable."

The scene outside the ship began to change, and Marianne realized they were in the air. But it was almost like a movie—she couldn't feel the motion.

"Laura, if you start getting nauseous, let me know," Ja'el offered. "But the flight is very stabilized, so I doubt you will be bothered by it."

The spaceship built up speed and flew relatively close to the ground for a while, until it was over the open ocean. Then something changed, and suddenly it seemed to shoot up into the sky. The sky quickly went from being blue to being completely dark and lit with stars.

"So that's how you avoid radar," David mused. "You just fly underneath it until you get out beyond the land-based radar, then go straight up. Our systems wouldn't catch that at all."

Rew'l nodded. The ship began to rotate, and Marianne could see a part of the Earth out of the rear windows of the craft. She realized that she was not weightless—they must have artificial gravity.

Diana said, "Wow!"

Ja'el looked meaningfully at Joel. "If you aren't convinced yet, there is far more to come."

The moon swung into view as they orbited around the Earth. Rew'l adjusted direction and began to fly directly toward it. The Earth got slowly smaller and smaller behind them, and the moon became larger and larger. In about half an hour, they were moving toward the dark side of the moon. Marianne felt the ship change its angle, and knew they were getting close to landing. Their only view now was of the distant Earth, and many bright stars. It reminded Marianne of "Earthrise," that classic image from one of the old Apollo missions, which she kept on the wall in her cubicle. It reminded her of why she did the work she did. As a child she had fantasized about becoming an astronaut, but she had long ago given up that dream, so she had never expected to be in space. Now she tried to contain her amazement. She was about to walk on the moon!

There was a tiny bump, and Marianne heard some sounds which appeared to come from outside. Rew'l explained, "That's the docking equipment engaging. We are docked, and ready to disembark onto moon station."

Laura and Diana were giddy. David was silent, swiveling around to take everything in and occasionally giving a long, low whistle.

"Well, Joel?" asked Marianne teasingly. "What do you think?"

"I really don't know what to think," Joel acknowledged. "I'm sorry, Marianne. I really thought it was a hoax. Now I'm starting to wonder if I'm dreaming instead. This is way beyond any technology I've ever heard of. If I'm awake, then I guess" -- he indicated Ja'el with a nod -- "the lady's story must be real. In that case, I owe all of you an apology." He pinched his arm a few times as he spoke.

Ja'el shrugged. "I have no—what is that phrase, Marianne? My feelings are not hard."

Marianne laughed. "She means she has no hard feelings. And neither do I. I knew this would be hard to believe, and I'm grateful to all of you for trusting me enough to come this far."

Ja'el motioned the group back toward the door they had come in through. "Well, how about I give you a tour of my current home?" They followed her back through the narrow mural-lined corridor, then out into a larger corridor, where a tall, very thin woman with curly white hair was waiting. Like Ja'el and Rew'l, she had light brown skin and multiracial features.

"My name is Erit'ala," she greeted them. "I am Ja'el's teacher, and the person responsible for the reunification program. Welcome to our moon station."

"Ja'el's teacher?" Marianne asked with surprise. "Is she just a student?"

Erit'ala laughed. "No, no, sorry. It is a translation that is not exact. In our culture, there are some we call 'teachers.' I believe you might use the word 'supervisors,' because they 'supervise' or 'oversee' the work of others. But we do not like those English words, because the relationship between such people is more like the relationship between teachers and students in your culture. It is our role as teachers to facilitate the process for which we are responsible, while at the same time fostering the continued learning and development of the people we 'teach.' Does that help you understand?"

Marianne nodded. "Yes, that actually makes a lot of sense to me, although that's rarely how it works for us."

"There are many strengths which your culture has yet to develop," Erit'ala commented gently.

Marianne nodded. "That's for sure. Sometimes it seems overwhelming, and I wonder whether people on Earth will really change."

Erit'ala nodded. "Yes, they will. It will be gradual. But people like you will be of great help in the process." She began walking down the corridor. "Let's start the tour, shall we?"

"This station was designed primarily to be the home base for Galactic humans who were making contact with the provisional species—those you call the 'dolphins'—as well as those, like myself and Ja'el, who are responsible for the reunification of the human species. It is largely made up of individual living quarters like this one." She turned and slid what looked like a standard pocket door aside. "Please, come in. This is currently unoccupied but will allow you to see what the living quarters are like.

The group filed into the room, which was surprisingly spacious. The walls were painted a beautiful, muted lavender, and there was a good-sized bed, a spacious area with pillows and a small low table, and another area with a medium-sized desk. There were also two comfortable chairs, and another small table nearby. The feeling was simple, yet so comfortable and well-designed that it gave the impression of luxury.

"Is this the living quarters for two, or someone special?" asked David.

"No, this is standard," Ja'el replied. "My quarters are exactly this size. Two people who wish to live together are given a suite."

"This is beautiful," Marianne said. "I think we've all gotten our ideas about these kinds of spaces from science fiction, where everything was so cramped. And even now, in real life, the EU Space Station is very small."

Erit'ala nodded. "Earth humans have lacked the technology to create these kinds of living areas in space. But for us, we have found it is essential to provide the best living situations we can create, given available resources and technology. It helps maintain the well-being of those who travel far from the open skies and lands of Casiti."

Erit'ala guided the group through the rest of the moon station. They saw the common dining room, which contained much more artwork on the walls and some three-dimensional sculptures and hanging pieces as well. Marianne noticed that a strangely beautiful music was following them, seeming almost to anticipate their movements as they walked from room to room. They toured the observatory, which had a glass dome through which they could see a large portion of the moon's surface.

"How long has this station been here?" David asked wonderingly. "And how have you kept it hidden?"

"Obviously, the placement of the station was carefully planned to be on the side of the moon facing away from Earth," Erit'ala acknowledged. "It was constructed about ten years ago. We didn't know whether or not you would have more missions to the moon, and we also wanted to evade detection by any new moon mapping projects. We are well camouflaged, but currently available Earth technology could have detected us, with some concerted effort. But we needed a base close to you, and this was the most effective. An orbiting base would have been detected quite quickly."

She turned around, taking each group member into her gaze one by one. "So, are you ready to go back to Earth, and determine the best way to tell the rest of the world what you now know?" Heads nodded.

"Will we be able to come back here?" Marianne asked.

Erit'ala smiled. "Of course. You may return as often as Ja'el feels it is advisable. And someday, perhaps, if you wish, you may even be able to work here."

"Wow—a job on the moon!" Joel sounded almost boyish in his enthusiasm for a moment. He really wasn't a bad guy, Marianne realized. His arrogance was mostly bluster.

"It's something to think about," Laura mused. "Of course, I don't imagine there's any human rights work to be done here," she grimaced ruefully. "But there's probably a lot to learn."

"This is all so astonishing," Diana said thoughtfully. "You're really turning us into emissaries between such radically different systems and cultures. I suspect that's a dream come true for each of us. Thank you so much, Erit'ala, Ja'el—and thank you, Marianne, for including me in this process."

"As with all Casitian efforts, we anticipate mutual benefit," Erit'ala responded simply. "We serve one another as we serve all of Creation and are served by it."

Chapter 5:
Evangelism

Moon Station, 138 Hevl, 780/May 29, 2011

Erit'ala and Ja'el sat quietly together, drinking the hot morning drink known as fuge. Neither sweet nor bitter, it had a creamy, slightly fruity taste quite different from anything Ja'el had encountered on Earth.

"What do you think?" Ja'el asked finally, although their conversation had been silent up to this point.

"There are some risks," Erit'ala responded gently.

"I know," Ja'el nodded. "I worry about how others will see it. But we have to find a way for the Earth humans to fully understand us. That cannot really happen through words alone."

"That is true," Erit'ala agreed. "And this feeling seems to have arisen naturally between you."

"Yes," Ja'el said simply. "Although she does not know our culture, she feels so much like one of us."

"You have my blessing," Erit'ala said, communicating her warmth and affection for Ja'el with a touch on her arm.

San Francisco, California, Earth, May 29, 2011

Marianne woke up exhausted. The group had talked for hours after getting back from the moon station, until they were so tired, they could barely think. Then Joel had gone home with David to crash on his couch, Laura had taken a cab to her friend's house, and Diana had retired to Marianne's study.

Ja'el had stayed behind on the moon station. She had taken Marianne aside for a few moments and explained that she felt the group needed to spend some time bonding as a team, and that that would be easier without her presence.

Back at her apartment, Marianne had ordered a couple of pizzas, and then had taken on the task of explaining the Casitian emphasis on consensus. That had led to a heated discussion, primarily between Joel and Laura. In moments those two appeared to be shaping up to become bitter enemies. It was clear that Joel's attitudes rubbed Laura the wrong way, and she responded by coming up with exceedingly well-worded arguments in response. Finally, in the end, they had agreed to proceed according to the Casitian model, although Joel expressed his doubts about whether the Casitians were truly culturally more advanced than Terrans.

"I've got to give them the technology piece," he'd said finally. "But *consensus*? And all that amateurish art everywhere? They're like a throwback to some cheesy hippie commune from fifty years ago! And how come they've got women in charge of everything? Did you notice that we have yet to meet a single Casitian male 'teacher'? Are they all staying home with aprons on, or what?" At that point the others just sighed and rolled their eyes.

Upon parting, the group had agreed to meet again this afternoon. They all felt it was imperative to begin work on the two key tasks they had identified: drafting an initial plan to create a larger team and creating an FAQ document to identify and address the kinds of questions Earth humans were most likely to pose.

Marianne was eager to have the larger team in place. It seemed quite clear that the work involved was going to exceed the capacity of the five of them. But she also knew that, for better or for worse, their five-person team was going to be under a lot of pressure over the next six months. They would be the point people, answering first to the larger team they assembled, and then to the entire rest of the world. It was this second thought that scared her.

Even through her exhaustion and fear, though, Marianne found herself thinking of Ja'el's face. She sighed and decided to indulge herself by letting herself remember, yet again, the feeling of Ja'el's fingers on her arm. As she did so, she felt her heart rate rise a little, and a tingle came into her body. She had known she was attracted to Ja'el ever since they had first met, although of course at that time she had had no idea of what was to come. Then, it had seemed like—well, like a relatively ordinary flirtation, one which might possibly have developed into the kind of relationship to which Marianne was accustomed. Now, of course, she knew that was impossible. But she didn't know what, if anything, might be possible between them. She thought again of Ja'el's green eyes, the depth of her gaze, and shook her head. She was used to being able to tell whether someone was attracted to her, but Ja'el was difficult for her to read. She felt Ja'el's affection for her, and her esteem. But she had to admit to herself that she hoped there could be more.

Washington, DC, Earth, May 29, 2011

Rita took a cab directly from the airport to the NPR building where her office was located. She'd loaded the photographs onto her laptop on the plane and had done some initial enlarging and image enhancement. Afterward, she'd been so excited she could hardly sit still. Although she wished she'd thought to take a video rather than still shots, what she had documented was still astonishing. That black oblong just sat there, with nothing else visible around it. People entered it and disappeared, and then it, too, disappeared. It was the stuff of science fiction, but there it was. She hoped that Rob, the science editor, could explain the technology to her. She couldn't quite believe her eyes, yet at the same time, she knew what she had seen.

When she got into her cubicle, she called Rob right away. "Rob, do you have a minute? There's something I'd like to show you." She waited impatiently for Rob's distinctive heavy footsteps.

"Hi Rita, what's up?"

"You won't believe this." She told Rob why she'd wanted to interview Marianne, and explained about the stakeout, and the photos. She swung her laptop toward him. "Look at these!" He sat in silence for a few minutes, moving his finger on the trackpad, clicking the button, checking out each one. Finally he looked up at her and laughed. "This is some amazing Photoshop work. How did you do this? You almost had me fooled for a minute there."

"I swear on a stack of Bibles," Rita said pleadingly. "Honestly, Rob, have I ever tried to fool you about anything? This isn't Photoshop. I saw it all with my own eyes."

Rob shook his head. "I don't know what you're up to, Rita, but this is just too weird for me. It's National Enquirer-worthy, for sure, but it's not NPR material. At this point no one reputable believes in that SETI signal, either, or in those supposed UFO sightings." He stood up, giving Rita a concerned look. "Hey, are you sure you're okay?"

Rita felt crestfallen and furious at the same time. "Yes, I'm fine! You're making a big mistake, Rob. This is big, really big, and we could be the ones to break the story. If you don't approve it, you'll be sorry later."

"Rita, I know your career is important to you..." Rob started gently.

"This has nothing to do with that! I mean, of course it does have to do with my career, but only because it's the truth!"

Rob shook his head. "I've got to get back to work. I'm sorry." He was still shaking his head as he left Rita's cubicle.

San Francisco, California, Earth, May 29, 2011

Diana bustled in, carrying a large bag. "Good morning! I thought I'd take a trip to the bagel place, for old time's sake. I got a few cinnamon buns, too."

"Mmmmm. I'm grabbing one of those before everyone else gets here!" Marianne smiled. "Thanks so much, Diana."

"No problem. You've done so much for all of us already. It's the least I could do."

Marianne grew serious. "I'm so glad you're part of this, Diana. This is going to be quite a challenge. I'm pretty worried about how we're going to be able to pull it off without unleashing World War III. This is going to hit an awful lot of buttons for people."

Diana said, "I think we can do it. I know some folks at the UN who should be able to help us out. I have a friend who does communications for the UN we should definitely include. She's a good egg, and she's got connections. But at the same time..." her voice trailed off.

"What?"

"Well, there's something bothering me about this. I feel like there's something Ja'el hasn't told us."

Marianne looked up. "What do you mean?"

"The timing seems fishy to me. Why did they pick this time in history to reunify the Casitians and the Earth humans? They've been observing us for hundreds of years, supposedly. They could have chosen any point during that time. They've certainly had the technology. And there have been some horrible things they could have stopped if they'd come sooner. Both World Wars, the Holocaust, a huge number of civil wars, AIDS... So why now?"

Marianne thought a moment. "Ja'el said the Sejo said 'it was time'—for both the dolphins and for us. What are you thinking?"

Diana paused. "I think it's mainly time for the dolphins. Humans have been destroying ourselves and the Earth for a long time, but it's only recently that we've really made serious inroads toward extinguishing dolphins. I'm wondering if maybe the Galactic government—is that what the 'Sejo' is?" Marianne nodded.

"I'm wondering if the Sejo doesn't care a whole lot about us. The human species is already part of the Galactic community anyway, and they see us as just a more primitive version of the Casitians, so what we do to ourselves probably doesn't matter much to them. It's what we're doing to the dolphins that matters. And when push comes to shove, it's the dolphins that will be the priority, not us."

Marianne nodded. "Yes, you're probably right. It's a little adjustment for us to think that way, because we're so used to seeing ourselves as the center of the universe. But ultimately, I don't think the interests of Earth humans and dolphins have to be opposed. If we can help people align themselves with what's best for the dolphins, it will work out well for everyone."

Diana nodded. "Well, that's what I've been trying to do for a long time."

The bell rang, and Laura, David and Joel arrived in rapid succession. Marianne noted an odd, almost flirtatious exchange between Laura and Joel as they bantered over a cinnamon roll. It surprised her, considering how completely at odds they'd been the night before. But then, she knew that Laura had recently divorced, and was now single for the first time in many years. And she remembered David mentioning that Joel hadn't been involved with anyone since his girlfriend had walked out on him during the SETI scandal five years before.

They had agreed to use the Casitian term, "joining," rather than "meeting," for their gatherings. Marianne suggested they begin by checking in.

There were a few moments of quiet, and then Diana began. "I'm excited. The Galactic humans are going to help create solutions to problems I've been working on my whole life. I'm going to get to work with people I like and respect in the UN. So overall, this feels to me like an amazingly exciting time. I'm tired, but happy."

Laura spoke next. "I'm happy and excited, too. I'm a little nervous about how some of the organizations I work with will react, but I'm glad I'll be in a position to help them. And, of course, I'm also tired. When you emailed me about this meeti... this joining, Marianne, I had a strong gut feeling that I should be here. But of course, I had no idea how it was going to change my life!"

Marianne waited a few moments before speaking. "On a personal level, I'm somewhat overwhelmed. I've realized that my career is over. There's no reason for us to proceed with the space program, and since the Galactic technology is already so far beyond what we've developed, most of my skills will be useless. I've decided to quit my job, and I'm glad at the thought of freeing up more time and energy for everything which is going to be involved in this endeavor. But I'm also worried, on a practical level, about how I'll survive. And like Diana and Laura, I'm excited about being involved in all of this—but I have to say that I also have some fear about how the rest of the world is going to react."

David spoke next. "I hear you, Marianne. I've realized that my career is over, too. And at the same time, I feel hopeful and excited. That Galactic idealism is pretty contagious."

They all waited, each involved in their own thoughts, until Joel finally spoke. "I don't really know what to say. This 'check-in' thing is a little, well, touchy-feely for me. But I'm glad to be vindicated, and to have proof that the thinking behind SETI was valid all along. And, frankly, I'm looking forward to watching this show unfold."

Diana began to speak, and then hesitated. "This is slightly off-topic, but I think it might be useful for people to hear. I'm in a position to authorize the addition of as many as four new staff people on my team, without much explanation. In other words, I can hire those of you who need it, so you can work full time on this. I think it makes sense, since our work will have direct impact on my program's central concern, the international treaties on fishing."

"Huh?" said Joel. "Did I miss something? How are we going to be working on fishing?"

"Well," Diana explained patiently, "One of our key tasks will be to communicate to people that our relationship with dolphins has to change—that we can no longer kill them, and that in fact we'll need to take immediate actions to improve and protect their environment. That is directly in line with the work my group has been doing for years."

"Why is that part of our task?" Joel countered. "I thought our job was to tell people about the Casitians."

Marianne stepped in. "You're both right. Ja'el explained to me that two things are going to take place: the dolphins are being recognized as full Galactic citizens, which means human beings will have to treat them very differently. And the Galactic humans and Earth humans need to become unified. Of course, both the technology and the attitudes of the Galactic humans will help Earth humans change our relationship to the dolphins. Both processes are very much related."

Joel looked skeptical. "I've always been interested in outer space, and in the idea of life on other planets. That's my connection to this whole thing. Frankly, I'm not much of an environmentalist. To be perfectly blunt, I don't really give a shit about dolphins."

Marianne felt her temper flare for a minute. Then she took a deep breath, let it out, and laughed. "Well then, you'll be a perfect 'focus group' for our efforts in that realm, Joel, since a lot of other Earth humans feel the same way you do.

"Thanks, everyone, for checking in, and thank you, Diana, for that information and that offer. I suspect that at least three of us will need to take you up on it. Now, we have a lot to figure out..."

Washington, DC, Earth, May 29, 2011

Rita dragged her suitcase up the front steps and unlocked the door. She wasn't surprised to see that Henry wasn't home yet. She figured he was probably still in the Fox newsroom. But she felt eager to have him get home, so she could tell him what she'd seen. She knew he'd believe her. He *had* to believe her. She paced back and forth from the kitchen to the living room, then sat down on the couch, opened her laptop, and looked at the pictures again. She thought about trying to do some Google research, but she didn't even know what search terms to put in.

She looked again at the pictures of each person in the group, wondering how she could find out who they were. Then she thought of Pierce. He was an attorney, he was well-connected, and he owed her big-time. They'd been lovers years ago, before she married Henry. Rita had finally ended it when Pierce refused to divorce his wife. Even though years had passed, Rita thought, she could call any one of a dozen reporters and blow the whistle, not only about their relationship, but about a number of Pierce's other activities. And of course, there was always the option of calling Pierce's wife and blowing his cover that way. It was only out of the goodness of her heart that she'd refrained from doing so, but she'd never really been sure if Pierce was sufficiently grateful. This would give him a chance to prove it to her.

Rita scanned through her phone, located his number, and reached him at the office. Like Henry, he was working late. She seemed to have a penchant for that kind of man, she thought ruefully. Pierce seemed glad to hear from her and promised to "do what he could" with the photos once she emailed them over.

Still musing, Rita boiled some potatoes and defrosted some steak for dinner. She was just setting the table when she heard Henry's key in the lock.

"Hi, honey," he hugged her. "How was the trip to Sodom and Gomorrah?"

Rita scowled. "Don't tease me, honey. This is serious for me."

"I'm sorry. So how was it?"

Rita sighed. "I didn't get the interview."

Henry was sympathetic. "I'm sorry; I know you were hoping that would be a big break for you."

"But I did get some pretty interesting photographs. Can I show them to you?" Rita grabbed her laptop from the couch and brought it over to the dining room table.

"Wow, these are strange," said Henry thoughtfully. "But there must be some kind of logical explanation. I know some people who might know, do you want me to..."

"No, no, I'll handle it." Rita suddenly had the chilling feeling that Henry might try to build up his own career by taking advantage of her big break. That was something she couldn't risk.

"Okay," Henry shrugged, smiling. "It's your call." They sat down to dinner, talking mostly about Henry's week at Fox. After dinner, Henry settled himself in front of the two TVs they had in the living room. One was set permanently on Fox, while the other roamed between CNN, CNBC, MSNBC, and then C-SPAN. They seemed to mostly be covering a Senate debate over a bill which would permit much more extensive dumping of chemical wastes into the ocean. Rita yawned, excused herself, and went upstairs to bed. She was asleep almost instantly.

San Jose, California, Earth, May 30, 2011

Joel and Laura had volunteered to work together to craft the FAQ document regarding the Galactic human civilization, and their purpose in coming to Earth. The two of them would draft a list of questions, incorporating suggestions from the rest of the team, and then come up with answers based on the information they had. They agreed that Marianne would then look over this draft, and then pass it on to Ja'el for further input and editing. They hoped to have it ready to distribute to the larger team, as soon as that team convened for its first meeting on the moon.

Joel found himself looking forward to working with Laura. He was primarily interested in questions about Galactic technology, and he knew that Laura's interest in Galactic culture was very different from his own. At first that had irritated him, but finally he had realized that the adage, "opposites attract," was at work again.

Joel set up instant-messaging on Laura's computer. That way the entire team would be able to connect that way, as well as via email. Ja'el didn't have instant-messaging, of course. But, through means Joel didn't understand, she actually had an email address. So they would all be able to email back and forth as they worked on developing the questions, and then drafting answers.

Joel opened his laptop and began to type in his own questions. He figured that was as good a place as any to start. "How many Galactic humans are there? Are they all on Casiti? What role have they played in developing Galactic technology? What are their plans for making that technology available on Earth?..."

Chapter 6:
Liaison

Diana had finally returned to New York, and it felt strange to Marianne to have her apartment to herself again, after their long days of joinings. But she felt satisfied with what they had achieved. David and Diana were assembling the list of prospective members to invite. Marianne would coordinate both the larger and smaller teams and serve as the liaison between both teams and Ja'el—who in turn served as liaison between the Earth humans and the Casitians. Marianne sighed as she thought of Ja'el. She knew it was time.

She took out the slim communicator and called Ja'el. In about two minutes, Ja'el's image appeared. "Hi, Marianne. How are you doing?"

"I'm fine—a bit tired but feeling like we accomplished a lot."

"Yes, you did. I am quite proud of you." Ja'el's image smiled perceptibly. "How can I help you?"

Marianne hesitated.

"Marianne?"

"Could I see you in person? I have something I need to talk with you about. I'm happy to come up there, if that's easier."

Ja'el seemed to be looking at Marianne, but it was hard to tell, given the perspective. "No, I can come to see you." She looked away momentarily, then looked back and asked, "Is tomorrow evening all right?"

Marianne nodded. "Yes, that's fine. I'll see you then. Thanks, Ja'el." Ja'el nodded, thoughtfully, and her image disappeared.

Marianne felt both excited and nervous. It was the same feeling she'd had before their second date, but it was much stronger now. She wondered how much she would be able to say to Ja'el about what she felt.

Fortunately, the next day was quite busy at work. She divided her time between catching up on what she'd missed while she was away and thinking about how to prepare to quit. She had no idea what to say in her letter of resignation. Moreover, she had no idea what she'd be doing long-term, although she was grateful for Diana's offer in the interim. Eventually she wanted to work for the Casitians in some capacity, but she didn't know what that might involve. And she knew it would take a while for the Galactic systems to become integrated with the economic realities of Earth.

She thought about Ja'el on the whole trip home. A knot had formed in her stomach, and she doubted she'd be able to eat dinner. Instead, she took a long, hot shower, letting the water sluice over her and breathing in the steam. Finally, she figured she'd better eat something, so she microwaved a frozen tamale—which, when eaten, sat heavily in her stomach.

She put on some music—Tuck and Patti. It was old, of course, but wonderfully romantic. She wondered what Ja'el would think of it, and realized, to her surprise, that she had never played any Earth music for Ja'el.

The bell rang, and Marianne watched as Ja'el mounted the last flight of stairs. She felt suddenly awkward, unsure. Should she hug Ja'el? Kiss her? Ja'el took care of that, by opening her arms for an embrace. Marianne returned the hug, and for the first time she allowed herself to really feel the sensation of touching Ja'el's body. Finally, Ja'el pulled back and looked at Marianne with a mixture of tenderness and concern.

"Are you all right?"

"Oh yes, I'm fine," Marianne responded, a bit embarrassed.

She had learned Ja'el's preferences. "Would you like some juice, or some tea?" Ja'el usually chose juice, so Marianne had taken to keeping a wider variety of juices in her refrigerator. Tonight, she had pineapple juice, which she knew would be new for Ja'el. Ja'el took the glass, sipped it, and smiled.

"Mmmm, this is wonderful. Thank you." She patted the couch beside her. "Come and sit down."

Marianne perched herself awkwardly several feet from Ja'el. She felt at a loss for words. Ja'el put her juice down on the coffee table and moved closer to her. They began to speak at the same time, both saying each other's names.

"Ja'el..."

"Marianne..."

Then they both laughed, and it broke the ice.

"What is it you'd like to talk about?" Ja'el asked softly. In that moment, Marianne realized that Ja'el knew exactly what she was about to say. Somehow, that made it easier. She took in a deep breath, and then allowed it to emerge in the form of words.

"Ja'el... ever since we first met, I've liked you a lot. I've felt... well, very drawn to you. And of course, I've gotten to know you much better, over these past few weeks. My feelings for you are very strong, and I would like... well, the truth is, I would like to be your companion."

Ja'el looked at Marianne and smiled gently, with her eyes bright. "Marianne, I have liked you since I began to observe you, even before we met. And I've been attracted to you since we met, as well."

Marianne was surprised. Her heart began to pound.

"But..." Ja'el continued. "I'm concerned that you may not understand what it would mean to be my companion. Also, we don't usually take companions when we're away from Casiti—it's not considered appropriate. And of course, I am serving as your teacher, which also makes it more complicated."

Marianne felt crushed. She realized that what Ja'el had said made sense. "I'm sorry I brought it up," she said quietly, not looking at Ja'el.

Ja'el placed her hand on Marianne's arm, and quite suddenly Marianne felt flooded with a gentle sense of hope, possibility, and well-being. "Yet," Ja'el continued, "These are unusual circumstances. I have discussed it with my teacher, and she has given me her blessing." Even before Marianne had time to fully absorb Ja'el's words, she felt Ja'el's body moving closer to hers. Then she felt her whole body respond as Ja'el took her face in her hands, moving her into a kiss. Marianne felt as if she was diving into the ocean of Ja'el.

Ja'el was the one to break the kiss. "Marianne, there is something I need to show you." Marianne felt puzzled. "Show me?"

Ja'el nodded. "Close your eyes, I think it will help."

Marianne sat back a little and closed her eyes. She felt Ja'el touching her face and felt the sense of calm and opening come into her. It felt as if Ja'el had actually transmitted those feelings to her with her fingers.

"How did you do that?"

"It has to do with focus, and intention. Basically, I am letting emotions move through my hands the way electricity moves through a conductor, in your system," Ja'el explained. "All Casitians learn to do that when we're very young. You could do it, too, if you learned how. It takes some practice, but it's a basic human ability."

"What if someone were to use that ability in a threatening way?" Marianne wondered aloud. "Could it be used to produce fear or intimidation, or to cause harm?"

"Yes, it could. In fact, Terrans do a lot of that, although often their techniques are less subtle!" Ja'el laughed. "This form of communication can transmit many of the same things that can be transmitted in words, or in touch. It's just a shortcut. And many of us find it more powerful." She took Marianne's hand in hers and held it lightly. Suddenly Marianne felt an intense sensation move through her body, almost as if Ja'el had begun to make love to her.

"That comes from my thoughts," Ja'el explained. "It appears that you are a very good receiver."

"Do you..." Marianne hesitated. "Do you also make love in the usual ways, with your bodies?"

"We do, but that is much less emphasized than it is here on Earth."

"I'm realizing I know very little about your customs," Marianne said thoughtfully. "I don't even know whether you lie down to make love, as we do, or whether you spend the night with your companion."

"Yes, we usually lie down—although not always, of course. I believe that is true here on Earth, as well." Ja'el looked at Marianne mischievously. "And yes, we sometimes spend the whole night together with our companions, although that is considered a very intimate act. There is much sharing that happens during the night, while both people sleep. It is not something we take lightly."

Marianne sat very still, holding Ja'el's hand. Suddenly she felt very shy again.

"You are shy," Ja'el acknowledged gently. "All of this is so new. But perhaps our bodies can communicate with more ease than our words." She held Marianne's shoulders in both of her hands, and again Marianne felt the calm and opening she had sensed before, along with just a hint of the more intense sensation. When she allowed herself to pay attention to it, the experience was exquisite.

"Would you like to invite me to your bed?" Ja'el asked. "We don't have to do anything you don't feel ready for. We could simply lie together."

At that, Marianne suppressed a grin. Knowing how she felt, she thought the odds that she and Ja'el would "simply lie together" were pretty slim.

"Come, then," Ja'el said, taking the lead. Hand in hand, they walked together into Marianne's bedroom.

Bahia de Los Angeles, Mexico, May 30, 2011

Raul and Paulo stood on the deck of the boat, preparing to drop their nets into the water. They had come out further than ever before, and there was very little fuel left. The winds would help push them back to shore, but the stakes were high. They both knew that if they didn't get a decent catch today, Raul would lose the boat.

Raul had inherited the fishing boat from his father, Fernando, who had bought it proudly thirty years before. Fernando had begun as a hired hand on a large fishing vessel out of Cabo San Lucas, and then moved to Bahia de Los Angeles to start his own business with a leased boat. Eventually, he was so successful that he became the owner of his own boat. Raul had worked with his father on this boat for many years, until Fernando's health no longer permitted him to fish. At that point, Raul had taken over.

But the business had hit its peak while Fernando was still fishing. Since then, things had gone steadily downhill. Five years ago, things had been so bad that Raul had been forced to take out a loan, using the boat as collateral. Now he was terrified of having to turn the boat over to his lender. He hadn't been making enough money to feed and clothe his family, let alone pay back the loan. He was months behind.

A very loud sound jerked him out of his thoughts, pulling his attention away from the nets and up to the sky. When he looked up, he saw a large ... thing. That was the only word that came to his mind. He didn't know what he was seeing. Paulo started to scream.

"Calm down!" Raul shouted, though he was far from calm himself. He ran into the pilothouse and grabbed some binoculars, so he could get a better look. The thing was roundish and appeared to have windows. As he looked more closely, he was almost sure he could see people in the windows, looking down toward the water. All of a sudden, another ... thing ... came up out of the water, hovering directly underneath the larger thing. Raul gasped as the smaller vessel kept rising, eventually disappearing into the larger vessel, which then flew off at an astonishing speed. Paulo was so frightened he was speaking gibberish and praying non-stop.

"Paulo, everything is fine. It's just some new thing the Americans are doing. Let's finish this," Raul said, trying hard to sound more certain than he felt.

Within a few minutes Paulo had managed to compose himself. Without speaking further, they dropped the nets into the ocean. But the day went as Raul had feared. The catch was dismal. They fished for as long as they could, hoping for a sudden break that never came.

Finally, after the sun had nearly set, they turned the boat toward the harbor and let the winds push them in. As they approached the harbor in the dim light, Raul saw Christofo, the moneylender, waiting there for him.

As soon as they docked, Raul dismissed Paulo. "Go get Ernesto. We need his help to unload the fish."

Paulo gave Raul a questioning look, then left.

Raul stood very still, looking straight at Christofo. "I've been expecting you. Have you come for the boat?"

"No, Raul. You can keep the boat. No one would want it now because there is no good fishing anymore, anywhere. But you'll still have to pay me back somehow. I'm taking this load of fish from you, and after this, every second load until you have paid what you owe."

"You can't! I have to feed my family! And Paulo! I have nothing to pay him with."

"I have no choice, Raul. I need the money." Christofo turned to another man, who Raul hadn't seen before. "Take this haul and bring it to Tulo for measuring," he said curtly.

Paulo returned a few minutes later, after the fish were all gone. He and Raul could barely look at one another. Paulo knew it wasn't really Raul's fault, but his own situation was dismal. Now he would have to beg for food. What would his wife say? She'd been urging him to move north to Tijuana for months now. The sea was in his blood and he hated the thought of working long days in a factory, but maybe she was right. It appeared he had no other choice.

San Francisco, California, June 4, 2011

The group had reconvened in Marianne's living room. Pizza boxes, soda bottles, scraps of paper and laptops were scattered all around. The place was a mess, but Marianne felt they had made some significant progress.

"Okay," she announced. "It looks like we're ready to assemble the larger team. We'll shoot for meeting all together on the moon, one month from today. Let's take the list that David and Diana have generated and divide up the contacts between us."

They had agreed that each one of them would make personal contact with four to five members of the larger team. They had even developed a basic script which each one of them would loosely follow. It was designed to convince listeners how important the issue was, and to provide enough information to be credible, without telling the whole story. They were prepared for the fact that not everyone would believe them, and that some people would decline the invitation to the meeting. But they hoped their personal connections would make most of their contacts set the day, and their reservations, aside. The trip to the moon and the meetings with Casitians would take care of the rest.

Together they pored over the list of names they had generated, dividing them up. Marianne spoke first. "I can be in charge of contacting Brit, the physicist, since I knew him at MIT. I can also contact Peter and Kyla; I have friends who know them. And Ginny Smith is an old friend. I'll contact her."

David volunteered, "Okay, I'll take Joanne, the dolphin scientist. I can get her number from one of my other contacts, Maria Gomez. John is a friend, and Patricia is my pastor, so those are easy, too."

"My contacts are all people I deal with on a regular basis, no problems there," said Diana.

"I might need a little help getting through to Nicholas, the TV producer," Joel mused. "Anyone know someone who knows him?"

"I think Gerard was interviewed by him for some documentary. I'll ask him," David offered.

"Thanks, dude, that might help."

"I've spoken to all my contacts in the last few months," Laura said. "So I'm covered."

Marianne closed her laptop, feeling exhausted but pleased. "Okay, then, it looks like we won't need to meet again for several weeks—I think we can do everything by email and IM. Then we can gather once more to finalize the agenda for the large team meeting and make any last personnel changes that are necessary for that team. Any other issues or questions?"

As she looked around the room, she realized that everyone else was as exhausted as she was. It had only been a week since that fateful first meeting with Ja'el—a single short week made long by all the joinings, emails, instant messaging, phone calls, thinking, writing, talking. Essentially, in addition to all the strategic planning, they'd been working separately and together to adapt to a whole new understanding of life on Earth. And of course, Marianne had been doing all of that *plus* getting used to a wonderful new relationship with—she laughed silently to herself—a woman from another planet. It was no wonder she felt tired!

Without talking much more, everyone got up, cleaned up the room, and filtered out. Marianne yawned and headed to bed, knowing she needed the rest. After all, she'd be seeing Ja'el again the next night.

San Francisco, California, Earth, June 4, 2011

Gerard sat at David's desktop computer, feeling both guilty and enraged. He'd been spending so much time away from David that he was pretty sure David must be seeing someone else. He'd mentioned Joel a few times lately, but Gerard knew it couldn't be him—Joel was too straight.

Gerard couldn't stand the thought that he might be losing David. He needed to know who it was that was taking his lover away. He hesitated, then quickly typed David's password in. They'd exchanged email passwords years before, back in the days when they'd sworn there would be no secrets between them. Of course, Gerard had changed his password immediately, but he figured that David—sweet, trusting David—had not. And he'd figured right.

Opening David's email box, Gerard scanned through the list of messages. There were a lot from Joel - that was odd. So maybe Joel wasn't as straight as he'd always claimed. Randomly, Gerard clicked on an email headed "Questions, Draft One." What he saw made no sense to him whatsoever. "How many Galactic humans are on Casiti? Are all Galactic humans bisexual?" What was this? He clicked on a second email, labeled "Draft talking points." Reading it, he couldn't believe his eyes. David involved in something that had to do with humans from another planet coming back to Earth? What was this, some kind of science fiction club?

Gerard looked at his watch. It was just past 9:30, and David had said he wouldn't be home until at least midnight—he'd claimed he had a big project to finish up. So Gerard had time. Methodically, he went back to the beginning of the emails with Joel and read through every one—not just the ones to and from Joel, but the others as well. As he did so, the story emerged.

It was even worse than Gerard had feared. The betrayal was far bigger. Although there was nothing to suggest that David had a new lover, he had been working with Marianne, Joel and others to create a team to "tell humanity" some very dramatic, fairly unbelievable things. He had kept all of this from Gerard, excluded him from important information—this, after having pledged so many years ago that there would be no secrets between them! Worst of all was that David had obviously not recommended Gerard's inclusion on the larger team. Gerard could barely contain his rage. Here he was, a rising political star in the dominant political party in the nation, and his own lover was leaving him out—in favor of Joel Gugenthorn, a Democrat?!

Gerard switched off the computer, then the light. Sitting alone in the dark, he rubbed his temples and tried to decide what to do.

He always did his best thinking in the dark. The urge to confront David was strong, but as he sat, he realized he could do something even better. He could take the information he had learned and use it for his own political gain. There was no telling how far he could go with this information—in fact, he probably could win the presidency. The timing was perfect. David's "team" - Gerard winced as he thought of it—had planned to release their information to the general public just a month before the beginning of next year's primary season. All of the other candidates would be taken by surprise—but not Gerard. He would have his entire platform prepared. He would make the most of it. David's betrayal would backfire. He would get in touch with Pierce—together, they could find out everything. Yes, this was going to mean that Gerard would become the next President of the United States. The thought of that eased the sting of losing David and replaced it with a fiery hot throbbing of adrenaline in his veins.

Still sitting in the dark and rubbing his temples, but gripped with excitement now, Gerard realized he would need to leave David immediately, live permanently with Juliana. After all, the United States would want a happily married president.

La Jolla, California, Earth, June 5, 2011

Something strange was going on. Joanne sat at her computer, looking over GPS data on the three dolphins they had tagged last year. They were part of a pod of offshore bottlenose who generally stayed close to the Hawaiian island of Maui. Suddenly, in the past month, they had left that area and swum all the way over to Baja Mexico. Now they were spending their time in the Sea of Cortez, the body of water between Baja and the Mexican mainland. This was extremely unusual behavior for *Tursiops truncatis*, who rarely strayed far from their home waters.

This might make a good paper for the upcoming conference, Joanne thought—but she'd need more information. What could have caused this? Weather? Water temperature? It was true that the temperature of the waters off Hawaii had increased, but that had happened everywhere. Joanne was just starting to look up weather patterns in the Pacific area near Hawaii over the past few months, when she noticed she had some new email. It was a message from her old thesis advisor, Blix, who'd been studying Atlantic *Tursiops* for years. He wrote that the pod he'd been studying, which frequented the waters off the Georgia Sea Islands, had suddenly disappeared. Unlike Joanne, Blix relied on old radio tagging, so when the dolphins got out of range, it was impossible for him to know where they were—but they'd been heading south, toward the Caribbean Sea. He'd written Joanne to find out whether she had any ideas about what might be going on.

Joanne decided it was time to do some informal information gathering. She emailed five colleagues, representing many different geographic areas: Thomas, who studied dolphins in the Indian Ocean; Alex, who was from New Zealand, and followed at least three or four pods in NZ and Australia, Kevin who followed dolphins off of Madagascar, and Andres from Chile, who followed dolphins in the Pacific off of the coast of Peru. She hesitated about emailing Gustavo. The last time she'd seen him at the International Marine Mammals conference, he had come on to her, and she knew he was still interested. She, on the other hand, had no interest in him at all. She sighed. She really needed information on the Mediterranean dolphins he tracked. She added him to the list. She was a bit vague in the email—just mentioned that she and Blix had observed strange behavior on the part of the pods they were tracking, and she wondered whether or not they had noticed anything odd. Thomas, Alex and Andres used modern GPS tracking, so they could easily find out where their dolphins were, if they left their home waters. Kevin and Gustavo, she remembered, still used radio tracking. Because dolphins were generally so bound to their home waters, radio tracking had been fine for most scientists, and the small power radio transmitters that had been in use just prior to the advent of GPS tracking devices were small and easy to use. It was completely understandable that they would still be in use. However, in this situation, it made things more difficult.

Just a few minutes after she sent the email, her phone rang. "Joanne? It's Kevin. I just got your email."

"Wow, that was fast. Hi, Kevin, how are you?"

"I'm fine, really fine. I've been spending the summer at Harvard, working with Harold on some genetics stuff. But I got an email two weeks ago from my student, who was going to spend the summer in Madagascar tracking the dolphins we'd tagged last year. She said the dolphins they had been tracking had disappeared. She was finally able to schedule an afternoon on the ship to do some dolphin hunting, so she could track some more, but there were none left in the home waters, so she went home."

After talking more with Kevin and getting emails back from the others, Joanne had her confirmation. Indeed, something very strange was going on. Everyone's dolphins had left their home waters at approximately the same time. Her stomach started to grumble, and she realized she hadn't had lunch. Since it was way past dinnertime, she decided to head home. She left her office and got in her car. As soon as she got into her car, her cell phone beeped to let her know she had a message.

"Hi, Joanne, it's David Lopez. I got your number from Maria. We met briefly when you two were together, when you visited here a few years ago, but you probably don't remember me. Anyway, some things are happening right now, and I remember that you study dolphins. There is something very important I need to speak with you about. Please call me as soon as you can. My number is ..."

Joanne's mind flashed first back to Maria. Their brief, fiery relationship had taught Joanne a lot about herself, including the fact that she preferred relationships with men, after all. But Joanne still thought the world of Maria, and still loved her. She remembered David only vaguely and wondered what he could possibly want. And why had he mentioned dolphins? Well, she was too tired and hungry to call him back right now. She put the car into gear and headed home.

Moon Flyer/Moon Station, 1 Gont, 780/June 5, 2011
K'flef greeted Marianne with his broken English. "Hi Marianne, how you?"

"I'm fine, K'flef, thank you. And thank you for this ride to the moon."

"Oh, pleasure mine, yes." K'flef turned toward the controls of the small aircraft, and they took off. This was Marianne's second trip to the moon, the first in a small craft. It was just as smooth, and the view was just as wonderful. She took it in, wondering at the beauty of the Earth.

"Is Casiti this beautiful?" Marianne asked K'flef.

"Sorry, it more beautiful!" K'flef grinned, and Marianne nodded.

"Of course, it's your home." Marianne smiled.

Ja'el greeted Marianne in the corridor as soon as they landed. They embraced, and then Marianne followed Ja'el back to her quarters, where they half-sat, half-lay on a mound of soft pillows in one corner of the room.

"I've been missing you, Marianne," Ja'el said, stroking her hand.

Marianne was surprised. She had assumed that her feelings for Ja'el were stronger than Ja'el's for her.

"I've missed you too, Ja'el. But I've been so busy with all of the preparations that I feel like I haven't had time to integrate everything that has happened—including, well, including you."

Ja'el smiled. "It's fine, it will take some time. We have plenty of time." She leaned forward, allowing her lips to lightly touch Marianne's. "So, how are the preparations going?"

Marianne forced herself back to cognitive thinking. "They're going pretty well, I think. We've decided who's going to be on the larger team, and we're almost finished with our list of questions. We'll be in good shape for the meeting next month. How are things going here?"

Ja'el looked serious. "They are fine, really. But we are more worried about the dolphins than we were at first. From what they have communicated, their situation is rather dire. We're still gathering more information from them; we'll brief you at the meeting next month. But the timetable is probably going to be much tighter than we thought."

Marianne nodded. "Okay, we'll take that into consideration. It will be easier to know how all of this will go once we have the larger team working together. We have a dolphin scientist on the team—she can probably be of help."

Ja'el looked puzzled. "It's not really necessary. Our contact with the dolphins is—direct."

Marianne was surprised. She thought back to Diana's comments, and wondered how much to say.

"I want to change the subject," Ja'el said in a different tone. "Close your eyes. Okay, now put out your hand, and place it right over mine, but not touching."

Eyes closed, Marianne stretched out her arm and put her hand over Ja'el's.

"Imagine energy from your heart pouring out of your fingers. How does that feel?"

At first, Marianne felt nothing. Then, slowly, she started to feel a bit of a tingle in her fingers. It was almost imperceptible, but there. She opened her eyes, looking at Ja'el.

"That's the first step. I'll teach you more. But you have the same abilities I do, Marianne. I know you find that hard to believe. Just for your information, we call this 'lyre'es'gkin.'"

"Yes, I do find it hard to believe that I have the same ability you do." Marianne cocked her head. "But, having experienced your ability, I would certainly like to think that I could return what you're able to give to me."

Ja'el smiled, reaching out her arms. As they embraced, then kissed again, lingeringly, Marianne let herself lose track of her sense of time and place, giving herself over to the pleasure of Ja'el's presence, their touching, their not-touching, and the power of lyre'es'gkin.

Chicago, Illinois, Earth, June 6, 2011

Pierce sat at his desk, thinking about what he'd heard from both Rita and Gerard. He had realized fairly quickly that they were both telling him pieces of the same story—like mosaic pieces which fit together to give a greater intimation of the whole. He wasn't sure what his role was to be in all of this, but he figured that aligning himself with Gerard would be a good bet. He could use the information he'd gotten from Rita to help Gerard, and Gerard would do all sorts of favors for him, in exchange. Rita, on the other hand, had nothing to offer him—so there wasn't much point in keeping her in the loop. But he would tell all he knew to Gerard. The five people, the other people they had contacted, the relationships between them...everything. He'd paid a cracker to tap into David's email on an ongoing basis, so they'd have that steady source of information coming in.

He'd thought of something else, too. Joel's friend Dwight owed money to someone who, by coincidence, owed a lot of money to Pierce. So it had been easy to convince Dwight to be their mole in the upcoming meeting. He'd attend it wired for sound and video, with the most sophisticated equipment in existence.

Moon Station, 32 Gont, 780/July 2, 2011
They had decided to have the final joining of the small group on the moon, since Marianne was spending more time there than in her own apartment. David had thought it really strange the first time Marianne emailed him and told him she was on the moon. He wondered exactly how the Galactics had been able to tap into the internet, but Marianne hadn't found out yet.

Everyone was seated at the table in the small joining room. It had a view of the moon's surface, which seemed to be teeming with activity at the moment.

"What's going on there?" Joel asked.

"We're starting up mining activities, so that we can be self-sufficient here on the moon," Ja'el answered matter-of-factly.

"Self-sufficient? How is that possible? There's no water here."

"There's ice in craters near the poles. We've been melting it and piping it to the station. This mining operation is for building materials, and for creating fertilizer for the plants we grow. We expect to be fully self-sufficient in a year."

Marianne said thoughtfully, "Yes, I remember a few years ago the Lunar Prospector sent back some data suggesting that there could be ice. That's fantastic, to be self-sufficient on an airless moon!"

"The Galactic community has a lot of technology resources. You'll be exposed to more of them as time goes on," Ja'el said.

"Let's start this joining, shall we?" David said, taking charge. "The agenda for the first joining with the larger team is drafted. Has everyone had time to look it over? Any comments?"

"I think you need more time for the team members to get to know each other, and to talk about what implications they see in their own spheres," Ja'el responded.

Marianne nodded. "Yes, I agree with Ja'el about that. This agenda only allows for brief introductions. Remember, they will have just arrived on the moon -- they'll probably be in shock. Let's give them some time to verbally process this."

Joel furrowed his brow. "Do we really need to spend time on touchy-feely stuff? Aren't these people professionals? We won't have a lot of time at this meeting, and we really need to get down to business."

Laura, who was seated next to Joel, put her hand on his arm. "Joel, calm down. You're right that there's a lot to do, but not everyone is like you. Some people need time to let it all sink in, and to reorient themselves. We need to provide space for that. If we don't, our later steps might not work as well."

Joel's face softened as he looked at Laura, and Marianne realized suddenly that they must have gotten involved. "Okay, Laura. I hear you. I'm just worried about the time factor."

Diana spoke up next. "I'm worried too, but I'm more concerned about the point of no return—that is, the moment when this information gets leaked, and things get beyond our control. The more we can do before that happens, the better off we'll be."

"We also need to talk about the budget," Marianne commented. "We've been using our own resources for things, but that's going to have to change as the group gets bigger. Also, Silandra and Ja'el are thinking about how to interface with Earth economic resources. Does anyone have any ideas about this?"

"Well, I do have some funds we can use," Diana offered. "By the time the budget review gets done, a few months from now, the world will know what's happening, so I can't imagine my supervisors will object to the expense. I can contribute 100,000 euros or more without much problem."

Marianne nodded gratefully. "Thanks, Diana. You've definitely been our economic benefactor."

Diana smiled. "Well, it's really the World Trade Organization at your service. They just don't know it yet."

They moved through the agenda fairly smoothly, checking in about the contacts they'd made. "From my list, Ginny refused to come,"

Marianne reported. "I think she thought I'd had a psychotic break. But I got in touch with Ira, who was an alternate, and he agreed."

Diana spoke next. "I had to do a bit of fancy footwork. One of my contacts got fired the day before I was going to call him, so I had to pick an alternate. Apart from that, they were all eager."

Joel reported, "Amazingly, enough, I was able to get Nicholas Johnson to come. And all of my other contacts are coming too."

David looked pained, and Marianne wondered what was up. "All of my contacts are coming," he said softly. "Joanne, the dolphin scientist, got very interested once I explained the dolphin connection. It turns out that the cetacean science community has been noticing strange events and was starting to investigate. So it's a good thing this is going to get out soon."

Laura spoke last. "We're all set from my group. I think the Lama is coming just to humor me, I don't think he actually believes what I've told him. Jerome from the Kinsey Institute is quite intrigued, especially after I told him about Galactic human sexuality."

Ja'el looked toward Laura. "What is the Kinsey Institute?"

"It's named after a researcher, Alfred Kinsey, who was the first person to really explore human sexuality from a scientific perspective."

"Ah, that makes sense, then," Ja'el nodded. "I will look forward to joining with them."

As the joining came to a close, Marianne caught hold of David's arm. "You don't look so good. What's going on?"

He avoided her gaze. "Gerard moved out last week."

Marianne raised her eyebrows. "Oh, I'm sorry. But I thought you'd wanted to ask him to do that anyway...?"

"Yes, I thought I did too. I guess I didn't realize how it would affect me. I really love Gerard. I want him to come back. I'm willing to stick with him through his campaign and everything."

Marianne put her hands on David's shoulders. "David, that's crazy and you know it. Yes, you love Gerard. But he was also making you miserable. Let him go. You'll be better off."

David hung his head. "I know. I just hate losing him." He straightened a little and looked into Marianne's face with just a hint of a smile. "And by the way, your relationship with Ja'el has not gone unnoticed."

"I told Diana. Does everyone know?"

David nodded. "Why didn't you tell me?"

"I was worried about what you might think. I'm worried about what everyone else might think, too."

David's smile grew bigger. "I don't think you need to worry. If Laura weren't involved with Joel, I think she'd be looking for a Galactic herself. Joel, on the other hand..."

"Do you think he's going to be a problem?"

"I hope not. But his reactions are making it clear to me that it's pretty likely the world will be divided into two groups: those that welcome the Casitians, and those that will oppose the Casitians with everything they have."

"David, we won't have a choice, you realize. We can't fight the Galactic Community. If we tried, we would lose, terribly."

David nodded, "I know, I know. But that doesn't mean people won't try."

Chapter 7:
Betrayal

San Francisco, California, Earth, July 2, 2011

There were two types of people who had clustered around Gerard. The first group was made up of people Gerard trusted completely -- people who were fiercely loyal to him, who would align themselves with him no matter what. The second group was made up of people whom Gerard knew he could trust to follow their own self-interest, no matter what. So, as long as Gerard's interest was in line with theirs, he could trust them, too. He went to the liquor cabinet and got out a bottle of his best 15-year-old Scotch, and offered it around.

"I want to thank you all for coming. Pierce, please start your presentation."

Pierce, a tall, lanky man with a bit of a pot belly and a small mustache, went to the front of the room, and pointed a remote toward a projector. A photograph of a dark two-dimensional oblong, with people entering it, came up on the screen. Using the photo for emphasis, Pierce told the assembled group everything he knew.

Gerard got up again. "Thank you, Pierce. So, you can see, we are heading into a very interesting time. And I have more information than anyone else except the small group in the photograph. With your help and support, I can become President of the United States, which will, of course, benefit you greatly."

The only woman in the room, who was medium height, and wearing a business suit, said "What is your strategy going to be, Gerard? How will you use this information to become President?"

"Most people in this country will oppose these alien humans, these Casitians, they call themselves. They will think their culture is decadent, and they will oppose any off-Earth governance. It is these people I will represent, and they will vote for me."

"What if your opponents also voice their opposition?"

"I have had more time and information to craft my message. I know about the sexuality and parenting habits of the so-called

Galactics. We can be in the position to expose what they don't choose to tell the world."

The woman nodded, but something in her manner sent up a red flag for Gerard. She might not be so trustworthy, after all.

San Francisco, California, Earth, July 2, 2011
Anna realized she would have to think fast. She sensed that Gerard's plan was likely to work, but the cost to the American people would be enormous. Anna was only the third woman to head a Fortune 100 company, and she had used her political savvy to help Biosis Pharmaceuticals reach the top of the industry. She had always supported Gerard; even now, she knew that as president he would represent her business interests. In the past this had mattered to her. But the information revealed at the meeting had changed her thinking. She had realized very quickly that big pharma was dead. All the major companies would undoubtedly be supplanted by the Galactics' superior medical technology. Not just her company, but her entire industry would be ruined. She was surprisingly philosophical; she had come to terms with that quickly. Since her career no longer mattered, it seemed right, at least, to try to save her country.

She remembered a few of the names Pierce had mentioned. Marianne Michaelson -- she'd heard of her in connection with the SETI scandal a few weeks back. Anna wanted to make contact with Marianne, but she would need to be careful. Gerard might be watching her now.

La Jolla, California, Earth, July 9, 2011/Moon Station, 35 Gont, 780
Joanne picked up her briefcase and stood at the curb outside her house. David had told her someone would pick her up promptly at 10:00, but it was 10:02 and there wasn't a car in sight. She shifted impatiently, then felt a sudden gust of wind. She looked up, but nothing was there. All of a sudden, a dark oblong shape, looking to be a doorway, appeared next to her driveway.

"Joanne Henry?" A man appeared inside the shape. Joanne got up and walked toward him. He held out his hand. "Hi, I'm K'flef. Come with me?" He had a heavy accent of some sort. She followed him, and realized she was in a small vehicle of sorts, with only two seats. It looked, oddly enough, like a spaceship.

"Welcome. Please sit." She heard a low whooshing sound behind her. When she turned around, the oblong door had shut. The view outside shifted as they started to fly over houses and trees, then into the open ocean off of La Jolla. They flew over the ocean for a while. Then, suddenly, they were flying straight up.

"I was told to, uh, let you enjoy view for a bit."

Joanne was indeed enjoying the view. She had never in her wildest dreams expected to be in space. The moon came into view, and they shifted direction to fly towards it. Slowly, the moon got larger, and the Earth receded behind them. This gave Joanne a bit of time to let the new experience sink in. She hadn't completely believed David, but the new dolphin behaviors made his story more compelling, so she'd figured she should at least attend the meeting. But David hadn't told her that the meeting would take place on the moon!

They touched down, and K'flef led her out of the vessel, through corridors with lovely paintings and drawings, into a large conference room where others were gathering. He then turned and left, presumably to pick up other people. Two more people arrived, and she noticed there was food in one corner. She saw David talking to Maria and went up to them.

"Ah, Joanne, it's great to see you." Maria gave Joanne a big hug.

"Thanks for coming, Joanne." David hugged her too.

Joanne saw Kyla Morgenstern across the room, who was coming their way.

"Hi Joanne, it's great to see you!" Joanne had last seen Kyla at a climate conference at UCSD. Joanne had wanted to know more about global climate change because of how that might affect the dolphins, and climate change was Kyla's specialty. They'd spent several hours talking over drinks.

"Hi Kyla, I'm so glad you're here."

"It was hard not to come."

As they all caught up with each other, more and more people filled the room. Finally, a tall African-American woman stood up on a chair and said loudly, "Thank you all for coming. Please take a seat."

They all filtered around the very large conference table and sat down. Apart from David, Maria and Kyla, all of the faces were new to Joanne. There looked to be quite a range of people present, men and women of varied ages, races and nationalities.

"Hi, my name is Marianne. We have a very interesting story to tell you, some of which you may already know, since we're here on the moon. We have a big job ahead of us, and a short time to do it in, and we'll be hoping for help from all of you. So, without further ado, I'd like to introduce Siladra z Vezeldame, who will head up the Casitian team, and Erit'ala z Helhum, who is the primary liaison between us and the Caraj, which is basically the Casitian government."

Erit'ala was a tall woman with striking white hair, who spoke with a light accent. "Hello, and welcome to moon station."

Moon Station 35 Gont, 780/July 9, 2011
Dwight was sweating. It always happened when he was nervous, and he just hoped people here wouldn't figure that out. He regretted having agreed to come to this meeting wired, but he had felt he had no choice at the time. He owed Enrico a lot of money, and it was probably the only way to prevent getting both his legs broken -- or worse. He tried to bring his mind back to the present, to listen to what the Casitian women were saying.

Silandra was standing up now. "Before we proceed, we have one small thing to bring up. We are choosing to attend to it publicly, so that all of you understand the gravity of what is involved. Dwight Marks, please stand up."

Still sweating, Dwight looked helplessly at Joel, hoping he would intervene. Joel shook his head. Dwight was trapped. So, avoiding Silandra's eyes, he stood up.

"Please take off your shirt."

"Why?"

"You know exactly why."

"How did you know?"

"We have sophisticated technology that you don't have. We knew that you were wearing taping equipment from the moment you arrived at the station," Silandra answered calmly.

Dwight realized he'd been busted. Very, very busted. What next? Were they going to kill him? Kick him off the moon? He unbuttoned his shirt and took it off. Everyone in the room could see the set of wires that went from the microphone and camera in his shirt to the recording devices underneath his pants.

"Why have you done this?" Silandra asked, still seeming surprisingly calm.

Dwight looked at Silandra. "Someone I know - um, someone I owe money to, this guy Enrico, asked me to wear it to the meeting. He wanted to know what was going on."

"Who is Enrico? Why did he want you to record this? Do you know how he knew this joining was happening?"

Dwight was embarrassed. He'd really had no idea how Enrico had found out about the joining, or why he cared. All he'd thought about was the fact that he owed Enrico money, so he'd better do what was asked. Now that he thought about it a little more, it made sense that Enrico was probably working for someone else. But Dwight didn't know who.

Dwight decided he couldn't possibly get in any more trouble by being honest. "The truth is, I really don't know. I'm just afraid if I go back without information, I'll get hurt."

Now Silandra looked both perplexed, and a little sad. "Why would you get hurt?"

"I owe Enrico a lot of money. He's the kind of guy that hurts people that don't pay him back. I thought I could pay him back, but I couldn't. So he asked me to do this."

"What if you come back with money instead?"

Dwight looked confused. "I don't know. I guess he might leave me alone."

"Please remove the device and give it to Marianne."

Dwight removed all of the wiring and the recorder, and handed the bundle to Marianne, who looked like she didn't want to touch it.

"How much money do you owe Enrico?"

"Twenty thousand dollars."

"We will provide you with that amount before you go back."

David was shocked. He stood up, getting a little red in the face. "You mean you're not only going to let him stay, you're even going to give him money? That's like saying what he did was okay! And how do you know he won't still betray us?"

"You don't think this is the right approach?" Silandra asked with some surprise. "I believe we are running into what you might call a 'cultural difference.' Joel, he is your friend, is he not? How would you suggest that we handle this?"

Joel hesitated. "Yes, he's my friend, or at least he was. But he betrayed me, and all of us. I really don't know what to do here."

Silandra looked at Marianne next. "What do you think?"

Marianne said, "I don't see what good it would do to kick him out at this point, anyway. He already knows plenty. Dwight, if we let you stay, will you promise not to tell anyone?"

Dwight, relieved, nodded vigorously. "I really didn't want to do this in the first place. The only reason I agreed was because I was scared of what Enrico would do to me. I won't tell a soul."

Silandra folded her hands. "I think that is sufficient."

Dwight could tell that David was still fuming. Silandra looked back toward Marianne. "Do you have any other information to share that might relate to this matter?"

"Yes, Silandra. I got a phone call from a woman named Anna Gezelle. She had been to a meeting with Gerard, David's former companion. From what she said, it appears that Gerard has obtained quite a lot of information, which he is planning to use to try to win the Presidential election. I wonder whether perhaps 'Enrico' is somehow connected with Gerard."

David put his face in his palms and was shaking. Dwight sensed a change in David's emotions, and he could imagine why.

Silandra sighed. "I see the larger picture now. It is important for all of you to understand that we find this kind of behavior both troubling and mystifying. We understand that it will be difficult to avoid this sort of, what do you call it, 'intrigue.' But this is not how we operate. And this is not how we want you to operate, either. You have been called together to work as a team and given the task of conveying very important information to the world. At every point, and at every level, you must be completely honest and straight-forward. Is that clear?"

Silandra looked around the table. Dwight got the message, and he imagined everyone else did, too.

"Okay. So let's get started, shall we? We have a lot to accomplish."

Moon Station, 35 Gont 780

Ur'lef sat in front of a three-dimensional display of the Earth that showed the gatherings of the species that the Earth humans called dolphins. Of course, the dolphins had a name for themselves that could not be heard by human ears. The Casitians also had a name for the dolphins, which was "parn'litd'shoms," or "parns," for short. The rough English translation was "swimmers in wisdom." Ur'lef's students were at each gathering, communicating with the parns. The parns had become aware of the Casitians very soon after first contact—a fact which had not surprised them at all. However, Ur'lef imagined that the Earth humans would be astonished, considering that most of them considered dolphins to be good at acrobatics and not much else. Ur'lef shook his head sadly. He was glad that he had been assigned to work with parns rather than with Terrans. He lacked the great patience of Erit'ala, Silandra and Ja'el.

He brought his attention back to the display. The parns were in the process of choosing their representatives to the Galactic community. Two or three parns from each of the twelve gatherings would go to the main station to further solidify the relationships between the Galactic community and their home system. Ur'lef wondered whether or not Silandra had told the Terran team that from now on it was dolphins, in collaboration with the Galactic Community, that would determine the fate of Earth.

Moon Station, 35 Gont 780/July 9, 2011

After the break, Marianne stood up. "You've now heard everything we know. We would like to give you time to talk about how you're feeling about all of this. We know it is a lot to take in all at once."

Kyla, the climatologist, raised her hand, and spoke a little nervously. "I'm excited about how the Galactics can help us clean up the environment. But I'm worried about how much obstruction and resistance we'll encounter."

Joanne spoke next. "Yes, I'm worried about that too. I think there are a lot of people who will avoid making changes. I'm sure there are people who couldn't care less about dolphins, and that won't change overnight."

A short balding Asian man in a suit said, "I work for a company that has championed dolphin-safe tuna - I believe many companies will try to comply, as long as they understand that it will benefit them to do so. I think that's the key -- making sure that everyone understands the benefits. Once they understand the benefit..."

Another man raised his hand. "I'm an economist, and I'm concerned about the massive shifts in the economy that will result from the changes proposed by the Galactics. Between the potential shutdown of so many companies and the re-orientation of so many others, and all of the associated job losses and changes, I think we're in for some serious economic quakes. I don't know how individuals and countries will deal with that."

An older woman with graying hair raised her hand. Marianne recalled that she was Patricia Warren, the pastor of the church where she'd taken Ja'el on the first day they'd spent together.

"This will lead to a complete upheaval in terms of religious belief for many people," Patricia was saying. "As a reflex, some might consider this a deception of Satan. It's also possible that people may lose their faith entirely. I also wonder how the Pope will respond—a lot of people listen to him."

Jal'end'a said to Patricia, "I would love to spend some time talking with you about these issues. I've been doing research and thinking a lot about what I've learned. I think perhaps we can help each other."

A slight, bald man in saffron robes, who Marianne remembered was the Tibetan Lama Chatral Nangwa, smiled, "Yes, there is much to learn, for all of us." Marianne noticed a look of recognition pass between Jal'end'a and the Lama.

The conversation continued, with many in the room expressing both their concerns and their excitement about the future. A few seemed to have deep reservations about the culture of the Casitians. They discussed the things that some Earth humans might find the most difficult, and also explored the things that most Earth humans would have a more positive view toward.

Marianne said, "The Casitians have come to realize that complete re-unification of our two branches of the species isn't going to happen as quickly or as easily as they had thought. They imagine that Earth culture will remain fairly different than Casitian culture for many generations to come. I agree with them on that."

They took a short break so that people had time to stretch their legs, eat some snacks, and talk a bit with each other. After the break, Marianne stood. "We have some things to hand out that will make our tasks a lot easier."

Marianne turned toward the door, where a Casitian man was standing, with a large carton in his arms. She motioned him to come to the table. He put the carton on the table next to Marianne, and she pulled out a thin, metal object.

Marianne said, "This is going to be your primary tool for work and communication. It is, of course, of Galactic origin, although it is designed for us. Galactic technology might be hard for us to use initially, but this will be a gentle start. You can think of it as a very souped-up laptop. There is no keyboard, because you can speak directly into it, as well as use the touch screen. It will display whatever you would like or need. All of these units will be keyed to your own identities, so that they will be inert without your voice signature. They will allow communication between the units and to the moon. They also can connect to the Earth Internet."

Marianne and the man started to hand out units. "The first thing you need to do is just speak into it. The unit will instruct you from there."

Some aural cacophony ensued as people spoke into their units and followed instructions. Marianne had already worked a little with hers—it was very intuitive and amazingly capable. The sounds in the room died down, as people had completed the first stage of using the devices.

Marianne stood up again. "Once we break for the day, please spend time with the device, and get used to working with it. Our next step is to lay out the detailed process for how to break the news to everyone on Earth. We have come up with a tentative plan; we want everyone's feedback on this plan as soon as possible. Please look at your units, they now should be displaying the tentative plan for dissemination of information regarding the Galactics, and your role in that plan."

Marianne asked, "As you can see, there are different teams—governmental, commercial, public and NGO, and scientific. We'll be doing a lot of this in parallel, until it all has to come together when we finally go public. Are there any immediate comments on this draft?"

Gita Padath, a UN communications official, looked up, and raised her hand. "I'm concerned about the vulnerability of the UN to the US government, given that the physical location of the UN is on US soil. If the US government decides that it is uninterested in UN oversight relating to environmental issues, it will be in a position to cripple the UN efforts. I am worried about possible violent conflict."

Silandra stood. "We understand that it is possible that violence will occur because of this process. It is important that you understand that Galactic ships have no weapons. We have no military. However, we do have technology far exceeding what you even would expect. We can, and will, if necessary, make it impossible for the US military, or any military for that matter, to interfere with these plans. We need to communicate this clearly to all governments."

John Gugenthorn, who had been a congressperson several years ago, spoke up, "Unfortunately, Silandra, you may well be tested on this one, especially by the US government, and possibly by the Chinese."

Silandra nodded solemnly.

Marianne asked, "Any other comments? The details of this plan are to be hashed out in teams. If you look at the display, you will see the team you are assigned to. If you feel that is in error, check with me."

Marianne paused, and looked around the room. "I think it's a good time to break for the day. We won't be meeting together for quite a while. We'll be doing everything in smaller teams and electronically. We have a very tight timetable. We start the UN dissemination process in two months, and let the press know in about three, if we can hold it off that long. It's going to be quite the ride for a while. Also, there are detailed guidelines in your unit about press contacts, and the like. The more people that know, the more chance that this will get out, so please limit the number of people you tell —for example, please wait as long as you possibly can to tell spouses and family."

People started to get up and move around, and as Casitian pilots entered the room to announce rides home, they filtered out, and the room emptied, except for Marianne, Ja'el, David, Laura, Joel, Diana and Silandra.

"How are you all feeling now?" Ja'el asked.

Joel looked at Ja'el. "I'm overwhelmed. I don't know how I'm going to manage to lead the science team. I know I can do it, but there feels like so much to get done. Just to let you know, Joanne is feeling very left out of things. I had a talk with her at the last break. She feels that she should be involved in dolphin contact—because she feels that she's knowledgeable and can help."

Silandra laughed, realized that might seem rude, then looked solemn. "No Joel, there is nothing she could do to help. Her understanding of the dolphins is not as advanced as she thinks it is. There is nothing she knows that we do not. I'm sorry that she feels left out, but she has no role to play except as one of the dolphins' advocates among humans."

Joel looked at Silandra with some degree of suspicion. "OK, I'll tell her, but that won't make her happy."

Diana leaned forward and spoke "I'm actually in pretty good shape. Gita and I have talked a lot about the UN issues, and I'm confident that everything will be in place within our deadline, especially if we've got some Galactic help."

Ja'el nodded, "That's good to hear Diana, thank you." She turned, "David, what do you think about contact with corporations?"

"Well, I'm worried. Corporations, especially in the US, are used to operating with little oversight. I'm not sure how they will respond, especially if they have to radically change their practices. And those that will simply go away because of Galactic technology will create a lot of disruption that we have to prepare people for."

Ja'el nodded, "Yes, there will be disruptions in a lot of different places and for a lot of people. We'll have to find ways to minimize that. I'm sure, though, that there will be some things we can't anticipate." She turned toward Marianne. "Marianne, how are you feeling in your leadership role?"

Marianne hesitated. "It's alright. I was cornered a lot at breaks, and I imagine I'll be getting a lot of email and phone calls. David has been helping a lot as my primary, um, student, and this team has been working quite well together." Marianne smiled, "Everyone has been a great support for me."

Silandra nodded and said, "You all have done incredible work here. Congratulations on making it to this step. Two more months, and we will be in a different season, as it were. Thank you all for a great joining, as well." She smiled, got up, and left the room.

K'flef came in, and said "David and Joel, I'm ready to take you home. R'ewl will take Diana and Laura."

"Are you staying here, Marianne?" Joel asked, suspiciously.

"Yes, Joel, I am staying for a day or two." Marianne looked Joel straight in the eye, as if in challenge. He backed down.

They all walked out of the door, with those going back to Earth following their rides, and Silandra going back to her quarters. Ja'el and Marianne walked back to Ja'el's quarters.

As they opened the door and went in, Marianne sat heavily on the pillows. "I'm worn out, Ja'el. I don't know how long I really can handle leadership, and the shuttling back and forth from the moon to home. It feels overwhelming at times."

"Would living here help? You'd be free of the distractions of the city, and I'd be here." Ja'el smiled. "I would enjoy having you here."

Marianne looked up at Ja'el, who was approaching the pile of pillows she sat on. Ja'el moved to sit down next to her, and began to massage her head, which made Marianne feel so much better. "Yes, it would be nice to live here with you. Would that be OK with everyone on moon station?"

Ja'el said, "Of course. Everyone understands what's happening. We could move into one of the suites, where there would be plenty of room. You could communicate with everyone on Earth just as easily from here.

Marianne felt relieved, and started, in her head, to move out of her apartment, put everything she owned in storage, and move to the moon. On one hand, it sounded completely absurd—living on the moon! On the other hand, she rather liked the moon station, and she loved being with Ja'el. And it would provide her with some insulation from the chaos that was going to happen on Earth. She was going to need all the insulation she could get. It was going to be a wild ride.

Chapter 8:
Secrets

Gita Padath rode up the elevator to the twenty third floor. They had finally reopened that floor, after months and months of renovation. The communications office had rented space on Park Ave. and 48th street, a full six blocks away from headquarters, which had been completely inconvenient. She guessed, though, that she had gotten some very good exercise over those months, since she was back and forth at least twice a day.

Gita had a difficult time at home, after her day on the moon. She had to lie to her husband about where she had been, which was impossible—she was a terrible liar, and they both knew it. He had finally said that she was lying, and she admitted it, and told him that she would be able to eventually explain where she had been, but for security reasons she couldn't. He didn't buy that, because he worked at the UN too, and he knew procedure; he also knew exactly what she was privy to. She promised him that everything would be alright, but he had decided that it was something she was purposefully hiding from him, like an affair. The argument that ensued agitated their daughters, ages five and nine, and it ended up being a miserable night.

She was glad she could escape their apartment. She wondered when she could finally figure out how to tell him, and how long she would have to endure his anger until she could. Ever since he hadn't gotten the last promotion, and she had, putting her at a higher pay grade than he was, he had been oversensitive and angry. She didn't know what she could do about it. He was trying hard to not bow to traditional Indian ideas about gender, but she could tell that this had been very difficult for him. This secret she held made it worse.

She walked down the hall, and past the main receptionist, who greeted her warmly. She went down to her office and sat at her desk. She had quite the task ahead of her. Do her regular job, as if nothing were happening, and, on top of that, help to plan how to tell the UN about the

Casitians. She had begun to articulate some ideas that her team, which included Okolo from UNICEF, and Gunther from WHO, had hashed out a bit over email. It needed a lot more work, but she thought the basic idea was viable. Orchestrate a series of meetings with the highest officials before informing any of the ambassadors and set in motion the process of mobilizing the UN to respond to the Casitians, and their conditions for environmental cleanup. Then call a general meeting with all the ambassadors, with the full details, that they would then communicate to their heads of state. The heads of state would probably not be happy finding out about this via their UN ambassadors, but the team all felt that was the best way to secure the UN's role. That large meeting would include a visit from Casitians, with open dialogue between all parties. It would also include video footage that the main communication team was working on. She was sure this video would be convincing—Nicholas Johnson, a famous documentary video and film producer was part of the video production team. She knew they were working on two videos, one for the general public, and one for governmental agencies, organizations and corporations. This second video would have much more detail on the steps that needed to be taken. Yes, she thought, it would be possible to alert a small cadre of high officials, and have it not get out. She started to consider the options, and the ways that she would put together this group. She also needed to put in place a contingency plan, in case of a leak, which she thought was not unlikely.

San Francisco, California, Earth, July 11, 2011
David walked into what felt like a completely empty apartment. Gerard had moved out two weeks ago, quite in a hurry. David was feeling devastated, betrayed and angry. He would always be in love with Gerard and would always wish they could be together. David loved Gerard even though he had always known about Gerard's ambition. It was, of course, that very ambition that had caused Gerard to spy on and betray David. David wished, in retrospect, that he'd seen that coming. But that was water under the bridge. Gerard knew what was happening, and knew about the Casitians, and planned to use that knowledge in order to win the presidential election.

They had recently discovered that someone had an ongoing tap on David's email. It had been impossible to convince Silandra, Ja'el or Erit'ala that it was a good idea to send emails that looked authentic to that account so that Gerard and the others would not find out that the tap had been discovered. But there was really no way to convince them—they were completely committed to truthfulness, disagreeing with any level of misleading information whatsoever. So they had shut the account down. David figured that whoever was spying on him had enough information at this point, and it was important to be prepared for what they might do with it.

David's role was to lead the team that was responsible for contact with corporations, particularly those that had large effects on the oceans, such as companies that caught, packaged and sold fish, companies that dumped waste of any sort into the ocean, and petrochemical companies that explored the oceans for oil and gas reserves. Some of these companies would have to be shut down, or their activities in the ocean discontinued. The Galactics were going to provide for alternative energy, so that eventually oil, gas and coal would no longer be needed. All fishing that wasn't limited kinds of fish farming would be shut down. No waste of any type could be dumped into the ocean anymore. David did not in any way relish the thought of being in boardroom after boardroom explaining why they had to radically change their business or go out of business altogether. He knew that he would be the target of many angry executives and workers who realized they had no future. He could relate: his career also had no future. But it was going to be a tough slog. It helped that Sunan Chulaborn, an executive of the BanPad Group, which packaged huge amounts of fish, was upbeat, and thought that his company would be able to adjust and be a model for others. He and David had talked about the idea of writing up a report, and perhaps doing a documentary on the changes that his corporation did, with the hope that such a report could help other companies along. But both David and Sunan knew how difficult this was going to be.

David turned on his Galactic information unit and asked the Artificial Intelligence to make a list of all companies that had anything to do with catching, packaging or selling ocean products. This was the first group that he and Sunan were going to work on. On the corporate team was also Maria Gomez, who owned a PR firm, and was going to help them shape their message most effectively. Primarily, that message was shaped around the big opportunities for Galactic commerce. David only half believed that Earth businesses could begin to enter the Galactic marketplace, but it was a good way to start. He'd had a frank conversation with Erit'ala about that. She assured him that she knew there were things that Earth humans would have to offer the Casitians in particular. She talked about food and food products as one large area of possible offerings. David didn't quite know how many companies would go into those realms and couldn't quite understand the economics if the Casitians didn't have any money. David suspected that given the advances in Galactic technology for energy and growing food, a lot of people would be happily unemployed.

San Jose, California, Earth, July 12, 2011

Joel sat at his desk, feeling uncomfortable. Laura had just left, and they were arguing bitterly about Marianne. Joel felt that it was a problem that Marianne was living on the moon, and involved with Ja'el, which meant that Marianne was probably more Casitian than Terran, and when push came to shove, which Joel thought that it would, Marianne would choose the side of the Casitians. Joel had thought that since she was the nominal leader of those who were responsible for letting the world know about the Casitians, that she compromised the whole endeavor. Earth humans had to be the priority. Laura had felt that Joel was overreacting. Laura felt so strongly about it that she had decided that it might be a good idea for them to stop seeing each other, which made Joel even more angry at the Casitians.

Joel had been far more suspicious of the Galactic culture than Laura was, and the more he learned about it, the less he liked it. Joel felt that a planet full of mostly pansexual people was not something that he was comfortable with. He imagined that most people on Earth would not be either. And, well, they didn't *do* anything. They sat around, growing their stupid little crops for themselves, and, from what Joel could tell, hung out and just simply took advantage of Galactic technology, but didn't do much themselves. They hadn't developed any new technology, the science they seemed to do was completely dependent on other Galactic species. What was wrong with them? And they wanted Earth humans to be like them? Joel shuddered. This was not what he had thought aliens would be.

He opened up his IM client, and looked to see if Dwight was around. He was available. "Dwight, how's it going? I need to talk with you."

A beep. "Yeah, I'm here. I'm surprised you are still talking to me."

Joel typed "Look, just meet me at Archie's at 7:30, OK?"

Words appeared on his screen, "OK, I'll see you then."

Joel left his computer, and went to take a shower, and get ready to meet Dwight. He felt nervous about what he was about to do, but he felt that it was important. No, it was necessary. He had to oppose the Casitians, even though their arrival had vindicated his career. He realized that he could use that to his advantage. He left behind the work of creating a plan to disseminate information to the scientific community. He didn't care much for that anymore. He got dressed and walked out of his apartment.

"Dwight, I need you to go back to Enrico, and find out who hired him." It was a dimly lit bar, and Dwight and Joel were in a back booth. Joel had ordered a whiskey on the rocks, Dwight was drinking a beer. The Giants–Yankees game was playing loudly on the big screen on the side of the room.

"You are crazy. Enrico had a hard enough time with the twenty-thousand. I don't think he ever wants to see me again."

"I need to talk with them. I'm not happy with this situation, and I want to help oppose what's happening."

Dwight peered into Joel's eyes. "What's wrong? They seem cool."

"Are you nuts? Have you read the cultural summaries that are being prepared for the UN Ambassadors?"

Dwight sighed, "No, I haven't. I've been busy researching our big database of UFOs and linking them with known activity of the Casitians over time. They match really well."

Joel yelled at Dwight, "Dwight, this is important! Don't you get what's happening? This so-called Galactic 'civilization' is going to take over Earth civilization unless we stop them! We have to stop them!"

Dwight looked surprised. "OK, OK, I'll have a look at the cultural summaries. But anyway, I'll talk with Enrico, and give him your number—right?"

Joel nodded, "yes, that's right. Thanks. We'll be in touch."

Joel quickly got up, left a partially finished drink, and walked out of Archie's, fuming. Why didn't people understand?

Moon Station, 41 Gont, 780/July 18, 2011

Jal'end'a looked out the window, as K'flef piloted the small shuttle. She had waited about as long as was possible to take this trip—it was time for her to visit Earth in person, meet with spiritual leaders, and better understand Earth human spirituality. She had come to realize that doing research on the moon wasn't going to be enough.

Her first stop was to visit with Lama Chatral Nangwa at his monastery in Dharamsala, India. She had decided to begin, and end, her tours at contemplative communities. The end of her tour was to visit a Camadolese Benedictine monastery in Big Sur, California. Patricia, whom she had already spent some time with, knew one of the monks there, and had gotten her invited. In all her research, she had felt that the contemplative and mystical traditions on Earth were the closest to what she had come to, in her own path. Spirituality on Casiti was a far less structured and organized thing: there were "schools" and traditions, and she was a part of the Gultur'we school, which was contemplative, and focused on understanding the mind and the heart by looking within, and by experience. Other schools were different and had different foci and different practices and rituals. Some schools were much more focused on rational and scientific thought and practice. But people came and went from each school freely. Even teachers might start teaching in one school, then move to another, or even mix schools in how they taught. Some of what Jal'end'a did in her own practice came from a different school, the Habi'ru school, which had specific holidays that she liked to observe.

She was brought out of her reverie by a soft jolt. They had landed, right in front of the main building. She got out of the shuttle with her small bag, and she felt a brief wind, as K'flef took off. He would pick her up in a couple of days.

She walked into the main building and saw the Lama walking toward her. "Welcome, welcome, Jal'end'a. I am so glad you have come. We are just about to start the afternoon sitting period, then after that, you can watch the dharma combat. I'll do my best to translate—but you'll probably miss some. I'm glad to answer any questions you have."

A very young monk walked in, and the Lama and that monk exchanged a few words Jal'end'a didn't understand. "Jal'end'a, this monk will take your bag to your room. I'll show you where it is later. Do you need anything else before we sit?"

Jal'end'a smiled, "no, I'll be fine." Sitting in meditation was exactly what she needed right now. She was also looking forward to talking with the Lama about some of the more interesting and complex parts of Buddhist philosophy she'd come across. She expected that this would be a good trip.

Moon Station, 50 Gont, 780/ August 1, 2011

Marianne felt like she was swimming up to the surface of her consciousness when the waves of pleasure finally subsided. There was Ja'el's face, looking at her with care. She bent down to kiss Marianne.

"It's wonderful to be here, Ja'el."

Ja'el smiled, and kissed Marianne again. As she opened her mouth to speak, a soft chime sounded on the desk. Marianne groaned.

"That must be Gita, getting back to me on the final timing of the meeting I'm supposed to help facilitate at the UN." Marianne got up from the low bed, put on her robe, and walked over to the desk, sitting down in front of the display. Gita's face appeared in the display. It appeared that she was in her car, and she looked worried.

"Hi Gita. What's going on?"

"Marianne, things are not going well. Somehow, someone leaked the information about the content of this first meeting to the US Ambassador, who is insisting on being at the meeting."

Marianne groaned. "He believed it?"

"Apparently he has some inside information from some other source that I don't know about."

"So what do you think?"

"We can't invite him. It would decrease the authority of the UN, and it would also raise the ire of a dozen other Ambassadors. I think the only thing we can do is skip the first step and move onto the big meeting."

Marianne turned to Ja'el. "Did you get that? What do you think?"

Ja'el inclined her head slightly. "Well, it sounds like the original intentions of the first meeting are now unattainable. I think it makes the most sense to move to the big meeting."

Marianne turned back to the display. "Gita, do you think you can get all of the Ambassadors as well as the high UN officials to the meeting? And set up a follow up meeting for just the officials?"

Gita nodded, "Yes, people can feel the tension in the air. The buzz is growing."

"Let's get this set up as soon as possible, before the press gets hold of this on their own."

Gita said, "OK, I'll keep you posted on the meeting schedule, so that Ja'el and Silandra can be there. Is the video ready? And what about the basic materials for the UN?"

Marianne nodded, "The video is just about done, and the basic set of documents for the UN are complete. We'll be ready to go when you are."

Gita nodded, then signed off. Marianne turned to Ja'el. "I expect that within a week, this will be public, one way or another."

Ja'el said, "Yes, I imagine you are correct. Erit'ala, Silandra and I had a joining with Ur'lef's team. They feel prepared. The first teams of dolphins are now at the station, and discussions about the needs of the dolphins have provided all of the details that are necessary right now. The AI's have adjusted all of the documents regarding human use of the oceans. Tell me more about how the, what did you call them, 'public interest spots' are going?"

Marianne thought of her joining a few days ago with Nicholas Johnson, who was producing the videos with a combination of Casitian and Terran crew and cast. "He'd screened some of the first cuts with me, and I was impressed. His expertise, and his work with Maria, the PR woman, has helped them to create very compelling videos. I really think that that these will be convincing. When I checked in with Maria, they were in the last phases of editing."

She worried a little bit about what they didn't talk much about. They had decided not to discuss in the first level of videos Casitian sexuality, in particular. They did decide that the basic family structure, which was similar to that of some cultures on Earth, would not be so foreign to people of Earth, and would be a good place to start. But they did intend to do interviews with the press and be clear about all aspects of Casitian life. People would find out, eventually. But their most important focus was the beginning of the cleanup of the environment and oceans.

Marianne looked at Ja'el, who looked back with a smile. Marianne got up, shed her robe, and got back into bed, kissing Ja'el. They lay together, side by side for a while, until they could stand it no longer. They embraced, and moved together in rhythm, as the moon continued its endless journey around the Earth.

La Jolla, California, Earth, August 2, 2011

Joanne was frustrated. She was part of the team planning the process of making liaisons between the Casitians and the scientific community. Primarily, the role of this team would be to help coordinate efforts among scientists to facilitate the cleanup of the ocean. Then, after that, their role would be to do information sharing—facilitate educational processes for Terran scientists to learn from Galactic scientists. Joanne had been excited to be on this team that was headed up by Joel, and included herself, Brit Morgan, who was a physicist that studied gravity, Kyla Morgenstern, the climatologist, and Hassan Jammar, who was a radio astronomer like Joel.

The problem right at the moment was that Joel seemed to have dropped off the planet. He wasn't answering his emails, both his home and cell phones had been disconnected, and apparently he hadn't been home in days. She'd contacted Marianne, who was trying to find out what happened. In the meantime, they could do nothing.

Further, Joanne had felt completely out of the loop in terms of the contacts that the Casitians were making with the dolphins. Joanne felt like there was so much that she could share, and explain, but they were completely uninterested in her input. She felt insulted and belittled.

Unlike many scientists studying *Tursiops*, Joanne had been convinced of their advanced intelligence very early in her career. She had to keep that understanding close to her vest. But now she was being lumped in with those who continued to promulgate the assumption that humans were the only intelligent species on the planet.

The team had a joining in two days, and unless Joel re-appeared, Joanne had no idea what would happen at that joining. She hoped that they would be able to move forward.

Moon Station, 109 Wend/August 2, 2011

"He is where?" Marianne spoke to her AI.

"Washington, DC. He is staying at a townhouse that is owned by Gerard Hopkinson."

Marianne sighed. Damn. Joel had defected. She wasn't really surprised—but she was saddened, and Joel had a lot of information that would be very useful for Gerard. She wasn't sure how she was going to explain it to Ja'el. Casitians were terrible at understanding things like this. She also had to figure out what to do with the team of scientists—they were going to be very important. She considered the options to replace Joel as leader. Joanne had an axe to grind and had been clearly angry at having been left out of conversations regarding the dolphins. Kyla, however, would make a good leader. She was as rising star in climatology and had a good dose of common sense. Marianne spoke into her unit. "Please advise Kyla Morgenstern that I'd like to speak with her at her earliest convenience."

The AI spoke "it is presently 2:45 AM in her time zone. I will leave her a voicemail message."

Marianne heard the meal chime, put the unit down, and walked out the door.

Chapter 9:
Uproar

New York, New York, August 8, 2011

The large hall was in chaos. Silandra and Ja'el had just finished their presentation. The video had been shown, and for the ambassadors and the UN functionaries the enormity of the situation was beginning to sink in. The Secretary General banged a gavel. "Please be seated" boomed out, amplified. Marianne knew that this would be projected into the earphones of participants in many different languages at once.

"Please be seated!" The sound slowly began to die out. He said, "There is one more speaker, Marianne Michaelson. She will describe, in detail, the proposed next steps." Marianne got up from her seat at the front and moved to the podium.

"Ladies and gentlemen, I know that this has been quite a shock. I know that some of you probably still don't believe this. I know that many of you are wondering what this means for the future of Earth. Let me say that I believe that the future of Earth is much more secure than it was before the Galactic Community decided to intervene. We will have help cleaning up our environment. There will be no more reason for war. Galactics have superior medical and agricultural technologies, so no one on Earth, no matter what country they live in, need die of starvation or of a disease such as Malaria or AIDS.

Yes, in the process there will be a lot of disruption. Whole industries will cease to exist. Many industries will need to radically shift the ways that they work. Many people will lose their livelihoods and careers, as I have. As Galactic culture begins to shift the way that we live and work, there will be even more changes. I imagine it will take until your children or grandchildren grow up for the changes to be complete."

Marianne looked at the audience, who were, for the moment, attentive. "But we must start, and we must start now. For the good of ourselves, as well as the good of our compatriot species, the dolphin. It is our first priority to reverse the severe damage to the ocean that is threatening the lives of the dolphins. So I will now outline the steps that we propose the United Nations take in implementing the requirements that the Galactics have placed on Earth.

First, these requirements are broad-brush requirements, and it is up to humans on Earth to implement them. But they must happen, within the timeframe specified by the Galactic Community. There are three basic requirements we must meet: a decrease in atmospheric carbon to 1960 levels, a decrease in a specific list of air and water pollutants down to levels specified, and an increase in ocean biodiversity. The good thing is that we have Galactic scientists to help us meet our deadlines—we would be completely unable to do so with our own technology. Even though it seems impossible, it can be done, but we must start now.

It seemed to make sense to us, the initial team responsible for being the liaison between the Casitians and the Earth, that the United Nations was the body that was best in position to facilitate the implementation of a plan to reach these goals. We suggest that the United Nations be empowered by the nations of the world to act to reach these goals. However, it is ultimately up to the individual countries to make those decisions, and to empower the UN to act in their territories.

You have been given a set of documents which outline and detail the goals, and the timeframe for these goals, as well as suggested steps for implementation. We are leaving the implementation in your hands. We have liaison teams for the scientific community, corporations, and the NGO sector to help facilitate their role in this transformation. There is also a leadership team, which consists of myself, David Lopez, Diana Westinghouse, and Laura Hernandez, whose role will be oversight, direct liaison with the Galactic community, and press contact. Diana will be the UN contact person.

We would, at this time, welcome any questions you'd like to ask, or concerns you want to raise."

The Secretary General stood up. "We will take a 15 minute break. We will entertain questions from the ambassadors after the break. If you wish to have time to speak, to ask questions, or raise concerns, please add your name to the list, and we will give each the floor to speak."

The din was deafening as people got up and started to talk with each other, and to talk on their phones. The word would be out in minutes. Luckily, they had arranged a full press conference after this session was over. But at this point, it was unclear how long the session would last. They had decided to delay the broadcast or webcast of the session until tomorrow, after the news broke. Marianne imagined that almost every ambassador would have a question or a concern. She wasn't looking forward to it. She thought she'd take this time to go to the bathroom and get a moment out of the din.

She walked toward the back of the hall, where she'd been told the restrooms were. She rounded a corner, and saw the large door, with the standard symbol for women on it. She walked in and was in momentary quiet. She washed her face, and as she stood upright to find a paper towel, a hand was at her right, holding one. She looked at the woman whose hand it was, smiled, and took it, and dried off her face.

"You must be under a lot of stress right now," the woman said, with a heavy accent.

"Well, in some ways, yes. It is going to be a long week. I don't think I know you."

"My name is Ritva Söderström. I'm the Finnish Ambassador to the UN."

"Hello, Ambassador Söderström. I guess you already know who I am." Marianne smiled, and put out her hand. She clasped it enthusiastically and shook it.

"It is very nice to meet you. Please call me Ritva. I just wanted you to know that there is at least one country that will be in full support of the Casitians."

Marianne smiled. "To be honest, Ritva, there are only a handful of countries I'm especially worried about. Finland wasn't on that list. But I appreciate your telling me, in any case."

"Yes, I imagine you will have your hands full with the US and China."

Marianne grimaced. "Yes, indeed, we will. Well, I think it's time to go back."

They turned toward the door, and made their way out, and back to the assembly hall.

New York, New York, August 8, 2011

Kirk Angler had made sure he was first on the list to speak. He had done some quick work, and made some important phone calls, and pulled all the strings he could. He even used some of his well-earned political capital. He had quite a bit to say, although he was saving most of it for the press conference afterwards. He had gotten the White House to schedule a very quick press conference the next day, to completely own tomorrow's news cycle.

He'd known about this all along. He had been at that early meeting with Gerard. He was an old political ally of Gerard's, and he'd decided that it made sense to hitch his wagon to his. He thought that Gerard could, if he used the information correctly, become president in this next upcoming election. And Kirk was going along for the ride, which is what he always did. He was going to use this to help Gerard and help shape the opposition to the Galactic takeover of the world. He fantasized a cabinet position, or perhaps even chief of staff.

The moderator spoke. "The representative from the United States is first."

Kirk moved forward into his microphone. "With all due respect to the Galactic community, to which Earth has not been invited, I would like to voice a real concern about the effect that these changes will have on the lives of millions, in fact billions, of people. You can't just yank out their livelihoods and lifestyles from them. This has to happen much more slowly. Give us 50 years. It can't be done in the 5-year timeframe that is required by the Galactics. The United States will not agree to this, no matter what."

The woman named Marianne looked at one of the Galactic humans, who nodded. Marianne then stood. "Believe me, I understand the kind of disruption that will happen. But no one will starve or die, because of these changes. Everyone's needs will be taken care of. We don't need 50 years to accomplish these goals."

Kirk then said, "Well, whether we need them or not, we are going to take longer."

Marianne said, "You have no choice. You must implement these changes immediately and meet the 5 year deadline."

"Why? What will happen to us if we don't?"

Marianne then looked toward one of the Galactic women. Kirk had forgotten her name. She spoke.

"If you don't implement these changes, the Galactic community will implement them for you. This will be far less pleasant to your governments."

"Well, how can you force us? Will you go to war with us?"

The woman smiled. "We do not go to war. That is uncivilized. Suffice it to say that our technology is far beyond what you can imagine. These changes will be implemented."

"So if you can implement these changes without our support, why are you bothering to go through all of this trouble in getting us to implement them?"

The woman smiled again. "Because we believe in free will and do everything we can to allow species the will to determine their own fate. However, your fate happens to include the fate of the dolphin, who is a newly introduced species in the Galactic Community. We are giving you as much room as we can, given that reality."

Kirk then said, "So in effect, what you are saying is that dolphins are more important than people. We will not stand by while this happens. We will fight, if necessary. The American way of life and freedom is at stake here." Kirk was angry, and he let it show. He got up from his chair, and stalked out of the room, into the crowd of reporters. He had plenty to tell them.

New York, New York, August 8, 2011

Marianne watched Kirk leave the room and sighed. She thought that there would be half a dozen countries that would, in fact, fight. The good thing was that they didn't realize it didn't really matter. As long as the majority of the countries gave the UN the authority to act, the technologies involved in cleaning up the environment would work fine, even if a few large countries didn't get involved. There would be the mess of the selective disabling of industrial technology in those countries that did not agree. But that was the price those countries would pay, and the Casitians would make sure that they fully understood that before it happened.

The rest of the questions were mostly mundane. China also made it clear that they would not agree with the UN. The representative from Russia, surprisingly, seemed to indicate that their country would go along. Most countries, it seemed, would need time to figure out what was best. The predictable allies of the US, including the UK, Israel, and Australia, all made noises. Marianne was reminded of gorillas beating their chests. It would be interesting to see how the countries finally made up their minds.

So, what remained was the press conference. The press didn't yet have as much information as the UN delegates had. But Marianne was sure that information was making its way already out into the press, and then into the world. She realized, in retrospect, that the minute they were forced into making this large assembly meeting, instead of having the smaller meeting with just the UN staff and officials, that was the moment it all got out of their hands. Marianne chuckled at herself. All of the time they had spent preparing for it were basically of no use. The moment had passed them by without notice. Well, here they were, and she had to make the best of the chaos.

New York, New York, August 8, 2011

Silandra watched the proceedings with interest and concern. She could see an emerging pattern. Larger, more powerful countries would resist, and most of the world would not. It was the larger countries providing a nexus of resistance that Silandra found troubling. In her many hours of analysis, Silandra had mostly been puzzled by Earth politics, and although she was learning much more as this went on, but she didn't feel like she understood it any better. Certainly, the Galactic community had its politics. She remembered the dispute between the Grentia and the K'l'l'iilith about the planet they both claimed. Some species thought the Grentia had the best claim, others felt that the K'l'l'iilith were the best stewards of the planet. There were some heated discussions, and some favors exchanged. But, in the end, the Galactic community decided that they should jointly control the planet, and both species had settlements on it, that were in harmony with each other.

Silandra was beginning to predict what Marianne had called "a mess." She tried not to encourage that set of thoughts in herself, but as the patterns began to emerge, she could see that there would be large groups of people that would be adamantly opposed to any changes in Earth societies or industry. She had known all along that there would be some resistance, and a few problems and chaos. But the patterns emerging suggested much worse. She thought that a conversation with Erit'ala was in order, as soon as possible.

New York, New York, August 9, 2011

Rita stood in the middle of the room, waiting for Marianne Michaelson and the Galactic humans to enter. Henry was also in Manhattan, having just been given the promotion to anchor a Fox news segment that was late at night. They had decided it would be best to share a hotel room, so they had booked a room at the Transcontinental, which was one of her favorites. She knew that he would be anchoring during this press conference. She hoped that she would be able to ask her questions so that he would see her.

She had tried valiantly to get people at NPR to believe her story, but no one would. Then the story broke. Because of this, she was catapulted into being the primary reporter for NPR on this story. That made her very happy. She expected that perhaps this would mean big things for her career.

She looked at her watch. It was 1:35 AM, and they had given her until 5:00 AM to get a report into NPR for Morning Edition. She was worried. If she had to, she had enough information to make a short report, but excerpts of the press conference would be key.

Another hour went by, and then she heard a lot of noise outside the room they all had been in. This suggested that the Casitians and Marianne were arriving. She had her questions ready and was hoping that one of the Casitians would be fielding questions, because she knew that Marianne would not be likely to call on her.

A large crowd burst into the room, with Marianne's tall figure obvious in the middle, and the Casitians next to her. They all arranged themselves behind the long table in the front and sat down. One of the Casitians said, "We have a short statement, then we will take questions."

The statement was very much like the information she'd gotten from that UN staffer that she had talked with. There was no information she didn't know already.

"Why are dolphins considered intelligent enough to become Galactic citizens? Our scientists don't think that is possible."

One of the Casitians said simply, "Your scientists are wrong. You did have some scientists that insisted upon the intelligence of this particular dolphin species. Most other scientists didn't listen."

Another hand went up, "Why is it that since there are more humans on Earth than on Casiti, that Earth government doesn't become the representative to the Galactic community?"

Marianne answered, "Because human civilization on Earth does not fit the criteria for membership in the Galactic Community. The environmental degradation that we are facing is only one of a number of factors disqualifying Earth society from Galactic representation."

Questions like this continued, and they were deftly answered by Marianne, or by one of the Casitian women. One of them said, "I think we've answered enough questions for tonight. It has been a very long day, and we are all very tired. We have given out information to all of you for interview scheduling, as well as more general information sharing. Please refer to those. Thank you very much for your patience in waiting until the UN assembly was over."

They all got up and left the room. Rita rushed to her sound man, checking to make sure he'd gotten a complete recording. They then both got in a cab and went to the NPR studios, where they could edit the recording, and Rita could prepare her report.

When she was done, the exhaustion that she had been pushing back finally made her stumble as she walked down into the street. She wanted to grab a cab to go back to the hotel, so she could get a little sleep. It would be a busy day of getting and lining up interviews with a variety of people, watching the news coverage, reading what was being said online, and putting together another story for the evening show. She expected that it would be important for her to file two stories a day on this for at least a week. Then, perhaps, she hoped she'd finally be moved up to a host position. She knew at least one person on Morning Edition who was leaving to join CNN. At the very least, she would be the primary person who they would depend on for news and analysis about the Casitians.

She arrived in her hotel room, to find Henry sleeping on the bed. She quietly undressed and slipped into bed next to him. She was almost instantly asleep.

She woke to the sound of a news show. She saw Henry sitting in front of the large TV in the room, watching MSNBC. That was odd, when they were somewhere with only one TV, Henry always watched Fox, or perhaps CNN, but he never watched MSNBC.

"Henry?"

He turned and looked at her. "Hi honey. Sorry to wake you. I had to see what they were saying this morning."

"Why MSNBC? I thought 'liberal wingnuts' was how you described them."

"Well, right now, they seem to be having the most reasonable coverage of this whole thing. Fox is getting weird."

"Weird?"

"Well, yes, more than usual. They are talking about the US destroying the UN as a threat to US security, and suchlike."

Rita thought a moment. "Well, I could see how they might think that. These Galactics are a real danger!"

Henry frowned. "A danger? How is that? They don't even have weapons, and what they are doing doesn't sound so bad."

Rita scowled. How could he be so naïve? "Henry, that's ridiculous. They are lying to us, and they will continue to lie to us. They are hiding some things; I just know it. I don't think the world will end up the rosy place they say it will be. They want to control us."

Henry got up. "I'm going to take a shower. There is no point in arguing about this now." He went into the bathroom and shut the door. Rita lay back in bed, pondering. She was surprised at Henry's reaction. He was usually so reasonable. So, well, conservative. She didn't like this, not at all.

Jefferson City, Missouri, Earth, August 9, 2011

Yolanda watched her sister on TV. Marianne had called her the day before, to warn her that something big was happening, and that she'd be on TV. Yolanda hadn't really believed it. But here it was: her big sister, on the TV, talking about Galactics, humans, and dolphins.

Yolanda had spent most of the past 10 years paying more attention to diapers, toys, scrapes and teaching her kids to read than she had paid attention to the world.

She was wary, though. She wondered what kind of culture those Galactics had. Especially given that there was Marianne, telling us all that Galactic human society was better than Earth human society. Yolanda didn't judge her sister, really, but her sister didn't live the lifestyle she wanted her daughters to live. She wanted them to live in a comfortable town, go to church, marry, have kids of their own. She didn't know whether this would be the kind of life Galactics lived. She doubted it. She would talk with her pastor. He would have a good answer.

The phone rang. "Hi Yo, it's mom."

"Hi mom. Did you see Marianne on TV?"

"Yes, isn't that great, my Mari on TV!"

"I don't know mom, I'm a little wary of all that."

She heard silence on the other end. "Yo, I think it will be good for all of us."

"I'm going to talk with Pastor Richard. Then I'll know."

More silence. "Yo, I think you should think for yourself sometimes."

"Mom, please, not this again."

"OK, Yo, I'll leave you alone. I have to go anyway. How are Bee and Leet?"

Yolanda sometimes hated her mother's penchant for abbreviating names. Beatrice and Leticia were her daughters. "They are fine, mom. When are you coming over to visit?"

"This weekend honey, OK?"

"OK mom. Bye.

"Bye." Yolanda heard the click and put the phone down. She could tell this might get tense between them. It didn't help that Yolanda felt that Marianne was her mother's favorite daughter, having gone to MIT and gotten a hot shot job in a big city. And all Yolanda did was stay here and have children. She sighed. Well, best not dwell on that. She had to pick up Leticia from ballet, and she knew she'd be petulant. Yolanda wanted Leticia to grow up to be a cultured woman. Leticia seemed to only want to play basketball with her friends. She said that she hated ballet. She gathered up her keys and walked out the door.

Washington, DC, Earth, August 9, 2011

Joel and Gerard sat in Gerard's living room, which had been newly equipped with several televisions, each tuned to a different news channel. Gerard had just formed an exploratory committee, a fancy term for a group of people who were going to start to raise money for his presidential primary campaign. He was coming into the race late; the primaries were only a few months away, and the other candidates had been campaigning in Iowa and New Hampshire for months already. But Gerard thought he had an advantage. Especially now that all of the Republican candidates were voicing what he would call "lukewarm" opposition to the aliens. That's the word that Gerard was going to use. Aliens. Heck, if they could use "aliens" as a term for Mexican immigrants, he certainly could use them for the Galactic humans, and their truly alien Galactic community.

Joel had turned out to be quite useful—not only as a source of information—but in other ways. It had become clear that having a scientist bitterly opposed to the Galactic community connected to his campaign was a real asset. Gerard couldn't believe his luck in connecting with Joel.

During the coming weeks, Gerard would pull out all the stops. He had a lot of information about the alien lifestyles that the press hadn't gotten yet. For some reason, the press wasn't asking the important questions about what life was like on Casiti. Some press were going to Casiti, but by the time they got back, Gerard would have told the public everything they wanted (or, really didn't want) to know about the Casitian lifestyle. Once they knew that, Gerard felt confident that the Presidency was his.

Chapter 10:
Coalescing

Moon Station, 71 Gont, 780/August 25, 2011

Marianne sat at the desk, with the large display showing multiple news shows. She was carefully observing how this was playing out. She wasn't too surprised by the range of reporting, and the way some networks were stridently opposed to them, and others much more supportive. She asked the AI to put up the most recent tally of countries that were going to work with the UN to implement changes to help reach the required goals. Very predictable, Marianne thought. Small, southern countries, with nothing to lose and everything to gain, had agreed. Nations like Finland and Sweden, more aligned culturally, saw the reasonableness of what was happening, and had also signed on, some quite enthusiastically. There were a few surprises. Russia and Israel decided to go along, and China seemed to be backpedaling from its initial stance as opposed. Marianne would be very interested to see how that finally resolved itself. India, Australia, the UK, and the Philippines hadn't decided yet. She expected them all to eventually go along. She'd had private meetings with of those heads of state and knew that their private opinions and public stances were somewhat different, given US pressure. They were on their way to signing on as well. What they were mostly concerned with was the United States, and what it would do. She had, she thought successfully, explained that it really didn't matter. The US remained staunchly opposed, as did Iraq, Afghanistan, Pakistan, Iran, North Korea, and Saudi Arabia, among others.

She sighed. She'd had a long joining with Silandra, Ja'el, and Erit'ala earlier. They had spent some amount of time talking about Silandra's concerns, and the probability of some major problems, both at a governmental level and at the societal level, primarily in the US. The election was coming up, and it was clear that Gerard was going to run and provide a major focus for the opposition to the Galactic plans. They had decided to have Marianne and Ja'el give an in-depth interview on the lifestyle of the Casitians, to take the surprise about those particular issues away from Gerard. They thought that would help, but they doubted that it would be enough. The unrest and chaos that would ensue from a US with Gerard as President was troubling.

She looked over at Ja'el, who was sleeping on the bed. One of the hardest things for her recently was knowing that this relationship with Ja'el couldn't be very long-lasting. Ja'el seemed to be very much interested in continuing the Casitian habits of having a new companion every Casitian year. Yes, that still meant that she and Ja'el had some time together, but Ja'el was due to return to Casiti in about an Earth year, in Casitian winter. And after the spending the winter together, that would be the end of her relationship with Marianne. Marianne understood this at one level, and at another found it very difficult. How could all Casitians live that way?

Marianne then thought about her own future. What was she going to do? The work on Moon station, after the chaos died down, would be mundane—even boring. She needed new challenges, new things to do. But she didn't have any of the skills Casitians had. She had been meaning to have a conversation with Erit'ala about it.

In any event, she had plenty to deal with right now. She shut off the display and slipped into bed next to Ja'el. Ja'el stirred, turned, and gave Marianne a kiss. Marianne drifted off to sleep.

San Francisco, California, September 4, 2011

"Thank you so much, Jal'end'a for coming to visit me."

Jal'end'a smiled. "Patricia, I've wanted to see this church of yours, dedicated to a mystic, for a while now. It is quite beautiful."

Patricia smiled in return, exuding quiet pride. "Yes, it is, isn't it? Thank you. It was quite the challenge to raise the money to get it built—but we finally did it." They finished the tour, then went into Patricia's office. "So, not to change the topic but... I need to ask you some questions."

"Sure, go ahead."

"We've already talked in detail about the different religious traditions of Casiti and Earth. I'm finding myself in a place where I'm having to describe Casitian religions, and I am not sure that I am doing them justice. I also have been faced, primarily by very conservative Christians, with the questions about what this means in terms of who Jesus Christ was, and who he died for. This is a very big issue for many Christians. If God is God, that means that God created all Galactic species. Some Christians think that this means that only humans fell, so Jesus only died to save humans. But that, of course leaves out other species. Others say that all intelligent creatures fell, and Jesus died for all of them. But then how do you deal with any being, human or not, who never did hear about Jesus—since, basically, the whole galaxy hasn't heard of him. Some, like the Calvinists, don't have a problem with that. Anyway, it's created quite the theological conundrum for Christians, especially. I think that Jews and Muslims have a different set of theological issues. Anyway, I have to figure out how to explain what Casitians think about who is chosen, or who is saved."

Jal'end'a was quiet for a moment, then spoke, "Patricia, we haven't ever had theologies like those that suggest that some are 'saved' and others damned. These are foreign to us. No Casitian school has a theology which suggests that some beings are 'saved' and others not, no matter what the criteria. We do have theologies of evil, and we have struggled with why evil exists in the universe. As you might imagine, given our history as slaves, that struggle with the presence of evil in the universe was a very important question for us for a long time. Different schools have settled that question differently."

Patricia sighed. "Yes, I imagined you would say something like that."

"All Casitian schools basically believe that the divine is present in all beings, small and great, all over the universe. We believe that we must respect the divine presence in all beings, and work to deepen our understanding of the divine. Some schools do that by contemplation, others by ritual and worship, others by scientific investigation. Does that help?"

Patricia nodded. "It helps, I think, but it won't help those who are conservative theologically. I do have a question, though. Would you be willing to meet with the Pope, and with the Dalai Lama?"

Jal'end'a smiled. "I would love to meet with both leaders."

Patricia furrowed her brow. "Don't think meeting with the Pope will be a cakewalk. He's very conservative." At the puzzled look on Jal'end'a's face, she said, "I mean—don't think it will be easy."

Jal'end'a grinned. "I didn't think it would be."

New York, New York, September 5, 2011

Marianne and Ja'el sat at a comfortable distance apart, obviously intimate. The producer had been very intentional in the setting and arrangement. They had explained that they felt that it was important that people know that they were involved. The interviewer, whose name was Cate Ricouki, walked into the room, and smiled at them, and sat down in her chair.

"Are you ready?"

Marianne nodded, and Ja'el smiled, "Yes, we are ready."

Cate then signaled to the producer, who looked at all of the crew, and said "We're all set, Cate."

Cate said her introductory comments, and then started the questions.

"So, Marianne and Ja'el, why are you doing this particular interview?"

Marianne said, "We felt that it was important that people learned as much as possible about life on Casiti, and how humans have been living in the Galactic community for thousands of years."

"Would you say that the lifestyle that is led today on Casiti is similar to that of a thousand years ago?"

This time, Ja'el answered. "We have been living in very similar ways for approximately twenty-five hundred years. It took us about five hundred years after being given the planet of Casiti to stabilize our society."

Cate decided to shift the questions a little. "So, give me some details of how Casitians live, then."

Ja'el then talked about basic family structure, explaining that most Casitians spent almost three-quarters of their year in their own dwellings, working, growing food, and possibly raising children.

"And the other half?"

Ja'el said, "The other part of the year is from very late Casitian fall, after the end of the fall harvest, through early Casitian spring, before the beginning of planting. During that time, Casitians who are not in the early stages of raising children, or in the later stages of their lives, find a companion to spend that time with."

"So you are telling me that Casitians spend a quarter of the year with a "companion"—would that be a lover?"

Both Marianne and Ja'el nodded.

"And then you move on, the next year? To more work, more planting, then, a different companion?"

Ja'el said, "for most, yes, basically. Remember, the Casitian year is four Earth years."

Cate nodded. "And I am to understand that at the present time, you are companions?"

It was Marianne's turn to speak. She had rehearsed this part. "Yes, we are. It was a somewhat unusual circumstance, since we are not on Casiti. Both Ja'el and I have had previous women companions, or what I would have called lovers."

"Do most women on Casiti have women companions? And I guess that also includes the corollary question, do most men have male companions?"

Ja'el shook her head. "No, not at all. Almost all Casitians have companions of both sexes during their lives."

Cate looked surprised. "So you are saying that most Casitians are bisexual?"

Ja'el nodded. "Yes. There are a few who choose companions of only one sex, but most have had companions of both sexes, and continue in that way. I've had two male companions, and three female companions."

Cate went deeper. "So do the Casitians who choose to have companions of only one sex choose companions of the same, or opposite sex?"

Ja'el shook her head, perplexed. "Why does that matter?"

Cate said, "I think our viewers will be interested."

"I'm not even sure I know. I've known people who choose to have companions of either the same or opposite sex. I imagine it's about even."

Marianne jumped in. "Actually, Kinsey would be completely unsurprised by Casiti. It's what he discovered about human sexuality

50 years ago. Most humans are bisexual, with a few on either end who are exclusively heterosexual, or exclusively homosexual."

Cate said, "Well Kinsey was somewhat discredited in his time, and people nowadays don't pay too much attention to that research. Do Casitians expect Earth humans to adopt Casitian social norms?"

Marianne had also rehearsed this. "We assume that most people in most countries will continue within their own social structures. We have no intention of imposing Casitian culture onto Earth. However, we also expect that some people on Earth will find Casitian social and family structure to be better suited to them and will adopt it."

"Don't the Casitians have anything to learn from Earth social structures?"

Ja'el visibly blanched, and Marianne looked surprised, and said, unguardedly, "Like what?" She realized her mistake too late. She knew already that the producer and Cate were interested in making the most out of the cultural clash between the Casitians and Earth humans. And that exchange was going to make it worse.

Cate said, "Well, I think that in certain circumstances, Earth humans have done well. I have come to understand that your technology hasn't improved over three thousand years, and that you depend on Galactics for all of your science and technology. It seems to me you could learn something there."

Ja'el said, "As for science and technology. Well, we were doing complex quantum physics and computational biology when you were still writing on stone tablets. Yes, most of that comes from Galactics, but we live in a Galactic Community that cooperates."

Marianne jumped in, "You wouldn't say that it was a problem that American scientists used research from other countries, like Germany or the UK, would you? I don't think they have anything to be ashamed of."

There were more questions, but Marianne realized that this was not going to be the positive interview that she had thought it would be. She had been naïve about the intentions of Cate Ricouki, and she thought that it was possible that the interview would end up being divisive. She hoped not.

Detroit, Michigan, September 5, 2011

David and Sunan were cooling their heels in the waiting room outside the boardroom. David was nervous about this board meeting. Except for the US, every country in the world that produced or bought cars, under UN leadership, had now adopted CAFE standards for cars that were dramatically better than previous standards. Some in the US car industry had called them draconian. The UN CAFE standards were such that no car sold could get less than 150 miles per gallon. The Galactics had given all of the car companies of the world a host of technologies that would allow the creation of cars that used alternative fuels, electricity, or used very little gas.

The trick would be to convince the US car companies to use that technology, and sell cars throughout the world, including inside the US. But Motors Universal, and other US manufacturers, were up against both the US government, which was asking it not to use Galactic technology, and unions, who felt that it was too much of a burden to ask their members to get re-trained so that they could build these cars. David had to first try and convince the board about the reasonableness of the new standards, the ease of transition, and the increased markets overseas, which had the higher CAFE standards. If he couldn't convince them that way, he then had to tell them that if they did not adopt the new technology, they would be shut down. He hoped he didn't get to that part.

The doors opened up, and someone beckoned them inside the room. David started the presentation he'd given to two other auto manufacturers already, to positive responses. He was stopped half-way through.

"There really is no point in trying to convince us. We've made our decision already. We will not be using Galactic technology. Period. We can still sell cars in the United States."

David sighed. "I think you need to reconsider. It really would be in your interest..."

"Save your breath. Is that all you have to say? If there is nothing more, you can leave now."

David held his breath for a moment. "Well, there is one more thing. If you choose not to adopt Galactic technology, you will be shut down."

"Who is going to shut us down? The US government is behind us!"

"The Galactics will shut you down. We cannot have cars that get less than 150 miles per gallon of gasoline on the roads. They will prevent you from making any new cars as of December 31st, unless you choose to implement the new technology."

"They can't do that! We'll get the government to intervene."

David sighed again. "There is nothing you, nor the US government, can do about it."

The chairman got up angrily. "You have no right to threaten us! Get out of here."

David and Sunan got up and left quickly. In their vehicle, they looked at each other. Sunan said, "That wasn't so surprising. They, on the other hand, will be surprised come December."

David nodded, and recorded the failure in his device.

San Francisco, California, Earth, September 9, 2011

It was late Friday night, and Patricia was writing her sermon. She hated when she had less than 48 hours for a sermon to percolate in her mind before she gave it. But in this case, she'd had no choice. The things that were happening were happening so fast. She was to give a sermon this week on the Casitians—and their spirituality. She really had learned a lot in her time with Jal'end'a, and she was becoming rather fond of Casitian theology. She was happy with the sermon, but she was not looking forward to tomorrow evening, when she was to be on a live news show opposite Jason B. Modes. He was a right-wing evangelical who had been all over the news and TV spewing hatred toward the Casitians and suggesting that they were a tool of Satan and a harbinger of the end times.

But she felt nothing except her continued sense of the mystery and wonder of God manifest in the new things they knew about the universe. And it was this feeling she was trying to convey in her sermon.

It was amazing to her how similar their views on God were to her own, and to a whole host of mystics of all traditions. Casitians did have a diversity of religious practice, but they seemed to be able to live with that diversity, and also live with a wide diversity of ideas about God and the nature of the universe. Her discussion with Jal'end'a had been fascinating, and one which allowed her to better understand why human societies ended up with such different beliefs and practices. Casitian approaches to understanding God were sometimes similar to those of Earth humans. Yet they held onto their own beliefs and opinions much less tightly than we did on Earth. She thought that perhaps we could learn something from them.

The next afternoon, as she was reading over a printout of the sermon, she heard a honk outside. She gathered up her things, walked out of her door, and into the car that had been sent to collect her. The driver greeted her, and she answered briefly. They spent the next twenty minutes in silence.

He then asked, "Excuse me, but aren't you going to talk about the religion of the Casitians today?"

Patricia smiled, "Yes, mostly. I'm also going to talk about how I think it impacts us, and our religion."

He nodded. "I think it's a good thing, really. I mean, there is nothing saying God couldn't have created more planets than this one. My pastor thinks this is all a ruse, all a big game that Satan is playing. But I just can't believe that."

Patricia answered, "I don't believe that either. The Casitians and other Galactic species have beliefs that are very similar to many of the beliefs that we hold. I think that it makes the most sense to go with a more expansive view of God. Don't you?"

He nodded. "I might visit your church sometime."

"Please do!"

They arrived at the building with the studio. Patricia thanked the driver and went upstairs to the studio. It was a surprisingly busy place, with people running to and fro, and rooms full of screens and equipment. She was guided to a smaller room that had a couple of couches, and a few people milling around.

"Reverend Warren, this is the Reverend Modes." She shook his hand, and he smiled. He seemed a nice fellow, although she knew that his ideas were far from her own. They made some small talk, as the producers and crew came in and out of the room. There was a TV monitor on the wall, with whatever was happening on the channel at the moment. It appeared to be a heated discussion between pundits about whether or not the US should oppose the Galactics.

Shortly after the makeup artist had finished with them, a producer came into the room, telling them it was time. They were directed to a larger room, with a couple of desks, and lots of cameras. She sat down where she was directed, as did the Reverend Modes, and the host, a younger man, asked them whether they were ready. They both nodded.

A crew member pointed at a digital clock on the wall behind the cameras, which was counting down from thirty. Patricia straightened up and looked at the host, ready for the conversation. She knew it was going to be difficult.

"Welcome all, to Point-by-Point. I am John Chan, and with me are Reverend Patricia Warren, of St. Julian's Episcopal here in the city, and Reverend Jason B. Modes, of Trinity Church of Christ, in Sacramento. I want to welcome you both to the show."

"Thank you, John, it's great to be here," said Jason Modes.

Patricia said, "Thank you very much, John, for this opportunity to talk about the religious issues around our new reality as a part of a Galactic community."

Jason frowned, but said nothing. John said, "Rev. Modes, may I start with you? What has the arrival of the Casitians, and the knowledge of a Galactic civilization taught you about what the truth might be, and about God?"

He straightened up, and said loudly, "It has taught me the length that Satan will go in the last days to deceive us and put in place the government of the anti-christ! Nothing that the Casitians say is true."

Patricia had to suppress rolling her eyes. She looked at him and mustered as much tolerance and compassion as was possible, given what he had just said. John turned to her, and asked, "What is your response to that?"

"What I have learned from the arrival of the Galactic humans is that God is a lot bigger, and a lot more interesting, than I originally thought. What I have learned from the Casitians is that all Galactic civilizations have some notion of the divine, or the supernatural. The structure of that belief and the structures of religious practice differ widely, just as they do here. And within most Galactic civilizations are individuals and groups with diverse notions about God.

What has been fascinating to me is that although the Galactic community has technology that is far beyond ours, and some of its societies have a recorded history that spans back from before we were even primates, they all still ask the same questions that we ask. Why are we here? How did we end up here? Who or what was behind the initial events that created the universe?"

Jason was clearly uncomfortable, and John called on him. "Reverend Modes? What do you think about what Reverend Warren had to say?"

Jason said, "I don't need Casitians to ask my questions for me. All of my answers are in my Bible. Anything that is not in the Bible is not of God, but of Satan, and a deception of Satan. God created only one Earth. Only one Adam and Eve. This is all a deception, and we will soon see what that looks like, after they have taken over the world."

Patricia looked at Jason Modes. "Excuse me Reverend Modes. The Bible says that God created the Earth. The Bible doesn't say that God didn't create others. Are you suggesting that we limit God to what the Bible actually says God did? Doesn't that limit God to human imagination? Don't you think God is bigger than that?"

When Jason pulled out his Bible, Patricia knew that she'd lost, even though most people in the audience would agree with her, in the end. But she couldn't win an argument with his worldview. The conversation continued along in that vein, with Jason quoting scripture, and Patricia having to be in the position of saying things like "Well, if you want to take it literally..."

John, thankfully, gave her the last word. "I think there is a lot to learn from the Casitians. Their systems of belief are remarkably similar to those of mystics of many traditions, including Christian. No, they haven't answered any big questions for us, but they have shown us that we have been asking the right questions all along."

She left the studio with a better understanding of what was going to happen next. Opinions were hardening. Opposition was growing, and fracturing relationships between people. Things were going to get much worse before they got better.

Tijuana, Mexico, Earth, September 12, 2011

Laura got off the plane and entered the airport. It was hot and stuffy. She remembered that the Mexican government had been having some trouble with its electricity grid. She hoped that the new Galactic power generating technology would be able to help them soon. She was in Tijuana to meet with a few NGOs, to talk about ways that they could tap into the system that the Mexican government and the UN had set up, with Galactic help, to provide people with adequate food, water and medicine. The Earth team agreed with the Casitians that this was a good avenue to provide everyone in the world the basics of living. Housing was going to be one of the hardest things to tackle. Water wasn't so easy either, but the Galactic desalinization technology could provide enough fresh water for everyone. They all knew that what was ultimately necessary was a decrease in population, but that would take decades to achieve.

A stocky man with a sign with her name on it was standing in the large group of people waiting for people to arrive.

She walked over to him, and said in Spanish, "Hello, I'm Laura."

"Hi, I'm Raul. I'm working with Citizens for Health here in Tijuana, and I've been assigned to take you to your hotel, and then take you to our offices."

"Thank you, Raul. Have you been working for CFH for a long time?"

"No, I'm new. I just moved to Tijuana about two months ago. I used to own a fishing boat and would fish off of Baja. But there was no fish to catch anymore, so I came up here. My cousin Panchita works for CFH, and when they got all of the new money from the government, she offered me a job. I like it a lot. I feel like I'm doing some good. And I can take care of my family."

"That's good to hear, Raul. We have a lot to do, of course."

Raul nodded, and showed her to his car. He opened the trunk and put her bags inside. She got in, and they started the drive to downtown Tijuana.

Rita turned the key in the lock of the door of their home. What a disaster. She slammed the door behind her and threw her bags on the couch in the living room. She'd eventually deal with them, but not now. It had been the worst month of her life.

First, Henry quit Fox. Quit! After working so hard, and getting an anchor spot, he decided that they weren't covering the Galactic story correctly. So he quit. And he got in touch with his old friend Maria Gomez, who owned a PR firm that had been working for the Casitians. She offered him a job, which he took. He had flown immediately to San Francisco, and would be living there. Rita had been taken off the Galactic beat on NPR, because, in the words of the news director, "she wasn't objective enough." In other words, she opposed the Casitians, and that showed. These things had been too much for both her and Henry, so they had decided to separate for a while. She hated how much he liked the Casitians, and she hated how much they had changed her life. She hated their lifestyles, and their smug self-importance. She hated their insistence that Terrans were inferior, and that they had messed things up for dolphins. Dolphins! What did she care about dolphins?

Erit'ala and Marianne were sitting at a table in the common dining room, having a cup of fuge. Marianne had come to like fuge. It was kind of like mocha, but kind of like tea. Maybe a mix of coffee and chai. And they used some sort of creamy thing, but she knew it wasn't milk, since they didn't have dairy products.

"Marianne, I don't think that you need to worry about your lack of scientific or technical training. Honestly, I think that the best role for you is to be involved in the human species relationship within the larger Galactic community. You have shown yourself to be quite good at organization, and good at talking to different people and helping them work together. I think you would make a very good student of the human contingent of the Sejo, for instance. When this has all settled down, and it is time for you to move on, I think you should visit Casiti.

You have done so well here. Working under one of the Sejo teachers for a time would be exactly the right thing for you. And they would appreciate your perspective and point of view."

"Thank you for your confidence Erit'ala. I am learning the Casitian language, so I hope that when I am able to go to Casiti, I'll be able to speak to everyone."

Erit'ala nodded. "Good, that's the most important part of your training at this point."

They finished their fuge, got up, and went their separate ways. Marianne felt better about things now. She felt like she had a future, apart from Earth.

Chapter 11:
Tursiops

Hol'venif, Casiti, 140 Gont, 780

Hetz'lef was in the process of harvesting his crops. He was happy with how this year's plan turned out. He had tried a couple of new varieties, and already it was clear that the result of those experiments had been quite positive. He realized that next year, quite likely, he would be trying some of the Earth food crops. He had been keeping track of what was happening in the Sol system. He had signed up to be part of a test group who would grow Earth plants next year. He had heard such wonderful things about Earth food.

He hadn't, however, heard much wonderful about Earth, although he thought that much of what he heard must be exaggeration. It couldn't possibly be that bad. People killing other people every day? Killing a more intelligent species, and a peaceful one at that? Making women act and live in specific ways? Limiting who people could become companions with? It all sounded, well, impossible. He looked forward to hearing from someone who had come back and had actually been on Earth.

In any event, he looked forward to next year, when he could try some Earth crops. The head teachers in agriculture weren't sure that the Earth plants would grow well on Casiti, but there was no way to finally know until experiments were done. They had suggested that perhaps there might be some limited tests during the winter in the communal greenhouses. Hetz'lef wanted to be sure to visit those when the time came.

He went inside his dwelling and noticed the message chime ringing. Two messages, one from Silandra, and one from Torf'ki. He read the one from Torf'ki first. Hetz'lef had brought up the idea of being companions this coming winter. Torf'ki seemed to be very interested. His message was a wonderful, playful one, full of affection, with a tinge of desire. Hetz'lef decided to set aside some time the next day to compose a message for Torf'ki. It was worth working on a good one.

He opened the message from Silandra. She was doing well and wanted to know how things were going back home. She wondered what things he was hearing about Earth on Casiti, and how people were reacting. He settled in to send her a message. He was glad they were corresponding; he was interested in her experiences and point of view.

Moon Station, 140 Gont, 780

Ur'lef got up from the display and went to the common room for the midday meal. He had been very happy about what had been going on with the parn'litd'shoms, or as the Earthers called them, 'dolphins.' Ur'lef had spent the last few days on Earth, at one of the gathering points. The AI's had finally gotten the last of the translation issues resolved, and it was relatively easy for the Casitians and the parn's to talk. He had spent a wonderful afternoon swimming with them, communicating what was happening, and describing what the next steps would be.

Ur'lef had a knack for working with other species, especially those that lived in different kinds of environments. He'd just finished work on the fifth planet of the Hulteron system. The planet was a gas giant and had a species that they called the Gl'liferon. They were a lot like the parn's in a way. They swam in the atmosphere, especially deep down in the lower layers. He had been in a specially designed ship, so that he could communicate with them. They had been the newest species before the parn's to join the Galactic community. He was still in touch with a few friends he'd made among the Gl'liferon, especially AiiAooa, who he had become very close with. AiiAooa now lived on the station close to the Hulteron system and was working with the Galactic Community.

Ur'lef went back to thinking about the parn's, and the humans on Earth. He knew that there had been a diversity of opinions about the intelligence of the parn's, but there seemed to only have been feeble attempts to help them. And when human self-interest came into play, the parns always lost. Well, that train of thought was really not especially useful, Ur'lef realized. That time was over.

He walked into the common room, looking forward to the meal. He'd heard that the group cooking this week had incorporated some apparently very tasty Earth food into the meal. Like all Casitians, he had learned that they had a natural taste for food from Earth.

They had brought up an Earth agronomist, who had helped them establish an efficient hydroponics system, based on Galactic technology. It would soon generate enough Earth produce to feed the entire station. But for now, there were just tantalizing tidbits of food. They had also found an Earth chef who was interested in working on the moon station.

There were an increasing number of Terrans that wanted to work on the Moon. Last Ur'lef heard, there were 10 Earth humans living on the moon, including Marianne, the head of the liaison team. Ur'lef hoped that no more came up. He didn't much care for Terrans, for the most part, although he got along fine with Marianne.

He went to the large hot table and took samples of the varied food that had been prepared. It all smelled wonderful.

"Hi Ur'lef. Oooh, sweet potatoes! I have been craving them enough that I might have had to go back down to Earth for a meal!" Marianne smiled at Ur'lef, and added in Casitian, "They are really good, you'll like them."

Ur'lef was surprised. She was learning Casitian? That seemed so unlike the other Earth humans he had interactions with, especially the ones from that dominant country, the one Marianne came from. He said in Casitian, "I am grateful, Marianne, I'll try them."

He took some sweet potatoes, something that Marianne told him was a kind of steamed green, and something else he was told was fermented soybeans. He sat down at a table near one of the large windows, looking out at the new construction. Re'il came by, and, with an inclination of his head, wondered whether he could join Ur'lef. Ur'lef nodded, and Re'il sat down. They both sat for a bit in silence looking at the construction activity.

Re'il finally said, "Many blessings, Ur'lef. It's been a while since I've seen you." Re'il and Ur'lef had been companions, many years ago, back on Casiti. They knew each other well.

"Blessings on you, Re'il. Yes, I've been pretty busy with the parn's, and you've been busy with the new mining project. How is that going?"

"We basically have completed the first phase. All of the basic mining equipment is in place, and we are generating several tons of raw materials for the construction project each day, so we're ahead of their demand. It feels good to have completed it so quickly. I expect I'll be able to return home before the end of Paqn. And the second phase is so easy to handle that the students I've left here can take care of it."

"That sounds wonderful. I'm looking forward to some extended time back home. I had been on Hulteron before this, and I haven't been home in a couple of years. I want to spend a year at home before I go out and work again. Luckily, there aren't any new species on the horizon for a while."

Re'il said, "Well, this assignment certainly has been, well, like getting stuck in a northern cave for the winter and wondering if one will get eaten by the garl'olia!"

Ur'lef laughed. "You really don't like it here, do you?"

Re'il frowned. "The Earth humans are worthless. I can't believe what they have done to their planet, and what kind of society they have constructed."

"Well, remember that if our ancestors had never been kidnapped, this is all that humanity would be."

Re'il snorted angrily. "It is my contention that the Tud'scla took the most intelligent and wise of the humans to be slaves and left the rest."

Ur'lef furrowed his brow. "You know that is unlikely. Besides, we had the benefit of help from, the Galactic Community. Earth humans had no such help, until now."

"You sound like you are defending them!"

Ur'lef sighed. "Re'il, I don't like them anymore than you do, but we have to live with what exists. We have to help them come to a new place of understanding. My responsibility is to the parns, and if we don't get Terrans to understand, and change, the parns will suffer."

Re'il said, "Well, I don't envy you your task. I can just work with my students, and my mining equipment, and go home when I'm done." He seemed agitated.

Ur'lef put his hand on Re'il's arm, sending calm, and love. "Re'il, you think this won't affect life on Casiti? There are 60 million of us, and 7 *billion* of them. It is inevitable that this will affect life on Casiti, in some way, eventually."

Re'il said, "Ur'lef, there will be Earth humans on Casiti when I can grow crops outside during Klef. I can't believe the Caraj would allow any Terrans on Casiti, and I don't imagine many Casitians willing to have them."

Ur'lef sighed. "Re'il, first of all, not all Terrans are problematic. Take Marianne, for instance. She is learning Casitian, has Ja'el for a companion, and seems, from what I can gather, to much prefer our culture to her own."

"Yes, there will be a few of those, I'm sure, but not many. And I don't think that any should come to Casiti without having discarded Earth culture."

"I don't know how you can control that entirely, Re'il. I'm sure even Marianne has remnants of her culture that will come out now and again. Things will change."

Re'il scowled. "I won't like them, you can be sure of that."

Ur'lef said, "Re'il—if we go about this carefully, the changes might even been good ones. Change can be good. I think we've gotten a little stagnant, honestly."

Ur'lef could tell that Re'il remained unconvinced. They finished their meal, got up, and gave each other a farewell blessing and clasped arm hug. Ur'lef was troubled. He wondered how many other Casitians had the same prejudices against Terrans. He left the common dining area and went back to his quarters to prepare for another period of time in the Earth ocean.

Moon Station, 1 Paqn, 780

Erit'ala got up from her meditation and sat at her desk, requesting information from her AI about the status of the implementation of plans at the UN. Erit'ala had been worried early on in the process, when it looked as though many countries would go against the Galactic community. Now it seemed that the United States, together with a handful of small countries, would oppose the Galactic community. Otherwise, everyone else was willing to work with the UN. They had been able to start medical and food programs going in the poorest of countries, and also begin working with local organizations to improve overall conditions for people. Most of that hadn't required very much Galactic expertise—once people had been given the permission and resources, the technologies that were already in existence on Earth had been sufficient. A few desalinization plants, and some nanobot colonies—to digest large dumps, and reclaim the land and the materials, as well as clean up waterways—had helped quite a bit. The good news was it seemed that this had helped the world take the Galactics much more seriously.

All of the wars, except the one war the United States had with Iran, who had also rejected the UN and Galactics, had stopped. Erit'ala was scheduled to go to a joining the next day to discuss the war, as well as the general question of disabling US technology. They had already delivered to the current president their ultimatum, which he had considered. It seemed that perhaps he was going to give in, after all. Marianne and Silandra had many meetings with him, and it seemed that perhaps that was helping. Marianne had tried to explain to Erit'ala the "pressures from different constituencies" that the president had to deal with. It confused Erit'ala. She thought she never would understand Earth politics. It was clear what had to be done. People were being killed, and it was silly to continue to do that. Why couldn't they understand how uncivilized war was? She was mystified.

For the most part, it seemed things were going well. The nanobot colonies that they had released into the ocean were beginning to have their effect, as had the atmospheric scrubbers. She had gotten a report from the team responsible for that work, and it seemed likely that they would reach their goals well within the timeframe originally specified. She hoped the US would go along. If it insisted on obstruction, it would have to be disabled. She didn't like that possible outcome, and didn't like the attitude of the current president, and hoped that a new president would help matters. They had been unsuccessful in working with the front runners of one of the "parties" as Marianne called them, but were working closely with the candidates of the other "party." Erit'ala shook her head. She was glad that she had Marianne to help. This would have been an impossible task without someone translating what was happening for them.

A quiet chime beeped on her display. She had a new message from Gler'yon, her companion of last year. She wondered how he was. She listened to the message, which was created in Gler'yon's wonderful style. He was so artistic. She wished she had been able to create more than the generic messages to send. She could have had her AI generate something, but that felt like it didn't really reflect her. In his message he wished her well and wondered how she was doing. He had started on a new project, which sounded fascinating. He had read about the Terran art of plays and thought that if they created plays for Terrans using Casitian subjects and stories, that Terrans might understand them better. It was a wonderful idea. Casitians had never developed that particular art form, probably because "pretending" was so difficult for Casitians. He would be coming to the moon within the year. It would be nice to have Gler'yon here. She thought, too, that this would be a perfect kind of collaborative project for Earth humans and Casitians. She took the short synopsis of the project he'd attached, and sent it off to Marianne for her information, and comment. She looked forward to hearing what Marianne thought.

Erit'ala thought a little bit about the varied reactions that she'd encountered in Casitians about Terrans. It ranged from Re'il's—who openly hated them—to Gler'yon, who wanted to take an Earth art form, and help them understand Casitians using it. That sounded enlightened of him, especially given the preponderance of people like Re'il. She wondered what kinds of other artistic exchanges she could encourage. It might help both sides. It amazed her how divided they could be, even though they were the same species.

She realized that Casitians had 780 years, or about 3000 Terran years, of peace and unity, with virtually no hard and fast divisions between them that caused conflict. On Casiti, there were always differences of opinion about all sorts of things, but Casitians seemed to be able to take all of that in stride, in a way that Terrans were not. She wondered what Casitians might be like if they hadn't had the unifying experience of captivity by the Tud'scla. Would they be just like the Earth humans? And then she remembered the Za'aref, the accursed. She shuddered and drove the thought of them from her mind. It was something the Terrans didn't need to know about.

H'terinon sat at his desk, impatient. He asked his AI about the status of the Keeelo decks. "They are within 95% of completion." H'terinon was responsible for the entire station, and lately it seemed like things were going wrong. The decks for the Keeelo were taking too long to finish. The decks for the parn'litd'shoms were also not complete. Part of the problem was that the Caraj and the Sejo seemed to be at odds over how many resources to send to the station. The Galactic council wanted as many resources as possible, so that they could provide for the parns. The Caraj, on the other hand, wanted to limit the amount of personnel required at the station, because they were afraid of too much interaction between the Terrans and Casitians. The Sejo was bowing to what they felt was the greater wisdom of the human council, but H'terinon was on the wrong end of that disagreement. He needed more students!

And, in the last message from Ril'tor, his Caraj liaison, Ril'tor made it clear that he wasn't going to get them, and he would have to make do. He explained to Ril'tor that the Caraj and Sejo could not expect things to get completed on the same timetable as originally planned. Ril'tor had bowed to the inevitable delays.

H'terinon liked his role. He liked working with the Keeelo, and he was looking forward to working with the parn's as well. He hadn't yet met a Terran, but everything he'd heard about Earth didn't really make him enthusiastic. He had even watched a bit of "television" that had been translated by AI's. It was astonishing and confusing. He had read much of the recent analysis by Casitian healers and teachers, but that didn't help much. The writing of the historians was even more confusing. Ah, well, luckily that wasn't his job.

He turned back to his display and tried to work with his AI to figure out how to get the Keeelo decks complete before the shipload of Keeelo engineers showed up in a month.

Moon Station, 1 Paqn, 780

Silandra was happy they had decided to do this joining here, on the moon, instead of on Earth. She didn't much like going down for meetings. The noise, the heat, the crowds—it was often too much for her. Around her sat three Earth humans, Maria Gomez, Nicholas Johnson, and someone she'd not met yet, Henry Reid. Maria had given her a synopsis of his story, which she had promptly forgotten, something about a strange television network. Also with her was Jur'tic, who had worked with Nicholas on the videos to show to Terrans. And Erit'ala had wanted to sit in on this joining, even though it wasn't necessary. She was taking an increasing interest in the ways that Earth and Galactic humans were communicating with each other.

"Thank you all for coming. We're here to talk about the upcoming, what did you call them?"

Maria filled in, "Public interest spots. They will primarily go on the internet, some will be broadcast."

"Yes, the public interest spots. Thank you. I understand that you have a few done, around particular themes. Shall we screen them now?"

Maria nodded. She asked the AI to project the first, which had the theme of Casitian art. It was a nice overview of the ways that Casitian art was displayed, with comparisons to Earth murals and other forms of public artwork.

"We were careful to steer clear of one particular public art form that many Terrans find problematic—graffiti."

"I've seen some art that I was told by Marianne was considered graffiti. I thought it was quite creative and wonderful. Why do some humans dislike it?"

Henry answered, "Well, many people feel it is a defacement of public or private property."

"You mean they would rather look at blank walls? That seems odd." Silandra looked genuinely puzzled.

Erit'ala asked, "Is this because the artists were not given permission to do their artwork?"

Henry answered, "Yes, basically. People who do artwork in ways that are not permitted are considered criminals, not artists."

Erit'ala said, "As you know, this seems completely strange to us. Even beginner art is better than a blank wall in a public space!"

Maria spoke next, "Well, remember that on Earth, there are few truly public spaces. Almost every space is owned, or controlled by individuals, companies or governments."

Nicholas said, "Let's move on, please? We could get caught in this kind of discussion for hours, and I have to return to Earth soon."

Silandra was slightly insulted, but let it go. "OK, let's look at the second one. This is about raising children." Maria asked the AI to bring up the second video, which they all watched.

Silandra said, "I don't think it's clear enough that the parents are not also companions. Earth humans will make that assumption, and it's the wrong one to make."

Nicholas nodded. "I agree, except I'm not sure how to incorporate that in a way that won't be too awkward."

Maria suggested, "Why not include some shots of adults gathering, in ways that include the adults' companions—so it's obvious what's going on."

Silandra said, "that sounds like a good idea."

Nicholas agreed, and said, "why don't Jur'tic, Henry and I work on revising the script for this spot." Henry and Jur'tic agreed.

They went through the rest of the spots, suggesting changes and additions, and set a timetable for completion, translation to other languages, and netcast and broadcast. Most of the TV networks around the world had agreed to broadcast these. Some networks in the United States refused, but others agreed. They would go up on video streaming sites everywhere. Both Silandra and Erit'ala were interested in the results of the videos.

Maria said, "After the videos run, we have a series of evaluation studies planned. First, a large set of phone surveys, and then some focus groups, at varied intervals. It should be interesting to see how this works."

Erit'ala said, "I'm glad, Maria and Nicholas, that you had these ideas. We would have never come up with such a technique to inform, and, as you say, *persuade* people. On Casiti, we just inform, and assume Casitians will come up with the proper decisions. But Earth humans seem not to work that way. That said, I'm beginning to be afraid that some Casitians might need *persuading* to accept Terrans. Anyway, thank you all for your work, and for a good joining."

They said their farewell blessings and went their separate ways, Henry and Jur'tic to work together on the videos, Maria and Nicholas back to Earth. Erit'ala and Silandra stayed and talked a bit and switched to Casitian.

"Silandra, I was, for a while, worried about Terrans, and how they will respond to us. Now, I am worried about Casitians."

Silandra nodded. "I understand, but I am not so worried. I think that we will all come around, soon. Especially as the Terrans become more accepting of the future." Silandra placed her hand on Erit'ala's arm, sending her emotional and psychic assessment of the other Casitians she'd talked with. Erit'ala accepted the sending and incorporated it into her own sense of what was happening. It was encouraging.

"Thank you Silandra. I'll take this all into consideration. I told you about the upcoming joining that is about this topic. Will you come?"

"Yes, I'll be there. Blessings, it's time for me to go."

"Blessings, Silandra."

They left the joining room and went to their respective quarters.

Waters Off of Baja California, Earth, 6 Paqn, 780

He was getting splashed mercilessly. The parn' named Q'q'aaliiin, which was the AI's translation of a name he couldn't hear, was playing with him.

"So... you aren't so good in water! You people think you're good at everything!" Q'q'aaliin was teasing him.

"You know as well as I do that we aren't so good at things you are good at." He dived under the parn,' tickling him on the belly, and came back up.

"But I can tickle you!"

Q'q'aalin gave a sound that the AI translated as a laugh. Ur'lef was equipped with earphones and a subvocalization pickup, with the translation system the AI's designed, so he could freely swim, and talk with the parn's. He loved it. He had been swimming with this pod all afternoon. They would take turns towing him around, and then they would stop and play some, then tow him some more.

Parn's tended to have their most complex discussions while they were deep underwater. The surface was for play. He was also equipped with a gill system, so he could follow the parn's as deep as they went, as long as they towed him, and allowed him to come. This afternoon, they hadn't wanted to. He wasn't sure why—he'd dived deep with them before.

On that previous occasion with them, where he'd spent a full day diving and playing, he learned a lot about how they felt about Casitians. They thought of humans in general as less intelligent beings that they loved anyway, they could be a lot of fun to play with, but often did mean things, so they needed to be forgiven, because they didn't understand what they did. Parn's thought of Casitians as not any more intelligent, really, but more compassionate. It had sobered Ur'lef. They didn't think of the Casitians as their saviors in any sense. They'd known that they would be saved by the Galactic Community all along. It had come as a surprise to them that the agents were humans. Ur'lef wasn't sure why or how they'd known that they would be taken care of and would join the Galactic Community. He suspected that there had been more contact with the parns than some members of the Galactic community had admitted.

Ur'lef realized that the parns would find deep friends in some of the other species of the galaxy but would probably always regard humans paternalistically.

Ur'lef had tired of the play, and decided to call it a day. "Q'q'aalin, I need to get dry."

"You go get warm and dry, and rest. You humans get so tired in the water. See you another day?"

"Yes, Q'q'aalin, I'll see you another day." Ur'lef watched Q'q'aalin and the rest of the pod swim off, then dive deep. He signaled his flyer, which appeared above him in a few minutes. The ladder came down, and he climbed on it, and was taken up into his ship. After taking off all of his equipment and drying off, he flew back to the moon, pondering the day's events.

Waters Off of Baja California, Earth, 6 Paqn, 780

He dived, deeply, with the rest of his pod. They swam in their usual formation, with the younger ones inside the older ones for protection. As they got into the colder currents, they started to communicate. They communicated to each other in a combination of sounds, movements, and energetic patterns sent between them. The conversation would not have been intelligible to even the Casitians. The one the humans called Q'q'aalin wondered if they even understood how little of their language was communicated to the humans. He gathered the oldest in the pod around him, because it was time for them to decide who would go to the big station. He had described in detail what was needed. The most important thing was to make contact with the ancient ones, the species that the humans called Kwalloo. He felt that the Kwalloo would be in the best position to help them make their way in the Galactic Community. He appreciated the intent of the Casitians, but he realized they didn't have enough wisdom to really help them.

Moon Station, 26 Paqn, 780

Jur'tic was looking forward to the second visit by Henry, the Terran she'd been working with. She liked him, because he seemed very open and willing to look at himself somewhat critically. He took far too much personal responsibility for the things that Earth humans did, like the ways in which people in his country were acting. Jur'tic didn't hold any of that against him—she appreciated him for who he was. She also learned, at one point in a very brief moment when they touched accidentally, that he had a compelling energy about him. She was drawn to him. She thought it might be interesting to see what it was like to have an Terran companion. Ja'el seemed to like it.

She felt she should be careful, though. According to him, he still had one of those lifelong companions that Terrans seemed to prefer, although he said he was in the process of separating from her. But she didn't know what stage that was, or how serious he was about it. She didn't want to step on any boundaries of his. So she would just take it slowly.

She walked into the joining room they had been using for the work. It had been especially set up for multiple screens and had a special AI who was designed for video editing. Casitians hadn't developed this particular art form. They did send video messages—either simple video recordings of someone speaking or a joining. Some people send video messages that were a mix of a video recording and animation: an artistic rendering of a person or a situation. But Casitians hadn't developed an art of *creating* stories like this on video. It was a very interesting art form to Jur'tic.

Henry had already arrived and was speaking to the AI about putting together specific small pieces of video. He looked up as Jur'tic walked in. He smiled broadly. "Hi Jur'tic. I think I've got this part down, where we include the companions. Have a look and tell me what you think."

They had gotten a number of Casitians to "act" as they called it, in certain ways. It was a bit of a challenge for some of them, but others learned quickly. Jur'tic sat down in front of the display and watched the video from the beginning. She liked what she saw. It seemed realistic.

"Yes, Henry, that's exactly right." She pointed to the screen with characters talking. "I like the way that you put them in the right place. You seem to have a feeling for how the companion custom works."

Henry looked at Jur'tic and smiled, "Yes, I think I'm learning a lot about that custom. I had a long talk with Marianne about it, when I saw her in San Francisco a few days ago."

Jur'tic inclined her head. "You did? What did you learn?"

Henry blushed. "Well, I was just, well, curious, about what it was like for a Terran to have a Casitian as a companion. Marianne told me quite a lot. She told me about something you call lyre'es'gkin. It seemed like it made things, well, a lot more interesting." He blushed again.

Jur'tic leaned forward, and put her hand on his arm, sending him curiosity. He raised his eyebrows.

"Wow." She then sent him calm. "Wow again. How did you do that?"

"We learn when we are children. It is a human trait—it is not just confined to Casitians, although some are better at it than others. Some are better senders than they are receivers. Some are better receivers than they are senders. Some are balanced. I think that you are a very good receiver, because I'm not such a good sender, but you sensed what I sent. For some reason, on Earth it is not a talent that is acknowledged or cultivated."

She still had her hand on his arm, and she considered what to do for a moment. Then she sent him affection. It wasn't what she really wanted to send. She'd wanted to send what she felt: arousal and interest.

But she thought he might get scared at that. He looked up at her, and had this odd expression on his face, a mix of surprise and incredulity. Then he began to smile again. It was a smile that made it obvious how he felt about what she sent, about her. And then she picked up his arousal, his lust. She realized then that he was also a very good sender. She thought that this was going to be an interesting day.

Moon Station, 28 Paqn, 780/January 1, 2011

Marianne and Ja'el were sitting in their quarters, watching a display that had multiple video streams and news channels. About one hundred companies, primarily in the United States, had just been shut down, because they that had refused to change some aspects of their operations. It happened at the stroke of midnight on December 31st. All of the companies had been given multiple warnings, and had visits by David and Sunam, some multiple times. Some had even had visits by Marianne. They had all flatly refused to change.

Knowing that economic disruption would result, the Casitians had partnered with many nongovernmental agencies in the US to provide food, medical care, and housing vouchers that could be used to pay rent and mortgages.

Some of the news channels from the US had debates between this pundit and that, talking about the relative merit of the shutdowns. Others, however, were only covering one side, the side of outrage. There were speeches by the presidential candidates, many of whom suggested caution before jumping to any conclusions. A couple in the Democratic race were fully behind the Galactic actions, and explained in detail why they thought it was reasonable, and what they would do as president to rebuild the economy. One candidate in particular, Gerard Hopkinson, was virulently, adamantly against the Casitians, and used this shut down to further his point of view. It was gaining in popularity. Some polls put him in front of the rest of the Republican field. And many polls suggested that a match between him and most of the Democrats would slightly favor him.

Marianne was not happy about this scenario. It had been bad enough to have a government that was moderately against the Casitians. But a

Hopkinson presidency would mean all out conflict with the Casitians. That was not something that Marianne thought would be tenable.

"Ja'el, I hope that Gerard doesn't win. I know we have a while before that might happen, but it doesn't look good now. And with people feeling displaced because their jobs have disappeared…"

Ja'el reached over, and held Marianne's hand, sending calm. "Sul, I have confidence things will get better."

Marianne remembered when she learned the word 'sul.' It was an endearment used often on Casiti by companions. It was a mix of 'love,' 'friend' and something akin to 'darling.' She liked when Ja'el used it. She felt Ja'el's calm, but also still felt her own deep unease, which she sent back to Ja'el, to show her how she felt. Ja'el responded by taking her in her arms and holding her for a while. "I know that this is hard for you. But I think it will work out. In any case, you will be fine, here, or on Casiti."

"I know, but it's hard to watch this, even though I know it won't really affect me. I worry about my family and friends." They had taken to speaking Casitian to each other, as much as Marianne could handle, and understand. Casitian didn't really have a word that was the same as 'family.' But Marianne had adopted the Casitian word that signified the group one grew up in. In English, it had been translated as 'family group,' which wasn't quite accurate.

They held each other for a while, as Marianne let the scenarios play out in her head.

Moon Station, 28 Paqn, 780/January 1, 2011

Silandra had just disconnected with her contact at the World Bank. The process of translating Galactic technology and resources to actual money that they could use had been complicated. But the UN, the World Bank, and other banking institutions had been surprisingly cooperative. They now had all of the economic resources they needed to support what they were doing in terms of humanitarian aid all over the world. Some of it was raw materials from the moon. It also helped that Galactic technology made some things, like growing food, cleaning up the environment, and providing water and health care, so much easier and more efficient. Earth companies were beginning to buy those technologies.

Silandra did a crash course in Earth economics. Things worked so differently on Casiti, and in the Galactic community in general. There was no such thing as money, per se, which the people at the varied financial institutions had found very hard to believe. The closest thing that the Casitians had to money was their access to wormholes. Some individual species did have their own monetary system, but Silandra had never worked with one of those. Casitians shared everything. They collectively contributed to Galactic exports so that collectively, they provided Casitians as a whole with access to the wormhole. Individual Casitians traveled through the wormholes on assignments from teachers, or they might get on waiting lists for pleasure trips to one system or another. The average Casitian could expect to take four or five interstellar trips in their lifetime, unless their work was such that they were often needed elsewhere. But many Casitians chose never to travel from Casiti.

One of the bankers at a large American bank that was working with the Casitians had asked her once about private property and ownership of land. It was a baffling discussion. Silandra had replied that everyone had access to enough land to grow food for themselves and others they would gift food to. The banker then asked if someone wanted to have another person grow food for many people. Couldn't that lead to the owner of the land making more money? Silandra explained that they didn't have money, and asked, "Why would anyone want to grow more food than was needed?" It went back and forth like that, the banker not understanding why no one wanted to accumulate "things," and Silandra mystified as to why people would want to accumulate "things." They both agreed that they each needed to actually physically visit the other and talk more. But that would have to wait until things calmed down.

She was still not so worried about the responses of the Casitians to Terrans, but she did know, even after all of this calmed down, that it would be difficult for the two sides to really understand each other.

Chapter 12:
Shutdown

Jefferson City, Missouri, Earth, December 31, 2012

Stan had been asked to do the third shift this evening. He was respected as one of the best managers, and the higher-ups thought that there might be some trouble overnight, since the Galactics had threatened to close the plant down. It was 11:00, and everything was going perfectly smoothly.

Stan was glad that they had installed the new monitoring system—he could see all of the conditions of the varied processes right on his laptop. Before they'd installed the system last year, he had to physically go to each of the different parts of the plant, and manually check all of the varied heat exchangers and flow meters. He did miss roaming the plant, saying hello to the workers, and "feeling" the place. Sometimes he could tell something was going to go wrong before anything registered on the instruments. He decided maybe it was a good idea to go roaming, in spite of the monitoring system. But he could take his laptop with him.

He left his office and went down the metal stairs to the main plant floor, and started his tour of the plant. He ran into a few people along the way, who smiled and waved. He liked working here—it gave him a sense of importance. He'd started out at the plant right after high school, and he felt that he knew it better, perhaps, than he knew himself.

He looked at his watch. 11:50, and all was well. He figured he'd go back upstairs to his office and watch one New Year's webcast, or another. He sat on his desk started to check his email, when some of the readings on his monitor started to change, radically. The power going to just the production processes was slowing down, although the power to the exhaust systems were intact. The phone rang. It was one of the line workers.

"Stan, we have a big problem. The power supplies to all of the production processes are, well, not working right. They aren't failing—

they are just dropping in amperage gradually. They'll be out of power in about five minutes."

Stan figured he should go down and see if he could re-start those power supplies. If that failed, he'd have to call the engineers in—that would be lots of fun. He ran downstairs, and into the room with the power supplies. By the time he'd gotten there, they were completely shut down. Then, an alarm rang, loudly. He recognized that one: the exhaust power had failed, which could lead to a deadly buildup of gases. Except—there hadn't been any production in several minutes because of the power failure of these units—so nothing bad would happen. Stan was puzzled. He then realized that what had just happened was the standard procedure for bringing plant production to a halt—except that they hadn't done it. He called the exhaust section and told them to turn off the alarm.

He went upstairs, and then called his boss. It seemed the Galactics had made good on their threat.

Jefferson City, Missouri, Earth, January 6, 2012
Yolanda hung up the phone. Her attempts to reach Marianne had not been successful. She'd left several messages over the past few hours, to no avail. Marianne's strange voicemail system sometimes baffled Yolanda. She decided to try sending an email. As she walked over to the desk that had the computer, Stanley walked into the living room. "Have you gotten hold of Marianne yet? We really need to speak to her. She's got to change the Galactics' minds about the plant."

"No, Stan, I haven't yet. I'm still trying. I'm about to send her an email."

Stanley shuffled back into the room with the TV, to continue to watch the news, nonstop. Yolanda sighed. She hated to see him this way. He was always so anchored to work, and without it he didn't know what to do. He had worked at the chemical plant since he graduated from high school fifteen years ago. He had progressed from an entry level job to managing a whole department. It had been devastating to him when the plant was shut down five days ago, on midnight of New Year's Day. She sat down at the computer, and logged in. Leticia bounded into the room.

"Mom, dad won't let me watch my show. He only wants to watch the news."

"Leticia, your father has had a horrible thing happen to him. You have to be patient."

"Well, then can I get my own TV?"

"Leticia, we don't have any money right now, your father got laid off. I'm sorry. Can you see the show at a friend's house?" She hoped this would help get Leticia out of the house. Both Leticia and Beatrice were at their wits' end, with their father being at home. It would help when they went back to school in a week.

"I'll call Felice. She might want to watch it."

"Thank you, honey. You can go over to Felice's house to watch."

Yolanda went back to the computer and typed an email to Marianne. She had been answering her email lately. She couldn't understand why she hadn't called her back.

Moon Station, 30 Paqn 780/January 6, 2012

Marianne woke up, and Ja'el wasn't next to her. Ja'el liked to eat the first meal of the day much sooner than Marianne—Marianne could usually skip it, because she got up later, and she was never hungry in the morning.

Marianne heard the insistent chime, and the soft voice of the AI. "Bright morning, Marianne. You have one hundred and twenty-five messages on Earth internet email, forty-three Earth voicemail messages, and seven Galactic messages."

Marianne groaned. She said, "Can you prioritize them for me?"

"You do have three voicemail messages and one email from your sister, Yolanda."

Marianne sighed. She knew exactly what that was about. Chap, Cue and Dot Limited, a very big chemical company, had been shut down due to their lack of interest in making any changes in their procedures or processes. Stanley, Yolanda's husband, had worked all of his adult life at one of the CC&D plants, the one in the town that Marianne had lived in once.

She asked the AI, "Please try and connect a call to Yolanda."

There was a bit of silence, then she heard ringing.

"Hello?"

Marianne spoke, "Hi Yolanda, how are you? I'm sorry that I didn't get back to you sooner, it was sleep time up here."

"I figured it was something like that—you always were prompt before. I don't know how the time is different up there."

"Well, there is no exact correspondence, since we are on Casitian time, which is totally different. I just woke up. Anyway, I know this is about the CC&D plant."

"Marianne, I know you are in charge up there..."

"No, Yolanda, I am not 'in charge.' What I do is a lot like being an ambassador. I have no control over the decisions made by the Galactics. There is nothing I can do to help Stanley, except to tell him that he should get together with the other managers and workers, and pressure CC&D to do the changes necessary for them to be restarted. There wasn't much, really. They had to install some new equipment from the Galactics that would convert their waste into inert compounds and change a few procedures so that they didn't risk spills. That's all. It's not such a big deal and would not have cost CC&D a cent, except for some staff time to help with the process of conversion. If they would rather be shut down than change, then that's their choice."

"But Marianne, hundreds of people here have lost their jobs and livelihoods. Stanley is going around the house like a zombie. He has no idea what he will do."

"Have you been down to the local aid center?"

"I won't go there! I refuse. We can manage."

"Yolanda, they are providing replacement money, food, full health services, and counseling for people who were laid off, helping them plan next steps in their lives. This could be a great thing for Stanley. He's talked about wanting to go to college—he could now."

"We always took care of ourselves. I won't get in line for any government, or Galactic, handouts."

"But isn't that what you just asked me for?"

Yolanda sputtered. "I knew I wouldn't get any help from you. I hope you are happy with all of the chaos you have caused!"

"Yolanda..." but there was nothing but dead air.

"The other side terminated the connection," the soft voice of the AI said. Sometimes, Marianne thought her AI had a very strange sense of humor. Marianne decided she needed first meal before she could deal with any more calls this morning. She got up, got dressed, and walked to the common dining space.

Washington, DC, Earth, January 6, 2012

"The Iowa Caucus is three weeks away, and the New Hampshire primary is nearly four weeks away. How do you see the shutdown of hundreds of US companies affecting your chances?" The blogger asking the question seemed young and earnest. Perhaps a bit too earnest, Gerard thought.

"Well, since I've been the candidate with the most consistent message against the Casitian alien threat, I think that people know exactly who to vote for. I'm the one who can start the process of getting those companies up and running again. I'm the one who will get the Casitians out of our country once and for all. Did you know that they have made partnerships with some non-profit organizations in the US, and that they have a presence here, even though we have rejected them? I will use force, if necessary, to get them out of this country."

"That's strong language, Mr. Hopkinson."

"This is a big problem that needs to be solved. And I know there are a lot of Americans who feel the same way. And they will vote for me." Gerard looked at his watch.

"I need to end this interview—I have a plane to catch to Iowa this afternoon—and then it's off to Michigan and Georgia. I have a lot of ground to cover."

Gerard got up and waited for the blogger to rise. He grabbed Gerard's hand, a little too enthusiastically.

"Thank you so much, Mr. Hopkinson, for the interview. I know my readers will be interested in what happens here."

"You are welcome."

The blogger turned and walked out of the room. Gerard went to his phone and called in Joel. In a minute or two, Joel walked in. "Hi Gerard. How can I help you?"

"I need you to go to Arizona, and then California, and give some speeches on my behalf. Talk with Angela. She's made the arrangements. It's with some scientist crowds. She knows the details."

"OK, Gerard, I'm on it."

As Joel walked out of Gerard's office, he was annoyed. Angela was one of Joel's least favorite people. She used to work for a Christian right presidential candidate whose name Joel had forgotten, when he ran some years ago. She still believed he should have been president. She was very pious, and very conservative, herself. She and Joel had almost come to blows about Gerard's position paper on teaching evolution in schools. They had managed to be able to work together, but it was a challenge sometimes. Gerard was attracting particular kinds of people—the Christian right, the NRA, people Joel never would normally associate with. He sighed. It had been increasingly bothering him. Something was wrong if these people made up the majority of those opposing the Casitians.

Joel had had some conversations with other groups opposing the Galactics—some scientists who thought that the Casitian science was too spiritually-based. There were others, like the libertarians, who didn't like the idea of the UN running things. But these folks would not join Gerard's campaign because of the radical right wing support he had. He'd tried to explain to Gerard that moderating his tone on moral issues would broaden his base, but Angela refused to agree, and Gerard sided with Angela.

He left Gerard's office and walked down the hall to speak to Angela. As he walked into her office, she was on the phone. She waved his hand to come in, so he did, and sat down.

"Yes, Senator, I know that you have been opposing the Galactic threat as adamantly as the candidate. He's interested in your support. Yes, Senator, he is a little bit less conservative than your positions, but he really wants to protect American freedom, and I am sure that you can support him in that. Yes, Senator. He would be happy to. Indeed. That's wonderful. I look forward to our meeting in a few weeks. I'll talk with your people about scheduling. Thank you very much, Senator Grimsford." She hung up the phone smiling.

Joel cringed. Senator Grimsford was the most conservative Senator by far. Draconian in terms of law enforcement, he supported the death penalty for offenses short of murder. He was against abortion under any circumstances, even if the mother's life was at risk. Joel never liked him much, and although he came from his old home state of Texas, Joel never voted for him. That Gerard would be aligning himself with people like that deeply disturbed Joel. As Joel looked at Angela, he was sure his face showed how he felt.

"What's wrong, Joel? Senator a little bit too conservative for your taste?" It was a mocking tone.

"Well, honestly Angela—yes, he is. But I know he's right up your alley, so to speak."

Angela smiled. "Yes, in fact, he is, and I am thrilled that our candidate is getting his endorsement. It will make a big difference in the primaries."

"And sink us in November." Angela shook her head. "Joel, November is eons away from now in the public's mind. And who knows what the Casitians will pull next. I don't think it is a danger."

"Well, the press has a short memory, but bloggers don't. Believe me, there will be blogger after blogger who will drag this out in November."

Angela started to look angry. "Joel, I am the campaign director, not you." She shuffled some papers. "The candidate wants you to speak to the Union of Nuclear Scientists in Palo Alto, California, and then there is a conference of some kind of scientists... oh, the Public Health Association, in Scottsdale Arizona. Here are the talking points." She handed Joel a piece of paper.

Joel looked them over, dismayed at their tone. "Public Health Association? Are you sure? Those people are basically pro-Galactic, because they have managed to wipe out most infectious disease in the world already! I can't use these talking points there!"

"If you feel you can't speak for the candidate, then perhaps you should find a new line of work."

He was furious. He couldn't possibly use these vitriolic talking points with a crowd of people who honestly thought that the Galactics were a positive thing. Over the past few weeks, as all of the good things that had happened in the world because of Galactic help and technology were becoming known, and started to sink in for Joel, and he had gotten less and less enamored with being in opposition. He still didn't much like Casitian culture, but it was hard for him to keep up the idea that they were a bad force. He realized that, when push came to shove, he couldn't hold the radical opposition corner. And he felt bad about the things he had done for Gerard's campaign. It was time to leave. It had been brewing for weeks, but here it was, out in the open.

"Well, I might indeed have to do just that. Goodbye Angela, I think it's time for me to quit. Give my regards to Gerard, will you?" He spun on his heel before Angela could speak, and walked out of her office, to his desk. He quickly gathered a very few personal items, feeling something vaguely familiar about all of this. He stuffed them in his backpack, and walked to the elevator, where Gerard was waiting.

"Angela tells me you are leaving us. Joel, I don't think that's a good idea."

"Gerard, I'm sorry. I've been feeling uneasy about this for a while. I'm beginning to think that perhaps the Casitians aren't so bad after all. I can't go and speak to hostile audiences with your rigid stance toward them. Plus, I can't deal with the people you are gathering around you. This whole thing is not working for me, Gerard."

"I understand what you are saying Joel, but I truly think that the Casitians are a threat to American freedom. They have a communist, morally decadent culture. I can't let our country succumb to that. And I know that there are people I would normally not agree with on my side, but we've got to find friends where we can. And I think I am the best person to lead this opposition."

"Gerard, you know that even your 'friends' would hate you if they knew the real truth about you."

Gerard's face went white. "You wouldn't..."

"No Gerard, your secret is safe with me. Just be careful about what you are doing."

"I see. Well, I'm sorry that you are leaving. I wish you the best. I do appreciate all that you've done for me, really I do."

Joel said, "Good luck, Gerard," even though he didn't really feel it.

They shook hands. Joel punched the elevator button and took the elevator down to the first floor. He went to the Metro station in order to find his way home. He'd rented a small apartment, and he had no idea what he was going to do with his life now. He couldn't go back to the Casitians, and he couldn't in good conscience belong to the opposition anymore. He needed to think.

Birmingham, Alabama, Earth, January 6, 2012

Patricia was at yet another town hall meeting of religious leaders and the public. She'd gone to more of these than she could count, all over the country. Today's meeting was in Birmingham, Alabama. This was the first one she'd been to in the South.

"I think that the Bible doesn't talk about a situation like this and can't address it. We have to use our minds and search our hearts to find the answers here."

A tall, stocky man, with balding blond hair stood up. Patricia knew him to be Reverend Jackson, the senior pastor of one of the largest churches in the United States, here in Birmingham. She thought she'd heard they had 25,000 members. Churches of that size simply staggered her.

"The Bible does talk about the lengths Satan will go to deceive, and test, mankind. Take Job, for instance. Satan took everything away from Job, to test Job. This is our test."

Patricia happened to know the book of Job well. She had taken a course on Job by a noted Job scholar in seminary and had read the book in the original Hebrew. She thought a minute how to say this so that the audience could understand.

"Reverend Jackson, using Job as an example of how far Satan will go is not appropriate." She turned to the audience. "As many of you might know, translations of the Bible from Hebrew to English are not always exactly accurate. Jews, who wrote the Old Testament, didn't have a being called Satan. The real translation for that would be "the adversary." Jews thought of "the adversary" as one who was, in a sense, like a prosecutor. One who would challenge God. And it was not capitalized. It was a generic term, not meant to be a specific being."

Reverend Jackson countered, "Well, here is these fancy-dancy people who went to fancy-dancy seminaries talking about things you can't really understand. You don't need to understand all that. The Bible says exactly what it means and means exactly what it says. Satan is Satan. Satan will deceive, and will twist, and will test us. We must not give in to Satan's deceptions. And what better way for Satan deceive us, than to supply us with cures for diseases, and all sorts of food, and good things, and leisure. And what's bringing that? A host of communist homosexuals! That is Satan's work!"

The meeting went downhill from there. The other clergy, who included a Catholic priest and an African-American preacher, who tried to be a little more conciliatory than Reverend Jackson, but they basically had the same, or similar things to say. The morality of the Casitians was suspect, and we should not adopt their values, their perspectives on God, or, really, anything they could give us. It was the road to hell. Patricia could tell that her moderate tone, and her positive perspective on the Casitians, was lost on this audience.

She walked out of the building toward end of the parking lot, where a Galactic flyer was waiting for her. She heard footsteps behind her, and she turned to see a young man trying to catch up to her. "Reverend Warren!"

She stopped. "Yes, can I help you?"

"Hi Reverend Warren. I just wanted to tell you that I appreciate your being there. There are more people than you think that agree with you, but it's just hard for people to show their support."

Patricia smiled at the young man. "Thank you, I do appreciate hearing that. It felt pretty hopeless in there."

He smiled, "I understand. Some of those people are, well, a bit out on the edge. But so many others are simply scared, and they will believe their leaders."

Patricia nodded. "I know. I hope that changes."

"So do I. Anyway, thanks!" He turned around and walked quickly back to the building. Patricia finished her walk to the flyer, and climbed in. Re'wl, her favorite pilot, was going to take her back home.

Rita entered the large corner office nervously. Here was the news director of Fox, and she had to make a good impression. She wanted this job so badly she could taste it.

"Hello, Ms. Reid, please have a seat."

"Thank you, Mr. Moore. How are you today?"

"I'm just fine, thank you. I see that you were let go from NPR a few months ago. Can you tell me about that?"

"Mr. Moore, NPR, as you know, is a news organization that has decided to not tell the public the truth but has sided entirely with the Casitians. They felt my reporting was biased, so they fired me."

"And why do you want to work here?"

"My husband always told me what a stellar news organization this is; sir, and also, I think that your reporting and opinions on the Galactic threat are really right on the money. I'm a good investigative reporter—it was me who first alerted NPR to the Galactic threat."

"Yes, Ms. Reid, I know that story, thank you. I have to tell you that there is some concern about hiring you, because of what happened with your ex-husband. I understand that he now is working with the Casitians?"

"Yes, he is. He joined the PR firm of an old friend of his, one that has been hired by the Casitians to produce public interest video spots."

"Have you spoken with him recently?"

"We talked last week. He asked to start the process of finalizing a divorce." Rita had been surprised. She had thought that perhaps it would have been possible for them to have gotten back together, even given his change in views about the Casitians. But he was not at all interested in that. He wanted a clean break. He had even mentioned something silly about visiting that Casitian home planet. Rita had been angry at him.

It seemed that Mr. Moore had possibly picked up on Rita's anger. "Ms. Reid, are you sure you are in a position at this time to report on this issue?"

She nodded. "Yes, yes, Mr. Moore, I am completely ready."

He nodded, and said, "OK, Ms. Reid, we'll give you the position. You will be on a 30-day probationary period before we will sign a contract. Is that agreeable to you?"

"Yes, yes, that's fine. I completely understand."

He got up and extended his hand. She hastily rose and extended her hand out, and they shook.

"Please go to the Human Resources department, and go through all the paperwork, when you are done with that, please show up at the Galactic news desk, on the 4th floor, to find your desk and your assignments."

Rita smiled, possibly too broadly. "Thank you so much, Mr. Moore. You won't be disappointed." She turned, and walked out of his office, and could almost whistle. A job reporting the Casitians! She could really uncover the truth. It was her wish come true.

She walked down the hall and found the Human Resources office and spent an hour or so there filling out and signing various papers, showing identification, and giving a retina scan and a fingerprint. She then went down to the fourth floor and found the head of the Galactic newsdesk, who was a very young-looking man, named Peter Tinch.

"Hello, Rita, welcome to Fox News!" He was very enthusiastic.

"Hi Peter. I'm looking forward to working here."

"Follow me, I'll show you your desk." Peter turned and started to walk back into the newsroom. Finally, they arrived in front of an empty cubicle.

"Phone, computer, etc. Probably everything you need. Your first assignment will be to research Marianne Michaelson. I understand you have a personal connection to her. We want to know everything about her. Basically, we want to do an exposé on her—how she couldn't possibly be the right kind of person to be doing what she's doing. How's that?"

Rita thought that was a project she could really do well. "Thanks, Peter, that's fine. What's the deadline?"

"Next week, on Thursday. We'd like to run it during our Friday afternoon Galactic roundup. Sound OK?"

"Yes, sounds good."

Peter smiled and walked away, leaving her to her desk and to her assignment, which she relished.

Los Angeles, California, Earth, January 6, 2012

Kyla realized that she was enjoying herself. She had the rather enviable job of contacting the scientific community, and of sharing with them the science and technology of the Galactics. This was going to allow them to catapult themselves several millennia forward in science and technology. Her team was also tasked with the process of introducing the concepts of individual and small-group farming, which was the basic way that Casitians grew their food. She was working with Gretchen Polhey, who was connected with the Food and Agriculture organization of the United Nations. It wasn't nearly as complex a problem as Kyla had originally thought. A large percentage of people in the third world already were doing it that way, and they were so happy to get new tools and technologies that made their work easier. They were able to grow enough food for their extended families with about 20% of the effort.

The first world, however, was a little harder. The increased popularity of farmer's markets, community supported agriculture, and organic produce, as well as the already popular hobby of gardening, made it easier than she had expected, especially in rural areas. And it would be many years, if ever, before most people in urban areas grew much of their own food. A small migration outward to more rural areas was needed, but not enough of a migration to strain the sustainability of those areas. Increasing the efficiency of those who provided food to urban markets, plus the introduction of rooftop gardens, and small garden plots within cities, would provide the gradual steps.

Kyla thought that it would take decades for the kinds of values that caused the Casitians to do their own farming to make their way into the minds of many people, particularly those in developed countries. She was trying, with efforts such as the video she and Gretchen were working on today. They were sitting in Kyla's office at USC.

"I don't want to be too, well, pedantic." Gretchen looked up from the video editing screen. "I think we need to cut out that short lecture on the planetary spirituality of Casiti. I think we should highlight the stuff that's Earth-based."

"Yes, I guess I see the point. Perhaps we'll also move that short piece by Patricia, the Episcopal priest, up closer to the beginning, then add that small piece on the pagan group."

Kyla liked working with Gretchen. She seemed very straightforward, and they had a lot in common. Kyla thought that this video would work well as one of the many public interest commercials that were being produced by the Casitians.

Moon Station, 30 Paqn, 780/January 6, 2012
Marianne started to wade through the large number of voicemail and email messages. They were mostly from harried UN officials, who had been harassed by varied levels of US bureaucrats, who had, in turn, been harassed by CEOs and board members of corporations that had been shut down. She kept repeating the same information, over and over again. For a few companies, shutdown was permanent and irreversible. Something that they did was completely incompatible with the environmental cleanup, and the health of the dolphins. Whalers, large fishing operations, coal and oil-based power plants, and some others were included in that list. Some companies on that list were shut down because they refused to change their operations. Motors Universal had refused to change and build cars that met the UN CAFE standards (although all of the other US car manufacturers had complied). CC&D, the chemical company that Yolanda's husband Stanley worked for, had also refused to comply to changes mandated by the Galactics.

Then, of course, there were all sorts of downstream problems. Some of the oil refiners that refused to use Galactic anti-pollution and anti-spill technologies were shut down, creating shortages of gasoline for cars and trucks.

Basically, the United States was slowly grinding to a halt. It was all preventable. Government officials, company executives, workers, and the general public were all notified, and the companies had been given almost five months in which to make these changes. There really was no excuse, except that they didn't want to change, and didn't see that the requirements that the Galactics imposed upon them as important enough. They somehow thought that there was no way that the Galactics would be able to do anything. They had vastly underestimated them.

Marianne remembered meeting after meeting where she had explained all of this. She was honestly frustrated and out of patience. Some of the voicemails were from company officials who had changed their mind and were going to implement the changes that were required. This felt good to Marianne. Perhaps, she thought, it will all work out in the end. She did wonder how long it would take, though.

One of the last voicemail messages was from the President's office, asking for a meeting. She sighed. That was one of the parts of her role she had liked the least. The current president clearly hadn't felt like Marianne was someone who should be in her role (he had, on more than one occasion, suggested alternatives). And it always felt like he thought he was talking to an inferior. But she had no choice but to answer the call and schedule a meeting with him.

"Please put a call into the President's office and set up a meeting with them according to what makes sense for my schedule," she asked the AI.

"You have several meetings in Northeastern North America scheduled three Earth days from now. Would that be a good time?"

"Yes, thank you, that's perfect." Her first work with this AI (that was, officially Ja'el's AI) had been rough, because its English hadn't developed too far. Over time, though, this AI had come to speak virtually perfect English. She didn't think that the President's office had any idea that they were not even speaking to a human being.

She liked the Galactic AI's. They seemed to be amazingly intelligent and resourceful, but at the same time there was strong consensus about their lack of consciousness. She remembered reading all of those science fiction novels about Artificial Intelligences, and emerging consciousness. What she hadn't known was that many species had tried many, many times to create intelligences with consciousness, but had uniformly failed. The current theory among the Galactics was that consciousness required biological life to emerge and was not something that could be created by any species, no matter how intelligent. This was presently a very active area of Galactic research.

"The President's office has confirmed a meeting with the President and some of his staff on the day that is Earth Monday, at 9:00 am. That will be your first meeting on that trip. For your information, that is the 32nd day of Paqn, at 3rd hour."

"Thank you. Can you set an alarm for one hour before that meeting, and set up a transport for one quarter hour before?"

"Certainly, Marianne."

She thought that the hour (which was three Earth hours) would help her get prepared. She had quite a number of meetings, mostly with varied officials at the United Nations. There was a lot to talk about these days.

Chapter 13:
Chaos

Columbia, South Carolina, Earth, January 8, 2012

Laura Hernandez sat in the too-cold office of the Columbia, South Carolina aid office. She was there as a part of her team's work monitoring the use of the aid offices and making sure that people who needed to get help were getting it. Her team's work, which theoretically encompassed the nongovernmental sector of all countries of the world, had, of late, shrunk down to working specifically in the US. Things in other countries had been handed off and were working smoothly. A few countries had inexplicably chosen to oppose UN and Galactic authority, and had excluded any UN, Galactic-related, or international aid organizations from helping people in those countries. It was frustrating to Laura, because there was no reason that the people of those countries needed to suffer. But they would.

Conversations regarding those situations were ongoing on the moon, but no decisions were being made yet. The Casitians were, it seemed, very much in favor of giving countries the right to self-determination when it did not interfere with the environment or the well-being of the dolphins. The Terrans on the team were trying to convince the Casitians that it wasn't fair for the people of those countries to suffer for the decisions of their leaders, and that the Casitians needed to step in, which they were capable of doing.

There was going to be another joining about this issue in a few days, which Laura looked forward to. She was going to try and really push the Casitians on this issue. In the meantime, she was in South Carolina, freezing to death. It was January, and because the local electric plant had just begun to make the changes necessary to keep from being shut down, it wasn't able to put out very much electricity, and there were rolling brownouts and blackouts. She was glad that all of the electric companies in the northern part of the US had agreed months ago to comply with the necessary changes. Otherwise, there would have been a very hard winter for many.

"So, we've had a steady stream of families here, and most have been eligible for replacement income and health care." The small, African-American woman, whose name was Wanita, was running this center, and had been a pleasant change from some of the other people she'd been dealing with lately. She seemed keenly interested in making sure that people in her district got the aid they needed.

"How have they seemed, coming in here? Disgruntled? Upset?"

"Most of them, yes. But many, once our caseworkers talk about the educational programs, and the fact that the replacement income is for as long as they want, until they find another job, or move onto a different career, they soften up. They are realizing that their lives actually might be better now than they were before."

Laura smiled. There was so much bad propaganda floating around, that people were taking in, hook, line and sinker. That the Casitians were lying, and would never help them, or worse things. So, it seemed, finally, that perhaps the beneficence of the Casitians was sinking in.

"Is there anything that you need, besides heat?"

"No, we are all set. We have finally gotten our quota of doctors and nurses for the health center, and we have been able to hire enough case workers and train them. I want to thank you for this visit. It's nice to know that people are paying attention."

Laura smiled. "We are trying. We've greatly increased the size of our team, so that we have enough people to travel around and see how things are going. So far, we have seen very little government interference, which we've been very happy with."

"Yes, I had been prepared for that, especially given the President's stance. But I'm getting the impression that his position is softening somewhat."

Laura nodded, and rose. "Yes, we hope so. Thank you so much for taking time out of your busy schedule here. We will be in touch. And please don't hesitate to ask for anything." She put out her hand to shake, and surprisingly, the woman grasped her forearm, and embraced her in the Galactic clasped-hand embrace. Laura had known that this was a spreading custom but was surprised to find it here.

She smiled, and said, "Farewell blessings."

"Farewell blessings to you too."

Laura walked out of the office and into her car, which she quickly started to blast the heat in. She was cold! Her next stop was Charleston. It would take her a couple of hours to get there, and she could check her email and get a bunch of work done in the process. She loved the new AI that had been installed in her car. She didn't have to drive anymore. Just tell the AI where she's going and watch the landscape roll by. She was looking forward to getting one of those new vehicles that had seats that moved and rotated, so she didn't have to feel like she was stuck behind the driver's seat. She told the AI her next destination and started on her backlog of email.

Washington, DC, Earth, January 8, 2012
"Thank you for taking the time out of what I know is an incredibly busy schedule, given all that is happening right now." The President seemed different today. Almost, well, respectful.

"I am happy to be here, Mr. President, if it will help us figure out how to get the US out of its current predicament."

"Yes, well, this is why I've asked you to be here. I have decided that it is time for the US to work with the UN and the Galactics. For one, I've been impressed by the aid that has been given to all of those that have been displaced by the shutdowns, as well as the changes in living standards for those in the third world. And, quite honestly, the fact that the Galactics were able to selectively, and completely, shut down certain companies exactly on schedule was, well, impressive."

"Mr. President, I'm glad that you have begun to change your thinking—we tried to explain all of this in detail over the past five months. But I know that sometimes it takes actual experience to change people's minds." Before this meeting, Marianne had done a perusal of the varied polls that had come out in the wake of the shutdowns. She was surprised that on the whole, especially in the most recent polls, the majority of Americans were pro-Galactic. She imagined that this was a big part of what had changed the President's mind.

"So, I've been calling quite a number of executives of the companies that were shut down and have been urging them to contact you and set up plans for accomplishing the changes required. I've also talked with some of those that were permanently shut down, to discuss plans and help on how they can find new areas of revenue generation."

"Thank you, Mr. President. Many of those companies have had departments, or units that were not affected by the shutdowns. We would be happy also to work with those companies to help them rework what they are doing. The Galactics have been very willing to lend any technologies that they have to help the Earth economy be sustainable."

"I will be giving a press conference this evening, where I will make it clear that the US government is now fully cooperating with the United Nations and the Galactics, in terms of the requirements published a few months ago."

Marianne was relieved. She had been afraid that would be another meeting full of bluster and arrogance. It was so nice that this was different. And she was gratified that basically, the last big hurdle had been jumped. Perhaps, maybe, the worst was over.

"Thank you, Mr. President. Is there anything more that I can help with?"

"No, Marianne. Please send my regards to..." he paused, thinking. "Silandra and Erit'ala."

Marianne nodded, and rose. They shook hands, and she was ushered out of the oval office. The chief of staff, John Worden, whom she'd met with several times, sidled up to her in the hall as she was making her way toward the main exit.

"Marianne, the Vice President is visiting the UN next week. Would it be possible to get a joint meeting with Silandra or Erit'ala and the Secretary General at that time?"

Marianne remembered that the VP was one of the Republican candidates challenging Gerard in the primaries. Any help she could give to him would help. It was essential that a pro-Galactic candidate won the presidential election, and the VP defeating Gerard in the primaries would basically seal the deal.

"Yes, certainly, I think we can arrange that. You know the number to call my staff, right?"

"Yes, yes, I do. I'll call. By the way, about your 'staff'.."

"Yes?"

"Well, I always seem to talk to the same person, who seems quite pleasant, and always knows who I am, but..."

"But what?"

"There is something, well, kind of funny about him."

"'Him' would actually not be accurate, although he has a male voice. 'It' would be. It is an Artificial Intelligence."

John's eyebrows raised. "Ah, I see. A computer."

"An extremely advanced computer. Yes. But it takes care of everything quite efficiently, doesn't it?" Marianne smiled.

"Yes, indeed it does. Thank you for that information and clarification."

"Certainly. I look forward to working with you, and with the rest of the White House staff."

John smiled. "As long as we're here."

Marianne walked out to the lawn, where her flyer, and K'flef, waited to take her to New York, to meet with UN officials. She could give them reassuring news about the US, finally.

Washington, DC, Earth, January 8, 2012

Gerard watched the news conference, and worried. He had been meeting with his pollster earlier today, and they had made it clear that he was likely to be able to win the Republican nomination on his anti-Galactic platform, since a majority of active, voting republicans agreed with him. But the general election would be difficult. The majority of Americans were pro-Galactic or neutral. The shutdowns had had the reverse effect than he expected, because of the availability of aid. People were taking vacations, deciding to go to college, changing their careers, and starting new businesses. In general, the shutdowns were mostly good for people. In addition, most of the companies would be up and running again quite soon, now that the president had come out pro-Galactic.

He was frustrated, and he worried about his campaign. Maybe he shouldn't be so strongly anti-Casitian. Maybe he should change his tactics. But he realized that he couldn't do that. There was no way he could win anything if he became less strident in his approach. So many of the other candidates had more governmental experience than he did, like the Vice President, who was the current favorite to win the presidency. And most of his supporters would abandon him, and perhaps even pick another, if he changed his position. He had no choice. He had to stay on his present course or drop out. He'd come so far. Dropping out just didn't seem like a reasonable option.

He called in Angela, who appeared almost instantly. Clearly, she had been waiting for him to call her in.

"Angela, I need you to contact our supporters. I need you first to assure them that I maintain my stance of being anti-Casitian. And also let them know that I will need more support—we have to begin to mount an enormous ad campaign. We need to activate Plan B."

Angela nodded. "I'm sure we'll have no problem getting them on board. Also, I am having our pollster do an independent poll, asking deeper questions, like how people feel about Casitian lifestyles, or possible hidden agendas of the Casitians."

Gerard smiled. Angela was always so on the ball. "Thank you, Angela. That will be wonderful. And contact our PR firm, and our ad agency, and have them start on the Plan B publicity. We want this to coincide with the early primaries."

"Certainly, Gerard. I think that will be in place in time for Iowa, certainly."

The Vice President was from New Hampshire, so Gerard had basically written that primary off, and hadn't even campaigned in that state, like most of the other Republican candidates. His focus was on the following week, on the Iowa caucus. If he could come in second there, he had a good chance of continuing on to win the nomination.

He remembered he had to prepare for the Republican candidates' debate, which was happening next week. "Angela, how is the debate team going? I think we set aside this weekend for preparation?"

Angela said, "Yes, and we've got everyone and everything in place so that we can be sequestered in preparation for two solid days."

"Thank you, Angela. I think that's it for now. It's late, I'm going to head home."

Angela left his office. He was tired and needed to sleep. But he also realized that he would be going home to an empty house. Juliana, his wife, was on vacation in the Caribbean with her lover, and was away for the next week and a half. And it didn't matter anyway, since he and Juliana were in a marriage of convenience. He sometimes missed David, and part of him felt terrible for what he'd done. But he couldn't let go of his ambition. He got momentarily angry. He would show everyone that he could go as far as he wanted to.

Gerard realized there was no profit in going down that road. He thought perhaps he could go down to that park he used to go to, before he met David—but it was too risky. He couldn't take any risk at all. He sighed. He was tired of satisfying himself with videos, but he felt that was the only thing he could do until he finally got into the White House. Then, he could do anything he wanted. He grabbed his briefcase, in which his assistant had put things to read for debate preparation, walked to the elevator, and out of the building to his car.

Moon Station, 32 Paqn, 780/January 8, 2012

Marianne was lying down on the pillows, her head in Ja'el's lap. A recording of one of her favorite Casitian composers was playing. She loved Casitian music. It was unique, and yet familiar. It used some of the same rhythmic structures and tones as Earth music, but in different kinds of combinations. This particular composer was one that liked to use rhythms and scales that were found in very early Casitian music, which, Marianne supposed, would be most like Earth music. This composer, H'jrefli z Wold'rene made music that was melodious and calming for Marianne. It was just what she needed.

It had been a long couple of days. She had started out her visit to Earth with a meeting with the President of the US, which had gone very well. She'd watched the news conference that evening at her mother's house, with the entire family there: Yolanda and Stanley, Leticia and Beatrice, and her mother and father. They were all glad to see her, and she was happy to hear that Stanley had decided to go to college, instead of going back to the CC&D plant, which was scheduled to re-open in a few weeks. She had always thought that Stanley had a lot more in him than being a simple manager. He had been excited to think about studying architecture, which had always interested him.

Yolanda, though, seemed unhappy. She kept talking about her pastor, and what her pastor said about the Casitians. She frowned when their mother asked Marianne about Ja'el, and Leticia then asked Marianne the innocent question of what it was like to live with Ja'el on the moon. Yolanda chose that exact time to hurry their whole family out the door. Yolanda clearly didn't want Leticia to talk much with Marianne about the moon, or about Ja'el. Marianne saw a budding tomboy in Leticia, and was reminded of herself, at that age.

Then, she'd spent the next day in more meetings at the UN, and with a few large corporations in New York. She met with the CEO of Travelbank, one of the largest banks in the US, who had some good questions about Galactic economics, questions she couldn't answer. She promised to get a joining with him and one of the Casitian economists.

She got back to the moon completely exhausted, and ready for a break. Ja'el had been so wonderful. She'd gotten some food from the common dining hall and had created a soothing atmosphere for them to eat in, and then suggested they spend some time just relaxing, and not think about anything going on. Although she'd arrived late in Earth evening, it was the middle of that Galactic day. One of the things that Marianne had the hardest time getting used to the time difference on the moon they used the Casitian system: a Casitian day was divided into eight hours, each lasting the equivalent of three Earth hours, resulting in a day cycle lasting 32 Earth hours. Because the station was on Casitian time, it was completely out of sync with Earth time. She had slowly begun to get used to it, but it was also nearly impossible to explain to people on Earth the difference in time. And the Casitian sleep cycle went along with the Casitian day. They spent about 20 Earth hours awake, and 12 asleep. When she was on the moon for extended periods, she got used to that pattern. But whenever she had to go back and forth between the moon and Earth, everything got messed up in her body and head, and she ended up exhausted and cranky.

Ja'el massaged her head, and she calmed down. She wasn't ready to sleep yet, and she was happy just to be in Ja'el's presence. In all of her meetings, she was beginning to get the sneaking suspicion that things were not going to be as smooth as she'd hoped after hearing the President tell her that the US would cooperate. There were still very solid pockets of resistance, and those were coalescing and strengthening. She knew that she needed to have a joining with Silandra, who was good at seeing patterns, as well as Ja'el, Erit'ala, David and others, to talk about what she was seeing, and to think about things they could do. But all of those thoughts began to melt away under the gentle touch of Ja'el's hands, and her lyre'es'gkin, sending calm, and something else... Marianne looked up at Ja'el and smiled. Ja'el bent her head down to kiss Marianne, who became lost in the sensations between them.

San Jose, California, Earth, January 20, 2012

Joel sat across from Dwight, who was busily eating his french fries. "Dude, are you listening to me?"

With a stuffed mouth, Dwight looked up and said, "Yes, yes, Joel, I'm listening. I just don't know what to tell you. I don't think that Marianne will ever trust you again. But then again, she forgave me, so I guess you never know."

Joel sighed. "I know, I know. I just need to figure out a way to make better what I screwed up. I really screwed up. I don't know what I was thinking."

Dwight said, "I know what you were thinking. You were jealous of Marianne, and you were pissed off at Laura. You were thinking with your..."

"Alright, already! Look, can you talk with Marianne for me? Tell her I don't expect her to forgive me, or take me back or anything, but if she can think of a way I can help, I'm willing."

"OK, dude, I will. I'm sorry that you haven't been with us. It's been fun working with the scientists. I'm almost, like, well, respected now that they realize that there really were UFOs."

Joel smiled, and was genuinely happy for his friend, who had survived years and years of abuse for being a UFOlogist. They finished their meal and said their goodbyes. Dwight took Joel in a clasped-arm hug, which surprised Joel, but he went through it. Joel walked to a house he was presently sharing with a bunch of other people. It had seemed to make sense for him to move back to San Jose, since he was so familiar with it, and most of his friends lived here. He hadn't liked DC much anyway. He got back to his house, and didn't know what to do, so he started surfing the web, the news sites, and blogs he usually read. One blogger, whom he'd started to read while working for Gerard, was talking about a new organization—the Front for Liberation from Galactics, or FLG. Joel didn't think this was too serious, but he went looking for it anyway. He found an incredibly well done website, with bulletin boards, a blog with about ten authors submitting articles, and an upcoming conference.

Joel had a thought that took him by surprise. He was a known anti-Casitian. He'd worked for Gerard, he'd made statements. He could infiltrate this organization and find out how serious they were. That was something that perhaps Marianne and rest of the Casitian team would appreciate. And he was going to be careful. He sent an email to the owners of the FLG website, indicating his interest. He started his own blog, which was something he had wanted to do for a while, and his first post was about the FLG, and other opposition bloggers and websites. He went out of his house, and walked down to the local library, and signed up for an anonymous account. He then sent Marianne an encrypted email, with a short message, that basically told her what he was going to do, and that he would contact her on a regular basis using this email account, with any information that he felt was useful to her and the Galactics. And he apologized. He felt better. Maybe he could make up for the mess he'd made.

Lubbock, Texas, Earth, January 20, 2012

Dennis' email beeped. It beeped constantly these days. He figured it was time to turn that notification off, since he was getting several hundred emails a day, now. But for some reason, he was curious what the next batch of emails had in it.

One stood out, from Joel Martin. That surprised Dennis. He knew Joel's story pretty well. SETI scientist, discredited in what was called, at the time, SETI scandal number two, but which turned out to be a signal from the Casitians. Joel had been vindicated, and had started to work for the Casitians, but had become disillusioned, so he started to work for Gerard Hopkinson, who was running on an anti-Galactic platform. Then, all of a sudden, he disappeared. He had stopped working for Gerard, but no one knew what had happened. And here it was, an email in his box, suggesting they work together.

The explanation Joel gave for why he left Gerard's campaign seemed reasonable. Joel felt that it was likely that Gerard would not win, and he felt a need for more direct action. Dennis was hearing from people all over the country, in fact, all over the world, who wanted to be involved in direct action. He wanted to meet Joel in person, and if he felt comfortable with him, he would introduce Joel to the key players of FLG. The website of FLG was designed to make people feel like the FLG was well organized, but it was mostly for show. But Dennis had put months into going into the underground of a variety of already existent movements, getting them on board. He had made contacts with conservative religious leaders, such as evangelical preachers in the US and Catholic bishops from around the world. He had connected with mullahs from a variety of Muslim countries as well, so that when the movement went international, they would be ready.

There had been planning meetings, and assessments of Galactic technology. They had come to the conclusion that they could not use any advanced weapons. They had made the assessment that Galactics likely could not deactivate firearms that did not have any electronic components. Dennis had gotten funding from a number of sources, and he had contracts with several arms manufacturers for weapons that were, in some senses, vintage. No special sights, none of the new technologies available for firearms. But there were a whole host of firearms they could use, including machine guns.

One of the ongoing disputes was how to start. Some felt that it made sense to take over the Galactic aid offices. Others thought that a takeover of the UN was a good first step, although Dennis was doubtful about that. There was a week-long retreat of the highest FLG members set up for a few weeks from now, and he hoped to get more information in preparation for that meeting. He wondered whether Joel could help with that.

He responded to Joel's email with a suggestion that they meet in person. He gave Joel a time and a place. The location was close enough to Dennis' home so that it wasn't much of a burden for him, but far enough away not to clue Joel in on where he lived. He gave Joel enough time to arrange a plane, since Dennis lived in Texas. He sent off the email and wondered whether or not Joel would choose to make the meeting.

His phone rang. "Hello."

"Hi Dennis, it's Thomas." Thomas was chair of the FLG board. He was a member of the state senate in South Carolina.

"Hi Thomas, what's up?"

"Well, you'd never believe this, Dennis. I had a brief meeting with some of the leaders of the state senate and house, and, well, a bill with a lot of co-sponsors is making its way through the system. It basically repudiates the President's position on the Galactics and solidifies an opposition to it in South Carolina. It criminalizes any Galactic funding of any program, provides for state trooper and South Carolina National Guard protection from Galactic influence of any sort. It provides for the immediate imprisonment of any Galactic agents."

Dennis was amazed. "What prompted this?"

"People down here are pretty angry at the President for going off and just caving in to the Galactics. And the Governor is willing to sign this bill—he is angry that the president never consulted him on that decision."

"How can I help?"

"I think this can spread, Dennis. I think we can pass this bill, and there are other states that can use it as a model. I think we can get at least six or more states to get on board."

Dennis didn't want to get too far into politics, though. "Thomas, you know how I feel about politics. The FLG is about direct action."

"Yes, yes, I know. Once we get a good number of states in on this, we can mobilize the FLG to help with the situation in other states. This bill, by the way, will provide for what we're calling a 'citizen militia' to fight the Galactics. That's going to be the FLG."

Dennis realized what a sea change this might cause. He suddenly wondered whether or not they could actually win.

"That's great, Thomas. Thanks for the info. Please keep me posted. We'll incorporate this into our planning at the retreat."

"You are very welcome, Dennis. Goodbye."

"Bye."

As Dennis hung up the phone, his brain started to work very fast. And he realized how Joel could be of help to him. He hoped Joel would agree to a meeting. He heard another beep of his email, and saw a reply from Joel, that was simply, "See you there, then." Dennis was elated.

Washington, DC, Earth, January 22, 2012

"I think it is of the utmost importance that we are very sure that the Casitians are truly trustworthy, and benevolent, before we agree to let them rule our country, which they are doing now. I have not seen enough evidence to convince me yet." Gerard used a strident, but measured tone to reply to the question put to him by the debate moderator.

The moderator said, "Mr. Vice President, do you have a response?"

"Yes, certainly, I do. Mr. Hopkinson, you don't take the virtual elimination of the scourges of Malaria, AIDS, and Cholera as evidence for the benevolence of the Galactics? What about the systems they have put in place to provide clean water? What about the aid centers in the US which are providing superior health care, free education, and replacement income for those displaced by the company closures? There is, in fact, not one shred of evidence that the Casitians wish us harm. They seem to be interested in our welfare. They are human, after all, and Earth is the home of their ancestors. I can't see why they would not be completely interested in our well being. And they seem willing to let us run our own country, except where it conflicts with the requirements that provide for the healthy environment for dolphins, which, I might add, provides a healthy environment for humans as well."

Gerard watched as the other candidates made similar statements. The moderator asked the next question of the Vice President. "Mr. Vice President, how do you think the Galactic environmental requirements are going to affect the economy long term?"

Gerard loved this question. This would allow him to focus on the uncertainty, because there was a lot of uncertainty in the future. The

Vice President answered it in a predictable fashion. With Galactic help, and modifications to their economy, they could get back to where they had been, or even better.

"Mr. Hopkinson, do you have a response?"

"Yes, I do indeed. We have no assurance that they will provide the kind of assistance which would allow us to fully regain our economy. First of all, Casitians are, basically, communist, and don't understand or approve of market capitalism. Millions of people have been displaced by the shutdowns, and by the downstream effects of those shutdowns. Some will be getting back to work, but many will remain outside of the economy for years. People are being encouraged to leave the economy—to go to school, or just, well, not work. That will not be good for the US economy in the long term. The environmental regulations are extremely strict and will continue to hobble companies from making useful products and providing shareholder value. There is no evidence I've seen that we will ever recover from this debacle."

This was, in fact, the truth, and they all knew it. They all were doing their best to work their way around this elephant in the room, but it was plain to everyone. Their economy would never be the same. This was one of Gerard's main points, and he had honed this particular part of his message very well.

More questions about the economy and other things related to that were asked, and answered—predictably, as Gerard thought.

"Last question, to Mr. Hopkinson. You have stated on many occasions that you felt that the lifestyle of the Casitians provided a particular danger to the United States. Can you elaborate a bit on that, please?"

This was Gerard's favorite question, and it was another question he felt that he could work well with. "Yes, I'm happy to. The Casitians have a stagnant society. They have lived in the same way for over two thousand years. They have not improved their technology, explored new galaxies. They have basically done nothing except sit around idle, grow just enough food for themselves, like poor subsistence farmers, take advantage of Galactic technology that they did not invent, and practice immorality and promiscuity. I hardly think that this is the kind of model we would like to have for our society."

"Mr. Vice President—a response?"

"Yes, thank you. Mr. Moderator, ladies and gentlemen, we are not suggesting that we adopt the moral values of the Casitians. We think that they can learn a lot from us. But we feel that the positive work that the Casitians have done here on Earth outweighs the negative aspects of their lifestyle."

The rest of the candidates had similarly weak responses, Gerard thought. Luckily, this was a Republican contest, after all. None of the candidates were going to suggest that the Galactic lifestyle was superior to ours, like some of the Democratic candidates had.

After the debate, Gerard watched multiple reactions and analyses. Fox news, of course, thought he had won the debate, hands down. Other networks, like CNN and MSNBC, were less certain. Bloggers were all over the map, but the prominent conservative ones were on his side. But they all thought that the Vice President had not held his own as well as they thought he should have. And they were all acting as if this was now a race between the Vice President and Gerard. That was good news for Gerard, as well.

Moon Station, 35 Paqn, 780/January 30, 2012

Rita's voice sounded very strained. "Henry, have you spoken to the lawyer about the house closing?"

Henry had not been looking forward to this conversation. He had been, frankly, avoiding it for weeks. "Yes, Rita, I have. She seems to think that it will all progress fine. The buyer is using cash, apparently, so the closing should happen within two weeks. Once it happens, she will add that amount to the escrow account. She will then do the final split of the escrow. She has all of your financial information."

Rita sounded as if she was going to cry. "Henry, please, is there any way we can talk about this. We need to sell the house anyway, I understand, since you are living in San Francisco, and I am living in New York. But I'd like you to reconsider making the divorce final. I love you, Henry."

Henry sighed. He still cared a lot for Rita, even given her limitations. And, ultimately, the major difference of opinion that they had about the Casitians was only the final straw for Henry. And, of course, it didn't help that he had Jur'tic to compare Rita to, which was, in a sense, completely unfair. But Henry had been unhappy in their marriage for years. He realized that it was mostly because he had been unhappy in the role he had assigned himself. Their marriage was wrapped around that role. He'd tried to be the perfect upright, conservative man that his parents had expected. He went to the right college, studied all of the right things, got the right jobs in the right places, married the right woman. Henry was happy they hadn't had children.

"Rita, I'm sorry. I still care a lot about you, but our marriage can't work. I'm not the same man you married, and, honestly, I don't think you'd like the man I've become. I can't fill that role that I so carefully made for myself. It never really fit me, and I see that now. I'm sorry that I hurt you in the process of discovering this. Someday, perhaps, you'll understand."

Henry could hear Rita crying on the other end of the phone. He hoped she didn't realize that he was on the moon. He'd been spending more and more time here, and he expected to move here in the next few weeks. He was in love with Jur'tic, and he liked being on the moon, and being among the Casitians.

"Rita, I need to go. Please take care of yourself. I know that your job at Fox will be good for you. I hope that you eventually will forgive me."

Henry waited a little bit for a response, and when none came, he indicated to the AI to disconnect the call. He worried a little bit about Rita, but he knew she would bounce back.

Chapter 14:
Opposition

New York, New York, Earth, February 1, 2011

Rita was nervous, but she tried not to let it show. She had an on-the-air report that was part of the show called, "They're Here!" The show focused on the Casitians, or, in the words of the show, the "alien threat." Her special report on Marianne Michaelson, was something she had worked very hard on. Amazingly, Marianne's sister, Yolanda, had agreed to an on-camera interview. She would only show a short excerpt of it. She was trying to get the network to set aside a half-hour slot to show the whole thing. It was pretty damning, from Rita's perspective.

Make-up had spent far too long on Rita. That made her feel, well, not photogenic. They had fussed over her hair and put on tons of different kinds of makeup. She didn't like the way it felt. She received the signal from the producer—thirty seconds. She straightened up, did a last quick check of her notes, and then waited.

"Rita Reid reports on the Galactic ambassador, Marianne Michaelson. Rita, what did you find?"

Rita looked toward the camera and did a good job of pretending that she was talking directly to the host. "Keith, what we've found was quite disturbing. Marianne has had, of course, no diplomatic training whatsoever. She graduated from MIT with a degree in Computer Science, and then worked for a large database company in Boston. She was interested in the space program, and vied for a job with APSS, or Applied Precision Space Systems, based in the Bay Area. She has held only two jobs since graduating from MIT, and both of them were jobs doing low-level computer programming. There was little management involved there, and certainly no negotiation skills or diplomacy of any type.

Marianne's only qualification seems to be that she has been connected to the space program, and, perhaps, is similar to the Casitians because she is a lesbian. We did an interview with her own sister, and here is what she said about Marianne's role:

The screen cut to Yolanda, on her couch in her home. "I really have no idea why they would have chosen Marianne. She doesn't know anyone in government, or any diplomats. All she did all day was sit and do that programming stuff. I guess maybe because those Casitians are all, well, you know they do all sorts of immoral things, and Marianne has sort of always been that way, you know."

"What do you mean?"

"Well, I remember when she was fifteen, our parents found out that she had a girlfriend. Well, it was quite an issue, I remember. Mom and Dad forbid her from seeing that girl, of course. That's what I would have done."

"Any other reason why you think the Casitians might have chosen your sister?"

"I can't think of one reason. It seems to me they should have chosen someone, well, with a bit more importance or something."

The screen with Yolanda Jones switched back to a side view of Rita, who turned her head to look into the camera again.

"Keith, we can't figure out why the Casitians would have chosen Marianne to represent them, except that, perhaps, they knew she would easily become loyal to them, which she has. I talked with several CEOs and federal officials, who felt that Marianne was not taking their concerns seriously enough. It is a disturbing issue. Requests to Marianne and the Casitians for an interview have gone unanswered."

"Thank you, Rita, for that information. You can get more in-depth information and an interactive feature on our website. Next, why you should not let that garden grow. The aliens think you should grow your own food. We think that's a throwback to the Middle Ages."

They cut to commercials. Rita relaxed, and gathered up her notes. She walked out of the studio and ran into Peter Tinch. "Nice job, Rita. I have a new assignment for you. We need to understand better this whole thing about how they raise their children. What do you think? Talk to some child psychologists, that sort of thing?"

"Sure, I can handle that. For next week's show?"

"Yes. Thanks Rita. I think you'll do fine here."

Rita smiled. She thought so too.

London, England, Earth, February 5, 2012

Augusto Sanchez paced in the hotel room. The name the public knew him by was Papa Ioannes Paulus Tertius, or Pope John Paul III. He had been elected Pope just last year, after Benedict the XVI's relatively short reign as Pope. He was the first Pope ever elected from the developing world. Of course, like all spiritual leaders in the world, he had been caught completely flat-footed by the Casitian arrival, by and all of the changes and challenges they had caused. Because he had been Pope for only a few months when the Casitians arrived, he had kept a very low profile, waiting to see what developed. His home country, Argentina, had enthusiastically embraced the Galactics, and had benefited greatly because of it. This had made Augusto even less inclined to oppose them. He had done a lot of research and had kept a careful eye on the Galactics. He didn't think it was possible to oppose them. He did have to admit he liked their stance on non-violence.

But the cardinals were having fits. Most of them, because of moral reasons, had opposed the Casitians strongly, and they wanted Augusto to publicly make the same stand. And, for the most part, Catholics from most of the world agreed with the cardinals. Augusto felt he had no choice. At the moment, he was waiting to meet a group of religious leaders who were in opposition to the Casitians. Among them was Imam Ayatollah al Kalyani, who had lately gathered together a large group of conservative and fundamentalist Muslims to fight the Casitians. Al Kalyani was from Iran, one of the few countries to oppose the Galactics, and they were working on gathering forces to actually fight them. Augusto thought this was a very bad idea. Another of the other people at this meeting was Jason B. Modes, who was becoming the leader of the fundamentalist and conservative Christian opposition to the Galactics.

One of his assistants came into the room. "Your Holiness, the meeting is ready." Augusto turned, and followed his assistant out to the hotel elevator. Waiting next to the elevator was his secretary, who inclined his head. These days, Augusto felt it hard to trust those around him. He said nothing to the secretary but did smile. The elevator came, and took them up several floors, where the meeting room was. His assistant preceded him into the room. When he walked in, everyone stood, and bowed. He sat in his seat.

The Imam started speaking in Arabic, and his translator started after a short pause. "Good morning to all of you. We join together in the knowledge that the Casitians, and the Galactic Community, are not good for the Earth. We have, perhaps, different perspectives on why this is true, but we all agree that it is not God's will that we bow to the Galactics."

Jason Modes started to speak. "I think we can all agree that the Casitians do not obey the God we obey, do not worship the God we worship. We need to make sure that they leave this planet alone."

Augusto felt called to a moderating tone. "Gentlemen. We really can't say anything about the God the Casitians worship. We differ between ourselves on this matter. I do think it is important for us to limit the influence of the Casitian culture on Earth culture. But I think expecting that they will leave this planet is rather unrealistic."

The Reverend Modes looked upset. "Excuse me, your Excellency, but I know that we can oppose them. I am in contact with a group of people who have been researching the aliens, and they feel confident that with the right tactics, we can kick them off of Earth."

Augusto shook his head sadly. "I'm afraid, Reverend Modes, that you are misinformed. Have you looked at the reports of how precisely, and completely, they were able to shut down hundreds of companies? I think you are underestimating them."

The Imam cleared his throat and started speaking. His interpreter started, "Please, each of you. Ultimately, we all agree that the aliens should not be on Earth. We all agree that we must do something to at least limit, or, perhaps, eliminate their influence on Earth. And, ideally, we can try and eliminate them. What we need right at this moment are public statements that are in solidarity against the aliens. Can we do that?"

The conversation continued, and finally a draft statement that they all agreed with was finished. They would print a full-page ad in all major world newspapers, in every language. They agreed they would get as many religious leaders as possible to sign on to the statement. The Imam and the Reverend Modes seemed gratified, and satisfied with this as the first step toward, as Reverend Modes said, "Kicking the aliens back to their stupid cold little planet." Augusto was not so sure.

Joel parked his rental car in the parking lot of the restaurant. It was a little run-down sort of place that clearly had seen better days. It was on the old Route 66, east of Amarillo. It was basically in the middle of nowhere, surrounded by nothing but cattle. There were lots of trucks parked, and a few cars.

He wandered into the restaurant, looking for Dennis. Dennis had refused to describe what he looked like but had asked Joel to send him a picture.

A muscular man, with dark red hair and stark blue eyes, came up to Joel and put his hand out.

"Hello Joel, I'm Dennis."

"Dennis, hello, good to meet you." Joel shook his hand. Dennis looked to be in his mid-40s, although he had a full head of hair, without gray. He was wearing a pretty standard Texas outfit: jeans, a western shirt, and cowboy boots. His accent sounded like he was from Texas.

"I've got a table over here." Dennis led him to a table in the back. They sat down, and a waitress came over to them quickly.

"What can I get y'all? We have a great special on T-bone steaks tonight."

Joel looked at the menu and decided that a steak would be a good idea, even though he didn't really like steak much. But he wanted to make a specific impression. "Yes, the T-bone sounds great. Medium-rare please."

Dennis looked up. "Yes, darlin', I'll have the T-bone as well, thank you. Well done, please."

Joel inwardly cringed. He could have ordered his steak better done. He wondered whether he really knew what he was doing. The waitress asked about drinks, and took their order, then took their menus and walked off.

"So, Joel, how did you find the FLG?"

"Well, as you know, I'd been working for Gerard Hopkinson, but had been frustrated by politics. First, it's not clear that he can win in November, and I think we need to do something direct, something that will have an effect. Even if he won, I think that it would take a lot to get congress to reverse what the current President has done. I felt the need to find people who are working to really get these aliens out of here. There is a blog I was reading a lot, and they mentioned you. So I looked the FLG up. I was impressed, frankly, and glad that you exist."

"So why did you defect from the Casitians in the first place? You were working with them for a while."

"Well, not so long actually. When I first heard about the whole thing, I was very skeptical. Then I heard about their lifestyles, and I really didn't like it. But I wanted to be vindicated, so I helped with that initial process to get the word out. But I was disillusioned by them, and I don't trust them. I left, and Gerard seemed the best bet at the time. But I think the FLG is better."

Dennis looked at him, weighing what he said. Joel could tell that Dennis wanted to believe him, but that there was a part of him that didn't trust Joel. He didn't know what he could do to make Dennis trust him.

The waitress came back with their steaks, and the beer that they had ordered. Joel was hungry, and the steak, even though it was less well cooked than he generally liked it, was quite tender and tasty. Joel and Dennis talked about the Casitians and about Joel's life. He didn't mention Laura. He thought it would not be a good idea to let Dennis know that there was an emotional tie to the Casitians. He had thought of Laura often, and hoped that whatever he did, he would be able to get back together with her someday.

"Well, Joel, I have an assignment for you, if you're willing. You can, if you want, see this as a test. I need to know whether we can really trust you."

Joel nodded his head. He was a bit afraid of what this assignment would be. He hoped he could actually do it.

"We are doing a raid on a small aid facility in Louisiana. We want to shut it down and see what the Galactics will do when that happens. I want you on that team. The raid will be during the business day. I have information that there will be a Galactic agent visiting that facility on a specific day. We want to kidnap the Galactic agent, and get information from them."

Joel was worried. It seemed straightforward. The question was, how to warn Marianne about it, and not tip off the FLG that the Galactics had been warned. He'd have to discuss that with Marianne.

"OK, sure, I can do that. How many others on the raid?"

"There will be three others. It will happen in about two weeks. And you will be staying with Albert Festulo, in Shreveport. He'll be expecting you 12 hours from now. Here's his address, and directions." He pushed a piece of paper with a printout of directions.

"Please give me your cell phone." Dennis put out his hand. "You'll get it back when this assignment is over."

Joel realized that he was stuck. He either could forget the whole thing, and walk out the door, or go through with this. How could he warn Marianne? He would have to figure it out, while he was driving. The good thing was that he knew no one from the Galactic team would be calling him. Joel took his phone and its holster off of his belt and handed it to Dennis. Dennis turned it off.

"OK, well, I'll either see you in a few weeks at the FLG retreat, or I won't ever see you again." Dennis had a crooked smile on his face. Joel nodded. Dennis got up from the table and walked out of the restaurant. It was clear that he did not want Joel to follow.

Joel finished his steak, took a pit stop in the bathroom, then got into his car and started driving. He realized that he could get one of those pre-paid cell phones at most convenience stores. He did a good job of making sure he wasn't followed, and in about 3 hours he found a store that had them. He bought one, and then as he was driving, called the number he knew for Marianne.

A voice he did not recognize answered. "Hello, this is the number for Marianne Michaelson, liaison to the Galactic community. How may I help you?"

Joel explained patiently who he was, and that he needed to speak to Marianne within 5 hours. He felt he needed to ditch the phone at least 3 hours away from Shreveport.

The voice said, "Please wait a moment, I will find her." He heard silence, then "Joel? It's Marianne. I got your email. What's going on?"

Joel explained what was happening, and what was going to happen. "I don't know exactly when it is supposed to take place, or which aid center in Louisiana. And I don't think I will be able to tell you, either."

"Actually, that's easy. It's the Shreveport office. Laura is the only Galactic agent slated to visit an aid office in Louisiana this month.

Thanks, Joel. We can handle it fine, it will work out, without them figuring out you warned us."

Joel heaved a sigh of relief. "Thanks, Marianne. I need to ditch this phone."

"Good luck. I look forward to hearing your report after the retreat."

"Thanks. Goodbye."

Joel took the next exit and drove down one road for just a little bit. He took the phone and used the tire iron in the trunk to smash the phone to bits. He then took some of the bits and buried them next to the road. He scattered bits of the phone over the course of 100 miles. He'd paid cash for the phone. He figured there was no way that anyone in the FLG would know he'd bought or used a phone, or that he'd called the Casitians.

He cruised fast, to make up a bit of time. He arrived at the house he'd been directed to in 11 hours and 12 minutes, with plenty of time to spare. He wondered whether or not he would get to talk to Laura.

South San Francisco, California, Earth, February 5, 2012

Henry carried the last box into the little storage pod. That was it. Most of the possessions he had taken with him after separating with Rita were in this little pod. He had no idea whether or not he would ever get this stuff out of storage. He was moving to the moon, and moving in with Jur'tic, which made him very happy. He liked the moon, liked Casitians, and finally felt useful in a way he'd never managed to feel as a journalist. He thought that perhaps he would even move to Casiti, when things on Earth settled down. He got out of the pod, closed the door, and locked it. He took out his cell phone and called the storage company and told them that it was available for pickup. He went back into his house, looked down, and saw the three bags sitting on his living room floor. That was everything he'd need for quite some time. He took out his slim Galactic communication device and called Rew'l, who had promised him a ride up to the moon. Rew'l appeared.

"You're ready?" Henry nodded.

"I'll be right there."

Henry wandered around the house for a while, remembering the short time he'd lived there. He moved out to the Bay Area to work with

Maria Gomez only four months ago and rented this little furnished house in South San Francisco. He'd never really settled in; he never really got to know the neighborhood, or the neighbors. He spent most of his time either in San Francisco, at the offices of Maria's company, or on the moon.

He picked his bags up and left the keys on the table in the hall. He closed the door and walked out toward the street. A gust of wind signaled the arrival of the flyer with Rew'l. An oblong door appeared, and he entered it.

Moon Station, 46 Paqn, 780/February 5, 2012

This joining was turning out to be much more difficult than Marianne had anticipated. She kept forgetting, for some reason, the Casitian's aversion to subterfuge. They couldn't understand Joel spying on the Earth organization for them, they couldn't understand why Marianne wanted to set things up so that the people doing the raid would fail, but also would not be able to tell that it was because the Casitians had been warned.

Silandra said, "Marianne, we don't understand why we should not just shut down that aid center, now that we know it is a target."

"Because then they would know that Joel warned us. That would put him in great danger."

"Why? Would they hurt him because he told us the truth?"

Marianne was exasperated. Ja'el tried to come to the rescue. "Why don't we not worry about the reasons, and just try and do what Marianne wants."

Silandra shook her head. "That would be against our principles, and we have been told quite strongly by the Caraj that we cannot act in ways that are against our principles. I cannot allow it."

Marianne said, "So what can we do?"

Silandra looked sad. "We need to simply shut down that office, now that we know it is a target. Laura cannot visit."

"But they might target other aid centers. If we don't have Joel to warn us ..."

Laura spoke up. "What if we do nothing?"

Marianne looked at Laura, surprised. "But you would be at great risk."

"I trust Joel. I think he would prevent anything horrible from happening."

Marianne said, "But Joel will be with other people, people he doesn't know. I don't think he will be in control."

Laura looked at Silandra "Is there something that you can give me that will protect me?"

Silandra thought a moment, then nodded. "Yes, we have a device that will basically put everyone within a given radius to sleep immediately, except the person using the device. And there is an antidote, to wake selected people up."

Marianne had her answer. "Then we should do nothing but give Laura this device to use as she sees fit. That would still be within your principles, wouldn't it?"

Silandra looked doubtful but nodded slowly. "Marianne, I don't like this very much, but I will allow it. Laura, talk to G'rrilzi, He will show you the device."

Marianne thought that perhaps, in the end, this might all work out.

Shreveport, Louisiana, Earth, February 6—17, 2012

Joel had company almost all of the time. They clearly didn't trust him. He wondered whether they thought that perhaps he'd made some contact with people during his drive here, but they didn't ask, or mention it. They had, however, searched him and his car.

They hadn't told him yet which day they were going to do the raid, but he had been briefed about the procedure. They would go in with their weapons concealed, acting as if they were trying to get aid. They would then take over the center and find the Galactic agent. Joel, it turned out, would be securing the door. He didn't like that he might be far away from Laura, but Marianne had been warned, and he would do what he could to protect Laura.

The days wore on, and more than a week had gone by. He was starting to get bored. One day, he was shaken awake. "Today's the day, dude! Get up! We're leaving in one hour."

He showered, got dressed, and went to the living room to get his firearm. He'd had to practice at a firing range, since he'd never used a gun before. He went outside, where the other men were gathering and getting into the car. He got in the back.

It was a short drive to the center. They parked the car in the back, in an alley behind the aid center. They walked around to the front. The center seemed deserted. Joel saw a flyer parked on the lawn across from the center. So, they hadn't shut the center down. He'd been afraid that the Galactics might do that, instead of helping him.

They walked casually into the center, as they'd discussed. Joel looked around. There were two people waiting in the waiting area, and one person talking to a caseworker. The rest of the building seemed to be empty of people.

Albert, who was the leader of this group shouted, "Everyone! This is a raid! Hands up in the air!" One of the other men had plastic handcuffs, which they used to tie the hands of the caseworker and the three clients. Joel stood just inside the door, guarding it and looking out in case someone came in. The last man, someone named Leo that Joel had not liked at all, went into the back. In a few minutes, Joel saw a woman and Laura walking into the front. They were both quickly tied with handcuffs.

Leo said to Joel, "Which bitch is the Galactic agent?" Joel was surprised. There wasn't necessarily any reason that Joel would know who it was. He had told Dennis he had worked for the Galactics for a very short time and had gotten to know only a very few people who were agents. But in this case, he knew very well who it was. He struggled, and looked at them both, pretending to try and figure it out. He didn't want to give Laura away.

"I don't know, Leo, I don't know either of these women. Sorry."

Leo looked angrily at the woman who was not Laura and held his gun to her head. "I bet it's you, is it?"

Laura intervened. "No, it's me. I'm the Galactic agent. My name is Laura Hernandez." Leo threw the other woman down, and pointed his gun at Laura, who looked surprisingly calm.

"Good, good. Joel, you have your assignment, and I have mine. He pulled the safety off of his gun, and Joel began to leap in his direction, when everything went black.

He had a splitting headache. Everything was swimming in front of his face. He heard in the background "Shit, shit, shit." He tried to get up, but he couldn't really see anything. He heard sirens. Oh, no, the police. He was carrying a weapon, and he'd been part of a raid. That woke him up more, and he took in what was in front of him. The only people in the center were the four men. Everyone else—Laura, the caseworker, and the clients—were gone. Joel stumbled up and lurched toward the back door, and the others seemed to be following. Albert had been driving, and he got into the car, and got it started. They drove into a different alley, and slowly emerged onto a street a couple of blocks away from the center. Albert tried to nonchalantly drive the car toward the highway and back to his house. Joel was shaking uncontrollably. What had he gotten himself into?

Moon Station, 50 Paqn, 780/February 18, 2012

Laura was sitting with Marianne in the common dining room. "It was awful. There was no question that Joel had been misled about the purpose of the raid. It wasn't to get information. It was to kill me. And they would have succeeded if Joel hadn't warned us."

Marianne said, "Well, I am glad that you engineered it so that Joel didn't get caught. But I'm not so happy about the rest of those people walking around. It sounds like they have a pretty nasty agenda."

"Yes. I think we need to give all of our agents this protection."

"I agree, and I imagine Silandra will agree as well." Marianne sighed. When would violence stop?

Chapter 15:
Conflict

Near Lubbock, Texas, March 3, 2012

The gathering was impressive, Joel thought. Several hundred people, almost all men, gathered at a large compound in Texas, owned by some old oil gazillionaire. There had been meetings, and talks, and lots of informal conversations over beers or martinis. There was golf and target shooting, and even some quail hunting. He saw Reverend Jason B. Modes, and a number of other prominent Christians who were against the Casitians. He had gone to a presentation that Modes did, which talked about the meeting he'd had with the Pope and some Imam from Iran, who had all agreed on a statement strongly opposing the Casitians.

Joel had come to realize that the information that he could gather here would be enough. He could be done with all of this. He hoped that he would be able to move to the moon—for one thing, he had come to realize he might actually prefer it there. And, of course, once he skipped out on these people after this retreat, he was going to be a marked man. The moon would be the safest place for him.

"Joel, so good to see you again."

Joel turned toward the hand on his shoulder.

"Hi Dennis. Good to see you."

"I hope you are not angry at me."

Joel had been extremely angry, but he couldn't let it show. "No, not really, Dennis. I understand. You really don't need information from the Galactics, you wanted to make a point. I get it. It's just that perhaps you underestimated them."

Dennis looked at Joel, as if to examine him. "Yes, well, you are right. We did underestimate their capabilities. I guess it makes sense, of course. But we think that we can circumvent their protections."

"How? That's pretty good protection they have."

"It won't protect them against snipers, or against rockets, will it?" He had a smirk on his face.

Joel raised his eyebrows. "No, I guess it wouldn't."

"That, my friend, is what's next. We did hope that the death of a Galactic agent in the raid would send a message. But there will be other messages we'll be sending. In fact, one is being sent right now." He smiled. And pointed toward the TV screen. "Any moment now, there should be a very interesting story reported. Keep watching." He walked away.

He wandered around the compound, noticing who was here, who was talking with whom, and what was being said. He was filing it all away. He had lots of information for Marianne and the rest of the team. Also, Albert had given him access to his laptop, and Joel had surreptitiously copied an enormous number of files onto a thumb drive. These people trusted him now, which was their mistake.

He heard a shout and walked quickly toward the sound. Dennis was in front of the large screen TV in the main gathering room.

Dennis smiled, and said, "Yes! It worked!" CNN was showing a large building that was a smoking ruin.

The anchor said, in a droning voice, "At least 20 staff members were killed in a rocket attack on a Galactic aid center in Columbia, South Carolina. An organization called the FLG, or Front for the Liberation from Galactics has assumed responsibility for the rocket attack. More people would have been injured or killed, except the center had been closed that day for a staff meeting."

Joel mentally prepared how he was going to get himself out of this group. The retreat would be over in a couple of days, and he would ask for a little bit of time off, to take care of things at home in San Jose. He would pretend he was moving to Shreveport, which was one of the main centers for the FLG. He'd then contact Marianne and get transport to the moon.

Moon Station, 61 Paqn, 780/March 3, 2012

The AI disconnected the call, and Laura was stunned. How could they do that? How could they just send a rocket and kill people? She cried for the life of Wanita, who she had visited a number of times. The Columbia center was one of the best run of all of them. She'd met the doctors who worked there, and the caseworkers.

She hoped that Joel had managed to get enough information out of those people to stop them. Laura had been unsure of Joel, until that day in the center, when he had chosen not to identify her, and she saw him so clearly about to jump in to save her life. During the raid, she hadn't been able to risk waking him up separately and talking with him. But she knew she'd be able to talk with him again soon.

Columbia, South Carolina, Earth, April 15, 2012

Dennis was wilting under the abuse of Thomas' ranting. Thomas was chair of the board of the FLG. He had been quick to remind Dennis that Dennis was simply an employee of FLG, not it's leader.

"I can't believe you actually let that man into our retreat! How could you be so stupid? You should have known that the reason he left the Hopkinson campaign was to go back to the Casitians. Hell, maybe he never left the Casitians, but was a spy all along! What an idiot you were! And why didn't it occur to you that the reason why the raid in Louisiana failed was because they were warned? Yeah, I heard, you took his cell phone! So what? You can pick up a phone anywhere these days. You are such an idiot!"

Thomas stopped shouting, but Dennis realized that there was nothing he could say in his defense. He had been stupid. It had all been wishful thinking. He'd gotten virtually no information on the Casitians from Joel, and Joel had managed to get an incredible amount from them. Albert had finally confessed to Dennis that he'd given Joel his laptop to borrow, which contained a lot of inside information about the FLG. It had been a complete fiasco.

"So now, what are we going to do? Every single bombing since the first bombing in South Carolina has failed. There has been no successful action in weeks. They know too much!"

Dennis said, "They have no way of knowing what actions we are planning—that wasn't in any information Joel might have gotten. They have technology superior to what we knew. We have to rethink our approach."

Thomas got up. "Yes, we need to rethink our approach. I think we also need to rethink our staff." Dennis knew that meant that Thomas would have the board get rid of Dennis. It was time, he supposed, to go find another avenue to fight the Galactics. Perhaps one of the other organizations he'd made contact with could use some help.

He made himself sound conciliatory, even though he knew it was futile. "Thomas, I made a mistake, and I intend to do everything I can to make up for it. Yes, it was stupid. It will not be repeated."

"Yes, Dennis, in that you are correct. It will not be repeated."

Thomas turned, and walked out of the restaurant, leaving Dennis to pick up the check. He was glad the FLG credit card was still good.

Washington, DC, Earth, May 15, 2012

Gerard got out of bed, and immediately turned on CNN. He hadn't gone to bed last night until they had proclaimed him the winner of the California primaries. That primary was one of the most important, because California had the most delegates to the convention. It was late in the game, and Gerard was only slightly ahead of the Vice President in the delegate count. California carried him over the edge. He was going to win the nomination.

It had been a slog, these last couple of months. The bombing of the aid center in South Carolina had come just after "Super Tuesday," which was fortunate. Super Tuesday had given him a lot of delegates, but he'd lost several primaries the weeks after the bombing. He vociferously spoke against people who would become terrorists and kill innocent civilians in order to fight the Casitians. Eventually, he had turned the opinion back in his favor. California had been the big ticket he needed.

He would campaign for the rest of the primaries, but for all intents and purposes he was the Republican nominee for president. It was clear from CNN's reporting that they thought so as well. It felt good, but also daunting. He had to begin to position himself to win in November.

Moon Station, 130 Paqn, 780/May 15, 2012

Marianne was deeply worried. Gerard had all but won the Republican nomination for President. There were full page ads in hundreds of newspapers around the globe from religious leaders of many faiths that talked about how Earth needed to rid itself of the "evil influence" of the Casitians. The FLG had bombed an aid center. The information from Joel about the extent of the FLG, and who was involved in it, was staggering to look at. It went so much farther and had many more government officials involved in it than Marianne had even thought possible. Public opinion continued to be basically in favor of the Galactics, yet there were very strong pockets of opposition to the Galactics. South Carolina had a bill that was still pending that would criminalize all Galactic activity in the state. The Governor said he would sign it.

Once the bombing of the South Carolina aid center had occurred, the Galactics had considered releasing a kind of nanobot that would incapacitate all projectile weapons, including guns and rockets. What they did instead was set up AI observation of all aid centers and monitor activity within a 10 mile radius. That sounded impossible to Marianne, but they had already found, and inactivated, another possible rocket that was aimed at a center in Louisiana.

Marianne thought that the time would come when the Galactics would have to do something. She'd talked with Silandra and Erit'ala, who seemed not to understand. They thought that since public opinion was in their favor, it would all eventually work itself out. Marianne knew better.

Los Angeles, California, Earth, July 25, 2012

Gerard walked slowly onto the stage. He could hardly believe he'd gotten here. He had managed to get enough of a majority of delegates that he would be the nominee without a floor fight. It had been a long, long road. He had managed to come in second in New Hampshire, and he had won the Iowa Caucus. It had been touch and go for months. The other candidates besides himself and the Vice President had backed out, and most throwing their support to him. The base of the Republican party—the white, middle- and upper-class conservatives, most of whom were Christian—were deeply troubled by the Galactic threat, and threw their weight in his direction. Some conservatives, particularly the neo-cons, were much more lukewarm towards the Casitians, and aligned themselves with the Vice President. But that hadn't been enough. And the fact that most industries in the US had bounced back from the shutdowns hadn't mattered, either.

As he walked to the large central part of the stage at the convention center, he could hear the crowd yelling and clapping, and shouting his name: "Hopkinson! Hopkinson!" He was elated. He was one small step away from the White House, the goal of his life. He wished his father were still alive, to see him on his puny television. He remembered how his father used to sit in front of it and say to him, "Look there, that's a man you'll never be like. You'll never amount to anything."

It gave Gerard some small sort of satisfaction to know that his older brother, who shared his father's opinion of Gerard, was still alive, as were the rest of his siblings, and his mother. It didn't matter that he hadn't spoken to them in years. Here he was, on this big stage, almost President of the United States.

He got to the podium and raised his arms wide and flashed a broad smile. He let the adulation of the crowd wash over him for just a minute, as he took in all of the signs, and banners, and buttons with his name on them.

"Hello, my fellow Americans, and fellow Earth citizens." At that, the crowd went crazy with claps and yells. He raised his arms again, to try and quiet the crowd.

"Thank you, thank you all. Tonight is an historic moment. Tonight is the beginning of the process to take this world back for Earth!" More claps and screams.

"Tonight, ladies and gentlemen, we will fight to make the United States a safe haven for the people of Earth who want to live their lives the way *they* want to! People of Earth who believe in the American dream of freedom, and an enjoyable life. People of Earth who do not want to live by the arbitrary strictures of the Galactic requirements. People who think that humans are more important than big fish!" The crowd again went wild. He waited a bit to let it quiet down.

"People who don't believe a life of subsistence farming and immoral liaisons are the kind of life they want for themselves or their children! My candidacy is about living the Earth lifestyle, the lifestyle that the United States is known for, and the lifestyle that was emulated all around the world. There are many people who agree with us. Even this President has caved in to the immorality of the Casitians, and decided that it was better to go along with their 'requirements' than to fight them. Well, if you elect me President, I will fight. I will use the might of the United States to fight the Casitians, to oppose them wherever they are! We can win! We can send them back to where they came from!"

The crowd erupted. He knew he had them. And he knew he could tap into the deepest part of the unease that many felt about the Casitians. He could win, he knew it.

Moon Station, 40 Musb, 780/July 25, 2012

Marianne, Silandra, Ja'el, Henry, Jur'tic, Joel, and Erit'ala sat in the joining room, looking at a large screen, which showed Gerard speaking. They silently watched him as he gave his speech, full of triumph and vitriol. Marianne was stunned, and unhappy. She had known for weeks that Gerard was going to win the nomination. But the way he spoke was chilling. She knew that it would tap into the fears and uncomfortableness that Americans had felt towards Casitians, even as the Casitians had made their lives better. There was an increasing amount of nostalgia present in society for the "good old days" before the knowledge of a Galactic civilization, and before the knowledge of the greater intelligence of the dolphins—the time when humans were at the top of the totem pole, instead of low down in the hierarchy of sentient species.

At the end of the speech, Silandra spoke. "Dear ones, I am quite worried. The patterns I am beginning to see in the Earth community are quite troubling. He is just a small part of the pattern. My AI has been doing some analyses of Earth public communications. At this moment, there is the full spectrum of opinion present, but there is more and more weight at two disparate ends. For a long time people were undecided, or could see both the advantages and disadvantages to aligning Earth with the Galactic Community. But increasingly, people are making choices. And there is a strong coalescing force on the anti-Galactic end. I don't think it will take over, but it is very strong, and we have to find a way to deal with it."

Joel said, "I'm not sure that there *is* a way to deal with it, Silandra. The people that I interacted with in the FLG would die to get rid of the Galactic influence. They will stop at nothing. They can't be reasoned with or given anything—they have made up their minds, and they will die trying to get you off of this planet."

"But don't they understand that the Galactic Community cannot, and will not, leave? This is the home planet of the parn's, and the parn's are a represented species in the Galactic community. They take precedence."

Joel shook his head. "Silandra, all of that is lost on them. For them, Earth is the human planet, and always has been. Earth is for humans, Earth was created by God for humans. They don't care about the dolphins. To them, dolphins are still just big fish."

Ja'el sighed. "So what is possible, here? What can be done?"

Joel said, "I don't have any idea. They won't back down. They might just all have to die trying."

Marianne spoke up. "Well, that's not going to happen. The Casitians won't kill people."

Joel said, "But Earth people kill people. I imagine that what might happen is that pro-Casitians end up fighting anti-Casitians."

Silandra looked shocked. "We would never let that happen!"

"How will you prevent it?" Joel asked.

Silandra was silent. Marianne said, "What if, instead of them kicking the Casitians off of Earth, which is, as we've said, impossible, we kick them off?"

Joel turned to look at Marianne in shock. "What do you mean, kick them off?"

Marianne turned to Erit'ala. "Erit'ala, are there planets without sentient species that could support human life?"

Erit'ala nodded. "Yes, there are quite a few. The Galactic community controls colonization and keeps track of planets that are habitable for a variety of species, but have no sentient life. That is how we were settled on Casiti. What are you thinking?"

"What if we offered the holdouts a brand-new planet for them to colonize?"

Joel laughed. "Forget it, Marianne. They would never agree to that."

Ja'el said, "That may well be, Joel, but I think we should leave it on the table as something we might possible want to think about."

Erit'ala said, "I'll talk to my contact at the Sejo. Perhaps they'll have an idea for us."

Chapter 16:
Campaign Trail

Chicago, Illinois, Earth, September 20, 2012

The campaign was grueling for Gerard. They had a plane and several buses, and it seemed that he spent all of his time in the plane, or in a bus, or on a podium. He hadn't been home in weeks. Juliana accompanied him at times on the campaign trail, but only minimally. She clearly hadn't thought he would get this far and hadn't been prepared to play the Presidential wife quite so soon. Gerard thought she was having second thoughts about the whole thing, but he knew she wouldn't leave until after the election.

He was, at this moment, on the plane, going somewhere. "So where are we going today?"

Angela looked up from her notes. "Ohio, sir. First stop is Cincinnati, at a rally for Veterans. Then we drive to Columbus for a conference—you are the keynote speaker for the conference on 'Opposing Alien Influence in our Schools.' On the way, we'll stop at as few towns—Lebanon, Wilmington and Octa, and you'll speak at rallies that we have set up. We should arrive in Cincinnati in about an hour."

"Do you have my speeches?"

"Yes, sir, the speechwriting team is working on them now. We'll be all set."

For Gerard, this was all beginning to run together. He knew he'd been in Ohio before, but Ohio was a critical state, and campaigning there was crucial.

They arrived, and when his feet had just touched the tarmac, one of his assistants came up to him. "Sir, I have an urgent phone call from Thomas Martin."

Gerard had been introduced to Thomas Martin. He was a state senator from South Carolina, a big political power player there, and increasingly elsewhere. He was strongly anti-Galactic, and had thrown his weight, power, and some money, in Gerard's direction. He had to take this call.

"OK, where can I take the call?"

"In the bus, sir."

They walked toward the bus. Gerard loved the buses. His name was in huge letters on the bus, and it was festooned with lots of red, white and blue. They got on the bus, and Gerard found his way to the back, where the office was. His assistant gave him a cell phone.

"Hello?"

"Hello, Gerard, it's Thomas Martin."

"Yes, Thomas, sorry to keep you waiting."

"It's no problem. I made this urgent call because the governor is about to sign that anti-Galactic bill, and I thought that you might want to bring your campaign here for that. The governor wants you at the signing, which is tomorrow morning."

"He wants me at the signing? Yes, we'll make it happen. We'll rearrange whatever we need to so that we can be there."

"And Gerard, we need to have a private meeting while you are here, the two of us. I have some very important things to discuss with you. There are some very important things coming together now, and you need to know about them."

"Thank you very much Thomas. I'll make room for that as well. My people will be in touch."

"See you tomorrow." The call ended.

"Please get Angela in here, now!"

The assistant scurried off, looking afraid. Angela appeared soon after.

"We need to reschedule tomorrow. The governor of South Carolina is going to sign that anti-Galactic bill, and he wants me at the signing. Can you work all of that out?"

"Gerard, we don't need to be in South Carolina. We already have those electoral votes in the bag. We had planned to go to California, there are some important rallies, and you were invited to speak at the AFL-CIO conference. We can't miss that!"

"Angela, we are going to the signing in South Carolina tomorrow, and I need you to set up a private meeting with Thomas Martin after the signing. There is no conversation here. This has to happen."

Angela furrowed her brow and stared at the schedule, deep in thought. "OK, Gerard, whatever you want. I'll set it up. But I think it's a mistake. That bill is very extreme, more extreme than even many anti-Casitian people are."

"That bill is a model for bills around the country, and I want to make sure that it spreads."

"But Gerard, you want to win in November. This will alienate voters who might be swayed in your direction."

At that moment Gerard realized that he had come to fully believe in the things that he said. Yes, he wanted to win in November, and he was sure that he would. And he wanted the Casitians off of Earth.

Columbia, South Carolina, Earth, September 21, 2012

Thomas Martin was taking a risk. Telling Gerard Hopkinson about the FLG, and about the coalescing opposition to the Galactics and the actions they were beginning to take, seemed to make a lot of sense. He wanted Gerard to be in place as an ally when he won the White House. If he didn't win the White House, well, it would all be moot anyway. He didn't know how Gerard would react. He imagined that Gerard would be on their side, based on what he had said.

The signing ceremony had gone well. Gerard had played his part perfectly. Thomas knew that Gerard would get some bad press because of it, but he was gratified that Gerard realized how important it was to be here. The same bill was already pending in Georgia, Mississippi, and Louisiana, and he was working hard to get it introduced in Texas, Oklahoma, Utah, and Missouri.

He heard a knock on his office door. "Yes, come in." His secretary entered, with Gerard in tow.

"Welcome, Gerard. I'm glad you came to make this meeting." Thomas got up and extended his hand. Gerard took it, and they shook hands. None of that clasped-arm hug business, never for Thomas.

"Thank you, Thomas, for all of your support. It will be critical to our victory in November."

"Yes, yes, Gerard, you know I believe in your candidacy, and that we share the same cause—to get the aliens off of Earth. I wanted to talk with you in more detail about what I've been involved in, and what's happening, and get you and your organization connected to what's going on. What's amazing is that there is an incredible coming together of the varied threads of alien opposition, and I felt that you needed to know about this. I feel that if, in a month, you win the presidency, you need to have all of this in place."

"Thank you. I'm glad to know what's going on. You've clearly been a leader in a lot of the efforts against the aliens, haven't you?"

Thomas was gratified that Gerard understood his role. So many did not and didn't give him credit for all that was happening. But he was the man behind it all. "Yes, Gerard, I have been a leader, and I continue to be."

"I think you might be quite helpful in a Hopkinson administration, Thomas."

Thomas smiled. Yes, Gerard got it. "So let me tell you about three different, but connected, efforts you should know about. First, the political. The bill that was signed into law today, which takes effect immediately, is a model for bills now pending in three states, and it is in the process of being introduced in at least four other states. I have a whole group of people working to spread that bill as far as possible, so that as many states as possible criminalize the alien influence."

Gerard smiled. "Yes, I'm so glad that is happening. And, of course, when I win, we will press for a federal bill much like that."

"Yes, we will want and need such a bill. Also, these bills provide for what is called in them a 'citizen militia'—which might seem unclear, but actually is already set up. It's called the FLG."

Gerard was surprised by this. "The FLG? But that's considered a terrorist group. I mean, they were the ones that bombed the aid center in Columbia! How could that be?"

"We are in a position to put the FLG in place as the citizen militia that will enforce the law, in collaboration with the state and local police forces, most of which, at least in South Carolina, and increasingly elsewhere, are all FLG anyway."

"How do you know this, Thomas?"

"Because I am the chair of the FLG. It is a risk telling you, but I hope that you know that the FLG is on your side. We want the aliens off of Earth as much as you do, and we are willing to put our bodies on the line to make it happen."

Gerard sat back for a moment. Thomas wondered what he was thinking.

"OK, Thomas, this makes sense. I can go along with it. I can see how having the FLG would be incredibly useful."

"Now for the third piece of the puzzle. As you know, there is a network of religious leaders all over the world that are anti-alien. What you might not know is that they are talking to one another and coordinated. Their numbers include the major Imams of the Middle East, the Pope, and people like Reverend Jason B. Modes here in the US. And they are tied into the FLG. We've been meeting with them for months. They will be ready to act when the time comes."

"Act, how?"

"They will be ready to mobilize their followers and have them act when it is time for the uprising."

"Uprising?"

"Yes, the plan is that when you are inaugurated in January, and the US puts into place a process which pushes the aliens out of the US, then cells in every country of the world will begin to protest the aliens, and target their centers, and sabotage their facilities. We also have gotten in place hundreds of fishing boats, who will start a large dolphin hunt. We will overwhelm the aliens."

"This sounds like a good plan. And I imagine you will need the full might of the US military behind it?"

Thomas nodded. "That would be the key to success, yes."

"Well, then I can guarantee this. You'll be on my transition team. Is there someone from your staff you can assign to my campaign so I can keep updated, and we can keep in touch?"

"Yes, indeed, I have an assistant, Justin, who will be perfect. He is quite gung-ho for your campaign, as well. He'll be a real help to you."

Gerard smiled, and got up. "Thank you, Thomas, so much, for the information and the contact. This is very important."

Thomas rose and gripped Gerard's hand. He was elated. This was all going to work. "Thank you, Gerard. We will be in touch."

Gerard turned and walked out of Thomas' office. Thomas went back to his desk and started on his long list of phone calls and emails, in the wake of this meeting.

New York, New York, Earth, September 21, 2012

Marianne had gone down to Earth to meet with Laura, as well as meet with White House staff. Things were getting out of hand. "So we have to simply stop all of our work in South Carolina?"

"Yes, we have to fire everyone who works for us, shut down operations, and stop giving aid to everyone we've been helping. Anybody who works for us will be arrested, and anyone who is getting aid from us will be arrested. None of us can go inside South Carolina, or we will be arrested, and tried, and, I imagine, put away for a good long time."

Marianne groaned. "This is absurd!"

Laura nodded. "Yes, it is, but there isn't much we can do about it. And worse yet, this is spreading. This same bill is pending in Georgia, Mississippi, and Louisiana, and will almost certainly pass in the next few weeks."

Marianne sighed. "Well, do what you have to do? We don't want anyone to get arrested because of it."

"We'll set up extra aid centers near the borders of North Carolina, but not Georgia, since it's almost certain that we'll have to shut those down within the month. But people visiting those centers will be taking a risk, when they return to South Carolina. But I expect they won't bother people much. It's really us they want to get rid of."

Marianne realized that it was likely that her nightmare scenario would become true. Eventually, they would be forced out of the United States. There wasn't much that she could do about it. States that passed anti-galactic laws would be prevented from re-starting industries that were harmful to the environment, and they would be prevented from going back entirely to how things used to be. She didn't know how much they realized this. And criminalizing Galactic aid would simply make people impoverished. The US would become like a third world country, with an economy in shambles, no health care, and millions upon millions of people unemployed and hungry. But she knew that Silandra and Erit'ala would never agree to more forceful intervention.

"Well, I have to go to the White House to speak with some folks about this situation. Thank you so much, Laura, for filling me in. Let me know if there are things we can help with up on the moon."

Laura nodded. "Actually, I hope to make a visit in a week or two. Joel invited me up to have a long talk. I think we need it."

Marianne smiled. She always thought that Joel and Laura made a good pair, but she was pretty angry with Joel when he skipped out on them. But he seemed to have more than made up for that early mistake.

"Farewell blessings, Laura." Marianne and Laura embraced in a clasped-arm hug.

"Farewell blessings."

Marianne got up, went out of Laura's office, and rode down to the ground floor, where she got out of the building. Her flyer was waiting outside. She got in, and Re'wl asked, "Ready for the White House?"

Marianne smiled. "Yes, Re'wl, let's go." The flyer rose up, and flew straight south, toward Washington DC. She imagined the meeting with the White House chief of staff would be a doozey.

Moon Station, 126 Musb, 780

Erit'ala's AI spoke softly. "There is a message from Galactic central that just arrived." Erit'ala had been waiting for this message. Messages from other star systems had to be carried by ships through the wormholes and were then transmitted from the large station by laser to the moon.

"Display, thank you."

The message was straightforward. The Sejo did, in fact, consider the solution of moving intransigent humans to another planet to be preferable to other avenues. Other solutions seemed to jeopardize the safety and quality of life of the parns. There was a planet that they considered perfect, although a bit on the warm side, and rather large, that was available for colonization by humans. Research suggested that not only were most of the plant and animal species on this planet compatible with human biochemistry, but that the land would likely support many Earth plant and animal species. There were a large number of colony ships that had been in storage for hundreds of years, last used to move a large population of F'zziliard, a banned species, out of a system that had a population of a particularly peaceful and passive species. Those who knew about these sorts of things thought that it would take approximately six Earth months to take those ships out of storage, prepare them for humans, and get them to Earth. They thought that the whole group of one thousand colony ships would hold close to 100 million humans. It was always possible for the colony ships to do multiple trips.

Erit'ala, however, did not like this solution. She wanted to find a way to let the humans of Earth determine for themselves how to live, within the constraints that the Galactics had set. She thought that perhaps it would take a few generations, but eventually, Earth humans would come to appreciate the Galactic community of which they were a part.

But she felt it was good that this option existed. She would wait some time, however, before telling them to send the colony ships through the wormhole to Earth.

Philadelphia, Pennsylvania, Earth, October 30, 2012

"The polling numbers don't look good, Gerard. I'm just being honest. With only one week to go in the election, and with the double-digit lead in most states that the Democratic candidate has on you, it's just not likely that you can pull this off."

Gerard was angry at his pollster. Didn't she ask the right questions? Ask the right people? "I'm sorry, but I just don't believe that. I've talked to people all over, and they are so against the aliens. There must be something wrong in your numbers!"

"Gerard, it's not just my numbers. It's also CNN, The New York Times, Fox, even, has you from 50 to 80 electoral votes behind the Democratic candidate. I'm sorry, Gerard."

"Get out! Get out of here. I'm not going to lose, and I don't want to hear what you have to say!"

The pollster was startled, and gathered up her papers, and ran out of the room. Angela came quickly into the office. "Gerard, are you OK?"

"I'm not going to lose, Angela, I refuse to lose. Please get Justin in here, will you?"

Angela looked at Gerard in a way he thought might be a bit worried, then turned and left. He needed to talk with Thomas Martin. He figured that there was a lot Thomas could do to turn this around. Justin came in, after a few minutes.

"Hi Justin, I need to set up an in-person meeting with Thomas. I'll fly down to South Carolina, if necessary."

"OK, Mr. Hopkinson, I'll set it up, and arrange scheduling with Angela."

"It needs to be very soon, like tomorrow, or at worst, Friday."

Justin nodded. "I understand, sir, I'll make it happen." Justin left the room, and Gerard was alone. He didn't want to give into the fear that he would lose. If he lost, all was lost. Yes, four more states had passed the anti-alien bills. The FLG was getting stronger, and opposition to the aliens was getting stronger in other places in the world. But they needed the US military, he was convinced.

After a few minutes, Justin came back. "Sir, we can fly to Columbia tomorrow morning, and meet with Mr. Martin at 10:00 AM."

Gerard nodded. "Thank you, Justin."

Angela came into the office. "Gerard, we don't need a new trip to South Carolina.

"I need to meet with Thomas Martin, Angela, it's important. He can save this election for me."

"Gerard, we need to stump in California and New York. We only have a few days left, and wasting a day in South..."

"It will not be wasting a day! You don't understand! You never did understand, did you?"

Angela looked shocked. "Gerard..."

Gerard's voice moderated. "Angela, please just trust me. I need to talk with Thomas."

Angela backed down. "OK, but we'll be flying up to New York by noon tomorrow."

Gerard nodded. He would have enough time. Thomas would make sure he won.

Thomas watched Gerard leave his office and shook his head. There had been no way to promise Gerard a way to save the election. He knew it was lost. He'd thought that they could tap into the fears and uncertainties that people in the US had. It turned out, that passing those bills criminalizing the aliens had worked against them. People liked getting free education, and more leisure time. People seemed to like... *gardening*, and all of that silly new public art work that the aliens had promoted. People seemed to be taking to the alien culture. Thomas shuddered. Well, they would not win the election, but they had a Plan B. And he decided that Plan B should go into effect as soon as possible after the election was clearly lost by Gerard.

The good thing was that he got Gerard to promise his voice and aid for Plan B. Gerard would be the rallying point for all of the opposition, as it gathered force across the country and around the world. Thomas had confidence in Gerard as a leader, and Gerard seemed to realize that he could do something that, in the end, would mean more than being President. Gerard would be an emperor of a new Earth, the Earth united against aliens, and without aliens. If they had to fight those who supported the aliens, they would.

Chapter 17:
Election Night

Moon Station, 136 Musb, 780/November 6, 2012

Marianne had decided that the certain election loss by Gerard would be a great way to introduce the Casitians to an old-fashioned Earth party. She had gotten a bunch of varied alcoholic beverages up from Earth, got the AI's to load up on great Earth music, and set up the large common dining room with all sorts of decorations. A large screen on one end of the room showed the election results. They were going to have a blast.

She had been surprised to learn from Ja'el early on that Casitians didn't have the equivalent of alcohol. There were a number of plants on Casiti that were soporific, euphoric, or hallucinogenic, and they used those on occasion, but no one had managed to invent alcohol. Some Casitians had sampled alcohol, and some liked it and some didn't. She figured that she'd give them the widest array possible, from beer and wine, to varied mixed drinks and liquors, and see what they thought. Gerard's loss to the very pro-Galactic Democratic candidate would be a good reason to celebrate.

She walked into the common dining room, and the party had clearly already started. Most of the larger team from more than a year ago had come up for the party. They had been working hard over the past months. She saw Laura and Joel dancing in one corner, looking very much in love with each other. Marianne was glad that particular story had turned out well. She saw Kyla, and Gita and her whole family. She waved to Sunam, who had come with his family. This was an international affair. The polls on the East Coast were just closing, and they had already called all of the New England states for the Democrat. They had also called the states of South Carolina, Georgia and Mississippi for Gerard. No surprises there, although what was a surprise was how narrow the margins were. The Democrat almost won South Carolina. New York and New Jersey were heavily in the Democrat's favor, but not enough precincts were reporting in, so they hadn't called it. The same was true for Pennsylvania and Florida. This looked to be a rout. She had seen an electoral map a couple of days ago. The only states that Gerard was likely to get were all of the states of the south, except Florida, and North and South Dakota, Utah, Indiana, maybe Colorado and Arizona. Not California, not New York, not Florida, not Ohio. There was no way he could win.

She joined the party and had a beer, and walked around talking with people, feeling happy. She thought, this is going to be the end of it, finally. Gerard loses, the opposition loses its force, it all works out. She had been foolish to worry about it, and foolish to suggest the idea of getting people off of Earth. Over the past month, things had been quiet. No more attempted bombings of centers, not much activity in countries overseas. She had overreacted. Already, voter rebellion in the states that had passed the anti-Galactic bills were likely to precipitate new administrations in those states, which would reverse the bills.

As they partied, slowly, but surely, Gerard lost states. The very instant that the polls closed on the West Coast, every single news outlet, even Fox News, called the election for the Democrat. Gerard had lost and lost decisively. Marianne was elated at this final news. She hung around the party for a while, as many did, waiting for Gerard's concession, but it didn't come. She wasn't so interested in waiting around anymore. She sidled up to Ja'el and whispered, "I'd really like to get out of here. What do you think?"

Ja'el turned toward her and smiled. "Yes, I think we can find better things to do than wait for Gerard." They said their farewell blessings on the way out and went back to their quarters.

They had told the AI to not disturb them "unless very urgent," so it was a surprise, a few hours later, to be interrupted by an insistent, loud chime from the AI.

"What is it?" Marianne was annoyed.

"Silandra is calling a joining. She feels that it is an emergency."

"An emergency? What happened?"

"Would you like a run down of all of the events of the past three hours?"

Marianne groaned. "No, no, when is the joining?"

"In one tenth hour." Marianne always needed to do a translation to Earth time. 24 minutes until the meeting. Time enough for a shower.

Ja'el and Marianne arrived in the joining room, where Silandra, Henry and Jur'tic were sitting already. In very short order, Joel, Laura, and Erit'ala came into the room.

Silandra stood up. "I'm sorry to interrupt your festivities and relaxation, but some things have happened that are quite disturbing. First, I need you to hear Gerard's 'concession' speech."

She turned toward the display, and a scene of Gerard in a hotel ballroom appeared.

"I want to thank you all for the hard work that you did. We may have lost this election, but we have not really begun the war against the aliens. We will fight, tooth and nail, to get them off of our planet." The speech kept going in the same vein. It was not so surprising. Marianne didn't really think much of his blustering. What could he do?

The speech continued, "Join with me. We will fight the aliens. We will win against the aliens. You will hear more about how this will happen. We will win and kick them back to the cold planet they came from."

"This is a little unexpected, but what can he really do? It seems to me that he is in a position to bluster and bluff, but not actually take any actions." Marianne said.

Silandra spoke softly to her AI. "Display, thanks, the news story that followed the speech."

An anchor of CNN was reporting, "Apparently, just minutes after the concession speech by Gerard Hopkinson, hundreds of armed, uniformed men have shown up at most of the Galactic aid centers in the country and shut them down. This is also apparently happening in many countries overseas."

Silandra said, "We had detected this activity beforehand, and since the centers were closed, there was no danger to the staff. We decided to let this happen. We are afraid, however, about what will happen in a few hours on the East Coast, when morning comes, and people try and go to the aid centers. But there is more. Display, thanks, the next story."

Another anchor, speaking somewhat hurriedly, and seeming worried. "It seems that a number of churches and mosques around the world are becoming gathering points for people in opposition to the Casitians. We're not clear what's happening at those sites at the present time." He paused, and touched his ear plug, then looked up.

"We hear that there will be a press conference first thing tomorrow morning in Columbia, South Carolina, with members of FLG, as well as some religious leaders. We'll keep you posted." The display went blank.

Silandra continued. "We have detected a wide variety of activities, all over the world. Firearms are being distributed, people are gathering. It looks like this is coordinated and has been planned out quite far in advance. Finally, some of the patterns I'd been noticing over the past weeks are making sense. I wish I'd seen this more clearly."

Marianne shook her head. "Silandra, this surprises all of us, I think. I had hoped that this wouldn't happen, that..."

Joel cut in, "Marianne, you were always too optimistic. I told you how serious these people were. This actually doesn't surprise me in the least. I don't think there is anything we can do to stop them."

"Joel, I know, I realize now I was being optimistic, much too optimistic. Silandra, what can we do?"

Erit'ala and I have decided that we will release the nanobots that will prevent the use of any projectile weapons. We also will be activating sleep defenses where it seems that conflicts are going to start."

"That's a good start, but there must be something else."

"Marianne, we think that you should hold a press conference tomorrow, to answer any questions and respond to what has been said by Gerard and others. You have been almost invisible for the past couple of months, and we think it is time for you to make yourself known again."

"I think I should do that press conference together with the President, and President elect. I think that would have the most impact. I'll try to arrange that."

Columbia, South Carolina, Earth, November 7, 2012

Gerard and Thomas were about to enter the room with all of the reporters, along with Jason B. Modes, and the governor of South Carolina, who was about to declare the November election moot, and take his state out of the United States, joining the Federation of Free States, or FFS. Seven other governors were poised to do exactly the same, and together, they had chosen Gerard to be the President of the FFS. Columbia, South Carolina would be the new capital of the new country. And this new country would form the nexus of opposition to the aliens. It was a bold plan, a plan that Thomas had set up months ago, and it made sense. He expected that at least twenty states would eventually secede, creating a strong opposition.

They entered the room one after the other and sat at the long head table along with Reverend Modes and the Governor. The press was clearly jumping all over themselves to ask questions.

Gerard got up and read a prepared statement.

"Ladies and gentlemen, we are prepared to do all that we can to fight the aliens. We have concluded that the best way to go about this would be to become independent of the United States government. Thus, today, South Carolina is a free state, a state of the Federation of Free States. I have been asked to serve as the President of this new Federation of states. Other governors are now poised to join with us, and we will become a strong new nation, bound and determined to eliminate the alien threat from the world." He ended his speech, and the room erupted in shouted questions from the press. The questions were all expected: why, how they would be governed, what would happen to the aid centers. They had planned out the answers to all of these questions very carefully. But then, a question came from a reporter that surprised Gerard.

"We have reports that all projectile and explosive weapons, which include guns, bombs, rockets, and missiles, have been deactivated. They just don't work. In addition, we've heard of several incidents of conflict where, without explanation, everyone within a radius of about a mile just falls asleep for several minutes, and then they wake up, forgetful of why they were there, and go home. Do you have any comments about this?"

Gerard was stunned, and completely taken aback. He turned toward Thomas, who had become quite pale. He turned back, "I haven't heard these reports, and I would have to assess whether or not they were valid. In any event, we can find ways around any technology that the aliens have. We are resourceful, we can win."

Gerard realized he had to end the press conference immediately. He had to find out more and, he couldn't have the press asking him any questions along those lines. If what the reporter said was true, that would radically change what they could do. It scared him.

They all got up and walked out, without much warning. The press yelled and shouted after them, but they did not pay attention. On the way out, Thomas hissed, "That reporter was lying, it's not possible." Gerard wasn't so sure.

Washington, DC, Earth, November 7, 2012

The press were far more deferential toward Marianne and the President and President Elect. Marianne got a question about whether or not those reports of inactivated weapons and sleep defenses were real. She acknowledged them.

"The Casitians, as you know, have no weapons. However, they do have technology that can be used in defense. They are completely committed to having no one hurt or killed in any kind of anti-Casitian/ pro-Casitian conflict that Earth humans might have. They have implemented a number of defensive technologies, including nanobots that deactivate all explosive and projectile weapons, nanobots that deactivate all chemical and biological weapons, and sleep defenses that are automatically activated in a conflict situation."

A reporter stood up. "So, Mr. President, you are going to depend on Galactic technology to defend people from the FLG and secessionists?"

"Well, honestly, the Casitians can do a much better job than we can. And if they have deactivated all weapons, there isn't much we could do in any event. We've sent some national guard to guard the aid centers that were not taken over, and we will stand by to move into areas where we can be in a position to provide protection. But I think, honestly, the Casitians are best at this."

More questions came at them, and they answered them in turn. Marianne felt like a broken record. She said, "We will make sure that no one is hurt" over and over again. She wondered, though, whether they could actually follow through that promise.

Vatican City, Earth, November 9, 2012

Augusto had finally been stretched beyond his ethical bounds. He could not find a clear way to align himself with the likes of Reverend Modes and Gerard Hopkinson, and still feel he was doing God's will. He thought back to that conversation he had with the Galactic contemplative, Jal'end'a. He had truly liked her, and their discussion had been wide ranging and deeply theological. He had learned a lot about Casitians then, and he could no longer agree to continue this present course.

He had gathered his closest associates and cardinals and had told them that he was making a statement to the world, to welcome the Casitians. He was completely distancing the papacy from the anti-Casitian movement. They had all agreed and encouraged him to include something about limiting the influence of the Casitians for the good of Earth, which he did. He did still feel that the Galactic moral influence was problematic.

He wrote his encyclical, which was short and to the point. He denounced the actions of anti-Galactic groups all over the world. He welcomed the Casitians, and he expressed a wish for a peaceful reunion and gentle coexistence. He put his weight behind the UN, he wished the best for the dolphins, and, finally, he wished for a minimization of Casitian cultural influence because of what he described as immoral cultural practices.

He felt it set the right tone. He asked Catholics to play nice but stay Catholics. And he made it clear that the single largest group of people of the Christian faith had decided to peacefully coexist with the Galactic Community.

After two weeks, it was clear that the whole situation had gotten completely out of their control. Since the FLG and others couldn't shoot anyone, or gather in groups, they would harass people individually, with knives and clubs. Anyone who had gotten aid from the Galactics, or was known to be sympathetic, was a target. Anyone who didn't agree to join them was harassed. A number of people had been stabbed or clubbed to death. It was impossible for the Casitians to keep track of everyone, everywhere. They had taken to giving sleep defenses to people who volunteered to patrol their neighborhoods and protect people. It helped but didn't do enough to stop the violence. Everyone was afraid, and many were hiding in their homes, or moving north or west. The number of refugees from the FFS was increasing. And the harassment wasn't limited to the FFS. There were harassments everywhere, all over the world, in many countries and cities. It was clear that the FLG tactic was to simply scare people into agreeing with them about the Casitians. It was largely not working, but it created a climate of fear and uncertainty.

Marianne, Joel, Ja'el, Silandra, and Erit'ala were in a joining. Marianne spoke. "We have to end this, Silandra. There is just no way that this will end well, as long as these people continue to be able to do this. And honestly, we can't stop them."

Silandra said, "Yes, indeed, it does have to end. I spoke with Ur'lef last day. The parn's have been disturbed by the energetic patterns they are picking up from the humans. They explained to Ur'lef that the current situation was not acceptable to them, that it must change."

Marianne's mouth was wide open. She was completely taken by surprise by this. She had no idea the dolphins had that sort of ability. And no idea that they would demand something of this sort from them.

Marianne said, "So we really have no choice, do we?"

Silandra shook her head. "But the question is, how do we get them to agree?"

Marianne said, "I think we just tell them what we can offer them and see what they say. We can explain that we have a number of plans in place to cut off food, water and energy going to the FFS states and to the countries that have opposed us, and any to cities that are presently in the hands of our opposition. We can tell them that will be permanent. They know there is no way they can survive under those conditions. Giving them their own planet would seem, I think, to be the best option for them. I think they might even see that."

Silandra asked, "So how do we offer this to them? Have a joining with them?"

"Yes, I think that's what we do. Tell them to gather anyone they would like at a meeting, and we'll be there. Tell them we have something to offer them."

"I sent a message to Galactic central to send the colony ships through the wormhole. They should arrive at the station in a few days. Luckily, the space docks where they were stored are close to that system's wormhole. They will be at Earth within twenty days."

Joel, who had been quiet, spoke up. "What if they don't agree? What if they completely refuse?"

Silandra sighed. "We will have no choice but to force them. It won't be easy or fast, but it is possible. We can do it."

"But why weren't you willing to do that sort of thing earlier?" Joel was clearly both angry and perplexed.

"Because the parn's did not ask us, and we would have preferred a solution that preserved Earth human autonomy. But, in the end, this is the parn's planet, not ours, and not yours. They are the final authority. They are asking us to do this now, and so we must."

Marianne nodded. "I'll try and set up a meeting. We'll see how this goes."

Columbia, South Carolina, Earth, November 30, 2012

Marianne, David, and Joel were in the flyer, piloted by Re'wl. They were flying to Columbia, South Carolina, where they would meet with Gerard, Thomas Martin, and others, including an Imam from Iran. They had no idea how this meeting would go. Marianne was pretty nervous. They were carrying sleep defenses, and other precautions had been taken, although Marianne didn't think that they would try anything. She looked down, and the city came into view. As they flew low over the city, they saw abandoned and gutted buildings and people in the streets, picking over garbage. There was debris strewn everywhere. Marianne knew that many people had fled South Carolina for other places such as Florida and North Carolina and other states, because people couldn't stand the harassment and lack of resources.

They flew over the statehouse and landed on the lawn in front. A number of people came from out of the statehouse toward the flyer. They looked like staff. Marianne, David, and Joel left the flyer, and walked toward them.

Joel said under his breath, "That is Angela, who was Gerard's campaign manager, and the kid is Justin, who works for Thomas Martin." Marianne nodded.

Angela said, "Hello Marianne. I'm Angela Johnson, Gerard's chief of staff. Welcome to the capital of the FFS."

Marianne looked at Angela and said "Thank you. Please direct us to the meeting."

Angela nodded and said, "Please follow me."

They walked up the stairs and into the statehouse. They went down a long corridor and arrived at a set of double doors. Justin opened the doors and waved them inside. Neither he nor Angela followed them into the room. Justin closed the door behind them.

Marianne looked at the men assembled in the room. She recognized almost all of them. There was the Reverend Modes, Thomas Martin, Gerard, and a man whom she recognized as the Imam from Iran, with an unknown man next to him. She assumed that man was his translator. She looked carefully at Gerard, who seemed to be frightened. She had brought David completely on purpose, but she hadn't quite expected this reaction from Gerard. He seemed petrified.

"Hello gentlemen. This meeting, I hope, will be short and sweet. I bring an offer from the Galactic Community."

Jason Modes stood up. "An offer? What kind of offer? There is nothing we need or want from the Galactics. We are solving our problems ourselves."

Marianne laughed. "Oh, really? People are starving in the FFS and there is virtually no energy. People are leaving FFS states in droves. You won't have much left."

The Imam started speaking, and his translator said, "The United States is unfortunately undergoing some problems. But there are many places in the world where opposition to the aliens is strong."

Marianne sighed. "Look, let me just make this clear, before you all start telling me what it is you can do. This is the offer. There is a very nice planet, uninhabited by any intelligent species, that the Galactic Community is offering to the anti-Galactic population of Earth. This includes anyone anywhere in the world who doesn't like it that Earth has become a member of the Galactic Community. We have a large fleet of colony ships waiting to take people to a planet that is twice the size of Earth. You can do whatever you want on that planet, the Galactics will not intervene in any way."

Thomas spoke, "And why would we accept that? What's in it for us?"

"A whole new wonderful planet to colonize as you wish. Plenty of room, plenty of food. You can do what you want, and you'll never be visited by the Casitians, or by any member of the Galactic Community, if you don't want them."

"Why would the Galactics do that?"

"Because, frankly, the dolphins, want you off the Earth."

Jason Modes stood, red faced. "This is the planet that God gave us. God created this planet for human beings to live on, to be in dominion over. This is our planet, no other. Those fish are not going to force us off of our home planet."

Marianne looked Modes in the eye, and decided it was time to play all of the cards. "Reverend Modes, God is not calling the shots right now. The dolphins, and the Galactic community on behalf of the dolphins, are in control here. If you don't go willingly, you will be forced to go. You basically have no choice. Forcing you to go is not something the Casitians like to think about. But the dolphins have made it clear. This conflict must end. As they say, harmony and quiet must finally be present on Earth, now that they have a say in the matter. Apparently they are getting tired, or perhaps bored, with Earth human conflict. They have been living with it for a long time."

"And how would they force us? We can stop them!" Modes was still red-faced.

"And how much luck have you had stopping them so far, eh?" Joel seemed to be toying with Modes, who got even more red in the face, if that were possible.

Spittle started to come out of his mouth as he said, "How dare you! You traitor to your country!"

"OK, please, everyone calm down. Look, I've put the offer on the table. You have 72 hours to decide. If you don't simply agree within that time frame, the Casitians will begin putting in place the processes necessary to gather up anti-Galactic individuals and put them on the colony ships."

The Imam started speaking again. "How much geographic space would Muslims get?"

Marianne shrugged, and thought fast. "The planet is rather large and would be divided up proportionately by population. I imagine that it would be divided up by original country, and population."

The Imam smiled. "How much bigger than Earth is it? What kind of planet is it?"

Modes interrupted. "It doesn't matter, we won't ..."

The Imam rose and shouted in Arabic. His translator spoke quietly, "If we wish to go to this planet, we will go. That is not up to you to decide." He turned to Marianne and spoke. The translator said, "Please, continue."

Marianne took out the flash chips that she had prepared for them. "This has all of the information you want on the planet. The planet has a diameter that is approximately twice that of Earth, which means that the surface area of the planet is much larger. Further, Earth's surface, as you know, is 70% water. This planet is mostly land. Only about 30% of the surface area of the planet is water, and all of that is fresh. The planet is a mix of rainforests, arboreal forests, mountains, and prairie. There are no deserts. I would bet that Iran, for instance, would get the equivalent of ten times the amount of land that it presently has. The planet is abundant in all sorts of things that you would need to create a successful society of any type."

She handed the Imam a chip, which he took eagerly. She held out the other chips to Thomas, Gerard and Modes, but they did not reach for them. She put them on the table in front of them. She had a suspicion that the Imam, and his followers, would agree to go. She imagined that Erit'ala and Silandra might even be willing to give them a few extra incentives. She looked over at Thomas Martin and Modes. They, she thought, weren't going to budge. Then she looked at Gerard. He was staring rather obviously at David. He had a look on his face that was unreadable. David said nothing.

Marianne broke the tension. "Look at the information on the chips. It's really a nice planet, and you are getting an incredible break here. Just go for it. I don't think you want to go through the process that the Casitians will have to implement in order to force you on those colony ships. And they will, I guarantee it.

We are going to webcast and broadcast this offer to everyone, everywhere, after your 72 hours are up, so that your followers can make up their own minds, if you don't go along with this. As you know, that might put your leadership at great risk. That's something to think about, isn't it?"

Gerard seemed to come alive at that moment. He leaned forward and grabbed one of the chips. Modes looked at him sharply. Thomas Martin said to him, "Gerard, we can't agree to this. We will not leave Earth."

Gerard looked back at him. "I don't think we'll have a choice. Listen to what she says about all of that land. People would like it, and we can create a society without any Galactic interference at all."

Chapter 18:
Decisions

H'terinon stood, looking out of the observation deck, toward the wormhole. He knew that the colony ships would be coming any minute now. The wormhole was far enough away that he wouldn't see the ships for a couple of hours, but he looked in that direction anyway, knowing that they were on their way.

It had been a good thing that they'd been able to finish the Keeelo decks before all of this chaos was about to descend on them. The Caraj had finally allowed the Sejo to bring more staff here, including some very industrious Twaddlego. H'terinon loved the Twaddlego. They were a short, squat humanoid species, very intelligent, amazing at engineering, and very industrious. They had a spirituality that was hard for H'terinon to grasp, but in his talks with Tywo76, he was learning. A contingent of Twaddlego were sent here to facilitate the completion of both the Keeelo and parn' decks. And just in time. Everything was in place, and the large contingent of Keeelo had arrived only 10 days ago.

H'terinon was not looking forward to the thousand colony ships docking here. The station was well able to handle a thousand ships—in fact, it was designed to handle several thousand at any one time. This was the true test as to whether all of the systems H'terinon had put in place were going to work, since they would now have more ships than had ever docked since construction began. Each colony ship had a crew of five hundred, of varied species. Mostly Topli, Twaddlego and Krumptia. Topli were the species that were the best navigators in the galaxy. They built most of the ships in the galaxy and were always in demand. They also ran the premier astrogation and piloting school in the galaxy. The Krumptia were adept at management and bureaucracy. Casitians found the Krumptia to be annoying, largely because of their need for hierarchy, but from what he knew, H'terinon figured the Terrans wouldn't mind them so much. The station would be inundated with half a million beings of different species, all at once.

Luckily, they would only be staying a few days, then they would be off to Earth.

It was also time for H'terinon to take more of a management role, like that of a Krumptia. He didn't like that much. Luckily, he only needed to fill that role for a short time. A Krumptia would be taking his place, once the station was put into standard operating mode. H'terinon's specialty was getting stations up and running. Running them long term was something he had no interest in. He thought it was getting near time for him to request his replacement. Once the colony ships had finished all of their necessary runs, and things were settled down, it would be time for him to leave.

New York, New York, Earth, December 1, 2012

Marianne had decided to spend the 72 Earth hours waiting for the answer from the anti-Casitians on Earth. She was in NYC, staying with Diana, whom she hadn't seen in a while. She hadn't realized how badly things had deteriorated in the US. It was sad.

She'd recently visited Geneva, Beijing, and Kampala, which were cities that were greening, bustling, and happy. Visiting NYC was troubling. All of the US was suffering from the decisions of the FFS. There were disruptions in food and fuel supplies, and there were refugees everywhere. There were a lot of Galactic agents and aid centers, and they were doing their best, but the situation was unstable and deteriorating.

Diana and Marianne were sitting in front of Diana's video panel, watching CNN's webcast. It had only been a day since Marianne, David, and Joel had delivered the ultimatum. She had decided to keep the whole thing very close to her vest. Everyone in the original team knew what was happening, but they had told neither the larger team, nor the UN, nor the White House. Marianne had realized that a press leak about this could lead to disaster.

A commercial for a new Galactic device was cut off in the middle, and a harried news anchor appeared. "We have just learned from Al Jazeera News, that Imam al Kalyani has made a statement to his people in Iran, and Muslims worldwide. We are going to play this statement in its entirety, then come back. We are gathering some experts who can talk about what this all means. It's staggering."

The screen went momentarily blank, and the familiar form of the Imam appeared. He started to speak, and then the translator began.

"Asalaam alaikum. Greetings to all in Iran, and the world. The Galactic community has made an offer that we will not refuse. They have offered us resettlement on a beautiful planet that is much larger than Earth, with plenty of food, and water, and space. They have offered to let us live there completely free of Galactic influence. We have decided that we will create a new Iran, and we invite all of those in the Muslim world to create a new Islamic world with us."

Marianne groaned. "Oh, no, now I have to make it clear that they don't get the whole planet!"

Diana said, "That was quite brilliant of him. He knows you won't give him the whole planet, but he's put you in a tough position, and will likely get more out of you than he would if he hadn't said that."

Marianne nodded. "I should have thought of that."

Diana smiled. "Well, you are thinking more and more like a Casitian these days, it's no wonder."

They continued to watch the statement, and the coverage and analysis of it. Marianne made some phone calls, first to the White House and UN officials, to calm them down and explain. Then, to get interviews on some major programs, to clarify what the offer was. They were eager to have her speak. She called K'flef and 5told him she'd have some trips to make over the next hour or two. He said he'd be in DC within the quarter hour.

While she was waiting for K'flef, a news anchor said, "We now have a report that Gerard Hopkinson got a similar offer from the Casitians of land on that planet, and he will lead as many Americans who wish to follow him to that new, Galactic-free frontier. Rita Reid is reporting from South Carolina. Rita?"

Marianne was surprised to see Rita on CNN. She'd thought she'd been on Fox most recently. Marianne had never forgiven Rita for that terrible exposé which included an interview with Yolanda. She hadn't talked to Yolanda since that interview, because she really hadn't forgiven her, either.

"Hi Chuck, I'm here in Columbia, the capital of the FFS. Gerard Hopkinson, president of the FFS, has said that he will lead as many Americans as want to go to this new planet, to create a new United States, free from Galactic influence, with plenty of land to go around. He likened this to a new era of the frontier. There will be lots of space to grow and expand, and, as he put it, no 'Injuns.'"

"He didn't actually say that, did he?"

"Yes, Chuck, he did. I think he's trying to connect to the American frontier spirit, which he thinks still exists."

"Thank you, Rita. We now know that we will have an interview with Marianne Michaelson, a few hours from now."

Marianne wondered about Reverend Modes and Thomas Martin. She had expected that Gerard was already leaning in this direction, and that the Imam's statement pulled the rug out from under Modes and Martin, so that Gerard won the argument.

K'flef signaled that he was arriving in NYC, so Marianne got up.

"Diana, it was a great, but brief, visit. It will take me a while to get all of this straightened out. Hey, visit the moon sometime soon, OK? I've missed you."

Diana smiled. They said farewell blessings, hugged, and Marianne went downstairs to catch K'flef.

Hol'venif, Casiti, 13 Klef, 3146

Hetz'lef had been keeping close tabs on the Earth situation. He worried about Silandra constantly, although he knew she would be fine—she was on the moon of Earth, after all. He had been amazed at the kinds of things that the Earth humans would do. It baffled him, frankly. What was happening on Earth was the talk of Casiti. You couldn't go anywhere where people weren't discussing it. Sometimes arguing about whether the Earth humans were really the same species. Which was an assertion everyone knew was ridiculous. But it didn't stop people from suggesting such a thing.

Hetz'lef thought that what most mystified the Casitians was the Earth penchant for violence, and for hating people who looked, or thought differently. Hetz'lef looked forward to a long conversation with Silandra, or perhaps Marianne, the woman that had become a companion of Silandra's student, Ja'el. He felt, for some reason, the need to understand these differences between the different branches of humankind. What was behind those differences? How could Earth humans become more like Casitians? Would they want to?

Hetz'lef had been very happy to be part of the first experiments in greenhouses growing Earth plants. They had done quite well growing a large number of Earth crops, including peas and beans, squash, potatoes, onions and all sorts of other root vegetables. Some crops— such as tomatoes, some herbs, bananas, and other more warm-weather crops—were complete failures. Hetz'lef and the others working on these experiments were fairly sure that there just wasn't enough light and heat coming from their star for those crops.

He had given a presentation of the results and had accompanied that with a feast of all Earth foods. It was a total hit, and the number of people signed up for the next round of growth experiments, where they would try these crops in the Casitian soil, instead of in greenhouses, was staggering. People really liked the taste of the Earth crops.

It had also taken some time and work to adapt the Galactic agronomy technologies to the Earth crops, but the group felt that they had come most of the way, and that the second group would help to finalize how those procedures would work. They would be working harder that growing season, but many felt that the result would be completely worth it. Hetz'lef wished that everything coming from Earth would be as positive and trouble-free as the crops.

Columbia, South Carolina, Earth, December 3, 2012

The interviews and the follow-up meetings at the UN and White House went very smoothly, although there were some noises about feeling insulted for not being in the loop. She let those pass. She then had been asked to go to Columbia, to discuss issues with Gerard. As she prepared to leave the flyer once they had landed in Columbia, she turned to K'flef and said in Casitian, "You have gone far beyond Kren'a in helping me, K'flef. Many blessings and thanks for your piloting."

K'flef smiled. "I feel as if I am doing Pho'sia's work here, Marianne."

Pho'sia was one of the manifestations of God that one particular school of Casitians worshipped. Pho'sia was a female aspect, one that was the holder of peace and wisdom.

"Yes, K'flef, I think you are correct. Blessed be Pho'sia."

Marianne got up, and left the flyer, turning around to face K'flef briefly. "I should be back in about one-half hour or so. I'll signal you if it will be much longer."

K'flef grinned. "I brought a giv of Ul'tretor." A giv was the Casitian equivalent of a very long biography. Ul'tretor had been one of the earliest Casitians and had been responsible for the origin of much Casitian culture. She had learned that K'flef was a real fan of Ul'tretor. There were about a hundred givs of Ul'tretor, some better than others. Marianne wondered which giv K'flef had chosen to read. Someday soon she would read one.

"Enjoy." She walked out of the flyer, into the cold winter of South Carolina.

Columbia, South Carolina, Earth, December 3, 2012

Gerard was pacing. He had been planning to come out first with an announcement, but that darned Imam beat him to it. He wanted to make sure that his 'New America' would get enough land, and prime land. Martin and Modes had left him, and he had no idea what they were planning, but it didn't matter. He knew that most people would agree to leave and go to this new land. And he would lead "New America."

The door opened, and Marianne walked in. "Hello Gerard." She reached out her hand. Gerard hesitantly took it and shook.

"Marianne, you know that I was quite concerned about the Imam's statement on Al Jazeera. He cannot create an Islamic world! We deserve at least one half of it!"

"Gerard, we will be as fair as possible. The land already has some natural boundaries. There are several groups of people wanting to settle on the new planet, plus hundreds of thousands of individuals. All of the land on this planet is prime. It's almost all arable, there is adequate water and food everywhere. There are no polar ice caps, and it is only 30% water, so there is an enormous amount of space for people to inhabit.

"The Casitians do not want to be in the position of making decisions about who goes where. So we have come up with a plan. A leader of every identifiable group will come to a conference that we are holding at the UN. At that conference, you all, with the help of the UN Secretary General, will hash out what pieces of land go to whom. The amount of land will be directly proportional to the population in your group. For you, that is the remaining population of the FFS.

"People who are not attached to any group will be settled in an independent zone, and they can find the land that they want as they land in the colony ships. There are hundreds of billions of acres of land on this planet, which means more than enough room for everyone. You really don't need to worry about this, Gerard."

Gerard was reassured, but he still was troubled by the fact that there were so many other groups, and that he would be competing with them for space. But he knew that his group was the largest next to the Muslims, which made him happy.

"Well, I guess that all sounds reasonable. I'll be at the conference. I want you to know that Jason Modes has decided not to leave, and some of his followers are staying."

Marianne shook her head. "No, Gerard, they are not staying. They will be forced to leave."

"Well, good luck with that. They are holing up at a compound in Texas."

"Thank you for that information Gerard. The conference will be in one week. Here is a list of things that you will have to have prepared by then, and other directions and instructions." She handed him a flash chip and looked at him. "Is there anything else, Gerard?"

Gerard smiled. "No Marianne, there isn't anything else. I want to thank you, and the Galactics, for this opportunity. It's the right choice, and I see that now."

Marianne got up, shook Gerard's hand, and left the room. Gerard put the flash chip into his laptop and opened up the list. It was a very long list. He needed to identify one representative for every 10,000 people. They didn't care how it was done, but it had to be done. And then, another representative for each 1,000 people, who would answer to that leader. There would be 100 groups of one thousand on each colony ship, and there was a lot to coordinate. Luckily, the trip to the planet was only a couple of weeks long. But there was food to produce and coordinate, determinations of what things people could, and could not, bring, how much they could bring, and how they would be gathered, and placed on the ships. Gerard started to think about who he should tap to start organizing all of this.

The ships could hold 100,000 people, and about one ton of cargo per person. It sounded like a lot, but then it wasn't so much if they were bringing things like horses and cows, or heavy equipment. It was clear that they would receive little, if any help or support from the Casitians. That wasn't what they wanted, anyway.

San Jose, California, Earth, December 15, 2012

Hassan and Joel sat at a café in San Jose, which was crowded at this time of day. San Jose, like all of the Bay Area, was mostly insulated from the chaos happening elsewhere in the US. Hassan Jammar was a radio astronomer like Joel, although he hadn't been involved in the SETI program. Hassan had been tapped by Joel to be on the larger liaison team.

"My father called. He has decided to follow his Imam to the new planet. I'm not happy about this."

"I've been reading about the divisions in the Islamic world about this whole thing. It seems like conservative Muslims are mostly emigrating, and moderate or progressive ones are staying. It's actually pretty similar to what's happening in the Christian world."

"But my father has been a moderate Muslim all of his life, even though he is very observant. I think that for him, the romance of living in a completely Muslim environment really appeals. His Imam has likewise been moderate. I'm worried that moderate Muslims will be drowned out in the new place. What's worse is that it's splitting my parents up. My mother refuses to go."

"I can certainly understand her desire not to go."

"She is bucking a trend, though. It seems that Muslim women are going with their husbands. I probably will never see my father again. All of the people emigrating there agree on no contact with any Galactic community civilization. That means no messages, no visits, nothing. I don't know whether they will open again, but it means a one-way ticket to a black hole."

Hassan looked disturbed, and Joel could understand. Joel wondered what kind of life people would have on this new world. No Galactic technology or contact to help them.

Joel said, "I'm sorry about your father, Hassan. I hope that you get to spend time with him before he leaves. On a different topic—what are you up to these days?"

"Ah, mostly spending time with the Galactic stellar databank, which is an amazing resource. I don't know where my career will take me. Somehow, the funding for our program at Stanford has been maintained, so I will have a job. And my tenure review is next year. It shouldn't be a problem. What have you been up to?"

"Not a whole lot. I've been living on the moon, which has been wonderful. I've been involved with emigration logistics, but that's coming to an end. All of the original team have been offered the opportunity to visit Galactic worlds, to tell the story of the Casitians' arrival. Diana declined, she wants to stay on Earth and continue her work with the UN, strengthening the world government. Marianne also declined. She decided to move to Casiti with Ja'el. I expect she'll stay there. David, Laura, and I agreed, and we'll be traveling together, along with K'flef, who is David's new companion. We've been given this really cool ship, and we'll be traveling at least for the next Casitian year. I don't know what will happen after that."

Hassan looked surprised. "I'd heard that all requests of Earth humans to move to Casiti were being denied. I had toyed with it until I heard that."

Joel nodded. "All of them except Marianne. I don't think they would deny her anything. But I have heard that will be relaxed in the future, so it's not permanent. They are quite wary of the influence of Earth humans on Casiti. I am not so surprised about that."

Moon Station, 40 Klef, 780/February 21, 2013

Silandra was looking at her AI's analyses of the preparations for the new Earth colony. The resourcefulness and cooperation that Earth humans had shown in this process was, for Silandra, a complete surprise. She felt that she was finally seeing more of a Casitian side to Earth humans. Once the land mass of the new planet had been equitably divided by the United Nations, different groups that were emigrating started cooperating with other groups, and they collaboratively planned how to bring equipment, animals, and food crops. All conflict, except for small pockets of anti-Galactics who were refusing to leave, had stopped. Earth humans who were not leaving were helping those who were leaving. Since the humans remaining on Earth would have the help and support of the Casitians, they were being surprisingly generous in giving planetary resources to those who were colonizing. In the US, 35% of the soldiers in the armed forces were interested in going to the new colony. Those who volunteered were being discharged so that they could provide logistics for "New America."

The different analyses that Earth news organizations had were similarly fascinating. It seemed that a consensus was emerging among the humans that would stay. They hoped that the new colony would be created in such a way as to make the Earth humans proud of what the emigrants had accomplished.

Those emigrating, however, had a completely different consensus—one that was less surprising to Silandra. It was primarily one of complete self-interest, or, in the case of select groups, interest in the group welfare over all others. Silandra thought that all of this, the colony preparation and formation, as well as the next decade or so both on Earth and on the new planet, would be a subject for both Earth and Casitian researchers for a very long time.

Everything was smooth, and on schedule. There would be four waves of colony ships. The first wave, which would include half of the ships, would take the "New Americans." The second wave would take most of the Islamic emigrants. The third wave, which would include most of the returning ships from the first two waves, would include the rest of the Islamic immigrants, and the many smaller groups and independent emigrants. The final wave, of just a few ships, would carry all of those that were being forced to leave, which included the twelve enclaves of fundamentalist Christians, about 95,000 in total led by Reverend Jason Modes, and a few other small enclaves of people.

Silandra had spent many, many hours over the past few months trying to understand Reverend Modes and the people who followed him. Patricia and Jal'end'a had helped, a little. She understood that their rigid belief system dictated that they would try their utmost to stay on Earth. But she didn't really understand their beliefs. Every time she read something about him, or heard him speak, she was completely flummoxed. She knew that his thinking wasn't logical, and that using logic to understand it wouldn't work. But she couldn't get her heart to understand it either.

They had gotten the help and support of the UN peacekeepers and the US National Guard, to gather those who were resisting. The plan was to put them all to sleep, and physically carry them and the contents of their compounds onto the colony ships. They would wake up on route to the new colony. The US was going to provide them with logistical help, food, water, and all of the necessary tools for survival on the new planet. But they were going to be at a major disadvantage compared to the others that had prepared.

Silandra and Marianne had actually argued about whether to put them with the "New Americans" or in a separate area. Silandra felt that all the anti-Galactics were pretty much all the same. Marianne argued that this group would severely undermine the ability of "New America" to get off of the ground without too much conflict. These folks needed to be on their own land. Silandra had finally agreed.

Chapter 19:
Emigration

Moon Station, 110 Klef, 780/May 10, 2013

Marianne watched the first wave of ships leave from a display on the desk in her and Ja'el's quarters. Ja'el was in another part of their suite, reading some reports from the initial loading of the colonists. Marianne thought that the whole first wave had gone very smoothly. The second wave of ships were starting to load up and would be leaving in about a week or so. The first wave ships would be back in about a month.

It all would be over in about three months. The most surprising change was the followers of Jason Modes. Just about all of them had decided, pretty much at the last minute, to join the "New Americans." This hadn't made Marianne happy—she worried about their influence, but Gerard was happy to take them in, so they were added to the first wave. In the end, she expected that the few hundred left in the one enclave that Reverend Modes lived in would also leave him, and the UN peacekeepers might just have to carry only a few people onto the last ships. The other enclaves that had been holding out had similarly emptied and joined one group or another of emigrants.

Marianne didn't really have a job to do anymore. The UN was becoming quite a strong government. People were adopting some Casitian customs, like the clasped-arm hug, different greetings, growing their own food, and other things. They were using Galactic technologies, listening to Casitian music, and doing public art. Some groups were going much more slowly than others. Marianne could tell that Earth culture was always going to remain different from Casitian culture. But the point had never been to make Earth into Casiti.

Interestingly enough, there were quite a number of Casitians that wanted to live on Earth. About five hundred had emigrated to Earth, mostly choosing to live in Europe and Asia. But some were living in some very unlikely places. Marianne wondered how they were doing, and what they would do as time went on. She'd heard that as many as five thousand Casitians might move to Earth.

Ur'lef had come back from a long stint with the parns and had expressed their relief at the huge changes in the energy of the planet. They were grateful for everything we had done. They were beginning to take their place as a Galactic species.

She thought about her future. She and Ja'el were moving to Casiti and would arrive in the middle of winter. Ja'el had rights to a dwelling that they would share for the winter. But Marianne had no idea what she would do once she got to Casiti. She also knew, and Ja'el and she had discussed, that she and Ja'el would part perhaps not at the end of this winter, but certainly by the end of the next one. She didn't really like that idea, but she knew that was Ja'el's custom. Even so, she would have been with Ja'el longer than any other companion Ja'el had before. It was something that would take time for Marianne to get used to.

New York, New York, Earth, August 15, 2013

Diana was putting the finishing touches on the report about changes in agricultural practices in western Africa, when the phone rang. "Hello?"

"Hello, Diana, this is Doug Williams, at the emigration office. How are you today?"

"I'm fine, Doug. How can I help you?"

"Well, I need to talk with Marianne, if possible. Something rather odd is happening."

"Something odd?"

"As you know, we were getting ready to wind down, since all four waves of emigration had been planned, and filled."

"Yes, and?"

"As you know, the first wave of ships has been back for a few weeks. Apparently, several people came back from the planet, and have been publicizing it."

"Yes, I've heard that."

"The requests for emigration have gone from a small trickle each day, which we deal with fairly easily, to thousands a day."

"Thousands?"

"Yes, thousands! We have received over 25,000 requests for emigration in the last four days, and the trend is upward."

Diana wondered about this. Well, lots of land, people could spread out, something new. It wasn't too surprising.

"OK, Doug, I'll call Marianne, and get her in touch with you. I'm not sure what she'll say."

"Thanks, Diana, I appreciate it." She hung up the phone, then called Marianne's AI on the moon.

Moon Station, 40 Wend, 780/August 16, 2013

They sat in the joining room: Marianne, Silandra, and Erit'ala. Marianne said, "It seems that finding out how wonderful and big the planet is has made more people want to move."

"But do they understand that they will be cut off from Galactic contact?" Silandra asked.

"Apparently, they do, and they want to go anyway. There is plenty of free space. Most of the planet hasn't really been allocated."

"About how many are we talking about?"

"It looks like about another 10 million, only 100 or so ships. We can easily add that to the fourth wave."

Erit'ala said, "But we must publicize that they will be cut off from all Galactic contact."

Marianne nodded. "I talked to Henry and Jur'tic—they are preparing a video, and getting it translated into many languages. Plus, we've told the emigration office to make that entirely clear. Everyone will know."

Chapter 20:
New Beginnings

New America, New Earth, November 12, 2013/Month 3, Year 1

Gerard looked around him, quite satisfied. Here were his leaders, his two hundred men, who were creating the New America. They listened to him, they trusted him. He was the leader of the new country. He listened to their reports, all of them favorable. This planet was a paradise. There were abundant edible plants and game and lots of fresh water. It did get hot, and there were some nasty biting insect-like things. But all in all, it was easy to survive here, and he thought they would thrive. They didn't need Galactic technology.

One particular man, Dennis, was a good leader. He had already put together a team of people to build the capital city. They were investigating the different kinds of trees, to determine how good they would be for building. They were all in pre-fabs and tents and would be for quite some time. He admired Dennis. He was also quite handsome, and definitely Gerard's type. Gerard hoped sometime to figure out what Dennis' story really was.

The colony was going very well. Planned communities were forming, farmers were beginning the process of figuring out how to grow crops and raise farm animals. Companies were forming and developing and finding markets. It was coming together in ways that made Gerard happy. The whole development process showed off his leadership skills. He could have been President of the United States, but President of New America was a lot better.

Independent Christian State, New America, New Earth, Month 3 Year 1

Yolanda walked out of the tent and looked around. At least she could stand inside the tent. Poor Stanley was always stooped down. It was Sunday, and time for church. Her pastor and virtually all of the congregation had joined a large group of Christians forming a state within New America. Yolanda was glad that she had come. Her daughters, however, had not been so happy. Leticia had run away at the last minute, but she had been found by a friend. Neither daughter could understand why Yolanda and Stanley wanted to come to the new planet.

Of course, Marianne hadn't understood either, nor had their mother. But Yolanda was determined to raise her children in a place that was free from Casitian influence. She thought this was the best thing she could do for them, even if they didn't understand.

New America, New Earth, November 12, 2013/Month 3, Year 1

Rita had managed to snag one of the large pre-fab units, which were much more comfortable than the standard size. She was a minor celebrity here. She was one of the very few journalists to come to New America, and she'd been known for her anti-Casitian reporting. She was the only reporter for a new paper that her boyfriend, Frederick, had started here. She had bought a new laptop just before she had left, which was chock-full of Galactic advances. But she was really happy with it. It would help her reporting immensely, given the primitive nature of New America. It would take years, she suspected, for many of the things that they took for granted back on Earth to be available here. But she was willing to wait. And as one of the few journalists here, she would be going places.

New Aard, New Earth, Month 3, Year 1

Abdul Jammar thought briefly of his son Hassan back on Earth and wished for a moment that he hadn't left. It was a regret that he could do nothing about. His decision had been irreversible, which he had known when he made it. He also missed his wife, but he was now glad that she hadn't come. Women were not being treated well here.

He heard the call to prayer, got up from his tent, and made his way to the makeshift mosque. His Imam, a moderate, had been replaced by a much more conservative Imam. This had happened all over the colony. The conservative Imams had made sure that their influence was strong. Abdul had yearned for a new way to live his Muslim faith, but he feared that he was only going to find the old ways. He hoped that someday he could find a way to make his dream happen.

Interstellar Transport, 120 Wend, 780

It was strange, finally leaving. Marianne had not been on Earth for weeks, and now she was leaving the solar system entirely. She was in a ship with a large contingent of Casitians, on their way home. The moon station was now populated primarily by Terrans, who had been trained by Casitians. Some Casitians remained on the moon for the time being, but eventually, most of the Casitians would go home. Silandra and Erit'ala, as well as Re'wl, Ur'lef, and many others, were on this ship.

She was sitting in the observation bubble, watching Earth and moon recede quickly from view. They were traveling amidst the last wave of colony ships bound for the new planet. She had never quite gotten an appreciation for how enormous they were until now, when she could see the bulk of her ship and compare the size. She never lost her amazement at Galactic technology.

She didn't know what Casiti would be like—except, of course, cold. Ja'el kept telling her she would get used to it, and that people spent the entire winter indoors anyway. She had a lot to learn about Casiti. She was looking forward to meeting Ja'el's family group, and her friends, and seeing more of Casitian art, and hearing Casitian music in person. She had become fluent in Casitian, and people to seemed always commend her on her great accent.

She found it almost impossible to believe that she was on the way to another star. She found it hard to believe all that had occurred since that single melodic "Hello" three years ago. But she had no choice but to believe, as she was watching her home fade into a canopy of stars.

###

The Story of New Earth

Chapter 1:
Under Tulip Trees

"Those who settled Casiti tried hard to understand those who wanted to stay behind. In the end, that understanding did not come, and in its place, came the name: Za'aref." – Ul'tretor (20)

Independent Christian State, New Earth, Month 1, Year 3

Leticia sat brooding under her favorite Tulip tree in a grove she'd found about a mile from the edge of their settlement. It had become her refuge very soon after they had landed. She was unhappy, again and still. She felt, yet again, her anger at her mother and father's decision to move here. She didn't understand why her parents wanted to leave Earth, and she hadn't wanted to. It had been two years, or one Earth Year, and it seemed to Leticia like forever. And she knew she'd never get to go back home, or to Casiti, where she really wanted to go.

It was getting toward fifteenth hour, and she knew her mother would be wondering where she was, so she got up, and made her way home. As she walked in the door, she saw her mother cleaning up their dwelling, and her little sister Beatrice was playing with her toys.

"Leticia, your father and I need to go to a church meeting now. I need you to stay here with your sister."

"OK, mom, that's fine. See you later." Leticia was happy to get some time without her mother around. She could spend the time compiling the notes she'd been taking on her explorations, and the plants and animals that she'd found.

The next day, Leticia sat at the back of her classroom, restless and uncomfortable in the all-in-one desks of the small classroom. It was inside one of the prefab buildings that had been put up just after landing. The new school hadn't been built yet. Of course, churches were first, and next were the houses of the powerful people in the settlement.

Her ninth-grade science class was boring, and she knew it was all wrong. She didn't understand why her classmates just went along with it. She'd read a lot of science before they moved to New Earth. She'd even read parts of Darwin's *The Origin of Species*. But this class was all based on the Bible's origin stories. And she tired of hearing things that were patently ridiculous, parroted by a teacher who clearly didn't comprehend a whole lot of real science.

She knew that she didn't have any choice. All of the schools in the Independent Christian State were run entirely by a group of ministers. All of the schools taught, as they called it, a "Biblically-based education." They read the Bible in English class, studied the history of Christianity in Social Studies, and then what she felt was pseudoscience in the Science class. Leticia hated all of that. Luckily, her math teacher had realized how talented she was, and had taken her under his wing, and she was now doing much more advanced math than the other students in her class. She felt that was keeping her from complete insanity.

"Leticia?"

She raised her head, realizing that she had not been paying attention at all to what her teacher had been saying for the last while. She looked at what was on the board. Oh, talking about fossils back on Earth. She dredged up her knowledge about the reasons why these people thought fossils weren't as old as they really were. She scratched her short Afro, as if in thought. She looked down at her notebook, as if looking at her notes. But there was only a blank page.

"Because it is impossible that the earth is older than about 6,000 years, so the dinosaurs and humans must have coexisted," she said it with certainty, emphasizing the "impossible" and "must."

The teacher smiled, nodded, and said "yes, Leticia, thank you very much."

Leticia had realized a long time ago that this teacher really didn't care what you said, as long as it fit into her paradigm. And Leticia thought it was even stranger that they insisted on teaching this, even when they were on a completely different planet than Earth and had learned much about the galaxy in the last few years.

The bell rang, and she put her notebook into her book bag, and walked out with the other students. She was on her way to her required class in sewing. She was getting into a foul mood, when Susanna ran up to come beside her, her long blond hair waving.

"Leticia, come over to my house after school? My parents won't be home until right before dinner."

Leticia smiled. She really liked spending time with Susanna. Susanna was a good friend. She had liked the Casitians too, and had come here against her will. Her father was the pastor of the one of the local churches, the largest in this settlement. They had gotten so large that they had been given special dispensation to build a new building. And that made her father powerful in the settlement. Susanna, though, didn't like it.

"Yeah, OK. My mother won't mind. It will be fun!" She wished for the days when she had a cell phone, and she could just call, and ask. But her mother liked that she had a friend who was the daughter of someone so powerful, so she knew that it would be fine.

"OK, I'll see you after school!" Leticia watched Susanna bound off, to get lost in the crowd of students going to classes.

New America, New Earth, Month 1, Year 3

Gerard got up from his midday sleeping period disturbed. He'd had another nightmare, which seemed to come to him only during his midday sleep. It had taken him a long time to get used to days that were more than twice as long as days on Earth. The accommodation that New America had come to was to simply divide the day into two effective days, with two sleep periods. But most people had been finding that they didn't sleep as well during the mid-day sleep, nor did they work as well during nighttime. He had resisted any adjustments in the daily schedule. Gerard wanted an efficiently run, well organized society. Farmers, however, had completely rebelled. They wanted to spend as much of the day working as they could. They were busy raising crops for biofuel to run vehicles of all sorts, since food was so easy to get, at least now. Gerard knew that in 10 to 20 years, when the population was much larger, large scale agriculture would become a necessity. Gerard had let the farmers off the hook, as the only exceptions.

He was working hard to make himself lifetime leader of New America. Luckily, everyone was too busy starting to build their own homesteads, learning the new planet, and starting new businesses to think much about things like elections. And he got things done for people. Dennis had come in quite handy. He was good at being secretive and setting up structures that would build and maintain Gerard's power. And, of course, Dennis was good in bed.

But Dennis' complex about their relationship kept it secret. The truth was, the last thing Gerard wanted was for people to know. And Dennis was busy making alliances all over New America, particularly in the Independent Christian State. The ICS had their own government that took care of just about everything, and they had power and resources – it would be important to keep them part of the fold.

He got up, got dressed and left the prefab he lived in, and walked the few feet to the prefab that was serving as the government center for the time being. About 1/2 kilometer away, the new "White House" as well as the adjoining government buildings, were under construction, and nearing completion. Gerard had let Dennis do all of the coordinating work of the construction – Gerard was busy with keeping people as happy as could be and fulfilling promises that he and Dennis had made.

As he walked in, one of his aides came up to him and said, "Gerard, the gentlemen that you gathered as your economic advisory council have all arrived."

"Thank you." He had been looking forward to this meeting for days, now. His advisers included John Mitchell, head of the brand-new New America Bank, which acted much like the Federal Reserve Banks back on Earth, except that it was completely privately owned. Keith Harrington had been an economist at Harvard and was slated to head the economics department at the first university in New America when it was finished being built. Ralph Merill had brought his entire company to New America. It had been the third largest farm implement manufacturing company in the US and was now the largest corporation in New America. Finally, there was Timothy Christopher, a successful steel manufacturer who had his pulse on industry in New America. He was now advising Gerard on all things related to industrial infrastructure.

He walked into the conference room, and saw the men seated around the table. They suddenly became silent as he walked in. Gerard wondered what they had been talking about.

"Hello gentlemen and thank you for agreeing to work with me."

John, head of the Bank, stood up. "I think I can speak for the group - thank you, Gerard, for choosing us to advise you - you made wise choices." A chuckle went around the room.

Gerard sat down. "So, let's get started, shall we?"

New Aard, Month 1 Year 3

"How are you, Olam?" Abdul Jammar looked at his friend.

Olam shook his head. "Not well, Abdul. Ever since our old Imam was asked to resign, I've felt at odds with everyone."

Abdul felt a deep sadness. "The new Imam is quite strict - I had originally hoped that our mosque could be a model for others in the area, but those from New Islamabad must have other ideas."

"I don't know how long I can survive here, Abdul. They are always giving preferential treatment to the conservatives. I might end up living in a tent for the rest of my life." Olam put his head in his hand.

Abdul touched his friend's head gently. "Olam, Olam, we will get out of here at some point. We will find a way to create that settlement that we have talked about." Abdul knew that it would take some time.

Abdul watched his friend Olam leave. Abdul had become an important person in his mosque because he was a fluent speaker of Arabic and was quite good at administration. He had realized, right after his moderate Imam was replaced by the more conservative Imam, that if he did not act as if he towed the party line, he would be in a lot of hot water. Already, a couple of more vocal moderate members of the mosque, like his friend Olam, had been ostracized, and were living on the outskirts of the settlement in tents, and not given work. Even though getting food in the surrounding wilderness was easy the ostracism was hard. Abdul had decided to keep his mouth shut for the time being. Olam stayed in his house quite a bit, and Abdul helped him out as much as he could. He was glad that Olam didn't resent him but understood that this was only a means to a greater end.

Abdul eventually became head of administration for his mosque. His mosque had quickly become the largest in the region, so he became a powerful man. This didn't sit well with him, though, since he knew that by being silent, he was basically lying about how he felt about the policies of New Aard. It was a good thing that they weren't quite as bad as the legendary Taliban on Earth, but they were far more conservative than he was. He didn't understand why this was necessary. They had a whole large territory to settle, most of which was still wilderness. Why not allow for Muslims of all stripes to follow their own hearts?

Abdul's eventual goal was to create a new, progressive settlement far away from the original settlements. But it would take a lot of doing, and a long time. The Imams had already carved up the territory of New Aard and were making plans for new settlements. Abdul had obtained, at great cost, a map of the entire world, and there was a lot of territory still unsettled. He thought that perhaps, soon, he could gather with him people who were progressive like him and settle in a new place.

Outside New Columbia, New Earth, Month 1 Year 3

Timothy looked over the latest batch of mining reports. He wasn't happy, not at all. His company had just begun the manufacturing of steel that would be needed all over New Earth for a variety of purposes, but in other kinds of metal production he was stymied. Getting iron wasn't the problem. The rock below the soil of New Earth was extremely rich in iron. In addition, one didn't need to dig too deeply: New Earth had a lot of iron-rich laterite soil. There were also deposits of hematite in many areas – another source for iron.

With the available iron ores, they could make most kinds of steel very easily. The problem was there were virtually no sources of titanium, platinum, zinc, silver or gold. He was in the process of equipping an expedition group to go up north above the Chalcedon River to look for sources of these metals, but he wasn't especially optimistic.

He heard a knock on his office door. "Come in."

His assistant poked his head in the door. "Mr. Christopher, I just got a message from John Culvert."

Timothy sighed. He was getting tired of John Culvert. Culvert was working on getting an electronics manufacturing operation off the ground and had been pestering Timothy pretty much since they landed for raw materials.

"What does he want now?"

"He wanted me to tell you that he had been talking with some banks and the like, and some financing could be on its way."

Timothy shook his head; he would have to visit Culvert personally and give him the bad news.

"Ah, Timothy, come in. So nice of you to visit."

Timothy walked into the ornate office. Clearly Culvert had used up most of his cargo allotment in furniture and furnishings, rather than anything that would actually help him start his business. They shook hands and sat down.

"Anything to drink?"

"No thank you. I'm fine."

"So, I imagine you are here to talk about that financing that I'm working on."

"No, John, I'm here to deliver some pretty bad news."

"Bad news?"

"We've surveyed 50 sites over every area of New America, as well as several sites in both Independent Zones. We've started several iron ore mining operations, and are producing lots of varied kinds of steel, as you know.

We've also located at least one source which will provide us with tin and aluminum. It's a large formation of granite in the southwestern part of New America. But the granite present on New Earth seems to be bereft of other metals. And we have yet to find any significant sources of titanium, zinc, platinum, silver or gold. And the Rare Earth elements aren't so rare on Earth, but they sure are rare here."

"But without those metals and others ..."

"I know, you have no business."

"We have no electronics manufacturing capability at all! And without that, we can't begin to have any advanced manufacturing of anything."

"I am aware of this dilemma."

"What are you doing to solve it?"

Timothy was angry. Who was this guy to demand anything of him? Despite his anger, he answered Culvert.

"I am sending out expeditions up north toward the poles. Based on my reading of the Galactic reports on this planet, if we don't find what we're looking for nearer to the pole, we won't find it anywhere."

Dlejon, New Earth, Month 2 Year 3

"Is there anything else anyone wants to share?" Douglas' booming voice carried over the quiet but insistent din of the gathered group.

Joan, a short, compact woman with dark hair, stood up. "We have already been in contact with the Lakota nation next door to us to the west, and I think there will be a lot of fruitful dialogue and trade. We have chosen, at this time, to not engage in a dialogue with our neighbors to the east. I think, however, that it might be time to start. We have much to offer many of the settlements along the river, and they are quite an independent and varied lot."

Some in the room nodded, others shook their heads. Douglas had been considering whether or not to create relationships with those settlements that were a part of the Southern Independent Zone. He agreed with Joan that it would be to their advantage and help with their long-term goals. Douglas pointed to a tall man in the back.

"Peter, you have a comment?"

"Joan, I understand why you think this is a good idea, but many of the settlements in the SIZ are allied with the New Americans. I think we need to understand much better what those relationships look like before we plunge in and start trade. I worry what might happen if the New Americans find out much about our settlement."

Douglas said, "OK, we need to wrap this up. Clearly this isn't something that is going to be resolved today. Thank you all, for a wonderfully productive council joining. Third meal was postponed until we finished. I think it's probably ready now. Farewell blessings."

Everyone in the room got up and filtered out of the meeting hall. It was a wonderful day in Dlejon. Doug looked up at the orange tinted evening sky. Doug had fallen in love with New Earth the minute he stepped out of the colony ship. It felt so much like home to him.

He had started out being very doubtful of his mission in life. He had realized, when he first heard about the Casitians, that he really was a lot like them already. He had become so committed to the Casitian way of life that he first had wanted to move to Casiti. But then the moratorium that stopped emigration to Casiti from made that impossible. He could understand that, even though at the same time it angered him. He imagined that it would eventually be lifted, but there was no way for him to know when. So he thought he could stay on Earth, and live in a community that was committed to Casitian culture.

But then, one day, he and a group of friends were hanging out at his house talking about Casiti, Earth, and New Earth, when an idea was hatched. He remembered the conversation vividly, as though it had occurred yesterday.

"Louis, are you nuts? Create a Casitian-like settlement on *New Earth*? Most people settling New Earth hate Casitians and want to get as far away from Casitian culture as possible! They will hate a community of people who want to live like Casitians."

"Douglas, have you read the most recent emigration reports? It looks like 75% of the people emigrating from Earth are small, independent communities that are going primarily for the adventure, and for space to grow. I talked to an old friend of mine who is going to settle in the Northern Independent Zone, as part of a new community they are calling 'Burning Man' – a bunch of artists and such who have been involved with that gathering for years. They want to create a permanent 'Burning Man', basically. That's hardly a bunch of folks who will hate us."

Sally chimed in, "I think it's a great idea. There are abundant resources, and we could really create an environmentally sustainable community. And I bet the Casitians would really like having a reliable community that they knew could contact them if necessary."

They were easily able to recruit several hundred people to come with them, and they came to New Earth. Once they landed on New Earth, they called their territory Dlejon, which, in Casitian, meant "spirit ground."

Knowing that people of New Earth could contact them was something that had been important for the Casitians. The Casitians did appreciate their presence and had entrusted them with a one-way communications device. The Dlejonese had promised never to use it to contact the Casitians unless there was complete consensus of all communities on New Earth that it was time.

Their eventual goal was to unite New Earth into a society that could be in contact with the galactic community again. Douglas knew that subsequent generations of New Earth people would not feel the same way as the original colonists who had wanted to escape the Casitians. He realized that it was likely his children's children that would be the ones to reunite New Earth with the galactic community, and Casiti.

Chapter 2:
Grapeberries

"We had great courage. We had the courage to stand by the beings who were our friends, allies, and mentors" — *Jlir Nern Klaft (1st age)*

Independent Christian State, New America, New Earth, Month 1, Year 7

"Don't you think he's so totally cute?" Susanna asked Leticia, as they sat in Susanna's bedroom. Susanna went on to describe Kurt, her current crush. He was blond like her, tall, and had what Susanna thought was a "gorgeous body."

"Um, well, I guess so, sure." Leticia had honestly been finding it difficult to find any of the boys at school cute, even though she understood it was expected. She had never really been drawn to boys. It was something that seemed to really bother her mother, which Leticia couldn't understand. Why would her mother care? It had come to a bit of a head around the Junior prom. Her mother had asked her whether any of the boys had asked her to the prom. She had lied and told her that none of them had. In fact, four different boys had asked her, and she'd declined.

Susanna, on the other hand, was ecstatic about going, and excited that the boy she had a crush on had asked her. Her mother had sewed her prom dress. Leticia just couldn't get her mind around it – she'd much rather sit under a Tulip tree and read.

"So you really don't want to go to the prom?" Susanna looked puzzled.

"No, I really don't. I'd rather be doing almost anything else."

Susanna nodded. Leticia thought that even though Susanna knew her well, she sometimes didn't really understand. But Susanna was very accepting anyway.

Leticia got up from sitting on the floor. "Well, I should get back home. Dinner is going to be soon. And I promised Beatrice I'd help her with her homework."

"OK, see you Thirdday? We were going to explore the ridge."

Leticia smiled. "Yes, the ridge it is! See you at first light." She walked out of Susanna's room, and house, and turned toward the street that her house was on. It was pretty quiet after everyone got home from the work periods. Leticia hated the rigidity of the ICS. She knew that other states in New America were much more fluid and flexible. But people in the ICS were following the Bible, or, as Leticia said to her mother one day, what particular people thought the Bible meant. That had generated a severe punishment from her mother. She'd been grounded from doing anything except go to school and church for weeks, and she had been sent to a church class for recalcitrant kids where they spent a lot of time trying to scare them about hell.

The one thing that she was glad of was that there was a lot less school here than on Earth. School was only three days a week and lasted for about six hours a day. That gave them three days off a week. One of those days was invariably the sabbath day, which rotated, since the Bible said that there had to be a sabbath every seventh day, but New America had six-day weeks. Sabbath days were filled mostly with church things. But the other two days Leticia had free to do whatever she wanted, since her parents were usually working. She used to have to babysit Beatrice, but now that Beatrice was 13, or, rather, 26, she didn't need to anymore.

She had to admit there was one thing she loved about New Earth: it was the planet itself. She had spent countless hours explored the landscape around the settlement. She kept notebooks filled with the new things she'd found and questions about them she wanted to research more. She once asked her science teacher about some of what she'd found, thinking that perhaps her teacher had gone to one of the workshops she'd heard about for people who wanted to learn more about New Earth. But the teacher hadn't. Leticia knew more about the planet than her teacher did, by far.

It was Leticia's dream to eventually see the whole planet. She knew that the only way she'd be able to do this was to escape from the ICS. She knew she had to escape from the ICS just to be able to live in the way she wanted to. She had found out about maps that existed of the territory beyond New America, and she was saving up to buy one. She was learning about all of the edible plants, the small animals and water creatures (they really can't be called fish) that could be caught and cooked. She was learning that some plants had medicinal uses. She was surprised by how many of them existed, and how few people knew about them. She had already begun to gather together things she might need for her trip, and was hiding them under the bed, and in the back of her closet. When the time came, which she thought might be soon, she'd be prepared.

New Columbia, New Earth, Month 1 Year 7
Sean looked over the epidemiology reports he'd managed to get from the few health care practitioners in New America, and some beyond. They had spread slowly, so most of them were months old.

It was an interesting mix of things. Accidents were common, which was to be expected. Infectious diseases, primarily of Terran origin, were growing alarmingly, some of them quite dangerously. That was going to be something that needed close attention.

The strangest thing was that cancer diagnoses were ... well ... non-existent.

Cancer had seemed to simply disappear. Although Sean's specialty on Earth had been oncology, he had been spending all of his time in general practice since he moved to New Earth. He had imagined that eventually, he would be able to return to his specialty, but the disappearance of cancer would mean that would never happen.

He wanted to spend time working out what was going on, but he doubted he'd find space in his schedule for that any time soon. He indulged himself in a little bit of consideration on it. He thought that it could be selection bias – those who had chosen to leave Earth were healthier. He then thought that perhaps, he needed to give more credit to the idea that the environment caused cancer. But he had a sneaking suspicion that there was more. People came to New America as smokers, and they were already raising tobacco. But there had been not one new lung cancer case diagnosed since they landed. This seemed rather unlikely to Sean. Some people must have arrived on New Earth with cancers that were at an early stage - why hadn't any of those shown up?

He looked at the epidemiology report he'd gotten from some people in New Calgary in the NCIZ. They had a preface which at first Sean ignored, but now he went back to read it. Apparently, they had found very active antiviral and antioxidant activity in a large variety of local plant life, including grapeberries. Sean wondered whether this was part of the key. He also wondered whether he could get more information from them to help New America.

He looked at the clock. It was time to leave to go to his meeting with the President. He gathered his notebook and got up from his desk. He walked out of his office to start the relatively long walk to the White House. Sean didn't really regret the lack of a real transportation system – he knew that would come in time. As he walked, he noticed how quickly things were changing. New buildings were being built at a rapid pace, now that building materials such as granite, steel and brick were in much greater supply than they had been at the beginning.

He walked into the White House, registered with the desk, and was met by an aide, who led him into the Oval office. Sean had heard about how large and ostentatious it was, but he wasn't quite prepared for what he saw. He was almost ashamed.

"Mr. President, Dr. Sean Joseph," his secretary intoned in a way that suggested she was bored.

Sean turned to the aide, "Thank you."

He then turned to the President, holding out his hand. The President shook it, and then motioned Sean to sit.

"I have heard good things about you, Dr. Joseph."

Sean felt uncomfortable. "Thank you, sir."

"You have a report for me?"

"Yes, yes, Mr. President. I have some sobering news about health in New America..."

"Well, go on, then."

He looked briefly down at his notes, and looked back up at the President, whose face was hard to read.

"After seven New Earth years, it has become clear that the life expectancy of people in New America is going to be much lower than it was in the United States. We certainly came with the full spectrum of Terran medical knowledge. But we haven't been able to begin production of either vaccines or antibiotics, or really any of the advanced pharmaceuticals that we had on earth. Plus, new ailments from the natural environment here are cropping up, and the few medical and scientific people we have haven't had enough time to figure them out. The good news is cancer has seemed to disappear, but infectious diseases that we brought with us are growing in frequency, and in some cases, virulency."

"So the rumors and scattered anecdotal reports I'd been hearing are true, then. What does this all mean?"

"I'm sorry Mr. President, but unless some large-scale efforts are put in place, people just aren't going to be as healthy here as they were on Earth."

"What are the steps you will be taking to create these efforts?"

Sean looked down again at his notes, feeling nervous.

"First, we need to find ways to encourage the beginning of a pharmaceutical industry. We need incentives from the government, for this to happen."

President Hopkinson said, "incentives are not the problem, Dr. Joseph. The problem is the lack of raw materials."

"Lack of raw materials?"

"Yes, apparently, we don't have the materials needed to manufacture most kinds of electronics, which makes pharmaceutical manufacturing extremely difficult."

"Honestly, Mr. President, without electronics - it's nigh on impossible."

The President nodded. "Indeed."

"Second, we need to train more medical professionals – from public health professionals, doctors, dentists, scientists, the whole gamut. We just don't have enough. We need you to set aside money to start schools for this."

The President shook his head. "Dr. Joseph, you know the story. This is a pure laissez-faire government. We don't do schools, we don't do health care, we don't really do much of anything except protect people's right to property, do policing, provide transportation infrastructure, and patrol and protect our borders. Local communities, if they wish, can deal with health education. We are trying to keep this as small a government as possible. You'll have to look elsewhere for money for schools. I'm sure there are some enterprising people see the value in this."

Sean sighed, and felt exasperated, "Mr. President, small communities can't shoulder the burden of medical and dental schools - it's just not possible."

"I'm sorry, but that's the way it is. The one thing I can do is call a meeting with those that I know that have some capital to throw around and see if I can get them on the bandwagon."

"Thank you, President Hopkinson, I appreciate that." Sean got up from his seat, shook the President's hand again, and made his way out the door, and back home. As he walked home, the unease at the pit of his stomach grew; he knew that things weren't going to get better any time soon.

Dlejon, Rec'jeter'she, Month 1, Year 7

"Feeling better?" Theresa looked into Douglas' ears. "Looks like your ears have cleared up tremendously."

Douglas nodded. "Yes, I feel so much better. No more pain or dizziness."

"Great. I'd say take the infusion for another week, then stop."

Douglas nodded, got off of the examining table, and gave Theresa a clasped arm hug. "Thank you so much Theresa."

"No problem, Doug. You realize that you are somewhat of a guinea pig. There haven't been so many cases of adults getting ear infections, and so we're trying out larger doses of the same infusions that we've been giving the kids. This seems to work fine."

Douglas nodded. "I am so glad that we started this program of investigating the health benefits of the local plants. It seems we are learning some very useful things."

He gave Theresa farewell blessings and left the medical compound to go back to the central coordinating compound. He realized he had been spending too much time in the central compound working. He needed some time off. He decided he would spend the next half-month in his cabin in the hills. Or, he should say, in his construction project in the hills. The foundation was in, and he had begun to put up the walls.

It had turned out that the most common tree in this part of New Earth, the Tulip tree, made great wood for buildings. Based on their studies, Tulip trees did not grow quickly, they needed to find ways to use them sustainably. They had calculated that each person could only use two Tulip trees in a lifetime. Luckily, older Tulip trees were very large, and one tree would provide enough wood for the basic necessary framing of a small house. But they had needed to find another possibility where wood was usually used for things like the framing of the walls, windows, the floors, etc. No other type of native tree would work. So during the first two years, they had experimented with creating small bamboo plantations. It turned out that the bamboo grew very well, and as long as they were careful because it could be invasive, they could use bamboo for all of the other needs they had for wood, including furniture.

Douglas had gotten his allotment of Tulip wood, in the form of big beams, which were all up. His next task was to use the bamboo planks to frame the walls. Douglas liked construction, and he liked the idea that soon, he would have a retreat in the hills he and his companion could enjoy. He thought that perhaps he could convince his companion to join him for a few days.

He thought, briefly, about his daughter, Mira, who was now sixteen (or thirty-two – it was hard for him to adapt to the new numbering scheme.) She'd been living in the youth settlement for a couple of years now, and only heard from her once in a while. When he did, it seemed she was really enjoying herself. He felt a twinge of guilt. She had said that she missed her mother. Her mother hadn't wanted to emigrate, and she hadn't wanted custody of Mira, so Mira came to New Earth. Douglas suspected that Mira would, in fact, have done better on Earth, but at least here, she was part of the New Casitian settlement.

Independent Christian State, New America, New Earth, Month 2, Year 7

"Leticia, where did you get this book?" her mother looked really angry. It was the book about Buddhism that she had gotten from Susanna. Susanna had picked it up surreptitiously during a trip her family took to the capital. She wasn't about to give Susanna away.

"It was in a trash bin, Mom. What's the problem?" Leticia knew what the problem was. There was a relatively short list of books that were allowed to people in the ICS, and her mother was petrified of being caught with a book that wasn't on the list. It could result in all sorts of punishment – ostracism, privileges being revoked, even, in extreme cases, time in a re-education program.

"You know darned well what the problem is. This book is going in the burn bin right now. You will march it to that bin and give me the receipt."

Leticia knew that she didn't have a choice. She would have to apologize to Susanna for getting caught with it. She'd been careless in hiding it, and her mother had begun to search her room. Leticia didn't know whether or not she suspected something, but she realized that she could no longer hide her stash of supplies and information in her room. She would have to find somewhere in the places that she explored with Susanna – a place to hide it all. She thought of the deep cave she and Susanna had discovered on the ridge. Yes, that would be the place. It was on the eastern side of the settlement, in the direction she'd have to go anyway when she escaped. She would have to slowly and carefully move items from her room, and hope that in the meantime, her mother didn't discover anything.

She took the book from her mother's hand, and walked out the door, toward the central government building of the settlement. It was a good thing she'd read the book already. As she arrived at the building and was going to the side with the burn bin, she heard a voice that brought her to attention.

"What's that?" She looked over, and saw Maybell, one of her least favorite people.

"None of your business, excuse me."

"Looks like a banned book to me."

"Go away, please." Maybell was the daughter of the pastor of the church they went to. She was also in her grade in school. She had been the one to tell the school principal that the math teacher was tutoring her in calculus. It was because of her that the teacher was fired, and she was disciplined to three weeks of church class, which had primarily consisted of learning and reciting verses from the bible such as I Corinthians 14:34 "women should be silent in the churches. For they are not permitted to speak, but should be subordinate, as the law also says." This, of course, simply made her hate Maybell even more.

"Well, I'm going to tell my dad that you have a banned book!"

"I'm burning it, OK? Leave me alone!"

"My dad might have something to say about it!" Maybell walked off, looking triumphant. Leticia sighed, and wished she was able to demonstrate the kind of tolerance and love that the book she was about to have burned had espoused. Right at the moment, she hated Maybell and her father, her own mother, and everyone in this stupid place.

New America, New Earth, Month 2, Year 7

Gerard woke with a start, and then calmed down, realizing he'd had another nightmare. He hated the nightmares – they were getting more and more frequent, and had moved to all of his sleep periods, whether mid-day or night. They had the same motif: someone threatening his power, and taking over, and him not being able to do anything about it. But it was silly. He was still firmly in control.

He remembered what was going to happen today and groaned. He had the meeting he'd been dreading with Robert Hurler, the current governor of the ICS. Maybe that was the source of his nightmares. The ICS was becoming more and more powerful and demanding more and more from New America. Primarily, they were most interested in making New America a lot like the ICS, which Gerard resisted as much as possible.

He got up and saw Dennis in the bathroom cleaning off his face after shaving.

"So what are you up to today, Dennis?"

"The usual, Gerard."

"You've given me that answer for months. But I don't even know what the usual is."

Dennis flung the washcloth into the sink. "Why does it matter to you? You don't really care what I do."

"But I do care – I need you to help me keep things in check."

"Things are fine, Gerard. Don't worry about it."

Dennis walked by Gerard, quickly finished getting dressed, then walked out the door.

Gerard got on his shirt and suit, and walked into his breakfast room to eat, hoping that Dennis would be there drinking his standard cup of coffee. But he had left the residence already, so Gerard had breakfast alone.

After breakfast, he walked down the long hall from the residence to the Oval Office. It was, in fact, larger than the Oval Office in Washington, DC on Earth. He'd commissioned a portrait of himself, first President of New America, and it dominated one of the walls.

Lately, there had been some agitation for elections. People were beginning to feel that since almost four Earth years had elapsed since they settled in New America, it should be time for elections. He knew that sooner or later they would have to hold them. But he was doing his best to work on how he would maintain power even with elections. There were several ideas, one of which included the ICS. If he could give the ICS what it wanted, he would own the presidency, since more than 35% of the population of New America now lived in the ICS.

"Mr. President, your first meeting of the day is with Dr. Sean Joseph." Sean, who was now the head of the New American Medical Association and had organized the doctors in New America. Gerard knew what he was going to ask for, and knew he would say no. His government was laissez-faire, and he was going to keep it that way. Tax money went to transportation infrastructure, defense along the border with the North Central International Zone, and internal law enforcement, and nothing more. And all of the major business leaders were in agreement with him. He had the chance to remake the United States the way it should have been, before things like the New Deal.

Gerard nodded at his secretary. "What's after that?"

"You have a meeting with your economic advisers, then with the governor of the ICS, Robert Hurler. After that, interviews with potential interns."

Gerard nodded. It was going to be a long day. Meetings mostly with people he had no interest in talking to. His economic advisers were likely going to give him news he didn't want to hear. Robert Hurler was going to make demands, and the stupid little interns were going to annoy him.

Gerard sighed. His secretary said "Dr. Joseph is waiting, shall I show him in?"

Gerard nodded, as he looked at his secretary who was a lean, tall woman and always wore severe dresses and high heels, he was suddenly reminded of his mother. He shook that thought away as Dr. Joseph walked in the room.

He looked terrible. It looked as though like he hadn't gotten much sleep in the past week or so.

"Hello, Mr. President. I'm glad that you could see me. We have a problem on our hands, a big problem."

Gerard looked at him with some suspicion, wondering what kind of problem it could be.

He nodded, and said, "go ahead."

"There is a growing epidemic of a new strain of polio in western New America. It clearly is a result of some sort of mutation - people who had been vaccinated as children seem to be still susceptible. And it is very virulent – many people are getting paralyzed and dying – possibly as many as 30% of those infected, although it's hard to know. We've had ten deaths from polio in the past month. We need some resources to be able to begin to research and manufacture a vaccine. If we don't get on this now, we could be decimated by this."

"There is nothing I can give you, Dr. Joseph, I'm sorry."

"Well, perhaps there is one thing you can do."

"What would that be?"

"Apparently, people both in the Southern IZ as well as the Northern IZ have been studying the medicinal properties of many local plants. We need their expertise. Can we ..."

"Dr. Joseph, New American stands or falls on its own. I will not have influence from outside this country, no matter what! Anyway, thank you, Dr. Joseph, for that report. I'll keep in touch." It was a dismissal. The doctor turned and walked out of the office.

Gerard walked around his desk and sat down. There were several bills he hadn't signed yet. A bill that finally divided up all of the land in New America, and made it open for sale. A bill to prevent private citizens from complaining about industrial waste that might end up on their land. A bill to define marriage as one man, and one woman.

Gerard looked at that bill, and for a moment, had some hesitation. But if people wanted to get married in some other configuration, they could always leave, and go to an IZ, where there were settlements and communities that fit anyone.

"Sir, your economic advisers are here."

"Thank you." They walked in, all four of them. He'd been meeting with them regularly for years now and knew them well. They all sat down on the couches, and Gerard sat in his signature chair.

He'd never actually be to the White House and had never seen the real Oval Office. He remembered what the office looked like on that old TV show, *The West Wing*. He'd liked an old-fashioned looking style, and he did his best to make his office look majestic. He did his best to act presidential, even though sometimes in New America that seemed, well, overly formal.

"Gentlemen, thank you for coming today. I have a couple of specific items I would like to discuss with you, after I hear your assessments of New America's economic situation."

He pretty much knew what they would say – he knew them well and had taken care to learn what was most important to each of them. He figured that Ralph would be happy – people needed the equipment his company made and were willing to pay for it. He was fiercely against any sort of government regulation of his, or any, business. George and Keith were worry warts about the diversity of the New America economy, and the fact that there was little trade between NA and the burgeoning economies of the Independent Zones and New Aard. And Timothy would wax on and on about the lack of supply of raw materials.

Ralph cleared his throat. "Well, Mr. President, what is most on my mind right now is that I can't get enough workers, and the ones I have are out sick far too often. And further, I thought that the training programs I'd put in place were going to be enough – but the schools here are not enough preparing students for the jobs I have, and the older, more experienced workers keep getting sick. You are going to have to do something about this situation."

Gerard was taken aback. "Ralph, you have been fiercely in favor of the kind of government that I have put together – we only deal with infrastructure issues, defense, and defending property rights – you didn't want the government to start a pharmaceutical manufacturing facility, or any medical facilities at all – you wanted that to be private. And schools – last I heard, you wanted all of the schools to be private schools.

Keith spoke up "I think many people have come to realize that the health issues are creating serious difficulties for everyone. We need government leadership."

"Well, government leadership requires taxes. You're suggesting that we start corporate taxes, and increase the personal tax rate?"

Ralph said, "Gerard, if I knew that paying my taxes was going to help my workers stay healthy, it would be worth it to me. Otherwise, I'm going to go out of business."

Gerard looked at Christopher. "Any changes?"

"No Mr. President. We're going to be stuck in the early 20th century, possibly forever. There just aren't any of the necessary precious or rare earth metals we need for advanced technology. People have been working on alternative methods for manufacturing things like chips and the like, and there are some positive results, but it's going to take a long time.

They talked more about taxes, and about the government's role in health care, and the general economic status of New America. By far, the most pressing issue was health care – Gerard would have to get Sean back in his office, soon.

North Central Independent Zone, New Earth, Month 2, Year 7

"It's amazing, isn't it? We've so far been able to demonstrate antibiotic properties in five native plants, antiviral activity in six, and anti-cancer activity in twelve. There are four food plants that have more antioxidants than all of the fruits and vegetables from Earth we can grow..."

"Too bad they taste so bland." Jeffrey laughed.

"You love grapeberries, though, don't you?" Thomas walked over to Jeffrey, and affectionately rubbed his hands over Jeffrey's naturally kinky hair. Thomas and Jeffrey had been lovers for years, and had decided to settle on New Earth, simply because of the adventure. Thomas had been interested in medicinal plants on earth, and it had turned out that he was really in his element here. Jeffrey, an epidemiologist, had been able to help Thomas document the benefits of the plants. Their settlement and the ones surrounding it had benefited greatly.

"Now the question is, how do we publicize this all over New Earth?"

"Well, publicizing it in this part of the Independent Zone is easy. The new widenet has been up now for a couple of months, and most of the settlements around here have at a cybercafe. We can put up a website and get the announcement on the newsgroups and email lists. But outside of that..."

"I heard that there are noises about expanding the widenet, and connecting our net, to some others, like the Southern Independent Zone in particular. That would help."

"But Tom, that will take months or longer – I hear there has been a lot of trouble getting electronics for the widenet. People need to know this, *now*. I'm thinking I need to start to travel."

Thomas groaned. Sometimes, Jeffrey's sense of doing anything he could for the common good made their life difficult. Back on earth, Jeffrey had gone to sub-Saharan Africa about a year after they became partners, to spend three years helping to get people treatments for HIV/AIDS. Thomas had visited Jeffrey about five times in Africa, but it had been a strain on their relationship. Traveling around New Earth would be worse. Thomas realized that it meant that if he wanted to see Jeffrey anytime in the next couple of years, he'd better travel with him.

"OK, I'll come with you. It would be good to find out the range of all of these plants anyway."

Jeffrey smiled. "Besides, admit it, you love adventure!"

Thomas couldn't help but agree. "Alright! Let's start planning..."

Independent Christian State, New America, New Earth, Month 1, Year 8

"OK, so do you remember how I factored that last equation?"

Leticia and Beatrice were sitting at the kitchen table, hunched over Beatrice's Algebra 1 assignment. Leticia had gotten a chance to learn calculus, and math came fairly easily to her. It was a struggle for Beatrice, although Leticia was always surprised by how Beatrice was able to analyze people, situations, and their motivations far better than Leticia could.

Beatrice started to write on the page. "OK, I think I get it – the x squared minus 6 becomes x minus three ..."

"Yes, there little sis, you got it."

At that moment, Yolanda came into the room.

"Leticia, I need to speak with you now."

"Mom, I'm helping Beatrice with her algebra homework."

"It's important."

"Oh, OK." She turned toward Beatrice, and rolled her eyes, tilting her head toward her mother, "I'll be right back."

She followed her mother into the living room. She knew exactly what it was going to be about.

"So, Leticia, I was wondering whether there were, you know, any boys you liked at school."

Here is was again. Her mother's angst and stress about the fact that she didn't really have any interest in a boyfriend.

"No, mom, I don't right now. I don't even want to think about it. I have my studies, and I'm exploring ..."

"But Leticia, you *have* to get married. You will be thirty-two very soon. The new guidelines say that women have to be married by thirty-six, so that they have time to produce a lot of children before they get too old."

"Mom, I've already told you, I don't want to get married, and I don't want to have children. Why don't you just leave me alone?"

"Leticia, you don't have a choice. Get married or join the Mission Society. You have only two months before your thirty-second birthday, which is the end of school for you."

This particular rule, enacted last year, had really made Leticia mad. Not that she liked school all that much, but that there was a difference between boys and girls. Boys could graduate from high school, and even attend the new Bible college or the new technical schools in the ICS. Girls, on the other hand ...

"Look I can get a job or something, until I'm eighteen, then I can find a place on my own, I don't need to live here"

"Leticia, you are not on Earth anymore. Single women live at home or in the Mission Society. There are no other choices." That was another new rule. Leticia knew that her days of stalling her mother were coming to an end.

"Mom..."

"Leticia, this is your choice. Sign up for the Mission Society this week, or I will go to the marriage matching service, and find a husband for you. You are still a minor, and still have to do what I say. What are you going to do?"

Leticia knew what she was going to do, but she wasn't about to tell her mother. "I'll think about it, OK?"

Yolanda nodded. "OK, but this is it, Leticia. I'm not even sure the Mission Society will take you, given how many disciplinary problems you've had at school and church. But if you don't want to get married..."

"Alright Mom. Will you leave me alone now?"

Yolanda nodded, and walked out of the room. Luckily, she and Susanna had already planned an exploratory trip on Thirdday that her mother had approved of. That would be the last day her mother would ever see her again. She regretted having to leave Beatrice behind, and even thought for a minute of bringing her, but then she realized it would never work – Beatrice wasn't old or strong enough.

North Central Independent Zone, New Earth, Month 1, Year 8

Thomas and Jeffrey sat in their living room, with notebooks, and paper and maps strewn all over the floor. They had been planning this trip in earnest for about two weeks, spending much of their waking time on figuring out logistics. Thomas was a better planner for trips of this sort than Jeffrey, even though Jeffrey had done more of it. Thomas had an idea of how long they were going to be away, and what sorts of things they would need. Jeffrey was in charge of letting people know what they were doing and finding people who might want to join them.

Thomas picked up one notebook and looked at his notes. "So I contacted several guides, and one of them said he could take us from New Calgary to Dubuque. He was sure that there were plenty of river guides to take us down the Mississippi river once we got to Dubuque."

Jeffrey nodded. "That sounds good. What did the guide say about places to stay along the way?"

"He said we'd need the full spectrum of camping equipment, although there were a number of settlements we will be staying at with inns or hotels. We'll be spending plenty of nights in our tent, though."

"That's fine. I like our tent." Jeffrey smiled.

Thomas flipped the page. "It seems the best route will be to go from here overland to Dubuque, then down the Mississippi river to New Orleans. At that point, we can start with New Aard settlements along the Nile river. We can then go back down the Nile to the Mississippi, down the Mississippi to The Great Western River, and travel that along the South Central IZ, and then up into New America. From there, using the River Chalcedon, we can visit settlements both in the Independent Christian State, as well as the settlements of Mormons and Seventh Day Adventists. "

"Yeah, it's those last three I'm most looking forward to," Jeffrey said with a wry look on his face.

"We don't have to tell them anything about ourselves, Jeff. It will be fine. Don't worry about it."

Jeffrey picked up a sheet with notes that he had written. "OK, so it looks like we have gathered our team. Leonard, one of the people who started the widenet wants to come so he can help connect the unconnected settlements, and then also perhaps work with folks in the other territories."

Thomas nodded, "great idea. And we can use his help in spreading the word."

Jeffrey nodded. "And then there is Johanna, the anthropologist, she's pretty keen to find out how the cultures of these isolated different groups are evolving. We can definitely use her in the epidemiology studies, as well."

Thomas nodded. "Keep going."

"Georgia and Chuck want to come."

"You're kidding! She's going to get Chuck out of New Calgary? I guess he's running out of material now that he's interviewed every single New Calgary resident on video."

Jeffrey chuckled. "And she's ready to write the great New Earth travel guide! This guy Jon contacted me, from the next settlement over. He's a geographer and wants to do as much mapping and exploring as possible. He wants to know how far and wide people had managed to settle and put those settlements on the maps. I thought he would be a great fit."

"Wow, it is sure going to be a motley crew."

Thomas was excited. He liked adventures, and this would certainly be one. And he did like that it would end up helping a lot of people, and that made him feel good.

Independent Christian State, Month 1 Year 8

Leticia, Susanna, Susanna's boyfriend Kurt, and Leticia's friend Terrance sat down in the grass in a small area just outside of their settlement. Leticia could see the stakes and strings in the ground, suggesting that someone was planning to build here.

"So I have to leave sooner than I thought. My mother is threatening to send me to the Mission Society or a marriage matching service, neither of which I want. I've been gathering my supplies up in the cave that we've already explored. I'll have to leave when we are supposed to be exploring thirrday."

Susanna seemed positively excited. "Kurt and I have also been stashing supplies – we're ready to go whenever, and thirdday is as good as any, as far as I'm concerned."

Leticia looked at Terrance, who if anything looked terrified.

"I'd ... I'd like to come. I have some things I've stored in my room that I'll bring with me."

Kurt snorted, "are you sure you can handle what we're going to do?"

Leticia was about to come to Terrance's defense, when Susanna said, "Kurt, he's a strong kid, like all of us. He'll be fine – won't you Terrance?" She smiled at him.

He smiled back. "Yes, I'm ready. Really, I am."

Leticia wanted to get back to planning their escape.

"So this is what I think we need to do..."

Casiti, 18 Klef 781

Marianne was fertilizing her greens in the greenhouse alongside Ja'el, and she was thinking about New Earth. She wondered how her sister and nieces were doing. By now, she hoped things had settled down. Leticia and Beatrice would be in school, still. Marianne wondered what colleges had started, and where Leticia might end up going.

The Casitian winter had been both hard, and wonderful. It was cold and going outside for even a little bit was brutal. She spent her time with Ja'el, gardening, writing about Earth. She was in the middle of a very long and engaging discussion with Diana back on Earth about politics and the future of Earth now that what they were calling "The Casitian Crisis" was over.

She knew that in a relatively short time, at the end of this Casitian winter, Ja'el would leave. She was getting used to the idea, but she knew that when it happened it would be difficult. She thought that she'd probably go back to Earth – Casiti hadn't been the haven she'd thought. And she'd faced more anti-Terran prejudice than she'd ever expected. The very few Terrans on Casiti talked together often. They all experienced pretty much the same thing as she, although it seemed that some were better able to handle it. One of her fears was a slow separation over time between Terrans and Casitians. Casitians weren't allowing any immigration, and few Casitians were living on Earth. That made her sad.

"Penny for your thoughts?" Ja'el's beautiful voice brought her out of her reverie. That wasn't at all what Ja'el had said, since they always spoke Casitian these days. But it was Marianne's best internal translation of the Casitian colloquialism that was often used to mean pretty much the same thing. Money, of course, was not part of the Casitian phrase.

"Just thinking about the future, love. And wondering how Leticia and Beatrice are doing on New Earth. I sometimes regret not trying harder to get Yolanda and Stanley to stay..."

"You did your best, and they really wanted to join the ICS. It's understandable."

"I know, but I hate to think about what Leticia is going through. And worse yet, I'll never know how things turn out for them."

Chapter 3:
Tato Root

"We must never forget the experiences of slavery that have shaped us." –
Ul'tretor (20)

Independent Christian State, New America, New Earth, Month 1, Year 8

She was lying in bed, waiting for her alarm to ring. She had finally told Beatrice what she planned, and Beatrice had promised not to tell what she knew. The conversation had been difficult for Leticia.

"Bea, I just have to leave."

"I'm going to be lonely without you, Leticia. Mom is going to go crazy when you leave."

"No she's not. She knows I can't fit in here, not the way she does, or the way you can."

"I don't really want to fit in, but you're right. I actually want to get married to Craig. But I hate the ICS. I know we'll leave soon after."

Leticia grinned. She liked Craig – thought he was decent, and she knew that he and Beatrice would make a nice couple. Craig had been Beatrice's best friend since the first day that they landed on New Earth. They'd met on the colony ship. He became "officially" her boyfriend last year.

"But Leticia, things are bound to change. I've been watching the way the ICS government is working, or, really, not working."

"What do you mean?"

"I can see that there are not enough resources to do the things that need to get done, and people want more freedom, even people who follow the faith. There is a lot of stress on the system – things will have to change. But I know you can't wait. Don't wait. I'll miss you."

"I'll miss you too."

She tossed and turned in bed, not able to sleep. Susanna was coming with her, of course. So was Kurt and Terrance. Kurt and Susanna had gotten involved, but they both knew they couldn't live in the ICS. Terrance was a slight boy, with piercing eyes, and very soft features.

He had been teased terribly in school, and Leticia and he had become good friends.

She looked at the clock and saw that there was only fifteen minutes before the alarm. She could see the first beginnings of light showing in the sky. She got up, turned off the alarm, and went to take a shower. She suspected that this would be the last shower she got in a while. As the water washed over her, she thought about what lay ahead of her. She, Susanna and Kurt had done a lot of exploring east of the settlement. Kurt had taken a five-day canoe trip a while back, and had heard about the river network that lead to the big Chalcedon River. That river, Kurt was told, lead to the River Nicea, which was the borderline between New America and the Independent zone.

The hardest part was going to be getting out of the ICS. Once they got into New America, they would probably be left alone. But no one was allowed to leave the ICS. They would travel over land or follow some rivers on foot until the border with New America, then keep going until they got to the border with the Independent Zone.

She finished her shower, dressed, put the last of her things in her day pack, and walked downstairs. She smelled breakfast cooking.

"Leticia, I'm glad you are up. I'm sorry, but you have to cancel your exploration trip."

"What do you mean?" Leticia got panicked.

"I managed to get us an appointment with Maria of the Mission Society. She was so gracious. She said that it might help you to decide to talk with her."

"But Mom, Susanna is expecting me!" Invoking Susanna had worked less and less over the past few months.

"I'm sorry, but you can't go, and that is that."

"Mom, at least let me go to Susanna's and tell her? I'll be right back." Leticia hoped that her mother would allow this. Otherwise, she would have to quickly figure something else out.

"OK, go right this minute before breakfast."

"I'll be right back." She picked up her bag and began to walk out the door.

"What do you need that bag for? Leave it here."

"It has something of Susanna's I need to return. I'll be right back, Mom." She gave her mother no chance to protest further, as she bolted out of the door, and down the street.

She ran to the gathering point, which was at the end of a dead end street, on the east side of the settlement. She saw Susanna, but not Kurt or Terrance.

"I have to leave and meet you at the caves. My mother made an appointment for the Mission Society for today, and I was supposed to be going to your house to tell you I can't come today. But if I take too long, she'll probably start looking for me at your house."

"Oh no! I should go too, then, but then what about Kurt and Terrance?"

Just at that moment, they saw Kurt rounding the corner. Leticia ran to him. "Kurt, wait here for Terrance, and then meet us at the caves. It's a long story, I'll tell you later."

Kurt looked startled. "OK, meet you later."

Leticia ran back to Susanna, and they started running toward the ridge. Luckily Leticia had never told her mother about the cave in the ridge, and she had told her mother that she and Susanna were taking a trip southwest, to Lake Timothy. Hopefully both of those things would mean that they would never be found.

They slowed down once they had lost sight of the settlement. The hills leading to the ridge were steep, and it was slow going. Usually, the cave was about a two-hour hike. She hoped they could make it much sooner. They decided to take the lesser used trail, which lead around the ridge from the north, and was steeper, but shorter. They knew that once they got to the cave, they would be fine. It was easy to see anyone approach from quite a distance, and they had found another exit from the cave far to the northeast, where they would go to start their trek to the river.

They finally arrived at the ledge that had the cave entrance and decided to wait there for Kurt and Terrance. It took a while for them to catch their breath.

Finally, Leticia said, "I was so scared that I wouldn't be able to leave today. I think somehow my mother knew."

"Yeah, it seems pretty convenient that she made that appointment for today, huh?"

"Well, we managed to get away. I can't imagine that they will be able to find us."

"No, they'll never find us. I'm really confident we'll get out of the ICS."

"What about your dad? Are you worried that he will get a huge search party going?"

"I don't know, but we can evade them. We know this territory better than they do."

Leticia nodded and smiled. "And we're younger."

Susanna laughed.

"What's so funny?" a deep voice asked. They heard scuffling, and then saw the figures of Kurt and Terrance appear around the corner of the ledge. Susanna got up, and hugged Kurt. "I'm glad you made it. Any signs of pursuit?"

"Nope, everything was all quiet. I only had to wait for a few minutes."

Leticia got up. "Well, shall we? We've got supplies to pack, and a long trip ahead of us."

They all started to walk toward the cave, and once in it, they stopped for a moment to let their eyes adjust.

Terrance asked quietly, "so what happened, Leticia?"

"My mom canceled the exploratory trip – I was supposed to go meet with the mission board. So we don't have the benefit of a whole day's lead time."

He replied, "yeah, and my dad forbade me from coming, which is why I am empty-handed. I had to sneak out, too."

Kurt said, "OK, it looks like the adults will know soon that we're missing. We have our work cut out for us. The question is, should we stay here for a while, or start?"

Leticia said, "Start. They might eventually find the cave. I want to put as much space between us and them as possible, as quickly as possible."

They all agreed, and moved into the cave, to the small side tunnel was that held all of the supplies they had been accumulating. There was an extra pack for Terrance, and they arranged all of the supplies, and divided them up. Once they were set, they lit one of the torches, and started to walk northeast, to the other entrance to the cave.

"Any other details we haven't thought of?" Thomas looked around the room at his traveling companions. They were, in fact, a motley crew. Jon, the geographer, was an intense older man, who wore glasses, and was balding. Thomas worried a little about whether or not he'd be OK on the trip. Chuck was another worry. He sort of reminded him of a version of that famous filmmaker who used to do liberal exposé films back on Earth. Chuck was quite heavy, bearded, and obstreperous at times. Georgia, his wife, was a good moderating influence on him, though. Leonard was what Thomas would think of as a real geeky type. He was thin, had long, stringy brown hair, and could hardly speak a sentence without several words Thomas could not understand. Johanna, the anthropologist, seemed a bit of a mystery. Thin, wiry, with long hair and glasses, she said very little.

"Well, Tom, if we haven't thought of them, who is going to talk about them?" Jeffrey asked, playfully.

Thomas frowned. "I'm just trying to tie up loose ends, here, Jeff, making sure we have everything we need."

Georgia smiled, and said calmly, "Thomas, Jeff, I think we have everything we need. We're just about finished packing everything up. Our first few stops are all in relatively civilized parts of the Independent Zone. I'm sure we can get what we need if we find we need something else. We've got a good supply of money and items we can barter. We'll be fine."

Thomas nodded. She was right, of course. He was just nervous. It was going to be a long trip, taking several years out of his life. He wanted as much as possible to go well. The meeting broke up, and they all went their separate ways, until Firstday, SecondMonth. That was the day they would leave, at first light.

ICS – New Earth, Month 1, Year 8

"Don't tell me she didn't say where she was going!"

"Mom, she didn't tell me. I have no idea what direction she was headed."

"You know where she used to explore – where would she go?"

"Mom, she explored everything all around the settlement, she knew every inch of land within 20 miles of here. How would I know where she went?"

Beatrice was surrounded by a group of very agitated adults, sitting in the living room of Susanna's house. Susanna's father, a powerful pastor, had been pacing. He was livid with rage.

"I know this all was Leticia's idea. Susanna would never have left without some kind of instigation."

Beatrice looked at her mother, who at first appeared as if she was going to defend Leticia, or, more accurately, herself, but then thought the better of it.

"Yes, Reverend, Leticia was always a troublemaker. I imagine it was her idea."

"Mom, that's not fair!"

Yolanda glared at Beatrice, "Shhhh. be quiet now. We adults have to figure out what to do. She told me she was going south and visiting Lake Timothy. We could go search in that direction."

Stanley said, "no, I think we should search in the opposite direction."

"There isn't going to be a search," the Reverend said.

"What do you mean?" Stanley looked angry.

"They will all reap what they sow. We need to focus on those that are here, like your daughter Beatrice, who I hear is a very good girl." He looked at Beatrice cloyingly. Beatrice managed a thin smile, and realized that Leticia had, indeed, successfully escaped from the trap.

Independent Christian State, New America, New Earth, Month 2, Year 8

"Shhhhhh. Be quiet!" Kurt whispered very loudly to Terrance, who was walking through the brush with a lot of noise. Leticia could hear it all the way back where she was, and she winced. They had almost run into someone who was camping along the river, and they were relatively close to a settlement. Kurt had insisted on taking the lead and wanted Terrance close behind. Susanna was in the middle, and Leticia was acting as rear guard.

They had been traveling now for six days. They had been long days, although Leticia felt more rested than she had when they started out.

They chose to travel for as long as possible during the daylight, so they would often try and walk for as long as 20 hours at a time, with some rests. When they stopped, they would rest for the entire night period. They had moved far fairly quickly and were about half of the way from where they started to the border of the ICS. Luckily, their settlement was on the eastern side of the ICS. The ICS itself was more than two thousand miles wide.

There was no indication whatsoever of any sort of pursuit. There was an outpost settlement that they had passed just after getting off of the ridge, and Leticia had taken a huge risk, and walked down to it during a night period, and sat next to the police shed, to listen to what they were saying. There was no mention of runaway teenagers from their settlement, or any sort of search for missing people.

They felt that their only worry was going to be simply running into people who might want to report teenagers who were traveling without adult supervision. They had decided on a strategy that might help them evade trouble, especially now that they knew that there had been no alert out for them. They would play two young married couples who were on their way to start a new outpost settlement. It wasn't out of the realm of possibility, and likely people would fall for it. But they hadn't yet had need of it, since they avoided people and settlements as much as possible.

As they came down from a hill, they came into view of the place where the Nicea River and the Chalcedon River came together. The sun had begun its very slow descent into the west, and they had been walking for close to twenty-one hours. Leticia moved ahead to where Kurt was, and suggested a halt for the day.

"This seems like a nice place for a stop. We can see everything around, there doesn't seem to be anyone close by. I think we can stop for the night here."

Kurt nodded, "sure, I think it's a good time. I'm pretty beat. I wish Terrance would be quieter!"

Leticia put her hand on Kurt's shoulder. "Give him a break. He doesn't have the experience you have, and he's really tired. We're all really tired."

Susanna went up to Kurt, and together, they went to a small group of trees at a short distance to set up their tent. Leticia went up to Terrance, who was sitting on a rock, looking dejected.

"Don't worry about Kurt – he's just a bit too bossy – and he does worry about us being caught."

"Do you think I want to be caught?" His features screwed up as if he was about to cry but didn't want to. "We have to get out of here, I can't live here, I'll die if I stay. I don't understand why Kurt is so mean to me."

Leticia sighed. Kurt tolerated Leticia, barely, but he seemed to have no time or patience for Terrance. She didn't really understand what it was about, and she'd worried a little bit about it over the past couple of days. But it really didn't matter. In another week, they would be out of the ICS, and could, if they wanted to, go their separate ways. Apparently, Kurt was trying to convince Susanna to stay in New America. Leticia wanted as little to do with New America as she possibly could. New America was a country that allowed something like the ICS to exist. The Independent Zone was her goal, even though she knew nothing about it. Independent sounded really good to her.

"Well, try not to worry about it too much. It will work out fine." Leticia put her hand on Terrance's arm, and got up to find a spot for her tent.

After she had set up her tent, and begun to find a place for the fire, Kurt walked up to her and said, "you take first watch, Terrance second. Susanna and I will take third and fourth."

Leticia was annoyed. "Um, don't you want to ask me and Terrance what watches we might prefer before you simply decide unilaterally? You aren't the leader, Kurt."

"Well, from my perspective, it's just easier for me to decide, than for us to have another darned meeting about what to do."

"Kurt, it might be easier, but that doesn't mean that's what we should do. You are not the leader. Anyway, I can't take first watch, because we had already decided the dinner rotations, and it's my turn to cook dinner. Or did you completely forget about that?"

Kurt rolled his eyes and stomped off toward Terrance. He turned back, and said "OK, you take second watch."

Leticia decided that sooner rather than later was a good time to straighten this out. It wasn't that she wanted to be leader, instead of Kurt. It's that she wanted them to collaboratively make decisions, instead of having Kurt act as though he was the leader. She walked toward Susanna, who was just getting out of the tent she shared with Kurt.

"Susanna, can we talk for a minute?" Leticia and Susanna had broached this subject before, Susanna had said she would try to talk with Kurt about this situation, but nothing had changed.

"Sure, Leticia, what's up?" Susanna stood up fully and looked toward Leticia.

"Kurt is being bossy again, and I think it's time for the four of us to have a meeting and make some clear decisions about things. Is that OK with you?"

Susanna nodded, and looked sad. "Yeah, it's OK. Honestly, Kurt is starting to really bug me with the way he's been acting since we left. I don't really know what to do. But having the meeting is a good idea."

Susanna and Leticia walked back toward the center of the camp, where Terrance was gathering stones to build the fire circle, and Kurt was standing over him, telling him what to do.

Leticia said, "Kurt, Terrance, we're going to have a meeting now, to talk over issues about decision making."

Kurt looked up, with anger on his face. "I'm getting this fire circle set up, we don't have time for a meeting."

Susanna looked at Kurt, clearly annoyed. "Kurt, it looks like Terrance is setting up the fire circle. We have plenty of time. Let's all just sit down, OK?"

Terrance stopped what he was doing, and sat cross-legged on the ground, pretty much where he had been. Leticia and Susanna sat down across from him, and they waited for Kurt to join them.

"I have no interest in a meeting, and I don't think it will at all be useful. I'm going to do first watch, since no one else seems interested."

Susanna rose. "Kurt, you are being an idiot. Sit down right now, and let's talk about this. We still have at least a week until we get to the border with New America, and then probably two weeks after that before we make it to the Independent Zone. We have a long way ahead of us. It makes sense for us to work out how we are going to make decisions, and how we will divide the work."

"I'm not going to the Independent Zone. I'm staying in New America, and I thought you were staying with me."

"Alright, Kurt, let's not talk about that now, let's just figure out how best to handle the next week, OK?"

"No, I want to know, are you, or are you not, staying in New America with me?" Kurt looked at Susanna with his blue, piercing eyes.

Susanna's face started to harden in a way that Leticia had never seen before. She combed her long blond hair away from her face with her fingers. "I'll stay with you in New America if I want to stay with you. But the way you have been acting in the last week is suggesting to me that I might not want to stay with you."

Kurt looked stung and stepped back a couple of steps. He then turned on his heel and stormed away from the campsite. He quickly came back, went into the tent he shared with Susanna. The three of them were stunned enough that they just watched the tent. After a while of movement, he came out of the tent with his pack.

"I've had it with the three of you. You don't know how to follow orders; you seem to think that it's better to come to idiotic consensus. I wanted to leave the ICS, because I wanted the freedom to do whatever I pleased. I didn't leave the ICS to join a bunch of *Casitians*. And you, Susanna, have been a complete disappointment, in *every* way." He turned away from them, toward the river, and walked off. Susanna got up and went into the tent.

Over the past few years, the word "Casitian" had become a swear word in the ICS, and all over New America. It was a word that suggested that people were lazy and immoral, but in reality it was used to harass people into conforming to the norms of society. Leticia had been called that word countless times by her classmates.

Leticia looked at Terrance. "Well, let's get this circle set up so I can cook dinner, shall we?"

Terrance smiled, got up, and grabbed a stone. "I have to admit, I won't miss him."

Leticia started to move some stones into a tight circle. "Neither will I, but I think it will be different for Susanna."

Leticia decided to give Susanna time until she'd finished cooking dinner to be in her tent, but Susanna came out of her tent well before then. She looked like she had cried but had reached some sort of peace. She sat next to Leticia, who was cutting some tato root and psuedopeppers for the stir fry. Terrance had managed to get to the river, and catch a few gumbys, which were four legged aquatic animals that looked a lot like an old earth toy, but tasted kind of like fish. They would have a really nice, hearty dinner. There were also a few cone nuts left from a few days ago. They'd found a small group of cone nut trees, which were pretty unusual. Cone nuts were very sweet and had a taste reminiscent of chocolate. They also had picked the deeply purple grapeberries, which would make a wonderful dessert with the cone nuts.

"How're you doing?" Leticia asked Susanna.

"I'm OK. He is such a jerk, and I think the thing I most hate is that I didn't see that sooner."

Leticia shrugged. "Well, he did seem nice enough at school ..."

"There were things that I should have seen, really. Maybe he's always been a jerk, and I just didn't let myself see it."

"I don't know, Susanna, he must have some redeeming qualities. Anyway, we'll be OK without him, and he'll be OK without us. I'm just sorry that it didn't work out for you."

"Don't be. So, how's dinner going? Can I help?"

NCIZ, New Earth, Month 2, Year 8

The wagon was rocking back and forth a little too much for Thomas' stomach. The two horses pulling the wagon didn't seem especially sure-footed. It could hardly be their fault – the road badly rutted, and sometimes almost completely washed out. Their guide had told them that after this next settlement, the road to the river got better. Thomas was looking forward to that.

They had been traveling for a slow two weeks, or that's how it seemed to Thomas. Jeffrey and Thomas' home settlement, New Calgary, was settled by a mix of Canadian and US citizens in the foothills of a large mountain range. It was a well-developed inland settlement

– one of the largest in the North Central IZ. New Calgary, and the half-dozen settlements near it, had created a large, well developed economy of its own.

The first stops after leaving home were all well-populated settlements that were fairly well-advanced. Thomas and Jeffrey had spent time with a number of public health, medical, and alternative medical practitioners, and had shared what they knew. Many of those they spoke with had already had some experience with the antibiotic properties of plants in their area. Thomas learned more about other plants and took many samples that he had to carefully either dry, or make into an infusion, for later testing when he got back home, whenever that would be. He felt sometimes like a naturalist. So many of the native plants weren't cataloged, and their relationships to one another not known. He felt like he had a lifetimes worth of work to do.

Once they left the immediate area around New Calgary, most of the other settlements they had passed through were pretty marginal. The settlements ranged in size and character. So far, they were traveling between settlements made of people from the United States on Earth. But they were all strikingly different. Thomas' favorite settlement so far, called "Burning Man" was made up of a large group of artistic, creative, and counter-cultural types. They were certainly making an interesting community. Thomas did wonder why they chose to come here, given that they would have been welcome on an Earth made more Casitian.

Thomas' least favorite by far was "New Reno." It was like a mythical Wild West gambling town, with men riding horses and carrying guns, an active group of brothels, some with girls far too young, and huge casinos that people came to from miles and miles around. The medical people at New Reno were too busy sewing up stab wounds and burying people who had gunfights to worry much about plants with medicinal value, although they did pay special attention when they heard about the powerful analgesic in spider flower infusion.

Their original plan to go to New Aard had changed. They had gotten information from other travelers that New Aard was advanced in using plants for their medicinal needs. It sounded like they might have gotten even further than Thomas and Jeffrey had. As well, New

Aard was not welcoming what would have been, on Earth, "Western" influence – it took very special dispensation to travel there, and Thomas didn't think they would get permission. So they decided to skip New Aard entirely for now. They had decided to go west and then south, and cross into southern New America, before going into the south central Independent Zone. They would then travel north from there, back into New America, across the Independent Christian State, up north to the settlements above ICS, then back home.

There were a lot of settlements in the North Central Independent Zone along the river that was called the Mississippi. It was a broad river that flowed from the northern lake, called Lake Superior to the southern lake, called Lake Maracaibo. Thomas expected that they would spend quite a while along this river. It was a good thing – he liked rivers and was looking forward to traveling on the river.

But before then, they had a slog. Between their home settlement and the river was a vast expanses of plains, with not much in the way of interesting landmarks. Thomas' point of view as that this was the completely boring part of the trip.

"Can we take a break?" Jeffrey asked their guide, who was a grizzled man, with gray hair, and arthritic joints. Thomas wondered how old he was. The man called the horses to a halt.

"Alright, take a break, not too long – we need to get to Albertville by dark – and that's not many hours from now."

Thomas got off of the wagon and went to find a semi hidden place to relieve himself. Luckily, there were a few trees around that provided convenient concealment. Albertville was next. He'd heard some things about Albertville. He'd heard that it was very closed off, insular, not welcoming. It had been started by a single family from Ohio. It had only one inn, and virtually no commerce. Their guide didn't like Albertville much, but it was the only route to the river settlements. Their guide's home was Dubuque, which was one of the more northern settlements along the Mississippi. Many of the settlements had named themselves after well-known cities that were on the Mississippi of Earth. There even was a settlement down south, called New Orleans, in a space where two great rivers met – across the Nile River from New Aard, and the Mississippi river from the South Central Independent Zone.

Their guide named Gunther said that it would take them another two weeks to get from Albertville to Dubuque. There were about five settlements along the way, all increasingly large and developed.

They got back in the wagon after a short break and a snack. In a few hours, they reached Albertville just as the sun was beginning to get its orange tinge in the blue-green sky. The town looked terrible. The prefab houses were in serious disrepair, and some were demolished. There looked to be only a few newly and poorly built buildings. It was eerily quiet.

The rutted road they had been traveling on became a flat, dirt road: the main road into town. The town was completely empty. The guide turned a corner and stopped the wagon in front of a large prefab building with a sign "Inn" scrawled in paint. It was deserted. Gunther got out of the wagon, and went up to the door of the inn, and opened it. It came off the hinges in his hands, and dropped to the ground, creating a cloud of dust. It was dark inside. Jon got out of the wagon, and walked to the door, and peered in.

"It's empty, there's no one here."

Gunther scratched his head. "I was out here just'a bout a mont' ago. There were some people here, really."

Everyone else got out of the wagon. Thomas said, "maybe we should look around. See if anyone is left."

Thomas went toward what looked to him like the main intersection, which had some large buildings, one of which looked to be some sort of central administration building. It was similarly empty, as was every building he looked into. Chuck got his cameras out, and started to walk around, getting footage outside, and inside of buildings.

They eventually re-gathered next to the wagon to talk about what to do.

Chuck said, "Obviously, we can't keep going to the next town, it's too far away. I guess we might as well camp here."

It'sa creepy here, idn't it?" Gunther spat. "I'd rather camp outside o' town, be honest."

Jeffrey said "well, actually, I think that's a good idea. We don't know what happened, and we should be careful."

Gunther pointed to a hill toward the southwest that looked like it had some trees. "We can get there by full dark."

Thomas nodded. They all got back into the wagon, and Gunther took them to their camping place for the night.

In their tent, Jeffrey and Thomas were discussing what they thought happened. Jeffrey thought that perhaps they got sick, and tried to go somewhere to get help, and never came back.

Thomas said, "well, maybe they just got sick of being so isolated, and went to settlements closer to the river."

"But they were supposed to be a very insular family, not welcoming much to anyone."

"Well, who knows, I imagine the people of Graceland know what happened. It wouldn't be a surprise, really, smaller settlements dying, and merging with larger ones."

They settled into their sleeping bags, and as Thomas drifted off to sleep, he wondered what the settlement called "Graceland" was going to be like. He wasn't sure he wanted to know.

Independent Christian State, New America, New Earth, Month 2, Year 8

"I don't see anyone. It seems quiet out there." Leticia, Terrance and Suzanna had gotten up to a small hill overlooking the Chalcedon River. Leticia knew that the border of the ICS and New America was where the Chalcedon and Trinity rivers met. She hadn't seen anyone on the rivers, or near the rivers. There was a settlement on the other side of the Trinity River, but they had decided to avoid it by crossing the river to the south of it, just in case. They had done fine traveling in the wilderness. Leticia was really enjoying it. She was enjoying learning about the many new plants and animals they were coming across and enjoying getting to know the territory.

They had only been traveling for an hour or so that day, so they figured they would be able to cross into New America that day. It made all of them much happier that they were going to be, finally, out of the ICS. They started their walk down toward the Trinity River, which they would need to find a way to get across it.

They made it down to the bank of the river, where there was a small beach full of large pebbles. The river looked quite broad, and quite deep. Swimming it seemed to not be a great option, but it would do if they had to. Leticia looked around and wondered whether they should build a small raft.

"Looking to cross the river?" A voice came from out of nowhere. Then, all of a sudden, a small boat appeared from behind some trees next to the riverbank. In the boat was a slight, small woman, who looked to be pretty old, older than Leticia's mother, certainly.

"I saw you when you were on that hill." She pointed back to where they had been standing a while ago.

"I know, I know, you don't want to answer me, because you are worried that I'll turn you in." She laughed. "I live on the other side, and I help people cross from that godforsaken state all of the time. It'll only cost you twenty dollars.

Leticia had thirty, and she knew Susanna had more. She looked at the woman, who seemed nice enough. "Why help us?"

"Well, I make a bit of extra money this way. And I help people leave that place. It's an awful place, I know. I escaped my husband a year ago."

"You take the risk to help people? What if they catch you?"

"No one cares, really. They tell you over and over again that no one can leave, and they lie, and tell stories about people going to prison and all. But they just let people go. Think about it. They'd rather people who really wanted to leave, left."

Leticia nodded. It made sense. "OK, we'll come with you. Can you drop us off on the bank south of that settlement?"

She raised her eyebrows. "You're avoiding civilization?"

Leticia nodded. "Yes, until we get to the Independent Zone."

She shook her head. "OK, that's fine by me, but you don't need to worry. And the IZ ain't no place for three nice young people like you, I guarantee you that. But anyway, come on in the boat."

They gathered up their belongings and entered the boat with the woman. "Name's Muriel."

"I'm Leticia, this is Susanna and Terrance."

"Nice to meet you all."

The boat drifted away from the bank, and downstream. Muriel paddled a little bit, but mostly just steered the boat toward the far shore. After a time, they arrived at another small beach on the far shore, where she let them get off. They did a quick negotiation about money – Terrance had come empty handed, so Susanna and Leticia split the twenty dollars, and gave them to Muriel.

"Thank you, Muriel, you've been a real help."

"Well, dears, you've helped me too, in more ways than one. Travel blessings on you."

Leticia reached out to Muriel, who gave her a clasped arm hug, which she then shared with Susanna and Terrance.

Leticia said, "blessings on you, as well. Thank you again."

They parted ways, and Leticia looked back, seeing Muriel paddle her boat back upstream, to her home.

NCIZ, New Earth, Month 2, Year 8

Thomas groaned. "OK, we've been here for two days, and I'm *sick* of Elvis. Can we leave tomorrow?"

Jeffrey smiled. "Come on, Tom. First off, we've been able to help a lot of people. Second, well, I like staying in Elvis' bedroom. Isn't that cool? And besides, Chuck is getting great footage, Georgia is writing up a storm, and Johanna is learning a lot. But the plan is to leave tomorrow anyway."

Thomas had never had any patience for Jeffrey's love affair with the dead rock star, and he never understood it, either. Luckily, Jeffrey had been to the Graceland on Earth years before they had met. Thomas did have to hand it to the people who settled Graceland. Somehow, they managed to have an incredible amount of Elvis memorabilia, although he truly doubted any of its authenticity. But that didn't seem to matter to either Jeffrey or to anyone else in Graceland.

They had, however, solved the Albertville mystery. Albertville had been settled by a family of three generations. The older generation was the one that was the most insular, and uninterested in anything outside of the family. An infectious disease struck the settlement, and everyone in the older generation died. Those that were younger decided to disband the settlement and move elsewhere.

"I wish we'd gotten here earlier," Jeffrey said.

"We would have prevented the deaths, but only postponed the inevitable, Jeff." Thomas answered.

Jeffrey nodded. "I guess that's true. But I hate to see people die unnecessarily."

They did leave Graceland the next day, and travel on the road to the river was much improved. Gunther said that they would make it to Dubuque in a week, just at the beginning of ThirdMonth. They would stay in Dubuque for a while. Leonard, the techie, planned to establish a network along the river settlements, and it would take a while to get everything set up before they traveled on. They also had supplies to purchase for the trip and would need a new guide. Gunther only did trips between New Calgary and Dubuque – they would need to find a river guide to take them down the Mississippi.

New America, New Earth, Month 3, Year 8

The bridge was huge, and surprising. It reminded Leticia of bridges she'd seen back on Earth. She wouldn't have thought there would be anything on New Earth like it, but here it was, right in front of her. The bridge spanned the broad expanse of the Mississippi River, and the settlements of New Richmond and Dubuque were on the New American, and IZ sides, respectively. They had walked into New Richmond and joined the small but steady stream of people walking across the bridge into the IZ, with a few wagons and trucks passing by them. There seemed to be a small checkpoint, but they didn't turn anyone back. Leticia did notice vehicles moving in the opposite direction, passing from the IZ side into New America, but no people walking.

As they walked across the bridge, and reached the checkpoint, they could see several men in camouflage, holding rifles. This scared her a bit, but as she watched people go up to the gate, and then be passed through, she realized that there didn't seem to be much to worry about.

"State your reason for leaving New America." The soldier asked the woman ahead of her.

"My cousin is in Dubuque, and I'm going to live with her."

"Name, please."

"Joan Graves."

The soldier looked down at a clip board, with a sheaf of papers. He flipped up some pages and ran his finger down what looked like a list of names.

"OK, fine, you're fine, please move on."

Leticia at first thought she'd fake a name, but she realized there was no reason to.

"State your reason for leaving New America."

"I have an aunt who lives in Dubuque. I'm going to live with her."

"Name please."

"Leticia Green."

After looking at the list, he told her to move on. Susanna and Terrance similarly got through the checkpoint.

Leticia was relieved, and excited. They were now in the IZ! They could do whatever they wanted, however they wanted. She knew she wanted to travel more, and she was happy that finally, she was free of her mother, and of the ICS. She could live as she pleased.

They walked into Dubuque and asked at a small general store about a cheap place to stay. The man behind the counter told them about a small inn about four blocks away. Leticia also asked about a river guide, to take them down river, one that was reasonable in price.

"My daughter does that. She's really good. I don't think she has any clients right now."

He scribbled her name and address on a small piece of paper and handed it to Leticia. "She'll be good."

They walked out of the store, to the inn. They got two rooms, for a very good price.

"Why don't I go check out the river guide? You two can explore the town." Leticia was not really all that interested in the town, although she could tell that Terrance and Susanna were. They seemed to be in their element in this large settlement, which was much larger than their home settlement in the ICS, and, of course, much more interesting.

"Can I ask how much we can spend? I had originally brought 30 NA dollars – and we spent 10 of that on the river crossing, and five more on the rooms. That only leaves me with fifteen, and I don't want to use it all."

"Well, why don't we just stay here for a while?" Susanna asked. Why go down the river? This seems like a great place."

"I want to explore – I want to see what's out there in the IZ before I decide where to stay."

"I need a break from traveling. I think I'm going to look for a job here."

Leticia was disappointed. She had hoped that they would stay together. But Leticia had the exploratory itch. She wanted to see as much of New Earth as she could.

"OK, well, I guess I understand. I'll go check out the guide anyway." She didn't know how she would manage to pay the guide, if Susanna didn't help. She grabbed a couple of things from her bag and started to walk out the door. "I'll be back in a while. Let's have dinner together, OK?"

Susanna nodded. Leticia walked out of the room, and down the stairs, into the street. She was assaulted by the noise and business of the settlement. She figured that it was at least four or five times the size of their settlement, which had about ten thousand people. The settlement seemed very crowded to her. She looked at the map they had found of the settlement and wound her way toward the address of the river guide, which looked to be only a block from the river.

North Central Independent Zone, New Earth, Month 3, Year 8

"Yes, well, I can take you as far as New Orleans. I've been doing this for a few years, and I know the river settlements well. I just got a larger capacity barge as well. We'll still need to camp on the river where there are no settlements, but during the day, it will be a comfortable ride." Keitha, the river guide was speaking to Thomas, who had been given instructions from the rest of the group about what they wanted.

"There are seven of us, with a fair bit of equipment. Can you handle it alone? We need help with food and camping logistics as well."

Keitha nodded. "Yes. I need to hire one assistant, given the duration of the trip. It will take me some time to prepare everything. We'll leave in three days, at first light. I do need a deposit, so I can purchase the things we'll need."

Thomas nodded. "How much?"

"Twenty-five percent of the final cost, which will be eight thousand IZ units, so I need two thousand."

Thomas nodded, and pulled out his wallet. They had raised a lot of money for this journey, between the money that each of them had contributed, and the settlement's contribution. He took out two one-thousand notes, and handed them to Keitha, who looked a bit surprised.

"Well, these are large bills, I don't often see bills this big, honestly." Keitha smiled.

"We've been well funded. Thanks, Keitha."

"Where are you staying?"

"At the Bear's Den Inn, on Dodge Street"

"OK, I'll be in touch. I'll likely come by tomorrow to discuss some of the logistics."

Thomas nodded. They shook hands, and he turned, and left the courtyard. As he was walking through the gate, he saw a very young, tall, muscular, woman with a medium-dark complexion walking toward the gate. She looked travel weary, but Thomas thought he saw excitement in her eyes. Thomas detected a bit of worry, perhaps, in her face.

"Hi there. Does Keitha live here?"

Thomas nodded. "Yes, indeed she does. She's in that courtyard."

The woman nodded and smiled. "Thanks." She walked into the gate.

Thomas walked back to the inn, feeling like he knew he would see this woman again soon.

North Central Independent Zone, New Earth, Month 3, Year 8

Leticia passed the tall, thin man, with a feeling of familiarity. But she knew she'd never seen him before. He seemed nice enough. She walked into the courtyard, to find a stocky woman of medium height, pale skin, very obvious muscles and dark hair, writing on a pad of paper. She stood a while, as the woman had not noticed her presence.

"Uh, Keitha?" she said tentatively.

Keitha looked up in surprise. "May I help you?"

"Your father told me about your river guide business, and I was wondering if you are taking any trips down the river soon. I just arrived in Dubuque, and I want to explore. But I don't have much money ..."

The woman seemed to be assessing her.

"How much camping have you done?"

"A lot – I just traveled from the Independent Christian State in New America."

The woman looked surprised. "You traveled all of that way by yourself? Walking?"

Leticia all of a sudden felt very proud of her accomplishment. "No, there were two others. But yes, we walked, found food, and camped. We traveled during the day times and rested all of the night."

Leticia could tell that Keitha was impressed. "Why did you leave?"

Leticia decided honesty was best. "I didn't want to get married or join the Mission Society. Those were my only options."

Keitha smiled. "I'd heard the ICS was a crazy place, but that's really nuts. Well, welcome to the IZ."

Leticia smiled. "Thanks. But now I want to explore it, find a place I can call home."

Keitha looked at Leticia again, as if making a decision. "OK, how about this. I was going to hire someone I had worked with before, but I like your look and you have a lot more experience than anyone else I know. I'll hire you as an assistant. We'll try this out just for the first leg of the journey down the Mississippi – to Bellevue – the next settlement down the river. If that works, you can come with me as far as you want. But this is the thing, I'll only be paying you twenty IZ units a day, and, of course, food and lodging are included."

Leticia made a quick calculation. They'd had to exchange their NA dollars into IZ units, and the current exchange rate seemed to be about two IZ units to each NA dollar. So she'd be making ten dollars a day, which seemed, to her, to be a fortune. She didn't want to sound completely enthused, though.

"Sure, that will do fine, thank you. When do we start?" She realized a bit of excitement was creeping into her voice.

"We start today, actually." Keitha looked down at her pad. "If you wait here for about an hour, we're going to need to go to town and pick up a lot of supplies. The trip starts in three days, at first light. I think it would be best for you to stay here, though, we'll have some short sleep periods in the next two days. I've got a spare bed in my office."

"That will work fine. I should go get my stuff and come back – I'll be back soon."

"That sounds good." Keitha got up, and walked toward the back of the house, where the door to the office was and pointed. Leticia followed. "Here's the office. You can put your stuff in that far corner."

Leticia nodded. "Thanks. I'll be right back." She turned, and walked back toward the gate, then ran back to the inn, and bounded up the stairs. She was ecstatic. She had a way down the river, and she was going to be paid for it! She opened the door to the room she shared with Susanna, who was sitting on the bed, looking pensive.

"Susanna! I got a job helping a river guide go down the river! I'm so happy."

Susanna looked up, seeming to have been drawn out from being deep in thought. "That's great Leticia. I got a job, too."

Leticia was surprised. "Wow, doing what?"

"I got a job waiting tables downstairs in the restaurant."

Leticia thought that seemed, well, not up to Susanne's ability, but, if she wanted to do it... "Is that what you want?"

"It's great pay. Three units an hour, plus tips. Plus free room and board."

Leticia whistled. "That's good pay. Congratulations."

"Thanks. It's just a first step. Terrance found a job, too, at a bookstore."

Leticia remembered that she'd wanted to stop at a bookstore before she left. "Where?"

"On White street and 14th. It's a cute little store."

Leticia realized she probably didn't have time to get there before she went back to Keitha's place now, but perhaps later today, or tomorrow.

"I gotta pack up and go, now." She started to gather her things and put them into her pack.

Susanna said, "so will I see you soon again? When are you coming back?"

Leticia stopped packing for a moment. "I don't know, Susanna. It might be a long time. I might choose to stay somewhere else. But I'll come back and visit sometime." She went to Susanna, and they hugged. "I'll miss you."

"I'll miss you too. It's hard to imagine not having you around."

"I wish you wanted to come with me."

"This seems like a good place to stay for a while. Not forever, but ..."

Leticia nodded. "I understand. I still have the travel bug, I guess." She went back to packing. When she was done, she hefted her pack, and started to walk toward the door. "Tell Terrance I said goodbye. I'll try to get to the bookstore before I leave."

Susanna nodded, and Leticia walked out the door, down the stairs, and back to Keitha's place, by the river.

Chapter 4:
Greenwood Leaves

"In the end, all humans want power. Power over others, and over their circumstances. It is the ultimate aphrodisiac." — Jlir Nern Klaft (1st age)

New America, New Earth, Month 4, Year 8

The message he'd received from them was cryptic, but Dennis couldn't ignore it. He needed to follow up on any promise of power, and the promise of precious metals was irresistible. If he could be the source of a supply of these metals, Dennis would have the power and influence he needed. Dennis was eager to find out what these people had in mind.

He got out of his four-wheel drive vehicle and walked the final mile to the rendezvous point at the top of a small peak about fifty miles from New Columbia. It seemed an oddly isolated place for a meeting of this sort, but he figured they wanted secrecy.

He reached the rocky peak, and didn't see anyone else there, so he sat to wait. In a few minutes, he felt a cool breeze, which seemed odd to him in the stillness of the hot day. He heard a sound that he couldn't identify, and then from some trees a bit downslope, he saw two men walking up toward him. They were both tall, slim, and had very short hair. Their coloring and features reminded him of Casitians for a moment, but they didn't have the manner or dress of Casitians.

He got up. "Hello. I imagine you are ..."

"Hello Dennis. My name is John, and this is Mark."

Dennis noted they had very strange accents, accents he'd never heard before. They were most definitely not Casitians.

"Where are you from? Where do you live? I haven't seen you around New Columbia."

"We travel a lot."

"I see." Dennis was wary.

The one whose name was Mark was hefting a medium-sized box, John pointed to it.

"In here are five pounds of titanium, five pounds of Palladium, four pounds of Gallium, two pounds of Gold and seven pounds of silver, all in small, one ounce bars. There are also some plans for advanced manufacturing technology that will be helpful given your lack of some materials. In this other box are bags with a number of important rare earth elements."

"Titanium? Palladium? Gold? Rare Earth elements? Where did you get those? No one has been able to find any of this on New Earth!"

"We have our sources. Let's just say we brought them with us."

"Ah, that was smart of you to add them to your cargo allowance. No one else thought of that."

John looked at Dennis enigmatically. Dennis was definitely suspicious, but he wanted what was in their hands more than he cared about the truth of how they had come to have these things.

"We are giving these to you for free. And there is much, much more of all of this and other things you'll need."

"What do you want from me in return?"

"For now, we want nothing. We want you in power in New America. That's all. When we need something, we'll let you know."

"Why? Why me? And how could you want nothing now?"

"You'll be in the best position to provide us with what we need. But don't worry, it won't affect your power. We don't want it. We have other things in mind."

Dennis wondered what those things were. But he didn't really care. All he wanted was to be in charge.

North Central Independent Zone, New Earth, Month 4, Year 8

Leticia sat at the rear of the river barge they were traveling on, holding the rudder. She looked up and saw Thomas grinning at her as he walked toward the back of the boat. Leticia and Thomas had already become fast friends, even after only a few days on the river. It was funny to Leticia – Jeffrey wanted to act like her father, and Thomas just wanted to be her friend. Most importantly, though, Keitha thought that Leticia was a good worker, and decided to keep her on for the entire trip down to New Orleans. Leticia liked Keitha a lot, and also liked the entire group traveling with Thomas and Jeffrey. They all seemed to get along fine, although Leticia thought that sometimes Thomas would get a bit too stressed out by things. Lately, she had been making it her mission to make him lighten up, which he seemed not to mind.

They'd left Dubuque a week ago, and had passed through Bellvue, and were headed south toward Moline, one of the larger settlements on the Mississippi. Keitha said that it would take about two weeks to get to Moline. They got into a routine, traveling on the river, stopping at each settlement along the way. Most often at night they would camp, or, if they were lucky, they found an inn. Sometimes people would invite them to stay in their modest homes. Since the major reason for their trip was to share information about native plants, Jeffery and Thomas had to find the medical practitioners of whatever sort in each settlement. At the same time, Leonard was busy taking notes about where to place widenet antennas and talking to folks about how the new widenet would work, and Johanna was doing interviews with a few willing individuals about life on the river. Georgia and Chuck were busy filming various activities. It was hectic, and Leticia was enjoying every minute.

She worked hard assisting Keitha with equipment and logistics. She did most of the cooking, when it was needed. She was responsible for gathering or buying food when they stopped. She had a lot of time to herself, though, while the others were talking with people in the settlements, or when they were just cruising downstream. Every step further away from the Independent Christian State she got, the more relaxed and happier she felt. It had finally sunk in that she was free and could live her life as she pleased.

What she had seen of this Independent Zone so far had been educational. She was astounded by the range of settlements that she'd gotten to visit, as well as the ones she had heard about from Thomas. She thought about where she might want to settle eventually. Thomas and Jeffrey's hometown of New Calgary sounded very attractive to Leticia, but even though she knew she wanted to settle down at some point, she wanted to see as much of the new world as she could before then.

"You seem to be enjoying yourself, finally," Thomas said. He had commented to her that sometimes she seemed sad or on guard.

"Yeah, I guess it has finally sunk in that I'm really gone from that horrible place, really finally free. I don't have to worry about my mother forcing me to get married or anything."

"It's about time! Do you know how many miles from the ICS we are now? Hundreds!"

Leticia smiled, and said "I know, I know – but sometimes when I wake up in the morning I'm afraid that this was all just a dream, you know? But finally, I woke up realizing that it really is real. You have no idea what it was like to live there – a total nightmare."

Thomas nodded. "You've told me. I have to admit it's hard to believe, but I do believe you. Have you thought more about that letter?"

Leticia had been thinking about writing a letter to her mother. Apparently, mail along this route to Dubuque was quite reliable, and it was very likely that the letter would be delivered.

"I don't really know what to say to her – 'Goodbye and I hope to never see you again?'"

"Thomas shook his head emphatically. "No, Leticia – your mother is probably worried about you. Just tell her that you are doing fine, and happy, and leave it at that. Just reassure her that you are OK."

Leticia looked at Thomas. "I don't even think she cares really about me. But maybe you're right. I'll write her a short note and drop it off at the next settlement.

"If you want, you can tell her to write you in New Orleans. I've heard that post offices most places will hold mail for people to pick up."

"OK, that's worth a try. I know you are trying to be helpful, Thomas."

Leticia started to compose the letter in her head. What would she say, exactly? Part of her did really hope that she'd never see her mother again.

ICS, New America, New Earth, Month 1, Year 9

Beatrice relaxed into Craig's arms and looked up at the sky.

"I wonder where Leticia is, and how far she has gotten."

"I'm sure she's fine. Do you envy her?"

Beatrice laughed and looked up at Craig. "Of course I do! But it's not so much that she gets to see more of New Earth – it's that she gets to meet people who have made different choices than my parents did."

Craig nodded. "We'll be OK, Bea. We'll have the ICS marriage everyone will envy, then we'll say we're going off to start a new settlement and sneak out. Maybe we'll even run into Leticia someday."

"I know, I know, I'll have a chance to see all of that. I'm glad that we feel the same, Craig. I love you."

"I love you too."

Dlejon, Rec'jeter'she, Month 1, Year 9

Mira looked a bit exasperated to Douglas. "They will be short trips, Dad, and anyway, I'm an adult now! And it's an important part of my training."

Douglas sighed. "Yes, Mira, I know that. I guess I'm still not used to the fact that you're growing up. I'm glad that you've decided to get medical training. And I know that Theresa will be a great mentor and will take care of you on this trip. I just can't help worrying. Forgive me."

Mira jumped up, and hugged Douglas. "Dad, I'll be fine. And I'm so looking forward to learning more about other parts of New America and telling people about what we've learned about the plants here. We can really help."

The Dlejonese had spent years cataloging and studying the wide range of plants on New Earth and understanding their medicinal properties. From what they could tell so far, either individual plants, or combinations of them could treat much of what they brought with them. There were a few illnesses that had cropped up that they hadn't yet been able to find treatments for, which sometimes worried them. But, in general, the people of Dlejon were healthy.

Douglas was proud of Mira. He lost his regret that she had come along – she was doing very well here, and the community could really use her growing talents as a doctor.

"So tell me more, Mira. Where are you headed?"

"The first trip is to the Lakota community, west of here across the river Ul'tretor."

"Ah, yes, we've had a bit of contact with Wachiwi, the chief of the tribe."

"Theresa knows that they have already done some of their own studies of the native plants, so we're looking forward to exchange of information more than anything. The second trip is to go to the South Central Independent Zone. That's going to be longer, and we'll be doing a lot of dissemination of the information about medicinal plants."

"You'll need to be careful. I understand that some of the northern most settlements of the SIZ are talking a lot with the New Americans."

"We'll be careful. Remember, Dad, we're just a big settlement of hippies." Mira smiled.

St. Louis, North Central Independent Zone, Month 1, Year 9

"So you're saying that you think that it's those strange amino acids that bind up all of the free radicals?" Leticia and Jeffrey were sitting at a table on the pier in St. Louis, one of the larger settlements along the Mississippi.

"Yes, I do. I wished we'd had access to more equipment to do mass spectroscopy and NMR, but it was clear from the electrophoretic analysis we did that these different amino acids are getting incorporated into our proteins. It appears that at least two or three of them are similar enough to ones that we have but aren't present here. It also seems to be those proteins with these amino acids function quite normally. But there seem to be some additional characteristics – like this antioxidant behavior, and some others."

Leticia was fascinated by all of this. During her spare time, she had spent time reading books Jeffery and Thomas had about epidemiology and medicine, and both of them had been teaching her about the medicinal properties of the native plants. In the process she'd learned a lot of medicine and had decided to train as a doctor. She realized that it suited her, and she could also be of help to many.

Both Jeffrey and Thomas were encouraging. All the way up in Dubuque they had heard rumors of a new medical school in the South Central Independent Zone, and the further south they got, the more they heard about it. Leticia was excited. She knew there were other ways to get trained on New Earth, but a real medical school sounded like a good idea.

"I was reading your report about the combinatorial antibiotic effects of the grapeberries and greenwood leaves. It's amazing that the combination of the two has about five times the antibiotic effect than either one alone. I don't really understand what you meant in the conclusion – how do you think the grapeberries potentiate the greenwood leaves?"

"Well, we think it's the greenwood leaves that have the real antibiotic effect – but the grapeberries are very rich with enzymes for some reason, and we wonder whether the enzymes help release whatever is antibiotic in the greenwood leaves. But of course this is all speculation – we just don't have the equipment to figure it out. We're not sure we ever will."

"Well, if we can keep doing empirical research on what works, then we'll at least be far in figuring out what will cure people."

"That's the plan, Leticia. Our job is mostly to be naturalists and empirical researchers for a while. The real analysis is going to have to wait a long time."

Leticia heard Keitha and Thomas talking as they approached. Leticia had to switch modes from student to assistant guide. There was a lot to do, since it was just about time to leave St. Louis, and move down the river to Memphis. Because of the size of the settlement, they had stayed here for a few days, and besides, they all felt they needed a break. But they knew it was time to get moving again and keep going down to the next destination.

New America, New Earth, Month 2, Year 9

Dennis left the meeting with the New American power brokers he had begun to gather, and he was excited and satisfied. He got into his car for the drive to his new house. He had most people who were important in New America on his side, now, since he had been providing them with precious metals and plans for new technology. Those things had helped them to build their wealth and power immensely, which had helped Dennis build his wealth and power, too. Several people had already started new businesses manufacturing such things as chips and circuit boards with the materials and plans Dennis had provided and were profiting from it.

He was also aware that people were beginning to notice who was "in" and who was "out." He was being careful to leave "out" those currently close to Gerard. Dennis was glad that he'd finally broken the ties with Gerard. Gerard had been stunned at Dennis' decision to leave. Dennis figured Gerard assumed he had Dennis in his left pocket. Dennis had been slowly building his own power base from almost the moment he stepped off the colony ship onto New Earth soil. With the help of John and Mark, Dennis had consolidated his power base, and Gerard would find himself without support.

Dennis arrived at his house, one of the most magnificent on the edge of New Columbia, the capital of New America. It had been designed by the hottest architect in the country – a specialist in the newest neo-classical architecture. He had spent a lot of money to buy it. It came up for sale because the previous owner had decided to move further into the country. The house was large, with huge columns in the front, and even a carriage house.

He walked into his house, and for a moment felt its emptiness. He had gotten all of the furniture in the right style, imposing, dark wood, with curvy lines and stern upholstery. A part of him missed being with Gerard, but he knew that leaving Gerard had been the best thing for him. He brushed his loneliness aside and resolved to find someone who could complement him.

New Islamabad, New Aard, Month 2, Year 9

"I have a hard time believing you." The sheik spoke in Arabic to the two visitors, who called themselves Hassan and Rafi.

Hassan said, "Why? Here are the metals and resources you need, right here. You can start to manufacture vaccines quite soon. Your people are dying, don't you want the vaccines?"

"Of course we want to manufacture vaccines! But I want to know ahead of time what it is you will want from us. I don't even know who you are, or where you are from. What settlement are you from? Who are your families?"

"Does it matter?"

"Yes, it does! If you are not willing to tell me more, then please, leave me. I have enough business to attend to, without mysterious people with what seem to be unbelievable promises."

The sheik turned to his aide, and said, "please escort these men out."

Twenty meetings, with almost the exact same dialogue went on in numerous settlements of New Aard. The results were the same. The men who called themselves Hassan and Rafi walked out holding exactly what they came in with. No one wanted it.

New Aard, Month 2, Year 9

Abdul could see the sun come into his tent through his closed eyes. Reluctantly, he opened them, and looked around his tent. It was small, and his varied personal possessions littered the floor. Although he had slept through most of the last dark period, he was still exhausted. And it would be another long day of travel today.

It had been a long haul. Abdul had bided his time, and slowly put together a small group of liberal-minded people within New Aard who were willing to take the big risk of breaking away from the mullahs, and form a community far to the south, where no one had yet settled. In the end, a group of 75 people traveled south with him, far more than he had ever expected. They had traveled separately or in very small groups, to make sure they weren't followed or captured. Unfortunately, their plan had been unveiled when a group of married women who had decided to leave their husbands were discovered trying to leave. It had been a close call, but in the end, they were allowed to escape. That's basically how Abdul looked at it. He imagined that it would have been impossible for them to have made it out otherwise.

Abdul didn't want to push his luck. Finally, just about everyone had made it to the rendezvous point, and they had to push south. They would travel close to the river for about 1500 kilometers, over a small group of mountains, to a part of New Aard that was unsettled, and close to the South Central Independent Zone. They would settle right across the river from the small Baha'i territory. Abdul had planned it this way, so that if, for some reason, the mullahs of New Aard decided to not allow this settlement, and try to invade it, they could flee across the river and be safe.

He rolled out of his sleeping bag and got up, got dressed and left his tent. Standing in front of his tent, as if waiting, was his longtime friend Olam.

"Hi Olam. I'm getting the feeling you were waiting for me."

Olam grinned, "Asiya arrived yesterday, in the dark."

Asiya was Olam's fiancee. Olam had been worried that they would have to leave before Asiya could make it to this point.

Abdul clapped Olam on the back and smiled. "That's such great news Olam. We need to start packing up and get going."

At that minute, Abdul realized that there was a lot of activity in the camp. "What time is it?"

"Third hour."

"Third hour! Why did you let me sleep?"

"Abdul, calm down. I knew you could get your things together quickly, and you have been working so hard for all of us. You needed your rest." We'll all be ready to leave by fifth hour, I'm sure.

Abdul sighed. "OK, Olam. But we have far to go today. How many are missing?"

"Seven, in total, mostly women, including Najla, Khadija, and Diane, the ones who were caught before we left. I will be surprised if any others make it out. But we'll leave the coded message anyway."

"Thanks, Olam. I guess I should get packing." Abdul turned and went back in his tent to gather his belongings. Abdul realized that it would be another long haul, but soon, soon, he could settle down, and relax.

New Orleans, NCIZ, New Earth, Month 4, Year 10

She watched Keitha's barge leave the dock, to go back up the Mississippi. Keitha was headed back to Dubuque, having brought Jeffrey and Thomas' team down the river. The team had spent three weeks in New Orleans, talking to people, gathering information, and making their plans. There had been a very informative and surprisingly friendly meeting at the New Aard Embassy in New Orleans, and there was a promise of future information sharing.

Leticia had been sorry to leave Keitha, but she wanted to go to San Antonio, a large settlement in the South Central IZ. Very early on, Jeffrey and Thomas invited her to accompany them into the South Central IZ, and really insisted once they'd learned that there was a new medical training facility there. Leticia had been glad to find out about that facility – and Jeffrey and Thomas were also quite excited to share their knowledge with the physicians there.

It was going to be a long trip, almost as long as they'd already traveled. First, they needed to go downriver trip to New San Francisco, a settlement among a group in the SCIZ called "New California." They would be, for a short time, in a stretch of river with New America on one side, and New Aard on the other. They had plans to stop at the few New America settlements along the river and share what information they had found. Next there was an overland trip north to San Antonio.

Going into New America made Leticia a bit nervous, but she realized that it wasn't really reasonable. She knew that no one was going to be interested in dragging her back up to the ICS. After all, she had been gone for almost 3 years now.

She heard footsteps behind her and turned to see Thomas. He sat next to her on the dock. "Penny for your thoughts."

"I'm a little sad to see Keitha go. I really enjoyed working under her. And I was thinking about New America and the ICS."

Thomas nodded. "I've been thinking a bit about New America, too. I can't understand what we keep hearing about it. Their epidemics are getting better, faster than anywhere else. It sounds strange. New America was founded by people who intensely disliked, and actively opposed the Casitians. There were few doctors or scientists among them, because most of them realized how good galactic technology and science would be for human beings. I'd bet that the vast majority of scientists and doctors that emigrated to New Earth ended up in the Independent Zones. I'm actually surprised they have *any* doctors in New America. So the fact that New America is doing better is puzzling.

"Anyway, they still might want our knowledge, and maybe we can learn more about what's happening there. I'm hoping that we can find at least a few medical people in New America. Anyway, it's time to go – our new guide says the barge is all packed up."

They got up from the edge of the dock and walked further down the pier to where their barge was tied. Leticia had been glad that Thomas and Jeffrey were happy to let her stay a student, instead of having to help with the logistics of the trip. That gave her a lot of time to keep reading. She'd gotten some chemistry and physics books from a bookstore and had been sobered in realizing how badly she had been educated during her time in the ICS. She had a lot of catching up to do.

Outside of New Columbia, New America, New Earth, Month 4 Year 10

"I'm missing something. You are trying to sell me advanced computer components?" Timothy was skeptical.

"Yes, I have a source."

"What source? From these specs, these are not stock from someone's colony ship cargo store."

"No, no, I told you, they are newly manufactured."

Timothy had let this man into his office, even though he thought he was a shyster, but he was curious about what he had. Now, he was sure he was a shyster. Timothy's son Joseph was in the office today, and Timothy thought this might be a good lesson for him. Joseph had just turned 32 years old, in New Earth years, and he had high hopes that Joseph would follow him into the business; he seemed interested and engaged. And his son was very good at electronics – he had been making all sorts of things when they were back on Earth.

"Look, sir. I don't care what you are telling me. These components cannot exist. Believe me, I know."

He laughed and took out something that looked like a circuit board wrapped in an anti-static bag.

"Here. Look at this." He handed the bag to Timothy. Timothy took the bag, and opened it, and slid the small looking board from its bag. It was a circuit board, alright. It looked newly manufactured and had some components on it that were unfamiliar. It also had stamped on one side "NewAmerica Electronics." It looked to match the specs he had on the sheet in front of him.

He handed it to his son, who looked it over and said, "dad, this is definitely new manufacture."

This was disturbing to Timothy. Given his position in New America, a wealthy industrialist, he had heard rumors about new raw materials being available in New America, but every time he tried to find out how to get his hands on some, he hit dead ends. It was almost as if his influence was preventing him from obtaining anything. Now he had absolute proof that these raw materials existed, and that someone could get their hands on them, and they were using them to manufacture electronics.

He needed to follow this up the food chain.

"OK, I'm interested. I'd like to buy a lot of these, but I need to have a conversation with your boss first."

After a few days of negotiation, and dogged determination to get to the top of the food chain, he finally got a call from Dennis Hickler. He knew that Dennis was a serious power broker in New America and had recently broken from the President. Somehow, Timothy was not surprised that he was the original source. He went to meet Dennis at his house.

"Please, have a seat. What's your poison?"

"Scotch."

"Straight up?"

Timothy nodded.

"Kurt, please get Mr. Christopher a glass of my best single malt? And pour one for me as well."

A slight teenage boy scurried out of the room.

"I understand you are interested in getting your hands on some Nickel and Platinum."

"Yes. Without some precious metals, we are limited in the kinds of steel we can produce. I'd like to expand that capacity."

Hickler nodded. "I see, I see. Well, I believe I can help you out there."

The teenage boy named Kurt came back into the room with a silver platter, and two cut glass tumblers. He handed one to Timothy, and the other to Hickler.

Hickler raised the glass. "To a new business relationship."

Timothy nodded and took a sip. He immediately knew this scotch. It was his favorite, one he could only have on extremely special occasions. He'd done well for himself on Earth, but even then, a bottle of this scotch was something he treated himself to once a year. The 16 year old Balvenie Rose 1st release was rare. He had seen a couple of bottles at auction last year, and he couldn't afford one.

"You have good taste in Scotch."

Hickler nodded. "I can get you a bottle of this."

"I'm listening."

"I have made my acquaintance with some travelers who have precious metals and rare earth elements. My current theory is that they are with a group who secretly brought many tons of these items on the colony ships. It doesn't matter, really. I have control of the sole source, and I'm happy to sell you whatever you need, at a reasonable cost."

"Such as?"

"15 units per ounce of Nickel, for instance."

"I'm missing something here. That's very high, by Earth standards, of course, but considering how little of this material could possibly be on this planet, that cost is, well, almost free. What's the catch?"

"I'm working to depose Hopkinson from the Presidency. I need support. I know you are friends."

"You are mistaken. We have never been friends. I advise him. That's all."

"Well, then, this particular cost shouldn't bother you."

"No, not particularly."

Hickler stood up, and Timothy drained his glass, slowly, and also stood. They shook hands.

"Let me know what you'd like to order, and I'll have it fulfilled right away. And, I'll send you a bottle of the 16 Balvenie Rose, on me." Dennis was smiling in a way that made Timothy's skin crawl. He nodded and left the office. He noticed the teenager looking at him, as if to evaluate what he would do.

Casiti, 2 Wend 782

Marianne sat paralyzed while Ja'el was gathering her things from their dwelling. It had been a brutal few days for Marianne, even though she'd known it was coming for months. Spring had arrived on Casiti, and with it, a new season of change. Ja'el had been clear with Marianne when they first arrived on Casiti almost a year ago, that she would be staying with Marianne only through the following winter.

And here it was, the end of the following winter. Marianne hadn't really let Ja'el know how she felt. She understood Ja'el's desire to move back into the regular rhythm, especially now that the crisis was long over, and she was back home. Ja'el was moving to a community in the next valley over, the community she grew up in. Marianne would be driving her there tomorrow morning.

"Marianne, do you know where I put my toolbox?"

Marianne got up and went into the small ante-room next to the greenhouse, and picked up the toolbox, to bring to Ja'el.

"Here it is, love. It was near the greenhouse."

"Thanks." Ja'el didn't even look up.

Ja'el and Marianne had shared only words of necessity of late. Marianne couldn't quite understand why Ja'el had been so quiet - it seemed uncharacteristic of her. Perhaps she was picking up Marianne's distress, although Marianne was trying her best to hide it. It was getting late, and Marianne's stomach started to rumble. She'd planned a fairly elaborate final meal for them tonight and got up to start preparing it.

"Well, I guess I'm packed. What's cooking? It smells heavenly."

"I learned that kwelis goes really well with sweet potatoes, so I'm making a casserole. And we're finally getting some eggs now, so I made a pepper zucchini soufflé. And there are some great greens in the greenhouse, so we'll have a salad."

"Sounds wonderful; I have been spoiled by your cooking all this time, Marianne."

Marianne looked up, and Ja'el was looking away, as if she was looking for something. Marianne finished the food preparation and set the table.

"It's ready."

They ate in relative silence. Ja'el complimented her on the food and made small talk. Marianne didn't say much. She didn't have much to say except to ask Ja'el to stay, which she wouldn't do.

"So, Marianne, what have you thought of your first year on Casiti? Is it what you expected, or hoped for?"

Marianne decided to answer the question directly, and honestly. "Ja'el, it's been neither. I've been glad to have been able to work with a wide variety of Casitians to help them understand Terrans better. I find it promising that Casiti has decided to consider the idea of immigrants from Earth, and I'm looking forward to those conversations continuing. The trade talks between Earth and Casiti have been going well, and that has been quite gratifying. But culturally, I thought I was a lot more like you than I seem to be."

Ja'el looked down at her plate for a while, then looked directly at Marianne. There were tears in her eyes. "You don't want me to leave, do you?"

"Of course not. But I would never ask that of you, Ja'el."

"I have to go. I'm Casitian."

Chapter 5:
In the Horsehair Grass

"Casitians have learned that nonviolence is the only route to lasting harmony among humans. It is a supreme effort, but without it, we remain bound to a cycle that will inevitably end in our species' demise." – Ul'tretor (21)

New Columbia, New America, Month 1 Year 11

"Gerard, there is nothing I can do. Your polio is progressing rapidly, and there are no treatments I have that will help."

"You are telling me I am going to die?"

"I'm sorry to say this, but every other case I've seen at this stage has been fatal. You are in God's hands, now."

Gerard lay in bed, where he had been for the last week. He had lost control of his lower body, and he was beginning to have trouble breathing. He knew that he didn't have much time left. Sean Joseph, who had become his personal physician, looked down at him, with sympathy.

"I'll be back to see you tomorrow, Gerard." He looked sadly at Gerard, turned, and left the room. Gerard watched his departing back, both angry and sad at how things were turning out.

Everything was falling apart. Everything he had worked so hard for was crumbling in front of his eyes. New America was doing well, mostly. All of a sudden there seemed to be a lot of wealth and power in New America, but people were turning away from him. He had lost all of his advisors, and he could no longer demand any attention from anyone. It was as if he didn't exist anymore.

Gerard drifted into an uneasy sleep, where he dreamed of his father, sitting in his tattered recliner, with a beer in his hand, television on in front of him. "So, you think you did so great, did you? Turned out bad, just like I knew it would. You never had the smarts or ability, did you? Stupid boy." Dennis walked in, looked at Gerard, and spit at him, then walked away. Gerard stumbled through buildings searching for something, but not able to find it.

He woke up, sweaty and gasping. He realized there was one more thing he could do. He hated Robert Hurler, governor of the ICS. But he hated Dennis more for completely betraying him. He was going to hand power to Robert Hurler.

"Jason," he gasped.

Jason, his lover and personal attendant, got up from his chair, and came next to the bed.

"Jason, I need to dictate a statement that I want read and spread widely."

Jason went to get paper and pen, moved the chair next to the bed, and sat down, ready to dictate.

"My fellow New Americans. We are in dire times. And I, your President, am dying ..."

Nytt Grier Nro, Cfro 40, 1157/Eastern Wilderness, New Earth, Month 1, Year 11

"Ngellin, you have first watch."

He bowed. "Yes Fourth Chief."

Ngellin moved to the perimeter of the camp. Watch was sort of a silly thing, he thought, because there were absolutely no people out here. And no dangerous animals, either. They could all be sleeping soundly in their tents if it weren't for silly Kinder military rules.

The one good thing about doing first watch is that it gave him a chance to see the sunset. He'd seen it for the first time yesterday, their first day on this planet. It was spectacular, much more spectacular than any sunset on Hilcyon Ngellin had ever seen. It made him wish for his paints.

Well, no hope for that. His paints were light years away, in a place he wasn't even sure he wanted to return to. He hated his home planet, actually. Having a tiny glimpse of life on this planet during the study for the invasion made him plan to desert - to leave the instant he was able to.

He watched the sunset in peace, sitting on a small boulder, getting absorbed in the pinks and blues, and purples of the sky.

"Ngellin." He jumped and turned around.

"Lren! Don't scare me like that."

"You are supposed to be on watch."

"Watch from what? There's nobody here."

Lren sat on the ground next to him. "I know. It's silly isn't it? This sunset is amazing."

"It is." They sat in companionable silence for a while.

"You are leaving, aren't you, Ngellin?"

"Yes. I am. Will you ...?"

"No, your secret is safe with me. Besides, I might join you."

New Columbia, New America, Month 1, Year 11

Kurt walked into the room, with the paper in his hand. Kurt had been living with Dennis for two years, and it was a better life than he could have expected to live otherwise. But it had gotten old.

He had already begun to regret his long ago decision to stay in New America. It had seemed so full of promise, so ready to fulfill his dreams of wealth and power. He had come to see that realizing those dreams, as Dennis had, didn't necessarily lead to happiness.

Once he left Susanna, Terrance and Leticia, he headed directly to the capital, where he thought that he would have the best chance of understanding how the government worked, and how to find the right people. He found Dennis by accident. Well, no – Dennis found him. Dennis thought he would make a good aide. Kurt had, at first, looked up to Dennis, and would do just about anything for him. Eventually, that included sharing Dennis' bed, which Kurt had liked. Kurt was now Dennis' lover, and right hand man.

But over time, Kurt had begun to realize how self-centered Dennis was. Anything he did, he did for himself, and for his own benefit. Dennis was fabulously wealthy, and very powerful, but he had become that way because of these men he called John and Mark. Kurt was deeply suspicious of John and Mark. They looked alarmingly like Casitians, had odd accents, and strange behavior. They didn't seem to act or speak like Casitians, though, which was puzzling to Kurt.

"What's that in your hand?" Dennis' grating voice yanked Kurt out of his reverie.

"You'll love this. It's a proclamation from Gerard." He handed the paper to Dennis, who looked it over. As he read it, Dennis smiled, then started to laugh.

"This is too funny. Gerard thinks that he is taking something from me. Little does he know that Robert Hurler is in my back pocket. I'll be President quite soon."

At that moment, John and Mark walked into the room. They seemed to just show up, if by magic. He'd asked Dennis about that, but Dennis didn't seem to care, and, in fact, told Kurt never to tell anyone about John and Mark.

John said, "Dennis, it seems that power in New America will be yours."

"Yes, it seems that way. I'll be in contact with Robert Hurler and let him know that I will be taking the Presidency. I don't imagine anyone will mind." Dennis smiled.

Mark looked at John, then spoke. "Dennis."

Dennis looked shocked. "Uh, yes?"

Kurt realized that he had never heard Mark speak before.

"Dennis, it is time for us to explain what we want from you."

Mark's accent was strange, like John's.

Dennis answered, "what is that?" Kurt felt concerned.

"You need to identify all people, both boys and girls from the ages of 30 and 38 New Earth Years, who are strong and healthy."

"Why do you ... ?"

"You need not ask. And you need not know. Just give us names, and where they are settled. They will not be harmed, we promise. We will supply New America with all of the metals it needs, as well continue giving you advanced technology. New America will soon dominate New Earth."

Dennis looked thoughtful, then smiled. "That's all?"

John nodded. "For now."

"That's easy."

John and Mark left the room.

Kurt said, "I'll be right back."

He walked quickly out of the room, and then ran to a room upstairs with a back window. Out of the window, he could see the figures of

John and Mark walking away from the house, across the yard toward a line of trees in the back. They stopped, seemed to climb into an invisible door, and disappear. A gust of wind kicked up where they had been. Kurt then thought he knew exactly who they were.

Independent Christian State, New America, Month 2, Year 11

Beatrice was asleep in her bed, and was having a dream about Leticia, when a sound woke her up. She sat up, looking around at the dark. She saw a figure in the door, and before she could speak, some sort of netting wrapped itself around her, binding her tight. She couldn't see or hear, make a sound, or move at all.

She was picked up roughly, and felt herself being carried, but she could see nothing. After a while of bumping and movement, she felt herself being dropped on a padded surface. There was a long time of quiet, which gave her some time to think about what was happening. She remembered her mother crying hysterically after reading a letter in the mail. She'd asked her about it, but her mother wouldn't tell her.

She didn't know whether this was related, but it made sense. Ever since Leticia left, her mother treated Beatrice like a precious piece of china. She was controlling and wanted to know everything Beatrice did. She hardly ever let Beatrice spend time with her friends, except, luckily, Craig. It made sense to her that somehow her mother knew that something was going to happen, and that made her upset.

But Beatrice had no idea what was happening. There were a few movements now and again, but mostly quiet. Beatrice fell asleep, but then was awaken when she was again roughly picked up and carried. She was again dropped onto a surface that was not very padded. She was sure she would be bruised.

All of a sudden the netting loosened, and fell off. She opened her eyes, but there wasn't a lot of light. She was in a huge room with very high ceilings, no windows or doors, and there were hundreds of kids – all about her age, mostly in their pajamas. All around her were a group like her who had just arrived and were taking off their netting. Others were sitting in varied places all over the room, talking, walking around, or sleeping.

She got up and went to someone who was beyond her group. "Where are we?"

He looked up at her and shrugged his shoulders. "I've been here for longer than you, and all I know is that we're in this room, and more people keep being dropped here. That's all I can say. If you're hungry, there is something over there in the far corner that might possibly be called food, but it tastes like, well, cow turds. And the bathrooms are over on the other side."

Beatrice wasn't hungry, but she did need a bathroom. On her way over, she looked all around. The only thing she could think of was that it reminded her of the large cargo hold of one of the colony ships, but that didn't make any sense to her.

As she came out of the bathroom, she saw Craig, and ran over to him.

"Craig!" They hugged and kissed. "I'm so glad you are here!"

"Beatrice – you are the first person I've seen that I recognize. I wish I knew where we were."

They walked over toward the large tables which had small, brown, squares on it, that people were taking, and eating. Craig said, "these fill your stomach, but they taste bland and chalky."

"Where are we, do you think?"

Craig shook his head. "I have no idea, Beatrice, I wish I did."

New Columbia, New America, New Earth, Month 2, Year 11

Timothy was desperate. He had bidden his son Joseph good night last night and woke up in the morning without a son. All of his son's belongings were in his room, but he was nowhere to be found. Neither his wife nor either of his younger daughters had seen or heard anything. Timothy knew his son wouldn't just disappear like that.

He'd talked to a number of people on his street who had also had their teen-aged children disappear last night. It was such a strange thing. They had all gotten that silly letter from the "Office of Volunteer Corps" about a volunteer opportunity for children from the ages of 30 to 38, but everyone had ignored it. Joseph wasn't interested in going to the hinterlands.

He was on his way to talk with Dennis Hickler. He figured if anyone knew anything, Dennis Hickler would. As he was walking toward Hickler's house, he saw that teenager, Kurt who he'd met there. He had a small pack on his back and looked to be in a hurry. He hurried toward him. Kurt was looking down and hadn't seen Timothy yet.

"Hey, Kurt." He looked up and backed up a little looking scared.

"I won't hurt you."

"Look, I'm in a hurry, OK?"

"Where are you going?"

"Dubuque. Getting out of here.

"Look, I need to understand something. My son disappeared last night."

"Yeah, yours and a lot of people's."

"You know about this?"

"Where do you think we got all those metals from? The Casitians took your kid. Don't expect to see him again."

"What in God's name are you talking about? The Casitians?"

"Two guys, named 'John' and 'Mark' have been providing all of the materials and technology to Dennis so he could get rich and influential. In return for all that, Dennis gave them the names of all of the teenagers in New America and the ICS. They aren't from here. I saw them leave in a cloaked shuttle. And now they are gone."

Timothy was speechless.

"Look, I gotta get out of here. I'm sorry about your son."

Kurt walked past Timothy and started running toward the train station. Timothy watched him go and realized that nothing added up. He didn't much like Casitian culture, but he'd come to know them well in working with them to modify his plants on Earth. They would never do such a thing. He knew that for certain.

Jerome, New America Month 2, Year 11

"Thanks, but, really, no thanks. We don't need it. Our rates of new polio and other diseases have gone down dramatically."

Thomas said, "don't tell me, you've got the vaccines."

Thomas was sitting across the imposing desk of a doctor who was the head of a very small clinical practice in Jerome. Jerome was a large settlement in the south of New America. They had 3 doctors and a few nurses, for a population of over 30,000. The doctor was an older man, with graying hair, and thin lips that were pulled taught.

"Yes, we finally got our vaccine production facility going in New Columbia."

"Can you please get me in contact with ..."

"No, no, I'm sorry, this is New America exclusive vaccines. I am not authorized to give it to anyone who is not a New America citizen. Look I have a lot of patients to see."

It was clearly a dismissal. Thomas got up and left the office. As he was walking out of the clinic, a nurse looking furtively at him from her desk in the waiting room.

He walked up to her, and she whispered, "there is something I need to tell you."

He whispered back, "meet me at the Jerome Hotel lobby at second hour tomorrow."

She nodded and turned back to her work.

All of his meetings in New America had been the same. New America's epidemics were under control, and vaccines were being manufactured in the northern part of New America.

But Thomas found it hard to believe that someone in New America, or anywhere on New Earth, could manufacture vaccines in such a short time period. He had known for years now that advanced manufacturing was going to be extremely difficult because of the lack of precious metals. But he had no way of knowing how it had been done.

The next day, Thomas and Jeffrey sat waiting for the nurse in the lobby of their hotel. They started to talk about what they'd found.

"It's mighty strange, Jeffrey, this whole thing doesn't make a lot of sense."

"I agree. You want to know something else kind of strange?"

"What?"

"Have you seen very many teenagers?"

Thomas thought for a minute. "Hmm, now that you say it, I haven't seen any."

"Right. When we were at the first settlement, it seemed odd. I had even passed a school that was in session, and I saw plenty of pre-teens, but no teenagers. None."

At that moment, the nurse walked into the lobby, looked quickly to her left and her right, and walked up to Thomas and Jeffrey.

"Can we talk in your room, please?"

Jeffrey got up and motioned to the stairs. They walked up the stairs to the room they were staying in, opened the door, then closed it behind them.

"So what is it you have to tell us?"

"All of our teenagers have disappeared."

Thomas looked at Jeffrey, who said, "What do you mean, disappeared? Died? Ran away?"

"No, no, simply disappeared. Not all at once, but over the course of about a month. We were warned..."

"Warned?"

She nodded. I have a son, he's 34. There was a letter in my mailbox which told me that vaccines were available in New America, and a new prosperity would be starting. But that all teenagers between 30 and 38 would be asked to join a new volunteer corps. I didn't like the idea, but I assumed the word 'volunteer' meant that my son would have a choice. Anyway, he wasn't interested, but it didn't seem to matter."

"Did someone take him away?"

"No. One morning, I woke up, and he was simply gone. None of his stuff, just him. Gone. I talked with other parents, who had similar experiences. Their children just disappeared without a trace."

Hol'venif, Casiti, 2 Hevl, 782

Marianne had put all of her energy into her garden this year. These days, there seemed to be less call for her expertise and advice about Terrans and Casitians, so she plunged herself, rather uncharacteristically, into growing food. It was absorbing, engaging, and took her mind off of Ja'el, and her future.

When she had moments to think, she was sure that she was leaving Casiti permanently before next winter. She had spent some time with a woman named Yulse'lor, who she liked a lot – they had much in common, surprisingly, and they had talked a little about becoming companions, but Marianne couldn't see herself staying another winter.

Oddly, every time she tried to picture what her life might be like on Earth, whether she'd go back to the Bay Area, or somewhere else, the picture wouldn't come, and images of her sister and nieces and what she imagined New Earth was becoming would be there in her mind. She shook it off every time as worry about what was happening there. She knew she could never see them again.

She bent over her raised beds and kept fertilizing the beets and potatoes.

Independent Christian State, Month 2, Year 11

Yolanda sat in her living room, staring at the wall. She'd been that way for days, after Beatrice's disappearance. She held the letter in her hand, which she'd read over, and over again. Beatrice had been taken by the Mission Society to do God's work in other places on New Earth that needed to hear the word of the Lord. She wished she'd had some warning, or some time to tell Beatrice how much she loved her. First Leticia left, now Beatrice was gone.

Some small part of Yolanda knew that something was wrong, but she didn't let herself feel that. Some small part of her knew that Leticia was actually the safe one and had escaped before this all had happened. Yolanda hoped that someday, she would be able to see both of her daughters again.

San Antonio, Month 2, Year 11

Leticia sometimes could hardly believe her luck. She was sitting in a classroom again, but this time, it was one she liked a lot.

"This new combination of horsehair grass roots, grapeberries, and cone nut oil seems to be working some against new polio infections. So far, 65% of those with defined new polio have completely recovered on this combination. We don't know whether we can reach 100% recovery rate, but many are trying different kinds of combinations. And horsehair grass roots alone seem to be fighting Influenza infections, but not as well as we'd like."

Their teacher was in front of the room and had been showing slides of the newest studies on the treatment of the new polio epidemic. One of the students raised their hand. The teacher pointed to him. "I've heard a rumor that new polio and the other epidemics have been controlled in New America, and they have vaccines."

"Yes, we've heard that, but we have been unable to get any supplies of these vaccines. But our vaccine studies are coming slowly. We have begun to have access to some components we need to make our own vaccines, and we hope to ramp up vaccine production in the next few years."

Leticia stole a look at Mira, sitting a few seats away, the beautiful woman she'd met a few days ago at orientation. She was just so different than everyone else here. She was confident and outspoken. She was from a community called Dlejon. Mira claimed that wasn't a Casitian word, but Leticia knew better. She wondered what that community was like. Perhaps sometime she would get to find out.

"OK, class is over. You have a lot of homework, people – I want to see everyone's epidemiology analysis of Influenza Virus tomorrow!"

A collective groan went up in the class. Leticia was loving medical school, but it was a lot of work. She was already behind in anatomy and physiology, and the class on acupuncture was going to kill her. They needed doctors desperately, and at the same time, the founders of the school were determined to teach the students not only western medicine, but epidemiology, Chinese medicine, other health traditions, and, of course, the new science of the use of local plants. She felt proud that she knew Jeffrey and Thomas, who had contributed key knowledge to that science. They were doing the whole education in four New Earth years, half of the time of normal medical school back on Earth. Leticia wondered if she would make it through. But everyone felt that way, so she definitely had company.

This school had started the second year of settlement – but it had taken a few years to really get going. This class, the ninth and largest, had almost one hundred students, mostly from the North and South

Central Independent Zones. She was one of the first students of the school to come from New America.

As they all got up to go to the next class, Leticia walked up to Mira.

"Hi Mira, how are you today?"

Mira looked at Leticia and smiled broadly. "I'm doing OK, but this homework is going to kill me. I can't keep up!"

"Maybe we could work together on the epidemiology report – the prof said it would be OK to work in teams."

Mira looked a bit surprised, as if she wouldn't think Leticia would ask. "I'd love that, Leticia, that's a great idea. How about we meet in the upper lounge after dinner?"

"See you there." It made Leticia's heart dance to think of getting to spend more time with Mira.

Chapter 6:
Burger and Fries, Please

"We are small in number, and our planet poor. We must be strong and make our mentors proud." – Jlir Nern Klaft (1st age)

Dubuque, North Central Independent Zone, Month 3, Year 11

Kurt walked into the restaurant, looking for dinner. He'd had a hard day at work in his new job working for the local widenet provider. He was glad to have gotten that job, and he had a lot to learn.

His first month in Dubuque had been an education. No one wanted to hear what he had to say about his suspicions about the Casitians being here. No one believed him, and he thought that even if they did, this lot wouldn't care.

When it had been time to emigrate to New Earth, Kurt had been happy to come with his family. He thought that the ICS would be good for him. He lost that illusion quickly, which is why he left the ICS. But in New America, at least, people hated the Casitians. He hated the Casitians. Kurt could only imagine that Dennis would conspire with them because he was blinded by his own ambition and didn't really know who they were.

After unsuccessfully trying to get people to listen, he decided he might as well get a job. Kurt had been somewhat of a geeky kid back on Earth before his parents migrated to New Earth, and he was happy to be working on the widenet. The widenet had spread all across and down the North Central Independent Zone, as far east as the settlement of Bonjour, which was on the river bordering the unsettled lands to the east, and down as New Orleans, the southernmost settlement in the NIZ. Charlie had Kurt working hard – installing and configuring computers in the cafe, in government offices, and beginning to install widenet antennas in individual houses.

The ironic thing about his job was that Charlie had been able to order some electronic parts from New America that Kurt knew were manufactured using the raw materials provided by the Casitians. But Kurt mostly ignored that irony.

"Kurt?" He heard a familiar voice and looked up to see Susanna looking at him. He smiled, tentatively. He had assumed Susanna hadn't stayed in Dubuque.

"Hi Susanna! How are you? It's good to see you."

Susanna looked doubtful.

Kurt said, "Really, it is. I was a complete jerk back then. I should have never been the way I was. I'm sorry."

Susanna smiled. "I have to admit I'd pretty much forgotten about you. What brings you here?"

"Dinner?" Kurt grinned. "It looks like you're working ..."

"I'm the manager – I can take a bit of time off. Here, let me find us a table toward the back."

They walked toward the back, and Susanna whispered to a waitress, and pointed to one of the small tables. They went to sit down at that table, and the waitress brought a menu, and put it in front of Kurt.

"Have whatever you want – it's on me." She looked up toward the waitress. "Illia, I'll just have a coffee, and a slice of Joe's grapeberry pie."

Kurt looked at the menu quickly. "A burger and tato root fries, and just some water, please."

The waitress took the menu and walked toward the kitchen.

"So you manage this place?"

"Yes. We arrived here and I decided that I'd had enough travel for a while. So I stayed, and found the first job I could, which was waitressing here. I moved up to manager after a few months. It's a job, it pays well, but I'm getting ready to move on. I'm tired of standing still."

"Where's everyone else?"

"Leticia got attached to a river guide and went off down the river. I got an email from her just a few days ago. She's in medical school in the SIZ now. Terrance is still here – he worked at a bookstore for a while, but now he's working in the local government – I've forgotten what he's doing, I haven't seen him in a year or so. So what have you been up to?"

"Well, I ended up in New Columbia, and got involved with this guy, Dennis, who was a real wheeler dealer – he used to be lovers with President Hopkinson, believe it or not. He wanted power for himself, really. Selfish prick. I lived with him for a while, but ... then I left."

Susanna looked at Kurt with a puzzled face. "Wait – is that Dennis Hickler – the new President?"

"Yes, that one."

"And you were involved? Like you were lovers?"

Kurt said manner-of-factly. "Yeah, Susanna. I'm gay. I was doing my best to ignore that while I was in the ICS, and that's why I was such a jerk toward Terrance, and all of you. I really thought that I could suppress it or ignore it. And I thought New America could fulfill my silly dreams of wealth and happiness or something. I was so wrong, on so many counts. I hope you can forgive me."

Susanna laughed. "Yes, Kurt, I can forgive you. I knew you had a sweet side, but you just hid it so well, back then. So what are you doing now?"

"Well, for now, I'm working with Charlie, the widenet provider. But I actually have something I need to tell you."

Susanna looked puzzled. "Need to tell me? I don't understand, you weren't looking for me..."

"I know – I need to explain why I left Dennis." He described exactly what had happened over the course of the months he lived with Dennis, and his suspicions about John and Mark, and the things that John and Mark had given Dennis that could not have originated on New Earth, and the vaccine production and electronics production in New Earth.

Susanna listened, then shook her head. "It doesn't make sense, Kurt. Think about it. I know you hate the Casitians, although now that you say you're gay, I can't ..."

"Leave that out of this, please?"

"OK, OK, anyway, Kurt, the Casitians cannot lie. They don't do duplicity. Even you, who hate them, should know that. They would never do what you are saying. And why teenagers? It just doesn't add up. I believe you, really I do. But those people aren't Casitians!"

"Well, if they aren't Casitians, who can they possibly be?"

New Columbia, New Earth, Month 3, Year 11

Dennis looked at John and Mark. "So, you should be happy. I'm in power of all of New America, and you have your teenagers."

John said, "Yes, Dennis we are happy. We are interested in helping you move your power beyond New America, into the Southern Independent Zone."

Dennis had been thinking a lot about that. He was almost getting bored by how well things were going in New America. There had been a few complaints from the parents of the teenagers, but mostly everyone had been happy to be done with the epidemics. Everyone had a job, there was plenty of building and new industry. New America was thriving, thanks to Dennis.

"What did you have in mind?"

"You should start offering vaccines and precious metals, and some of the other goodies we have given you to the border towns first. Then, let the news spread, and offer settlements protection and citizenship in New America. You'll soon have settlements begging to join."

"That sounds like a wonderful plan."

Southern New Aard, Month 3, Year 11

"You need a vacation." Olam looked sternly at Abdul. They were sitting in the prefab that had served as the central administration building of the new settlement for almost a year. The settlement across the river had completed all of their building projects, so they were able to obtain it. It was one of the last prefabs standing. The new administration building was almost complete.

"It's fine, I'm fine, really."

"You need a vacation! Get out of here. Go take your old tent, and go to the lake, like you have been threatening for the last month! You have been working nonstop since we left, and that was more than two years ago. The settlement is fine, we're all fine. We're building up a storm, trading with the Baha'i across the river, we even have managed, thanks to you, a friendly relationship with the settlement up north of us across the mountains. They are tolerating our existence, we are living well, and everyone is happy. I even got a honeymoon. You can get a vacation!"

Abdul nodded. "OK, OK, I'll go. You are right, everything is working well, and you'll be fine in my absence. I'll be leaving tomorrow morning."

Olam smiled "That's good to hear. You'll enjoy it, I'm sure." Olam waved, and left the prefab.

Abdul had been training Olam to replace him ever since the beginning. His goal had long been to get the settlement up and running, then retire to become Imam of the new mosque they had created. He already was the part-time Imam and spiritual head of this community. It was time for him to let Olam govern, and for him to turn to do Allah's work.

They had accomplished much. Their settlement had grown from the 70 or so people at the beginning, to 300 people now, with increasing migration out of the northern parts of New Aard, into the south. All manner of people, from Sunni Saudi Arabians, to people from the old territories of Palestine, to Shia Iranians, had come down to the southern part of New Aard to start a new life in a progressive Islamic community. Women especially were coming in large numbers, sometimes convincing their husbands to come, sometimes leaving them. And many young people, as well.

The last meeting he had with the leader of the community north of them, across the small mountain range, had been especially cordial. This leader had apparently communicated directly with the capital about the progressive community, and the capital had given him clear orders to be friendly. At first, it puzzled Abdul. But then he realized that they were, in a sense, a pressure valve. It was a way for the mullah's up north to keep their power intact. He started to clean off his desk in preparation for his vacation.

Mississippi River, Month 1, Year 12

Kurt and Suzanne were sitting on the edge of the quickly moving river barge, traveling down the wide Mississippi river. They left this morning and would be in San Antonio in five days. They would get off this barge at New San Francisco and take one of the new trains to San Antonio.

Kurt was happy that he had gotten to spend time with Suzanne again. Suzanne had gotten tired of his apologizing so much, and they had dropped into a quiet, amiable relationship.

"I can't quite believe I let both you and Leticia talk me into traveling down to San Antonio with you."

"C'mon, Suzanne! It will be fun. Never know who'll you'll meet there."

"Well, yes. It's already fun. I haven't been traveling in a while, and Leticia wanted me to travel with her. It will be good to see her again. And besides, there is now lots and lots of time for you to tell me what happened between the time you left, and when you got back to Dubuque. Nothing happened for me except I got promoted and got some raises – I've been living and working in the same place since we got here. Is that boring?"

"No Suzanne, I can understand that."

"Well, you did all that stuff in New Columbia, Leticia saw the world *and* is in medical school."

"Suzanne, have you thought that maybe you're stable and sane, rather than unstable and crazy?" She grinned.

"Anyway, the story, man!"

Kurt told her his travels into New America, getting his first job at this small electronics plant, and having a visiting Dennis Hickler hire him on the spot as his assistant. He talked about sharing Dennis' bed, and how much of a problematic character Dennis turned out to be. He was glad to have decided to settle in Dubuque. He'd had enough of New America, even though he wished things could be different.

"I want to talk with Terrance, ask his forgiveness."

"Good luck. That one harbors a grudge against you, my friend."

Kurt sighed, and felt bad. He had been so unkind, and he didn't know a way to undo what he'd done.

San Antonio, South Central Independent Zone, Month 1, Year 12

"Thank you for that report, gentlemen. It was quite informative, and, sobering. It fits with the information we have received from other sources, it does appear that the presence of precious metals and the missing teenagers is linked."

The mayor of San Antonio was a stocky woman, with dark brown hair, streaked with gray. Her office seemed very down home, with a large quilt on the wall, and stuffed animals on the couches.

"You've gotten that information from other sources?"

"Yes, a man named Timothy Christopher, who used to live in New America, met with me about a week ago. He gave me a lot of information on the whole thing. He lost his son, apparently."

"Can you give us information on how to reach him?"

"Certainly." She fished around her desk for a book and wrote down an address on a piece of paper.

"Here you go."

"Thank you very much."

Jeffrey left the mayor's office, feeling like there were too many puzzle pieces that didn't fit. Perhaps somehow, they could find an understanding of it. He walked back toward the medical school, to where he was supposed to meet Leticia.

When she saw him, Leticia ran to Thomas, and gave him a big hug. "Thomas! It is so great to see you!"

Thomas smiled as they broke the embrace. "How's medical school?"

Leticia smiled, "It's really, really hard, and really really great."

"Well, I'm happy for you. Have you made some friends?"

Leticia blushed, then tried to hide the blush. Thomas caught it. "Aha! You've made more than a friend, haven't you?"

"Yes, Thomas, I have. Her name is Mira. She's from Dlejon. She's amazing. She is smart ..."

"It's OK, you don't need to wax on. I'm sure she is. When do I get to meet her?"

"Well, tomorrow night, Kurt, Terrance, Susanne, and I are having a bit of a reunion party, and you are invited. They also apparently have some interesting news, but they wouldn't tell me what it was yet. We're going to a restaurant on Alamo avenue, called 'Taco Maybe.' Meet us there at 28th hour?"

"That sounds great. I've got several meetings to go to, Leticia. There is a lot going on. I'll see you then."

San Antonio, Month 1, Year 12

Kurt, Susanna, Leticia, Mira, Thomas and Jeffrey were seated around a table at 'Taco Maybe' – a busy restaurant in San Antonio. They had chosen a table in the back, to get some privacy, but the restaurant was so loud, people wouldn't be able to overhear them anyway.

Leticia had heard Kurt's story and put it together with Thomas and Jeffrey's story. It was strange, for sure.

Leticia said, "OK, let me review the facts. Kurt says that there are two people who look a lot like Casitians that are providing precious metals and other resources to New America. Thomas and Jeffrey have learned that the vaccine production in New American could not have been done with materials available on New Earth. They also confirm Kurt's story from that guy Timothy, who Kurt also met, who has very detailed information on the materials and metals that showed up in New America. But Casitians working with New Americans just doesn't add up. Timothy was adamant that this wasn't done by Casitians. And Kurt, you said they didn't actually have the same accent."

Kurt argued, "no, they didn't, but I really still think they are Casitians. Dennis was power-hungry, he would sell his soul to the Casitians to gain power in New America."

Leticia, "but what about the missing teenagers? It makes no sense whatsoever."

Thomas said, "I agree, it doesn't make any sense at all. But the problem is, Hickler's power is spreading. I've already heard of settlements on the northern edge of the SIZ joining New America."

Susanna said, "well, we have to do something! We can't let this keep going. What can we do? Warn people?"

"We can ask the Casitians what's going on."

Everyone turned to look at Mira, who had been completely quiet up till this point.

Kurt said, "what? We can't contact them!"

"Yes, we can. It's a long story, and my father would kill me if he knew I was telling you..."

Thomas said, "your father?"

"He's the leader of Dlejon. The Casitians wanted to give us a communications device, so that if sometime in the far future, New

Earth humans wanted to reconnect with the galactic community, they could. We accepted."

Kurt said, "Yeah, OK, but why would the Casitians tell you anything?"

Mira said, "They don't lie, Kurt, they would tell us if they were involved, or who might be."

Kurt shook his head, doubtfully. "I don't really believe you, but I guess that's better than nothing. I guess if it isn't them, maybe they can help. But I still think it's them."

Thomas said, "So, it's time for a trip to Dlejon, eh? I'm sorry that we will have to pull Leticia and Mira from medical school, but this seems important."

"It's OK, Thomas, we can always come back."

Suzanna said, "y'all have fun. I'm going back to Dubuque."

Kurt said, "what about that cute guy Geoffrey you met?"

"Turns out he's on his way to Dubuque, too. I'm hitching a ride with his family on their barge." She smiled.

Southern New Aard, Month 1, Year 12

Olam just looked at Ahmed, stunned. "You saw what?"

"Troops."

"Troops? How many?"

"How should I know? I'm not a soldier. A lot. More than I could count, that's for sure."

"On the eastern slope? Not the northern slope?"

"I was on patrol on the eastern range, Olam, you know that. These troops are not from New Aard, but are from the eastern territories."

"I don't know who had settled out there, maybe Abdul does."

Ahmed was dusty, and still clearly out of breath from his fast trek down the hills to town. Olam looked at him, unsure of what to do.

"We need to speak with Abdul. Come with me."

They left the administration building, and went straight to the mosque, looking for Abdul. They found him in one of the small classrooms, teaching a group of young men and women the Koran.

Abdul looked up, to see Olam and Ahmed. "Hello, Olam, it has been a while since you've visited the mosque for prayer."

"I'm sorry Abdul, I wish I had time to discuss my spiritual state with you. However, we have much more pressing problems. We need your help."

Abdul turned back to the students. "That's all for today – remember the assignment for tomorrow – that packet of poems by Hafiz I gave you to read. You'll like them, I promise." He smiled.

After the students had trickled out of the room, Abdul motioned Olam and Ahmed to sit. "So, my friends, what is so urgent?"

They remained standing. Olam turned to Ahmed, who said, "Abdul, I was on patrol this morning, on the eastern range, as I usually am on the third of the month. I saw what I thought might be a dust storm on the horizon, but I got out my binoculars, and I saw a large mass of troops on their way to the hills. I don't know how large, but I couldn't count. I didn't wait long, I just ran here."

"The eastern slope?"

Ahmed nodded.

Abdul said, "As I recall, there aren't any settlements to the east at all. That seems very strange. You must evacuate the settlement, now! I will stay behind."

"Yes, we will evacuate, but Abdul, you can't stay behind!"

"I will be fine. I can handle it. I will meet you across the river when all is done."

Olam wondered whether or not this was meant as a metaphorical statement. "Abdul ... OK, you'll be stubborn, anyway. We'll start the evacuation."

Olam and Ahmed left the mosque, to put in motion evacuation plans that they thought they would never need. Olam estimated that they had less than five hours to get everyone across the river. They had to act fast.

Abdul watched them leave, and made his own, internal preparations. He didn't know what he was going to face, but he feared the worst.

He walked out of the mosque after many hours and could see the dust settling from the road leading to the river. He expected that his people were safe on the other side now. Just as he turned to go back into the mosque, he could see the troops arriving at the far end of town. He walked slowly back into the mosque, and sat down in his customary place, with his eyes closed.

He heard voices, and the scuffling of many shoes, and looked up to see a large group of men enter with weapons drawn. He then heard a shout in a language he could not understand, and the men surrounded him. One struck him so forcefully that he was forced from his sitting position and sent sprawling onto the floor. He could only see the floor tiles that were in front of his eyes.

"Where are they all? Tell me!"

"I don't know where they are. They left me here alone."

Another one struck him in the head, and he started to get dizzy.

"Tell me the truth, this time!" Abdul had imagined this scene just a little bit differently, but he knew that it was possible that it would turn out this way. Even in his pain, he could register that the accent of his captor was strange. He realized that it didn't matter if they knew where his people were.

"They are across the river, in the Independent Zone."

He felt another kick to his stomach, then his body erupted in pain when a kick was aimed at his groin. He heard lowered voices in that language he did not understand. Then, a sentence that he could easily translate, "Kill him."

Abdul heard shuffling, and a small metallic snap, which was the last thing he was aware of.

Chapter 7:
The Accursed

*"We must be the model for all humans in the Galaxy. All of them." —
Erit'ala (775)*

Hol'venif, Casiti, 50 Gont, 782

A chime woke Marianne. She didn't think it was morning quite yet, and as she opened her eyes, she realized that it was still dark out. Fall Harvest was at its peak, and she'd worked hard yesterday bringing in and preserving some of the harvest from her garden.

She got up from her bed and sat at her desk. "Thanks, display alert."

A dulcet voice spoke in Casitian, "activities on Rec'jeter'she have reached the threshold level for attention."

Marianne sighed. She had been afraid of this moment. They had promised that they would never contact people on New Earth. But the Casitians didn't want to leave the New Earth people completely on their own, so they had planted many listening devices all over the settled areas, which beamed data constantly to an unmanned satellite that was orbiting Rec'jeter'she. AIs monitored activities, and when a certain level was reached, basically showing a crisis, they would let her know. She had been given authority to act, or not. It was power she wished she hadn't had.

"Thanks, display basic data from the last ten timecycles."

She looked over the data in some dismay. Population counts were ... simply weird. The population was growing in New America, at about the rate that would be expected, except that over one New Earth month, the population of New America shrank by a large number, and only on one age range. The populations of the other areas were not growing anywhere nearly as fast. Could there be epidemics? There was definite evidence of troop movement, especially in the far southeast. Troops? The closer she looked at the data, the stranger it was. Satellite images of buildings in New America showed radically fast growth – faster than any other area of New Earth.

It was certainly strange, but she couldn't quite figure out why the AIs had sounded an alert.

"Thanks, please explain alert."

"The analysis of random samples suggests the presence of some elements on New Earth does not match their availability."

"You are saying some elements appeared there but shouldn't be?"

"That is correct. These specific metals and Rare Earth elements appeared about four New Earth years ago."

"Please explain."

"Between these elements being present so suddenly, troop movement which cannot be explained by movements of the current population, and the unusual development trends in New America, there is a very high probability of foreign influence on Rec'jeter'she."

Marianne was stunned. "Who could it possibly be? All galactic species know that Rec'jeter'she is off limits."

"There is no data to know definitively. More investigation must commence."

Marianne sighed. She'd have to go.

"Thanks, please send a message to the AIs at Illsenor station to begin activation for human habitation." They had left an unmanned station in the New Earth system. The star was called Illsenor by the Casitians. They had imaged at some point in the far future that perhaps the people of New Earth would want to rejoin the galactic community.

"Thanks, what is the soonest I can arrive at Illsenor station?"

"Approximately eight days. Should I order a shuttle?"

"Thanks, yes. And send the following message to Erit'ala, Silandra and Ja'el, and David, Laura and Joel, wherever they are. Include the data packet. 'Things on New Earth seem to suggest foreign intervention. We need to investigate. I suggest a meeting at Illsenor station, to discuss options.' And send a message to Diana on Earth: 'I'm on my way to New Earth. Things are weird there. I don't know what exactly I will find, but I will keep you informed. We'll be keeping this secret for a while, but as bad as it is getting I'm imagining people on Earth will want to know, sooner or later.'"

She sent a message to her friend Torf'ki, asking if he would gift all of the food she'd harvested and preserved. She wouldn't be needing it. As she started to pack her things, she knew that she would not be coming back to Casiti after this. Being on Casiti had been surprisingly difficult for Marianne. She had assumed that she would fit in, but it hadn't quite worked out that way. Casiti had a culture was different than she'd expected. Ja'el and Marianne had an amicable parting, but Marianne could never really understand why they had to part, and Ja'el could not really understand why Marianne had trouble with that particular aspect of the way things were done on Casiti.

Another chime sounded, and Marianne looked up to see Ja'el's face. She smiled. "Blessings, Ja'el. Thanks for calling so soon."

"The data you sent was sobering. I will definitely come with you. I suggest we take Yulse'lor. She's been studying the Rec'jeter'she immigrants. She has some interesting insights that might be helpful. I also suggest that we bring Gila'ndor, who is very knowledgeable about all of the galactic species."

Marianne nodded, "I've been in contact with Yulse ... 'lor, and I agree, she has some interesting insights. It would be great to have her along. I'll contact Gila'ndor." Marianne omitted what Ja'el probably already knew, Marianne and Yulse had discussed the possibility of becoming companions for the upcoming winter.

"You've arranged a shuttle to Illsenor station?"

Marianne nodded.

"We'll meet at the space center in the morning."

Kinder ship, Month 2, Year 12

It was impossible to tell time in the huge room. Beatrice had decided that her sleep cycles were as good a way as any. After about ten cycles, no more teenagers arrived in their room. They counted themselves, and there were 1728 of them.

Many of them were strangers to one another. They had started to gather in small groups, mostly by settlement area. There were about 80 of them from the ICS, and Beatrice knew a few of them in addition to Craig. One of the strangest things they had learned was that those who were not in the ICS had been told they were joining some sort of teen volunteer corps. Most of those from the ICS could only remember tearful parents without reason. Some said their parents were told they were required to become part of the Mission Society.

The tables with the food would periodically drop into the floor and come back filled with new food cubes. At a point where Beatrice thought that another 15 sleep cycles had passed, a large projection of a man appeared on one wall, and he started to speak.

"I am First Chief Jgadi." Beatrice thought he had a very strange accent.

"You have noticed that all of your needs are taken care of. There is ample food, plenty of water for drinking and washing. I do imagine, though that you are bored."

A laugh erupted in the room.

"You don't need to know where you are, or why you are here, right now. But you do need to organize yourselves, in the way we are organized."

Craig looked at Beatrice. "But who are they? He looks kind of Casitian, but he talks differently, and he's bald. I don't think I remember ever seeing a completely bald Casitian."

The man started speaking again. "There will be a competition. The rules will be projected after I finish speaking. The winner of this competition will be your Second Chief, and he will answer only to me. He will divide up the group into 12 groups, and he will choose a Third Chief for each of those 12 groups. Each of those Third Chiefs will divide their group into 12 groups and choose a Fourth Chief from each group."

"You must obey your Chiefs completely. Punishment for disobeying your Chief start with no food rations and get more serious as the seriousness and frequency of the offense increases."

He stopped speaking, and the rules were projected, for all to read. Beatrice could hardly believe her eyes. Only men could compete to become chiefs. The competition was one of strength, endurance, and, from her perspective, brutality. The game was basically kick boxing, and the only rule was that the winner had to knock the loser out.

It sounded horrible. Something from those old movies from the 80s about apocalyptic Earth she'd watched once with Leticia. She looked at Craig. "Are you going to compete?"

He shook his head. "No, Beatrice. I can't. I hate to fight. I hate it."

The man who was speaking came back. "One more thing. Every man must compete. If they do not, their Fourth chief will determine a suitable punishment."

Some amount of chaos ensued. There were arguments about whether or not the group would follow the orders. A girl climbed up on one of the tables and shouted "We don't have to follow this nonsense. Why should we have to fight?"

A tall boy got up on the table next to her. "She's right. We don't need to fight. Why don't we divide up into groups, and democratically elect representatives. We can let those representatives talk to this big chief guy."

There were murmurs of agreement around the room. No one seemed to be arguing or agreeing they should fight. They started to move around, to divide themselves into reasonably-sized groups. As this was happening, the projected man spoke again. "You have no choice. For every timespan you delay, there will be a punishment."

The tall boy got back on a table again. "Folks, look, how are they going to punish us? We don't have to listen to them."

The wall where the projection had been went blank, and people continued to divide up the groups. They had about 50 groups, with about 30 or 35 each. They decided that the 50 representatives would choose one representative to talk with the First Chief.

It took some time, but eventually they had one representative, a likeable girl named Hilda. She had been helpful and friendly and had started several activities to keep people busy and entertained before the edict of the First Chief.

Beatrice was among a group of the representatives talking at one side of the room, and Hilda was with them. Suddenly, a door opened up, and several men walked in and grabbed Hilda. Beatrice and a few others tried to follow them, but they were prevented, and the door closed.

In what seemed only a few minutes, the door opened again, and two men carrying Hilda walked in, dropped her on the floor, and left. Beatrice ran over to Hilda, who was motionless. Someone kneeled down, and tried to wake Hilda up, to no avail. They listened to her heart.

"She's dead."

The First chief was on the screen again. "More delays mean more punishment. Commence the competition at once."

There was utter silence.

Illsenor station, 60 Gont, 782 (Month 3, Year 12)

Marianne was pacing in the joining room, waiting for the others to arrive. David, Joel, Laura and Kf'lef had been visiting a planet on the far side of Orion's arm, and had not been especially happy to end up at New Earth, but they realized they were needed. Silandra had come out from Casiti with Marianne and Ja'el along with Yulse'lor, Gila'ndor and a number of other Casitians who they thought could help.

During the trip to the station she and the others had studied all of the data. The devices planted on New Earth had worked well, and there was an enormous amount of data for the AIs to process. The basic trends and analysis were clear, as well as the current dilemma. They had been able to finally tap the new "widenet" and had learned much from it.

People started to drift into the joining room. Silandra, Ja'el and Kal'or walked in first, followed by Yulse'lor and Gila'ndor, then Joel and Laura, and finally David and Kfl'ef. There were some happy greetings – Marianne hadn't seen David, Joel or Laura in years. She was happy to see them, and happy they were here to help.

"Blessings on all. I'm glad that we are all here. We have a lot of work to do."

Joel spoke first, "the data is kinda scary, Marianne. We need a lot more information, and fast."

Marianne nodded. Silandra said, "we will send an array of three satellites. In addition, we will re-tune the listening and watching devices to more easily pick up what might be foreign activities."

Marianne said, "contact with some on New Earth might be a good idea. We should send a shuttle down as soon as possible. I imagine those in Dlejon would be the best folks to talk with first, although they might not know what's going on."

Silandra nodded. "They have the communications device. They know they can use it to contact us. What they don't know is it works both ways."

Marianne looked at Silandra, "works both ways? You never told me that – and you didn't tell them either, did you?"

Silandra shook her head. "We didn't think they needed to know."

South Central Independent Zone, Month 3, Year 12

Olam and Ahmed had been running for days, and Olam was exhausted. Once they had evacuated the community to the east side of the river, the decision had been made to continue the evacuation, including the community of Baha'i, and go all the way upriver to New San Francisco. Olam and Ahmed had volunteered to be in a small forward contingent, warning communities along the way. Olam was looking forward to letting New San Francisco know about the invasion – he assumed they would be able to help.

Olam had held in his grief for Abdul, who he was sure had perished at the hands of whomever was invading. He knew that Abdul would have done what he could to protect them, and Olam knew he had suffered greatly for it. He looked forward to a time when he could grieve properly.

They really didn't know much about the invasion force except that it was large. Olam had gotten a glimpse of them at one point when he and Ahmed had climbed a mountain just north of the Baha'i territory. Olam was a little better at estimating the size of a crowd – he thought there were probably twenty thousand troops.

This puzzled him. Abdul had said there were no settlers east of them. So where did those troops come from? At one point, they had traveled far enough north along the river to be right across it from Jal'alam, the southernmost "real" settlement in New Aard. Olam crossed the river to warn them and suggested that they evacuate north. The leader of the settlement was doubtful but promised to post a sentry high in the hills south of Jal'alam, so they could have enough warning if an invasion came north to them.

As they kept running and crested a hill, Olam could see the large settlement of New California below them. Finally, their running was over. Hopefully, they could rest, and those in charge would listen to what they had to say.

Dlejon, New Earth, Month 3, Year 12

Douglas looked at Mira with dismay. "You told them?"

"Dad, no one else knows."

"It was Dlejon's secret to keep, Mira. I know that what you have heard sounds disturbing, but it is not enough for us to make contact with the Casitians. And now, non-Dlejonese know our secret. This was not wise."

Mira sighed. "Dad, I don't understand! We have clear information that someone outside of New Earth is doing things – making teenagers disappear, giving New America all of these new resources. We can't just sit idle and do nothing!"

"Mira, we are going to do just that. We can't interfere."

They heard an insistent knock on the door. Joan poked her head into his office.

"Douglas, I'm sorry to bother you, but ..."

"What's the problem?"

"Miriam asked that you come to her office, immediately."

Douglas furrowed his brow. *"Miriam?"*

"Yes, Miriam."

Douglas looked at Mira. "This is certainly odd. I haven't spoken with Miriam in months."

"Dad, who is Miriam?"

"Miriam is the designated keeper of the communications device. Her 'office' is actually quite a distance outside of the settlement. I can't imagine why she would want me to come out there. But out there I must go. I'll be back in a few hours."

"Dad, bring me."

"No, Mira, you have already done enough damage."

Douglas left his office and took one of the electric overland vehicles to Miriam's office. Her office was a small, nondescript dwelling, about

50 miles northwest of the main settlement of Dlejon, inside protected wilderness land. While he drove, he had time to ponder all that Mira had said and wonder what he was going to do about the situation. Their mandate had been clear – only use the one-way device to send a message to the galactic community when the New Earth population was united in the desire to rejoin the galactic community. He had made a solemn promise, one he took very seriously.

He reached the dwelling, got out of his vehicle, and knocked on Miriam's door.

"Come in, Douglas."

He walked in to see in the center of the room a holographic projection of Marianne Michaelson.

Miriam said, "I think you'd better sit down, Douglas, you look a little weak."

He found a chair and sat down. The image didn't move for a while.

"Hello Douglas, I hope you are well."

"Where are you?"

There was a delay. "At Illsenor station. Douglas, we have a lot to talk about."

"Well, Marianne, I have a lot to tell you."

Miriam looked at Douglas with increasing concern as he began to tell the tale brought to him by Mira.

Illsenor station, 60 Gont, 782 (Month 3, Year 12)

Joel was in charge of the satellites orbiting New Earth. They finally had made it into orbit, and he was beginning the testing process. Two of the satellites would be trained at the ground, one he placed in geostationary orbit above the southeastern part of the settled lands, one was in north-south orbit, and was going to spend a lot of time following action along the large river they called the Mississippi. The third satellite was in orbit around the equator. That satellite was the one Joel was working with at the moment. It would be focused on looking for spacecraft.

Once testing was complete, he would be putting AIs to work on pre-programmed monitoring routines. It seemed fairly straightforward to Joel. He'd learned a lot about galactic space technology in the time since he left Earth.

A chime sounded. "Signal detected."

"Signal? What kind?" He asked his AI

"Communications beacon, from orbit to land."

"Point all cameras toward the source of that beacon."

After a delay, an image began to form. It was a big ship. It looked about one half the size of the colony ships. The AIs zoomed in on the ship automatically. The image came into focus, and Joel panned back and forth, to record as much of the ship as could be seen. Just as he was ready to do another pan, the image dissolved into static, and he was faced with a blank screen.

"What happened?"

"The satellite was destroyed."

Illsenor station, 61 Gont, 782 (Month 3, Year 12)

Marianne sat at the table, recalling her conversation with Douglas.

"So, it's all very confusing. Kurt, the one who actually saw these men called 'John' and 'Mark' is sure that they were human. He said they even looked Casitian, although he did say they had a different accent. He was sure that they took off in a cloaked shuttle."

Joel piped in, "the image that was taken before the satellite was destroyed was not identified by the AIs. It was strange – the AI didn't say that it could not identify the ship – it said it *would* not."

Marianne looked at Joel. "That sounds weird, Joel. Perhaps the Tud'scla managed to escape their isolation, and they are up to their old tricks of kidnapping humans? But there seem to be massive numbers of troops of humans moving in southeastern New Earth, more than could possibly be accounted for by the population. I don't understand how the Tud'scla would have made contact with those on New Earth, and where all of these human troops came from. And who is 'John' and 'Mark', who seem to be the source of the foreign metals and materials?"

Marianne looked at Ja'el, who had an odd look on her face. She then looked at Yulse'lor, Gila'ndor and the rest of the Casitians, who all had similar, odd looks. They looked a lot like looks of regret and consternation to Marianne.

"What's going on?"

Ja'el sighed. "I hoped we would never need to explain this. I left something out of the story I told you a long time ago. The majority of humans who had been enslaved by the Tud'scla settled on Casiti. The rest, who were allied with the Tud'scla, were given yet another planet, called 'Hilcyon'. They were separated by force from the Tud'scla when the Tud'scla were banned. We call them 'Za'aref'. It is Casitian for 'accursed'. They call themselves 'The Kinder'. The ships here are definitely not purely Tud'scla design but are similar to ships we've seen of Za'aref design."

Marianne was stunned. "What? They were allied ... with the Tud'scla?"

Ja'el nodded, "yes, there were war-like, they had organized themselves like the Tud'scla, and would have stayed with them if the Sejo hadn't ordered the Tud'scla isolated as a species."

"You, you never told me this! Why didn't you tell us?"

"We didn't think you needed to know."

Yulse'lor said, "Marianne, we are in great danger here. We have already started evacuation planning. We need to leave this station in the next cycle. It's quite possible that the ship that destroyed the satellite would come to find this station, and I'm sure that ship has offensive weapons that can destroy it. We don't have any defense mechanisms here. We need to leave."

"We should contact the Sejo immediately! When can the galactic community come to the rescue?"

Ja'el and Silandra looked at each other, as if weighing something. Silandra finally spoke. "Marianne, unless there is clear evidence of the presence of actual members of the Tud'scla species, this is a matter not for the Sejo and the galactic community, but for the Caraj, and the human community. And the Caraj has given us very clear indications that we will not get involved."

"What? Thousands of people could die or be enslaved. How could the Caraj just let this happen? We have to do something."

Marianne looked at her Terran compatriots, who looked as shocked as she felt, and then looked at the Casitians in the room, who all of a sudden seemed foreign. "You don't really care, do you?"

Silandra said gently, "It's not that we don't care – but we cannot come in contact with the Za'aref. Any contact we have with them increases the chance that the Sejo will begin to see all humans as problematic and ban the entire species. We cannot let that happen."

Joel said, "Can't we get the galactic community ..."

"They see this as a conflict within our species. Any conflict within a species is a bad thing. They will not come to our aid."

Marianne said, "I don't want to leave. I want to be on New Earth. Leticia is down there, and this planet was my decision, my making. I'm responsible for it. I can't just leave."

Joel spoke, "Marianne, it's suicide. It is going to be a horrible mess down there."

"I know, but I'm staying."

Silandra spoke again. "Marianne, we have to place a lock on the wormhole. Once we leave, it will prevent any new ships from coming into the system, and it will prevent anyone from leaving. At least that way no more Za'aref can come here. At some point in the future, someone from Casiti will return."

Marianne nodded. "I guess I'd better be going, since it will take me some hours to get down to New Earth."

Marianne got up and left the room. She was feeling a wide variety of feelings, anger at the inaction of the Casitians, sadness at what had happened with Ja'el, fear about what she would find when she landed.

As she was gathering her things and asking her AI for specific items she would need, there was a chime. "Come in."

Ja'el pushed the door aside, and walked in. She closed it behind her.

Marianne stopped what she was doing and turned to face Ja'el.

"You are angry with me."

"Yes. Why can't you help?"

"Marianne, we cannot – the Caraj has given us strict instructions to stay out of this conflict. Listen to me. Don't stay here. Come back to Casiti with us. The lock on the wormhole will mean that all of this will work itself out. It will take many, many years. You don't need to be here."

"What about my sister, and nieces, and the Dlejonese? What about everyone else?"

"They will all have to figure this out on their own."

"I can't leave them, even if it means my own safety. Ja'el, I'm sorry. Don't you care about these people? They are humans! Just like us! They are part of our species, like 'The Kinder' too. We can't just abandon them!"

"We must. We have no choice, Marianne. We cannot risk the status of humans with the Galactic Community."

"You mean the status of Casitians, don't you?"

"Marianne, you aren't seeing the larger issues – we Casitians hold the place for all humans in the galactic community. We cannot be tainted by the Za'aref."

Marianne hung her head and moved one of her folded shirts from her bed to the duffel bag.

"Ja'el, sometimes I really don't understand Casitians, even though we were companions. And I didn't really do so well on Casiti, did I? And I still don't understand why we couldn't stay companions. I miss you, Ja'el." She looked up at Ja'el, feeling the tears in her eyes. Ja'el had an odd look on her face.

"Marianne, we did not have a completely a regular companionship."

"What do you mean?"

"It was sanctioned, officially."

"You're telling me it was part of your *job*?"

"In a manner of speaking, yes."

Marianne was stunned, and silenced. "I see. I guess I have even more to be angry about."

She turned away from Ja'el, hoping that she would leave. Ja'el said, "Marianne, don't ever doubt that I loved you." She heard Ja'el open the door, and leave. She felt tears dripping on her hand, as she folded another shirt to pack.

Later, on her way to the shuttle, David and Joel caught up with her – David looked concerned.

"Are you really sure, Marianne? We have no idea how long it will take before the Caraj decides to send a ship. You could be stuck here for a long time. I might never see you again."

"Don't you see why I have to go? I'll miss you, but I have to..."

"Marianne, I feel as responsible as you do for New Earth, but ..."

David put her hand on Marianne's arm. "Marianne, really, please, don't put yourself in danger."

Marianne shook her head. "I'm sorry, David. I don't feel like I have a choice. Will you both do something for me, please?"

Joel nodded. "Anything."

"Go back to Earth. Tell this story. Everyone there needs to know."

David looked at Joel, and they both nodded.

Joel said, "Yes, Marianne, we'll tell the story. We have to tell the story."

She had plenty of time to ponder this situation, and her life, as the shuttle made its way toward New Earth. After five hours, the shuttle was about to make its final approach, and Marianne could see the planet filling the windows. She thought about how beautiful it was. She realized that she'd spent so much time planning and thinking about New Earth, but this was her first time actually seeing the planet.

She had come from the station in full cloak, running quiet, so that she wouldn't be detected. The trip had been entirely on autopilot. She was the only person going down to New Earth, and she had never learned how to fly a shuttle.

"We are about to enter the atmosphere. Prepare for turbulence." The dulcet AI voice was soothing, in its way. The shuttle reoriented, and they moved into reentry. The turbulence was actually minimal, and once they had gotten through the atmosphere, and were flying at high altitude, the AI said, "we are flying toward Dlejon. Payloads are now released." Marianne heard five small thumps in sequence. She looked outside, and saw small, black spheres floating down away from the shuttle.

"Thanks, what are the payloads?"

"Unknown. No record of what they contain exists."

Marianne had theories about what they were, and hoped they were useful nanotechnology parting gifts from the Casitians.

Southern New Aard, Month 3, Year 12

"Look, there is a whole planet for us to get lost in. Let's just start this now, let's just go." A muscle-bound man squatted in the tent, facing another man. Both were bald, clean shaven and of medium complexion.

"You're crazy, Ngellin. They will miss us, and they will find us, if not soon, eventually, when the immigration starts for real."

"Haven't you heard, Lren?"

"Heard what?"

"No one else is coming."

One of them, the one called Lren, sat up.

"What do you mean? How can that be?"

"I heard Second Chief Rmorter talking with Third Chief Jlec. Apparently, some Breft arrived and closed the wormhole. More ships aren't coming, Lren. And we are a small group in comparison to the population here. We can't win. You and I should escape, and just fade into the landscape."

Lren asked, "Which direction?"

The one called Ngellin looked at a small device in his palm. "We should go away from the conflict that is coming, toward the setting ninth moon."

"Isn't it strange, Ngellin, to be on a planet with no moon. I am disoriented."

"We have our navs, Lren. We'll be fine. Let's go."

Lren nodded. "I can think of at least four others we should ask. Kwelt, of course, Triz, Dfolt and Mner."

"Let's gather them together and leave at first light tomorrow."

Moon Station, January 3, 2019

David and Joel were sitting in a joining room on the Moon station, discussing their next steps. Joel had decided that he was the one to tell Earth the story. David was glad that Joel had volunteered for it – it wasn't something he would have looked forward to. Joel even seemed eager to get down to Earth and start spreading the word.

"So what are you going to do, David?"

"Well, I think it's time for me to spend some time on Casiti. Kf'lef wants to go back, and even though we won't be companions, I like hanging out with him, and I'd like to get to know Casiti a bit better."

"Even though Marianne had such a hard time?"

"Especially because of that. I want to live there for a while, see how it really is. It's likely I'll move back to Earth eventually."

"Laura is happy to be visiting home for a while, but once we're done here, we want to see more of the galaxy. We're going to do some more traveling."

"That sounds like fun. We did have a good time these last few years."

"It's amazing what's out there."

"Yeah, indeed it is."

"Do you think we'll ever see Marianne again?"

"Joel, logic tells me no, but my heart tells me we'll see her again sooner than we think."

Dlejon, Rec'jeter'she, Month 3 Year 12

"Please, quiet, quiet!" Douglas was shouting and trying to be heard above the din in the room. It slowly died down.

"I'm handing the floor to Marianne, who will fill us in on everything she knows about the current situation. Marianne?"

Marianne got up and looked around the room. Only two of the faces were familiar. She had met Douglas many years before, during the emigration phase. Leticia looked so different than when she saw her last.

"It seems we are pretty dire straits I'll admit." She explained everything. The Za'aref, the Caraj's inaction, the evacuation of Illsenor station, and the lock on the wormhole.

A large, bearded man got up toward the back of the room. "So, you are telling me that the Casitians left us at the mercy of a bunch of nasty humans with no support whatsoever? And that there are tens of thousands of troops of them invading the southeastern settled lands?"

Marianne nodded. "Whatever happens is up to us. We do know that no more Za'aref ships can arrive. We think there is only one, but we cannot be sure. We also know that no one can leave. We don't know when the Casitians will choose to unlock the wormhole and check up on us. Probably never, as far as this generation is concerned."

Douglas asked, "So what do you suggest?"

"We need to let everyone know what is happening. We need to find out whether or not New Aard has also fallen prey. We need to find ways to defend ourselves from the invaders."

As people started talking, and laying out plans and actions, Marianne looked around the room at everyone, and realized that this had been the best place to start, after all.

Later, she was sitting at second meal with Leticia. "I'm glad you made it out of the ICS, although I'm sure your mother was upset that you left.

"I've been worried about Beatrice. She's just the right age, you know, to get 'disappeared.' I hope that she'll be OK, wherever she is."

San Antonio, South Central Independent Zone, New Earth, Month 3, Year 12

The mayor of San Antonio looked at Dennis Hickler, the President of New America, and knew he was about to lie to her. What he didn't know was that just yesterday, she'd had a meeting with Marianne Michaelson, who told her the entire story. Marianne had asked her not to let Hickler know yet that she was here, and not tell him what she knew.

"Mr. President, I appreciate your visit, don't get me wrong. I know that several settlements to the north have chosen to join New America. I'm not interested in adding San Antonio to that list."

"I understand, Ms. Mayor, you want to remain neutral. But you yourself know how well things are going in New America. The epidemics are gone, industry is growing, our population is becoming affluent..."

"Will all due respect President Hickler, I know what is happening in New American, but we came to New Earth to be independent, and independent we will stay. Besides, as I imagine you've noticed, the epidemics seem to have disappeared spontaneously. So we don't need your vaccines. If you want to talk trade, I'm happy to talk trade. But threatening me won't get you anywhere."

Hickler looked uncertain. "I'm not threatening you Mayor, although some are – there seems to be a bit of trouble to your southeast, isn't there? We can protect you from that."

"We don't need your protection, thank you."

"So what is it that you want?"

"We have things to offer, as do you. Enter into trade with us, as friends, or leave us alone. We can take care of ourselves."

Chapter 8:
New Miners

"All humans must return to our nature. Humans are fierce fighters, men are stronger than women, and all humans need a mighty leader." – First Chief Glendr, 6th era.

New San Francisco, New Earth, Month 3, Year 12

Marianne had arrived with a small contingent of travelers to New San Francisco. The roads in the Independent Zones had gotten quite good, and it had been a two-day drive to arrive in New San Francisco. As they approached the settlement, they watched the other side of the road, as hundreds of evacuees left New San Francisco.

They were actually on their way eventually to New Islamabad, in New Aard, but they thought a stop at New San Francisco would be good for fact-finding. The troops from the southeast were massing on the river but hadn't started to cross yet. It was a small river, and wouldn't slow the troops down much, when they chose to cross. They had also received word that troops of another sort were beginning to move toward them from the north, from New America. They would soon be attacked from two sides.

People in New San Francisco had learned that projectile weapons no longer worked. New SF had a small stockpile that had been brought with gun club, and when they had first tried to use those, they wouldn't fire. They didn't know what kinds of weapons the troops on the other side had, but Marianne was confident that the Casitian "gifts" would de-activate them.

Marianne stood on top of the tallest building in New SF and looked at the massing troops with powerful binoculars. She was accompanied by a man named Olam, who had escaped these troops in New Aard.

"You are sure New Aard has not joined them?"

"Yes, ma'am, I am sure. The last meeting I had in Jal'alam, before the evacuation, the sheik there had mentioned a strange meeting with men promising precious metals. He said that he had been told that these men had traveled all over New Aard, and to not believe them. So he turned them away. This sounds a lot like the men that you described from New America, doesn't it?"

Marianne nodded. "We need to speak to the leadership of New Aard. Can you accompany me?"

Olam blanched. "I am hardly a worthy escort, ma'am…"

"Please call me Marianne."

"… Marianne. I was a defector, a progressive Muslim who could not live within the fundamentalist society. They would not want to see me again. Besides, my wife and child have already left for San Antonio, and I must follow them."

"What other suggestions would you make?"

"There is a New Aard embassy in New Orleans. You should start there."

Marianne nodded. "OK, Olam. Thanks."

New York, Earth, February 10, 2019

It seemed almost surreal to Joel, walking from the train he had taken from JFK spaceport, on his way to the subway to go to Diana's apartment. He hadn't been in New York City for a long time, in fact, many years before the Casitians had arrived. Different reactions were competing for space in his head – the massive changes in the city since he'd been here last, and just being back on Earth at all, after having spent so many years traveling around the galaxy. It was easy to find his way to the right subway, guided by the AI in his new phone. He finally walked up the stairs at the West 4th street station, to emerge in a completely familiar setting. It was almost as if nothing had changed in the 20 years since he'd been here.

He'd lived in The Village for a summer during college, working with an NYU professor who was studying the connection between tornadoes and global climate change. At the time, it was a contentious field. He'd stayed with a friend of his, who lived just a block from Washington Square Park, so it felt like he was back in his old stomping ground.

As he walked toward Diana's building, he noticed things that were indeed different – small indications of change and galactic influence.

Everything was spotlessly clean, there were no panhandlers, and it was eerily quiet. The few cars that drove by were silent, and there were no sirens.

As he walked down West 4th street toward MacDougal, where Diana had her apartment, he could pick out the small changes – new traffic lights, lights and transponders embedded in the streets and sidewalks, and the shapes and colors of taxis, that made it clear that this was, in fact, a new New York City.

He finally reached Diana's building, and the inner door opened for him automatically. He walked up the two flights of stairs and saw Diana's smiling face poking out of her door. She walked up to him and gave him a hug.

"God, Joel, it's so good to see you." She put him at arm's length, to look over him.

"You are looking good, my friend. Come in, come in. You must have important news to come all the way back to Earth to deliver it."

They walked inside the apartment, and Joel put down his bag.

"Let me introduce you to my girlfriend, Janie."

Joel looked at Janie, who looked like a reliable, sturdy companion for Diana. She had dark brown hair, with a shock of gray in the middle.

Janie walked up to Joel and gave him a hug without hesitation.

"You look famished. Diana, we need to feed this boy."

Joel in fact, was famished, and was happy to sit down over what looked like a wonderful meal. He had plenty to tell them, and it seemed like good food would help.

After telling the whole tale, Diana looked sad. "So we may never see Marianne again?"

"It looks that way. From the kinds of things that the Casitians have been saying about those Za'aref, I don't think that they ever want to open that wormhole again."

Far Southeastern New Aard, Month 1, Year 13

Ngellin turned on his sleeping mat, slowly waking up. He shook out the cobwebs and got up. Ngellin's small band of rebels had turned into a larger trickle out of the mass of troops. Most of them had found their place in smaller communities in New Aard. Some had gone away far to the southeast, to make their own new settlements. He imagined that now that everyone understood the realities, that there would be little reason to continue fighting.

Then he remembered First Chief Glendr. He was a determined fighter, and was sure that his goal, which was the unification of all humankind under the Kinder, or "righteous ones," was pure, and obtainable. Ngellin imagined that this current situation was simply a minor setback in the eyes of Glendr.

Ngellin had never felt he fit in – he'd never wanted a chiefdom, would have rather been watching Hilcyon's moons or even painting them, than fighting. He'd had no choice – he drew a low number in the draft and had been on the second ship to this place.

He liked the planet – it was gentler than Hilcyon, much warmer and wetter, with much more abundant food. He missed the nine moons, but there was plenty here to keep his interest. In all that he heard about the people, he knew he could find a place to call home, eventually. He was intensely curious about the other humans and expected that he would make his way toward them soon, leaving this group behind.

New York, Earth, February 20, 2019

Joel sat uncomfortably in the couch that was designed to be informal and relaxing, or at least seem that way for the audience. He was being interviewed by Joh Appel, who was the newest, and hottest host of the "Today" show. Joel felt some amazement at its continued existence.

Of course, there was no longer any such thing as a "TV network" – but the show kept going on the net and had millions of viewers. Joel, Diana and Janie had chosen this as the best first venue for getting the word out. They had planned many other interviews.

The face of the producer was in a screen facing both Joel and Joh, and she signaled when the live netcast was about to start.

"I'm here today with Joel Martin. You should all are quite familiar him with as one of the folks who helped us through the Casitian crisis. He has been away from Earth for a number of years and is back to tell us some disturbing news."

The "Casitian Crisis" was what people on Earth now called the few years between first contact with the Casitians, and the final departure of emigrants to New Earth. Things had settled down on Earth, and people had, for the most part, gotten back into more standard rhythms of life, even though things were different.

"Joel, please tell us the latest about New Earth."

Joel nodded his head, "certainly. Yes, this story is disturbing." Joel then told the detailed story as he knew it, about the Za'aref, the wormholes, what had happened on New Earth, and the actions of the Casitians.

"So Joel, let me get this right – the Casitians *locked* the wormhole to New Earth? No one can get in or out? They left the people on New Earth at the mercy of those Za'aref? They didn't try to help?"

Joel nodded sadly. "Yes, Joh, that's what happened."

Joel knew that this would cause a backlash against the Casitians, but he himself had come to feel betrayed by them, and it wouldn't surprise him if most other Earth humans felt the same way.

Kinder ship, Month 4, Year 12 /Cfro 20 1151

Beatrice ran to Craig, who had just returned from his meeting with the First Chief. He looked ashen and shaken.

"Are you OK?"

He looked up at Beatrice, shaking his head, and walked to the corner of the room, where he and Beatrice had been given a large space, now that Craig was Second Chief.

He sat for a while, silently, while people started to gather around their space, waiting for any information he had.

Craig, it turned out, was a very good fighter. He hated fighting because he had been forced for many years to fight with his father, who had been a championship ultimate fighter. Because of those years of training, he easily beat every opponent that faced him.

He looked up at Beatrice. "We are in deep trouble, Beatrice." He got up from the space, and walked toward the tables, and he jumped up on one.

"Please, your attention, please!" Quiet settled in the large room. "I spoke with the First Chief. I have information to share. We are no longer on New Earth. In fact, we are no longer even anywhere near New Earth." Murmurs and chaos had erupted.

"Please, please be quiet!" The murmurs died down.

"We are on a ship, heading for a mining operation. We will be working in that mining operation."

Beatrice looked around her. People were looking at Craig with disbelief and shock. Beatrice couldn't imagine how this could be.

"I have been told that if we work here for a while, and work well, we will be allowed to join the population on the planet here eventually. And we may be able to return home someday. But First Chief didn't tell me how long that would be, or what 'working well' meant. We have to cooperate. I need to announce my Third Chiefs, which I will do very soon. We will take it from there."

Casitian Cruise Transport, May 10, 2019

Joel and Laura were on their way again, traveling the galaxy. They'd hitched a ride with a Casitian tour of amazing sights. They were sitting in their quarters, relaxing after last meal.

"I feel like I left a complete uproar, but I'm glad we're gone."

"Joel, there is nothing you could have done about the uproar."

"I know. We told the story, and now we've left."

Laura put her head on his shoulder. "Glad to be heading to the Cat's Eye Nebula. I hear their hotel in space is amazing. Good thing we learned Casitian. I doubt they speak English."

Joel laughed, then sobered. "Somehow I doubt that anyone in the galaxy will be speaking English anytime soon."

They sat in companionable silence for a while. Joel thought about the weeks they had spent on Earth, on talk shows and interviews, and how much their news had tapped a current of anger Joel had no idea was there. The Za'aref were lionized as heroes, even though they were known to have invaded and kidnapped thousands of teenagers from New Earth. And the Casitians were villainized. Kurt could understand the anger toward the Casitians, but he could not understand why people were idolizing the Za'aref, or, as everyone now called them, "The Kinder".

Joel and Laura had decided to travel for another few years, then settle back down on Earth. They both had multiple standing job offers, which felt like nice security. They could imagine a quiet life on Earth.

Chapter 9:
Acts of Courage and Cowardice

"In my travels I have come to know that all humans, even if they reject it, have, at one point or another, felt the deep peace of the all." – Jal'end'a (781)

Casiti, 140 Gont 782

The insistent chime was annoying. Erit'ala had just fallen asleep, her companion stirred beside her. She rose, walked to her work area, and whispered, "Display, thanks, the alert."

It was a recorded message from Gret'lor, the human representative to the Sejo. She was stunned.

"Erit'ala, I am sorry to disturb you, but the Sejo has learned of some very disturbing events, and I need more information from the Caraj. The Keeelo say that there was some unusual activity at the Illsenor wormhole, which resulted in an unauthorized lock on the wormhole. This activity included first, two very large ships going through about one year ago, then a pause, then one of those ships leaving, and another arriving, then leaving and locking the wormhole. The lock has been identified by the Keeelo as of Casitian origin."

"I know of no Casitian ships going to New Earth last year. But I need more information, and I imagine you might have it."

The message ended. The news was sobering. First, it suggested that a ship left the system, presumably full of humans from New Earth. Erit'ala felt a moment of sadness for those humans. There was nothing they would be able to do about it, and the Casitians could not enter Za'aref space to retrieve them. Asking the galactic community to intervene on the behalf of those people would be tantamount to asking the Sejo to suspend human citizenship, and the Casitians could not afford that. Erit'ala was afraid that reporting what they knew to the Sejo would have exactly the same result.

She composed her message to Gret'lor carefully. She told him what she knew, that Marianne had stayed, that the lock prevented any more comings and goings to Rec'jeter'she. She did the best she could and hoped that it would be enough.

Kinder ship – Month 1, Year 13/Cfro 21 1151
Craig had just returned from another meeting with the First Chief, and he sat down hard on their sleeping mat, folding his frame into himself. Beatrice knew when he was feeling the stress of his position – she could see it in his body and in his face.

"Honey, what happened?"

He looked up at her, his eyes dark, with pools of tears.

"We're arriving soon at the Asteroid. The First Chief was giving me the lowdown on what will happen next."

"And..."

"We'll be assigned quarters as a group, with individuals having to share large dorm spaces, but couples will get small quarters of their own."

That made Beatrice happy – at least she and Craig could have privacy.

"What else? Why are you so troubled?"

"We will have a production quota to meet, with sanctions if we do not meet it. We won't have much time to learn how to mine before those quotas come into play. The schedule is brutal. They have a different calendar and time, of course, but I did some calculations. It looks like we will have 16 hour shifts, with only 7 hours off. And the equivalent of one day off every 10."

"How can they expect to keep us going under those conditions?"

"I'm not sure, Beatrice, I just don't know. It scares me. I also think that we'll never be let go."

Southwestern New Aard, Month 2, Year 13
Ngellin and Lren were talking in Ngellin's tent.

"Yes, Lren, this is the place. We're relatively close to New Orleans..."

"And that's a good thing?"

"Yes. From what I can tell, New Orleans has become a center of sorts."

"You scare me, Ngellin."

"Lren, our success depends on our willingness to work with the people here."

"I know, I know."

Ngellin liked Lren a lot but knew that Lren missed home. Ngellin, on the other hand loved this planet. He loved everything about it. He had no intention of ever going home, even if he got the chance.

Ngellin asked, "have you had time to send messages to many of the Kinder here? What have you gotten back?"

"Apparently, there was a Second Chief who was trying hard to gather up deserters, but now he has deserted."

Ngellin laughed. "And?"

"We think there are about 2,500 of us who have left. The rest seem to have been sent back to the ship."

Ngellin whistled. "That's quite a lot."

"Yes. It seems that Glendr is not willing to expend too much energy in finding us. And now that most of us are growing our hair and learning the local language…"

"We'll soon be able to simply fade into the background, won't we?"

Lren nodded. "Especially here. The people have similar coloring."

Ngellin nodded. "That's another reason why this is a good place."

Lren said, "people are looking up to you, Ngellin. Some have even asked me if you were going to make yourself Supreme Chief of the Kinder on Nytt Grier Nro."

Ngellin said forcefully, "I am willing to lead our people, Lren, but *never* as a Chief. Never, ever. Hear that? Tell everyone!"

Lren stepped back in response. "OK, Ngellin. I get it."

"We need leadership, Lren, but not like we've had it. I don't want to have leadership like we have it at home. It is stifling and stupid."

Lren nodded. "You won't hear different from me, Ngellin."

Kinder ship – Month 1, Year 13/Cfro 23 1151

Beatrice sat next to her new friend, Jasmine. They had been talking about what was coming.

"I'm worried, Beatrice. I have to admit to worrying about myself, and what will happen to me. It's scary."

"Yes, I understand. It feels a little better having Craig. Is there anyone you feel you can trust?"

"I can trust you."

"You know what I mean, Jasmine."

"No, Beatrice. None of my friends is in this room, and, well, I was a loner at school – people thought I was weird."

"I don't think you're weird."

Jasmine smiled. "Thanks. Anyway, no, I haven't found anyone. A lot of people have coupled up, but there isn't anyone I want to be with right now."

Beatrice thought Jasmine reminded her a little of her sister Leticia and wondered if she preferred girls over boys.

"Well, stick with us, we'll do our best to protect you."

Craig walked up and sat down next to Jasmine. Beatrice knew that he liked Jasmine a lot.

"Yup. We will. Actually, I have a job for you."

"A job?"

"Yes. The First Chief asked me to find someone to be the 'analyst' he called it."

"Analyst?"

"I'm not sure exactly how you'll do the job, but it's important. You'll be the lead on our team into mining areas, analyzing the rocks for their composition, to see if we should mine them or not."

"Sounds like a great job."

"It's dangerous, but I think you can do it."

"I'm happy to."

"I really want to have someone I trust in that position. I know they would expect me to choose a man, but I know you can do it – you're strong."

Jasmine smiled. "Thanks for your confidence in me, Craig."

They talked for a while, wondering what their future on the asteroid would hold.

New America, Month 1, year 13

President Dennis Hickler looked at the man facing him. He could see in his eyes that this was going to be tricky. He needed him as an ally, but he knew that going too far would lead to trouble. He had come to learn over time that peaceful coexistence with the surrounding communities was going to work much better than threats or conflict. He had seen that his power was greater when he gained influence not by intimidation, but by cooperation. Dennis was ambitious, but he was also smart, and willing to adjust his strategies to meet his goals.

"Mr. ... Bercyg, I do believe I can say that our army, which now numbers almost ten thousand, would be willing to help you in your efforts, depending, of course, on what you had in mind. We do want to continue the peaceful trade we have been building with our neighbors – it is providing us with needed goods and services."

"Well, President, of course we can't say at this moment what we will be using these troops for, but it is good to know they are available to us."

Dennis always felt strange when Bercyg called him "President" instead of "Mr. President," or "President Hickler." It was like being called "General" or "Sergeant" or something. And Dennis would have certainly preferred to have Bercyg call him by his first name. Dennis knew that Bercyg was doing his own dance.

Bercyg was a muscular man, with the shoulders of a soldier that has seen a lot of hand-to-hand fighting. Bercyg's head was completely clean shaven. John and Mark had very short hair, and no facial hair, but all of the other Kinder men Dennis had seen so far had their hair completely shaven.

"In addition, President, we would hope that you would return some of the favors we have given you and send a bit of your food production our way. We still have rations that will last many years, but fresh food from the planet would be greatly appreciated."

Dennis nodded. "Yes, of course, we would be happy to do that. How much do you need?"

Dennis was a calculating man, and realized at that moment, in a rush, that the Kinder had weaknesses. He was going to find ways to take full advantage of them.

"Keep moving forward!" the amplified voice grated on Beatrice's nerves. They had arrived at the asteroid and had left their room in an orderly fashion – in groups of 12 and 144. They had entered into a very large bay as big as an arena.

Speculation about who their captors were was rampant. Most people around her had assumed that they were Casitian, but both Beatrice and Craig didn't think that made any sense. They looked similar, but seemed to speak a different language, and certainly acted differently. The First Chief had refused to answer Craig's questions about it, so Craig had stopped asking.

"Follow your Chiefs. They know where your quarters are."

It was a bit chaotic at first, but then slowly, the large bay emptied, and they made their way to the section of the asteroid where they would stay.

As Craig's "wife" – even though it wasn't official, Beatrice got to stay with Craig. The "wives" of the chiefs were given special consideration, and the chiefs got better quarters than everyone else. This meant that many girls had been vying for the attention of those chosen to be Chiefs. Some girls had even tried to get Craig's attention.

Craig and Beatrice were at the head of their group, with the group of Third Chiefs behind them. The corridors were sparsely lit by small, yellow lights that cast a pale glow into the dark spaces between. There was a thin layer of water on the floor, which would be slippery if it weren't for the gravely surface of the floor. Beatrice could hear a steady drip somewhere, which seemed to follow them as they walked.

They finally arrived in a section labeled with letters in an alphabet Beatrice didn't recognize.

Craig said, "this is our section, and the section of Third Chief Jonathon."

The rest of the Third Chiefs and their groups kept walking down to other sections. They walked in, and down a last corridor. The corridor ended in a large room, with lots of furniture. There were chairs and couches, and assorted boxes and objects that looked like books and games. The Chiefs then arranged everyone and found the rooms that people were assigned to. Craig showed Beatrice to their joint apartment – it had a small bedroom, with what looked like a comfortable bed, and a larger living room, with a small kitchen alcove. She also found they had their own bathroom, which even had a shower, although it looked strange and unfamiliar.

"Well, this isn't so bad, although I'm sure we have the best of it."

Craig nodded. "Yes, we do. We'll make do. Unfortunately, work starts tomorrow. I need to gather the group of chiefs and let them know what to expect."

Craig walked out of their apartment, and she heard his voice amplified over a speaker system.

"All Third Chiefs please meet in the common room at 10th hour. There are clocks in each room. You have some time to get settled. You'll find sheets and towels in the rooms, and there are clothes of many sizes in the cabinets of the common room."

Craig came back into the room.

"Come lie down with me, Craig, for just a little bit."

Craig didn't argue, and the two of them lay on their bed, holding each other.

New Orleans, New Earth, Month 1, Year 13

It seemed odd to Marianne to be sitting with Douglas at a sidewalk cafe in New Orleans on New Earth, sipping coffee with chicory and munching on a beignet as if nothing was wrong. In some ways, nothing was, at least not here. Their short trip into New Aard had been fruitful. It was true that the Za'aref had visited New Aard, but they had been completely rebuffed. The leadership of New Aard was far from happy to see Marianne, but given the circumstances, they were conciliatory.

"Well, I think that things are coming to some kind of peaceful ... stability, don't you?"

Marianne nodded. "Yeah, it does seem that way. Everyone has realized that cooperation is better than conflict. The troops from the Za'aref seem to have left, and people have also come to respect the wishes of some, like New Aard, to remain distant from other communities."

Douglas nodded. "You haven't yet explained to me the whole thing with nanotechnology..."

"When I was coming down from the Casitian ship, they had placed several payloads on the shuttle. They'd not told me about them. You probably remember the nanotechnology that was released on earth to help clean things up, and, finally, to inactivate projectile weapons?"

Douglas nodded.

"The same kinds of nanotechnology must have been released from my shuttle. Cured the epidemics and prevented violence by guns or other weapons."

Marianne was glad for the parting gifts of the Casitians. There had already been too much death and conflict – it was good that it was coming to an end.

Douglas changed the subject. "So, Marianne, what's next for you? I know I have a community to return to on Dlejon. You are, of course, most welcome to settle there."

"Yes, Dlejon seems to be a good place to settle. I know that the Dlejonese will be involved in New Earth development, and I want to be a part of bringing people together as much as possible. It seems like Dlejon is a good place to do that."

"When do you think the Casitians will return?"

"I don't know, Douglas. Honestly, I don't expect to see them in our lifetimes. They seemed really clear that they wanted to get as far away from the Za'aref, or any other negative influence as possible. We are on our own, probably for a very long time."

Dlejon did seem a nice place to settle. She mentally prepared to make her way back there and find her place. But before that, she felt that she had a bridge to mend: she needed to visit Yolanda.

Kinder ship Month 1, Year 13/Cfro 35 1151

First Chief Glendr paced, a few minutes before his status meeting with his Second Chiefs. He was glad for a spacious office – pacing had always been the way he figured things out.

To get this job, he had challenged the previous First Chief, Proygy. It was too bad Proygy had a bad heart condition, and died during the fight, without succumbing to Glendr's weapon. Glendr had no intention of being challenged or deposed. Glendr intended to return to Hilcyon victorious and take the Kinder Supreme leadership when Vondryn died. But now, he was stymied.

The door to his office slid open and three men, all tall and broad-shouldered, walked into the room, and stood around the large conference table. There was only one seat. Glendr joined them at the end of the table and sat in the seat.

"Status reports, please."

The first man he looked at was Second Chief Jercyn. Jercyn sported a very small tuft of hair below his lower lip. It always irritated Glendr – it felt like a way to show Jercyn's contempt for the norms of Hilcyon society. Jercyn was also unusually light-skinned for a Kinder. Sometimes, there were children who ended up unusually light- or dark-skinned. But they were rare. He leaned a bit, his fists on the table.

"First Chief Glendr, we have, as of yet, been unable to break the encryption on the wormhole lock. It appears to be of a very high order, and we don't have the computing power to break it."

"Have you considered other strategies?"

"Yes, First Chief, but so far, nothing has proven likely to break the lock that the Breft left."

The wormhole had been closed by the Breft, or "Casitians" as they liked to call themselves. The Breft were supreme cowards. Of course, they ran, and of course they closed the wormhole behind them. Glendr was frustrated by this situation.

"You said you thought that you could break it within the year, Jercyn! Was that a lie?"

Jercyn looked very uncomfortable and shifted back and forth. Glendr could see sweat beads forming on his forehead. "No, First Chief. It was an estimate. I think now it was an underestimate."

"Be careful, Jercyn. There are others who might be interested in your position should you fail to deliver."

Glendr took his attention entirely away from Jercyn and looked at Second Chief Retyl. "Retyl, what bad news do you bring me?"

Retyl, if it were at all possible, looked even more uncomfortable than Jercyn – as if he wanted to run away from the table. He stood at a bit of a distance from the table, not touching it.

"First Chief Glendr, as you ordered, we have removed our forces from ground for the time being. However, it seems we have lost 12-15% of them. They have either disappeared into the wilderness or joined the other side."

"And how did you let that happen, Retyl? You clearly did not choose the right Chiefs to keep everyone in line!"

Retyl almost looked defiant, but then Glendr could see him think the better of it. He finally said, weakly with his head down, "First Chief, I bow to your greater wisdom. I am willing to go down to the surface and lead the efforts of bringing the deserters to justice."

Glendr knew that Retyl had no such plans. He knew that Retyl planned to disappear himself. He wondered how he had ended up surrounded by such weaklings. Glendr was not going to give him the chance to desert. The First Chief knew about one of Retyl's Third Chiefs who would be more than happy to take Retyl's place.

Glendr then turned his attention to the last man, Second Chief Bercyg. Glendr had great hopes for Bercyg. Bercyg was strong, loyal, and, most importantly ambitious. Bercyg knew that long term loyalty to Glendr was his ticket to higher, better things.

"First chief Glendr - I have very good news."

Glendr nodded. "Go ahead, please."

"Our alliance with the group that calls itself New America is still strong. The man who is now Supreme Chief, or 'President' as he calls it, is firmly in control, and he has gathered around him a group of loyal, hard working men. We will have New America as an ally in whatever efforts we wish to engage in. And, further, the first shipments of fresh food from the surface have begun. I know that you enjoyed your breakfast this morning."

Glendr nodded again, smiling. "Yes, indeed I did Bercyg. This is very good news. Has this 'President' raised an army yet?"

Bercyg said, "yes, First Chief, he has. From what I understand, he has approximately ten thousand troops at his disposal."

Glendr frowned, and he could see Bercyg's face shift. "Ten thousand? That's all? We lost two thousand at least, and there is no way we can conquer this planet with so few troops. We need more!"

Bercyg began to look uncomfortable himself. "First Chief, it is simply a limitation of population. New America is the only country that is our ally, and they have a small population. And fifteen thousand strong, young people are now at our disposal back on Hilcyon – so they are unavailable to us here. It will take more time to raise a bigger army."

"They are using conscription?"

Bercyg shook his head. "No, First Chief, they are not."

"This would be a good test of how cooperative they could be, isn't it? Tell 'President' Hickler to initiate a conscription program."

Bercyg's face went white. "First Chief..."

"I want no excuses! None! All of you, don't you have work to do? Go do it!"

As the men left the room, Glendr had the distinct feeling that he was seeing little creatures scurrying out of sight.

Casiti, 5 Paqn 782

Erit'ala, Silandra and Ja'el sat together with cups of fuge. They were all in a very somber mood. Erit'ala had been delivered some devastating news, and she had to share it with everyone. Silandra and Ja'el didn't know the details of her news, but she could tell from their demeanor that they knew it was serious.

Erit'ala spoke first. "The Sejo has decided on a full inquest."

Ja'el asked, "What does this mean?"

"It means that all humans materially involved have to show up at the Sejo council in one Casitian year for the inquest."

"What could happen?"

"From what I've read, the pending action could include probation or possible restriction for the human species from the galactic community."

"They wouldn't..."

"I can't see how they could, but the fact that they wish a full inquest is troubling."

Silandra, who had been quiet thus far, spoke. "Erit'ala, what can we do?"

"We need to prepare our case. I'm about to send messages to everyone, including Joel and Laura, David, Kf'lef, Yulse'lor, and Gil'ander. We'll need the help of many people to work this out."

Ja'el said, "I'll get some space in the galactic center reserved for us and assign housing near there for the Terrans."

Erit'ala nodded. "Thank you, Ja'el, that sounds like a good idea. I guess the best thing we can do right now is to get started on our defense. We have a lot of work ahead of us."

Hilcyon Asteroid Mine – Month 3, Year 13/Mrontl 10 1151

Craig climbed the stairs to the First Chief's office. He wasn't looking forward to this meeting. After landing on the asteroid and getting settled in, the teenagers from New Earth were a uniformly unhappy lot. Craig did the best he could, as did his chiefs, to provide what was needed and soothe raw nerves, but the first few weeks of actual mining work had been hellish. They had managed to meet 2/3 of their production goal, which Craig thought was quite good, considering none of them had ever mined before. Jasmine had been invaluable. She had quickly learned what tunnels would help them meet their goals, and which ones wouldn't. That had been the only way they were able to come close to their production goals. The next period had been better, but it was difficult to figure out how things were going to smooth out.

He knocked on the door. The gruff voice of their new First Chief, Krellen made it clear that Craig should come in. Craig opened the door and walked into the grimy office. He noticed pieces of mining equipment strewn about, and other odd, assorted things. There was a layer of dust, the same dust that got into everything in the asteroid. You could even taste it in the food. He obviously didn't even attempt to clean any of it off of anything.

Words started to come out of the First Chief's mouth, then the translation plug Craig had in his ear started to kick in.

"I just got the production reports today." Krellen looked up, right at him, piercingly.

Craig waited.

"One-half goal." Craig was puzzled.

"Sir, we produced at least twice this period what we produced last period – how can that be half of the goal, if we were almost at 2/3 goal last period?"

"Goal has changed. The production goal goes up every period for 10 periods."

"No, you can't do that – we can't possibly produce twice what we did this period – then keep producing more – we don't have enough people, and we don't know enough yet."

Krellen chuckled. "No, it's not that. You are too soft. You let people take sick days, you *talk* to people who aren't producing, instead of punishing them. Punishment is all people really understand."

"You are asking me to do something that I will not do."

Krellen laughed even louder. "I know. You are dismissed. Go."

Craig stood there for a moment, puzzled by Krellen's behavior. He turned around and opened the office door. As he opened it, he saw a man he recognized. He'd met him at a meeting once. He was a Third Chief of a well-established mining group. He had something grey and cylindrical in his hand that moved quickly. Craig felt a piercing pain in his midsection, and everything went blank.

Casiti, 7 Paqn 782

David and Ger'lier were wrestling on David's bed. He liked wrestling with Ger'lier – it was great foreplay. Ger'lier had managed to get him in a headlock, with his leg around David's torso. He was licking David's ear.

"OK, I give up! You win."

"What do I get?"

"Whatever you want." Ger'lier let go, and Ger'lier shifted David so that he faced him. Just as he was about to kiss him, they heard the insistent chime of an urgent message from David's AI.

"Crap." Ger'lier let him get up to pick up the message.

"Display message, please."

It was a video message from Erit'ala.

"I'm sorry to disturb you, David. I need you to come to the Galactic Center within the next few days. Expect to stay a while. The Sejo has requested a formal inquest into the situation on Rec'jeter'she. We need to appear before them in one Casitian year." There the message ended.

"Oh, shit."

"You said that in English! What's the problem?"

David switched back to Casitian. "I don't need to deal with it right now. Where were we?"

Hilcyon Asteroid Mine – Month 3, Year 13/Mrontl 11 1151

Jasmine brought Beatrice some tea. She had been sitting on the bed she shared with Craig. She had been sitting there motionless ever since she returned from seeing Craig's body.

"Beatrice, here, have some tea."

Jasmine worried about Beatrice. She hadn't moved for hours. But she looked up at Jasmine and had a small smile on her face. She took the tea.

"Thanks. You are a good friend."

"Do you know what happened?"

"I haven't been told. All I was told was he was dead, and that I'd be assigned to a new husband in a few days."

That had become standard. Jasmine had managed to escape the fate of being assigned to a husband by being willing to work in very dangerous conditions. Otherwise, all women were subject to that arrangement. Some of the women who came with them on the ship had been assigned to Kinder men. Jasmine had heard about horrible things happening to them, including being forced upon and beaten. The women who had attached themselves to the New Earth men were in much better shape.

She was afraid for Beatrice, but she didn't say anything to her about her fears.

"You'll be OK. I'll look after you."

Beatrice smiled a very sad smile. "Thanks, Jasmine."

Hilcyon Asteroid Mine – Month 1, Year 14/Wtler 27 1152

Beatrice woke up to the clang of the morning alarm. Mornings were the worst. It was when she woke up in the morning when she remembered everything. Being taken from New Earth, being on a ship for weeks, ending up here in this horrible place, and then, worse yet, losing Craig, and New Earth people having been largely broken up as a group. She had been assigned to be the wife of a Kinder man named Pkygy, who had been here long before they arrived. He was a very kindly man, quiet and respectful, and he hadn't forced himself on her – he seemed content to let her cook and clean for him, although even that seemed to make him uncomfortable. From him Beatrice had finally heard the entire story – who their captors were, where they were, how this all had happened. Beatrice hadn't really figured him out yet – he had been so different than the other Kinder men she'd met so far. She even realized that she was beginning to appreciate his presence, even though it had only been a couple of months since Craig was killed.

Beatrice was learning the language, and could understand more and more before the translation device kicked in. She figured that in a few weeks, she'd be able to turn it off.

She got up off of their uncomfortable sleeping pallet. Pkygy was washing up. She had learned he liked a certain kind of food for breakfast – it was a strange looking gruel that she had finally figured out how to make to his liking, although he would just as often be up making it for himself and making her toast of the bread she had learned to bake. She went to the side of their small quarters that held the single burner stove and small sink and began to prepare breakfast.

"Beatrice, we need to talk about something."

She turned around slightly and looked at him. "What is it Pkygy?"

"We are rewarded if we have children – more children mean more miners. More miners mean more production. More production means more points for our group. More points for our group mean bigger quarters, more food, more supplies, you know."

Beatrice shook her head. "Pkygy, it's not that I wouldn't want to ever, well, you know, make love with you. It's that I can't bring a child into this – to be a miner all their lives? Or worse still, die like so many children I've heard die here? We had been told that if we worked hard, in a few years we could go back to New Earth. Almost no one ever leaves this place, do they? I can't do that to a child. I'm sorry."

Pkygy nodded. "I understand – and I agree. But ..."

"But?"

"Second Chief Zlgyzo threatened me. You see, you aren't my first wife. My first wife died about 3 years ago, but we never had a child. He said that if I did not get you with child within the next year, he would send me to the prison asteroid, and give you a new husband."

Beatrice had heard about the prison asteroid. It was, apparently, worse than this one. She had a hard time imagining anything worse than this. And the idea of being assigned to a man that might end up being more traditionally Kinder...

"What can we do Pkygy? Can't we fight this?"

"Fight? How? I hate this as much as you. I was born on Hilcyon, but you've heard the story of how I ended up here – publishing dangerous writing."

"This system only works because people cooperate. We need to find a way to stop cooperating. But that requires a lot of people. We need to find people, and then when we have a critical mass – we can stop cooperating."

"Beatrice, we might die doing this."

Beatrice nodded. "Pkygy, I think I might rather die than keep living this way."

Pkygy nodded sadly. "How do we start?"

Chapter 10:
Change is Possible

"One cannot argue with a sword. It is a sword that conquers all." – Dver Wrdnyz, historian, Hilcyon (3rd era)

Southwestern New Aard, New Earth, Month 4, Year 14

"Settle down, everyone, please!"

Ngellin was having a hard time being heard over the din that Grezl had created. What an idiot! He needed to stop this craziness right now, before it went any further. He found a plastic carton, and he banged it with a rock. That made a difference; people became quiet.

"Look. Let's be clear. This is not Kinder Home. We all left for a reason. We left because we hated the way that we were forced to come make war, and we wanted to be free."

A cheer started.

"And..." He raised his voice higher. "And..." Finally, there was quiet again. He continued, "we will not return to chiefdoms. I have a suggestion." He was surprised that he hadn't created an uproar again.

"We do need to organize. Here, I have learned something about 'elections.' We are spread in many settlements out all over this part of New Aard, and into the Independent Zone. We should have each settlement elect a representative to a council. The Kinder council will make decisions together."

There was a little murmur in the room, and a lot of nodding heads. He liked to see nodding heads.

It took them another few days of meetings to iron out the details, but they had a plan. Soon, the Kinder of New Earth would be organized.

Hilcyon Asteroid Mine – Month 3, Year 14/Lykl 1 1152

A long time ago, Beatrice had read a spy novel which she loved so much she she it read over and over again. And then she read every spy novel she could get her hands on. Those spy novels were coming in very handy right now. One of them had detailed the use of "covert cells" for revolutionary action. Beatrice realized that a structure like that would be perfect here. She doubted, based on what she knew of Kinder hierarchical culture that anyone had ever tried anything like this – and she bet it would work. She realized she was betting her life on it.

She started small – with people she knew well, and people Pkygy knew well. She created a beginning cell, and then got those in her cell to start new cells. When she or Pkygy had been approached for recruitment by a few people they didn't know well, they knew that the cell structure had penetrated far enough. But she realized they needed a test – something that would allow them to see how many people were on their side, but would not put anyone in danger, or even raise much suspicion. She decided that she would send a simple command out to the cells – work an extra 10 minutes on one day. Then, once they could see their power, they could plan for an asteroid-wide shut down.

"Pkygy, do you think we're ready?"

"I've been thinking, Beatrice – I think we should use our power to get some of us off of this asteroid and spread the revolution to Kinder Home. The asteroid is just one part of the whole system. We'll need help from Kinder Home to get everyone here home anyway."

"Do you think we could get to Hilcyon?"

"I do. I know that there are already some Second Chiefs involved in our plans. They could get a ship and get a small group legitimately off of the asteroid. Then, we could settle on Hilcyon, and keep going. I don't know that I can rest until all of Kinder Home is free."

"But Pkygy, you don't even know what it means to be free."

"I learned from my gamma's writing, and I've learned from you, Beatrice – I've learned what freedom is. It is something I want for all of our people."

It took a while, and some scary moments, but one of the Second Chiefs they had recruited got a small group as official passengers on a cargo ship headed for Ghedro, the main city of Hilcyon. Pkygy had somehow managed to be assigned to a low-level plumbing position, which was his previous occupation. It was going to be the beginning of a long period of work for both of them.

New York, Earth, January 12, 2020

Diana put the newspaper down in disgust, wishing she hadn't seen it. These last few years of Casitian influence hadn't changed much. Now that humans on Earth had found out about the Kinder, they had become almost lionized. The Casitians had been vilified for keeping the existence of the Kinder a secret.

"Don't take it too seriously, sweetheart." Janie, Diana's lover, was sipping coffee. They had just started to spend most nights together, and Diana treasured the brief morning times they had before her hectic days began.

"It's hard to deal with. Marianne is stuck on New Earth, Joel and Silandra are defending our species in front of the Sejo, and I feel helpless."

Janie smiled. "You are far from helpless, Diana. You've been great as the Casitian Liaison and people seem to want to draft you for World President."

Diana raised her eyebrow. "Me, President? I'd be nuts to run for President, especially now. I'm happy to let Nicholas do it. He certainly keeps the cameras clicking."

"Sarkozy? Come on, he's not a very serious candidate. Do you really want him to be the first President of the World?"

"Well, OK, maybe not. What about Davies? She has been the best Prime Minister Canada ever saw. She'd make a good World President."

"Yeah, I like Libby a lot, but still I think you should be President. So do a lot of other people. You'd have full Casitian support, which is more than any other candidate could say."

"Let's talk about this another time, shall we? I need to get to the office..." Diana got up from the small table in her breakfast nook, and kissed Joanna goodbye and started to walk out of her apartment.

She called back, "I'll come to your place tonight? We said we'd stay in and watch an old movie."

Janie smiled, and called after her, "sounds good. See you later." As Diana walked out the door, she wondered how long their quiet life would last.

"Pkygy Hostro Gnova and wife." The booming voice over the loudspeaker in the shuttle waiting area brought Beatrice back to attention. She had been drifting, again, in that sad mist that sometimes came over her when she thought of Craig. Even now, all this time after his death, she still missed him desperately.

"Come, Beatrice, it's time for us to get on the shuttle." Pkygy was always gentle, and he understood her sad moods. It was the second leg of their trip. They had been passengers on a cargo ship headed for the Hilcyon station, and after days of waiting they had finally gotten on board a shuttle that would take them to the surface. Once they landed at Plrody, the largest city on Hilcyon, they had a relatively short train ride to Ghedro, where they would be living.

The mass of people started to shuffle through the doors, and Beatrice was afraid of yet another trip with no windows, and no idea of where she was going. But when they entered the shuttle, she was surprised to see comfortable looking chairs, and nice full windows. She could see the station they were attached to, and the large planet below. It was the first time that she'd seen anything except walls since she was kidnapped. She didn't even know how long it had been. She knew she had been on the asteroid for about three-quarters of one of their years, but she had no idea how long that was in relation to New Earth years, or Earth years. It had felt like eons, and she thought that it was possible that she had been gone from New Earth for a long time.

They found seats, and Pkygy gracefully offered her the window seat. She thankfully took it. Her window faced away from the planet, and she could see two of the moons clearly. They were stunningly beautiful.

"Pkygy, you described the moons to me, but I had no idea..."

"Yes, aren't they beautiful? Wait till you see the other seven!"

The shuttle slowly started to move, and then accelerated, and she could see the station recede into the distance. As the shuttle swung toward the planet, Beatrice could see the planet in full view. It was so different than either Earth or New Earth. There were no clouds, and no oceans. The planet was a dull orange color, with very large polar ice caps on each pole – they extended well into what she would have thought were temperate zones. As the shuttle started to enter orbit, she could see part of the night side, and the sparkling shapes she assumed were cities.

As they got closer, a voice spoke over the loudspeakers, "preparing for re-entry. Please put your harnesses on."

All of a sudden, shutters came down over the windows. Pkygy was showing her how to put the harness on. "The windows will open again, but this part can be a little rough."

Beatrice could feel a deep rumble underneath her, and the shuttle shook, and bucked for about 20 minutes. All of a sudden, things smoothed out, and the shutters came up. Beatrice looked down at the planet surface, and seeing the harsh reality of it, understood the Kinder people a bit better. It was clearly a harsh environment. Pkygy had told her about it, but it was so much more stark when flying above it. It reminded her of the short trip her family once took to visit Utah, when she was very little.

She could see no water at all. They flew over canyons and deserts, with very small hints of green now and again. Once in a while, they flew over what looked like a settlement, where there would be large green patches, and lots of buildings that looked like greenhouses. Pkygy had mentioned that because the surface was relatively cold for most of the year, many food crops were grown in the greenhouses.

"Pkygy, where do the food crops come from? This planet looks like it's never had any significant vegetation."

Pkygy was used to her nonsequitors – questions and comments that seemed to come out of thin air, but he could follow her train of thought. It was something she really appreciated about him, and one quality Craig hadn't had.

"They were imported from the Breft planet." He let that fact hang in the air for Beatrice to absorb.

As the shuttle slowed and was making its final approach to the space port at Plrody, Beatrice began to see what looked like small hexagonally shaped hamlets, with about twenty or thirty dwellings, built close together, around what looked like a square. What Beatrice would have expected was for the hamlets to give way to suburbs, and then city, but what actually seemed to happen was the hamlets just got jammed closer and closer together and were more tightly packed.

The demarcations between hamlets remained obvious, even from the air. This gave Beatrice some pause. Close knit families, insular, self-protecting. This would be a challenge to their goals, certainly. But there were also advantages to this – it might be possible to sway whole families at once.

Independent Christian State, New Earth, Month 4, Year 14

Marianne and Leticia had traveled quite a way from Dlejon to visit Leticia's mother Yolanda in the ICS. Leticia had been very reluctant about going back; she worried that she could get stuck in the ICS again. New America and the ICS had finally opened themselves up to dialogue and trade, and there had been a return to normalcy over the course of a few months. When travel to the ICS seemed safe and relatively easy, Marianne suggested that they go. There was a new train linking parts of the SCIZ, and travel to New San Francisco by train was fairly quick. But then they still had to do a river trip up to New Richmond – there hadn't been much in the way of development of easy north-south travel except by river. Then, from New Richmond, they got on a somewhat rickety bus for the rest of the way to Yolanda's settlement.

They all sat in Yolanda's living room: Yolanda, Leticia, Marianne and Stanley. Yolanda had been surprisingly happy to see Marianne.

"I heard you were on this planet – it was all over the widenet. I wondered if I'd get to see you."

"It's good to see you Yolanda. You've been through so much. I'm so sorry about Beatrice. I'm sure she's still alive, I'm just not sure if we'll ever see her again."

Yolanda hung her head in sadness, then looked at Leticia, and a smile started to slowly come onto her face. "I'm so glad to see you Leticia. You have grown so much. And a doctor? That is so wonderful."

Leticia looked a bit uncomfortable, but then smiled. "Yes, mom, I'm enjoying my life in Dlejon, although I'll be moving to the Northern Independent Zone to live in New Calgary.

Marianne remembered the conversation she'd had with Leticia and her partner Mira. Mira was ready to leave her home of Dlejon and find her place elsewhere. They had decided to take up the offer for them to join Jeffrey and Thomas in starting a new medical school in New Calgary.

As if Yolanda were reading Marianne's mind, she asked "so, are you married? Do you have a boyfriend?"

Leticia looked uncomfortable, and then looked to Marianne, somewhat pleadingly. Marianne gave Leticia as much of a "go ahead, tell her about Mira" look as she could muster.

Leticia looked back at her mother. "I have a partner, mom. Her name is Mira, and she's also a physician. She's from Dlejon."

Marianne could see a wide range of emotions move over Yolanda's face, but the last one was one of peaceful acceptance. "That's good, Leticia, I'm glad you've found someone to love. I know that I was hard on you when you were here, but I wanted so much for you to fit in, even though deep down I knew that you never could."

Marianne could see everyone in the room relax. They spent the rest of the afternoon and over dinner reminiscing about Earth, talking about the realities of life in New America, and talking about the future of New Earth. Marianne had been increasingly feeling hope that there could be peaceful coexistence among the people of New Earth continued to grow.

New York, Earth, September 4, 2022

Here I am again, Joel thought, sitting in Diana's living room, delivering bad news. This was getting to be a bad habit.

Janie asked, "do you think humans will get probation?"

Joel said, "it's hard to know. The Casitians don't think so, but I'm not so sanguine. From my perspective, they actually did make a big mistake in locking the wormhole. But of course, they spent the last year trying to figure out how to make a defense which makes them look innocent."

They kept talking, and, in particular, talked about how to tell people on Earth.

Diana said, "I think we need to tell them before the Sejo acts. Because if the Sejo acts in a way that will affect us, it won't be such a surprise – people need to be prepared."

Joel nodded. "I agree. I'm happy to be interviewed by the press, again, and basically lay out what's happened so far. I hope they aren't getting too sick of me."

Diana smiled, and put her hand on Joel's arm. "Silly boy, the press absolutely loves you. I guess you don't hear how much they miss you when you're gone. I'll make contact with the folks I know, and we'll start from there. This is going to create a bit of a storm. How long can you stay?"

"I have to be at the council world in about 5 months. There is a ship that is scheduled to leave Sol station for the council world in 2 months. So I have about 4 weeks before I need to leave for Sol station."

"That's enough time."

Chapter 11:
The Unthinkable Happens

"We cannot express how much Galactic citizenship means to the us. And we must do everything we can to maintain it." Erit'ala (782)

Wuj'tren (or <u>Upsilon Andromedae</u>) March 5, 2023

Joel had arrived on Wuj'tren, the third planet of the sun the Casitians called Yrel, a few days ago. Terrans had named this star Upsilon Andromedae. Joel had been awed by the planet, its verdant, but foreign landscape, and it's majestic, yet in some ways understated architecture. Because it was the Galactic capital, it had representatives of all of the species in the community. He and the group from Casiti entered the building that held the Council offices and where the Council met. He was completely overwhelmed by the scale of the Council room. "Room" was hardly a reasonable term. It was huge, as large as a coliseum, tiered, with light streaming in from above. There were balconies that jutted out at various angles from the tiers of floors, and some had bridges between them where beings who he assumed were aides of varied sorts would scurry from balcony to balcony. Their group were all far down below, in a small circular depression with very comfortable seats. He couldn't help the feeling that he was about to go to jail.

Eventually, things settled down. He was handed a small device, which he was instructed to place inside his ear. He assumed this was the translation device. A loud, booming voice came from above. A creature he could only describe as a mix between a kangaroo and a cat seemed to be speaking from a platform in the center of the chamber.

After a small delay, he heard, "Welcome, members of the council, staff, and guests. We must begin these proceedings."

There were small murmurs around the chambers, then silence.

"The Keeelo have brought a filing against the human species. Based upon the findings, the council will vote for continuation of human citizenship, probation, or restriction of the human species from the galactic community."

"Will the Keeelo representative please come forward."

A white translucent cube that Joel had not noticed started moving toward the center. He could see a little movement within it. Eventually, it stopped, close to the center.

"Please state your case."

The strangest sounds Joel had ever heard started to emanate from the cube.

A translation came through his earpiece, "We hold the wormholes, hold them, keep them, we hold the wormholes. Those who disrespect the wormholes must not be a part, must not be us, aren't us. They disrespect the wormholes again, another time, it is enough."

Joel was puzzled. Disrespect the wormholes again?

The cube returned to its previous position.

"The Keeelo have chosen intermediaries to argue their case. Will these intermediaries please come forward?"

A small group of funny-looking beings Joel had learned were the Krumptia walked into the center of the area close to them. They were natural bureaucrats and lawyers, and Joel had met some in his travels. That they were going to argue against the humans sobered him greatly.

"You are ready to make your case?"

"Yes, we are ready to make our case."

"Will the human representatives please step forward."

Erit'ala, Ja'el and several other Casitians he didn't know got up and moved toward the center.

"Are you ready to defend your species?"

Erit'ala nodded. "Yes, we are."

"Do you understand the possible consequences?"

Erit'ala nodded again, this time it seemed sadly. "Yes, we do."

"Then let us begin."

New York, Earth, March 5, 2023

"Hello world! I'm Joh Appel, and I'm here with two experts who will help us figure out our future with the Casitians. First, we have John Bulmeister, Professor of Sociology from University of Arizona. Also with us, is Gina Winthrop, Professor of Psychology at the New School for Social Research, here in New York. Thank you both for being here with me today."

"Thank you, Joh."

"Thanks, Joh, I'm glad to be here."

"So, first, Professor Bulmeister. What have you made of this whole issue of the Casitians vs. the Kinder?"

"Well, Joh, it's simple. The Casitians are xenophobes. They proved it while they were here, and this is the ultimate proof. Thousands of years ago, instead of uniting the Human race, they chose to separate it."

"Professor Winthrop, your opinion?"

"Professor Bulmeister, Joh, that is a complete oversimplification of the issues here. Remember, the separation of these two groups happened after a period of two thousand years of slavery. We can't even begin to understand what the dynamics were."

"Professor Bulmeister, do you have an opinion as to what will happen at that Galactic Council thing?"

"Well, if I were them, I'd come down hard on the Casitians. They clearly were at fault here."

"Clearly at fault?!?"

"Professor Winthrop?"

"The Kinder invaded New Earth. That happens to be a planet with our people on it, Professor Bulmeister!"

"They Casitians locked the wormhole, leaving our people ...."

"The Kinder invaded..."

"Please, please. Don't interrupt each other. Professor Winthrop?"

"Look, I think there is probably enough fault to go around. I don't know what the Galactic council will do, but it can't be good for any human beings, Casitian or Terran."

Wuj'tren (or Upsilon Andromedae) March, 5, 2023

"So what is the basic procedure?" Joel was curious. He wasn't part of the defense group – that was made up of Casitians that knew galactic law. He was simply a witness that would be called on at some point or another. He wished Marianne was here. Joel was not at all sure that things were going to go well.

He was sitting comfortably with Silandra and a few others in a room that had been given to the human defense team. It was sumptuously appointed, with lots of food which seemed custom made for them – some of the food even came from Earth.

"The Keeelo will make their case, through the Krumptia. Then we make our case. Then the Sejo will adjourn to make the decision on the verdict."

"Do the Keeelo and human representatives on the Sejo get a vote?"

"No, they must recuse themselves, and will not be present during the deliberations. The Krumptia must also recuse themselves."

"The Krumptia are on the Keeelo's side?"

"Well, the Krumptia and Keeelo have a very long history together, and they support each other."

"How long will all this take?"

"I the inquest will take several days, plus several more days of Sejo deliberation on the verdict. The sentencing can take years. They don't take the probation of a species lightly."

"Is that what you expect – probation? The Keeelo seem to be asking for outright restriction."

"I'm hoping we don't get probation, and I can't imagine the Sejo would suggest restriction."

Joel fervently hoped not.

Wuj'tren (or Upsilon Andromedae) March, 7, 2023

Joel had listened carefully to the case that the Keeelo and Krumptia had been laid out. It had been very short, and, he had to admit, devastating. Galactic law was quite particular about the qualities of a species that would assure galactic membership, and the qualities of a species that would result in restriction. Qualities that included harmonious relationships between individuals of a species and groups of individuals within a species were, in the eyes of the galactic community, paramount. Armed conflict, and, more particularly, the use of wormholes for armed conflict were enough to restrict a species for 1000 years. Armed conflict where one species attacked other species, as the Tud'scla did, generally resulted in permanent isolation and restriction.

Joel thought that the Krumptia were meticulous in making their case. It rotated simply around two particular events: the use of the wormhole by the Za'aref to invade New Earth, and the locking of the wormhole by the Casitians to prevent the Za'aref from leaving. The Keeelo saw both of these actions as use of the wormholes for acts of violence against other members of the human species.

Joel wasn't sure what the Casitians would use as a defense – the case the Krumptia had laid out was rock-solid. The Casitians could hardly use as a defense that it was the fault of the Kinder, since the Kinder were human as well, and the actions of the Kinder clearly were considered by this body as an act of the human species. As he sat in the lounge chewing on some sort of exotic vegetable, he looked over at Silandra and Erit'ala, who were deep in conversation.

"We have decided to call Grel, the Tvierl representative – I can't imagine any other way to defend ourselves. The Tvierl understand humans better than any other species."

Erit'ala sighed. "I'm not sure that calling the Tvierl in is going to make much of a difference. The galactic policy is clear, the Za'aref violated it, and there isn't much we can do. But it will be good to have a species on our side."

Joel walked over to the pair. "But the case also hinges on your decision to lock the wormhole. It seemed to be that, more than the use of the wormhole by the Za'aref, that the Keeelo objected to."

Erit'ala shook her head vigorously. "We acted in the only way we could to limit the damage. They've got to understand that!"

The doors to the lounge opened, and one of the odd-looking robots came in. "The Sejo is re-convening – please return to the council room."

They filed back into the council room, and Joel sat down nervously. He knew that in this next phase, he would likely be called upon to testify.

R'terin, the main Casitian running the defense team, rose, "august members of the Sejo, we now begin our defense. We understand why the Keeelo were upset by the use of the wormhole by those we call the Za'aref. The Za'aref have been separate from the rest of the human species for a long time, and we intend to keep their influence from contaminating the vast majority of humans – those who live on Casiti and Earth. Casitians have come to an easy, companionable relationship with the people of Earth, the homeworld of humankind. Earth and Casiti are without warfare or conflict of any kind, and in harmony with our worlds, and with the universe. We have no reason to believe that this will not continue indefinitely, and humans should, therefore, continue to be a full member of the Galactic community."

"I now call Erit'ala to describe the events surrounding the current crisis."

Erit'ala got up and sat in the witness chair. R'terin asked a series of questions, which she answered. Joel could tell that this was a very well-orchestrated dance. Some facts were left out, and some glossed over. The whole thing made him nervous.

One of the most interesting ways that this "trial" differed from ones he was used to was that there was nothing like a cross-examination. R'terin had not been allowed to ask the Krumptia or Keeelo any questions, and, likewise, they were not allowed to ask any of their side's witnesses anything.

After Erit'ala stepped down, R'terin stood up, and turned toward Joel. "I would ask that Joel Martin, from Earth, come forward."

Joel stood up, and walked toward the witness seat, and turned around, and sat down. He could look up and see the tiers of beings of all sorts looking down at him (some of them he had to imagine looking down at him – he couldn't see any identifiable eyes.) Joel had not been coached, which worried him a little bit.

"Joel, please explain the status of the human species on Earth. Has there been any conflict?"

"No, not since the colony ships left. People have been very happy with the new technology and points of view. They have been happy with the environmental cleanup, with a more egalitarian culture, and with no poverty or hunger, and more ease. It is a good life on Earth now."

"And this is due to the work of the Casitians?"

"Yes. We were going to hell in a handbasket before they arrived."

"And how do you see the future? Will Earth and Casiti coexist peacefully?"

"Yes, I can't imagine why it would change. People on Earth have been very interested in visiting Casiti, and there are Casitians on Earth, and I expect that Earth will continue to be peaceful."

"Thank you, Joel. You may go back to your seat."

Joel walked back, happy it was over for now.

Wuj'tren (or <u>Upsilon Andromedae</u>) March, 8, 2023

"We now call Grel, the representative of the Tvierl."

A very tall being came forward, with no clothing on. Joel could swear he looked just like a very tall human basketball player, lanky, with long legs and arms. Except that his skin was a greenish blue hue, his eyes were all blue pupil, and he had webs between what looked like seven fingers on each hand. He walked a bit awkwardly, as if that was not his most comfortable way of traveling. Joel realized that although the Casitians had called Grel "he" in conversation, Joel couldn't see any evidence of male-like genitalia. The nose was a bit odd, too – much larger and longer than a human nose, with only one large nostril, that Grel seemed to open and close when he breathed. He sat in the chair, which had grown a bit to accommodate him.

"Grel, I thank you for being willing to act as our witness."

Grel seemed to nod his head, but it was slight. He looked toward R'terin, waiting.

"You have heard these events, and the Tvierl have been advocates for humans over the years. Will you vouch for the human species?"

There was a pause – it felt to Joel that it was far too long. He could see Erit'ala move uncomfortably in her seat.

"No, we cannot at this time."

There was a stunned silence in the room. Joel looked over to Erit'ala, who had her head in her hands. Silandra had lost all color in her face. R'terin stolidly continued, "please, Grel, be clear with us why this is so. The Tvierl have always supported humans – you were the ones who supported our joining the Galactic community so long ago and have always been our ally."

"We have supported the human presence in the Galactic community because we felt that the Casitians were fit for Galactic citizenship. And we still would be supporting continued human presence if the Casitians had chosen to act with the whole of their species in mind, not just themselves. From our perspective, their actions to lock the wormhole at New Earth, instead of finding ways to mediate the difficulties, and provide leadership for all humans, was not in keeping with the behavior of a galactic citizen. We suggest a 1000-year restriction. We expect in that time, the humans will return to us whole."

There was a lot of conversation in the room, some hushed, some loud. Joel knew that at this point, the fate of the human species, at least for the next 1000 years, was sealed.

R'terin rang a bell, and the room became quiet. "We ask the Sejo for a recess. We have much to consider."

"Recess granted."

They eventually ended up back in the lounge and sat down close to each other. R'terin stood up first and spoke. "I talked to Grel before the trial started, and he seemed, at the time, to be sure that they would support us. I don't know what happened, but clearly, they decided otherwise. I suggest that we suspend our defense."

"Suspend our defense?" Silandra looked shocked. "That would mean that we would have to agree to being restricted for 1000 years! We must defend ourselves, and at least try to get probation."

R'terin replied, "I think the best we can do at this point is to hope that we can soften the terms of the 1000-year restriction."

Erit'ala said in a pained voice, "How do you soften isolation from galactic contact and loss of representation? It is the worst possible outcome – the outcome we have been working to prevent for the last three thousand years!"

A light went off in Joel's brain. Somehow, now, the behavior of the Casitians made more sense to him: the reason they guarded the wormhole from Hilcyon, the reason they kept the information about the Za'aref from Terrans and their behavior at New Earth. It was this fate that they had feared from the beginning.

Transport from Casiti to Earth, March, 20 2023

Joel was dead tired. He and Laura were finally on their way back to Earth after the debacle on the Council world. The Terran group had taken a transport from Wuj'tren to Casiti with the Casitian defense team, who basically refused to talk with them. It was almost as if the Casitians blamed them for everything – it was infuriating. And the worst thing was that it wasn't over yet. The Sejo had officially given their verdict, that humans had acted in ways that were counter to galactic standards. The regular sentence for that was 1000 restriction, but the Sejo was to deliberate to fully consider the sentence. Erit'ala had told him that it could take years. He and Laura had decided to go back to Earth to figure out what they were going to do next. Their galactic traveling days were over.

He thought that the Casitians were overreacting. He'd certainly enjoyed his jaunts around the galaxy, and he knew that galactic technology was always getting better, but it seemed that it wasn't that big a deal. He and Laura were thinking that it was time to get on with their lives, no matter what the Sejo did, and it seemed Earth was the best place for them to do that.

David was going to stay on Casiti. He liked it there, and seemed to prefer Casitian boyfriends, for reasons Joel couldn't quite understand. He was happy that David had found his place, though. And he missed Marianne more than he imagined he would. He missed her reasonableness, her steady hand, her quiet leadership.

As he drifted off to sleep, nuzzling in Laura's arms, he had a short, strange, dream of large colony ships. Then, just blissful sleep.

New Orleans, New Earth, Month 3, Year 23

This meeting had been a long time coming, Marianne thought. It had been over ten New Earth years since the Kinder deserters had begun to form collection of small settlements in the southwest corner of New Aard, as well as the southern part of the SCIZ. She had watched the developments from afar, and she was glad to finally get to meet the Kinder leader.

Marianne and the Kinder man called Ngellin sat across from each other at a table in a New Orleans Cafe. It seemed that he had gotten used to the setting.

He said, "I like New Orleans, quite a lot."

"Really? It's becoming my favorite New Earth city. Your English is very good."

Ngellin smiled. "Thanks. We learned some on the way here."

"Really? How?"

"There had been infiltrators for years, learning the lay of the land, and learning your languages. Those of us who were going to go down to the surface were required to learn one of them, and English was the one I was assigned."

Marianne thought that made sense. They could have disguised themselves as someone from New Aard, for instance, who didn't know English.

"We'd like to learn more about you, and the Kinder, Ngellin. But I have a tough question for you."

"Please ask."

"What will happen to those teenagers who were kidnapped?"

Ngellin looked sad. "They will work in the asteroid mines."

"That sounds unpleasant."

"It is. It's where all of the criminals and dissidents go, too."

"Is there any escape?"

Ngellin shook his head. "No, Marianne. A sentence to the mines is lifelong."

Casiti –130 Wend, 784/March 10, 2025/ Month 4, Year 24

Joel was in the room with Erit'ala and other Casitians, watching the holographic recording of the final verdict from the Sejo. It was the council's final sentence. The verdict had been determined two years ago when Joel had been on the Council world. He guessed the Galactic Council moved slowly during the sentencing phase.

Erit'ala had sent a message to him on Earth, telling him the sentence was in, but not telling him what it was. She had asked him to be physically present on Casiti to hear the sentence. He had to wait several days until he could get here to see it.

The Sejo council leader gave the official sentence of a 1000 Earth year restriction. It was a short little speech. Even though he didn't say it, Joel knew that it included not only lack of representation on the Sejo, and lack of involvement in the galactic economy, but complete isolation from all other species. The Keeelo would specially tune and lock the wormholes, so that no humans could use them to get into space other than that inhabited by humans. Joel understood that to mean that the wormholes would only work between the human worlds – between Earth and New Earth, Earth and Casiti, and Hilcyon and New Earth, and Hilcyon and Casiti.

But it looked like there was more coming. The weirdest looking creature Joel ever saw walked up to the front.

"I am Yuyuyuyuyu, representative of the Kwalloo. I speak for those who swim the waters of the planet the humans call Earth. They wish to make it clear that those waters are the waters they swim in. It is their home, and they should not be separated from it."

"What are they asking?" Joel said.

"This is the logical next step, and we fully expected this in the case of restriction. They are asking that human beings be removed from Earth."

"WHAT?"

"Yes, Joel. They have that right."

"But it's *our* planet!"

"No, it's not. It is the Dolphin's planet now, not yours."

Humans Untied

Chapter 1:
Four Whlis Leaves, One White

(AP) August 1, 2025

World Government Process in Chaos, Some Say

New York, NY – As the world prepares to unite under one government, some skeptics are pointing to chaotic procedures orchestrated by the United Nations, United States, and the European Union. "They really don't understand the complexities of the situation," said one participant, who wanted to remain anonymous. Although the conversion to the world currency, the Bancor, went without a hitch in 2017, many observers suggest that a one-world democracy, even without much of the rancor that preceded the Casitian Crisis, is a much more difficult arrangement. "Yes, we have some hurdles, but we've come quite far in working out the details, country by country." Diana Westinghouse, one of the top candidates for World President, is confident about the process. "Look, a lot of things we take on are complex, but we can do it, and we've got support and help from the galactic community. We'll do fine."

Hilcyon, Mrontl 5 1158

Hreller shook his head. "I don't think we're ready, Pkygy. We have, by our count, 120 cells spread out around the city. And we do know of cells in many other cities. We need a critical mass of cells in each city before a takeover will be successful – this just isn't widespread enough."

Pkygy nodded with what seemed to Beatrice to be reluctance.

"Yes, yes, you are right - I guess it was wishful thinking that we could get started now. I'm impatient. I can feel change coming."

Beatrice was in the back of the room, listening. She had felt out of the loop since they had started on Hilcyon. As a woman, she was considered simply Pkygy's wife – someone who cooked, cleaned and took care of him, and was going to have his babies – she wasn't someone who had a mind of her own, or ideas of her own. Pkygy respected her, but his friends and people they knew didn't know how to respect women. She had let Pkygy lead, and he had been a good leader. He took her ideas, added his own, and grew the movement they had started.

She had begun to focus more on working with women she found who were sympathetic to their cause. The Independent Christian State on New Earth was demeaning to women, but Kinder society took it one step further – complete disenfranchisement. It was at times very difficult for Beatrice to tolerate, or to abide by the rules.

Hreller said, "I have a friend who is starting a cell in Wlyntry, in the Central Valley – I hear there are many, many cells in the Valley. And I have another relative who happens to be moving to the upper highlands. This will spread, faster than you think – but we must be careful. I had a very close one with a suspicious Fourth Chief. He was playing sympathetic, but then I was beginning to tell it was an act. Luckily, I caught that before I invited him to the cell!"

Pkygy turned to the tall, broad-shouldered man next to him named Jren. Of his colleagues, Jren had been the most respectful to her.

"Jren, do you have anything to report?"

Beatrice thought his quiet voice belied strength of will that she had seen on occasion.

"Yes, Pkygy. As you know, I am being groomed to be promoted from a Fourth Chief to a Third Chief. My Second Chief had me over for drinks. When he was well into his cups, he let me know how unhappy he is with the way things are. I think he is a prime target. Like you, he respects his wife, and says he feels like we stifle creativity and waste talent, and we need to foster more independence to help the Kinder people grow and mature. He even confessed to me that he really wanted to be a storyteller, not a Second chief!"

"Yes, Jren, that sounds like someone who could be a great asset to the movement. Thank you all for coming. We will meet again next moon." The meeting broke up, and the men left the house one by one, leaving Pkygy and Beatrice alone in the house.

"I am quite optimistic, Beatrice. I keep being surprised by how many people are unhappy with the way things are. I look forward to flexing our muscle."

Casiti, 12 Nird, 784

Joel, David and Laura had been surprised to be invited to Casiti, given the frosty relationship between Terrans and Casitians that followed the Sejo's verdict and sentence. They had been asked to temporarily represent Terrans on the Caraj, the Casitian council. The Caraj was having many days of joinings to deal with the ramifications of the Sejo's ruling.

Joel felt that the whole mess was a complete catastrophe. Humans had three Casitian years, or twelve Earth years to completely vacate Earth because the dolphins had decided to claim Earth as their own. Terrans would have use of a very large fleet of colony ships, a fleet about five times larger than the fleet that brought humans to New Earth. But it would take many, many more trips to take all of the humans off of Earth. And there was no question that there would be conflict, perhaps even all-out war.

"We need you to create a plan to move Earth people to New Earth." Joel was yanked out of his reverie by Erit'ala speaking to him.

"You want us to create a plan? You're saddling us with all of this? We don't even know where to begin!"

Erit'ala looked at Joel with sad eyes. "Joel, I know how hard this seems, but you have to move forward – we have three years."

Joel sighed. "We can't do this alone, Erit'ala. We need your help."

"Of course, we will help as we can."

Joel thought that was an exceedingly weak promise of assistance. He decided to let it go for now. But he knew this would be revisited again.

"Well first, we have to tell people everywhere – on Earth, on New Earth, on ... what is that other planet?"

"We will not be communicating with the Za'aref. They are why we are in this situation."

Joel lost his patience. "No, it is not only their fault. Certainly, they precipitated this – but your actions were as much at fault as theirs. Face that. And we have 1000 years to get this right. Until we can unite the human race, and bring all humans to peace, we will never be re-united with the galactic community. Sure, 1000 years is a long time, but if we don't start out right, we're dooming the race to perpetual isolation. Is that what you want?"

David said, "Erit'ala, perhaps Casiti won't contact the Za'aref, but we will."

Joel knew that it was going to take a long time, way longer than he had to live, for the Casitians to own up to the mistakes they had made – in hiding the existence of the Za'aref from Earth humans, in trying hard to separate themselves from the more troubling members of the species, and in locking the wormhole. But Joel wasn't going to let them off the hook.

Joel added, "We have to tell them. We have to find a way to at least begin to coexist."

"It's just not possible. You all saw how impossible it was for some Terrans to go along with the changes that had to take place on Earth. The most conservative Terrans are nothing in comparison to the Za'aref."

David countered, "Look, we have three Casitian years, and we only have three planets, and a planet with seven billion people to empty. They have to go somewhere. I'm assuming that you don't want all that many to go to Casiti?"

Erit'ala blanched. "We think they all should be settled on New Earth."

"And how would that happen? There aren't any real cities built there yet – they have to be built. Fast. Casiti and the Za'aref planet are the only ones with already created infrastructure. My suggestion is that we place as many Terrans on each of these planets as possible, to lessen the problems that are going to arise with billions of people arriving on a planet with no infrastructure."

The room became suddenly quiet. Joel knew that the likelihood of many Earth humans ending up on Casiti was fairly slim. If there was one thing he had learned over the Earth year of this unfolding disaster, it was that the Casitians were truly human, after all. With all of the human frailties and tendencies. And somehow, he was going to have to convince the Casitians that their lot was finally, ultimately, tied to the lot of all of humankind, whether Casitian, Terran, or Za'aref.

Joel sighed and decided to change his tack. "Can we at least send a ship to New Earth, and make contact with Marianne again? There is no reason to keep that wormhole locked anymore."

A tall, broad-faced man named K'lellen raised his head from the tablet had been looking at studiously. Joel had first met him today, and he learned that K'lellen had been newly assigned as teacher in charge of all Casitian space flight.

K'lellen looked at Joel and spoke. "Yes, Joel, I agree. We should dispatch a couple of ships to New Earth – one to repopulate the New Earth station, and the other to defend it. We can at that point make contact with Marianne and the New Earth people, as well as the remaining Za'aref ship. We will still need to defend the wormhole from further Za'aref passages to back New Earth."

Joel got the uncomfortable feeling that K'lellen had been picked because he had characteristics that were a bit closer to that of a military man than most Casitians could ever be.

Joel nodded. "I think Marianne can help us strategize settlement on New Earth, since she's the only one of us that has spent time there. She'll understand how things are shaping up and help us to figure out where best to put people."

Joel saw David being busy on his small tablet. "David, suggestions?"

"I'm just doing a little math – I'll let you know what I come up with. I realized that a reasonable way to figure this out was to look at the available temperate acreage on each planet and come up with some optimal figures given some ideas also on spare resources. Erit'ala, I would appreciate some data from Casiti on carrying capacity, given the harsh winters."

Erit'ala nodded, although Joel wondered what kind of data the Casitians would actually provide. He knew that one of the biggest parts of this battle with them was going to be convincing them to take a significant number of Earth humans.

Krely took the water off of the top of the cook oven, just as steam began to rise from its surface. Perfect. Hot enough to drop the curlick eggs into for a slow cook. She thought that they will be perfect for last meal, slightly warm to the touch and solid inside. She put the pan on a small wooden table next to the cook stove. One of the things she liked so much about the new house that they had built was that she convinced Sadre to make the kitchen large. The cook stove sat on one wall, with small tables on either side. The iron sink which sat on another wall had shelves above it where many of her cooking implements were kept. In the middle of the kitchen was a large table she used for preparing food, and it had some trell leaves soaking in salt water. She and her daughter ate here when Sadre had guests for dinner.

Krely tried her best to keep herself busy and out of trouble. She did this by cooking as much food as she could, as often as she could. She loved to cook and loved the results of her hands. The fresh breadmufs, the steamed trell leaves, which most cooks made tough, but in her hands were so tender, they almost melted in one's mouth. The baked jeltors she made were juicy and flavorful. People always loved her cooking, and they almost always had guests for dinner.

She learned, very early in her life that she might as well do the one thing that was a part of "women's work" that she enjoyed – and do that so well that the rest that she didn't do could go without notice. It worked. She managed to be married to a man who tolerated the fact that she always had to ask someone else to sew his clothes. That the house wasn't ever especially clean, and that most of their children had largely been raised by other hamlet women. But she cooked for the entire hamlet often, and it seemed that the rest of the women held no grudges against her for the things she did not do.

Sadre walked into the kitchen.

"Krely – a special visitor is coming tonight. What can we serve him?"

"Who is it, Sadre?"

"Does it matter? You're always asking me questions like that!"

"I'm just curious."

"Women aren't supposed to be curious. But he's important."

"Sadre, he will be treated well, and stuffed with good food, I promise. That's all you need to know, right?"

Sadre smiled and waved his arms toward Krely. "Yes, yes, woman! It's a good thing you can cook!"

Sadre turned and left the kitchen, leaving Krely to think about what she'd add to the menu for the evening. Perhaps an appetizer, and some flatbreads, and perhaps even a special dessert...

Jurrl pushed his chair back from the table, leaning back. "That was wonderful, Sadre. Your woman sure knows how to cook." Krely was listening to them from the kitchen.

"Second Chief Jurrl, tell me of the capital. You say you have news? And why have you come to me?"

There was silence for a minute.

"Yes, Sadre, I have news. There are rumors that there is a movement to take over the Kinder High Chiefs. All of the Second and Third Chiefs are now on alert, but there is a fear that it has gone quite far."

Sadre was a Fourth Chief – the lowest Chief rank. Krely knew that Sadre was ever loyal to his own Third Chief, Ceckzl. She wondered why this Second Chief – from the capital, had come here to talk with Sadre.

"I have heard nothing from Ceckzl."

"I assume has chosen not to tell his Chiefs."

"Why would that be?"

"Because, I am afraid, he is one of them: those who would take over the High Chiefs. We fear they have infiltrated very high up."

There was more silence. Krely imagined Sadre was thinking about what to say or do.

"Why are you speaking with me?"

"We know you are loyal to the Kinder way. We know you would never want to see things change."

"Yes, I am loyal."

"You must choose loyalty to the Kinder over loyalty to your Chief. You must watch him. Talk with him. Get us evidence that he is a traitor to the Kinder."

In that moment, Krely knew what she needed to do, and what her destiny was. She didn't know whether she would see the end of it, but she knew that if there was a movement to change the Kinder way, she wanted to be a part of it.

Hilcyon, Mrontl 12 1158

Krely knocked on the door of the small dwelling, and Tivyl opened it, welcoming.

"Krely, what a nice surprise. On an errand for Sadre?"

Krely shook her head. "No, no, I thought you and Ceckzl would appreciate this new kind of breadmuf I made. It has a lot of fresh spice."

"Ooooh, Krely, thank you so much. That is so thoughtful of you."

"Well, I know that Ceckzl is a very busy man ..."

Tivyl, Ceckzl's wife, looked at Krely as if sizing her up. Krely, of course, had known Tivyl since she had come to the hamlet to be Sadre's wife.

"Please, Krely, come in and sit for a while."

As Krely entered the house, she began to see some small details she'd never noticed before. She'd been in the house a few times, running errands for Sadre. It was very well cared for, and in good order. She knew that Tivyl and Ceckzl had never had children – she assumed, like many couples, that one or both of them were sterile, which was not uncommon on Hilcyon. What was uncommon was for men to stay with a sterile wife or for a wife of a sterile man to remain childless – there were always agreements made.

There were two large relaxing chairs, side by side, with a table between them – as if Ceckzl and Tivyl relaxed together! Krely's house had only one relaxing chair – for Sadre. The table between the chairs was bare on the top, but on a shelf underneath, there were many books in piles. There were a few paintings on the walls – but nothing she recognized. That seemed strange, since the only thing that she had seen anyone put up on their walls were the reproductions of the paintings of the big epics by either Qyren or Pemintel. These didn't look like anything in particular, but they were quite beautiful.

"Please, sit," Tivyl pointed toward the low bench with cushions, "can I get you something to drink?"

"Some jul juice, if you have it."

"Of course. I'll be right back."

Tivyl came back with two cups of juice and sat down next to Krely on the bench.

"How are you doing, Krely? How has life been for you?"

Krely was taken aback. What a question! It so surprised her, because she realized that not only had no one ever asked her that question, it seemed, in some ways, a taboo question.

"Well, I do what I can. I get by. What else would a woman say? Why ask this, Tivyl?"

"My husband and I have been doing some thinking – with the help of some others."

"What kind of thinking? I've been thinking, too."

"Thinking that it's time for things to change. We don't like the Chief system, and we don't like the fact that women don't have any say in things."

"Well, Tivyl, I don't like that either, but I worry that we can't …"

"Don't say 'we can't change anything'! Things can change. Things can be changed."

"Tivyl, I think I believe you, but the system hasn't changed since …"

"Yes, I know, since we and the Breft split."

"How long has it been now? Thousands of years? It's hard to imagine changing thousands of years of tradition overnight!"

"Yes, Krely, it is hard to imagine. But we have to start somewhere. And talking about change is starting somewhere."

Tivyl began to describe the small "cell" that they were a part of. Ceckzl had been recruited by a Second Chief who was an old friend, and they had decided quite some time ago that this hamlet was a good place to start a new cell.

"Tivyl, you must tell your husband that Jurrl was at my house last night – he has asked my husband to spy on Ceckzl, and report back. He is asking my husband to be loyal to Kinder, but not to Ceckzl."

Tivyl nodded her head. "Thank you Krely, for that – I saw Jurrl walking in the hamlet and wondered if that was why he was here. He has no idea how many Third and Second Chiefs have been moved over to our cause. Many, many!"

"I will be with you – but I must be careful. My husband is so loyal to the Kinder way."

"We must not think of the present system as the Kinder way. The Kinder can do so much better."

Hilcyon Asteroid, Mrontl 12 1158

The bell rang, and Jasmine slowly straightened from her stooped position over the instrument, feeling the pain in her back from being bent over it for so many hours. She was measuring the amount of certain key metals in this new part of the asteroid they were opening up for mining, to see if it was a promising area to spend effort on. She could taste the dust in her mouth today for some reason, which surprised her. She seemed to have lost her sense of taste long ago.

She'd been on this asteroid for so long that it felt like forever. She lost track of time a long time ago. She figured it had been at least three years, but it might have well been 10 years, or 30 for all she knew. Jasmine had gotten used to seeing her friends get sick and die, buckle under the load of endlessly increasing quotas, or become heartless to raise themselves as high in the ranks as possible. She had decided to bide her time, do the best she could without compromising her ethics. She thought, somehow, she'd get out of the mines, even though the avenue out hadn't yet shown itself.

One of the strategies she'd employed was to be willing to take on very physically risky tasks. It ended up putting her in positions where she didn't have to work as hard as most. She would be the first person inside of a newly opened cavern, measuring the ore. Or she'd be working alongside of the caver bots in a caved-in section, trying to rescue either equipment or people.

It made her invaluable to her Third and Second Chiefs, and she worked hard to stay that way by doing dirty, dangerous work that none of her male colleagues would do. And it allowed her to avoid the compulsory marriage and child-bearing that her fellow women faced.

She was hungry; it had been a long day. Even though most of the day had been spent in measurement – she rarely actually mined anymore. She, like the single men, ate in the main commissary –

having no one to cook for them. The food was barely passable. She enjoyed the rare meals when an old friend invited her over to dinner with their families. The food was always better prepared.

On her way to the commissary, she ran into William, who was a newly minted Second Chief, the first of their group of New Earthers to make that rank since Craig lost it (and died) very soon after they had first come here.

"Hello Jasmine. How were the measurements on the new mine region?"

Jasmine knew that this question had more to do with how he could position his crews. If it was bad, he'd avoid it, and good, he'd do what he could to get his crews there. Jasmine was a part of his crew, and as much as she hated it, her fortune rose and fell with his, and the more information she could give him to help him, the more she easily she could avoid things she didn't like.

"I'd avoid it, William. Very low on Titanium and Gold."

"Thanks, I appreciate the tip."

"No problem."

"Oh, and by the way, it's pretty likely that Gary will be your new Second Chief in a couple of moons."

"Why?" That statement puzzled Jasmine. Chiefs only took over by one Chief being killed or dying.

"I've gotten an assignment on Hilcyon. I'm leaving the asteroid." Jasmine was surprised by the matter-of-fact way he said it.

"Wow. Well, I guess congratulations are in order, then?"

He smiled a thin, humorless smile. "You would not believe what it's taken. Anyway, I'll make sure Gary understands how useful you have been to me."

Jasmine knew Gary and had no hope that Gary would listen.

"Thanks."

She walked past William, into the commissary.

Hilcyon Asteroid, Mrontl 25 1158

"Jasmine, may I speak with you?" Gary sat down across from her at the table in the main commissary. It had been almost a moon since he took over, and he was reshuffling everything. Jasmine had heard rumors

410

about his intentions for her but had tried her best not to get anxious about it. Jasmine knew that Gary was, like William, from the ICS, but she thought he was probably less willing to let a woman be the one doing complex, dangerous work.

"Sure. How's the new position, Gary?"

"Look, I know that for some reason I can't understand, William allowed you to avoid getting married. Frankly, I'm a traditionalist. I don't think a woman should be in the position you are in. There are several men who need wives, and here you are – available. We need more children since so many die."

"What are you saying, Gary?"

All of a sudden, the alarm klaxon went off. Cave in! Jasmine had always been first on call for any cave in rescue duty. She decided to sit still, to see how Gary would react. Gary looked at Jasmine, as if making a decision, and then sighed.

"OK, come with me, let's see who or what needs rescuing."

The next several time periods were a blur. Jasmine managed to rescue four miners alive, recover three bodies, and several expensive pieces of equipment, in varied states of damage. When that was done, she went to her quarters, showered, and fell into sleep.

The next day, she saw Gary approaching her.

"Jasmine, I can see that I really need you to be on rescue duty. John, Walt, Kevin and Marquez would not have made it if you hadn't been there – and that equipment..."

"You are letting me be?"

"Reluctantly, yes. I clearly need you as you are more than any of my men need a wife, or we need children. There don't seem to be any men who want to do what you do. Be warned, if you don't keep up your end..."

"Believe me, I know. I've known it all along." Jasmine walked past Gary, back to her quarters, back to the only peace she knew on this misbegotten rock.

Casiti, 16 Nird 784

Hetl'zef and Re'il were sitting in Hetl'zef's office, discussing the Earth emigration.

Hetl'zef said, "Re'il, aren't you being a little extreme? No Terrans on Casiti at all? In fact, all Terrans already here deported to New Earth?"

"As far as I am concerned, if we had never had to re-unite with Terrans none of this would have happened. We'd be living happily on Casiti and in complete connection with the Galactic community. I want those days back."

Re'il had called this joining with Hetl'zef, the head teacher of the Caraj. Hetl'zef had been appointed to this position by consensus after he had been serving on the Caraj for only a year. Hetl'zef knew that Re'il didn't really approve of him, having been a previous companion to Silandra, one of the key Casitians involved with the Terrans.

"Re'il, that's silly, we can't go back. I understand your desire to protect Casiti from Terran influence, but we have to be realistic. Besides, the Terrans who are here have been great. What has been a problem?"

"Oh, there has been talk. Talk of tearful break-ups at the end of Winters, talk of ..."

"Re'il, tell me you've never cried at the end of a Winter!"

"You know what I mean!"

"Let's be realistic. I agree with limiting the number of Earth people we can allow on Casiti. Erit'ala is working up some data for carrying capacity, which will only include Rel'toro. This will limit the number of Earth people who can emigrate to something like five million."

"Five million? That's an enormous number!"

"Re'il, there are seven Billion people on Earth. Even five million is a tiny number in comparison to what they need. And there are more than five hundred times that number of Casitians here. They will not have much of an influence on our culture, especially if they live separately."

"New Earth is big enough to handle them all."

"New Earth doesn't have much infrastructure yet. We're already in danger of relegating some people who go to New Earth to starvation. As it is, it's going to be a massive feat to get things in place in three short years. We have enough spare greenhouse capacity, as well as building materials and farming equipment to easily take care of that many Terrans with almost no effort. We should, honestly, take many, many more, but I think five million is the most that we'll get consensus on."

"Honestly, Hetl'zef, I don't care who starves. I don't want any Terrans here!"

Hetl'zef was taken aback. He was surprised by the vehemence with which Re'il was expressing his distaste for Terrans.

"Re'il, you don't really mean that! That is not the Casitian way. We must do everything in our power to make sure that all humans, no matter who they are, or what planet they came from, are taken care of. We cannot give in to the kind of hatreds that our other human brothers show."

Hetl'zef could see in Re'il's face that he didn't appreciate being corrected in this way.

"Thank you for seeing me, Hetl'zef. I'm sorry that we don't see eye to eye on this. I want you to know right now that I will block consensus on any Earth humans coming to Casiti."

Re'il rose from his chair, turned quickly, and walked out of the room. Hetl'zef sighed. He didn't like the potential outcomes he saw facing him, not in the least.

Hilcyon, Mrontl 25 1158

William had a hard time actually believing his luck as he strode out from the port, into the light of the Hilcyon sun. He'd spent so much time in the dark that the sun of Hilcyon made his eyes hurt. He knew this sun was less bright than Earth's sun. He looked up at the sky to see three of the nine moons – he knew that at night, whichever of the nine moons that were up would be spectacular. He looked forward to seeing that.

He was to report to Fourth chief Sadre for his assignment. He didn't much care what it was. He did whatever he needed to do to get ahead. He'd left his wife and child back at the asteroid- the first chief of the asteroid had been clear. They stayed behind, assigned to another man, while William started his new life on Hilcyon, free, apparently, to marry again.

He had committed the address of the Fourth chief to memory and was able to easily find it. He was gratified by the orderliness of the city layout – hamlets were clearly labeled, and streets numbered obviously. As he stood in front of the Sadre's door, he wondered what kind of stance he should take. Too deferent, he might be seen as weak. Too aggressive, he might be seen as a threat. It was a very thin line he had to walk on. He took a deep breath, and raised his fist to knock on the door, but before he could complete the motion, the door flew open.

"Ah, you must be ... Wllem? Sadre said that you'd be coming around now. Come in, come in, have a seat. I've got some breadmufs, do you like those?"

William was used to being called Wllem. He found that the Kinder all had short names, and a name like "William" was hard for them to pronounce, so they shortened it and took out most of the vowel sounds. He realized he had no idea what a "breadmuf" was - it was an unfamiliar word to him.

"Yes, thank you. Where is Sadre?"

"He's out doing his rounds. He'll be back soon. Come, please, sit here."

The woman, who William assumed was Sadre's wife, pointed him to a bench with some padding next to the window.

"Thank you."

He looked around the room, taking in details. William was surprised that Sadre allowed his house to get as dusty and cluttered as this. William had always been very strict with his wife around the cleanliness of the room they shared.

"My name is Krely. I hear you're just off one of the asteroids. Congratulations. I know it's quite rare to be let out the asteroid mines."

"Yes, it is rare."

Krely handed William a fist-sized thing resting on a cloth napkin, which looked a lot like the cinnamon buns he vaguely remembered from Earth. It was the first thing resembling real food he had eaten in years.

"Thank you so much!" He ate the breadmuf with relish - it reminded him of Earth food, and he was for a moment, transported back. He felt an old sadness tug at him.

As he was finishing the last crumbs, and wiping his face, the door opened and a squat man with gray hair and a pot belly came into the house and turned to see him.

"Ah, Krely, I see you are already stuffing the boy's face! Good!"

William was caught totally off guard. He rose, and wiped his hand on his pants, and put out his hand. He then realized his mistake, pulled his hand back, and bowed.

"Fourth Chief Sadre, William Harris at your service." Sadre nodded and looked at William with some curiosity.

"I hear you are not from Hilcyon, but from Grier Nro."

William had no idea what Sadre had said, but he surmised that Grier Nro must be either their name for New Earth, or Earth, so he nodded.

"Yes, sir, I was not born here."

"Well, Wllem, you'll get used to it. I already did my rounds this morning, but there are a few people I'd like you to meet. Let's go walking, shall we? Krely, you'll be feeding our guest this evening, and he'll be staying here – apparently his apartment won't be ready until tomorrow."

"Yes, Sadre, I'll get everything prepared, and we'll have a very nice meal." William followed Sadre out the door, and Krely closed it behind them.

"She's a wonderful cook, but that's about all she can manage. If she weren't able to cook as well as she can, or hadn't made a baby, I'd have given her up a while ago. OK, let's go down Tsrul Street. I want you to meet one of my assistants."

They had been walking for a few minutes when William saw an especially dark-skinned woman leave her house. She looked at him and started, clearly recognizing him. He recognized her as well: Beatrice! He knew that she had gotten off the asteroid with her Kinder husband. He never could figure out how they had managed to do that, but William always assumed that her husband had connections he could pull.

William saw her put her head down, turn, and walk back into her house, as if she didn't want to have to acknowledge seeing him, or talk with him. William was instantly suspicious. He was going to get to the bottom of this. He thought that if he did, he could possibly learn something invaluable to Sadre, getting himself in position to move up the ladder again.

Sadre seemed to have completely missed that whole exchange. One thing William knew that most Kinder men did not – women could not be taken for granted or expected to always be docile. William knew better.

Casiti, 22 Nird 784

Jal'end'a heard the light, quiet chime of her meditation bell. She emerged from her meditation uneasy rather than settled. The communications that she had received from the Caraj suggested to Jal'end'a that very few Terrans would be allowed to settle on Casiti, no matter how dire the need.

After she returned from Earth, she returned to her cloistered life. She was working on a book about Earth religious and spiritual tradition and practice. She had been honored to spend time among the most revered Earth spiritual leaders, and she had learned an enormous amount. There was much for her to process and to write about.

This new crisis, though, had been eating at her for days. She realized that she could not stand by the sideline. She came to a resolution, suddenly. She may not be asked for her opinion on the matter, but she would give it.

She rose from her cushion, and started to compose a letter to Hetl'zef, the new leader of the Caraj. She thought he was likely aligned with Re'il and others on the Caraj who wanted no Earth human influence whatsoever on Casiti. Jal'end'a knew that there was much to mend among humankind. Bringing Terrans to Casiti would be a good first step. She outlined a plan she thought made sense – to have Terrans settle on the other continents of Casiti.

Casiti had three large continents. The smallest was Rel'toro, the in the northern hemisphere. It had the largest band of temperate zones on Casiti. Although it was the smallest, it was a similar size to the Asian continent on Earth. Casitians were living all over Rel'toro, although it was much more sparsely populated than most Earth continents. Loc'deher was a continent also in the northern hemisphere, and mostly covered over with glaciers. There was a relatively small band of coastal land on Loc'deher that could certainly be settled. It was completely empty of Casitians. The largest continent was Jul'when. It like Loc'deher, had glaciers, but it had as much arable land as Rel'toro. Casitians used it almost entirely for recreation – camping, wilderness trips, etc. There were probably only a few thousand Casitians that lived there full time. There were a few monasteries and schools in remote southern reaches of Jul'when, but they would not be affected, since they were in regions of Jul'when that were not temperate.

In truth, Casiti could easily hold another billion human beings, without much effect on its environment. All Casitians knew this. But Casitians didn't want anything to change. The time for holding back change was done, closed off irrevocably by the judgment of the galactic community. Jal'end'a finished her missive, sent it along, and hoped for the best.

New Earth, Month 1, Year 25

Marianne was dreaming of Ja'el. She could feel Ja'el's soft skin against hers, her deep voice in her ear. She was brought out of that dream with an insistent low-pitched chime that she didn't recognize. It was dark out – it was the middle of the night. Marianne looked around her room and saw an orange glow in the far corner and realized that was the source of the chime. For a moment, she was puzzled, then she remembered – it was the communications device that had been given to the Dlejonese by the Casitians and was now in her care.

She groped to find the lamp on her end table so she could turn it on, and stumbled up to take the device out of the cubby hole that she had stored it in. It had only been about eight years since the Casitians had locked the wormhole. She had expected never to see any Casitians again in her lifetime.

She moved the device out from its cubby and saw that there was definitely an incoming signal. She ran her finger over the activation switch and stood back. A holographic image began to form in front of the device. It was none other than Ja'el. It felt odd to see Ja'el standing in front of her, after her vivid dream.

"Marianne. It is good to see you. You look well."

"As do you, Ja'el. I have to say, I'm surprised to see you."

"Yes, I imagined that you would be. I am at Illsenor station. The wormhole is open again."

Marianne let that sink in. "So soon? I didn't expect you to open it again in my lifetime."

Ja'el nodded. "Yes, it would have been many years before the Caraj would have chosen to regain contact with New Earth. But we were not given a choice in the matter."

"I don't understand."

"I can't explain now. A shuttle is coming to get you – it should arrive in about an hour. Please be ready. Joel, David and Laura, as well as Erit'ala, Silandra, and I are at Ilsenor station. We have much to discuss."

"OK, I'll be ready."

The holographic image faded, and Marianne realized she would need to wake up Douglas. She quickly got dressed, and walked out of her small cabin, down the dirt road to the more central part of Dlejon's main settlement. She turned down the small lane where Douglas' apartment was – a part of a small cluster of apartments where council members lived. She found his door and saw the bell. She took the mallet hanging next to the bell and rang the bell several times.

In a few moments, she heard the sound of muted voices, and footsteps on the way to the door. The door swung open, and Joy, Douglas' current companion, stood in the door, looking a bit disheveled.

"Joy, I am so sorry to wake you up. I must talk with Douglas immediately."

"Of course, Marianne, please, come on in. Have a seat. I'll get Douglas. Would you like some tea?"

"Thanks, but no, I don't really have time."

Marianne could tell that Joy was puzzled. Marianne internally chuckled. She was puzzled herself. Joy went into the other room, and Douglas came out of it, in the last stages of putting on a robe.

"I'm so sorry to bother you Douglas, but this is very important. Ja'el activated the communications device. The wormhole is unlocked, and they are coming to get me in a shuttle within the hour."

"What? How can that be? Why?"

"She wouldn't tell me – but based on what I know of them, she probably didn't want whatever the news was to spread out of their control. I expect it's fairly dire, but I can't imagine what it would be. Perhaps war broke out between the Kinder and Casitians? I just don't know."

"You'll find out. In any event, I think it's probably wisest not to tell anyone of the wormhole until you know more."

"Yes, I think that's wise. I don't know when I'll be back – probably tomorrow."

"Well, good luck. I do not envy being in your shoes."

Douglas saw Marianne to the door and gave her a hug. Marianne quickly walked back to her cabin, thoughts of what was to face her in her mind and heart. She felt more ready to see Ja'el, somehow – much of the hurt had healed. But she also was worried about what circumstances provoked this change in the Casitians behavior. It was ominous.

She gathered a change of clothes and assorted required odds and ends and put them in a small travel bag. She heard a rustle of wind outside and realized the shuttle must have arrived. She walked out to the small clearing across the road from her cabin and saw the characteristic open door in the middle of nothing. She walked up to it and walked inside.

K'flef greeted her. "Hello Marianne, it's been a long time."

They gave each other a clasped-arm hug.

"K'flef, I missed you. How have you been?"

"David and I traveled around the galaxy, then we were involved in the ... oh, you'll hear about that – I can't give it away yet. There is a lot to tell."

Marianne smiled. "OK, K'flef, it's fine. I can be patient."

K'flef got back in the pilot's seat, and the shuttle took off.

"It's about a five-hour ride. Tell me about New Earth. How have things been?"

Marianne settled in and told K'flef what she'd experienced in the years since the Casitians left.

Ilsenor Station, 22 Nird 784

When they arrived on the station, Ja'el met them at the shuttle dock, and came forward to give Marianne an embrace. Marianne felt enveloped in Ja'el's love. She lingered in the sweetness of the embrace for a bit, then they broke apart, looking at each other.

"Marianne, I've missed you. I'm glad that I am able to see you again."

"I truly never thought I'd see you again, Ja'el. It is wonderful to see you." Marianne paused. "So, tell me. What happened?"

"Come, Marianne, let's go to the joining room. Everyone is anxious to see you."

They walked down hallways that Marianne noticed were bereft of artwork. Clearly, they hadn't been here very long. Marianne wondered if they intended to stay.

They walked into a large conference room that Marianne recognized – the room they were in on that fateful day that she decided to cast her lot within New Earth. It seemed both so long ago and just yesterday.

David shot out of his seat to run up to her and embrace her, and before she knew it, she was surrounded by people she loved and missed. She'd assumed for so long that she'd never see them again. It was a sweet moment for all of them. Finally, after a while of greetings and hugs, they all sat down. Marianne was anxious to hear what had happened.

David cleared his throat. "It's pretty dire, Marianne. After the Casitians locked this wormhole, the Keeelo asked the Sejo to have an inquiry. The human species was put on trial. We lost. It was the combination of the Za'aref using the wormhole to promote conflict with New Earth, as well as the Casitian decision to lock the wormhole. We have been banned from the galactic community for 1000 years."

"Oh, my. Banned, huh? So we're stuck on four worlds. That's really sad, and I can imagine hard for the Casitians. But … why did you unlock the wormhole? That doesn't change the relationship between the Kinder and the Casitians."

Joel leaned forward. "It's because we don't have four worlds, Marianne. We have only three. The dolphins are kicking us off of Earth. We have 12 Earth years to move everyone."

Marianne was stunned. "Kicked off of Earth? But…"

"It's the dolphin's planet, too. The Kwalloo requested on the dolphin's behalf that we leave. The Sejo agreed."

It was going to take a while to let all of this sink in. Twelve Earth years to evacuate more than seven billion people? She found it hard to fathom.

"I guess we have our work cut out for us, don't we?"

Kinder Ship, Mrontl 25 1158

First Chief Glendr paced, back and forth first slowly, then quickened his pace. He was a patient man. But he was losing his patience after four long years. Bercyg, the one he thought had the most promise, had deserted him, to stay on that accursed planet. He had a new Second Chief in command of the troops, Krelso, who had so artfully disposed of Retyl. But he had had no more success in raising more troops from the New Americans than Bercyg had. In fact, the President they had been originally working with had died suddenly and had been replaced by someone who was insular and protective of New America and had pulled their army away from the border entirely and ceased most communication and trade with the Kinder. Krelso had also had no luck in rounding up defectors.

Worse still, Jercyn had still not gotten anywhere in breaking the wormhole lock - so they were still completely stuck here. He was running out of options, and worse yet, the ship was running out of food.

His door chime rang. "Come."

Jercyn burst in, out of breath.

"You finally broke the wormhole lock?"

"No, First Chief. It has been opened."

"Opened?"

"From the other side. The Breft are back."

Although he was shocked, his wits kicked in quickly. Glendr thought – this was his moment. He would go home and bring more ships and troops. Then he could take over New Earth, and finally be triumphant.

He turned toward his console, ready to command the movement of the ship toward the wormhole and being battle preparations when Jercyn said, "They want to talk with us."

Glendr snapped his neck to turn back to Jercyn. "What?"

"They initiated communication. They wish to talk with us."

"There is nothing for us to say to them, besides, get out of our way, so we can go home, or we'll destroy you."

"They didn't tell me any details, First Chief, but they wanted to speak to the commander of this ship, with the note that it was very urgent."

Glendr went back to his console, flipped a couple of switches. "To all personnel. We are leaving this system. All Second Chiefs please meet in my office in 30 time units." He flipped them back.

"OK, let's go to the comm center and see what it is that this Breft idiot has to say."

Ilsenor Station, 30 Nird 784

"I think I should do it." David was adamant. He had a strong intuition about this.

"Why you?"

"I think that Terrans will seem more threatening to them than you will. And they don't know us – but they know that we are different than you are. If I talk with him, he'll be disarmed, to some extent, and also probably convinced that he knows something he doesn't. You all are completely predictable and disposable to him."

K'lellen looked thoughtful. He finally spoke. "I believe you are correct. You will speak with him. Be careful, though."

David nodded. "Always."

A group of them were in a small space set aside for communications. They were waiting for the commander of the Za'aref ship to make contact with them.

A soft chime rang, and the AI's quiet voice spoke, "Za'aref ship requests comm connection."

David went to sit at the console. "Initiate connection." A face appeared on the screen in front of him. Clean shaven and bald, with a severe chin, and small lines in his eyebrows. He began to speak, and it took a few seconds for the translator to kick in.

"This is First Chief Glendr, commander of the Kinder ship 'Kingdom'. What urgent news do you have for me?"

"First Chief Glendr, my name is David Lopez. I am from the planet Earth."

Glendr's face changed. He clearly looked surprised. Then he laughed.

"What could you possibly have to tell me?"

"There has been a change in the status of human beings in the Galactic community."

"And I should care because?"

"Because all human beings, including Terrans, will be required to live on only three planets - Casiti, New Earth, and ... Hilcyon. We have been restricted as a species and need to leave Earth."

It was difficult to read Glendr's face. He seemed to be going through a number of thoughts and emotions at once.

"I see. In other words, you are telling me that there are many, many more humans on their way to New Earth?"

"Yes, billions of them. I'm also telling you that our three branches of humanity must find a way to coexist. We are all we have now. We need you to bring this message back with you to Hilcyon. We also wish to send both Terran and Casitian emissaries with you."

Glendr laughed. "No, that is not possible."

"Why not?"

"There are Kinder, and there are Breft. If you Terrans cooperated with the Breft, you are Breft. We have not had any diplomatic communication with the Breft since the betrayal of Klor, and that will not change."

His face disappeared from the screen. David turned toward K'lellen, shrugging his shoulders. "I don't know if that was any better..."

"Actually, I think it was. I don't think he would have even let me deliver the news."

"What was the 'betrayal of Klor'?"

K'lellen's face was a mask, and he said only, "just history." David didn't dare ask more.

"So what's next?"

"We let them go home."

Kinder ship, Mrontl 25 1158

First Chief Glendr turned off the comm device with one hand and sat motionless for a few minutes. He could feel Jercyn standing uncomfortably behind him, waiting for him to say something. But he was far from ready to let any of his nascent thoughts out of his mouth. His plans of finally conquering this planet were, he realized, for naught. Billions of new people from the planet Grier Nro (roughly translated to "Origin of Kinder") would be coming to this planet, overwhelming any possible force the Kinder could array against them. Hilcyon and all of its colonies had but 500 million people.

He must bring this news home and help Hilcyon defend itself against a likely invasion by Grier and Breft. He began to build a new plan in his mind – one that he thought would be even more likely to result in his ascension to Supreme Chief.

"We are going home now. Send out a message to any still on the planet that we are leaving. Send shuttles down to the planet now to pick them up. We leave in 3 days."

Glendr rose from the stool perched in front of the comm panel in one smooth motion, spun on his heels, and started the walk back to his quarters. He could feel Jercyn's incredulity behind him.

San Diego, Earth, August 4, 2025

"Ms. Henry?" The slight girl with pigtails and glasses in the front of the classroom raised her hand.

Joanne impatiently answered, "yes, Maria?"

"Ms. Henry, Question 5 on the quiz didn't seem fair."

"Fair, Maria? What do you mean?"

"Well, you asked about our understanding of Dolphin behavior, and my answer..."

Joanne got angry. She could feel her fatigue and her barely suppressed rage bubbling toward the surface. Better end the day.

"Maria, your answer was wrong, that's all you need to know." She raised her voice. "Everyone, remember tomorrow we'll be studying Jane Goodall's work. Please make sure you read Chapter 15 in your text. I'm letting you out early today."

The standard end of day chaos ensued. Maria looked as if she was going to come up and challenge Joanne further, but then thought better of it. Joanne gathered her things and walked out of the classroom.

"Joanne..." she heard a deep voice to her left and turned. It was the principal of the school, now called "head teacher" standing in the hall. Joanne felt far from ready to talk with Hank Peters, who was younger than she by a number of years and didn't have the education she did.

"Yes, teacher Peters? How can I help you?" Joanne figured that her voice sounded far from patient.

"Can you please come into my office?"

Joanne followed him into his office, and she sat down in the comfortable chair he had for guests. He closed the door, then swung his office chair out from behind the desk that faced the window and sat down.

"Joanne, I just got the annual reviews back on the teachers."

"And..."

"For the second year in a row, your evaluations have been far below average. This year, they are even worse than they were last year. I warned you about this last year. I'm sorry, but this year will be your last teaching here."

Joanne let the seething, bubbling anger surface. "Fine. Actually, today might as well be my last day. I'm done here."

"Joanne..."

"What, do you have something to say?"

"I'm sorry this didn't work out for you. You need to find some help - I can see you eating yourself alive."

She had nothing to say. She got up, left the office, and walked down the hall, knowing she'd never come back. It didn't bother her, really. She'd hated teaching high school since the day she arrived.

It had been the third of three post-dolphin careers she'd tried. After the dolphins became part of the galactic community, all dolphin research was stopped. So Joanne lost her life's work – her life's passion. Worse yet, there was no room for her in any sort of liaison position. The dolphins were adamant - people who had so misunderstood them could not be in a position to communicate with them. Joanne understood, but felt that she had been painted with the same brush.

She'd theorized for years, in private, that dolphins were in fact more intelligent than human beings.

She had tenure at UCSD - she could change her research subject and still remain on the faculty. She tried studies of other ocean mammals, but all of those avenues seemed closed. She, along with all other Marine mammologists were casting about for new research subjects. Others of her colleagues started looking at terrestrial mammals.

She just didn't have the heart for it, so she left UCSD after a few years to join a small startup using galactic medical technologies. That lasted about a month. She decided then, that perhaps teaching kids was the best idea. That idea was now at its end. She didn't know what she'd do, except go home and drown her sorrows as usual in the bottle of '10 Merlot she'd gotten at the wine store the other day. Drinking pre-Casitian vintage wine had become not only a habit, but somewhat of an obsession for her. She swore it tasted better.

New Calgary, New Earth, Month 1, Year 25

Mira, Leticia, Jeffrey and Thomas were sitting around Jeffrey and Thomas' dining room table in New Calgary, having a heated discussion over dinner.

"No way, no way, Jeffrey! Sean Joseph was the personal doctor to two New American Presidents. He even admits to immigrating to New Earth because he hated Casitians! You can't hire him for the medical school."

"Mira, he left New America, and he's been living here for more than a year. He's a nice man, and he cares a lot about people. He was one of the best oncologists on Earth, and he's clearly the best on New Earth. How can we not hire him?"

Mira countered, "but there isn't any cancer on New Earth!"

Leticia placed her arm gently on Mira's. "Love, we can't make political or cultural litmus tests for faculty of the New Calgary Medical School. We need to find the best physicians and other practitioners that are on New Earth, no matter what their political leanings."

Leticia could see Mira relax, and heard a quiet sigh. "I know, Leticia, it's just hard for me. He just seems so ... I don't know, emblematic of what's wrong with some of New Earth."

Leticia and Mira had graduated from the first Medical School on New Earth in the Southern Independent Zone and had moved up to New Calgary. Their goal was to create a second medical school to train a new generation of physicians in this part of New Earth. The four of them, along with a small nucleus of others, were beginning the process of hiring faculty, getting funding to build the school, and other endeavors. It would likely be two or three more years before they could have their first class. They also were soliciting funding to start an associated research institution.

Mira looked at Thomas. "Anyway, on a totally different subject, this was an amazing dinner. What you did with the grapeberries and chicken..."

Thomas grinned. "Thank you, Mira."

They started to clear the table of dishes. Leticia could not imagine being happier in her life. She had work that she loved, good friends, and a partner with whom she shared so much. A lot had changed in the years since she ran away from the Independent Christian State. She was even on good terms with her mother and got to see her Aunt Marianne once in a while.

Her one sadness was for her missing sister, Beatrice. She hoped, someday, to see her again, but every once in a while, she was afraid that her sister was lost to them. She knew her mother mourned for her as if she was dead, but somehow, Leticia couldn't fully believe that.

"Hey, Leticia," Thomas called from the kitchen.

"What?"

"Guess who I ran into yesterday?"

"I don't know, who?"

"Leonard Wilkins. Remember him?"

"Oh, the guy who came with us to help build out the widenet! How is he? Where is he living now?"

"He's fine. He lives in New Orleans. He was up here just visiting and checking out how the network is up here."

"I've been meaning to send him an email, actually. I was curious to see how far the widenet has made it so far."

"He says that wherever there is a settlement, there is widenet. It hasn't made it to many individual homes, though. He says his biggest problem is getting equipment - he has to hand-manufacture it, which takes a lot of time."

"Yeah, and he can't just order equipment from Earth, now can he?"

Hilcyon, Mrontl 26 1158

As the movement had progressed, more and more women were getting involved, and Beatrice had become the leader of the nascent women's movement. A few of the women leaders were gathered in the small living room. Pkygy was off at work. The morning was a great time to meet – all of the men were busy at work and a gathering of women would not be noticed.

There were about seven women present, of varied ages, from Klana who was the very youngest – a single teenager who was doing everything she could to avoid having to marry, to Jvly, an old, wizened widow. She had especially taken to Tivyl, who reminded her of her mother somewhat. They sat on the chairs and pillows in the small room, quite close to one another. Beatrice started to speak, raising her voice slightly so that all could hear.

"Thank you all so much for coming to this meeting today. We are at a momentous time. Pkygy estimates that we have about one half of the Second, Third and Fourth Chiefs at least sympathetic to our side. Additionally, he says have about 5 First Chiefs all around Hilcyon that we know we can count on. We are almost ready to make our first moves."

Tivyl asked, "what would those be?"

"Well, the first step is an action that is subtle enough not to be noticed by the enemy, but powerful enough for us to know that we had an effect. One of the things we did on the mining moon was to have an actual speed-up of work."

"Ah, I see. So we would do something like a minor change in schedule, or increase a quota, that sort of thing. To show ourselves our power and to confirm the extent of the growth of the movement."

"Exactly. As women, we have it a lot easier than the men – we are mostly ignored. My suggestion for us is that for Kyl holiday, coming up in two Zhurs, the women who are part of a cell put out exactly four

Whlis leaves on their doors, with exactly one being white, instead of the more usual random numbers and colors."

"Ah, Btric, that is a wonderful idea!"

"So we need to spread that word – four Whlis leaves, one white. And we watch. Our next action will mean something!"

They said their goodbyes, and left Beatrice's house, one by one. Krely hung back, clearly wishing to speak to Beatrice alone.

"Btric, I need to tell you about something."

"What is it, Krely?"

"There was a man at my house yesterday, a man named Wllem."

Beatrice tried her best to hide her reaction. "And?"

"Btric, he asked me about you, by name. He wanted to know how long you'd been here, and what you were like."

"What did you say?"

"I told him enough of the truth to try and ease his suspicions. I'm not sure if it helped."

"Thanks, Krely. I knew him on the asteroid. He's from the same planet I'm from. He knows me. I saw him walking with Sadre yesterday."

"Be careful, Btric. I feel like he is dangerous. I can't believe he asked *me* about you. It doesn't make sense."

"Krely, men from my planet do not ignore women, or expect them to always be docile. It's not the way it is anymore."

Beatrice could see the understanding dawning on her.

Krely nodded. "I'll keep an eye out for you."

"Thanks, Krely." Krely walked out the door, and Beatrice closed it behind her, feeling more worried than she'd felt in a while. William wouldn't ignore the women, or an action that women took. That could be dangerous for the whole movement. She needed to talk about this with Pkygy when he got home.

Independent Christian State, New Earth, Month 1 Year 25

The woman who was the host of the gathering was standing at the podium, gesturing toward him.

"I want to thank you, Parker, for being willing to tell us about your travels to New Aard, and even further afield. Everyone, Parker Hill."

As she took her seat, Parker stepped up to the podium, and looked out at his audience. It was a group of about 40 people, gathered at one of the churches in the settlement. They were curious about where he'd traveled, and what he'd seen. He suspected few, if any of them, had been out of the ICS, let alone out of New America.

"Well, friends, thank you for having me. I have a lot to share. I'll focus on two key highlights of my trip: my connections with the business leaders of New Aard, and the Kinder, who are a very interesting bunch."

Parker regaled them with his tales of the riverboat trip down to New Orleans, which is the only way to do north-south travel at this time. He talked about meeting in several communities in New Aard, setting up trading pacts, arranging buyers and sellers of goods for the ICS. He then shifted his talk to describe the meeting he had with the Kinder – a seemingly accidental meeting that was, in his mind, completely ordained by God.

"I had just finished a meeting in New Orleans, setting up buyers for our biodiesel, and as I was leaving the building, I literally ran into a group of men. They looked very unfamiliar, although they reminded me a lot of Casitians. Then I remembered hearing about the Kinder, and I realized it must be them. I greeted them and started talking with a few of them. As we were chatting, Marianne Michaelson walked up." He heard hisses and boos from varied points of the room.

"Yes, well, apparently she had been meeting with them. She wanted to know who I was, and where I was from, and I told her. She was perfectly friendly toward me and invited me to join them for a dinner celebration they were having with representatives from other territories. She said that there wasn't a representative from either the ICS or New America, and I certainly could serve as one. I agreed."

"So I spent the rest of the afternoon, evening, and into the night with the Kinder. They are noble, honorable people, with the kind of social order that we crave here in the ICS. They worship God, although they call Him the 'Exalted King.' I think we have a lot to learn from the Kinder. I invited them to come here to visit sometime." Parker could here murmuring in the room.

"I'll take questions."

A man in the back stood up. "Parker, I heard that the Kinder were just like Casitians."

Parker laughed. "Nothing could be further from the truth. The Kinder and the Casitians are the exact opposites. Where the Casitians are immoral, the Kinder are upstanding. The men marry ... wives ... for life." He heard snickers. "They have a highly ordered, society. Women bow down to men, men bow down to their superiors. Literally. They bow, no stupid hugs." Full out laughter.

Another man, closer to him this time, stood up. "I heard that these Kinder had originally come to take over New Earth. Why should we trust them?"

"You have a good point there, Donald. The truth is the Kinder didn't want to invade and take over. But they saw opportunity here. They learned that they could take advantage of that opportunity without a fight. So they are happy, now."

A woman, who was blond and short of stature, stood up. "I have heard that these Kinder know where our disappeared children are. I heard that their people took our children back to their planet. What do you know about that? It's been years! They aren't even children anymore. Why can't they come back?"

Parker knew that toeing the party line on this one was the right way to go. "Ma'am, I know that they are safe here on New Earth. They just are working outside of the range of communication and the widenet. They'll be back soon." Parker decided to cut the questions off there.

"Folks, thanks for listening. I'm sure you'll be hearing a lot more about the Kinder in coming months and years."

Everyone stood up and milled about. As the woman who had asked him about the children started to walk up to him, Parker decided to make a hasty retreat. He quickly thanked his host, and walked out of the side door, into the night.

Ilsenor Station, Month 1, Year 25/24 Nird 784

The discussions had carried on for what felt to Marianne like forever, but it was only a few days. Marianne was having a hard time with the strange, distanced stance the Casitians were taking with the Terrans.

They seemed to blame the whole thing on the Terrans, which made no sense, as well as leaving the whole thing to the Terrans to deal with.

After a long-winded lecture from Erit'ala about how the Terrans should take responsibility for their own people, Marianne lost her temper.

"Erit'ala, I have the greatest respect for you, and other teachers of Casiti. But frankly, you screwed up in locking the wormhole – something Terrans could never have been in the position to do. To blame us for this situation, and leave the huge task of getting Terrans off of Earth to us is not at all fair. We need your help. We don't have the expertise with Galactic technology that you do, we don't have the liaisons with the Galactic pilots. We simply can't do this without you."

Erit'ala was quiet for a moment, as if carefully considering what she was going to say next. What she did say surprised Marianne.

"You are correct. It is unfair for us to hand this burden to you. And I personally am clearly not the person who should be helping to make decisions about this at this time. We will do our best to make sure that you have enough Casitian help."

Ja'el said, "this is my suggestion: a Terran team should oversee the political process of the immigration to New Earth, and a Casitian team should oversee the logistical aspects of an infrastructure building process on New Earth, as well as be the liaisons with the galactic authorities who will be in a position to help. These teams will meet regularly together and share information and help problem solve together."

Erit'ala nodded, "yes, that makes a lot of sense." The other Casitians in the room agreed.

Marianne was happy things seemed to be moving forward again. She agreed with Ja'el.

"Yes, Ja'el, I think that makes the most sense."

Joel broke his silence, and said to Marianne, "I think you should be the head teacher of the Terran team."

That was not what Marianne wanted to hear at all. But then everyone started to agree with Joel, and there wasn't much she could do about it. She could see the logic in it. People mostly trusted her (except those who didn't,) and she had come to an unusual understanding of the populations of both planets during the initial crisis. She had to admit she was the right pick, even though it was not a job she wanted.

Chapter 2:
Twelve Fingers of the Tud'scla

(AP) October 1, 2025

Last Holdouts Agree to World Democracy. Elections set for July, 2026

New York – The last few countries that were reluctant to join the world democracy have relented, paving the way for the World Presidential and Congressional elections in 2026. It was an epic effort, led by the United States, the European Union, China and some others. There are three major candidates for World President, and campaigning for representatives to the World Government will start in earnest. Debates will be scheduled by a global media committee.

Dlejon, New Earth, Month 1, Year 25

After several days at Illsenor station, Marianne finally returned to Dlejon with a lot of work to do. She was spending some time in her cabin, arranging her thoughts and next actions. She wanted to contact the major leaders of the settled areas by audio first, so they heard directly from her, and not via the rumor mill. Then, she'd have to travel, and meet with people all over New Earth. The team at Illsenor, both Terran and Casitian, had agreed that the leadership role belonged to Marianne, and she was now in charge of the process of settling Terrans on New Earth, as well as the communication with the Kinder.

In general, she was pretty unhappy with the way that the Casitians were acting. Silandra and Erit'ala were leaving the system and going back to Casiti. They apparently had no intention of being involved going forward. Ja'el was also leaving, but Marianne was less sure about Ja'el's intentions – she expected to see Ja'el again on New Earth.

She had this feeling that they didn't want to deal with the consequences of their actions. They had promised her Casitian personnel - K'flef and Wren were staying behind, as was a man named K'lellen, and several others she didn't know. She appreciated that – but she felt she needed their leadership and leverage with the Casitian council. She didn't have a liaison she could trust with the Caraj, and she thought that might make things difficult.

In any event, she needed to talk first with Douglas, and have him tell all of Dlejon. Dlejon was still a tender issue. Her re-appearance on New Earth, especially after the promise that the Casitians would never contact the planet, was still, after all of these years, a sore spot, even though it meant that New Earth had been saved from invasion. That she had seemed to be in contact with those in Dlejon made others suspicious of them, and they could feel it. She had to tread carefully.

She decided to get it over with. She left her cabin, walked down the road again, this time in daylight, and rang his bell. It was a day off, so she knew he was likely to be home. He answered the door, smiling.

"Marianne! It was a few days, I expected you back sooner."

"It took a lot longer than I thought – there's a lot to deal with, Douglas. I have much to tell you."

"Well, then come in, take a seat. Tea?"

Marianne nodded. "Yes, Douglas, thanks."

As Douglas prepared the tea, Marianne told him the outlines of the story. He listened quietly, without interrupting. He brought two steaming mugs of tea to the table and sat down across from Marianne.

"I'm a little daunted by all of this. Dlejon is, as it goes here, a very small region. We're happy to take on more people. I imagine we could easily double our numbers without too much trouble in the short term."

"Thank you, Douglas. That's the kind of thinking I need. But I actually have a much bigger role in mind for you and Dlejon to play."

"Bigger role? Marianne, we need to tread very carefully."

"Douglas, remember, at least, 7 billion human beings from Earth will be emigrating here over the course of 24 years. We have a lot to figure out in that time, not the least of which is how to make sure that we build sustainably. Dlejon knows better than any other settled region how to do that. We need that leadership."

"You know I would do just about anything for you, so I'll do this. But I need to prepare my people first. There are several folks I know I can count on to help me work on the sustainability issues."

Kinder Settlement, New Earth, Month 1, Year 25

He liked the way this brush felt in his hand. He'd traveled all the way to New Orleans for it. He chuckled internally. That was not strictly true. He'd traveled to New Orleans to meet with some New Earth leaders, to tell them that he led all Kinder on New Earth and assure them that all Kinder were peaceful and would stay that way. It had taken him many moons to gather his people and to show them the wisdom of a peaceful coexistence on this planet.

While he was in New Orleans, he had been walking by a shop which had in its display these wonderful paints and brushes. He'd wanted to go back to painting ever since he'd left the Kinder invasion force and started to think about settling down. He didn't have any money, but Marianne, who happened to be walking with him at the time, saw the look on his face when they passed the shop, and went in and bought him what he wanted. He was stunned by her kindness and generosity. Ever since then, he was sure that it was the grace of the Exalted King that he'd ended up on this planet.

He liked painting the sunset best. It was certainly true that he missed the nine moons, but the sunsets made up for it. His tent was perched on a hill that faced west, perfect for watching and painting.

Ngellin heard the sound of rapidly moving footsteps on the gravely path on the way up to his dwelling. He wondered who had decided to make the wrong choice of bothering him at this moment. He realized his companions here knew him well enough that if they came up now, it must be important.

He saw the now tousled hair of Lren bobbing up and down before he saw Lren's face. It looked like Lren was running. Ngellin had also grown out his hair and grown a beard. He figured that it would disguise him in the unlikely event that any Kinder came back looking for him. In reality, he liked his new hair, although at first it had itched a lot.

Lren crested the small hill, out of breath. "Ngellin, I'm sorry to disturb you – I know how much you like your sunsets in peace."

"Thank you, Lren. I figured it must be important."

"It is. Marianne is on the audio link. She said it was urgent and insists on talking directly to you, and only you."

Ngellin wondered what this was about. "OK, I'll come down." He left his paints, and ran back down the hill, behind Lren.

They entered the building that served as a small central government office. In the corner was communications equipment, including audio transmitters, and computers that had become hooked up by radio waves to what had become called the "widenet". Ngellin saw the small, blinking orange light on the audio communications device. He picked up the handset.

"Hello? This is Ngellin. Marianne?"

"Thank you, Ngellin, for taking time out to talk with me. Lren was loathe to disturb you during sunset."

"I realize it must be important."

"Ngellin, I need your help."

"My help?"

"First, I must share the news. The Sejo, that is the galactic council, has banned humanity from the galactic community for 1000 years."

"So?"

"I know, Ngellin, that you don't care much – the Kinder haven't been in touch with the Galactic Community for all of this time."

"That's correct."

"But the problem is this – Earth is now the planet of the dolphins."

"Dolphins?"

"Dolphins are the species that now have galactic enfranchisement. They have requested, and the Sejo has agreed, to remove humanity from Earth."

Ngellin was stunned. "Aren't there billions of humans on Grier Nro?"

"Yes, seven billion. We need to put them somewhere. Most will come here, but we hope to put some on Casiti and Hilcyon."

"Marianne, I'm sure that my Kinder fellows won't want any Terrans on Hilcyon, even if the planet could hold them, but it can't. Hilcyon is already strained with the people it has – it couldn't take more."

"Really? I didn't realize that."

"Yes, Marianne – it doesn't have much water, and growing food has always been difficult because of that and because of the climate."

"Thanks for the information, Ngellin. Even if we can't settle any Terrans on Hilcyon, I do think we should still be in contact with the Kinder there, and I could use your help with that."

"I am, how did you say it, 'persona non grata' among Kinder."

"I don't expect you to be in contact with them, I just need some advice. I'd like to visit, and I'm trying to figure out the best way to get permission to show up there."

Ngellin laughed. "First, you can't go alone. You are a woman. You need to find a man to go. He needs to be the leader. You need to follow."

Ngellin heard Marianne sigh. "Marianne, you know I am different now – we have talked a lot. This isn't how I feel – it's the reality of Kinder life."

"I understand, Ngellin, I do. OK, I'll have David lead."

"David must do everything. Make contact, make arrangements, everything."

"OK, I understand. In fact, the Kinder already know David."

"What?"

"We had to tell first chief Glendr about the edict. David was the one to break the news to him."

"Marianne, have David promise technology, especially technology to help with water."

"But you've had access to galactic technology…"

"Not really. The Kinder are shortsighted. We use galactic technology for war making, big warships, etc. But we did not ask for and did not use much in the way of technology to help us with living."

"OK, thank you, Ngellin. I think I can figure out how to make some clear promises around water."

"So, there will be billions more here, then."

"Yes. It will be a chaotic, strange few years. They will probably start arriving in about four years. We have 24 years to empty Earth entirely."

"I don't envy you this task, Marianne."

New Columbia, New Earth Month 2, Year 25

Marianne spoke to David on Illsenor Station. "David, any news from Hilcyon?"

"No. There has been no response to our communiqués."

Marianne exhaled. She was frustrated. "We know they got it, because it is the same communications protocols they've used with Casiti in the past. I'm a little confused as to why they are simply not responding – not even saying 'leave us alone.'"

"Maybe there are internal struggles going on. Who knows? We just need to be patient. I'm expecting that our offers of technology will mean that they will eventually come to the table."

"I guess in the end it doesn't really matter. Settling any more humans on Hilcyon doesn't make much sense from what I understand of their resource issues. But I'd like to at least start a communications process with them."

"They'll come around, Marianne. The terraforming ideas will help as well. In the meanwhile..."

"Yes, David, in the meanwhile, I have some more traveling to do. I'm in New Columbia to talk with President Mason, and I'll be going up north to the ICS to see Governor Hurler. I'll cross the river and visit the settlements in the North Central IZ. I'm looking forward to being on the river again, and, of course, it will be great to see Leticia and Mira again. I've heard such great things about how the new Medical School up there is shaping up."

Kinder ship Mrontl 35 1158

Glendr looked down at the report in his hands. All in all, they'd lost over 2,500 troops to that damned planet. 2,534 to be exact. From what he could tell, only about 150 died in battle. The rest... the rest deserted him, including two Second Chiefs, 18 Third Chiefs, and over 70 Fourth Chiefs. The sheet in his hand was the only evidence of the desertion. The official logs all had the 2,534 lost as honorably lost in battle, and none of his remaining Chiefs had any reason to advertise the desertions. Those desertions looked bad for all of them. He took out a spark lighter and lit the page on fire. He watched the flame curl toward his hand, and the smoke rise to the ceiling of his office. He dropped the sheet and stamped it out before it set off the ship's fire alarm.

It was time to leave the ship and take his place among the Kinder leadership. He had an appointment in a few time units with Supreme Chief Vondryn, to give his official report, one he wished he could miss. He gathered his things, left the office, and walked toward the docking area to catch a shuttle down to the surface.

Hilcyon, Mrontl 35 1158

"Supreme Chief Vondryn will see you, Chief Glendr." The tall attaché to the Supreme chief wore a uniform so well pressed and starched, Glendr wondered whether he ever got cut while putting it on. He nodded his head to the attaché and walked into Vondryn's cavernous office. The office that Glendr knew he would have someday.

He walked toward Vondryn's desk, and stood in front of it, and bowed deeply.

"Supreme Chief Vondryn, Glendr at your service."

"Glendr, tell me of your time on that planet, the planet settled by the Grier." Like Glendr's office, Vondryn's office had only one chair, the one on which he currently sat.

Glendr told the whitewashed story that he had rehearsed over and over again. Vondryn listened and nodded his head at appropriate moments. When he was done, Vondryn steepled his fingers.

"First of all Glendr, you are a liar, and not a very good one at that."

Glendr could feel the color drain from his face, and he felt a tingle of fear move up his spine. How could Vondryn know?

"I'm sorry, sir, I don't know what you mean."

"Don't act stupid. Just come clean. There are Kinder down on that planet that deserted, aren't there?"

"Sir?"

"We have been in communication with the Grier on that planet."

Glendr could see something in Vondryn's face – he wasn't quite telling the truth. He thought he'd dissemble a bit.

"Yes, sir, yes, a few Kinder stayed, deserted. We chose to call them lost in battle so that their families would not lose honor."

"And so you would not lose face."

Glendr bowed slightly, raising his hands, palms upward.

"Yes, Supreme Chief." The fact that Vondryn had not said anything about his comment "a few" suggested to Glendr that Vondryn had no idea of the extent of the desertions.

"I don't exactly trust you. I never quite did. First Chief Ylen, who was to be on the ship after yours, was originally slated to complete the invasion. Of course, he was unable to, and you were left. And it is clear you were unable to do much of anything, even though you were there for more than four years."

"Sir, you heard my report. The Breft used..."

"Never mind. My attaché will give you your next assignment. Get out of my sight."

Glendr bowed and left the office. He felt ashamed and angry. He vowed that Vondryn would someday regret his words.

New York, Earth, October 15, 2025

Joel looked at Lwel'in, who was piloting the shuttle down to New York. Joel liked Lwel'in. He thought he had a great sense of humor, and also a good understanding of the issues currently facing humanity. He, along with a tiny contingent of other Casitians had chosen to assign themselves to duty on the Moonbase and Sol Station to assist with the process of evacuating humankind from the planet of their birth.

Joel was angry at the Casitian leadership, and this emotion was shared by most of the Terrans who had most closely worked with them over the past 14 years. They now were overprotective of Casiti and Casitian interests, uncooperative, and largely placing the responsibility for pulling off this evacuation of Earth onto Terrans, who were far from the most able. This undertaking required technology and know-how only very recently available to Terrans. And the worst of it was that they were acting as if it were Earth's fault, when, in fact, Terrans were the least at fault. The true fault lay in the millennia-long conflict between the Casitians and the Kinder.

Their next task was to tell Earth the news. That was going to be a huge and unpleasant task. But he was happy about getting to see Diana and Janie again. They had finally gotten married, and they lived together in a nice little brownstone in lower Manhattan.

He felt the soft change in movement that signaled that they'd landed. "We've arrived. You'll call me when you need a ride?"

"Yes, Lwel'in. I expect we'll be doing a lot of traveling using planetary transportation, but I'll let you know when we need a ride. I expect we'll be down here for a several weeks."

"Okee dokee." Lwel'in smiled. One of his favorite things was using American colloquialisms.

Joel and Laura disembarked into the street across from Diana and Janie's house, and he could see Diana in the doorway. He smiled.

"Well, Joel, that's quite the story. I'm not sure I know exactly what to say, except that they chose a hell of a time in Earth history. Just as we managed to get our act together to be collectively responsible for all of Earth's people, we have to leave. Damn."

"Diana, I know, really, I know. But I also think that the fact that you are running for World President is a good thing."

"Oh, you think so? Why in God's name would I want this job now? Earth's first and last World President??"

"Diana, you are trusted with stuff like this."

"Yes, yes I know. Well, let's talk about what's needed now."

"I don't want to go to the press until I've first talked personally to the world leaders you think I should talk with, and other leaders are told."

"Fair enough. I'll get my team in place to help you out with that - and I'll get you two an office to work out of."

Hilcyon, Rtlel 10 1158

An insistent chime woke him. He hadn't been sleeping well, ever since Vondryn had assigned him to be First Chief of the desert quadrant. The only worse place would have been a mining asteroid, and Glendr thanked the Exalted King that he hadn't been assigned to one of those. It would have made his work of seeing his plans through much more difficult. As his vision cleared, he saw the blinking light on his desk communicator. He got up and answered it.

"Yes?"

"Glendr, this is Hgliz." Hgliz was an old friend of Glendr's who was acting as a spy in the capital for him. Hgliz knew that when Glendr ascended to be Supreme Chief, Hgliz would rise as well.

"Hgliz, why are you calling now? It's the middle of the night!"

"Glendr, Vondryn is dead."

"Dead? Did someone...?"

"No. Apparently he died of a sudden brain hemorrhage. Natural causes."

Glendr's mind worked rapidly. He didn't expect this, and he worried about his physical abilities at this moment. He'd just begun the strict regimen that would have gotten him into shape for the inevitable struggle to gain the Supreme leadership. Well, there would be no help for it. It was now or never.

"I'll be in the capital by daybreak."

"Glendr, you should know..."

"What?"

"There are at least four First Chiefs who have already made it clear they wish to enter the ring."

"I expect there will be more."

"One of them is Rplic, another is Ylen."

"That doesn't surprise me. Does it surprise you?"

"No, but you should know that Rplic is ... he is very skilled. And his weapon of choice is the Klee."

"Thank you, Hgliz, that's good information to have. Do you know Ylen's weapon of choice?"

"He is a master of the circle blade, I've seen him train with it, and no other weapon."

"Ah, good. That's very good. I'll see you tomorrow."

Glendr got up and began to quickly put his things together for the trip to the capital. He would not be coming back here. He either would become Supreme Chief, or he would be dead.

Mexico City, Earth, October 16, 2025

Raul Garcia looked around his office. Sometimes he had to shake himself – it was hard for him to believe how he started out as a poor fisherman who lost his boat in Baja Mexico and became one of the leaders of the Environmental Green Party of Mexico. It all started with that day that he lost his boat. After losing his boat, he moved up to Tijuana, and worked with his sister, and got involved with the local Green Party, after learning that it really was environmental pollution and overfishing that caused him to lose his boat.

As it turned out, he was a great organizer. Between the new ideas and the new consciousness engendered by the Casitians, and a long-overdue change in the Mexican democracy, the Environmental Green Party of Mexico became one of the two major parties. Raul's role was to keep the on-the-ground organizing process going – in hopes of finally making his party the leading party heading into the new election process for world leadership.

His phone rang, startling him out of his reverie. He reached across his desk to pick it up.

"Hello?"

He heard a familiar voice on the other end of the line.

"Hola, amigo, es Laura Hernandez."

"Laura! Mi amiga! Como esta?"

"Doing fine, Raul. I have some very big news for you, and I wanted you to hear it from someone you knew, before you heard it on the news."

"Big news? I guess big enough to bring you back to Earth after cruising the galaxy..." He laughed.

"Raul, this is very serious."

"Sorry chica. Tell me."

Raul could hear the intake of breath on the other end of the phone line. He sobered up, realizing something quite dire was up.

"I know you probably kept up with the news that Joel had brought last year. Humans were tried by the Sejo, the galactic community council, for violations of the use of wormholes. "

"Yes, yes. Was there a sentence?"

"Yes. Humans, from all branches, Earth, New Earth, Casitian and Za'aref, have been banned from the galactic community for 1000 years."

Raul's heart sank. He realized he'd never get to see some of the more spectacular sights he'd heard about.

"Ah, that's bad. So we are relegated to our four little planets for a long time, eh?"

"No, Raul. This is where the really bad news comes in."

"What could possibly be worse?"

"We have been told we need to evacuate Earth."

"Say what?? Leave? But..."

"It's the dolphin's planet. They petitioned the Sejo to stay. There is no other alternative but for us to leave."

"Oh, no! How long do we have? 20 or 30 years?"

"No, Raul, we have 12."

"Twelve? Twelve? That's ... ludicrous."

"It's what they ordered."

Raul sighed, and mentally moved into problem-solving mode. "Well, tell me what you need me to do, and I'll do it."

New York, Earth, October 20, 2025

"I'd like to welcome Joel Martin and Laura Hernandez. They should be quite familiar to all of you - they were instrumental in helping with the Casitian Crisis. Joel, as you might recall, was the discoverer of the signal that lead to our introduction to the Casitians. He also was the one who told us of the trial of humankind in the Galactic Council."

Joh Appel turned from looking at the camera, to looking at Joel.

"So, I guess the trial didn't go well, did it?"

"No, Joh, it didn't go well at all."

"Can you explain how it came to be that we are being forced to leave Earth?"

"Well, it's fairly simple, really. Galactic law says that any species that is banned, either permanently, like our original slaveholders, the Tud'scla, or temporarily, like we are, can have no contact with any species in the galaxy that is either an official member of the galactic community, or is a provisional member species."

"I would hardly call 1000 years 'temporary'!"

"Well, yes, Joh, I agree, but in galactic years, it's not a very long time. Remember, the Sejo has been meeting regularly for more than 50,000 years. So 1000 years isn't all that long from their perspective.

The dolphins are now an official member of the galactic community. They have representation on the Sejo. Either they get taken off of Earth or we leave. There is no other possible answer. Since we are the species deemed guilty, and the dolphins didn't want to leave, the Sejo declared that we are the ones that have to leave."

"Well, of course, I don't blame the dolphins for not wanting to leave. But making us leave... Isn't there a way to limit contact?"

"No Joh, it's not just communication - species have to be separated by wormholes that can be closed."

"You understand that most humans aren't going to want to leave."

"Of course. Why should they? But it doesn't matter. We have no choice in the matter. We have 12 years to evacuate Earth. Just 12. Assuming, and this is a big assumption, that we could start the evacuation in 2 years, we would have to evacuate more than 700 million people per year, or almost two million people per day off of earth. It's an enormous task, and we have to start now."

"People will fight to stay."

"And they will lose. There is no way we can win this. We have to just bow to the inevitable."

New York, Earth, October 31, 2025

"Trick or Treat!"

Joel watched Janie give out candy to the latest group of kids coming by the brownstone. He was dead tired. They had traveled all over the world, been on countless talk shows, talked to countless leaders, and very few people were being realistic. He was frustrated. He was glad that he had such a strong friend and leader in Diana. Otherwise, he thought they would have been sunk. It scared him to realize that their only hope in making this happen in a fairly reasonable way was if she won the election.

He'd had a communication exchange with Marianne, where he asked her if she was willing to make an appearance on Earth. She declined. He knew she had enough on her plate – having to deal both with New Earth and the Kinder, but ... it made him think again about the absence of the Casitians, and the bile started in his stomach again. Let's not go down that road, he thought.

"Joel, you look positively terrible. What can I do to help?" Janie looked at Joel sympathetically.

"I feel kind of hopeless right now, Janie."

Janie sat down next to him and put her arm around his shoulders.

"Joel, you are putting all of this on your shoulders. You can't do that - you'll buckle. It's too heavy just for you. Let others take some of the weight. You know that there are people all over the world who will help."

"I know, Janie, but ..."

"But nothing! Face it – you alone cannot make seven billion people leave Earth. It has to be a collective effort."

Joel sighed. "I know, I know. It's just so hard to watch people resist the inevitable."

"Remember, Joel, you've had months to get used to this. We've had barely two weeks. Give it time."

Joel nodded. She was right, after all. It was time to return to Moon station and start the planning process.

Lakota Territory, New Earth, Month 1, Year 25

The sunset was magnificent, as usual. This time, the sky seemed to be florescent in its display of yellows, purples, greens and blues. Wachiwi thanked the ancestors again for helping his people find this new land. Tomorrow was a big day. Chiefs from other tribes over New Earth, the Blackfoot, Navajo, Western Apache, Cherokee, and Seminole were coming to Lakota Territory to meet, and discuss the news.

Rumors had been spreading all over New Earth, and it was time for the Tribes to unite and find homes for all their tribal brothers and sisters coming from Earth. Wachiwi knew that old enmities and rivalries would rear their heads. He also knew that there was plenty of space for the tribes to settle. All of the tribes now lived far west of the Southern IZ and New America. There was plenty of land further west of them – thousands of miles of unexplored, unclaimed territory. Wachiwi knew that there were many other peoples to be settled on New Earth, but he also knew that there would be enough. Enough for them to live a life of freedom, finally, from the Wasi'chu.

He had a brief talk by audio with Marianne. He knew that she would be back to help figure out how to settle people and divide up the land equitably. She knew of the dreams of the tribes, the dreams his tribe on New Earth had already realized. They realized true sovereignty, true freedom, and the ability to determine their own destinies. He had faith that she would hold her promises to his people.

Hilcyon, Rtlel 10 1158

"Come in, come in, Wllem. I keep hearing very good things about your work around the city. You'll be a Fourth Chief in no time at the rate you're going."

William walked into Jurrl's house. He'd only been here once, a few moons after he landed. Sadre answered only to Jurrl, not to his Third chief, Ceckzl. This was very mysterious at first but became much clearer as time went on. Sadre had brought William to the capital to meet Jurrl. Now, he was back on his own.

"Thank you, Chief Jurrl. I have some important information for you."

"OK, go ahead."

"When I first arrived, I saw a woman that I recognized - she also is from Grier Nro."

"What? You are supposed to be the first person here from Grier Nro."

"Yes, I know. She had been on the asteroid mine with me and had been assigned to a Kinder man. They had managed somehow to get off of the asteroid mine and make it back here.

This was pretty suspicious to me, so I did some digging. It turns out that the man, whose name is Pkygy, is very close with Ceckzl. Pkygy was arrested originally for publishing seditious literature -- a crime which should have assured him of permanent occupation on the asteroid planet.

I have seen Ceckzl at his house a number of times. I have also seen other Kinder men at his house, together. I did some more digging and found that Ceckzl was the one who managed to get Pkygy off of the mine. "

William could see Jurrl beginning to understand the gravity of the situation.

"There's more. Beatrice, Pkygy's wife…"

"I don't care about Pkygy's wife. What could she have to do with any of this?"

"Chief Jurrl, one of the biggest mistakes Kinder men make is to underestimate the ability of women to …"

"Stop right now. If you are suggesting that they are smart enough to orchestrate some sort of rebellion, I will have you arrested for seditious thought."

William shut up. He seemed to continually hit that brick wall. They would have to learn the hard way! He bowed.

"Of course, Chief, you are right. There is no reason to think about his wife. I think there is reason enough to arrest Pkygy."

"Yes, indeed there is. And…"

Jurrl walked to his desk and lifted up a piece of paper. "There happens to be an open Fourth Chief spot in the Wrzcol district of Wlentry. The poor sod got hit by a transport, and there really isn't anyone I trust there to take over. Interested?"

"Of course! Thank you for your faith in me, Chief Jurrl."

"I think you are going places, boy."

Hilcyon, Rtlel 14 1158

Glendr wiped the blood from his face as he sat down on the bench for the short rest period. The audience was raucous. He was exhausted from 2 days of fighting. First, he bested First Chief Ghnor, which was easy. Ghnor was out of shape, overweight, and slow. Next, had been Rplic. Rplic was harder. He was young, but inexperienced. He had more stamina than Glendr, but didn't know the weapons as well, and didn't have the moves. Glendr knew that he had to kill Rplic fast, before he lost his stamina. He'd managed, but barely.

Now he was facing his most difficult adversary, and he was afraid he was going to lose. Ylen was the same age as Glendr, and had about the same amount of experience, but Ylen was in superior shape, and clearly had been working hard with fighting coaches for this day. Had Glendr had time to train … but that didn't matter. He hadn't had time. And it was showing.

Glendr's weapon of choice was the circle blade. A wickedly curved blade at the end of a long staff. It could be a weapon to slice, or he could use the other end to bludgeon. Ylen chose a short sword. This was a surprise to Glendr, since Hgliz had told Glendr that Ylen was a master of the circle blade. A short sword was one of the few weapons that had an advantage against the circle blade. Glendr thought that Ylen had changed his blade choice, until he saw him with that sword. He was a master with it, and adept at avoiding either side of Glendr's weapon. So far in the three fighting periods, Ylen had been the only one to draw blood.

Glendr held out some hope. He knew some tricks with his blade that he hadn't shown yet, on purpose. It had always been his plan to get Ylen overconfident, then move in with some of his best moves for the kill. He had only one more fighting period left to do it in.

The loud bell rang, and Glendr took a last drink of liquid, and a last wipe of the towel on his face, and he got up again to face Ylen, swinging his weapon.

Ylen feinted with his short sword, and Glendr recognized the moves Ylen was making. Glendr laughed inside. He didn't think Ylen's fighting trainers were all that good, after all. Glendr started the first of his special moves, designed to draw Ylen closer to him in an unguarded way, and Glendr was happy to see that Ylen was following his lead, and doing what he expected him to do. Glendr thought, a couple of more moves, and he'd have Ylen.

Glendr shifted his weight, did the right feint, then the left, and watched Ylen follow. As he swung around to slice Ylen's exposed neck with his blade, he saw a glint of metal where he didn't expect it. His swing brought his midsection right into the blade, and before he could complete his swing, he felt a sharp pain and looked down to see the short sword's hilt in his chest. There was no time for regret. He fell, hearing the roar of the crowd, and then knew no more.

Hilcyon, Rtlel 15 1158

Ylen sat in his new, spacious office, writing a few notes for his speech to the gathered First Chiefs. In reality, he had worked most of his life for this day. It all started with his mother. He had been twelve. He had just come home from being beaten up by the local boys for being a weakling. When his father saw him, he beat him even more, telling him he would turn out to no good, unless he could best other boys.

After his father left the house, his mother bathed him, dressed his wounds, and began to read to him stories he would never forget. Those stories gave him hope: hope that someday he could make things different among Kinder. And every step of the way, he was blessed. Every barrier for him was easily jumped, or spontaneously disappeared. Yes, he trained, and worked hard, and told no one of his dreams. But they stayed with him, all this time. He wished his mother were alive to see him.

The subjects of those stories, the Breft and Grier, had always been so far away. But now, they had come into his life, and the life of all Kinder, with an unimaginable force. To Ylen, the timing was astonishing. Two moons after the Breft and Grier are known to them, Vondryn dies, and he became Supreme Chief. He knew this was destined by the Exalted King.

There was a quiet knock on the door, and it opened, with the face of his attaché, Hgliz.

"Supreme Chief, your audience awaits you."

"Thank you, Hgliz. And Hgliz?"

"Yes, sir?"

"Thank you for your service to me. I imagine I could have won against Glendr anyway, but your work with him made it easier."

Hgliz nodded. "Supreme Chief, I want to see the Kinder change. Glendr was more of the same. It was worth all the risk."

Ylen rose and bowed to Hgliz. "I am in your debt." They walked together to the room where he would face his First Chiefs.

As he spoke, he could hear the murmurs start. He knew would have to move slowly and be fierce.

He barked, "if you have something to say, say it to me."

The room went silent. He knew that many were already plotting his demise.

"The Grier are offering us technology to make our lives better. I am going to accept their offer. We need to make our lives better here. We have too many children who die and too many women who die in childbirth. We are crowded into smaller communities than we need to be. With water we can grow more food, and spread out, and finally grow our population and become more of a power among humans."

A hand went up. It was Rplo. He was going to be trouble, he knew. "Yes?"

"Supreme Chief, I worry about the influence of these people. We already have a growing rebellion on our hands."

"Yes, of course. We will keep contact between the Kinder and the Grier to a minimum." In fact, he had no such intention.

"But Supreme Chief..."

He raised his voice. "Do any of you question my leadership? If so, I hear that they have just finished cleaning the ring."

There was silence. He knew that all of the First Chiefs that had been inclined had already entered the ring. He was the only one left. None of these would try to best him anytime soon. And if his plans went the way he expected, he would be the last Supreme Chief of the Kinder.

New Aard, New Earth, Month 2, Year 25

Olam often thought of his friend and mentor Abdul. Abdul had dreamed of a day when the leadership of New Aard would soften and allow progressive voices. That time had come. He was a new member of the New Aard Parliament, and leader of the progressive coalition.

He was sitting around the table with other leaders, discussing immigration. He liked the vision of a unified Islamic state, with different regions governed autonomously, depending upon whether they were Sunni or Shia, with secular or sharia law. People would immigrate and migrate to the regions according to how they wanted to live. Olam imagined a varied, vibrant future where Turks lived with Somalis and Egyptians, and Iraqis and Iranians sharing regions, and more. National borders wouldn't matter anymore.

Because Olam was a political, rather than religious leader, the whole question of where Mecca would go was a conversation he was not privy to. He knew that they were doing varied calculations, trying to figure out where in New Aard Mecca would go. It was mind-boggling to think about Mecca. As it was, Muslims on New Aard now prayed pointing toward Earth, which could sometimes mean standing up looking at the sky, or prostrate, looking at the floor, through New Earth, toward where Earth was.

He didn't know how the Masjid Al-Haram and the Kaaba were going to get transported here. He assumed that the Casitians had the wherewithal to do it. He knew that some proposed leaving Mecca where it was and postponing the one of the pillars of Muslim observance for 1000 years. He wished that Abdul were here to tell him what he thought of the whole thing.

"Olam" Olam was shaken out of his reverie.

"Yes."

"We need you to join the committee to work with the Casitians on infrastructure building. That seems like it might be up your alley."

Olam nodded. "Of course. I'm happy to."

New Calgary, New Earth, Month 2, Year 25

Marianne and Leticia sat together on the bench in the park, across the street from where the new medical school was to be built.

"You're leaving again?"

Marianne gave a short chuckle. "Going to Hilcyon. It seems my destiny to do this shit."

Leticia smiled. "Not your destiny, Aunt Marianne, you're good at it."

"Well perhaps that's true. What's also true is that they were very clear that no Casitians could come. Not as if any Casitians wanted to! I'll go and talk to the new Supreme Chief guy. Well, no, I'm not going to talk to the guy, David is. It's infuriating."

"I can imagine. It's like they have stone-age patriarchy or something."

"That's exactly what they have. Anyway, I don't really expect to be gone too long. We're establishing communications and doing a technology transfer. Even though we know that Hilcyon can't handle them, I got the strange feeling that this guy would have welcomed some immigrants."

"Really?"

"I watched while David talked with him via video link. He came across as ... well, soft. Almost as soft as the Kinder I met with down south. Surprising."

"Maybe he wants change."

"It's hard to believe that someone who has attained that status in Kinder society wants change, but you never know."

Marianne looked up to see Mira approaching with bags of lunch in hand.

"I thought I should bring you both lunch. Leticia seems to forget to eat if I don't feed her."

Marianne looked at both of them and smiled. She was happy for Leticia. Happy that she'd found her place after a tough time in the ICS, and happy that she'd found Mira. They started to dive into the sandwiches.

"So, you two, I need your help."

Leticia started to talk around the sandwich in her mouth. "How?"

"I need you to be the coordinators for medical services in a zone of New Earth."

Mira looked up. "Zone?"

"This is an idea cooked up by David and your father, Mira. The idea is to divide New Earth into zones and regions, with equal amounts of natural resources. They thought that dividing up New Earth into zones, and then determining immigration patterns per zone would be the wisest course. There will probably be about ten zones and ten regions per zone. The zone I'm asking you to be in charge of will likely encompass all of the NCIZ, as well as a big area north of the Mississippi and Lake Superior."

"That area hasn't even been explored, let alone settled."

"I know. But it must be."

"OK! Count us in. I've always wanted to travel up north."

Mira rolled her eyes. "Oh, no. We just got started here, and you want to travel more? You are incorrigible. Of course, I have to come with you."

"I'm sure Thomas and Jeffrey would want to come too. There might be some other varieties of medicinal plants up there."

"Well, I'll leave this to you. I'll get Douglas to send you the plan for that zone when it is finalized. Oh, Leticia, go visit your mother before you go traveling. She misses you and wants to see you more often."

"OK, Aunt Marianne, I will. And let me know if you hear anything about the missing teenagers."

"They are one of the first items of our agenda with that Supreme Chief guy! No teenagers, no water tech."

Hilcyon, Rtlel 15 1158

The loud knocking on the door woke her up. When there was silence, she thought perhaps she'd dreamed it. But it came again, and then Pkygy awoke, and turned on the light. He looked at her with fright.

"Open up!" The banging continued, and Pkygy arose from bed and walked into the living room. Beatrice quickly put on a robe and followed, entering into the room to see five men storm in and tackle Pkygy.

"What are you doing?! Pkygy!"

"Shut up, woman; go back into your bedroom, now!"

One of the men shoved her ungently back, and she stumbled into the bedroom. She heard the door slam shut behind her. She didn't know what to do. If she opened the bedroom door again, she knew they might hurt her, so she went to the window, and began to open it. As she did, she saw the men walk by with Pkygy in tow, chains around his wrists and ankles. She sat down on her bed and wept.

She didn't know what else to do, so after the sun rose, she dressed, and went to see Tivyl... She knocked on Tivyl's door, and Tivyl opened it, looking as distraught as Beatrice felt.

"Oh no..."

Tivyl nodded. "They came and took Ceckzl last night. They took Pkygy?"

Beatrice nodded.

"We must find out how many other men were arrested. But we must be careful. Go home; wait for me or Krely to come to you. It will be fine."

Beatrice nodded, and turned and walked back to her house. She had no confidence it would be fine.

Hilcyon, Rtlel 30 1158

Marianne looked down at the planet's surface from the shuttle windows. It almost looked to her like Mars – dull, cloudless, and dry. There were no oceans, or even any rivers or lakes she could see. No wonder the Kinder were tough. She'd talked at length with W'ren, who had been unceremoniously yanked from the project terraforming Mars when the Sejo had made its decision. After that talk, she'd convinced members of the Caraj that in the long term, terraforming Hilcyon was going to be worth pursuing. It was a huge planet, with a lot of frozen water. W'ren was convinced that there were just a few small adjustments to be made, and Hilcyon could become as verdant as Earth in as little as 50 years. She knew, also, that if the Kinder could have done that sort of thing, they would have done it a long time ago. That was a piece of technology that they would be dangling in front of the Kinder at some point.

As she looked out the window, she could begin to see settlements – small hexagonally shaped hamlets, bordered with neat lines. She thought it was an interesting way for people to arrange themselves. She and David were coming to Hilcyon as official representatives of Earth. This was the third planet Marianne had been able to visit. She was sad that she never made it to any other non-human planets, and she could not imagine fitting in time to see any before the 12 years was up.

The Kinder were reluctant enough to allow Terrans access to Hilcyon – they absolutely forbid the presence of Casitians on the surface, people they called "Breft". Many hundreds of years ago, there had been an active trade between the two planets, although Marianne suspected that the Kinder were more in need of Casitian goods than the Casitians needed Kinder goods. Casiti had given the Kinder many food plants. At some point about eleven hundred years ago, that trade had come to a halt and there had been no Kinder/Casitian contact since. Marianne didn't know why that happened, and the Casitians refused to talk about it.

The shuttle was piloted entirely by remote control by W'ren in orbit. They were directed to land on a pad near a large building in the Capital. They settled down and opened the door to the hatch and stepped out. She had let David lead, and leave first. It was going to be a challenge for her to keep quiet, she knew.

It was cold, with a breeze blowing from the north. She could see two groups of people walking toward them, and as they got closer, she saw three men followed by two women. David walked toward the men, and Marianne realized she needed to wait for the women to approach.

One of the women started to talk, and after a short delay, Marianne's translator AI began to speak in her ear.

"Hello. My name is Wtric. I am Supreme Chief Ylen's wife. This is my servant, Jrlil. She will see to your every need. Please come with me, I can show you the quarters your husband has been assigned to, so you can prepare whatever he needs."

Marianne wondered what they would think of what the actual truth was. David and she were best friends, had been for years. David had a male companion, and Marianne ... well, Marianne would have a female companion if... She let that thought go.

"Thank you, Wtric. Let me get our bags..."

Jrlil quickly walked past Marianne and picked up both bags that were just inside the door of the shuttle. Wtric lead the way, and the three of them walked to a small vehicle, which took them through the city to a small dwelling tucked in the corner of a dead-end street. They walked into the dwelling and Wtric gave her a little tour.

"The bedroom is over here, and next to it is the toilet. The tub is on the other side, over here."

Marianne could not for the life of her figure out why the tub would be on the other side of the bedroom from the toilet. And she didn't understand why there wasn't a sink. But she didn't ask.

"The kitchen is here. There is a box full of food for you, and food in the icebox, here. Of course, if you don't want to cook, Jrlil here can cook for you."

"Thank you Wtric. I appreciate that. I do know how to cook..." she stopped herself. She realized that she would make a mistake if she revealed that she'd been on Casiti, cooking using the same vegetables and other ingredients that she knew they had here.

"I know how to cook for my husband."

Wtric smiled. "Well, there may be some things you'll need help with. I imagine the food is different on Grier Nro."

Marianne was already tired. "Wtric, thank you so much for the help. I want to spend some time preparing for my husband."

"Of course, of course. Forgive me. Jrlil is staying next door, and there is a bell here." She pointed to a small indent in the wall of the kitchen. "Ring it when you need her help."

"Thank you so much. I'm sure I'll see you tomorrow."

"Yes, you will. There is a large state dinner planned in your honor the day after tomorrow."

Marianne tried to smile, and saw them to the door, and closed it behind them. She wasn't looking forward to state dinners, or anything else, really. She sank into a chair.

After a long while, David walked in.

"Aye, aye aye."

"Yes?"

"This is going to be interesting, Marianne."

"Why do you say that David?"

"I spent what felt like forever with Ylen and five men he called 'First Chiefs.' In their presence he was bombastic, demanding, rigid and insulting. When they left, he was a completely different person. Marianne, he spent his whole life working to get where he is so he can change things. He is playing a very dangerous game, and we have to help him. He wants change, big change. He wants to be the last Supreme Chief of the Kinder to be chosen by death battle. He wants future leaders to elected."

"Chosen by death battle?"

"That's how leaders become leaders. For any Chiefs lower than First Chiefs, if a Chief dies, then the Chief above him can appoint someone. But anyone below a Chief can challenge a Chief to a battle to the death. The one who wins is now that Chief. The Supreme Chief is the worst. Apparently Ylen had to kill three men to get his current job. He said that he's killed seven in total."

"That's completely barbaric!"

"Well, as I said, he wants it to change. Anyway, this visit is going to be short, and not very productive."

"I'm confused."

"We agreed that he needed to play this slowly, and that we'd be backing him all the way. He said that there was a burgeoning movement among the people here, but the time hasn't come to link all of this up. Soon, but not now."

"So what are we doing?"

"We're going to go to the state dinner, pretend to be bored and bothered, stay a couple of days, and then leave empty handed. But not really, of course."

Marianne nodded. "OK, I can handle a short visit. In fact, I prefer a short visit. Did you ask about the teenagers?"

"Yes. I asked about them first in the presence of the First Chiefs. And Ylen blew up at me. But then, later, he told me exactly where they are. He said that he as operatives on all of the asteroids, and we can go and pick them up. There won't be a fight. We should signal to W'ren to get a ship large enough to carry them. He said there should be about 17,000 of them."

Marianne whistled. "I knew there were a lot, but 17,000? It will be good to see Beatrice again."

Casiti, 45 Nird 784

Jal'end'a rose, slowly, composing her thoughts. She was speaking to the Caraj, in a public, open joining. She knew that this moment could make all of the difference. There were hundreds of people in attendance, seated in the tiers of seats around and behind the central table where the 12 members of the Caraj met. She recognized members that she knew well, such as Erit'ala, Yr'len and Hetl'zef. She'd had less opportunity to get to know the others. She smiled, remembering the history of the 12 seats, and realized that it might be useful to invoke it.

"Honored members of the Caraj, and guests, I thank you for this opportunity to hear my voice. As you know, I have spent many years in silence, contemplating what it means to be human. I broke out of this life of silence once before, more than a year ago, to help us become united with the planet of our origin and learn about their lives and cultures. I am breaking out again, now, because this time is critical to human history.

I know that for many of you, it was a shock to learn how much humans from Earth seemed to resemble the Kinder, our fellow human sisters and brothers who we have been cut off from for hundreds of years. We saw them as warlike and patriarchal, greedy and full of hatreds. Of course, this is what it means to be human. And, surprisingly, we found many humans that were a lot like us.

Casitians like to say that we have evolved beyond these characteristics we find problematic. We've put away our warlike nature, we've eschewed violence and greed, and we support one another, and love one another equally. But, of course, the instant that we are faced with what feels to us like an existential threat – the threat of many humans here on Casiti – we balk. No, we don't balk, we become greedy and hateful."

There were murmurs in the room, and she could see several people with looks of disdain on their faces. She kept going.

"I have done a deep study of Earth spiritual traditions. Those qualities of hatred and greed are often decried on Earth. In one of their traditions, they are two of the 'Three Poisons.' We share so much with Terrans. Of course, we must – they are our blood, our genetic material. I also want to remind you of how much we share with the Kinder. Yes, I will call them 'The Kinder!' Our word for them, 'The accursed' comes only because we have chosen to curse them. We invested in them all of our faults, all of our shadows, assuming that we had none left. But now we see the shadows right in front of us."

"Do you know why there are 12 of you sitting around this table?" Jal'end'a paused. She didn't expect anyone to answer, even those who knew the history.

"There are 12 of you because the Tud'scla organized humans into groups of 12 for maximal control. And do you know why groups of 12? Is it some magic number that the Tud'scla came up with out of thin air? No, it's not. It is because the Tud'scla had 12 fingers!"

She heard more murmurings. "We can no more leave behind the history of that time that shaped us, that made us who we are, than we can turn away from the needs of our fellow humans. We are Casitians! We take care of each other, even if it means hardship for ourselves.

There are two continents on our planet that are free for settlement. One continent has abundant land for raising food. The other has abundant shoreline for harvesting the riches of the ocean. Casiti has benefited from the technology of the galactic community for hundreds of years. We can build cities, build dwellings, and build farms for the humans who need space to live. And remember, what we do here, now, determines whether or not the galactic community will welcome us in a quarter millennium. We are the leaders. We are the ones that can lead the Kinder and the Terrans to a kind of society that the Galactic Community will welcome back with open arms. I know that, and you know that. And you also know that the strategies of separation will not work – that is why we here, now. We must end them for the good of future generations. It is our duty."

She sat down, and there was silence. And then, the room erupted in applause and shouts, so loudly that it astonished her. She was overwhelmed by the response of the people. After a time, she heard the loud ring of the bell, calling everyone back to order. She looked around the room and saw a new kind of expression on the faces around her. Expressions of determination, joy and assurance had replaced the earlier expressions of fear and anxiety.

Hetl'zef began to speak.

"Thank you for coming to order. Thank you, Jal'end'a for your eloquent speech. We have much to learn from you, and we hope that you will be willing to lend us your wisdom now and again." Jal'end'a nodded her head once in response.

"We have before us a proposal sponsored by five members of the Caraj, to send to Earth details and data on Jul'when and Loc'deher, as well as to organize a task force to begin the process of building infrastructure on those continents for settlement by approximately one billion Terrans. In addition, this proposal includes the settlement of as many as five million carefully screened Terran settlers to live with us on Rel'toro. Is there discussion of this proposal?"

At that moment, Re'il stood up. "I wish to tender my resignation from the Caraj. In all honesty, I cannot agree to this. However, I cannot stand in the way - I can see that now." He turned and walked out of the room, not looking back. Jal'end'a could understand the bind he felt himself in and felt compassion for him.

After some discussion, questions, and some amendments to the proposal, the Caraj reached consensus. Jal'end'a was glad, and for the first time, she felt that the future status of humans was more assured than she'd thought.

Hilcyon, Rtlel 31 1158

The rumors were flying. Beatrice had been convening the women continuously, even though she feared for her life. She couldn't stop. Pkygy was imprisoned, and the work must go on. The rumors she heard from several women was that a man from Grier Nro, Earth, had arrived with his wife, and was meeting with the new Supreme Chief, Ylen. She was trying to figure out how she could get to the Capital to see them. She thought that if she could tell them who she was, they could help save Pkygy.

Beatrice had found her connection. Tivyl's sister, who Tivyl had recruited to the cause, was the wife of a First Chief. Her sister knew Wtric, the wife of Ylen. After some discussion, it was decided that it would be best for Beatrice to travel to the Capital and find a way to contact them. Wtric had said that there was a state dinner, and that she could arrange for Beatrice to be a servant at the dinner, giving her a chance to meet the Grier. Beatrice thought it was a good plan, and she was hurriedly preparing to leave to catch the next tram to the Capital city.

When she showed up at the back door of the large hall where the dinner was to happen, she was ushered in by Wtric, given a uniform, and told her job. She did it and kept working for hours. Finally, Wtric came in, and handed her a large platter, heavy with a sweet dessert.

"This is a special dessert for the visitors. If anyone questions you, tell them that I said the visitors specially requested it."

"Thank you, Wtric."

"Go, go."

Beatrice shouldered the heavy platter, and walked through the hall, toward the dais. She couldn't imagine how she was going to manage to talk with the visitors. There were far too many people around. She wished she'd thought of bringing a paper message. She kept walking, and then she looked up at the dais, and almost dropped the platter when she saw who was sitting there. She realized then that she likely didn't have to say much, if anything. Aunt Marianne would recognize her at once. Marianne hadn't looked her way yet, so she kept going. All of a sudden, a large man was in her way.

"Where are you going, woman?"

"To the dais, sir. Wtric said that this platter of sweets was especially requested by the guests."

He looked at her doubtfully, but then stepped aside. As he did, Marianne saw Beatrice, and she could see the recognition dawn. She saw Marianne stand up. The man next to her looked at her with alarm. She said something to him, and he responded, and she sat back down, still looking directly at Beatrice. It seemed no one else had noticed. She finally got to the dais and put the platter down in front of them. Beatrice thought quickly of what to say to them.

"Gift of Wtric. She knows. This is a very good sweet."

A booming voice, which belonged to the man next to the visitors said, "yes, my friends, this is the sweet called Htlendrz. If it was made with the direction of my wife, it will be delicious."

Beatrice bowed, and turned and walked back to the kitchen. She could feel Marianne's eyes follow her the entire way, but she did not dare look back.

Wuj'tren, 50 Nird 784

Re'alo looked across the table at the squat humanoid with the square face and no neck, hair that looked like flat ribbons, and a large protrusion where his nose should be. He'd gotten used to their appearance over the past few days, since he had been meeting with one Krumptia after another. But every once in a while, as he looked at one, he got this weird shiver down his spine.

Re'alo was the Casitian liaison to the Galactic officials who were overseeing the evacuation of Earth. There was a lot to deal with, and a lot at stake. He wished that the Caraj had seen fit to give him some help, but here he was, all alone on Wuj'tren, trying to figure it all out.

The Krumptian, whose name was unpronounceable for Re'alo, slid a tablet toward him, and started to speak. Then, the AI translator kicked in.

"Here are the data on all of the available colony ships. We have 4,200 currently in service. With those ships, we can evacuate Earth in about 16 trips per ship over the course of 10 Earth years."

"I don't know how realistic that is – is there a way to build more?"

"We have started to build more – we can generate another 2,000 ships over the course of the next 5 Earth years. That would mean that we could reduce the number of trips per ship down to about ten."

"That's more reasonable. When can the first colony ships be on Earth?"

"We can send the first 1,000 to Earth within this Earth year. The next 3,200 will arrive within 2 years."

Re'alo nodded his head. "I think that works."

The Krumptian slid another tablet toward Re'alo.

He said, "here is the technology transfer information you wanted. The Sejo has given us instructions to give to you all of the technology transfer information you desire. They understand the hardship that evacuating Earth is causing, and they want to make sure you will have what you need."

"Thank you. When can we expect those shipments that we've requested so far for New Earth and Casiti?"

"You'll have them within the Earth year."

"Thank you. Is there anything else we need to discuss? I think I'm ready to head home and work with my people to figure this out."

"We need to finalize the wormhole closure procedure."

"Now? We're still almost 12 years from the deadline."

Re'alo still could not decipher Krumptia emotions. He couldn't tell a laugh from a sigh, or anger from happiness. All sorts of strange sounds were coming from the Krumptian, but the translator wasn't kicking in. Finally, he heard, "It is our duty to get this right. You will not stand in our way by delaying the inevitable. The wormhole will be closed on schedule, and we need to finalize the procedure."

Re'alo knew by those words that it hadn't been laughter. He realized the Krumptia didn't trust him, or rather, didn't trust humans.

"Fine, fine. You tell me what you need from me to finalize the procedure."

After another long period of discussion, it was finally worked out to the satisfaction of the Krumptian. Re'alo didn't really know why it mattered so much, but then he realized that from the Krumptian's point of view, they were responsible for making sure that this big thing of isolating a species was done exactly right. Their reputation as the bureaucrats of the galaxy depended on it. Re'alo was looking forward to going home.

Beijing, Earth, October 20, 2025

Chin had been glued to her laptop and video screens for hours after the edict was announced. She had been only twelve when the "Casitian Crisis" first occurred in 2011. She had learned all she could about Casiti since then and had been on a very long waiting list for permission to emigrate to Casiti.

Pundits were saying that the Casitians wouldn't want any Earth humans. Ever since the Kinder were discovered, many people had made conclusions about the Casitians that Chin didn't think were true. And they also seemed to idealize the Kinder, which she also figures wasn't the truth, either. Chin hoped that in this crisis, the Casitians would be willing to accept some Earth humans. She knew that they had space on Casiti to take at least some.

As she heard the analysis, and China's leader Leigin Shan, who wanted to fight the Galactics to stay on Earth, she realized that she wanted to be in the first wave of emigrants away from Earth. She had always wanted to leave, anyway, and she was afraid of what might occur on Earth. She was in good position to make that real as a highly sought-after agronomist who had done her Ph.D. Work on Casitian methods for growing high-value food in harsh climates. She had begun to use many of those techniques in the highlands of Tibet.

She needed to figure out who she would need to talk with in order to start her emigration process.

New Columbia, New America, Month 2, Year 25

Rita was having a hard time believing her eyes as she looked down at the unfolded flier. How dare these young upstarts and leaders from far flung settlements threaten what New America had built! How dare they use the excuse of the Galactic edict to cause unrest! She was incensed. Rita had spent most of the last 25 New Earth years making herself a central figure in New Earth politics. She never ran for anything, but was an insider, a behind-the-scenes dealmaker. Anyone who was anyone in New America had to go to her in order to win any seat they wanted. Even though she didn't work, she had everything she needed in life: a large, beautiful house, servants to help her, and many movers and shakers of New America at her beck and call.

She had to work fast. The first thing she would do is make sure that the venue these people had chosen would cancel. Then, she would make sure that no other venue would accept them. That would probably do the trick. She noticed several names on the organizer's list who were residents of New Columbia. She would have certain people pay them visits, and make sure that they understood the nature of their efforts.

"Ms. Reid?" Rita looked up to see one of her servant walk into the room.

"Ah, yes, Gloria, just in time. Can you ..."

"Ms. Reid, I need to speak with you."

"Does it have to be now? I have so much for you and Ronald to do."

"Yes, Ms. Reid, it has to be now."

"Well, then, make it quick, what is it?"

"I'm quitting, Ms. Reid. I can be here until the end of the day, if you need me..."

"Quitting? What on earth do you mean?"

"Isn't that self-explanatory? I'm quitting. Leaving. Ronald is coming with me."

"But I treat you both so well and pay you well." Gloria's face showed a contempt Rita could not understand.

"Ms. Reid, we are moving to the South Central Independent Zone, where I can use the skills I had when I immigrated to New Earth. We believed in New America, but all staying here has gotten us is menial jobs, barely decent housing, and no education for our college-aged kids. New America never really cared about making things work for the majority of its citizens. I've already accepted an offer to work in the Mayor's office of San Antonio, doing city planning. Ronald got a job in a construction firm, and my children are enrolling in SIZU this coming month."

Rita was insulted and realized that Gloria must have been brainwashed by the same people that were organizing that conference.

"Well, fine, go ahead and leave now. I don't care."

Without another word, Gloria turned from Rita and left. Rita went out to her foyer, and realized that she no longer had a driver, either. With a sigh, she went back into her office, and called the labor bureau where she'd gotten Gloria and Ronald a year ago. She heard the following recorded message:

"We're sorry, but we are currently closed. There are no laborers available, and there is currently a waiting list of more than 100 people looking for workers. If you wish to add your name to that list, please visit our site on the widenet. We are sorry for any inconvenience."

She went to their site on the widenet, only to be greeted by a message in large letters simply saying "Waiting list too full. No new workers have signed on in three weeks."

She wondered what was happening in New America – how could she have missed this? She made a few phone calls, and after speaking with several of her friends, it seemed as if this week was the week all of the servants decided to emigrate from New America.

Chapter 3:
The First will be Last

(AP) December 1, 2025

World Presidential Elections in High Gear as Earth Evacuation Debate Continues

Geneva – The debate about whether to fight the galactic edict to leave Earth or to evacuate has become the key issue differentiating the two primary candidates for World President, Leigin Shan, and Diana Westinghouse-Lewis. Ms. Westinghouse-Lewis, from the United States, was a key member of the team which introduced the Casitians to Earth, and prepared Earth for the new reality of the galactic community. She is adamant that we cannot fight the edict but must plan for a calm evacuation.

Leigin Shan, from the People's Democracy of China, was one of the key architects of the Chinese democracy and argues that we must fight to stay on Earth, and we can win.

The first debate will be in the New Year, on January 10, 2026.

Casiti, 55 Nird 784

Erit'ala had her hands around her cup of fuge and was remembering a conversation they had over cups of fuge four years ago. So much had happened since.

"I see you have come to the same conclusion as I have, Ja'el."

"Yes, I have. I can't see how it makes sense for me to be involved. My emotions are too ... too tied up to think clearly."

"We had our time, Ja'el. It's time for others to take over."

"I know. Re'alo and W'ren are so competent. Jal'end'a speaks so eloquently. There are others who are stepping up. They don't really need our expertise, anyway, this is such a different set of issues."

"Silandra, too, has decided to step out, and focus on writing the history from her perspective."

"There is much to learn. I feel that we made so many mistakes."

"How could we not? I feel that we are learning from those mistakes. I look forward to welcoming Terrans, and eventually... Kinder. Jal'end'a is right – we must be united as a species."

"I am thinking of spending some time on New Earth."

"Really?"

"Yes, Erit'ala. I'd like to learn more about what has been started there and visit Marianne again. I miss her, and I feel there are some wounds that I need to help heal."

Hilcyon, Wtler 30 1158

David and Marianne were back in their dwelling after the state dinner. Marianne was feeling a bit ill, and she didn't know whether it was from the food or from seeing Beatrice.

"So what do you want to do?" David was sitting in a chair that was far from comfortable in their shared quarters as Marianne paced.

"Honestly, go grab her and leave! But there's something strange going on. It seems that she's in danger somehow. We need to talk with Wtric."

"How in God's name did she get here?"

"Your guess is as good as mine."

They heard a knock at the door. They opened it, and Wtric entered.

"I shouldn't be here, but I wanted you to know that woman who gave you sweets..."

"We know who she is."

"I saw the family resemblance. It's a good thing Kinder men don't pay women any attention. If it had been your husband, you probably would all be in prison now. She's your...?"

"My sister's daughter."

"I see. Anyway, she and her husband have been organizing things she calls "cells" for change on Hilcyon. Her husband was arrested for sedition a moon ago or so. She needs help in getting him released. "

"Craig?"

"His name is Pkygy." Marianne let that sink in.

"Is there a way I can see her?"

"Not safely, no. But I will tell you where she lives, in case you have ways of getting around without being seen." Marianne realized that Wtric was much smarter than she'd given her credit for.

David said, "what about Pkygy? Can we figure out a way to have him released?"

Wtric looked at David with a look Marianne could not decipher. "You need to talk with my husband about that, I cannot say. I must go now. I'm sorry."

She walked out the door quickly, leaving Marianne and David puzzled.

New York, Earth, January 10, 2026

Diana was nervous. She didn't think she'd ever been this nervous in her life. She was running for first World President... so she could be its last. It was sobering and scary. Her opponent, Leigin Shan, had emerged from the new Chinese Democratic Party, to be a world leader that many people looked up to. He was adamant that humans fight to stay on Earth. Diana knew that was futile, and she knew that if she lost this election to Shan, there would be much bloodshed – bloodshed she wanted to avoid at all costs.

Joh Appel was moderating the debate. She could hear the producers in the background counting down the seconds to being live on the air.

"Welcome, World, to the first of four debates between the two candidates for World President, Diana Westinghouse-Lewis, from the United States and Leigin Shan, from the People's Democracy of China. The coin was tossed, and Ms. Westinghouse-Lewis won, but chose to have Mr. Shan start with his statement. Mr. Shan..."

Joh turned his chair toward Shan, who took a breath, and began to speak in Chinese. The translation started a few seconds later.

"People of the World, we in a perilous time. We have been asked to leave the planet of our birth. We were born here – our species evolved from others that were born here. We are of Earth clay. ALL humans, whether Terrans, Casitians or Kinder are of Earth Clay. We must stay here. We must fight to keep the planet of our birth."

Shan had much more to say, but Diana was filtering it out, working on her statement in her head. She knew what she had to say. It was painful and devastating, but the truth.

After Shan finished speaking, Joh turned his chair toward her. "Ms. Westinghouse-Lewis, your statement."

"Everything Mr. Shan has just said about the origin of the human race is correct. All humans are from Earth. Earth is our planet. We evolved here, from species that evolved here. We are inextricably linked to this planet.

But this is as true of us as it is of our Dolphin cousins. And, sadly, it doesn't matter. The Galactic government has given this planet to them, and we must leave. There is no choice here. None of this is truly our fault. It is the fault of a millenniums-old conflict between the Casitians and the Kinder. The truth is, that conflict is borne of the fact that human beings haven't yet learned to live with each other peacefully.

In any event, we must leave. You remember what it was like when the Casitians arrived. The Galactics are a force we cannot overcome, no matter what we do. They have tools at their disposal that will make leaving this planet far more unpleasant than it has to be.

I am running for World President so that I can oversee a peaceful, orderly, and compassionate leaving of Earth, instead of a violent, chaotic, and forced leaving. We have no choice in whether to leave. Our only choice left is how we leave."

Joh Appel turned to Shan. "My first question, Mr. Shan, is given the strength and power of the Galactic Community, exactly how do you intend to fight being removed from Earth?"

It was here that Shan stumbled. Interestingly to Diana, he clearly hadn't put much thought into logistics. He was simply thinking of the fight, but not how the fight could be won.

When it was Diana's turn, she made it clear that she'd considered, long and hard, all of the options. She laid out the options to fight, and the best strategies, then reminded the audience of the end of the New Earth emigration process. She then laid out, very clearly, her plans for evacuation. She said there wasn't really much else to call it, so we'd might as well get used to it.

When she was at home, later, she read the reviews of the debate. Most analysts felt that she'd won it, hands down, and polls agreed. She'd likely be elected. It's just that this wasn't a job she wanted.

Hilcyon, Wtler 33 1158

The effort had felt monumental to David. Messages to Ylen, waiting, then conversations with Hgliz, then more waiting. Finally, it seemed it was going to work out. Strings would be pulled, Hgliz and David would visit Pkygy in prison, and Pkygy would be released. Pkygy would go with David to the shuttle, where Marianne would be waiting, and then they would leave. They would then secretly drop back down to pick up Beatrice. It all made sense, but it made both of them nervous.

For now, David was waiting for Hgliz to arrive, and Marianne was pacing the floor of the living room.

"I've got a communications device to talk with W'ren if anything goes wrong, and I've given him the coordinates of Beatrice's residence. We'll easily be able to drop down cloaked and pick her up."

"This is making me nervous, David. There is just so much that can go wrong with this. I know we have assurances from Ylen that it will all work out, but..."

"Don't worry, Marianne. Before you know it, all four of us will be in orbit with W'ren, ready to leave this system and take Beatrice home."

There was a knock on the door, and David opened it to see Hgliz.

"Ready?"

"Yes, let's go. Marianne, I'll see you at the shuttle in a bit."

The two of them walked to the vehicle Hgliz had driven, and they drove down so many streets that David lost count. The vehicle stopped, and David could see a short squat building, with a guard in front, and words written on the top that he could not read, but probably said something like "Regional Jail."

Hgliz paused before leaving the car.

"I don't like this."

"Like what?"

"Seeing that guard. He's not one of ours."

"What do you mean?"

"I don't know him. He might not be aligned with us. We may have a bit of trouble."

David tried not to worry. They left the vehicle together and walked to the door.

"Hgliz Julset Frodr, attaché to Supreme Chief Ylen. We are here to see Pkygy Hostro Gnova."

The man looked at Hgliz with obvious disgust.

"Go ahead."

"Please see to it that no one else enters."

He saw the man nod, slightly, but David was not convinced.

They entered the building, and Hgliz greeted two men inside. David relaxed.

"Who is the man standing guard?"

"He is the son of Rplo. As Rplo is First Chief of corrections, he gets to assign anyone he wants at times. We were surprised by this change."

"Let's get this over with, shall we?"

They all walked back into the building and went to the cell holding Pkygy.

"Pkygy?"

A slight man curled up in the corner of the cell looked up and stood.

"Pkygy, we're getting you out of here."

"Out?"

"Yes, Pkygy, out."

One of the men took out his keys and unlocked the cell. David went in, and took Pkygy by the arm, and led him out. As they were about to open the door to the outside, David could hear voices.

"Just a minute," Hgliz said. Hgliz opened the door, and standing there were five men, all with weapons.

Hgliz shouted. "What are you doing here? I am Hgliz..."

All hell broke loose. Two men attacked Hgliz, and the others went for David and Pkygy.

He had nothing to defend himself with, and the only thing he could think of was to run, dragging Pkygy with him. He couldn't get past the men in front of him. He heard a grunt, and looked to his left, only to see Pkygy getting stabbed by one of the attackers. There wasn't anything he could do for him, and he needed to get out of there. He tried to tackle a man who seemed to be standing in the way between him and door and managed to bowl him over. He jumped over him, and made it out the door, and started running. All of a sudden, he tripped, was on the ground, tasting dust. He turned over to see one of the attackers jumping on him, blade down. He twisted and kicked, and felt a sharp pain in his side, and he got up, and ran. Only after running a long time did he look back, and he didn't see anyone following. He had no idea where he was. He felt warmth on his side and looked to see blood. A lot of blood.

He remembered that he had a communications device. He went into a small alley that looked hidden and switched it on. W'ren's face greeted him.

"W'ren, I'm in trouble. Pkygy's probably dead. I'm injured, and lost."

"I can see where you are, David. I'll tell Marianne. Don't worry, you'll be picked up in a few minutes."

The device turned off, and David slid to the ground, and fell unconscious.

Things were blurry as he woke up. He could hear voices, but he didn't know where they were. He couldn't understand anything they were saying, which made him think he was still on Hilcyon. He strained to sit up.

"David, don't sit up. You've lost a lot of blood."

David recognized W'ren's voice, and saw his face, and calmed down. He still could hear people talking in the background.

"What's going on?"

"Marianne is talking with Ylen. There is a complete disaster down there."

"Marianne's talking with Ylen?? What? You're telling me... Ow."

W'ren stood over David, and gently held down his shoulders. "David, be careful. Yes, Marianne is talking with Ylen. Apparently, Ylen is far more ... progressive than you even thought. We have

Beatrice. Pkygy was killed, as was Hgliz. Ylen is livid and has executed both Rplo and his son for attacking you and his attaché.

Apparently, the swift execution also managed to keep silent the fact that the attempted release of Pkygy was ... unorthodox. The official story is that Rplo and his son had been scheming to topple Ylen, which was probably true, anyway, and you had been offered a last-minute tour of some of the Capital, and they attacked you unprovoked. No mention of the prison or Pkygy was made."

David could feel himself falling into unconsciousness again. "Tell Beatrice and Marianne that I am sorry I couldn't save Pkygy."

Casitian Ship bound for New Earth, Month 3, Year 25

Marianne sat in the chair, looking at David, who was asleep. Beatrice was asleep in her quarters, and W'ren was also asleep. She seemed to be the only one who couldn't sleep.

Ylen seemed to have it all in hand. Marianne couldn't help but feel like he knew it could fail and had planned to do what he could to get the best out of a failed plan. It seemed that he'd managed to rid himself of a troubling enemy in the process. Marianne didn't fault him for this at all. He was clearly a very smart man. She had been stunned when he agreed to speak with her and surprised by how respectful of her status and intelligence he was. He somehow had instinctively known all along that it was she who was in charge.

She felt especially badly for Beatrice. This was the second husband she'd lost to tragic circumstances. She had told the story of losing Craig, and being assigned to Pkygy, and explained to Marianne that Pkygy was a gentle soul, and she had come to truly love him. Marianne she was happy that she was at least bringing Beatrice home. It also looked like 17,000 others of the kidnapped teenagers would be following her home soon. The ship to take them home was on its way from Casiti to the asteroid mines now.

Looking at David, she couldn't imagine what would have happened had she lost him. She had so depended on him lately, and she realized that she often took him for granted. Almost losing him had shaken something loose in her, and she knew, somehow, that she'd never be quite the same again.

She got up, dug around the first aid drawer for the magic Casitian sleeping pill, swallowed it, and went to her quarters.

New Columbia, New Earth, Month 3, Year 25

It had been a while since Leticia had been on this side of the Mississippi. She visited her mother once a year or so, but she'd been a bit neglectful, and it had been longer than that. After she and Mira visited her mom in the ICS, she traveled down to New Columbia, where she was meeting Kurt and Suzanna, and going to their conference.

Kurt and Suzanna, as well as some New Americans, had organized a conference in New Columbia with leaders all over New Earth and from both IZs, to discuss the implications of the current situation, and the changes that would be required in the governance of New Earth. It seemed that the current leaders of the large New Earth entities, New America, New Aard, and the ICS were ignoring the reality, and assuming that things would remain as they were. It was the leaders of the smaller territories, such as Dlejon, the tribes, the settlements in the independent zones, which were forward looking, and Kurt and Suzanna wanted to foster that thinking. Having the conference in New Columbia was a bit of a slap in the face to the government of New America, but they did that on purpose. The location was chosen because they wanted a large contingent of young, forward-looking leaders from New America to be here to get ideas from people from all over New Earth.

Leticia and Mira left their train transport at the New Columbia station, and walked toward their hotel, a small affair close to the conference venue. They were meeting Kurt and Suzanna for lunch, and would finalize the conference agenda in the afternoon. They walked up to the counter to check in.

"Mira Lindsey and Leticia Green."

The clerk looked at them with an odd expression.

"Traveling from outside of New America?"

"Yes, we're from New Calgary."

The clerk screwed up his face. "New Calgary? Where is that?"

"In the North Central IZ."

"OK, I see your reservation here. Our rooms only have one double bed. I assume you want a second room..."

"No, one room is fine, thank you."

The clerk looked disturbed to Leticia, but he didn't say anything.

"Here is your key. Enjoy your stay in New Columbia." The sarcasm in his voice was palpable.

"Thank you."

They walked up to their room in silence. Leticia was reminded, again, of what she'd left behind.

They sat around a table at the small restaurant that Kurt said had authentic southern food. Leticia hadn't had any since she left the ICS – her mother was a master cook, and made amazing greens, macaroni and cheese, and fried chicken. Leticia wanted to introduce Mira to this food, which she knew Mira hadn't experienced, since was born in Minneapolis, and grew up in Dlejon.

"I don't think I've ever had 'ham hock' before – what is that, besides some piece of a pig?"

Leticia answered, "It's a piece of a pig – don't worry about it, love. Just enjoy the greens; they are really good, and authentic."

Mira experimentally tasted a little bit, and then started eating with gusto.

"See, I told you."

They chatted amiably about their lives for a while. Leticia and Mira filling Kurt and Suzanne in on life in New Calgary, and the new medical school. Kurt was explaining his work with the Dubuque area housing authority, and Suzanne was describing the new business she and her husband Geoffrey had to manufacture solar cells. Geoffrey had pioneered a new methodology to maximally use the different kind of solar radiation coming from New Earth's sun. The solar cells they were producing were 50% more efficient, and they were doing more licensing of his technology to other manufacturers than producing cells themselves.

Suzanna had gotten married in Dubuque and had a toddler who was 6 years old. Geoffrey had also been an ICS escapee – he'd left the

ICS just a few months before they did. Leticia had heard Kurt say that he had been glad that he'd been able to return to New America again. He'd been persona non grata here after abandoning Dennis Hickler before he became President. Once Dennis died a year ago, Dennis' friends were shunned, and his foes were in favor, which made Kurt welcome again. He settled in Dubuque but had been thinking about a return to New Columbia, now that things were shifting. Leticia saw in place of the immature, angry, petty, annoying boy she had known, a mature, kind, and thoughtful man. She thought that he would make a good leader.

After the plates were cleared, Kurt broke into the informal conversation.

"People, we need to finalize the conference agenda. I reserved a room at the conference center for this afternoon. There are a few New America folks I know who will be joining us. Oh, before I forget, I heard from Terrance – he'll make it tomorrow with a contingent from his office in Dubuque."

Leticia had heard from Suzanna about the relatively new friendship between Kurt and Terrance. Apparently, Terrance had held a grudge for a very long time, but Kurt kept trying to cross the burned bridge, and finally Terrance gave in.

They all got up and walked together toward the conference center. As they walked, a short, slight middle-aged woman with long, graying hair that was tied up behind her head came toward them. Kurt, who was in front, greeted her.

"Rita, how are you?"

She frowned. "Hello, Kurt. I'm a little surprised you are showing your face here. There are still people who don't like you very much after what you did to President Hickler."

"What exactly did I do? Besides, I left before he became President, so whatever it was you thought I did, I did it to Dennis Hickler."

"I heard that you betrayed secrets to the enemy."

"And which enemy would that be, Rita?"

"You know what I mean..."

"No, I don't really. But I do have a little secret for you – you might find it interesting."

"Oh?"

"What I did, actually do to Dennis Hickler was break up with him." Kurt smiled, and walked on, leaving Rita sputtering. The rest of them kept walking.

"Was that Rita as in Rita Reid, that silly journalist that kept hounding Marianne on Earth?"

"Yes, indeed it is."

Leticia and Mira were exhausted after three days of intense conversations, meeting, planning and socializing before and during the conference. The night before they were to leave, they opted to bring take-out to their rooms for dinner and spend some time alone together debriefing.

Mira put down her burrito.

"I have to say, I do feel generally hopeful. There is true consensus in the IZs and other small settlements that we should do resource mapping and determine exactly how many Terrans each settlement can take, so they don't all have to go into the non-developed areas of New Earth. And that guy Harry, from Burning Man, had the great idea of publicizing the character of each community, so that the right people would end up joining these communities. My dad will be all for that. And Dlejon has a fair amount of space. They are already planning for new immigrants."

"I so wish that Aunt Marianne could have been here. We can certainly start the process – set up a site and recruit representatives from each settlement to post a settlement profile, as well as the resource mapping so that it is clear how many new settlers can join."

"The guy from New America ... what was his name?"

"Oh, James something."

"Yes, his comments about where he sees the New American leadership heading were troubling." Mira shook her head. "I can't believe that, all they are interested in is immigrants who can fill the jobs that people have been leaving in droves. I think New America is sort of destined to be a backwater."

"Something's got to change. No one in their right mind will immigrate to New America so that they can do menial labor, when they could go anywhere else and be part of building something they will have an investment in and can benefit from in the long term. Unless the New American leadership gets a clue ..."

"Well, if they don't, something else will arise from their ashes."

Leticia heard the beep of her widenet phone. She looked at her messages.

"Aunt Marianne is back! She says to meet her at mom's? That seems strange. Why there and not Dlejon?"

Mira shrugged her shoulders. "Maybe it's been a while since she's seen your mom, and she wants to see her again. Who knows?"

Independent Christian State, New Earth, Month 3, Year 25

The taxi stopped suddenly. "Here you go."

Leticia asked, "how much?"

"61."

Leticia thought that inflation in the ICS had gotten a bit out of hand lately. Mira opened the door on her side and got out, and Leticia handed the driver seven 10 unit bills.

"Keep the change."

"Thanks. Enjoy your visit."

Leticia got out of the taxi, closed the door, and watched it drive away. The front door of her mother's house opened, and her aunt Marianne stood in the doorway, with a very big grin on her face.

"I have a surprise for you, Leticia!"

Leticia couldn't for the life of her figure out why her Aunt should have such a huge smile, and then she realized what it was.

"Beatrice?"

Marianne nodded. We got here yesterday. She's inside resting. She's been through a lot, Leticia. Craig was killed just after they arrived in the Hilcyon system, and her second husband, Pkygy, was killed just a few days ago. And she and Pkygy were organizing a resistance, and from what I can tell, it was working."

Leticia smiled. "Why am I not surprised?"

They walked into the living room, where Leticia's mother and father were sitting on the couch. They got up, and hugged Leticia and Mira.

"It's so good to see you again, Mira. You know, you two don't visit enough! I haven't even had a chance to cook you dinner."

"Mom, you know we're busy..."

"Yes, I know, starting a new medical school, organizing conferences - you seem to be as busy as your aunt here. Anyway, tonight, we're feasting. Celebrating the return of my daughters! And, I heard from your grandmother, now that communications to Earth are flowing again."

"How is she?"

"She's fine, still healthy, thank God. She'll be on the first wave, she says. She's looking forward to seeing us all."

Leticia heard a bedroom door open, and saw Beatrice appear in the doorway to the living room. She was taller, which didn't surprise Leticia. Her face seemed aged beyond her years, and her expression seemed both very happy, and extremely sad. Leticia jumped up and enveloped her sister in a hug.

"Beatrice, I missed you so much!"

They hugged for a while, both crying. Finally, Beatrice broke the hug, and said quietly, "mom really likes Mira. She told me more about Mira than she told me about you!"

Leticia smiled. "I guess it took her a while to come around, but when she did - she was a champ."

They returned together to the living room.

Hilcyon Mining Asteroid, Wtler 40 1158

Jasmine heard the bell that meant the end of the shift, but she knew it was far too soon for that. She hadn't even experienced the standard mid-day hunger pangs that in a normal world would mean it was time for lunch. She hadn't heard an alarm klaxon, which meant there was no emergency. It was puzzling to her. She wondered if it were some other test the Kinder had decided to try on them, to keep them on their toes. But what would the right reaction be? Stop working to show her obedience, or keep working ... to show her obedience?

She was far away from everyone else. As usual, she was taking measurements in a new area just opened up by the digging machines, still dangerous before being shored up. She decided at least to go see what everyone else had decided. As she got closer to the entrance to this new section, she heard shouting. She ran toward them.

She saw Jamel who she knew and trusted. He was out of breath, as if he'd run from somewhere. He was surrounded by others.

"I'll say it again: they are here! We are rescued!"

Jasmine pushed inward to hear more.

Someone in the crowd said, "who is here?"

"The Casitians! There is a ship waiting for us."

"Why do we want to go with them?" Jasmine looked around, to see the speaker, who was Gary. Somehow, that didn't surprise her.

She spoke up. "Gary, you want to stay on this rock mining for the rest of your life? Be my guest. I'm happy to leave!"

"We've been promised that if we do well, we can move to Kinder Home."

"I'd rather got to Home Home, thank you very much." She heard laughter all around.

Jamel said, "c'mon, let's go."

They followed Jamel, who guided them back through the mine entrance, through their quarters, and back to a space that they remembered all too well – when they had disembarked from the ship that brought them there. It was surprising for Jasmine to realize that for all of the time she'd been here, she'd never returned to this space. As they entered they saw a group of people she thought must be Casitians, given their dress and demeanor, standing across the space from the group of Kinder chiefs that ran the mine. No one said anything. She couldn't figure out why the Kinder weren't putting up a fight.

One of the Casitians addressed the gathering group. "I need a head count. How many of you are here?"

Jasmine had kept track. She knew how many had died. "There are 986 of us here. We started with 1726. Most of the missing have died. Two left to go to Hilcyon."

He nodded. "There are nine other asteroids with New Earth humans. This is the second we've come to. I need some volunteers to go throughout the mines and quarters and get everyone."

Several people, including Jasmine, raised their hands. The Casitian man gave each of them a communicator. "As you find people, direct them to this space, and I will let you know how many are still missing. OK, everyone else please follow Jt'elor to the ship. We will count how many as you leave."

One by one, the rest of them went through the corridor. Jasmine realized that Gary was not here. The group of volunteers left the loading area and went through the quarters and mines. Jasmine sent about 50 people who were still working in the mines back to the loading area.

She was going through one last tunnel, when she heard from her communicator, "All are now accounted for. 983 will be leaving 3 wish to stay behind. Come on back to the loading area."

She turned and ran back. She'd be going home!

New Earth, Month 4, Year 25

Ngellin looked around the room. In it were ten of the leaders of the New Earth Kinder, and one woman. He was sometimes brought up short in his meetings with Marianne. She was the first woman he'd ever known that had leadership skills. Knowing her had made him realize that the Kinder made grave mistakes when it came to how they dealt with women. Had Marianne been a man on Kinder, she would have been Supreme Chief – Ngellin thought she was that good. But then, in a sense, she was certainly Supreme Chief here, on the planet of her making.

It had been a tense meeting. Marianne had sent word that the new Supreme Chief, Ylen, wanted change, and wanted the deserters to come home, and help. Marianne said that he gave assurances that they would be treated well, but Ngellin doubted that he could fulfill that, even if he wanted to.

"Marianne, I will agree that whoever wants to go home, can go home. I can't and won't stop them. I, however, have no intention of returning to Kinder Home."

He saw Marianne nod in that measuring kind of way.

"Certainly, Ngellin - it makes sense that some of you would want to return, and others... not. I have no interest in forcing anyone to do anything they don't want to do. But I would say one thing - the more of you that return to Hilcyon, the more likely Ylen is to succeed in his wishes to change Kinder society."

Ngellin said, "I concede your point, Marianne, you are correct. But frankly, there are many who won't care. We've found a comfortable life here, one without the constraints of the Kinder. I for one am loathe to give that up."

"I understand. We're expecting a large transport to arrive at New Earth in the next few days. Ylen would like that transport to return to Hilcyon with as many of you as wish to go."

Lren, who had been silent up until this point, raised his hand and spoke. "I for one, would like to return. If it is at all possible to achieve a new Kinder society while I'm alive, I'd like to help that happen. I'm happy to help organize those who want to go back."

Marianne looked a bit grim. "Thank you, Lren."

Ngellin could see why Lren wanted to go back. He'd been talking about returning ever since it was clear it might be possible. Ngellin was glad that some of them were less selfish than he was.

He added, "By the way, there is a small group of New Earth humans who would love a chance to move to Kinder Home."

Marianne had a look of pure incredulity. "What?"

"Yes, believe it or not. I've been in discussions with this man, Parker Hill, from the Independent Christian State. He's organizing a small group of people, mostly in his area, who want to leave New Earth, and move to Hilcyon."

"What is he, nuts?"

"From what I understand, he feels that Kinder Home has the society he wants to live in. What can I say, Marianne?"

"Well, I should have a talk with him to understand better what he's thinking. Can you give me his widenet address?"

Illsenor Station, 65 Nird 784/Month 4, Year 25

Marianne had made briefings at Illsenor Station a regular event. She sat in the briefing room, along with David, K'flef, K'lellen and W'ren. Also present were Torf'ki and Yulse'lor, who had both just arrived from Casiti with a very large team to help the New Earth effort. Marianne had been very grateful when they showed up. She finally felt like the Casitians were stepping up to the plate. She had heard from several sources that Jal'end'a had been instrumental in this change of approach. And seeing Yulse'lor again was a pleasant surprise.

These briefings were her chance to meet with the Casitians who had come to New Earth to help with the massive immigration from Earth. They would help plan and build infrastructure, monitor the environment to make sure there weren't too many people in some areas or others, and generally support New Earth in its evolution to be the primary home of Humankind.

The main subject of today's briefings was the impending arrival of the young adults who had been kidnapped by the Kinder to work on asteroid mines 8 years ago.

"Today we need to discuss the return of the kidnapped. What is the status of that ship?"

W'ren spoke first. "We just received word that they have picked up all of the passengers from all ten asteroids. They should arrive here on station in 2 days. We have a couple of large shuttles, but not enough to get them down in one trip – it will take several. Also, we need to prepare people – there were deaths."

"Deaths? How many?"

"17,280 teenagers were originally abducted. Apparently a few died on route to the asteroids. We have picked up 9,710. This means that about seventy-five hundred of them died. Four managed to make it to Hilcyon, and twenty wanted to stay behind in the mines, believe it or not."

"Four on Hilcyon? I know of two. One of them is my niece, who we rescued. The other is a guy named William, who apparently is now a Fourth Chief. I wonder who the other two are. Do we know the names of those who wanted to stay behind?"

"None of them wished to give their names. They wanted their families to think them dead."

Marianne shook her head. "I don't get it - but if that was their wish, so be it. My, this is not going to be a pleasant announcement. We don't have the names of the dead, do we?"

"They are trying to compile them now, but I don't know that it will be a complete list."

Marianne pondered how to deal with this. It was not common knowledge that the kidnapping was done with the full consent of the governments of New America and the ICS, or that had been in exchange for certain kinds of material goods. In fact, it hadn't even been acknowledged by these governments that the kidnapped were off-planet, although the return of Beatrice to the ICS had certainly caused rumors.

"I think my first calls are going to be to Governor Hurler and President Mason so that they know what's coming. I don't expect them to come clean, of course, but someone is going to get to the bottom of this eventually, and they are going to end up paying for it."

David leaned forward over the table. "Marianne, I think we can use this to our advantage."

"How?"

"Both the President and the Governor have been stick-in-the-muds about the immigration issue. Hurler wants only bona fide Christians, of his type, of course, to be able to immigrate to the ICS. Mason only wants immigrants willing to do menial labor. Neither of those conditions can, or should, be met. Both of those territories need to take more immigrants – we gave them a disproportionate share of the planet based on population in comparison to others, for reasons we all know well. We need leverage – either leverage to work to get them to accept immigration, or leverage to get rid of them. Their complicity in the kidnapping of their own population is leverage we can use."

"I hate to think of threatening them..."

Yulse'lor said in a quiet voice, "that would set a bad precedent, in my opinion. I would suggest something a bit different. I would suggest that you just simply let the facts be known. Even if the facts are just indirect evidence."

Marianne smiled. "I have far more than that, Yulse'lor. Supreme Chief Ylen, out of the blue, sent me the written logs of the then First Chief Glendr, who was in charge of the kidnapping operation. We have it all. I certainly could just publish it..."

Yulse'lor grinned. "Yes. That sounds exactly right."

David nodded. "It would definitely put them in an unstable position, and open to challenge from people who disagree with them."

Marianne said, "yes, indeed it would. OK, we've got our work cut out for us, and two days to get it done."

There were a few more agenda items, and then the joining adjourned. One of Marianne's first tasks was to call a few key people she knew who should know what was happening before it happened. She thought of Kurt and Beatrice, who were her moles in New America and the ICS respectively.

She had also struck up an odd friendship with an abbot who had settled in the far western corner of the ICS as a part of a small Benedictine community. He had been one of a very few Catholics who had left Earth. He'd requested a meeting with her soon after the news of the galactic edict went public. He wanted to make sure that the Vatican could move into the ICS. She thought that would be a fairly logical place for it, although she didn't think that the ICS leaders thought so. In the course of talking with him, she'd come to rather like him. He was unassuming, humble and kind to her. She wanted to help him in any way she could. She thought that this news might be of some use.

She walked to her quarters and sat at her desk. She realized that before anything, she had to contact Mason and Hurler. A joint communiqué seemed appropriate.

"Please record this video to be sent to President Mason, in New Columbia, and Governor Hurler of the ICS. Start now."

She told them the news, explained about the deaths, and also explained that the Casitians would publish on the widenet all of the information they currently had on the kidnappings, which included the full translated logs of the Kinder responsible for them. She was very matter of fact, and she knew they would freak out. She didn't care.

New Columbia, New Earth, Month 4, Year 25

It hadn't taken as long as Kurt thought it would to get back to living in New America. During the conference last month, Kurt had cemented his nascent friendship with Valorie Lira, who was the progressive mayor of New Richmond, the city on the New America side of the Mississippi River from Dubuque. When the news regarding the kidnapped teenagers was spreading, Valorie contacted Kurt, and asked whether he'd be willing to staff an office for her in the capital. He was ecstatic at the chance to re-enter New American politics, and do it backing someone like Valorie - a straightforward, down to earth progressive voice for New America, one who Kurt felt would handle the immigrant issues well.

Valorie didn't have much in her campaign budget, so he'd rented an apartment in a more modest section of the capital. But because of the flight of people from New America there was an incredible housing glut, and Kurt got the apartment for a song. It cost far less than his apartment in Dubuque. The apartment was big and Kurt decided he could work out of it for the time being, until they could build their base, and start getting support from folks around the country.

The clamor for a new presidential election was far too loud for President Mason to ignore. If he hadn't agreed to hold new elections, Kurt thought that he eventually would have been forcibly overthrown. The anger in the country about his knowledge of the kidnappings and his apparent complicity made his continued Presidency dangerously unstable.

The elections were set for Day 5, Month 2, Year 26. Kurt felt that gave him enough time to get enough support to get Valorie elected. She was beloved in New Richmond, the largest city in New America.

He had a lot to do: make connections in the ICS, re-establish relationships in New Columbia, and reach out to Jerome and other communities to the south. And, he needed to contact Leticia, so that she could get her aunt Marianne into the fray. Marianne and Valorie would like each other immensely, Kurt realized. It was time for them to meet.

Hilcyon, Sdert 18 1158

Ylen again mourned the loss of Hgliz. His current attaché, although faithful, wasn't very smart.

"Supreme Chief Ylen, there is an official complaint from First Chiefs Lkor and Jrem."

"And why are you telling me?"

"Supreme Chief, they are complaints to you."

"And I should care because?"

His attaché sputtered.

"Look, this is how it goes. You deal with them. I don't really care what you say. The only complaint that matters is one that results in my presence in the ring."

His attaché nodded.

"Besides, I already know the complaints. I removed 9,000 workers from the mines, and now they don't have enough people to mine. If you want, you can tell them that there will be plenty more coming." Ylen had plans to send as many of his opponents as possible to the mines.

"Now, onto other matters. What was the response of the First Chief's to my proposed rule changes?"

"Uniformly negative, Supreme Chief. The responses ranged from 'is he out of his mind?' to 'it's too soon to make such drastic changes.'"

"I figured as much. I need the new figures on water production, now that we have the new technology in place. Have you prepared the region-by-region report?"

"Yes, Supreme Chief. It's right here." His attaché passed him a folder, with a few sheets inside. He would read it later.

"You may go now."

His attaché bowed and left his office.

Ylen decided to look at the report before he moved on to other things. He opened the folder, and saw the figures he was hoping for. A 150% increase in water delivery to the Central Valley, a 100% increase in the capital region, a 15% rise in the Upper Highlands, a 120% rise in the lower desert, and a 15% rise in the Lower Highlands. The regions with First Chiefs that were loyal to him and had the most active resistance got the largest increases in water availability. He knew he was playing a dangerous game, but water was essential, and once the First Chiefs saw what loyalty to Ylen could buy, they would all come around.

Moon Station, January 30, 2026

Joel and Laura were lying next to each other in bed in the quarters they shared on Moon Station. Usually, after making love, Joel was out like a light, but tonight he was restless.

"Joel, I can tell you aren't asleep."

"It's OK, Laura, don't worry about it, I'll be fine."

"Darling, talk to me."

Joel turned toward Laura and propped himself up on his elbow.

"I'm losing hope that this will be anything like orderly. The invective spewed at us from the Australian Prime Minister, and the fact that more than 20 leaders refused to even receive a text message from us, let alone a visit..."

"Remember, Diana is going to win."

"Yes, I know, and that will make things better, but, did you read Dwight's report?"

Dwight was Joel's old friend who had been a mole for Gerard, the upstart Presidential candidate that eventually became president of New America. Dwight had gone on the straight and narrow ever since and was now working to map anti-evacuation movements. He had even recruited friends to infiltrate as many as possible.

"Yes, that was disturbing." Hundreds perhaps even thousands of formally and informally organized groups all over the world were planning on either passive resistance or active resistance to evacuation.

"I know that the Galactics have a lot of tricks up their sleeve, but..."

"Joel, you are doing the best you can. We are all doing the best we can. There isn't much more we can do."

Joel exhaled, and dropped back on his back. "I know. I just worry."

Laura put her head on his chest. She said quietly, "Maybe we need a bit of a vacation."

"A vacation?"

"Yeah, a vacation. Welen'da and her team just got here and are working on the big picture logistics of the colony ship use in evacuations. Gita and her team are here working with the countries that are fully cooperating to figure out how best to evacuate critical manufacturing resources. We'd be sitting here twiddling our thumbs for the month before either of them had any data for us to work with, and before Marianne finishes with her feasibility work on New Earth. Love, we need a break. We've been working non-stop ever since before the trial. Let's go somewhere else. Somewhere we won't be able to visit, after."

"Hmmm, like the planet of the Tvierl? I hear that the 12 moons are stunning, and their resorts are popular across the galaxy."

"Sounds like a plan."

A quiet chime sounded. "Uh oh."

Joel got up, and went to his desk, and asked the AI, "who is the message from?"

"Message from Marianne, on Illsenor Station."

"Play message, please."

"Joel, Laura, I know you've got a bit of a lull in things over there, can you come here for a bit? I need some help figuring out logistics for the immigration waves, and you guys know the data and situation on Earth better than anyone over here."

Joel looked back at Laura. "So much for the vacation idea."

San Diego, California, Earth, January 30, 2026

They met each week, on Sunday evenings GMT, by IRC chat. Ira, a programmer by trade, had set up a secret IRC server. There were more than 100 of them by now, from all over the world. They had most of the expertise they needed: a couple of geologists, a physicist, several people who knew how to grow food, people with repair skills – everything they would need to survive for an extended period underground, then survive on an Earth bereft of everyone except themselves.

Joanne was confident about this group: confident they could pull it off. She didn't think that the Galactics would be able to find them once they ensconced themselves in the deepest caves of Carlsbad Caverns National Park.

They estimated that they would have to hide for as long as 5 months. They were gathering instruments to look for radio signals and to detect various kinds of scans. They were preparing for every contingency any of them could think of.

One of them had purchased a large piece of land close to the cavern system. That would be their staging area. They would ferry their supplies at night into the cave system via a hidden entrance that few knew about. Joanne had spent much of the last three months learning spelunking, as had all of those who were involved.

They had also planned for the growth of their movement. 150 was the limit for this group, and once they reached that, they would spawn new groups, using the same knowledge and expertise being gained by this group. Joanne knew this movement would grow, it had to. Humans had to fight to stay on our own planet.

"Log started. Meeting beginning." The text from the current facilitator, whose nick was 'gigio' flashed on her screen. She waited for the agenda to scroll by.

"1. Results of geological scans of cavernous region

2. Seed supplies

3. Spawn criteria

4. Finalized personal skill building list

5. Agenda for next meeting"

The meeting, as usual, was orderly with few problems or sidetracks. She was happy to see that the personal skill building list that she'd drawn up was approved without much comment. They had 12 years to get this right, and everyone needed to be in good shape for what was coming.

Chapter 4:
Seven Waves of Knowing

(AP) February 10, 2026

Diana Westinghouse-Lewis ahead by 15 Points in Recent Polling

New York – Recent Gallup, Quinnipiac and Zogby global polls have all placed Diana Westinghouse-Lewis at 50-52%, 15 points ahead of challenger Leigin Shan who has 35-37%, and both are well ahead of trailing challenger George Hermsberger at 6-8%. Westinghouse-Lewis' strongholds are the US and Canada, Europe, Latin America, and parts of Africa. Leigin Shan has a strong showing in China, with 90%+ of the Chinese preferring him. He also has strong showings in the rest of Asia. George Hermsberger, a dark-horse candidate who also, like Shan, suggests fighting the galactic edict, is showing strongly in some sectors of Africa, as well as in his home country of Germany. Hermsberger has consistently polled less than 10% of the vote, eliminating him from participation in the debates.

Independent Christian State, Month 1, Year 26

Beatrice stood in the front of the group who had been chosen to greet the first returnees to the ICS. She was there because she knew some of those returning. She also suspected that it helped that she had become favored of the leader of her settlement, a relatively progressive man who wanted to be more open for immigration.

A hundred feet or so away from where she stood were the parents and relatives of those on this shuttle. She and her mother had talked about what it would have been like for her if Beatrice's name hadn't been on the list when these names arrived. She felt for all of those who had thought that their children were simply off in some unexplored and unreachable part of New Earth, to find out that they had been much, much farther away, and many were not going to return.

The publicity surrounding the release of the information about the kidnapping was ferocious. She knew already that the career of Governor Hurler was over – he had resigned yesterday, as had his

Lieutenant Governor. President Mason, who was not in power at the time, and had been in opposition to Dennis Hickler, was still in office. It was becoming clear that he had known what had happened, and never made it public. New America was in the process of a new election cycle, and Beatrice imagined they would finally vote Mason out of office.

She heard a sound above her and looked up to see the shuttle dropping down to land. It kicked up some dust on the ground and landed neatly in the center of the large yellow circle on the ground. The group of them walked toward the door. In about 30 seconds, it opened, and people began to leave the shuttle. Each were wearing sunglasses – she realized the Casitians understood the implications of living inside a rock for 8 years. As they stepped out, the small group greeted them and pointed toward the larger group with their families.

"Beatrice!"

"Jasmine! Oh my gosh, it's so good to see you!" They hugged.

"I missed you so much when you left. I'm glad that you are here - I was afraid you were still on Hilcyon."

"It's a long story. Pkygy is dead. Marianne rescued me when she visited Hilcyon. That's also how you got released I'll definitely tell you more soon."

"I'm so sorry, Beatrice. I know you came to love him."

Beatrice nodded. "Jasmine, go to your parents. Let's get together after you've had a chance to settle into life back here."

"Settle in here? Not a chance. I'm already plotting my escape to somewhere else."

"Wait a minute - things are changing here. Please, at least talk with me before you decide?"

"OK, my friend, for you, I will talk before I decide. Only for you, though."

Beatrice smiled, and they hugged once again, and Jasmine walked toward her family members. Beatrice saw them embrace and saw the tears on her mother's face. Her mother looked at Beatrice and mouthed "thank you." Beatrice guessed that it would be OK to be Marianne's stand-in here.

Casiti, 100 Nird 784

Re'alo felt that he'd been away for a year, but it had actually been less than a month. He was bringing back a lot of information, and news that three fleets of Galactic ships were on their way to Casiti and New Earth, brimming with critical technology for each of their planets. These fleets would arrive within the next two Casitian months.

Re'alo had brought with him W'ren's proposal to alter the climate of Hilcyon, and some of the equipment coming to Casiti was going to be for that purpose. There would be a crew whose role it would be to train Casitians in the use of all of the technology they were transferring, then those crews would leave before the deadline, since they weren't humans.

Re'alo overall had been appreciative of the approach of the Galactic council – the Krumptia in charge had been given instructions to be as helpful as possible to make sure that the coming isolation would not be a hardship for the human planets. Re'alo knew that they would have all that they needed.

The first colony ships were on their way to Sol station already. Re'alo had gotten the rather astounding message from the Caraj that more than one billion Earth humans were headed for Casiti. He did think that was exactly the right thing to do, but he had been surprised that the Caraj had been able to come to consensus around such a large number. He wasn't privy to the detailed plans, but he imagined that at least some of the first wave of immigrants would be heading to Casiti to prepare the way for others.

His AI spoke quietly, "arriving at Toleno station." It was time to gather up his things and go home. His first duty was to report to his Caraj liaison. After that, he needed to recruit a team to handle the arrival of the fleets at Casiti and recruit a larger team to be trained. He had some ideas of who might be interested in the team he'd have to send to New Earth. He'd be happy to leave to W'ren recruiting for the Hilcyon-bound fleet.

New Richmond, New Earth, Month 1, Year 26

"Marianne, come in, it is so nice to finally meet you in person."

Marianne entered an office that looked a bit cluttered and certainly well lived-in. Marianne realized that she was perhaps too used to the Casitian minimalist ethic. "Thank you, Mayor Lira."

"Please, call me Valorie. Everyone does."

Marianne nodded and smiled. "OK, Valorie."

Marianne looked at Valorie, who was medium height, with a small frame, and short graying hair. She was wearing the very utilitarian uniform of jeans and an oxford shirt. Marianne thought she was likely of Italian descent, especially given the name.

"I much appreciate your willingness to meet with me."

"It's funny, I was going to say the same thing. I've been hearing about you from more than just my niece's friend Kurt – you are seen around the region as a mover and shaker – and, most importantly for me, someone willing to come to the immigration table with reasonable ideas."

"Thank you. I do hope to bring those ideas to New America as its new President."

"Kurt told me. From what I can tell, it would be the right choice for New Americans to make."

Valorie smiled, and chuckled. "Coming from you, that's saying a lot."

"What can I do to help? I cannot officially or unofficially campaign for you or endorse you, obviously."

"I understand you are in a delicate position, especially regarding New America."

"Yes. But what I can do is publicize your ideas. Some of them are simply brilliant. The infrastructure proposals alone are fabulous. The Casitians have already been using them in part of their simulations of the immigration waves."

"Really?"

"Yes, really. And they seem to work very well in the simulations. Gradual infrastructure build out from the bottom up, rather than whole cloth infrastructure community by community seems to work better – it means that more people can be accommodated at a faster rate, even though the first and second waves will likely live in tents to begin with. But by the time the immigration is complete ... everyone will have what they need. How did you come up with this?"

"It's a funny story, really. I was a nurse before the Casitian Crisis. I worked with Doctors Without Borders, and I was assigned to Haiti after the earthquake. I was sitting at lunch one day, and next to me happened to be this group of architects and builders, and they were having a raucous argument about this very thing. I don't know why it stuck in my mind so, but the one who argued for ground-up gradual infrastructure won the argument. Of course, just because he won the argument doesn't mean that's what they did."

"Well, it's what we'll be doing in many regions of New Earth."

"Many? Not all?"

"First, we only have jurisdiction over the Independent Zones and unsettled regions. We can suggest to the other areas that they follow suit, but we can't make them. And there are some communities, such as those of the native and indigenous peoples, who intend to live much closer to the land, and won't be building much infrastructure on their land at all."

"How can that be? There must be limitations in the capacity of the land they are inhabiting."

"They are getting far more acres per immigrant than other regions, partially so that they can live as they wish to, and partially as reparations for hundreds of years of colonialism. They requested this of me, I conferred with the Casitian teachers, as well as Earth and New Earth leaders, and most agree it is a reasonable request."

"Some people, especially New Americans will be upset by it."

"I don't much care."

Valorie smiled. "I appreciate your willingness to do the right thing, even in the face of opposition."

"I suspect you would do the same."

Valorie nodded.

Marianne rose. "Thank you for this meeting. Feel free to be in contact with me. I very much look forward to meeting with you again, especially in your new office in New Columbia."

Valorie rose as well, and they embraced in a clasp-armed hug.

As Marianne walked from Valorie's office, she pondered this meeting. She knew, somehow, that Valorie would win. It would change everything in New America and make a New America radically different than it was when it started 26 New Earth years ago.

Illsenor Station, Month 1, Year 26

"Marianne, there will be no shortage of people wanting to be in the first waves. Between people who have relatives on New Earth, like your mom and my family, to people who see the writing on the wall, and want to be first on the ground here, we're going to be totally swamped with requests."

"Your suggestion, Joel?"

"My suggestion is that the first wave is only people with bona fide relatives on New Earth, and people with the kinds of skills we need to build infrastructure. We should space out the first few waves."

"Your calculations show that we need 7 waves per year for 10 Earth years?"

"Approximately, yes, with each wave having 100 million people, give or take. And of course 10 of those waves are going to Casiti."

"Right. What about country-based waves?"

"That would be way too chaotic. Imagine trying to empty out an entire country over the course of a couple of months? Can't be done. Has to be piecemeal."

Marianne was close to losing it. She couldn't keep all of it in her head, and she was having a hard time balancing the issues of leaving, with the issues of arriving. She finally realized that she was not the person to be dealing with this part of things.

"Torf'ki and Yulse'lor, can you both coordinate with Joel and Laura? I think my brain is shorting out on this one, mostly because I'm spending most of my time coordinating efforts here. Dealing with how people are going to leave Earth to match what's needed here is a bit beyond my ken right now."

Torf'ki nodded vigorously. "It's fine Marianne, it's just the kind of problem I love to bite into."

"This is what we'll do. I will be feeding you data on readiness for immigration of different zones. Readiness in terms of capacity, infrastructure, politics, etc. Coordinate with Joel and Laura and their team on Earth on who will leave when. How does that sound?"

Everyone seemed to be in agreement. Marianne was relieved. It was bad enough to try and manage expectations on the ground. She knew she could depend on these folks to handle other issues.

Independent Christian State, New Earth, Month 1, Year 22

Marianne felt like she was getting pretty tired of the ICS. She never understood why her sister insisted on living here, and every time she traveled here, she was subject to stares or outright hostility. Sometimes she wished the ICS women wore Burquas like some of them did in New Aard so she could travel unmolested.

She was in the ICS to meet with Parker Hill and his group, who, for reasons that were completely beyond her, wanted to move to Hilcyon. She'd communicated with Ylen initially about them, and he'd been clear about what he wanted. She was somewhat staggered by the number who wanted to go: Parker Hill had recruited more than 500 people, both men and women, to live on Hilcyon.

She'd picked up Beatrice on her way to the meeting. She wanted them to hear directly from her what life was like on Hilcyon, so they had no doubts about it. The teenagers, now young adults had returned to the ICS and New America, so knowledge of life on the asteroid mines was common knowledge.

Marianne and Beatrice got out of their car and walked into the large hall where the meeting was taking place. They entered the doors, and saw a couple of hundred people or more, milling about and talking. When they entered, the room got quiet.

A tall, slim man with a robust, bushy handlebar moustache came up and greeted them, "hello, Marianne, and this must be Beatrice? I'm Parker Hill. Glad to meet you."

Marianne nodded, and Beatrice looked disgusted.

"You know, they are going to make you shave that off."

Marianne looked at Parker, who was taken aback by that statement. "What do you mean?"

"All Kinder men must be clean shaven and bald. Just thought you'd want to know."

Marianne smiled at Beatrice, then turned to Parker. "Shall we begin the meeting, Parker?"

"Yes, yes, of course. Let's go to the front."

They walked up to the front, and Parker directed them where to sit. There was a microphone in front of each of their chairs.

"Hello, hello. We're going to get started. I would like to welcome you to this informational meeting about Hilcyon emigration. I would like to introduce you to Marianne Michaelson, who you all know."

There was silence in the room.

"And Beatrice ..."

"Hostro Gnova."

"Beatrice Hostro Gnova."

Marianne hadn't realized that Beatrice had decided to take Pkygy's name. It didn't really surprise her.

"Our purpose here is information sharing in both directions. Marianne has been instructed by the Kinder Supreme Chief to make sure that our motives are pure. And many of you here I'm sure are looking for information that will help you make your final decision. Marianne, will you start?"

"Actually, I'd like Beatrice to start. Beatrice lived first on the asteroid mines, then she lived on Hilcyon for a few years. Beatrice will tell you exactly what life is like there. Beatrice?"

Marianne listened to Beatrice's description of her life on Hilcyon. She talked about the Chief system, and the brutal ways men advanced in it. She explained the life of women and the complete subservience to men. She explained that if they emigrated as single women, they would be assigned to a husband, and expected to bear at least two children, preferably more. She explained that sterility was common on Hilcyon, for reasons that were not known. She told the story of her husband, and why he had been originally sentenced to the asteroid mine.

The more she said, the quieter the room got. When she was done, she turned to Marianne, who spoke next.

"I want to make something completely clear – Parker's comment about your motives being pure made it imperative for me to tell you this. Ylen, the current Supreme Chief of the Kinder, does not want you to emigrate if all you want is to be just like the Kinder as they are. And you've just heard the reality of who they are. Ylen is a reformer, and since he is a reformer in a society that has been calcified in its current state for thousands of years, you are entering a very dangerous game. If your plan is to become just like the Kinder, I can tell you Ylen doesn't want you, and I won't let you emigrate."

A man, toward the middle of the room, shot up, and shouted, "who the hell are you to tell me what I can and cannot do?"

Marianne said sternly, "I'm in charge of the relationship with Hilcyon; call me our ambassador to Hilcyon if you wish. I have no say over what you do on New Earth, that's for sure, but when it comes to going to Hilcyon, you've got to go through me, like it or not."

The room erupted. Parker was trying his best to calm everyone down.

"Please, please be seated. We will take questions in an orderly fashion." If you wish to ask a question, please form a line behind the microphone." The room slowly quieted, and people lined up behind the microphone placed in the audience area.

"This question is for Mrs. Hostro Gnova. Is it really true that in order to move up the chief hierarchy, you must kill?"

Beatrice nodded. "There are two ways to move up the hierarchy. One way is to be in the favor of a Chief above you, and when some Chief below them dies, they give you that Chiefdom. But there are two problems. One, in order to become favored by a Chief, you must be willing to be brutal, like being willing to kill someone the Chief thinks deserves it, or spy on people and turn them in, that sort of thing. A Chief is a Chief for life, and so you could wait a very, very long time before a Chiefdom opened up. The only realistic way to move up while you are young, and still able to fight, is to best the Chief above you by killing them in battle. It's not possible to move up the hierarchy without being willing to kill someone."

A woman took his place, and asked, "in the ICS, we have the Mission Society for women who do not wish to marry. Is there a similar society on Hilcyon?"

"No. Remember, infertility is common on Hilcyon, as is infant mortality. This means that in order to simply maintain the population, women must bear an average of about three children. I was married to Pkygy for five years, and the fact that we hadn't had any children was considered scandalous. He was told several times he should get rid of me and get a new wife who would bear him children. I was also approached by men who would help me bear children. I think that is the core reason Hilcyon society doesn't change – it takes so much to simply maintain the population, and if anything decreases the likelihood that women would bear children, that thing must be stamped out."

Marianne listened carefully to what Beatrice said – there was so much she hadn't heard before, and more about the Kinder made sense to her now.

Many questions followed, and all of them seemed to suggest that these people had no idea what Hilcyon was really like and had completely idealized the Kinder. Surprisingly, it reminded Marianne a bit of her initial idealizing of the Casitians, and her subsequent experiences that had shattered those illusions. There were no more questions, and Parker adjourned the meeting.

As they were leaving, Parker asked Marianne, "so what do you think?"

"I doubt any one of these folks is truly interested in emigrating. Am I right?"

"After that, I can say I'm not emigrating. I guess the Kinder men I met are different. It hadn't occurred to me that they should be, given that they had decided to desert. I was being naive."

"Ngellin and his people are great. I enjoy spending time with them. And they are happy here, which is telling, I think. These Kinder are different people from those on Kinder Home, although I do know there are many on Kinder Home who want change. Based on what I have heard here, anyone who wishes to emigrate to Hilcyon is doing so for the wrong reasons, certainly for Ylen."

"Agreed. Thank you both for coming."

Marianne nodded and they both shook Parker's hand and walked to the car. Marianne noticed that Beatrice was very quiet.

"What's up kiddo?"

"This was the first time I introduced myself with Pkygy's name. I had been considering changing my name in the ICS registry."

"If you feel it's right for you..."

"It feels right."

Casiti, 100 Nird 784

"Hetl'zef you are resigning?"

"Yes, Jal'end'a, I am. I have decided I would rather work with the agronomists on Jul'when, so we can feed everyone coming, than lead the Caraj. I think my talents are of better use there."

"What is it that you wish of me, Hetl'zef? I'm happy if you let the new head teacher of the Caraj know that I'm available for consultation."

Hetl'zef smiled. "It would be good for you to be available to yourself."

"What?"

"On behalf of the rest of the Caraj, I am asking you to join us as our head teacher. We have come to consensus on this matter."

Jal'end'a was stunned. This was not at all what she expected of this meeting. "Leader of the Caraj? Hetl'zef, I am a cloistered contemplative!"

"And a gifted spiritual leader. We need a spiritual leader now."

"But Hetl'zef, there are so many practical details..."

"... that don't need the Caraj leader to attend to. The Caraj head teacher has always been a role of guidance, not administration. There are talented administrators on the Caraj, as well as the Governing Council. We need a spiritual leader."

Jal'end'a happened to agree with him, but she didn't really want to be the spiritual leader in question.

"Give me a bit of time to decide, Hetl'zef. You are asking much."

"I know, Jal'end'a, but I think you agree this is right."

After they hugged and wished each other well, Jal'end'a let his last statement sit within herself. He was right, after all. She was the right choice to lead the Caraj at this time. She would, again, sacrifice her contemplative life for the good of Casiti.

Capital, Hilcyon, Brlew 12 1158

Jurrl was bleeding liberally, and out of breath. He ignored both and stood up tall. Mnib was down, his blood spreading over the ground of the ring. Jurrl was new First Chief of the Capital region. He never liked Mnib, or the way Mnib led. In the end, he hated Mnib's loyalty to Ylen, the traitor. Things would change in the Capital now that Jurrl was First Chief.

"Willm, come here." His protégé ran up to him with a towel and bandage, and helped Jurrl out of his shirt, and began to clean his wound, and bandage it.

"You know you have my Chiefdom now."

William, finished bandaging, and bowed. "Thank you First Chief."

"You deserve it. You have done well, and I have much work for you to do."

"Just say it, First Chief."

Two men came into the ring, followed by a woman. It must have been Mnib's wife. The men picked up the body, and carried it out of the ring, as she wept over it.

"I need you and your men to round up Mnib's allies in the Capital. I'm sure you can use your copious talents to find them."

"Yes, First Chief."

"Go. Now."

William bowed, and left the ring. He realized that as a First Chief, he needed an attaché. Willm would have been his first choice, but he rather would have Willm as one of his loyal Second Chiefs. He walked back to his house to rest, and to consider who to choose.

Capital, Hilcyon, Brlew 30 1158

"What do you mean the plants are dying?"

"First Chief, after the introduction of water tech from the Casitians, our water delivery increased dramatically, so we adjusted, and planted more, and changed the conditions of the greenhouses. We were assured this level would remain."

Jurrl was almost in the mood to grumble about the fact that Hilcyon had accepted the Casitian tech in the first place, but this wasn't the time, and his main green grower would not appreciate his sentiment.

"So, what happened?"

"About 15 days ago, the water delivery dropped by 40%."

"40%? Wouldn't that take it back to the previous level?"

"Very close. It's about 5% above the initial levels of delivery we had."

Jurrl knew why this happened. It was no coincidence that this happened two days after he bested Mnib for the First Chief position. Because of this, some people might go hungry in his district.

"Do your best to make do with this new level of water. I don't think it will change anytime soon."

"First..."

"Go."

The green grower bowed and left his office. He called in his attaché.

"Make an urgent appointment for me with Trill and Gvnor."

"Trill and Gvnor? Your fighting coaches?"

"Yes, my fighting coaches. Now!"

"Yes, First Chief!" His attaché bowed several times and scurried from the office.

Illsenor Station, Month 2, Year 26

David and Torf'ki were sitting together in a planning meeting.

Torf'ki asked in response to a comment of David's, "anger what?"

"Angkor Wat. It's the name of an amazing temple complex in Cambodia, in Southeast Asia. It's about 200 acres with many buildings."

"They want it moved to New Earth? How do they expect that to happen?"

"Torf'ki, I have no idea. That's why I'm asking you."

Torf'ki sighed. "Of course, this is only the sixth such thing I've been asked about so far."

"Sixth?"

"Yes, this after the Taj Mahal, the Pyramids, Mount Rushmore, the Eiffel Tower... and the whole city of Mecca!"

Pool Joel and Laura. Every country wanted their particular monuments moved.

"Well, Torf'ki, can you give me some parameters? Weight, size, etc.?"

"David, remember your physics. Galactic technology may be thousands of years ahead of human technology, but besides the makers of the wormholes, who are long gone, and their knowledge lost, the Galactics haven't learned how to change the laws of physics – like defying gravity. The heavier something is, the more energy it will take to get to orbit. There is nothing we can do about that. Some things that can be taken apart can be moved, but that will sacrifice the space needed for other things. Yes, they are good at harnessing the energy of suns, but it will never be enough for things like this."

"Of course, I understand."

"Let me communicate with Re'alo. He's in contact with the Krumptia, who have access to all galactic technology. My understanding is that they have been given instructions to be as helpful as possible. I'm not sure any of these things can be moved, frankly. But if they can, I'll figure out how, and what the parameters are, and I'll let you worry about where they go." Torf'ki grinned.

That, David would leave to Marianne.

David was about to leave, when Torf'ki shouted, "wait! I have an idea!"

"Yes?"

"It's a bit, oh, what is that weird English word ... 'hairbrained'."

David chuckled. "So far, I've liked all of your 'hairbrained' ideas."

"We have the ability to capture all of the physical details of something into digital memory. This can be done in enough detail to replicate that thing close enough to fool even the experts. The only differences are in the chemical makeup of the thing that is recreated. But to the eye and touch, they are exactly the same. Defects, wear and tear, erosion, etc., are all captured."

"So, you are suggesting..."

"One of the things on the long list I've been meaning to mention to you and the others was that I wanted to start the process of recording as many structures on Earth as possible. We could record these, and then recreate them on New Earth."

"I imagine that the idea will be hard for some to accept."

"It doesn't really matter whether they will accept it, does it? If we can't move it, there is no other choice."

"OK, let's meet with Joel and Laura, and they can coordinate with Casitians back on the Moon to get that party started."

"Party?"

"It's a colloquialism, Torf'ki."

Torf'ki smiled. "Ah, got it. All right, let's get this party started!"

Capital, Hilcyon, Brlew 15 1158

He looked with dismay at the report from Ceckzl that his attaché had brought to him. He had arranged to have Ceckzl released from jail moons ago after the debacle with Rplo and his son. Ylen had given Ceckzl a Second Chief spot in the Central Valley, underneath his most trusted First Chief, Wglurn. Wglurn had gone silent all moon, and Ylen had been unable to find out what was happening.

He got in contact with Ceckzl, who still owed him, to find out what had happened. Ylen feared the worst: that a rival chief had bested his trusted chief. What was true was worse. The entire Central Valley had decided to break away from his control, and create a separate, independent state. Ceckzl said in the report that Wglurn was impatient and didn't think that Ylen could create change.

Ylen knew that the Central Valley had been further along in the process of reform than any. All of the chiefs in the Central Valley had instituted changes on their own years before Ylen became Supreme Chief. He could understand their impatience, but this threatened him. If he let them be, he risked being challenged. If he tried to intervene, he risked the change he wanted.

He decided then to visit Wglurn, in person, and see what he could do.

Central Valley, Hilcyon, Brlew 20 1158

"You were silly to come here, Ylen." Wglurn sat in the chair opposite the Supreme Chief, in defiance of the usual protocol where all Chiefs below must stand. Ylen didn't care.

"You have put me in an extremely difficult position, Wglurn. If I let you do what you will, which, of course, I would like to, I am sure to be challenged by another First Chief. I already have heard that Jurrl is training hard. He's going to be tough to beat. He's younger, in better shape, and frankly, a better fighter than I. If he wins, everything we've worked so hard for is in jeopardy. If I challenge you to show my strength and 'loyalty to the Kinder way', what do I gain? Both of these outcomes are bad. Both of them result in things going backward."

"Ylen, the Central Valley is a different place than the rest of Kinder Home, and I intend to keep it that way. Because of the mountain ranges, once we shut off the train tubes, it is impossible for a force to get in here."

"We could cut your water off."

Wglurn smiled. "And many outside of the Central Valley would starve. Don't forget that 75% of the food eaten in the south comes from the Central Valley."

This was a fact that Ylen well knew. Because of its proximity to the equator and the protection from wind and dust storms that the mountains provided, the Central Valley was by far the most productive regions on all of Hilcyon. Ylen had looked at the numbers before he left. Fully 45% of all of the food of Hilcyon was grown here, and it was essential to the maintenance of the planet's population. And the recent increase in water availability from the technology delivered by the Grier was increasing production capacity. Soon, there would be no need for rationing.

Ylen knew that Wglurn was in a good position – as good as any. The Central Valley could be self-governing, and still provide the food that Hilcyon needed. There was not much the Capital could do.

"OK, Wglurn, you win. I'm letting you do what you will. Even though you will have my covert support, you will only hear my overt opposition."

"Understood, Ylen." Ylen nodded and stood up to leave.

"And one more thing."

"Yes?"

"If I am bested, please take my wife and children into your community, they'll do better here. Most importantly, my wife knows everything I know. She'll know what Chiefs you can trust, and what Chiefs you cannot. She'll know what kinds of strategies might be used against you. She'll know how you can best cope in my absence."

Wglurn stood up and bowed. "Thank you, Ylen. I will arrange for it."

Beijing, Earth, June 23, 2026

Chin's hands were shaking. She looked at her inbox, and one email was from the Casitian Emigration Team. This was it. This was her acceptance or rejection for emigration to Casiti. She clicked on the email and read.

"Dear Chin Lau, it is our great pleasure to offer you a berth on the first colony ship leaving for Casiti. We expect departure to be in early July of 2028. Your shuttle will depart from Beijing International Airport. Final date and time will be sent to this email address at least one week before departure."

The email went on and on, including lists of things that should be brought, and lists of things that should not be brought. Cargo limits, details, etc. She didn't care. She'd emigrate in her skivvies and sit on the cold Casitian ground if she had to.

Two years! She already felt the seconds ticking more slowly.

She looked again at her inbox and saw another message that looked a bit odd. It was from someone with a Casitian name!

"Dear Chin Lau, your application was forwarded to me. I'm acting as head agronomy teacher for the Jul'when settlement process, and I need to recruit a team to coordinate food production on Jul'when, using both Casitian and Earth crops. I looked over your work, and you are a great fit for our team. I'd like you to come up to the moon station to start this work in earnest. The team will be going to Casiti early. Please let me know when you can join us. The sooner you can join us, the better."

Chin got up from her chair and did a happy dance. Not only was she emigrating to Casiti, but she would get to be part of a very important team, right off the bat. She couldn't imagine being happier. She quickly composed her response, sent it, and then started to write her to do list. She had a lot to get accomplished in a few days, her last days on Earth.

Chapter 5:
One Hundred in the Highlands

(AP) July 31, 2026

Diana Westinghouse-Lewis Wins Landslide World Presidential Election. Pro-evacuation Candidates Sweep into World Office on Her Coattails

Ankara, Turkey – Diana Westinghouse-Lewis wins the World election with a landslide vote of 75%, with all districts and countries reporting. Leigin Shan received only 13% of the vote, and, most surprisingly, only 35% of the vote in his home country of China. Although polling before the election showed him with more than 70% of the Chinese vote, over the short history of the Chinese democracy, polling has proven to be extraordinarily non-predictive of victory or defeat of candidates in elections. Pro-evacuation candidates for World Congress won overwhelmingly in most countries, even though some countries still have anti-evacuation governments in place.

President-elect Westinghouse-Lewis is the first World President, and given the ten-year term of that office, she will be the last World President of Earth as well. She is also the first woman to hold any sort of global leadership position. President-elect Westinghouse-Lewis takes her office as of January first, 2027.

Dlejon, New Earth, Month 1, Year 27

Ja'el said, "I like this space, Marianne. I love the trees around the cabin. It feels so different than anywhere else I've been, although it seems more Earth-like than Casiti-like."

They were sitting at Marianne's small kitchen table, drinking cups of tea.

"Yes, I think that's true. This planet seems to agree with me."

"Do you have any plans to visit Earth before the end?"

The end. Marianne thought, yes, I guess it is the end.

"No. I have enough to do here, and from what I can tell, my presence would not be appreciated by many on Earth right now. It's in Diana's capable hands."

"Yes, indeed, her hands are quite capable. I've heard that she's working well with Welen'da and her team."

"The first wave of ships is due to arrive in a little over a year. I'm glad we're ready for them."

Ja'el looked at Marianne in a way that made her feel a little uncomfortable.

"Marianne, you look tired."

"I am. I've been working almost nonstop since you communicated with us 2 years ago."

"Maybe you should take a break."

"Actually, I am taking time off before first wave arrives. I'm joining Leticia, Mira and some others in their travels up north, to an area near-ish to the pole. No one has been up there. We're going to camp and explore. I'm looking forward to the quiet. Would you like to join us? You haven't told me how long you intended to stay on New Earth."

Ja'el looked away, and Marianne wondered what was going on.

"Marianne, I... I want to stay a while, if that's OK. I'd love to come traveling with you."

Marianne put her hand on Ja'el's arm and sent her love. She didn't quite know what else might be traveling in that sending. Ja'el looked at Marianne and started to cry.

"Marianne, I wish to ask for your forgiveness. I feel that I have hurt you, and I didn't really understand myself."

"I would forgive you anything Ja'el. But tell me more about what you mean."

"I was so intent on maintaining my ... my Casitian nature, that I ignored my own feelings. I missed you terribly in the time you were behind the locked wormhole. I struggled with the idea that we had done what was right for Casiti, even as I mourned my loss. Eventually I came to understand that I hadn't really wanted to leave you after our time together. I realized I left because I was trying to protect something that didn't need protecting."

"What about what you said the night I left?"

"I was trying to avoid feeling my own pain. It didn't work of course. I felt the pain anyway."

"Ja'el, I never stopped loving you, even when I thought you stopped loving me."

"I never stopped loving you, and I'm sorry that I made you think that I had."

Marianne got up from the table and took Ja'el's hand. "Well, I think we have a lot of years to make up for."

Ja'el rose from her chair, held Marianne's chin in her hand, and kissed her first on her cheek, where tears were falling, and then her lips. They embraced, and Marianne led Ja'el to her bed.

Independent Christian State, Month 1, Year 27

"Jasmine, you've been home for over a year now. I understand your need to recover, but it's time for you to get married."

Jasmine looked at her mother with confusion. When she first came back from the mines, her mother and father had asked Jasmine to stay because they had missed her and had been afraid she was dead. She hadn't wanted to, but they convinced her to stay a while. Then, about a week ago, the story had completely changed, and she didn't understand it.

"Mom, when I first came home, I explained to you that I was leaving the ICS. You begged and pleaded for me to stay, so I did, even though I didn't want to. Now, all of a sudden you want me to get married?"

"Jasmine, we want and need you to stay, and we could never understand why you would want to leave the ICS. Our pastor explained to us that the returning women didn't have dispensation indefinitely. The rule is that women over 18 must marry or join the Mission Society. We want you here, with us, so you must marry."

Jasmine shook her head. "Sorry mom. This means I'm leaving."

"But Jasmine..."

"Mom, I have explained this how many zillion times? I will not get married. Not to a man at least." She threw that last bit in just for spite. The truth was, she had no interest of marriage of any sort.

Jasmine got up from the chair in the living room and went into her bedroom to start to pack her bag. Her mother followed.

"Are you telling me you're... you're..."

"Yes."

Her mother's face was a mask. "It's better that you left then." She walked out of her room. Jasmine had figured that would do it. She couldn't stand dealing with her mother's inane requests anymore. And it wasn't really a lie, just an oversimplification. She happened to like men and women about equally well.

She finished packing and did a quick check of the bus schedule. She could catch the next bus headed for New Richmond in about half an hour. That gave her more than enough time to walk to the bus depot.

She left her bedroom with her bag on her shoulder.

"Goodbye, Mom. I'll send you..."

Her mother didn't look up from what she was doing. "Don't bother."

Jasmine nodded and walked out the front door.

New Columbia, New Earth, Month 1, Year 27

Kurt walked into the Oval Office in the White House of New America, remembering who designed it. It was much larger than it should be, with ostentatious furniture that would not suit Valorie one bit. As her new chief of staff, he needed to find someone to get rid of what was in here. The White House itself was quite small in comparison to the real thing. Kurt got an idea that maybe the office should be re-purposed to the conference room – the current one was far too small to hold the cabinet that Valorie had in mind to create.

He was happy to be Chief of Staff. Valorie had credited her victory to his work, and although he knew he contributed, she really was the one responsible – people just simply liked her, across the political spectrum. They could tell she cared about them, and she really did – it was not an act. She had traveled all across New America, from settlements scattered across the ICS, down to Jerome and cities close to the border with the IZs. Valorie had tapped into the anxiety felt all across New America about the inevitable immigration of the current residents of the United States. And unlike her opponent, who used fear of change to motivate them to fight the immigration, Valorie used their better natures to suggest how we could show leadership, and create a new United States that we all could be proud of.

In the middle of the campaign when emotions were running hot and all sorts of rumors were flying about where the U.S. population would be settled, many people started saying that they would be settled elsewhere. Marianne had to make an announcement to clarify that there would be no new US settled area save the areas dedicated to the native tribes. All U.S. citizens who wanted to immigrate to the US would be allowed to do so. Many U.S. citizens would choose to live in IZ settlements that matched their interests. She made it clear that no amount of protest or bargain would change her decision.

It had created an uproar, and had yanked the rug out from under current President Mason. And Valorie reminded everyone that New America and the ICS had more than the land area of all 50 of the current United States. There would be more than enough room for everyone.

President Mason tried to accuse Marianne of rigging the election, but Marianne had been extremely careful in her announcement. No one could suggest that she purposely favored Valorie, although Kurt knew that she did. Kurt smiled inwardly remembering that Valorie confided in him that she had a soft spot in her heart for Marianne. Kurt wasn't surprised.

Kurt heard footsteps behind him. "Good God, Kurt." He turned to see Valorie enter with another aide.

"I know. I'm going to get someone to get rid of all of this. I wonder whether this might work better as our conference room. There's another office down the hall that is a nice size, and has a great view – perhaps you can use that as your office."

Valorie looked thoughtful. "Kurt, I know this is going to surprise you."

"But?"

"This is going to be the office of the President of the United States at some point, not just the President of New America. We're going to need an Oval Office, Kurt. Let's get rid of most of this stuff, and find tasteful furnishings that would fit the real Oval Office, OK?"

Kurt nodded. Kurt and Valorie had a long talk about the change from New America to the United States of America on New Earth. He knew that she, unlike her opponent, took that transition utterly seriously, and would do everything in her power to make it as smooth as possible. She'd even talked with him about figuring out how to do trans-planet elections when the population of the US would be split evenly between the two planets.

"I think we'll need to start making expansion plans for the White House. We can get by with what's here for a year or so, but after that ..."

"President Hopkinson started a government that didn't really do much. We'll be doing a lot more..."

Valorie nodded. "Indeed."

Hilcyon, Mrontl 15 1159

"I'm sorry to give you this news. What you do is up to you. Moving to the Central Valley might be the best thing, but if you are willing to try and stick it out here with me, I'd be happy to have you."

Ylen was addressing the group of returnees from New Earth, who had just arrived. Lren considered the options. Ylen had made it clear in his address that he felt his leadership was in grave danger after the breakaway of the Central Valley. Their return from New Earth was considered suspicious. Ylen had said it was a direct prisoner transfer, that in return for the 9,000 or so from the mines, the prisoners that New Earth had supposedly kept were sent back. But many people knew that there had been deserters, and Lren knew he would not survive long under a conservative chief.

Five hundred of his fellow deserters had decided to come back. He imagined most would be doing the same calculus. He was happy that he didn't have a wife or family to worry about - he'd never married, and his parents and siblings were dead. He was free to go where he would.

"Supreme Chief Ylen, one question."

"Certainly, Lren." Lren had noticed that Ylen treated him with respect.

"Are there other regions like the Central Valley that are close to moving over to reform?"

Ylen closed his eyes for a moment. "There are two I can think of. The Desert Quadrant has always been a little wild. Their previous First Chief, Glendr, was a conservative, and uniformly hated by his Second

Chiefs. The First Chief there now is a close ally and trusts most if not all of his Second Chiefs.

"The second region is the remote Upper Highlands, near the glaciers. It's cold, and it's hard to grow much. But the Grier suggested that we try to raise buffalo, sheep and goats on the grasses that grow abundantly up there, and they sent us some. That has worked well so far. Since that change, the Chiefs up there have been very interested in reform. The supplies of food coming from that region to the rest of Hilcyon are becoming important. The First Chief is someone I trust, and he has the trust of his Second Chiefs."

"I suggest that some of us go to those regions. It will strengthen your hand should you be able to remain Supreme Chief. If you are not, they are regions not likely to bother the conservatives here in the Capital, but we can still work for reform."

Ylen nodded. "Yes, Lren, that is quite perceptive."

Ylen left them, and they started to discuss among themselves where they would go.

Upper Highlands, Hilcyon, Mrontl 25 1159

Lren left his dwelling to go check on the goats that were now in his care. He had moved up here with about 100 of his people. The rest moved either to the Desert Quadrant, or to the Central Valley. None of them chose another course. It was clear to Lren that the new herding programs could use more hands.

On his arrival, he had immediately been given a Third Chief position. He knew that he had made the right choice. He predicted that Ylen would lose his position, and reform from the top would stop. The only way reform could continue was from the bottom up.

Capital, Hilcyon, Mrontl 25 1159

Jurrl was out of breath, and the sweat was pouring down his face. He had to stop to wipe his brow before he wasn't able to see anymore.

"Ylen won't let you stop to wipe your face, Jurrl. He'll use any pause to try and end it."

"Yes, yes, I know. Let's go."

They had been at it for over two hours. Jurrl was in intensive training, spending several hours per day either in fight training or general athletic training. His trainers thought he'd be ready by mid-Sdert to best Ylen. He didn't want to wait that long, but he didn't want to die, either. They kept going for a while longer, and then Trill, one of his coaches, called a halt.

"Time for rest."

"No, time for work. I still am a First Chief, you know."

He grabbed a towel, and went to see Willm, who had just walked in.

"You have something for me?"

Willm bowed. "Yes, First Chief. I thought you'd want to know where the deserters went."

"Ah. yes, I do."

"As you expected, most went to the Central Valley."

"Not surprising. The rest?"

"This is where it gets interesting. I had expected the rest to scatter all over Hilcyon, to live with their families, or the settlements they came from. But none of them did that."

"None?"

"Not one. About a hundred went to live up in the Upper Highlands. The rest, about 20, went to the Desert Quadrant."

"What? The Upper Highlands and the Desert Quadrant? Why?"

"Well, my information tells me that the current First Chiefs of both are reformers, and that most or all of their Second Chiefs are as well."

"Ah, these are like the Central Valley, then."

"Yes. These are regions to watch out for."

"Nah, nothing is there. They can reform themselves into Breft for all I care."

"First Chief, the Upper Highlands now is producing those animals from Grier, with the meat and products everyone likes."

"Ah. Right. I see. But it is also a virtually impossible area to get troops into, like the Central Valley."

"Indeed. They have the advantage. They have abundant water, new sources of food, and it is remote enough to make taking it over not worth the trouble."

New Calgary, New Earth, Month 1, Year 27

Leticia was excited. She was going to go traveling again, this time in areas she hadn't been. Few had been where they were now planning to go. They would start by traveling east from New Calgary to the river that some had named the Missouri, since it was a tributary to the Mississippi. There were very few settlements east of New Calgary, so they would largely be on their own. They would take the river up to Lake Superior, the large freshwater lake near the pole. It was at least twice as large as all of the great lakes put together. Lake Maracaibo, near the south pole, was even bigger. One of these days, she hoped to get to visit that one, too. There were other lakes scattered around, the large ones all by the poles.

They initially had somewhat of a dilemma. They wanted to camp, and really get to see the land, and take samples, and do accurate mapping of the rivers, and such, but they also had an enormous amount of ground to cover. Because of its size and lack of oceans, New Earth had ten times the land area of Earth. Their present project was to map out an area that was larger than the size of North America. It wasn't going to be possible to do that all on foot in a reasonable period of time. So, they compromised.

Marianne told Leticia of these small overland vehicles that were used on Casiti. They were like a car, except that they could travel over rough terrain, as well as water. Marianne had known that they would be of great use here, and she put in a large order for them early on, and the first shipment had arrived a few months ago. They also would be supplied by shuttle, so they wouldn't need to carry a lot with them.

Leticia was happy that Marianne and Ja'el had chosen to come. Also coming were Jeffrey and Thomas, who wanted to do a lot of plant sampling, as well as a few other companions from that first trip Leticia took so long ago. It looked like they would need 3 of the cars. Leticia and Mira were in charge of the tents and equipment for cooking and the like. Jeffrey and Thomas in charge of the scientific equipment, and Marianne in charge of the logistics for use of the cars, and the shuttle supply. They would be gone for about 3 New Earth months. It seemed a long time to Leticia, but she was grateful for the break in her routine.

She knew that many other teams all over New Earth would be doing the same work in other unexplored regions, so that they could gain a complete understanding of the terrain, what places made sense for settlements, and what the weather was like.

She had realized just after he heard about the edict that the work that she'd been doing with the new medical school was moot. There would be thousands and thousands of trained doctors and whole medical schools making their way here. But she was, nonetheless, proud of their achievements. She didn't know what her future would hold, given that she didn't have the "real" credentials of a physician trained in the US.

New Columbia, New Earth, Month 1, Year 27

"Are you out of your mind?"

Valorie was taken aback by the question that came from Jerome Kramer, the new Governor of the ICS.

"Excuse me?"

"I understand that you want to come across as welcoming and touchy-feely and all, but we must protect our investments."

Valorie laughed. "Which would be?"

"Investments in infrastructure, in governance ..."

"Governor Kramer, the government that I just took over was a joke. Gerard Hopkinson refused to do anything except protect the privileged class, and Mason followed exactly in his footsteps. I don't even want to mention Hickler. New America has virtually no middle class to speak of, and most of the working class emigrated to the IZs last year. The rich are living off of the sales of titanium, gold, other precious metals, and materials and technology given by the Kinder to Dennis Hickler. New America has a little manufacturing, a little farming, and not much else. The 'riches' of New America came entirely from gifts given in exchange for 17,000 teenagers, many of whom died before being able to return. "

"Well, the ICS has fared better."

"Agreed. Because of your social structure, you have been able to retain a broader base of people and build some more infrastructure.

But it is not a model that can continue, and certainly is not a model that can be used for the rest of the country."

"What do you mean, cannot continue?"

"Governor Kramer, the ICS will be a part of the United States soon. As such, it cannot continue with its current model. It must be integrated..."

"Absolutely not! We left Earth because we didn't want to be tainted by the stink..."

"Please, be reasonable."

"Reasonable? We will not take any immigrants that do not fit our requirements, and we will not allow any governance over us that means we must abandon our Christian principles. Our only true leader is God, and that is the way it will always be."

He got up, and walked out of her office, without even a goodbye. Valorie went to her desk, picked up the communicator, and called Marianne.

New Columbia, New Earth, Month 1, Year 27

"Thanks for coming to see me on such short notice, Marianne."

"It's not a problem, and actually, I had a matter to discuss with you anyway. I feel for poor J'lera. He's my shuttle pilot. He hardly has gotten a chance to settle into his new dwelling in Dlejon. It seems every day someone somewhere on New Earth needs to talk with me. You know, I'll be off the radar for a while this year."

"I heard. Good for you. Get some R & R and some work done at the same time?"

"That's part of the idea."

"So, this is the problem. I had a very troubling conversation with Governor Kramer, which had been prompted by a complete failure of my aides to work with any in his administration. First, he blamed me for the problem, saying that my people were making inappropriate demands of his people, asking questions they shouldn't have been, etc.

"Then, he launched into this tirade about you and the Casitians, and how he had barely tolerated the presence of the IZs, and how troubling my winning the presidency of New America was, yadda

yadda. I mostly ignored it. Finally, though, he made it clear that the ICS was only taking immigrants that 'fit their requirements' and that they don't want to be part of New America."

Marianne sighed. She'd gotten a long-winded and angry missive from Governor Kramer, which, in the end, declared the independence of the ICS. That was the matter she had needed to discuss with Valorie.

"I got a long, angry email from Kramer. Basically, his demand is that the ICS become a truly independent territory, beholden to no one but God. I'm going to give him what he wants so he'll leave us alone."

"But he has so much land!"

"Yes, I know. However, the Western two thirds of his territory are largely unsettled. I'm going to tell him that he can have his completely independent country, but only on a third of the current land of the ICS. The rest will be given to you for the US."

"That seems like a proposal he won't like but can't possibly turn down."

Moon Station July 24, 2026/ 50 Gont 784

Chin Liau couldn't have thought of a better birthday present. Today was her twenty-seventh birthday, and she was sitting in her new quarters on the moon station, getting ready to work with a team on Casitian agronomy. She'd just arrived from Earth a few hours ago and had her first meal in space. She had been surprised by the station. She thought the architecture was beautiful, as well as all of the art on the walls. She had been told that most of it was from Earth artists, but some were also Casitian.

It had taken her a bit longer for her to finally get here than she thought. First, she had to take care of all of her belongings. Because of the upcoming massive emigration, it was hard to get rid of her stuff, because people had started dumping things all over the place, and new systems had to be put in place to prevent that.

She'd had to sell what she could, which wasn't much, and then take the rest to a new incineration facility, which would incinerate the stuff cleanly. There were extra clothes, books she had accumulated, all sorts of odds and ends. It took a while for all of that to be disposed of. Her landlord was angry that she was breaking their contract, and he knew he wouldn't find anyone to rent her place. But there was nothing he could do to her: she was an official member of the Casitian Agronomy Service (the Casitian name for it was one she could not yet pronounce) and was bound for Casiti!

Here she was, in her quarters, looking out at the moonscape after having unpacked her few things. Her first meetings were in about 8 hours – the beginning of the day here on the moon. It was morning her time right now, but she figured that getting at least a little sleep might be a good idea. A Casitian she'd met at the meal (third meal, she learned) gave her a few pills – she said that it was hard for Earth humans to adjust to the different length of days, since the moon station had always kept the Casitian clock and calendar, and that these helped. She took one with a bit of water from her sink, turned off the light, and went to sleep.

Moon Station July 24, 2026/51 Gont 784

"Hi. I'm Chin Liau, from Beijing. I did my doctoral work on adapting Casitian techniques for legume crops for high-altitude areas. We were able to get decent yields of navy and soybeans using these techniques. I'm excited to use this to help us grow crops on Jul'when."

Everyone in the room was introducing themselves. There were 12 of them on the team, from all over Earth. Collectively, Chin thought that they must be familiar with the widest possible range of cultivation methodologies and food crop varieties all over Earth. It was exciting to meet people from Africa who had worked with Casitian techniques to increase yields of crops in small plots, to people from the US and Europe who were familiar with cultivating warm weather vegetables like tomatoes and peppers. Chin took an immediate liking to Isidora, who had experimented with Casitian crops in Chile, with good results.

Ser'len'a was the Casitian teacher of their team. She was one of the stockier Casitians Chin had seen so far, and she had long, very black hair.

She said, "welcome, all to this program. You can't begin to know how happy we are to have you all, and to begin the process of working on growing enough crops on Jul'when to feed the immigrants that will be coming in subsequent waves. In the next day or two, please take time to read the rather extensive introductory material we've given you; it's a lot to digest. It includes the expectations for your involvement in this work, decision making by consensus, details about Casitian culture, as well as a large amount of scientific information about Jul'when. Also included are some logistical scenarios we are working on for the immigration process to Jul'when. Any feedback that you have would be appreciated. Please do read the cultural material. I know that most of you know a lot about Casiti - clearly you had wanted to immigrate there. But there are some details you might not know and will come in handy as you work among the Casitians.

Of course, there is learning our language. You'll find information on the options available to you. Some take longer than others, and people learn languages in different ways and at different paces. It would be good if you can take part in a fairly simple conversation in Casitian by the time we leave for Casiti in a month – a Casitian month, that is." Ser'len'a smiled and dismissed them.

Chin went back to her quarters, sat down on one of the comfortable chairs, and began to read the material.

Capital, Hilcyon, Pliert 12 1159

Jurrl was angry. He'd spent the last 24 hours recounting, over and over, the sins of Ylen. This was how he always geared up for a challenge fight. He started slowly, digging deeper and deeper into the ways his opponent was betraying the Kinder. He had Willm repeat the sins of Ylen. Ylen's willingness to talk to the Breft. Ylen not executing the deserters on the spot, Ylen's changing the water rations to support rebel regions. Now, a few minutes before he was to enter the ring, he was livid, the anger coursing through his body, streaming out of his hands – the hands that held the Hklef.

Early in his training, he'd considered other weapons. The short sword, the circle blade, the Klee, which was a weapon consisting of two sharp blades on heavy handles connected to a chain that was about an arm's span long. He chose the Hklef. It had many disadvantages. It was big and heavy and took work to move around. The main handle was thick, and couldn't be held by most men, but Jurrl had large hands. Each end had a heavy, round weight with 12 small but sharp blades sticking out from them.

It was a weapon both difficult and devastating. He'd used it each of the 5 challenge fights he'd fought. He had better upper body strength than most men, so the weight of the weapon was his advantage.

The door to the ring suddenly opened, and he heard the crowd roar. He walked into the ring, and the anger was running in his veins, ringing in his ears, and emanating from his body in waves. He saw Ylen enter from the other door. He saw the short sword in his hand. His face was a mask, but Jurrl thought he could see fear. He certainly felt Ylen's fear.

The judge, standing in the middle, began to speak. "Jurrl, you challenge Ylen's Supreme Chiefdom, is that correct?"

Jurrl had only to nod.

"Ylen, you accept this challenge?"

"Yes. Let's get this over with."

"There are four rounds. Jurrl, you must kill Ylen by the end of the fourth round. If not, your life is forfeit."

Jurrl nodded.

"Start!"

The judge left the center of the ring.

Jurrl started to slowly circle Ylen, sizing him up, looking at how he moved. His strategy was to take the first round to size up Ylen. He was simply looking at Ylen, moving his Hklef back and forth, when Ylen ran right at him with a yell, short sword forward. He was taken completely by surprise and didn't have time to bring an end of the Hklef to bear. Because of the weight of the Hklef, he couldn't move very fast. The best thing he could do was bring the handle of the Hklef up to guard against the sword piercing his chest.

The blade hit the handle of his weapon, and Jurrl twisted the handle to bring one side of it to hit Ylen's head, but Ylen moved forward and bowled Jurrl over. Jurrl fell to the ground sideways, and he heard some of his blades break when his Hklef hit the floor. He looked up to see

Ylen bearing down on him, and he saw the blade move quickly toward his midsection.

With a desperate heave, he pulled one side of the Hklef up toward Ylen, and he saw the blades slice Ylen's face, and all of a sudden blood was everywhere and Ylen was down. Jurrl got up to look down at Ylen. The blades had severed a main artery in Ylen's neck. Ylen was dead, his blood pooling below him.

It was only then that he felt the pain in his stomach, and the wound now bled freely. He looked at the wound in puzzlement, and the world started to spin, then went dark.

New Richmond, New Earth, Month 2, Year 27

Beatrice was in her new room, unpacking her suitcase in her new room. She didn't have much stuff. She'd brought with her one suitcase full of new clothes that she had gotten when she returned to New Earth, and one box of her belongings.

She opened the box, looking at the small, hand-bound books written in the Kinder language. They were the books that Pkygy had published of his grandmother's stories – the writing that got him imprisoned originally on the mines. She'd managed to find a complete set of copies on Hilcyon. Pkygy had been embarrassed by it – but she was glad she had something of his spirit with her. She intended to go to the Kinder settlement and get the book translated, because she didn't know how to read Kinder. She walked back out to the living room.

"Mom, I'm glad we left – things were getting so much worse there. Governor Kramer is getting more autocratic, there hasn't been much improvement in the local economy, and trade with the IZs is almost non-existent. And I've heard rumors that the ICS isn't going to take any immigrants except those that meet certain criteria – you know what that will be!"

"I know Beatrice. Your father is very happy we moved."

"And mom, grandma wouldn't have fit the criteria. She's not even Christian. Anyway, thanks for listening to me, mom. I think New Richmond will be a great place, and this house is big enough for all four of us."

"You know, I wouldn't mind if Marianne, or even Leticia and Mira wanted to ..."

"Dream on. They have their lives elsewhere, mom. Besides, they are about to leave on a big expedition, I hear."

"You didn't want to go?"

"No. I want to travel down to the Kinder settlement..."

"Why Beatrice?"

"I want to meet Ngellin. Marianne has told me about him. He seems like an interesting man. I want to find someone to translate the writings of my husband into English."

"So now that we've moved, mom, what are you going to do?"

"I don't know, Beatrice. Now that we don't live in the ICS anymore, I can work... although I don't know what I'd want to do."

"There's a lot to do around helping the new arriving immigrants, when they get here next year"

"That's a great idea, actually. Who do you think I should talk with?"

"I'm sure Aunt Marianne can hook you up."

"Maybe, but she never answers my messages!"

Dlejon, New Earth, Month 2, Year 27

Marianne got up from her desk and stretched. 600 widenet messages a day was brutal. She realized she needed to finally figure out how to get a Casitian AI to parse them - she would never be able to catch up. She thought that Torf'ki would certainly have someone on staff who could work this out. She made a mental note to ask him next time she was at the station.

As she went to her small kitchen and as she passed the dining room table strewn with maps of New Earth and Earth, she stopped and looked over it all. Her task was to balance a very wide range of demands of Earth countries, New Earth settlements and territories, native and indigenous tribes, and the assorted people, some sane, some nutcakes, who were requesting independent settlements. She thanked the God of Many Names that New Earth had ten times the land area as old Earth. Otherwise, her task would be impossible.

That still didn't make things easy. Earth countries, knowing that New Earth had ten times the land, expected ten times the original land area for their own countries. She had tried over and over to explain to all of them that because of the initial settlements of Earth, as well as the desire for many on Earth to live in Independent Zones, that was just not going to be possible. Incredulous and livid would be understatements of the response of some leaders to the idea that people would want to live outside of any country. She had several leaders who led democracies threaten war on independent zones if their people chose to live there instead of in their country of origin.

It was frustrating to say the least. But she wasn't giving in. The other big issue was borders. Countries would without doubt have borders that didn't have them on Earth. And that was an enormous issue for some countries. Australia didn't want to border any countries in Africa. Canada wanted to border only the United States, but that wasn't going to be possible. Europe wanted to be moved with the same exact borders they have now, except with more space, all Arab countries wanted to be on opposite ends of the planet from Israel, and Ireland wanted to be as far removed from England as possible.

Marianne took a deep breath. She heard some footsteps behind her, and felt Ja'el's soft hands wrapping around her torso, and her chin resting on her right shoulder.

"How's this going?"

Marianne sighed. "I guess as well as could be expected. I have less than a year to finalize this, and sometimes it feels impossible. But then I remember that I get to make the decisions. Then it feels easier, but somehow unfair."

Ja'el chuckled. "You always found leadership troublesome, even though you are so good at it."

Marianne turned around to face Ja'el. "Yes, you hit the nail on the head, as usual. It will all work out, of course, but it's going to be a bit hellish along the way. I think that our traveling will help clear my head so that I can finally finish it when we get back."

Ja'el smiled, and whispered in Marianne's ear, "I can think of something to take your mind off of it for the moment." She gently bit Marianne's ear, and every thought about maps and countries and priorities went out of her head, leaving only Ja'el.

Casiti, 5 Paqn 784

Jal'end'a sat facing Hetl'zef in comfortable chairs in one corner of her too-large office. All the official details of the transfer of power to her had been completed. This was the farewell meeting of the past head teacher and the new head teacher. Jal'end'a was calm, although she could sense the current of anxiety brewing within her. She would need to spend time in meditation soon.

"Jal'end'a, you know you'll have the help of assistants and the rest of the Caraj. Simply do what you know is best."

"Thank you, Hetl'zef. I very much appreciate your confidence in me. What are your plans?"

"I'll be leading the agronomy team on Jul'when. We're setting up some initial living quarters and structures for the team coming from Earth. I'm excited to get to live on Jul'when for a while. I've looked over the applications of this group of Terrans, and I am impressed by their dedication to creating a livable continent, as well as their interest in living here on Casiti. Most of them were on the Casitian immigration waiting list before the edict."

"I hear you expect to grow both Casitian and Earth crops."

"I know that some of the Earth crops will only grow for a very small part of our high summer, so they will be special treats. But many Earth crops will be able to be grown throughout the growing season, and indoors during winter."

Hetl'zef and Jal'end'a rose. "Blessings be upon you, Hetl'zef for your work with the Terrans. I'm sure you'll enjoy it."

"And blessings on you, Jal'end'a, as you lead the Caraj."

They shared a clasped-arm hug, and Hetl'zef left, closing the door behind him. A light chime sounded, and Jal'end'a went back to her desk to attend to a new message. The arts council had been in discussion with a small group of Terran museum directors that wanted their collections to end up on Casiti. They had requested that Jal'end'a mediate their discussions, as they had completely broken down.

Jal'end'a remembered that on Earth, most art was relegated to indoor spaces that relatively few visited. She wondered whether it would be at all possible to change their ideas about where art should go.

New Aard, New Earth, Month 3, Year 27

Olam read the missive for the umpteenth time from the Arab League on Earth. He was filled with dismay. Unlike the vision that New Aard leadership had of a new, united Muslim state, the Arab League wanted space for each of their countries. They hadn't heard back from any of the Muslim countries in Asia or Africa, but Olam could see their idea crumbling. If the Arab League refused to join in, then the rest would too.

His messages to Marianne had been answered by an AI who said that Marianne was traveling and exploring and would be unavailable for another two months. This meant that nothing could be done about this. Olam had no idea how this would affect New Aard, as it occupied a very large area – far larger than the area of the Arab League on Earth. Olam knew that Marianne would not give Muslim nations whole additional new space – it would come out of New Aard somehow.

And that would possibly be a disaster. The leaders of New Aard were not going to take kindly to dividing up their land so that existing Earth countries could fit inside. That would mean people would be forced to move.

Olam's role was to help build infrastructure in New Aard. He'd started that process, but now, with this uncertainty, he'd had to stop. And there had been frequent arguments among New Aard leaders for the last several days about what to do about the situation.

Olam had a plan, and he thought it just might work. He got out a piece of paper and started drawing possible territories and borders. Yes, yes, this was exactly right. And he could see how he could get both Marianne and his leaders to agree. In the end, though, he knew that Marianne had the final say.

New Orleans, New Earth, Month 3, Year 27

Torf'ki smiled. "Thanks, David for suggesting we come down here for a short break. I haven't been down to New Earth for a month or so, and it's nice to spend some time on the ground, for once. And I do love Earth beer."

David liked Torf'ki. He liked him a lot. This trip wasn't just to take a break, he had an ulterior motive, and he bet that Torf'ki had figured it out already. He was a smart one. But he figured he'd start on a somewhat innocuous topic.

"This isn't exactly Earth beer. It's not bad, but I'm looking forward to when real breweries make it over here. I like New Orleans. It reminds me a tiny bit of the old one on Earth. By the way, how is the memory capturing thing going?"

"It's going well, I hear. I haven't yet seen any of the results, but they've divided up earth into parts of about 100 square miles and are doing it piece by piece."

"All of Earth?? I thought it was just going to be ..."

"Welen'da decided that she had the time and the staff to get it done, and she thought that Earth humans would appreciate having the whole thing captured. Obviously, it can't all be recreated in physical form, but it will all be viewable holographically. We'll have to choose carefully what gets recreated, given the energy and materials it will take to for recreation."

"That makes sense. I never thought that I'd be able to, for instance, visit Ayer's rock, or the Grand Canyon after the end, but it looks like I will."

Torf'ki smiled. "It would be fun if you took me to those places sometime. I mean the real places. Since we're going to have to go back to Earth at least once or twice during this time, I'd like to see some of that."

David nodded. "Happily, Torf'ki. I would love to show you some of Earth."

They sat in companionable silence for a while, sipping their beers.

"Torf'ki, Musb is coming soon. Are you sad not to be on Casiti? Time to hunker down for winter, find a companion and all that?"

Torf'ki sat back in his chair. "Frankly, no."

David was a little surprised at the confidence of that answer. "Really? Why not?"

"A number of reasons. First, I don't really like the cold all that much. I've been enjoying New Earth's climate quite a bit. I want to go back to Casiti to visit sometime, but I'm already sure I want to make my home here. And I'm not alone. I've been hearing this from a number of Casitians working here now."

"Wow, Torf'ki, I had no idea."

"I really like the range of people here – it's much more interesting and engaging than on Casiti. Casiti got ... well, it got pretty homogeneous over the hundreds of years. I love the variety here."

"Anything else?"

"And I do have plans for Musb." Torf'ki grinned. "That is, if he agrees."

David raised an eyebrow. "He? And who would that be?"

Torf'ki leaned forward and dropped his left hand to sit lightly on David's thigh. David felt his desire. "What do you think?"

Wilderness East of NCIZ, New Earth Month 3, Year 27

They had been traveling for about a week, using some overland cars to get from New Calgary to the Missouri River. Marianne could see the river emerging as they crested this last hill.

Leticia turned backwards to face Marianne and Ja'el. "It's getting late. Should we camp by the riverside?"

"That sounds like a great idea, Leticia. Let's signal to the other cars and find a good place."

They turned the communicator on, and talked with the three other cars, and they agreed to meet at a small clearing right along the river. It would make a great campsite.

It had been a fairly uneventful week. There were 15 on the trip. Mira, Leticia, Marianne and Ja'el were in one car. Thomas, Jeffrey, Georgia and Chuck were in another. Leticia remembered fondly that couple from her first travels in New Earth. The third car had the three from Torf'ki's Casitian team, and the fourth car had the geographer

Jon, also from Leticia's previous travels, and his students from New Calgary University.

They rolled the cars to a stop at the end of the clearing. There was a bit of chaos as the supplies were taken from the cars, the tents were put up, and people went looking for wood for the campfire. They had worked things into a good rhythm over the week, with everyone pitching in to do their part.

After a dinner with discussions of their findings for the day and talk of tomorrow's plans to start moving upriver on the water, most everyone started to head off to their tents. Marianne and Leticia were left alone in front of the fire, as it died down to coals.

Leticia had wanted to talk with her aunt about something, so she was glad that she had this chance.

"Aunt Marianne, I'm glad Ja'el is here. You seem so happy."

Marianne turned from the fire to look at Leticia. "Yes, I am happy. It was kind of unexpected."

"Didn't you break up?"

"Well, it wasn't a breakup in the standard Earth sense. You know about how most Casitians only have lovers for small stretches of time."

"I do. I think I get it, and I can see how it might work out for a lot of people, but then I can't ever imagine being with someone else besides Mira."

Marianne smiled. "You and Mira are quite the pair, yes. I can't quite imagine anything else, either. Anyway, I'm not sure I understand it all completely, but basically at the time Ja'el felt the need to be Casitian – and give up our companionship as was traditional. It turned out in the end it wasn't what she really wanted."

"Do you mind if I ask you a pretty personal question?"

Marianne chuckled. "More personal than the one you just asked?"

"Yeah. I read about something I don't quite understand."

"What's that?"

"It's the Casitian word, lyre'es'gkin."

Marianne opened her mouth, only to close it again.

"Oh, boy. Let's see where to start on this one. Lyre'es'gkin is a word that doesn't translate to English, or any Earth language that I know of. It is a human ability that most Earth humans don't know about, or admit exists, although I think that's changing slowly."

"Yes, the article I read was from Earth. They were talking about new experiments, or something."

"That makes sense, although it seems to me they should ask some Casitians about that."

Leticia agreed with that sentiment.

"Anyway, it is basically a flow of energy, from one person to another. It can be very powerful. It's not hard to learn – it only took me a couple of months of Ja'el's instruction. Some people are more powerful 'senders' and others are more powerful 'receivers.' I'm a much better receiver; Ja'el is a very good sender. Others are pretty balanced. Close your eyes."

Leticia closed her eyes and felt Marianne's light touch on her arm. After a little bit, she felt this calm, peaceful feeling. It was hard to really grab on to - when she tried to pay attention to it, it wisped away.

"I definitely felt something."

"Remember I'm a better receiver than sender. You might be a better sender, so my sending and your receiving would be weak. Tomorrow I'll have Ja'el test it out on you, see what you can feel. There's one thing you really need to know, though."

"What?"

"Casitians take this very seriously. In general, it is used between loved ones and family members, maybe very close friends. None others."

"The article I read seemed to suggest it would make one's sex life better."

Marianne laughed. "That it will."

Chapter 6:
Treaty to Last a Quarter Century

(AP) July 20, 2027

First Wave of Colony Ships Leaves for New Earth

Earth Orbit – Yesterday, an historic moment occurred, when the first thousand colony ships left Earth orbit, bringing one hundred million Terrans to New Earth. This first wave of emigrants consists of only those who have immediate family on New Earth, and experts that will be needed to continue the infrastructure planning and building process already in progress on New Earth. Included in this first wave is a lot of equipment and parts that will assist in building manufacturing capacity on New Earth. Because the Casitian winter is starting soon, the first waves of ships bound for Casiti will not leave for another year.

North Wilderness, New Earth Month 1, Year 28

Leticia looked over the hillsides and saw the Chalcedon River split from the main part of the Mississippi. She knew the Chalcedon River was the northern border of the ICS. There had been several settlements of Mormons and Seventh-Day Adventists further west of their current position, north of the Chalcedon, but they weren't going any further west this trip.

Their trip was close to its end. They had traveled up the Missouri River, across the wide expanse of Lake Superior. They had discovered a large kind of fish-like thing - more like a shark, that were abundant in the lake, as well as other smaller creatures that were more familiar. The shark was most likely the largest animal on New Earth. They had then traveled across land west and north of the lake, mapping out regions, taking biological samples, sampling the climate.

It was significantly colder where they were, and the food plants were not as abundant in this area. One of Jon's students thought that it was likely that they could grow some hardy crops, like winter wheat, rapeseed, and cruciferous vegetables such as cabbage and kale, but not a whole lot else. Some on the Casitian team mentioned some Casitian crops that should be able to be tried up here as well.

Leticia had asked Marianne whether or not any countries were going to be placed up here, and Marianne said that it was likely that it would remain an IZ, like the other polar region. Leticia liked that idea, because she and Mira had found an amazing spot where they both thought they might want to live. It had a view of both Lake Superior and a part of the Mississippi River, as well as a small group of snow-capped mountains north of the river.

Leticia knew that once they returned to civilization, preparations would be in earnest for the arrival of the first immigrants. She knew that the first colony ships would be arriving at Earth in a couple of months, and in about one year, they would be here. She was nervous. She knew that one of the first groups of immigrants would be those who would be responsible for setting up the health care system on New Earth. She was glad she had been given responsibility for being the liaison for her zone, but she didn't have much confidence that it was going to be a smooth transition from the home-grown, cobbled together system they had, to what she expected the immigrants would be building.

She and Mira both were nervously considering what kind of role they might have in a New Earth full of old Earth people. She imagined this was true of many people on New Earth.

Capitol, Hilcyon, Lykl 2 1159

Jurrl looked at his First Chiefs arrayed before him. Most of them looked uneasy, shifting in their chairs. Others looked at him with barely concealed joy. There were a few absent. The First Chiefs of the Desert Quadrant and Upper Highlands had left - they insisted on governing themselves. Jurrl would teach them a lesson. Also, two other chiefs were missing, those who were loyal to Ylen were bested by some second chiefs. He was happy to know that most of these men fully supported him. The ones who did not, would pay.

He had already put Willm in place to determine who had been aligned with Ylen, so Jurrl could eliminate them by any means necessary. He would purge the ranks down to Fourth chiefs of those who were reformers. The time of reform was over.

Jurrl had been incapacitated for a couple of weeks while he recovered from his wounds in the ring. He recovered and was getting stronger and stronger. And he looked forward to putting things back in order after the chaos Ylen started.

"The first order of business is to bring the Central Valley to heel. They cannot go off on their own reform plan. The Kinder must be united. I am assigning First Chief Grly here to lead the charge and become War Chief. Grly will be recruiting from your ranks for the first assault on the Central Valley, to occur in one moon."

Grly moved forward and stood next to Jurrl. Jurrl turned to look at Grly, who had a smile of triumph. Grly was one of his most trusted chiefs, and he knew that if anyone could take back the Central Valley, Grly could.

After more discussion of the war, they all left the conference room, and he went back to his office to deal with an odorous task. He needed to communicate, one last time.

When he taken over Ylen's office, he found messages that Ylen had written to the three leaders of Breft, Grier Nro and Nytt Grier Nro. All of them were women! Jurrl couldn't imagine how Ylen could stomach that. He would have to, just to send his message to them.

Hilcyon would remain independent of Grier and Breft. Neither Grier nor Breft could visit or live in their system. They would find their own way, without any new technology, without any new people. They had lived without contact or trade with the Breft for more than a thousand years, since the betrayal of Klor. They would continue.

He spent a couple of time periods writing his message. He sent it along the communication channel, and then ordered the destruction of all Breft-connected communication devices. He also sent word to his First Chiefs in space to escort all foreign ships to the wormhole and create a wormhole watch system to destroy any ship that dared enter.

Ankara, Turkey, January 12, 2027

She was in her new office in the new World Capital, which was Turkey's old capital of Ankara, pacing. Pacing helped her keep calm. She felt like she was looking at an impending train wreck. China had completely withdrawn from the evacuation logistics talks, as had a couple of dozen other countries, including surprises like Brazil and South Africa. Work with the Casitians was going well but talks with Hilcyon had completely failed. Their new Supreme Chief completely refused to acknowledge that the leader of Earth humans was a woman and refused to talk to Diana at all.

The Galactic community had given them a lot of resources to quickly build infrastructure on New Earth, and that was occurring at a rapid pace. Also, previously un-assigned areas of New Earth were being bitterly fought over by various countries, all of whom were upset about the relative size of the regions that already existed on New Earth, such as New Aard and New America.

She had tried to explain, over and over, that those boundaries had been drawn before there was any idea that they would have to move most of the entire population of Earth to New Earth. She also kept reminding people that because of New Earth's size, no country would get space any smaller than the size of the country they had now – but somehow that didn't make them feel any better. She knew it really was all in Marianne's hands, and she was happy to leave it there.

The door opened, and one of her aides walked in.

"President Westinghouse-Lewis!"

The aide was Cecilia, who was always filled with enthusiasm, even when the situation didn't quite call for it. She was whip-smart, and that made up for the overabundant supply of jubilation. She'd been tasked with being the liaison to Logistics, so Diana was sure that it had something to do with the colony ships, or with emigration planning.

"Yes Cecilia, what's going on now?"

"I wanted to let you know that the first of the colony ships bound for New Earth are entering orbit!"

"Thanks, Cecilia, that's great news."

It wasn't great news as far as Diana was concerned. She knew it would finally bring home to everyone the stark reality of the task ahead of them. First on the list to leave were architects, builders, engineers, and scientists to build the infrastructure of New Earth, and those with relatives on New Earth. Then there would be a gap of about 2 years, and then the second wave of real emigrants would leave. They still hadn't figure out how they were going to order the subsequent waves of emigration. And people were getting restless about it.

New Richmond, New Earth, Month 1, Year 28

"I should have gone with that ship with the deserters, Marianne! Now, I can never get back to help."

Marianne was exasperated. Beatrice's knowledge of the Kinder had been invaluable during the last two years, but Marianne felt that Beatrice couldn't let go of Hilcyon because of the death of Pkygy, for which she seemed to take personal responsibility.

"Beatrice, this is not your fight. They are not your people. What could you possibly do if you went back? You are a woman, remember? Remember how they treated women?"

"But Marianne, I did so much..."

"And you almost ended up in prison or executed!"

"The Kinder are going to close Hilcyon off, aren't they?"

"That is the exact message I get from Supreme Chief Jurrl, yes. They have asked all Casitian and New Earth personnel to leave the system immediately and warned that any ships entering their space will be destroyed. Apparently, he's even destroyed all communications devices in the Hilcyon system capable of contacting Casiti or New Earth. There is a civil war going between one region that has broken away from the rest."

"The Central Valley?"

"Yes, that's what it's called."

"They were far along the path to reform when I was there - I'm not surprised. I hope they can prevail."

"In any event, Jurrl's side owns space and the wormhole, and they want nothing to do with the rest of humanity, from what I can tell.

W'ren's plans for modifying Hilcyon's climate are halted. The Kinder lost their chance for a verdant planet, at least for now. And we will have no way of contacting them until they decide they want contact."

Marianne could see the tears forming in Beatrice's eyes. "I never got to tell Pkygy that I loved him. I guess I didn't really know it until I'd lost him. Losing Hilcyon feels like losing Pkygy all over again."

Marianne drew Beatrice into her arms as she cried quietly. After a time, Beatrice wiped her face, and looked at Marianne. "Of course, Aunt Marianne, you are right. The Kinder are not my problem, and there is little I could do even if I went back. And I guess now that Hilcyon is closed, you don't really need my help anymore?"

Marianne nodded. "W'ren and his team have left Hilcyon and are going home to Casiti. There is no more we can do."

"Mom and dad are settling into life here in New Richmond. I'm thinking about what I want to do with my life."

"I always can use your help, kiddo. You have a gift for looking at how people think."

Beatrice smiled. "Yes, I do. I first want to talk with Ngellin and give him Pkygy's books to translate. After that, perhaps I'll come work with you."

"I'm sure he'd like to help with that translation. Ngellin is an unusual Kinder man."

"I'm looking forward to meeting him."

Earth Orbit, April 30, 2027

They were glad that they had been able to commandeer the shuttle so that they could watch the colony ships arrive in orbit. Like David, Joel had learned how to pilot a shuttle, and that definitely came in handy at times like this.

It was a spectacular sight. One thousand ships scattered all over Earth orbit. They were close to a few, and they were simply enormous. Galactic technology sometimes astonished Joel. These ships would take 100,000 people each, plus a lot of cargo. And the sheer logistics of getting the people and their stuff into orbit was almost unimaginable. Alongside the thousand colony ships were more than ten thousand shuttles that would ferry thousands of people and tons of equipment each trip. The amount of energy to pull this off was staggering, but the Galactics had harnessed the energy of suns in a way that Joel still didn't understand.

Joel and Laura had been spending most of their time on the Moon, working to figure out the logistics for the emigration from Earth. The preparations for the first wave were in such good order that he didn't have much to do anymore but observe. Which was, fine with him.

"Joel, have you thought more about where we should go when this is over, New Earth or Casiti?"

"I don't know whether I think my place is on New Earth, or on Casiti. I know you've been thinking a lot about Casiti."

"I have, and I'm torn. The idea of a yearlong winter..."

Joel smiled. "Well, if we got to snuggle up together for the whole time..."

Laura playfully pushed him, then smiled, and kissed him.

"Well, we'll figure it out."

Dlejon, New Earth, Month 3, Year 28

It was finished, finally. It had taken weeks and weeks of work, of discussions with leaders all over Earth and New Earth. She'd even consulted Jal'end'a on Casiti. She knew that no one would be happy. Even though every single country was getting more actual land than they had on Earth, she knew that it was less than they had expected.

The polar regions would be set aside as global parks. The near-polar regions would be independent zones. Although the climates of those zones matched many parts of the US, Canada, China and Russia in the early to late spring, depending on the altitude and latitude, they were colder than any part of the rest of New Earth and had very few of the standard food plants. In order for people to live there at all, they would have to farm or import food.

The United States would take up the land that was now New America. The ICS had been intransigent, so she had taken away two thirds of its land area, in exchange for making it an independent territory.

The situation with New Aard had been a train wreck. Originally, they had the vision of an Islamic territory, with different regions for different groups. The Arab League, as well as several countries outside of the League, had insisted on a nationalistic scenario, with each nation having its own space within New Aard. The New Aard leadership was adamant that there still be some space to allow settlements by Islamic sect. Marianne had compromised by expanding the size of New Aard and let them hash it out. She didn't want to have anything to do with it. She worried about the Christians, Jews, Buddhists, Hindus, Sikhs and other religious groups inside of majority Muslim countries. She had set aside sections of the NCIZ that were currently unsettled to give to them if they wished.

The large group of native and indigenous tribes had been given a very large territory west of the SCIZ and south of Dlejon, and they were going to figure out collectively how to divide up the land. She didn't want to be in any of those meetings, either.

The rest of the territories were given to the rest of the countries of the world in a way that didn't really satisfy Marianne's aesthetic, but which ended up being the fairest. The area was divided into regions with the natural borders like rivers and mountains. Just west of the ICS and New America was "North and Central America" which didn't, of course, have the United States. Below that was South America. West of North and Central America was "Europe and the Middle East" which was a bit strange, because the only Middle Eastern country in that region was Israel. Palestine was going to be part of New Aard. Africa was south of the Indus River, north of Lake Maracaibo, and east of the expanded New Aard. Asia was south of Europe, and Russia straddled both regions.

Countries and borders were very roughly analogous in shape with their Earth counterparts, but that wasn't always possible. Her AI had been invaluable in helping her make the borders, without it, she wouldn't have been able to figure it out without a lot of help. She had been really happy when one of Torf'ki's team had finally gotten an AI into her workflow. It made all the difference in the world.

She was sitting with Ja'el, looking over the map for the last time before she sent it to everyone.

"I know you aren't happy with it."

"Love, I wouldn't be happy with any map, I realize. But I'm as happy about it as I can be. I'm just bracing myself for the universal backlash."

"You might be surprised. Yes, there will be a backlash, but I think that more people than you think will be happy that it's done, and happy that they know what things will look like. And my bet is that the native people will be very happy with what you've given them."

"That is true, indeed. I might as well get this over with." She got up and went to her desk and spoke to her AI. "Send, please the map set to the predetermined list."

Her AI's voice responded. "Map set sent."

Ankara, Turkey, March 20, 2027

Diana pondered the current situation as she rode in the back of her limo on the way to the press conference. The final maps of New Earth had just been made public. Diana had been warned by Marianne via a recorded video message, as well as some assorted addenda to the maps that others didn't get. She knew ahead of time what was coming. She'd heard from the leaders of most countries, and their governments were surprisingly satisfied with the final maps and were already putting logistics in place for emigration from Earth. The Arab League and other countries that were majority Muslim, like Turkey, were happily splitting up the land given them collectively. Diana thought that Marianne and the Casitians had done a good job of weighing all of the priorities, and, ultimately, making everyone happy because no one was happier than anyone else.

What took Diana and other world leaders by complete surprise was the uproar created when the maps went public. Diana suspected that the primary issue was not the maps themselves, but that the maps made their predicament real in a way that it somehow hadn't been yet. People saw exactly what their options were for leaving Earth, and they began to understand they needed to make plans, and they didn't much like that.

The people that were the least happy were those in the island nations of the world. Diana could certainly understand that. There were no islands of any substance on New Earth because there were no oceans. The largest lakes, which were exceptionally large by Earth standards - larger than the Great Lakes, had some islands, but they were quite small.

The car slowed, and then stopped. Her security detail opened the door for her, and she walked inside a phalanx of security personnel into the building where the press conference was held. She had a small speech to give, and then she'd take questions. She wasn't much looking forward to this.

As she walked into the large room, she saw more press than she'd seen in a very long time in one place. Many were familiar: they were from her press corps. Many were unfamiliar. It reminded her of that first press conference 15 years ago when the existence of the Casitians and the Galactic Community was announced.

There was a bit of commotion as she walked in, and then a hush began to fall over the room as she walked up to the podium. She waited a moment while people settled in, and the teleprompter started to roll her speech.

"It has been a very momentous time in the history of our planet. We are faced, finally, with the reality of our lives. We must leave. The first wave of colony ships are in orbit, slated to leave in just a few months with the first emigrants, those with families on New Earth, and those who will be serving in a variety of capacities to help build infrastructure, governments, and settlements. There are teams of Terrans and Casitians working together on Casiti to build the structures needed for the emigrants to Casiti.

All global citizens have decisions to make. Join your country in emigrating to New Earth, find or start an independent settlement in the Independent Zones of New Earth, or choose to emigrate to Casiti, to either Loc'deher, or Jul'when. I know that these decisions are hard. They will be made individually, and by family. We will endeavor to provide each global citizen with all of the information they need to make the right decision for them and for their families.

It will be a long, as well as a very short ten years until December of 2037, our deadline to leave Earth. Each of us, not just those in the governments of Earth, have important roles to play to make sure that this evacuation is orderly and without conflict.

I will take your questions, now. Uh, Jim."

"Thank you, President Westinghouse-Lewis. One of the things we have heard is that many nations are telling their citizens that they have no choice but to immigrate to the same country on New Earth. What is your response to that?"

"With the new global government, every citizen of the Earth has certain rights. Those rights include the right to emigrate from their country of origin to somewhere else. Although there will not be the same kind of global government on New Earth, those rights are still in place during the evacuation process. This means that any citizen can choose to emigrate anywhere on New Earth or Casiti.

"Practically, though, since most countries and territories on New Earth will not be accepting immigrants other than those from their Earth counterparts, it means that people going to New Earth have the choice to immigrate to the independent zones or evacuate with their country. We are adamant that each global citizen has that right."

"Madame President, if I may, a follow up?"

"Certainly, Jim."

"How can you make sure that global citizens can exercise that right? What if I am a citizen of Turkey, for instance, and I want to go to one of the independent zones?"

"The colony ships are not going to be divided by country. For instance, if a person wanted to emigrate to the North Circum-polar IZ, they would sign up on the global evacuation website, and they would be given their colony ship assignment. Shuttles will be leaving from all over the world, picking people up where necessary. Local governments won't have a say in how this happens. Next question, please. Madelyn."

"Madame President, the maps have a very large area for Native American tribes, and other indigenous tribes in South America and Oceania. Our analysis shows that based on current census figures, those regions will have about 1/5 or less the density of other areas of New Earth. Why is this?"

"These peoples have requested their own space, so that they may live autonomously again after hundreds of years. They wished to live close to the land, in a largely hunter/gatherer mode. In order for that to be possible, we needed to give them more land per person than other regions. Please remember, the population density of New Earth is already going to be very much less than it is here on Earth. Next question... over there in the blue shirt – I'm sorry, I don't know your name."

"Thank you, Madame President. Gerhard Gronewald, Die Burger, Cape Town, South Africa. We have come to understand that there is a request from the African Union to allow the African region to be divided not by country but by tribal allegiance. Is this true?"

"Yes, Mr. Gronewald, this is true. There is an upcoming meeting in Kinshasa, which will try to hammer out agreements between the tribal leaders and the nations. I don't know what will come of this, but I expect there will be room for settlements based on tribal affiliation as well as nationality. Next question... yes, Katherine."

"Madame President, there has been some consternation about the fact that there will be no equivalent map building process for the two continents that we are settling on Casiti. Can you explain, please?"

"Of course. Casiti has its own system of government, and although the two continents that we will settle don't have many Casitian residents, those immigrants will abide by the system of government that the Casitians have."

"A follow up, if you please?"

Diana nodded.

"So how will people be settled on Casiti? Based on what?"

"That's a very good question, and I don't yet have an answer to it. Earth humans can choose which continent they wish to emigrate to, but the Casitians have not yet determined how new emigrants will be settled. That is up to them."

There was a big murmur in the room. Diana could tell that didn't sit well with this group. There were some more questions, mostly, at this point mundane. She wrapped things up and left the building. As she was riding in the car back to her house, she was thinking that it would be a very long ten years.

Jul'when, Casiti, 85 Paqn 784

Chin had been impressed by how much the Casitians had been able to put together in the first Jul'when settlement. Each of the team members had their own dwelling, there were a few community buildings, and there were about 20 large greenhouses already built. Hetl'zef, who she'd just met a few days ago when they arrived, had mentioned that there were very few large greenhouses on Casiti, because most people grew their own food. Any large greenhouses that existed were used for testing of new techniques and such, not for growing food for anyone.

Chin knew that Hetl'zef had realized that it was unlikely that all of the Earth immigrants would be able to start growing their own food immediately, so they needed to start some food production facilities in order to feed everyone at first. Chin thought that one function of the agronomy team could be to hold classes and teach people how to grow their food both outside during the growing season, as well as indoors year-round. She made a mental note to tell him about her idea next time she saw him.

Chin looked around her dwelling. She never expected to live somewhere that felt so luxurious. It wasn't an especially big space, although it was far larger than her small apartment in Beijing. It had a nice circular central room, with other rooms off of the circle. The whole dwelling was a large circle. On one side of the large central room was a beautiful dining table. She couldn't identify what it was made of, but it was clearly made with care. Near the table was the door to the kitchen, which also led to the door of her own small greenhouse, and the door to the back, which would have the garden. There were already structures in place on the ground for raised beds, although it would be more than an Earth year before she could use them.

On the other side of the room was a set of very comfortable chairs and a couch, and beyond that was the door to her bedroom, which had a large panoramic window looking out across the plain. There was also a desk in the large room, with a well-hidden computer system with an AI and display screens.

She knew that most of her time in the next few months would be to help create the plans for food production so that when the first wave of

Earth humans arrived, there would be something for them to eat, both Earth crops and Casitian crops. One of Chin's interests was how best to grow both Earth and Casitian crops in the same ground. Hetl'zef and others had done some work in this area years ago when the first Earth crops made their way to Casiti, but they had been working with a very limited number. They eventually wanted to know about how a much wider range of crops could grow here. They had traveled with the largest supply of seeds and seedlings to ever leave Earth. Of course, much larger supply would be leaving Earth for New Earth shortly.

San Francisco, Earth, July 19, 2027

Patricia's suitcases were sitting in the hall. She had set up the taxi ride to the airport for 3:00, about 20 minutes from now. She'd be picking up the shuttle to the colony ship carrying her to New Earth. It was with reluctance she was leaving now, and with some reluctance she was going to New Earth. The Presiding Bishop had asked her to emigrate to New Earth as part of the first wave, to begin the process of setting up the Episcopal Church in New America. She would be going with a small group of clergy and diocese staff to set up the office and start to prepare the way for churches to be moved or started.

She sat on the front pew, looking at the lit candles. Her church would still function. The associate priest would take her place until there were no more parishioners. Then he would himself emigrate. Patricia had been thinking she wanted to move to Casiti, but when her bishop made this request, she felt she could not refuse her. She hoped that someday she could at least visit Casiti, if not retire there. She felt that there was so much she wanted to learn from them.

She entered a time of prayer, asking for wisdom and clarity, patience and peace. She sat in silence until she heard a car horn coming from the front of the building. She got up, picked up her bags, and was soon on her way to the airport.

Colony Ship, Earth Orbit, July 20, 2027

Gita sat in her chair, fidgeting. It was going to be a long trip, if she was this restless the whole time. It would take them about 45 hours to get from Earth to New Earth, then probably another 10 hours to get off of the colony ship, finally. She had been on one of the first shuttle trips up to the ship, so she'd sat in her seat, or paced, for hours already before the ship finally left orbit. She turned on her tablet and started to read some of the preparatory material she had been given.

She thought that the colony ships were not designed for comfort. They were little more than human cattle cars. After a moment, she reconsidered. Her chair was certainly bigger and more comfortable than any airline seat she'd sat in, except perhaps that First Class trip she got to take once to Singapore.

The colony ship was enormous, full of rows and rows of seats with people. There were 100,000 people on this ship, a number which boggled her mind. She knew that there were few places on Earth where that many people would even fit. It was like she was riding a stadium in space. She couldn't see all of them, because the ship was divided into about 50 compartments. But she certainly could see a lot of people, many of whom seemed as restless as she.

There was a very large viewscreen that everyone could see. It showed the view outside the ship. There were one thousand ships leaving at the same time, and the juxtaposition of the Earth and a number of ships around them was frankly spectacular. It helped her to really feel the enormity of the project they were undertaking.

Gita, along with everyone on this particular ship, was going to New Earth to serve. To help create the structures that will be needed for everyone else immigrating. She had been recruited to serve as an undersecretary in Diana Westinghouse-Lewis' cabinet. She was responsible for setting up the communications system that the New Earth global government would need. It was a daunting task, but she felt up to it, and she had a large team of people at her disposal to help implement. She was glad that she was more of a technical bureaucrat this time around, rather than taking a diplomatic role.

She was looking forward to seeing Marianne again. She hadn't seen her since Marianne left for Casiti, at the very end of the Casitian Crisis. A lot had happened to Gita since then. She'd divorced her husband and her daughters had graduated from college and started lives of their own. She knew that both of them wanted to emigrate to Casiti. She hadn't had a substantive conversation with her husband in years. He had taken her initial involvement in the Casitian communications team as a betrayal, which she didn't understand. He answered that perceived betrayal with one of his own - he had an affair. That had ended their marriage of 10 years.

Gita was looking forward to settling down to a new life in a new place. The world capital had been identified as New Orleans, which because of its location had already evolved into a cosmopolitan city, with consulates for settlements, large and small. She had been given quarters in a new neighborhood of New Orleans, specially built for the incoming diplomatic and technical corps of the new global government.

She got up and went to an area she knew she could find some refreshments. There was a line ahead of her, and somewhat harried people serving up food from unfamiliar equipment. She saw a basket on the side of the counter that had the label "magic Casitian sleeping pills. Will knock you out for 8 hours straight, no side effects!" She grabbed a couple of packages. This would help a lot.

New Columbia, New Earth, Month 1, Year 29

Kurt walked into the office for his morning meeting with Valorie. She was already busy at work – had been probably since very early. She was one of those people who worked during the entire time of New Earth's almost 23 hours of daylight, and then napped, and worked a few number of hours during the night, then slept to start a new day. Having a day that was twice as long as Earth's day was proving difficult for many people to adjust to, and it seemed that people adjusted differently. It appeared that people who were born on New Earth naturally stayed awake for much of the daylight and slept for a large portion of the night. Kurt had begun to adopt his boss' schedule, which made their work easier.

"Good morning, Kurt, how are you?"

"I'm doing fine, Valorie. How are you today?"

"Nervous. I know that on the docket this morning is my first meeting with the U.S. President's office to start mapping out the transition. I have a feeling, just based on the little bit of correspondence we've already done, is that they are expecting to just waltz in here and take over. We've just gotten our feet under us here, with the government finally, really working. I don't want to throw all of that away."

"Just remember what Marianne said, Valorie. New Earth governmental entities have priority because we've been here on the ground for 18 Earth years. We know the realities of what needs to be done. We know the infrastructure issues. We know the relationships between territories."

Valorie nodded. "I know, but it's just that I think convincing them is going to be difficult."

"Agreed. But we'll do what we can. Our initial meetings with them are from 3rd to 6th hours, then we are giving them lunch in the gardens, and then they are splitting up, meeting with the infrastructure, communication, agriculture, and business committees. 8th hour you have a meeting with the ambassador from New Aard. 8:30 you have a meeting with your Secretary of Health."

Kurt continued the daily litany of meetings, and preparations for them. Sometimes, the work felt tedious, like now. But then there were always moments of everyday when he realized why he did this work, and why he enjoyed working with Valorie so much. He imagined the meetings with the U.S. President's office to be one of those moments.

They continued to discuss the day, when he heard a knock, and saw his aide poke her head in the door.

"Kurt, Valorie, the U.S. delegation is here."

"Well, let's show them in, shall we?"

Five people entered the room, four men and one woman. They all wore suits. Kurt stifled a laugh. He'd completely forgotten that those were the standard attire in the US government. Between the weight restrictions, the need to dress practically for the relative warmth of New Earth, and the rugged life that the settlers initially lived, Kurt guessed that there were exceedingly few suits on New Earth. Until now.

The man in the front stuck out his hand. "President Lira. I'm Kenneth Tirrel, Transition Director for the Office of the President of the United States."

Valorie shook his hand. "Nice to meet you. Please call me Valorie, everyone does. We don't so much go on formality here, as you can see."

"President Lira, I want to make one thing clear, before we start. This transition is the process of simply moving the U.S. government as it is on Earth, to New Earth. I'm glad you've had your time to be all informal and do whatever it is you wanted, but we've got 200 million people coming here, and this is very serious. We know how to run a real government."

Valorie took a moment. Kurt knew Valorie. Kurt knew that she was going to let them have it. He was looking forward to it.

"Kenneth, do you mind if I ask you a few questions?"

Kenneth looked surprised and shook his head. "No, I don't mind."

"How is polio transmitted?"

"Excuse me?"

"How is polio transmitted?"

"How the hell would I know that?"

"Polio was our worst epidemic, but it's gone now, so it's not that important. How about this question: how many Tulip trees can one person sustainably use in a lifetime?"

"What is a Tulip tree?"

"OK, never mind. What about this: how many people can an acre of wild land support at 45 degree latitude?"

Kenneth was silent.

"What methodologies exist for growing soybeans on New Earth soil? What do you think?"

He was still silent.

"How many train, truck and bus lines have we been able to build between New American cities? What capacities does our electric grid have, and how can we expand it? Or, let's see... what's the current relationship of New America with New Aard? New America and the Independent Zones? What forms of currency have we been using, and what are the exchange rates with other New Earth currencies? What is our balance of trade with other territories?"

As Valorie peppered Kenneth with the questions, Kurt could see his face get redder and redder. Kurt could tell she was enjoying herself.

"I get your point, President Lira."

"No, actually, Kenneth, I don't think you do. New Earth is not Earth. New America is not the United States, not yet. I am completely committed to a smooth transition from the governmental systems that we currently have in place, to one collaboratively created between our government and yours, and to a full democratic system for all citizens who will eventually live within our borders. You will have to live with the reality that two thirds of what you expect to 'simply move', will just not work here. I know that we have less than a million people here. But these people know what it's like to survive and thrive on a totally different planet, with no Galactic support. That is something you have no idea how to do."

Kenneth was still fuming, but the woman who had been with them stepped forward and put out her hand.

"Valorie, I want to introduce myself. My name is Wanda Holden. I am from the Department of Agriculture, and it is my job to make sure we can feed everyone when they get here. Our prepared agenda for this morning's meeting is clearly inadequate. I suggest that we go to the conference room, where we and our aides can hash out a proper agenda, and get this process started."

Valorie smiled, and Kurt saw in Wanda someone he knew they could work with. He wondered about Kenneth. Kurt even sensed something sensitive in him. He seemed all bluster, but no bite. Well, they'd see, wouldn't they?

Capital, Hilcyon, Cfro 35 1160

After the minister completed his last sentence, Jurrl looked at him with contempt. He was weak. That was the only thing he knew to say. Jurrl never liked ministers. They spent their time in big buildings praying to the Kinder Exalted King with women. They sang stupid songs. They served a necessary function in Kinder society, Jurrl knew, but he didn't have to like it. The chief minister seemed to worst. The most soft.

"I don't care who starves."

"Supreme Chief, you must. The lack of food from the Central Valley has meant that the number of children dying this moon has dramatically increased. If this continues, we will not be able to maintain our population."

"During war there are always casualties. This will end, eventually. Please leave. I have much work to do."

The minister turned and left, his robes swishing after him, Jurrl's contempt for him followed out the door.

A throat cleared, and Jurrl turned. "Yes, Willm?"

"Sir, First Chief Cntol is waiting to see you."

"Show him in, please."

Cntol was the War First Chief that took over when Hjryg, the previous War Chief was killed in battle several days ago. Hjryg took over after Grly, the initial War First Chief was killed a couple of moons ago. Jurrl had been frustrated by the lack of success of these Chiefs. No new territory had been taken. No damage had been inflicted on the enemy. The only result had been the death of more than 400 men on their side, plus the thousands hungry because both the Central Valley and the Upper Highlands had stopped all food shipments of food to everywhere on Hilcyon. Everywhere, except the Desert Quadrant. Jurrl had asked Hjryg and Cntol both for plans to attack the Desert Quadrant and the Upper Highlands, but they both felt that the cost would be far too high. Jurrl felt that the cost was never too high.

Cntol walked in, slowly, limping. He clearly had gotten injured in the last campaign.

"Cntol, what news?"

"Supreme Chief Jurrl..." Jurrl saw him hesitate.

"Go on!"

"Supreme Chief Jurrl, I recommend we stand down, and agree to the truce conditions."

"What?"

"We have lost another ..."

"I don't care how many more men you have lost. We will prevail!"

"We cannot, it just isn't possible. I've run all of the scenarios..."

"Are you challenging my leadership?" He could see Cntol cower.

"No, Supreme Chief, it's just..."

"Then go back out there and win this war. No excuses."

Cntol looked at Jurrl, seemed to pull himself together, and turned and limped out of the office, saying nothing more. Jurrl started to think who he would put into Cntol's place when the time came.

Capital, Hilcyon, Mrontl 3 1160

Jurrl looked down at the treaty on his desk. 45% of all food production guaranteed from both the Central Valley and the Upper Highlands. In exchange for a guaranteed water supply, and to remain unmolested by the Supreme Chief or Supreme Minister. Treaty was written to last for 200 years. Jurrl wondered why that length of time. It didn't matter. It was his only option.

The war had been costly to his side. He lost six First Chiefs, and more than a thousand good men. Thousands of people starved to death without the food shipments. Thousands more who lived downstream of the Central Valley's water supply died of thirst when they shut the water off.

Perhaps he should have listened to Cntol. He took out his favorite pen, signed his name, and waited for Willm to come to take the treaty to the other side.

New Richmond, New Earth, Month 1, Year 29

The spaceport in New Richmond had a kind of architecture Beatrice was beginning to see more of all over New Earth. It was of Casitian origin. Next to the large structure was a wide tarmac, where shuttles would land.

Beatrice and her mother stood on the second floor of the spaceport terminal and watched the shuttle land and saw a stream of people leaving and entering the terminal. They walked downstairs to meet her grandmother. She didn't know if she'd even recognize her grandmother. It had been more than 13 Earth years since she'd seen her last. They were among a large crowd of people, and they were lined up along the edge of the area that the passengers were entering from the outside. She looked at her mother, who was fidgeting, and looking at the stream of passengers entering. Finally, Beatrice saw a dark-skinned, short, stout woman with very short gray hair, walking with a cane. At that moment, her mother ran toward her. Ah, that was grandmother. Beatrice followed.

"Yo! And Let... no, Beatrice! Oh my God, you are..."

"I'm an adult, now, grandma."

They all hugged each other. Yolanda took her mother's small bag.

"Where's the rest of your luggage, Mom?"

"Apparently, we'll have to wait for a couple of days for them to offload the cargo. I left your address. They said they would deliver it."

"Well, then, let's go home."

"Where's Marianne? And Leticia?"

"Well, Mom, you know Marianne. She's busy running things. She said she'd be here later today And Leticia and her partner Mira are on their way down right now from New Calgary, where she lives. She'll be here later today. We'll have a big family reunion, and of course, a feast tonight when everyone gets here."

"I'm glad to be here, Yolanda. I missed you all."

They walked out of the terminal, to the tram station, and got on a very crowded tram to their neighborhood.

"Mom, how was the colony ship?"

"It was like a flying stadium, Yo. It was just amazing. I slept for a lot of the trip, except I had the unfortunate luck of being seated among a group of people headed for the ICS. I didn't know that until I let it slip that you'd lived in the ICS, then left."

"Uh oh."

"They were unpleasant. I was sort of surprised that anyone from Earth would still want to go to the ICS, but apparently some of them stayed behind to, in their words, 'convert the heathen left on Earth.'"

"Oh, my. I'm sorry, Mom."

"I won't go into any more of what they said. It was pretty horrible. Not very Christian."

"Well, Mom, they'll probably be happy in the ICS. It's a pretty horrible place."

"I'm glad you left, Yolanda."

They finally arrived at their stop and walked to their house.

"This is a little small, isn't it?"

"Mom, everything is smaller here. There's plenty of room. You'll have your own room."

"Where are you living these days, Beatrice?"

"I'm about to leave tomorrow to spend some time traveling, grandma. I don't quite know where I'll settle down, yet. Might be here, but it might be somewhere else."

"Tomorrow? I won't have much time to see you, then!"

"Grandma, I'll be visiting all the time, don't worry."

Stanley opened the door to the house as they walked up.

"Stanley! So good to see you!"

"Mrs. Michaelson, it's been too long. Come in, come in."

Lecheguilla Cave, New Mexico, Earth, August 1, 2027

Joanne turned her headlight toward the left. "OK, I think this is the right spot. I see the marker Kevin left us."

Joanne led the small group forward, deeper into the cave. This part was easy, it was relatively smooth walking, and the roof of the cave in this section was fairly high. For four long hours before getting here, they had a very difficult climb down and squeezed through many narrow sections, and even had to crawl on all fours at times. Ahead was the very deep cavern where they would store their stuff and live for a long time until the Galactics left.

This cave was strictly off-limits to the public, but one of their members was a speleologist, and had been given special access to this cave. They had chosen to enter the cave in a very remote area where few visitors or park service rangers ever went.

It was a brutal trip. They met in El Paso Texas, which had the airport they all flew into. They picked up a rental SUV and drove the 3 hours to Carlsbad Caverns National Park. They then had to drive for another hour to the spot where they parked the SUV. They then hiked for 2 hours to the entrance to the cave. From there, it was grueling 4-hour trip to this large cavern. If she wasn't utterly convinced that this would work, she didn't think it would be worth it.

They would have to slowly bring all of their equipment and food for the estimated 6 month waiting period by hand. It would probably take them the whole 10 years to do it. There was a lot of space in the cavern - enough for 100 people and their equipment and food. They would have to rig latrines of some sort, as well as sleeping quarters and living areas. Their speleologist was helping them to do this in a way that would limit the damage to the cave system, but some amount of damage was inevitable.

This particular cave system was chosen because it was the deepest in the US, and this cavern was the deepest large area of its size that was accessible. The physicists and geologist in their group assured everyone that the cavern was far too deep for the Casitian technology to find them. They would make sure to cover their tracks when they entered the cave for the hiding period. Their current plan was to hire drivers who were bound for New Earth to drop them off and drive the cars back to the city.

Joanne looked about the cavern. Yes, she thought, this was a good place. This would work.

Kinder Settlement, New Earth, Month 2, Year 25

Beatrice started her story, while Ngellin listened.

"Pkygy had a grandmother, whose name was Dbor. He loved to spend time with her, helping her bake bread, bringing in wood for her hearth when she could not. Her husband had died many years before, and she had only daughters, so all of her children left home to join the households of their husbands, and she was left alone. Pkygy's mother lived the closest – only a few houses away, and his mother was happy to have Pkygy take care of Dbor.

"Pkygy was with her in the last days of her life, and she had told him of her secret writing. He promised to burn all of the writing, and never tell anyone about it. After she died, he was going to fulfill his promise. He found the chest that was shoved into the corner of the closet of her house – there were a few undergarments laid on top, but underneath he could see thousands of sheets of paper."

Beatrice and Ngellin were sitting comfortably across from one another in Ngellin's living room, mugs of what passed for Kinder tea in their hands. Beatrice was telling him the story of her late husband. Ngellin was listening with rapt attention. He thought it was an amazing story.

"He gathered up a few loads of wood, and started a roaring fire, ready to burn the writing, but he sat down at the table next to the fire, and took a few sheaves of paper, and started to read. Many hours later, he told me, the fire was still burning, as he kept feeding it wood, not paper. He cried and cried. He couldn't possibly burn these writings. But he could do nothing with them. His family would be shamed horribly if anyone knew that his grandmother Dbor had written all of this.

"The stories felt to him like the door he had always been looking for, the way to find somehow else to feel, somewhere else to be, something else to do. He felt that these stories had to be heard and read. The only way he knew how to do that, was to tell people that he had written them.

"He decided to start with one of the most innocuous seeming of stories. This was the story of a Second Chief, and his loyalty to his First Chief, and the sacrifices that he makes. It seemed innocuous on the surface, but if you scratched it, it was a deep questioning of the way things are. He published that story first.

"She had other stories. She explored the Breft. The Breft who disliked order. The Breft who scoffed at the Exalted King's wishes for them – who, in fact, did not even believe in the Exalted King.

"Dbor had written stories that explored what life would be like without the strictures of Kinder life. What would it mean if women could operate machines? Or spend their time looking at the stars? Pkygy thought that she poured all of her longing for a different life into the pages, creating new characters.

"One character that she created was named 'Elfer.' Elfer was a woman who chose not to marry or have children. Elfer was a healer and teacher. She imagined Elfer's education, and Elfer's life. She wrote about Elfer taking lovers. She wrote about Elfer traveling from town to town, city to city, healing those who needed her help, and teaching more to heal as she did.

"Elfer was the story that ended it all for Pkygy. It was the story that his Chiefs finally could not tolerate. It's how he was sentenced to the mine."

Ngellin had been watching Beatrice talk, as she told the story in an animated way. There was something in the way she talked that reminded him of the better things of the Kinder, somehow, even though he well knew she was born here, and spent only a few years with the Kinder.

"Beatrice, thank you for the story. I would love to help you translate this writing into English."

"So you can do it?"

"Well, not alone. I never learned to write English. So basically, in order to translate it, we would have to work together. I would read the Kinder writing aloud, and we both would translate, and you would write the English."

"That would work. I would like that, Ngellin. When should we start?"

"Why don't we start first thing tomorrow? It's getting late, and I'm sure after such a long trip on the river, you are pretty tired."

"Tomorrow sounds good. Thank you. I have enjoyed your company. It is nice to meet more Kinder who are like my husband, and those I met and worked with to reform things. I often think of them, and wonder if they are alive, and how they are dealing with the current realities."

They rose from the table.

"I know it is not custom for Kinder to hug, but I thought..."

Ngellin smiled. "I have gotten used to new things, Beatrice. I would love a hug."

They shared a clasp-armed hug and said their goodbyes for the evening. Beatrice was staying at the small guest house in the center of the Kinder settlement that always housed visitors.

Ngellin was pensive after Beatrice left. He would enjoy working with her. She was the first woman Ngellin had met so far on this planet that he felt understood him, and he could understand.

Mexico City, Mexico, Earth, August 15, 2027

Raul and Laura sat companionably at an outside table of the restaurant that had a nice view of the Zocalo. It was a gorgeous day, high in the 70s and sunny. Laura was happy to have come down to spend time with her old friend. And she was also happy to get to eat some authentic Mexican food.

"So, what plans do you and Joel have for final emigration?"

"We've been debating that, Raul. Some days he wants to move to Casiti, other days, New Earth. I have those, too, but it seems that we're in those moods on opposite days!"

Raul laughed. Laura went on, "but, recently our Casiti days seem to outnumber the New Earth days. And we got a very warm invitation from Jal'end'a to move to Rel'toro and be a part of the inevitable changes in Casitian culture because of this situation. Both of us like that idea a lot, and we think we actually can be a good influence. Joel can't quite believe he's thinking of moving to Casiti after all of his anger at them over the years. But he's coming around, and he respects Jal'end'a and what she is trying to do. What about you, Raul?"

"My daughters and wife want to move to Casiti. They have fallen in love with this peninsula on the very southwestern end of Loc'deher, which bears a striking resemblance to Baja, both in shape and in climate."

"Climate? How is that possible?"

"It's one of the few pieces of land on the equator. So it doesn't really have seasons, and thus is also relatively warm all year round. It is also very dry, like Baja."

"Wow. That sounds interesting."

"It does. I am truly ambivalent, so given the desires of my family, we're moving to Loc'deher. When I put in my application, I immediately got an invitation for our family to be part of a group going over there before the first wave to help coordinate the set up. I am torn. There is so much for me to still do here in Mexico for the evacuation, but to be of service on the other end is tempting."

Laura smiled. "I can see why. What do you think?"

Raul had a wide grin on his face. "My wife wins again. She wants to get us there as soon as possible. I love blaming things on her."

They laughed together. Laura all of a sudden heard this strange quiet buzzing noise coming toward them. She looked in the direction of the noise, and saw a disk-shaped object, around the size of a Frisbee, making an odd path in mid-air across the street. It looked to her to be galactic technology, but she had no idea what it was. She then saw a Casitian she recognized following the disk.

"Heg'ell!" He turned and looked toward her, then ran over. They hugged.

"Laura! How are you? I haven't seen you in weeks."

"Busy, busy my friend. Although I haven't seen you on Moon station in a while."

"Welen'da has got me on imaging duty. This week is the sector with Mexico City in it."

"Heg'ell, I'd like you to meet my friend, Raul."

"Nice to meet you, Raul. I have to go, Laura, and keep track of my little toy there. I'll be back up on the moon in a couple of weeks. See you there!"

Raul had a puzzled look on his face. "Imaging duty?"

"Ah, yes. Believe it or not, the Casitians are taking incredibly detailed images of every square foot of the surface of Earth. Every square foot. It will be so detailed that things like, well, like the Zocalo could theoretically be recreated so faithfully that no one would know the difference."

"Really?"

Laura nodded. "Yes, really. So for the things we can't move, at least we'll have very faithful copies to view holographically, or eventually, to replicate in physical form."

"That seems good to me. I'll have to visit New Earth and see how they do that."

"They can recreate some things just as well on Casiti, you know."

"I love it. Maybe we'll have two Zocalos!"

New Orleans, New Earth, Month 2, Year 29

Marianne sat in the chair across from Cardinal McGinnis. He was a stout man, with quite the pot belly. He was balding and had a thin beard that was completely white.

"It was embarrassing. There I was, going to meet with the Governor of the Independent Christian State. How fitting the name was, I thought. That I was the official representative of the pope on New Earth was made clear. The Governor refused to even talk with me but sent an aide to tell me that the Vatican would not be welcome in the ICS."

"I'm sorry Cardinal. The have become extremely insular of late."

"Yes, apparently so. And the original agreement that was made is apparently null and void. Anyway..." he spread his hands.

"You need a place to locate the Vatican."

"Yes, we do."

Marianne had made contingency plans for just this situation. When Governor Hurler had agreed to have the Vatican locate in the ICS, Marianne had been quite unsure that it would stick when Governor Kramer took over.

"I have just the spot." Marianne smiled.

"You knew this would happen?"

"I suspected it would. There is a small area of land across the Chalcedon River from the ICS, west of the settlement of the Mormons. It's not huge, although it's probably about 100 times the area of the current Vatican, so I'm sure you'll make do."

"Have you spoken more with...?"

"Torf'ki. About recreating St. Peter's Basilica, and the Square?"

He nodded.

"I asked him to give me some reasonable estimates of time, effort and resources. He hasn't gotten back to me yet. He's a busy guy, as you might imagine. I would say don't expect to have any of that recreated before you have the entire people of the Vatican moved."

He looked troubled.

"What's wrong?"

"Marianne, I think you don't quite understand what's at stake, here. The Vatican is only the Vatican because it's... well... the Vatican. It's the holy ground, and holy buildings, not just the people. I don't know what we can possibly do without..."

Marianne leaned forward and put her hand on his shoulder.

"Cardinal McGinnis, the Vatican is not nearly alone in feeling this. Think about what Muslims are feeling about Mecca. What Hindus are feeling about Varanasi and the Ganges? All people of Earth have to mourn the loss of all that we know. It is a completely devastating reality we are facing. And we all are facing it."

"I understand. I'm sorry. I know we don't get any more special consideration than any others."

New Calgary, New Earth, Month 2, Year 29

Leticia was giving Theresa Bold, the representative of the Global Ministry of Health, successor to the World Health Organization, a tour of their medical school. Leticia decided that she would focus on the studies of indigenous plants, as well as the hospital they had built, which used complimentary, as well as Western medical techniques.

They were walking quietly through the acupuncture and Chinese medicine treatment center, the largest and best in all of New Earth. Leticia had been telling him about how they had incorporated many traditions, such as acupuncture and Ayurveda into the medical school curriculum, while giving students standard grounding in medical science, anatomy, public health, infectious disease and the like.

After they exited the acupuncture center, Leticia suggested that they go to lunch at the school cafeteria. Theresa agreed. After they got their food, they sat down to eat at a table near the large set of windows with a view of the mountains.

"So, Theresa, what are your thoughts about what we've done here?"

"Well, Leticia, I had known that very few physicians had chosen to move to New Earth during the first emigration, but when the wormhole opened again, stories of what you'd accomplished here made their way to me. That you have built such an impressive health care system in both Independent Zones is quite remarkable. And the way you have melded Western medicine with other traditions is admirable. We actually have some things to learn from you."

Leticia smiled. She was happy that they had made a good impression. One of her biggest fears was that the immigrating medical system would simply override everything they'd worked so hard for. Perhaps that wouldn't be the case.

"Do you have a feeling for how you want to put the new global health care system together?"

"Honestly, Leticia, that's not my role. Because we're reverting to largely autonomous governing of states and territories, each is taking their own path in this. We'll be primarily responsible for the Independent Zones, and in that, we're going to take your lead."

"Take our lead?"

"Yes, take your lead. You have built an infrastructure in the Southern and Northern Independent Zones that we should just build upon. I know that there need to be more hospitals and medical schools, particularly in the North and South Circumpolar IZs. I understand that you are in charge of coordinating the health care infrastructure for the Northern Zone."

Leticia nodded. "I am."

"Well, we have our work cut out for us, don't we?"

Leticia smiled. She couldn't have imagined a better outcome.

Dlejon, New Earth, Month 2, Year 29

Jasmine walked into Marianne's cabin.

"Thanks for agreeing to see me, Marianne." Marianne looked at the tall, well-muscled woman with very short cropped blond hair.

"Beatrice told me that you were friends and told me a bit of your story on the asteroid. It must have been quite an experience."

She grimaced. "One I'd rather not discuss."

"Understood. Would you like some tea?"

"No, thank you."

Ja'el emerged from the bedroom, and Marianne watched her introduce herself to Jasmine. She also watched Jasmine's response, out of curiosity. Jasmine seemed a bit in awe of Ja'el, but that was not an unusual response.

"So how can I help you, Jasmine?"

"I would like to be considered for immigration to Casiti. I've thought a lot about it, and I feel like that's the right place for me."

"Well, there aren't any plans in place at the moment for emigration from New Earth to Casiti."

"I understand it might be an unusual request."

"Not really. Do you feel like you'd rather live among Earth folk on Jul'when or Loc'deher, or on Rel'toro?"

"Rel'toro, absolutely." Marianne nodded. There was something a little troubling in this young person, something she couldn't quite put her finger on.

"So, tell me more about why you think it's the right place?"

"When we were on Earth, and learned of the Casitians, I actually felt like I'd found the people who I belonged to. I'd always felt like I didn't belong where I was. Everything was so inexplicable. But then you came." She was looking directly at Ja'el.

"Then everything made sense. It was like 'yes, these are my people, I was born on Casiti.' My parents were part of the wave of people leaving for the ICS. I tried to run away before we left, but I was caught."

"My niece did that, too."

"I was miserable. My parents love it, though." She shook her head.

"You could find your home here, Jasmine. Dlejon is a lot like Casiti, but it's not really Casiti. The real Casiti might surprise you."

"I'm prepared for that."

"OK. I'll let you know. But remember, Dlejon will always welcome you."

"Thank you, Marianne, I'll keep that in mind."

Marianne watched Jasmine walk out the door. She turned to Ja'el. "What do you think?"

"I'm not sure. She strikes me as someone who has not yet come to peace with what happened to her."

Marianne nodded. "Yes, and I think she needs to come to peace with it before she can go to Casiti."

Chapter 7:
The Twelvers

(AP) July 5, 2027

Shia Muslims demand their own states, outside of New Earth's New Aard

Tehran, Iran (AP) -- Shia Muslims are unhappy with the nation-based divisions currently proposed for New Aard, and want their own separate, independent territory outside of New Aard. President Westinghouse-Lewis has made it clear that the current maps, which have expanded regions for the Islamic countries, are the final maps, and any Shia state must be placed inside that region. Marianne Michaelson, who is the architect of the New Earth immigration process, has given the leaders of all Islamic states the power to determine the borders inside that territory.

In a related development, Ismaili Muslims, a minority branch of Shia Islam, demand their own state as well. "If the Shia are given their own state, we wish to have a separate state from the Twelvers." Imam Rahim Ali Tajdin, a very prominent Ismali leader said in a statement. "Twelvers" refer to name given to the majority of Shia Muslims, because they believe that there were 12 spiritual and political successors to Muhammad.

Lecheguilla Cave, New Mexico, Earth, September 12, 2027

They had just finished eating and were preparing to start setting up some of the new collapsible shelving they had carried down with them when Joanne heard this very low buzzing noise. She couldn't figure out where it was coming from.

"Quiet, everyone!"

Everyone was still. She kept hearing the noise but couldn't tell what direction it was from.

"Hear that?"

"Yeah, I hear it. It sounds like it's coming from the north entrance to this cavern."

"North entrance?"

"Yeah, on the far end over there is an entrance. I've been told that it probably leads to the other side of the complex."

"You mean the side that has the main entrance?"

"Yeah, but don't worry. The last expedition down south from the main entrance showed pretty clearly that all passages down south were too small for anyone to travel through."

Joanne relaxed. But she still heard the sound.

"Should we investigate?"

"I guess so."

They got up and brought one of the big lamps with them toward the northern part of the cavern. They could see nothing, although Joanne could tell the sound was getting louder. They kept going, and in the distance, Joanne could see some very small lights.

"What is that?"

"Let's go see."

All of a sudden, a beam of light came out of an object about the size of a Frisbee, shining away from them, illuminating part of the wall of the cavern.

"What the hell!"

The beam shut off, and the device swung around and the beam shone at them. Joanne shaded her eyes from the glare.

"What is that thing?"

"I have no idea. I think we need to destroy it."

As Joanne started to swing her lamp toward the object, the lights abruptly stopped shining, and the thing emitted a louder noise, and flew north quickly and disappeared.

"Shit, shit, shit. What was that thing?"

"I don't know, but I think we'd better get out of here."

They hurried back to the cavern and told everyone what happened. They decided that they should leave, in case it came back. They left the shelves and other gear behind and started to make the long climb and crawl back to the surface.

They emerged into the dim light of dawn. It was cold, and Joanne's sweat started to feel clammy under her clothes. They stopped for a brief break, and Joanne dug an energy bar out of her pack and started munching.

She turned to Kevin, and said, "what do you think that was?"

"I have no idea, Joanne."

"I wonder if they have any idea what we're doing."

"How could they?"

Kinder Settlement, New Earth, Month 4, Year 25

"Jlroteno erlywot ghtnazi nn brizil ..."

"Would that be translated as 'mouth took in her chest'? That can't be right, I've never heard that group of words put together."

Ngellin was embarrassed. He hoped that Beatrice hadn't noticed. The right translation of this phrase was actually, 'lips brought to her breast.' Ngellin had read the rest of the sentence silently, and it clearly was the beginning of an explicit love scene between two women. No wonder Pkygy got arrested for publishing it.

He wasn't embarrassed because of the content of the story. He was embarrassed because he had known for weeks now that he had deep feelings for Beatrice that he hadn't shared with her. And translating a love scene with her was excruciating.

"Beatrice, can we take a break? We've been working for several hours today, and my stomach is grumbling."

He looked up at Beatrice and saw her smile. He loved her smile. Every time he saw her smile, his heart did a little dance in his chest.

"Of course, Ngellin."

"Oh, I almost forgot!"

"Forgot what?"

Ngellin got up from the table and went into the kitchen and put the breadmufs that were rising into the oven.

"It's a surprise," he called from the kitchen. "Let me make dinner."

"Do you want help?"

"No, it's OK, I've got it. It's a pretty simple dinner. I've been really liking the new Earth plants I've been growing in my garden. We'll have a tomato and onion salad, some greens, and I made some beans and rice. And my surprise."

"Beans and rice? Really. Ngellin, you've really been learning to cook Earth food."

"It's hard not to. I love it. It's like the food I've been missing all my life."

"I've heard Casitians say that discovering Earth food was such a huge change in their lives."

"I believe it."

They talked companionably while Ngellin cooked dinner. When it was done, he brought it all into the main room. Beatrice had cleared off the table.

"The silverware, plates and napkins are on the counter, there."

Beatrice went in to get them. They sat down and started to eat.

"Mmmm, Ngellin, this is wonderful. Such good food. You are a great cook. I'm not much of a cook. I would have been a pretty big disaster on Hilcyon if Pkygy hadn't been such a sweetheart."

"Beatrice, do you mind if I ask you a personal question?"

"Of course not, Ngellin."

"Do you still mourn Pkygy?"

Beatrice looked at him, and his heart threatened to melt.

"No, Ngellin. I don't. It's been a long time, now. I think of him sometimes, but I no longer mourn him. I'm glad he was in my life. I feel some regret that I never got to tell him I loved him. I vowed never to make that mistake again."

Ngellin heard the timer ping.

"Just a second."

He pulled out the breadmufs from the oven, and dropped them in the basket, and covered them with a cloth napkin. He grabbed two wine glasses, and the bottle of Kinder wine his friend had started making.

"Ta da!" He ceremoniously put all of that on the table.

"Ngellin, what's the surprise?"

He uncorked the bottle, and poured the thick, brown liquid. He whisked the napkin from off the breadmufs.

"Some relatively authentic Kinder wine and breadmufs."

"Ngellin, you are so sweet. This is wonderful!"

Ngellin watched her face as she bit into the breadmuf. She closed her eyes and smiled.

"It reminds me of the breadmufs that this woman Krely used to make. Very good Ngellin. I'm impressed. The spices are a little different, but they are wonderful."

"Ngellin, can I tell you something?"

"Of course."

Beatrice reached her hand across the table to touch his.

"I think you are an amazing man. You come from Hilcyon, and yet you have shown such tenderness and thoughtfulness and you've been willing to show your creative side. It's all a pretty amazing package, Ngellin. I am falling in love with you."

Ngellin was speechless for a moment. He wasn't quite sure what to say.

"If you don't..."

"Beatrice, I ... I have been hiding from you a secret for the last several weeks. The truth is, I fell in love with you when I first met you."

New Islamabad, New Aard, New Earth, Month 1, Year 29

"I can't do anything." Olam was working hard to get this group of people to understand his predicament. "Until the internal borders of New Aard are finalized, I can't determine the proper placement of settlements and cities, or work with the Casitians on how to build the infrastructure. It's just not possible."

Olam was exhausted. He had been in hours and hours of meetings with his colleagues in the New Aard government, as well as representatives of many countries newly arrived from Earth. He felt that Marianne giving them full power to draw boundaries inside the expanded New Aard territory was both blessing and curse. Today, he thought it was mostly curse. And, cynically, he thought that most of what Marianne had done was dodge a bullet.

Olam was silent, as the others went back and forth and back and forth. The demands of the Shia and Ibadi Muslims were tossed around, as were the varied priorities of each country represented. Olam almost wished they would just divide the thing up by population. All thought in his brain came to a complete, total halt. Of course! Population!

"Excuse me." Olam interrupted the conversation, not really caring who he was stepping on.

"What?"

"Wouldn't it make our lives a lot easier if we simply divided up the available space by the number of people?"

He looked at his tablet. "Look we have about 30 billion acres of land in the expanded New Aard. The latest census of New Aard population plus the populations of all Muslims on Earth comes to approximately 1.7 billion. That's 17.4 acres per person, roughly. We take every entity that wants space. We allocate to that entity, based upon census figures, the number of acres appropriate. For instance, the Shia would get about 2 billion acres, the Ibadi about 100 million. Anyway, does that make sense?"

They all looked at him like he was crazy. This wasn't going to be a good day.

New Columbia, New Earth, Month 4, Year 29

"Let's see, the farm belt here..." Valorie pointed to a swath of land in the far west section of New America, near a rich valley full of rivers and streams.

"Yes, we'll need to make place the railroad lines through here..." Wanda pointed to a set of settlements that were fairly far apart from each other, east of the proposed farm belt.

"Sounds like a great plan. I'll let the farm team know where they can go to get started. The Casitians have these great pre-fab dwellings we can place the farmers in to begin with. We'll get the railroad lines extruded as soon as possible. It's amazing what the Casitian technicians can do with asteroids. Basically, they bring an asteroid to the surface, attach this thing to it, and ... out comes whatever you want. It's a bit astonishing."

Wanda chucked. "We need astonishing, Valorie."

"Indeed we do. Look, I think we've done way too much for tonight. I usually have a small snack and tea before 2nd sleep. Interested in joining me?"

"Yes, thank you."

"Just a second."

Her aides were gone for the night. She ducked out of the oval office into a side office that had the refrigerator, and tea kettle and such. She put together the snacks as the water for tea boiled. She brought in a tray with two small tea kettles, cups, and an assortment of snacks for both of them. She placed them on her coffee table.

"Please, help yourself."

Wanda smiled. "You know, I've been here for months, and I still sometimes get caught short remembering you're the President. It's such a different atmosphere than Washington. I like it a lot."

"Speaking of the Washington atmosphere, how is Kenneth doing?"

"He's pretty unhappy, and is sure Kurt thinks he's a jerk."

"Kurt doesn't think that at all, you know."

"I know. But I don't think Kenneth can see that. And Kenneth has built up a kind of defense system to get where he is, and he doesn't know how to let go of it. I do think he understands that he needs to, in order to get by here. His father's suicide made things even worse."

"Give it some time. And, if I know Kurt, he'll help."

Moon Station, September 14, 2027

Dwight was having more fun than he'd had in a long, long time. Not since the Casitian Crisis had he felt so involved with things. Joel had asked him to head up a small task force whose role was to track and potentially infiltrate as many groups as they could who planned to try and stay behind. He was given the resources of the global police force, INTERPOL, and lots of cool Casitian/Galactic gear. He was using his own knowledge of organizing, and the fringe groups that he used to be a part of.

His special interest was the group headed by the former marine mammologist Joanne Henry. They'd found out where the secret IRC meetings were happening, and had managed to hack into the server, and had full logs of all meetings. The basic strategy with all these groups was to let them go ahead and choose their hiding place, which then would be sealed and monitored.

The sad part was that these people had no idea how impossible it was to hide. Galactic technology was amazing. True, they couldn't scan too deeply into the ground where people were hiding themselves, but the trace of them going to wherever it was they were hiding was like a big neon sign to the galactic technology "they're in here!" The traces lasted for days and days, even in rain or snow. At this point, Dwight figured that they knew about 70% of the places people were planning to hide, and they were learning about more of them every day. And in the extremely unlikely event that someone managed to actually hide, the last bit of insurance was a very large array of listening devices all over the planet, which would pick up any signs of human activity on the surface. If they waited a month, six months, or even a few years to emerge from hiding, they would be found, and dragged to New Earth.

Dwight disagreed with the strategy of not sharing this information widely. Joel and others thought that if people knew this, then instead of hiding, they would choose to fight somehow, and more people would be hurt. Dwight thought that people would be logical. If they knew they could not hide, or fight, they would peacefully leave.

"Incoming message from Welen'da." Dwight loved his new AI. It was what he'd always wanted. He had been so happy when Joel suggested he ask for one from the Casitian team.

"Display message." Dwight couldn't for the life of him figure out why Welen'da would contact him. He'd never met her.

He read the message, and then viewed the attached holographic image. Joanne! With a crew of people. So that was where they were! He'd known the general location from the IRC logs, but they had been careful to conceal their exact location. It was a complete coincidence that the cave mapping process was happening the moment they happened to be in the cavern. How funny.

Dwight had to figure out what to do. Tell them? Have someone pick them up? They already had done significant damage to the cavern system, and Welen'da made it pretty clear she didn't want them to do more. All of a sudden, Dwight knew exactly what to do.

New Columbia, New Earth, Month 1, Year 30

"God, Kenneth, lighten up, will you?" Kurt was sitting with Kenneth at one of Kurt's most favorite restaurants. He had a plate of greens, macaroni and cheese, and fried chicken to die for. It had been a crazy day.

"I'm sorry, Kurt. I just don't know what you want me to do."

Kurt was about at his wits end. He liked Kenneth. He certainly was attracted to Kenneth. But Kenneth could be infuriating. He insisted on continuing to wear a suit, even after a year. He could never call Valorie by her first name. He even sometimes addressed Kurt by his title!

"Kenneth, look. This is not, and never will be Washington, DC. We have made great headway in figuring out what the government of the United States on New Earth is going to look like haven't we?"

He nodded and took a sip of his beer.

"But you, man, you still act like you are back on Earth. What can I do to convince you that you're never going back there?"

All of a sudden, Kenneth put his head in his hands. To Kurt, it even looked like he was crying.

"Hey, dude, I'm sorry. What did I say?" Kurt reached his hand out to touch Kenneth's arm. He could feel Kenneth sobbing. After a while, it subsided. He wiped his face off with his sleeves.

"I gotta go. Thanks for dinner." Kenneth got up and walked out of the door, leaving a full plate of food behind him.

Kurt was mystified. Out of pure curiosity, Kurt used his widenet phone to do a search on Kenneth's name. Earth's Internet was now mirrored on the widenet. There was about a 3-to-4-day delay, but it was good enough for government work. He went through a few pages of the search and found the key to the whole thing. He whistled. He wished he'd known this months ago.

He found the page that had the obituary for Kenneth's father, a prominent Senator from California who had committed suicide rather than get prepared to leave. No wonder Kenneth was having so much trouble. Kurt waved at a waiter.

"Please wrap these both up for me?"

"Sure thing."

He left the restaurant and walked to Kenneth's place. He didn't exactly know what he was going to say, but he hoped that he could be a listening ear for Kenneth. He walked up the stairs to Kenneth's apartment door and knocked quietly. There was no answer. He knocked again, a bit more loudly, and said, "Kenneth, it's Kurt. I know you're still hungry. I brought dinner."

The door opened, and Kenneth stood there, his jacket off, and shirt unbuttoned.

"Why did you come?"

"Because I want to make sure you have something to eat. I know you don't keep any food in here." Kurt pushed by Kenneth and walked into his apartment.

"I didn't think you liked me."

Kurt wanted to laugh, but realized it wasn't the time.

"Kenneth, I've always liked you, even that first day. You make it hard, though, I tell you. Will you let me in, just a little?"

Lecheguilla Cave, New Mexico, Earth, November 10, 2027

Dwight looked up at the shuttle leaving them behind. They knew that Joanne and five others were already hiking up to their position.

"Thanks, Jir'ell for accompanying me for this little expedition."

"No problem. I have to admit to some pure curiosity as to how this will turn out."

"What do you mean? It will turn out fine. Joanne will do the right thing. Let's get going."

Dwight and Jir'ell walked down to the small, hidden entrance to the Lecheguilla cave system that Joanne's group had been using. They entered it and walked a bit further to a small widening in the entrance.

"The entrance has been permanently blocked off about 10 feet from here, although you can't see it. They basically took an image of the tube leading downward to the first ledge and created a cement-like plug that they tell me can't even be blasted away without completely caving in this whole part of the cavern system."

"I don't think these people aren't going to be very happy."

"I'm sure that we can talk some sense into them."

"I hope so. I'm not sure I share your sentiment."

They spent some time talking about this, and about other groups they had been investigating, when they heard voices.

"Stop complaining, John. I know this is your first trip to the cavern, but if you are tired after two hours of a hike, just wait until..."

Joanne walked into the area that Dwight and Jir'ell were sitting, stopped talking and stared for a moment.

"Dwight?"

"Hi Joanne."

"What the hell... who is he?"

"I'm Jir'ell. I've been helping Dwight, here."

"Helping him do what? What's going on?"

Dwight stood up. "Joanne, your efforts to hide a group of people in Lecheguilla cave has been discovered. All entrances to the cave have been sealed."

"What?"

One of the team walked past Dwight and Jir'ell and went further down the entrance. He came back.

"Yeah, it's sealed. Completely. There's no way we could get through."

Joanne and the others walked further down as well, and Dwight could hear them shouting. Finally, it was quiet, and they walked back. Everyone except Joanne left the entrance to the cave.

"Joanne, you should know that any attempt to use explosives to get through that seal will result in the collapse of this portion of the cave system. All other entrances to this cave system are either sealed or monitored."

"Why?"

"What kind of question is that Joanne? I'd like to ask you the same question. You know my answer. The Galactic edict is clear. Not one human being is to be left on Earth. Period. That's all. It's my job to help make that a reality. Why do you think you can avoid this?"

"It's not fair! Not fair at all!" Joanne stamped her feet and became red in the face. All of a sudden, she swung at Dwight, and landed the punch on his nose. He fell back, and could feel his nose throbbing, and blood streaming from his face.

Jir'ell bent down to help him up. "Dwight, are you OK?"

"I think she broke my nose."

Joanne was gone. Dwight was feeling very lightheaded and was stumbling around. He heard Jir'ell speak.

"Come get us. Dwight is injured." Jir'ell put his arm around Dwight's back, and put Dwight's arm around his shoulders.

"Come on Dwight, let's get out of here."

San Diego, Earth, November 12, 2027

Joanne felt like shit. She groaned as she got up off the couch, to go relieve her full bladder. When she rose, she got dizzy, and felt nauseous. She remembered throwing up several times during the night. She took a few experimental steps, and almost tripped over the bottle of Jack Daniels next to the couch.

After the flight back to San Diego, Joanne had been part of a very vituperous discussion on IRC about what had happened. When things finally calmed down, they went through all of the possible other alternatives, and realized that there were none. If they could find them deep inside the Earth, there was nowhere to hide. They would have to leave, after all.

One of the members of the group shared the link to a list during the meeting. Another group had set up a wiki page of the known caves in the world and their current status. It was devastating. Every single known cave system either had monitoring or had some or all entrances sealed to prevent humans from entering - even caves in the remotest parts of the world.

During the IRC meeting, she'd been drinking some '10 Pinot Noir. When that bottle was gone, she went to her cabinet to get the '10 Riesling. After that bottle was gone, she got out the Jack Daniels. She'd said some pretty harsh things toward the end of the bottle of Riesling and didn't remember anything once she'd started with the Jack. She was regretting the whole night. She was regretting her whole life right about now.

Her phone rang. She considered not answering it but decided to go ahead anyway.

"Hello?" Joanne could hear her cottony voice.

"Joanne? It's Maria? Are you OK?"

Maria. She hadn't talked with Maria in years. Not since the Casitian contact team was disbanded at the end of the Casitian Crisis, when the last colony ships were leaving for New Earth. She'd often wondered how she was doing. Why would she be calling now?

"Hi Maria. What's going on?"

"Maria, Dwight called me. He saw that you were pretty upset..."

"Look Maria, I appreciate it, but I'll be fine."

"Are you sure? I want to help, if I can."

Joanne started to cry uncontrollably. "My life is a mess, Maria. I lost my research and academic position. I lost a teaching job, and the only reason I haven't lost my house is that no one is paying their mortgages anymore. I tried to hatch a plan to hide from the Casitians and failed miserably. I have nothing to live for."

"Joanne, that's not true. Look you got derailed for a while."

"It's the Casitians fault." She cried some more.

"Look Joanne, come visit me for a while. We've got a guest room, and I think you need some change of scenery."

Joanne sniffed, thinking. Yes, perhaps a change of scenery was exactly what she needed.

"OK, I'll come visit."

New Orleans, New America, Month 1, Year 30

Jasmine had contacted Beatrice because she thought Beatrice might be able to help her get to Casiti. She felt out of options. They met in New Orleans, where Jasmine was living.

"I want to go to Casiti, but I don't think your Aunt thinks I should go."

"Why do you say that, Jasmine?"

"I don't know, it's just a feeling I get. I've been very unhappy since I got back. First, my parents demanded I stay in the ICS, then they demanded I get married. So I left. Then, I settled in Jerome, doing construction work, but I hated my boss. He was almost worse than William."

"I find that rather hard to believe."

"Well, it felt that way. Anyway, so now I'm here, looking for more work, not having much luck."

Beatrice and Jasmine were sitting at an outdoor table at a cafe in New Orleans. She leaned forward toward Jasmine.

"Jasmine, you seem really angry and distant. I'm sure that comes across in job interviews."

"Why the hell shouldn't I be angry? The government of the ICS basically sold us in slavery to these people who promised riches. Sold us!"

Beatrice put her hand on Jasmine's arm.

"Jasmine..."

Jasmine pulled her arm out from under Beatrice's hand, and stood up. She was angry at Beatrice. She could tell that Beatrice was just like everyone else.

"Not even you understand!" She turned and walked away. What was she going to do next?

Oakland, CA, Earth, February 3, 2028

Joanne was sitting in a basement room, in a circle with about 15 other women. The leader started off the discussion.

"Today's topic is loss. We all have lost a lot, and, of course, we are all losing Earth. In what ways has loss affected you?"

There was silence in the room for a few moments. A woman across from Joanne started to speak.

"Hi, I'm Alice, and I'm an alcoholic."

"Hi Alice." The rest of the women spoke in response.

"A few years ago, when this whole evacuation thing started, my husband decided to use this opportunity to leave me and go off on his own. He said he was sure he wanted to be on a different planet than I was. He just left us, left our children, and left me with huge bills to pay. Then, I lost my job last year when the company I worked for decided to close down instead of move. After that, I started drinking again. It's hard to keep going with everything around me feeling like it's coming apart. I finally stopped again, but I know I need help."

Joanne felt a wave of emotion from hearing Alice speak. She felt compelled to speak herself.

"Hello, my name is Joanne, and I'm an alcoholic."

"Hi Joanne."

"I've lost everything. I lost my research after the Casitian Crisis, I lost my job." She laughed, once. "I've lost a few jobs. I lost the chance to stay on Earth. And with every loss, I drank more. Now I've come to realize that I am powerless over my disease, and I have to find a way to turn my life around, to turn those losses into paths to a new life."

"Thank you, Joanne."

There were others at the meeting sharing their experiences. She had come to realize, after 65 days of sobriety, that so much of what she was experiencing wasn't unique. She wasn't unique at all. She'd been harboring this idea that she had lost more than anyone. But other people had lost so much, too.

Joanne had moved her life to Oakland and was still staying with her ex Maria and her new partner. She was going back to San Diego to wrap up her life and prepare to be a part of the next wave of emigration. There was nothing she could do about the losses in her life, but she knew she could find some sort of redemption on New Earth.

Dubuque, New Earth, Month 4, Year 30

Marianne looked up. She was astonished at how tall the building was. She was standing next to the Dubuque area building inspector.

"Looks amazing, doesn't it Marianne?"

"Why so tall?"

"Dubuque wanted to distinguish itself architecturally. This is a design taken straight from the Tvierl, I hear. I recently saw some holo films of their cities. Astonishing."

"Straight from the Tvierl, eh? How do you do inspections if the architecture is so ... so unorthodox?"

"It's not hard. We've got all of the specs on file. The stress each strut is supposed to be able to handle, the angle of overhang allowable, etc. It's not hard. The Tvierl, while managing extraordinarily interesting architecture, are also sticklers for safety. What they design, they design to be extremely safe. Apparently, no Tvierl building has ever had damage from quakes, or burned from a fire."

Marianne was impressed. They kept walking to another area, with a different set of residential buildings. Dubuque was the only IZ settlement so far to be on target to be ready for the second and third waves of immigrants. All of the other settlements were woefully behind.

Back on Earth, a surprising 95% of the global population had already applied for emigration to New Earth or Casiti and been assigned to a wave. The first wave arrived early this year. The second wave was due to arrive in 3 years' time. The good thing was that this gap provided enough time to build the infrastructure needed to house and feed all of those coming. The bad thing was that once the second wave started, there would be no break. Three or four waves a year for 18 years, until Year 50. It was mind boggling.

Casiti had it easier. There would be far fewer people arriving, and because of Casitian winter, the first wave hadn't even arrived yet. But even Casiti was getting wave upon wave of immigrants.

She completed her tour and caught her shuttle back home. She was happy she got to have use of a shuttle, so she could be home every evening after a long day's touring of the varied IZs. During the first wave, most countries now had representatives and workers getting the building going, and didn't want her influence or, as they might put it, her interference. The rest hadn't sent any representatives, and there wasn't much she could do about that. Her primary jurisdiction was now the Independent Zones. That was enough on her plate; she was happy that was all there was right now.

Tomorrow she would be visiting some of the settlements along the Mississippi south of Dubuque, who she knew were not nearly far enough along. She'd bring some of the Casitian team members with her, so they could strategize on how to speed up the pace. In the meantime, she was going home to be with Ja'el, who had been spending most of her time writing. She had been surprised at Ja'el's insistence that she not get involved. She was just happy that Ja'el had chosen to stay on New Earth for a while.

Chapter 8:
A Warm Eighteen Degrees

(AP) August 15, 2028

"The Hiders" Give Up

San Diego, CA – Thousands of people had planned to hide from the Casitian and Galactic authorities during the last wave of emigration from Earth in the hopes of staying on Earth after the end of the evacuation and restarting human habitation. It has become clear to all of these groups that these plans were folly.

"We had no idea they had the technology to find our hiding places in the ways they did. We've also learned that they were going to plant listening devices all over Earth, so that when we emerged again, we would be picked up, whenever that was. There's no hope of staying. I'm emigrating on the second wave." Joanne Henry, leader of a failed "Hider" group was interviewed on Saturday. Other "Hider" groups have posted similar statements on their websites.

Paris, Europe, New Earth, Month 1, Year 31

The asteroid was in place, finally. Getting it down here had been more of a chore than he expected. The size he needed to do this particular re-creation was a bit bigger than any asteroid they'd needed to do buildings so far. But there it was, sitting in the middle of what would become the city of Paris.

Which large monument would be recreated first had been an epic argument between Marianne and every single world leader who had a monument. In the end, Marianne decided to take a poll of current residents of New Earth via the widenet, and they would recreate the one that was on the top of the list. The Eiffel tower won, so that was what he was recreating today. Where to put it in Paris they had left up to the French authorities currently on the ground.

The asteroid was placed adjacent to where the Eiffel tower would stand once completed. The extruder, which was currently sitting on the ground, between two very tall legs, would extrude materials drawn from the asteroid into the structures re-creating the tower, and would rise up into the air on the legs as the structure was created. This same extruder, which was the largest they had, had been carried all over New Earth to extrude quite a number of large buildings.

A crowd had gathered to watch the show. A perimeter of about 500 meters around this structure and the asteroid was put up so that the chance of anyone getting injured by the process was limited.

Torf'ki's associate let him know that everything was ready and in place. Torf'ki looked down at his tablet and gave the commands to his AI to start the extrusion process.

For Torf'ki, the process was relatively simple, but he realized that for Terrans, it was pure science fiction. He looked at the figures floating across his tablet. Everything was going exactly as planned. He heard an "oohing" sound from the crowd and looked up.

The extruder was about 100 feet off the ground now, and the very beginnings of the Eiffel tower were becoming visible below the extruder. It was fairly remarkable, he had to admit, and he knew that when the extruder was done, the result would be pretty much indistinguishable from the original. That is, the original as recorded just a while ago. It would not age in the same way, or at the same rate as the original, but then, that didn't much matter, since he doubted the original would still be standing by the time any humans got back to see it.

Illsenor Station, Month 1, Year 31

"I've done a detailed inventory, Marianne. It doesn't look pretty for a lot of the world."

"Tell me."

David, Marianne, Torf'ki and some others were sitting in a joining room discussing the current infrastructure efforts, and what would be ready for the next waves of immigrants. David had been collecting data, sometimes having to cajole and pry information out of people, over the past year, to determine what would happen when millions of people per day started descending on New Earth.

Marianne had been worried for a long time about how this was going to come together. She knew that once the next wave started, there was precious little time to do much infrastructure building. She had hoped that most regions would have tried to fill in as much as they could in the 4-year gap between the first wave and the rest. That wasn't universally the case.

"The North Central IZ is in great shape. The cities of Dubuque, New Calgary, Memphis, Baton Rouge, Vicksburg, St. Louis and Moline, as well as others along the Mississippi, in the plains and in the mountains, will be ready for all of the immigrants slated to arrive. In fact, I would say that there are only a few small settlements in the NCIZ that will be in trouble, and by just sending them either an extra extruder, or even dropping a few dozen pre-fabs, they will be fine. The North Circumpolar IZ is also in great shape. We've got a great team there, including your niece, who are doing yeoman's work helping the new settlements up there get ready.

South Central IZ is a bit further behind, but not really enough to worry much about. Again, for them, a few communities needing some extra pre-fabs etc. will do the trick. There are exceedingly few new settlements going into the South Circumpolar IZ. I think probably less than 100,000 people want to settle there, based on the data we have from Joel and Laura. We've been producing pre-fabs, and there are already enough down there for those folks.

The problems, of course, are coming from the countries. Olam, from New Aard and I have had several conversations, and they are still trying to figure out how to divide the land there. I'm thinking train wreck, truly. They haven't even begun to start building. New America is doing fine; Valorie and the team from the U.S. Government are apparently working well together and facilitating a lot of building of housing and commercial and government buildings. The ICS isn't talking with me, so I have no idea what they are doing. Our resources are at their disposal when they need it, but I doubt they will want it. I'm worried big time about India, China and Indonesia. They have some of the largest populations immigrating, and they haven't built much to speak of at all. In fact, China didn't even bring anyone on the first wave. Actually, Marianne, there are about 40 countries that didn't send teams for the first wave."

Marianne didn't want to think about what would happen when China's more than a billion people, plus the people from the other countries started to descend on those countries with no infrastructure.

"What can we do, even without teams?"

David looked down at his tablet. "Well, we've got a standard settlement that we are extruding a lot of places. It consists of basic buildings, stuff like libraries and a main street, plus residences for about 50,000. We can do this fairly easily, although we have to do it after the work to put the underlying structure in place - water, electricity, etc."

"Can we set enough of those up?"

"Not without help from the country representatives, we can't. We can set up some, but I can almost guarantee you it isn't going to be enough for the coming people."

"This doesn't sound good, David."

"It's not good, Marianne, but it's the best we can do."

"OK, that's housing, what about food?"

"Well, the good thing is that we've got those big swaths of land in New America and the IZ's, and the Casitian and Terran agronomy teams have been cranking for years now. We've already got a couple of years' worth of stores of rice, corn, wheat, and other grains, as well as soybeans and other legumes. Some challenge might come from distribution, but there are some great ideas from the Casitian teams on that. That food plus the indigenous food available means that no one will starve."

"OK, I can live with that. They might have to pitch a tent for a while, but they won't starve."

"The health care infrastructure is going well in places we're involved. We've been extruding and equipping hospitals by the hundreds. And we're also putting in water and sanitation infrastructure in as many places as possible so that even when people pitch tents, they will have clean water and proper sanitation."

"OK, last but not least... transportation."

Kil'ander, who was the Casitian in charge of the transportation infrastructure process took over.

"Not so good. We've been trying to focus on rail lines and light rail, but some countries are pretty committed to roads and cars, trucks and busses. We've tried to explain that New Earth doesn't have any fossil fuels. New Earth had a good biofuel industry, but most of the agriculture effort is now going toward food – we have very little in the way of biofuel reserves. I'm worried that some countries will be stuck without reliable transport for a while. They don't seem to get that long term, really all we have is renewable energy."

Marianne was tempted to say "let them learn the hard way" but she restrained herself. "What can we do?"

"Honestly, not much. If they insist on prioritizing roads over rail and light rail, they are just going to have to learn the hard way."

Marianne couldn't help breaking out in laughter.

Kil'ander looked at her oddly, while David had a smirk on his face. "What's so funny?"

"Nothing, ignore me."

"Alright. The IZs are in great shape, since they had prioritized rail and light rail to begin with. We're just expanding lines and building trains, which takes time."

"Let's do what we can to focus where we need to. Torf'ki, do you think we'll need more folks and equipment from Casiti?"

"No, Marianne, we're pretty saturated up here and on the ground. There isn't much more we can bring to bear."

Marianne nodded. "We've got one short year before another 100 million people knock on our door. And then, only a few months before the next 100 million."

New Orleans, New Earth, Month 2, Year 31

"They finally agreed to my plan because there was no other possible way. It was a nightmare few months, but finally, we've got the map of New Aard finalized. It's sort of a mess, but it basically means that the east and south of New Aard is dedicated to the countries, and we've given over the north and west to the NCIZ, to be dedicated to varied Islamic communities. It seemed the wisest course."

David and Olam were sitting in David's favorite cafe in New Orleans. Because it had become the de facto world capital, he was spending a lot of time here meeting with people from all over New Earth, explaining their infrastructure and settlement issues. It had become a huge job, one that David hadn't quite expected to take on. But he seemed good at it, and it needed doing. And the one perk was that since most people wanted to see David, he got to make them come to his favorite cafe, where he spent a lot of the day holding court. The proprietors loved him and gave him all of his drinks and snacks for free.

"Thanks for that update, Olam. So, you're now ready to start building. We've got the 'dozer bots ready for the piping, and the extruders ready to build what you need. In addition, I'll get the agronomy teams ready for you, once you all determine the farming belts. I'll get you in touch with the Casitian who has been in charge of New Aard's infrastructure, he's the one who will requisition everything you need."

Olam nodded. "He won't need to meet with any New Aard leadership, will he?"

David shook his head. "No, you can be the intermediary there, if anything needs to be ironed out. Are you worried about how your leaders are reacting to Casitians?"

"Quite honestly, David, although they know that they depend on the Casitians for much right now, it's rubbing them the wrong way. I don't want things to get too messy."

"It's been that way in a number of places. No worries, Olam. You should see what I have to deal with in the ICS."

Olam raised an eyebrow. "Oh?"

David chuckled. "I managed to get a meeting with them later this month, but they made me promise that I would not arrive in a Casitian shuttle, and that I would bring no Casitians with me. Apparently, they are forbidding the presence of Casitians in their territory."

"Wow, that's going to make building difficult."

"I'm going to explain that it will make it impossible. We'll see what they say in response."

Capital, Hilcyon, Mrontl 1 1162

"That's all you have for me?" William was irritated at this particular Second Chief. "I know there were more reformers in that part of town. You should find at least three cells."

"First Chief, these were all the names we got."

"I don't think you questioned your captives hard enough."

"First Chief, if we hurt them too much, they will be of no use in the mines."

William thought for a moment, realizing he had a point. And sending as many people as they had to the mines was definitely a strong signal he was sending to any reformers still around.

"Alright. Thank you, Jzrel. You are dismissed."

Jzrel bowed and left his office.

His attaché walked in. "First Chief, the green grower is here to meet with you."

"Show him in."

A slight man, with surprisingly muscled arms walked into his office and bowed.

"You have news for me?"

"Yes, First Chief. Our yields are down, I suggest that we return to rations."

"Rations? Even with the produce from the Central Valley?"

"For some reason, we have not been getting as much water as we had, and we can't keep growing the same amount of food."

William knew why this was true. He'd heard the report from Jurrl. The water technology that they had gotten from the Casitians needed maintenance, but they didn't have the expertise to maintain it, and it was failing. It was likely that over the years, they would have less water than they had before. It was infuriating. Another betrayal by Ylen.

"I'm sorry we can't do anything about that right now. Please send me the detailed numbers you have on production, and we'll figure out the rationing. You are dismissed."

He bowed and left.

William pondered the last few years of his life. Jurrl had become Supreme Chief almost three years ago. Somewhat unexpectedly, Jurrl had not given William a First Chief position off the bat. He wanted to know whether or not William was able to fight for one. He was and did.

He had married, and had a son, with another child on the way. He had become Jurrl's main ally and as such, was a very powerful man. He was certainly next in line for Supreme Chief when Jurrl died, which would not be any time soon. But William could bide his time. He wasn't in a hurry, and he kept up his fighting skills so that in case Jurrl did die suddenly, or was killed somehow, he would be ready.

His origin was still a secret. For reasons he didn't understand, Jurrl wanted it to remain so, which didn't bother William especially. William was unusually light-skinned for a Kinder, but there were some Kinder of his coloring.

Jurrl, William and some other allies had systematically purged all Chiefs of reformers, killing some, sending most to the mines. They sent more than 30,000 people who were suspected of being part of the reform movement to the mines, more than making up for those who had been returned to Nytt Grier Nro. This list he had been given was the last, and it didn't contain any new names. He crumpled it up and threw it in the trash.

He looked down at the new edicts. No gatherings or assemblies of more than ten without official permission from at least a Second Chief. Random searches of houses for forbidden writing. That one was important. The writings of that traitor Pkygy, Beatrice's husband, had somehow re-emerged, and were being copied around. They needed to stamp that out, and arrest and sentence to the mines anyone found with a copy. He knew that the random searches couldn't happen often, but the edict would be enough to frighten people into submission.

Jul'when, Casiti, 50 Wend 784

Hetl'zef walked out of the greenhouse, feeling satisfied that they were equipped to handle this first wave of immigrants. The greenhouses had been growing Casitian and Earth crops all winter, many were ready for harvest. The gardens in individual dwellings were ready for planting, and there was sufficient storage of grains and legumes.

He had worked harder this winter than he can remember working. Winters were usually easy. Times to write, make love, make art, and relax in the warmth inside. This winter he didn't have a companion, and he'd worked day and night with his team of Terrans and Casitians to get the settlements ready for the immigrants coming in spring.

He was lost in thought and ran headlong into someone.

"Forgive me."

"Ah, no problem, Hetl'zef. Did you hear that the colony ship is now in orbit?"

"No, I didn't. Thanks for letting me know!"

Hetl'zef walked back to one of the common buildings, which was serving as somewhat of a headquarters for the Jul'when immigration effort, and it was buzzing with activity. He heard someone say, "first shuttle due here in 10."

He realized that he was of no real use here right now. Until the immigrants settled down a bit, he wouldn't have anything to do. Silandra had been pestering him to come visit her new home on Loc'deher. She had decided she wanted to be among Terrans, and she moved her life over to the peninsula, which would have a large Terran community. Hetl'zef had wanted to visit for a while, and this seemed the perfect chance. Casitians had initiated regular shuttle service between continents, and high-speed rail networks on the continents, so getting there would be relatively painless. He started to walk home, to get prepared for a short trip away.

North Circumpolar Independent Zone, Month 2, Year 31

Leticia and Mira were touring one of the latest settlements built. Leticia had gotten used to it, but sometimes it seemed rather magical. The underlying infrastructure had been put in a long time ago - that had been a real focus early on, was to get the road, rail, electricity, and water/sewer systems in place all over the NCPIZ before any settlements were built. Because of that, building the actual settlement didn't take much time. One day, 'dozer bots were around to build the foundations, and the next few days, seemingly magically, there was a full settlement, extruded from materials gleaned from asteroids brought down to the surface.

This would be the large settlement they would be living closest to. They had scoped out the hillside they were going to build on, claimed it as a new small community, and recruited some friends from New Calgary and Dlejon to live there with them. They didn't want to use up resources to get their place built yet - they figured they could wait a while. But they were looking forward to being able to settle down sometime soon.

They liked what the NCPIZ was shaping up to be. The NCIZ was going to get pretty crowded, and some pretty interesting new communities were going to be placed in the NCPIZ, based on the data they'd seen from Joel and Laura back on Earth. Its climate was on the cold side, ranging from around freezing at night, and getting to around 18 degrees C during the day. Not many people wanted to settle in either Circumpolar IZ, when they could live places that were so much warmer. Somewhat surprisingly, a lot of people from Dlejon were going to head up to the NCPIZ. Both CPIZs were likely to have substantial numbers of Casitian settlers too.

They walked to the hospital, which was currently empty. As they walked through it, they both marveled at how many important components of the hospital were in place – operating rooms, beds, nurse's stations, exam rooms, etc. All of the plumbing, lighting, and fixtures got extruded with the building materials.

After they left the hospital Mira turned to Leticia. "Well, sweetheart, I guess it's time to go to the next one. Touring these is getting a bit boring. Do we really need to keep doing this?"

Leticia nodded. "I feel like I need to keep doing the due diligence on the communities under my jurisdiction, love. You know, you don't need to keep coming everywhere with me, you have enough on your plate back in New Calgary."

Mira smiled, and took Leticia's arm in hers. "I know, but I love spending the time with you, and if you were off doing this, and I was at home, we'd never see each other."

Leticia laughed. "Well, OK, then." She looked down at her tablet as they walked to the shuttle, figuring out which settlement was next on their list.

Kinder Settlement, New Earth, Month 2, Year 31

Beatrice opened the door to see Jasmine standing in it, looking a bit disheveled, with a large bag. She'd sent Beatrice a pleading message, asking to visit her. Beatrice didn't know what was going on, but she was always willing to help her friend.

"Jasmine! It's good to see you."

They hugged, and Beatrice showed Jasmine in, and told her where to put her stuff. "Would you like some tea?"

Jasmine nodded. "Anything but Kinder tea."

Beatrice wanted to put her fried at ease. "No problem. How's peppermint?"

"Thanks, that's good."

She brewed their tea and sat with Jasmine on the couch.

"Where's your husband?"

Beatrice smiled. "We're not married, Jasmine. We don't intend to get married, even though we live together now. Marriage seemed so ... Kinder to us somehow, and we decided we didn't want to go down that path. Ngellin is in New Orleans for some meetings. He'll be back tomorrow. I'm looking forward to having you meet him. How long were you planning to stay?"

"I don't know, Beatrice. I'm sort of at my wits end right now."

"What do you mean?"

"I feel stuck. I seem to fail at everything I do since I got back from the asteroid. And it's been years now."

"Jasmine, what you had to go through on that asteroid was truly traumatic - it was traumatic for all of us."

"I know. I've been seeing this therapist in New Orleans for the past year or so. I had PTSD. Apparently, a lot of the kids who were kidnapped with us have it."

"So, what do you want to do?"

"Honestly, I just want to be helpful, but the last three jobs with various immigration agencies went south, fast."

"What happened?"

She smirked. "Apparently, I am now allergic to taking orders."

Although Beatrice had been mostly involved in translating Pkygy's grandmothers' stories for the last two years, she had also spent a lot of time working with Marianne on immigration scenarios, helping Marianne plan for the varied possible outcomes of the waves of immigration coming soon. Beatrice knew what kind of work was being done, and what kind of work was needed. And one big need she knew of was monitoring.

"Jasmine, what about this: what if you were given a large zone, like several thousand square miles or so. And your only job was to see what was happening. You'd get one of the solar-powered overland cars; you'd visit settlements and outposts, and just do daily report backs of where you were, and what you found."

"That sounds like a job I'd really like. I could totally do that."

"That's a job I can get you!"

"Really?"

"Yes. My Aunt Marianne is looking for people to do just that. Most people don't want to do it because you'd probably not get to go home for years."

"I don't have a home right now, Beatrice. These days if you don't have a job to do, they kick you out of housing, since it is so precious."

"Well, it's settled, then. Let me send a message to Marianne."

They spent the rest of the evening talking about the ICS, about the asteroid, and Beatrice telling Jasmine about Hilcyon, and what it had been like there. It felt wonderful to share with Jasmine all that had happened. Beatrice hadn't keep in contact with any of the other kidnapped kids – Jasmine had been one of her only friends, and the others had died on the asteroid.

The next morning, as Beatrice was preparing breakfast, Jasmine came out of the guest room, holding in her hand a copy of one of Dbor's stories.

"Beatrice, a Kinder wrote these?" She seemed incredulous.

"Yes, a Kinder wrote those. You see why Pkygy was who he was."

Jasmine nodded. "Yes, I see. I can't wait to read them all. Are they all translated?"

Beatrice smiled. "Not quite yet. Ngellin and I are about 2/3 done with them. There were more than one hundred stories, in rather well-written Kinder language. The translation takes a lot of time, and we're not even sure that it reflects as it should. But we're trying."

"I think you should get them translated to Casitian."

"That is an interesting idea. I'll ask Aunt Marianne about that."

Kinder Settlement, New Earth, Month 3, Year 31

"... hlzrefzo ghler gg sarfy golm. Maybe 'he left the room, slamming the door?'"

Beatrice was sitting the long way on their couch, and Ngellin was sitting on one side, with Beatrice's feet in his lap, and the open book of Dbor's in his hand. She said, 'well, it could be translated that way, but the better way to say it, I think, would be 'he slammed the door on his way out.'"

"Ah, of course, that makes sense. I like that." Beatrice typed in the words.

Ngellin closed the book. "We're done."

"Done?"

"Done. That was the last line of the last of Dbor's stories."

Beatrice smiled at Ngellin. "It only took us two years. I guess it might have taken us less if we hadn't fallen in love."

Ngellin laughed. "True. But I think the extra time was worth it."

"Marianne says that she is interested in translating at least one story into Casitian, and perhaps more. I decided to send her 'Elfer.'"

"That's a good one to start with. I do hope we get them all translated to Casitian at some point. I'd like the Casitians to see what some Kinder could do."

"Yes, Ngellin, I agree."

"So, now that that is done, what are you going to do, Beatrice?"

"I want to figure out the best way to get these widely read. A friend of mine who knows these sorts of things to put together a widenet site for it. Another friend of mine who read a couple of the stories actually would like to make a movie!"

"A movie?"

"Don't you know what a movie is? I guess we haven't seen one together yet, we've been so busy. There haven't been many made here so far, but there are still movies being made on Earth. Tell you what, instead of explaining, let's just go to one next time we're in New Orleans."

Ngellin said, "that sounds like fun. I'm looking forward to it."

"But honestly..."

"Yes?"

"Honestly, I'm ready to have children."

Ngellin smiled. "You already know I would love raising children with you, Beatrice."

"Well, Ngellin, that's a good thing, because I have some news for you."

"Are you...?"

"Yes. It's a girl. Leticia did the honors of the first ultrasound."

"So that's where you went in the shuttle a few days ago! You were being so secretive about that trip."

"Yes. Being a Michaelson has its perks."

Ngellin smiled again, then stretched out on the couch next to Beatrice, and nuzzled his face into her chest.

"We're having a baby!"

Independent Christian State, New Earth, Month 3, Year 31

David was cooling his heels in the outside office of Bishop Kramer of the ICS. That's what he called himself now, Bishop. Democracy was gone from the ICS. They now had a council of Elders, chosen by the bishop from settlement leaders. The bishop, apparently, was leader for life, and his successor would be chosen from the Elders in case of his death. Funny that they didn't want the Vatican in the ICS, it was so similar.

David had whined and cajoled his way to this meeting. Kramer had refused to talk with him, until a few weeks ago, when the final tally of people entering the ICS was received by him. David guessed that he realized he couldn't possibly deal with that number without some help.

David, Marianne and some of the Casitian team had discussed the approach he should have with the ICS, and agreed that basically, they could get whatever they wanted. They all knew that they might not be able to give it to them. Marianne already felt a little guilty at taking 2/3 of their land area and knew that they would end up being a little squeezed for space.

"Mr. Hastings, Bishop Kramer will see you now."

"Thank you."

He walked into the now open door, to see Bishop Kramer behind a very large, ornate desk. David wondered where he got that thing. As David walked in, he noticed Kramer make no move to stand up.

"Bishop Kramer."

"Yes, please, sit down."

David sat in one of the chairs in front of the desk.

"I'm not especially happy we are having this meeting, but we clearly need your help. According to the final tally, more than 40 million people have been approved for immigration to the ICS. That is an enormous number, and it would double our population. We don't have the buildings we need, we don't have the food production we need, and we don't have the medical facilities we need."

"I am well aware of the situation, Bishop Kramer. We can build enough infrastructure, buildings and settlements, including hospitals and medical clinics to handle the load within a year. In addition, we can get the agronomy teams going as soon as possible on growing food for you. It's a little late, so some of the first immigrants might have to make do with tents and pre-fabs, but not for long."

Kramer looked at David with his eyes narrowed. "I assume that can be done without any Casitian presence within the ICS."

David was expecting this and assumed that he could sway Kramer. "Frankly, no. If you are not willing to have Casitian staff inside of the ICS, we actually can't do anything. Can't expand rail lines or roads, can't expand electricity or widenet, can't expand water and sewer, and can't build."

"Nothing, nothing at all? Somehow I don't believe that."

David shrugged his shoulders. "You can choose to believe it or not, I don't care. It's true. Even delivering pre-fabs requires Casitian-piloted ships to land. Look, what's the big deal? There will be some Casitians here for a few months, then gone. If you feel like you want to exclude any Casitians living here, that's up to you."

"You don't understand." There was a finality to that tone that David did not like.

"Obviously."

"We cannot abide by the presence of any Casitians within our country for any length of time, no matter how short. They are incarnations of evil."

David sat back. He wondered what Kramer would say if he knew that David spent a lot of his free time with Casitians. Male Casitians at that.

David said, finally, "I see."

"Good. So, now that that's settled, when can you start building for us?"

David rarely lost his temper. He didn't even really see it coming but was surprised by the vehemence with which he answered Bishop Kramer.

"Look, *Bishop* Kramer, that is the way it is. If you are unwilling to allow any Casitians inside the ICS, your people are going to go without shelter, food, sanitation, and medical facilities and staff. Many of them will starve and die of infectious disease when cholera makes its inevitable visit without sanitation facilities. I'm assuming you don't give a flying fuck about them, otherwise you would not be acting so stupidly. Call me when you change your mind."

David got up and started to walk out of the office. He was surprised when he got to the door and hadn't heard a word from Kramer. He looked back and saw Kramer with a set angry look on his face. 'OK' David thought. He left the office and left the building.

As he was walking to the train station, he was a little sorry he'd blown up like that, but not too sorry. Kramer wouldn't have budged, no matter how sweet David had been. And the ICS was going to become a backwater pit, with starvation, disease and homelessness. Probably the only one on this planet.

New Orleans, New Earth, Month 4, Year 27

David was happy to be back at his cafe. And happier still to be chatting with Leticia about the situation with the ICS.

"Any suggestions?"

Leticia sighed. "What an idiot!"

"Tell me about it."

"Well, this is the problem. In order to get them clean water and good sanitation, we need 'dozer bots. The only people that know how to run 'dozer bots well are Casitians. Luckily, though, Cholera and other diseases spread by inadequate sanitation are pretty easy to treat. My suggestion is we can recruit a corps of Terran doctors to go into the ICS with medical supplies. We can also drop lots of water filters. I think if we do those things along with the food drops you're planning, people won't starve, they can get clean water, and they won't die of nasty things. But that doesn't mean they will be happy."

"I can't do anything for their mood, anyway." David smiled. "Can you coordinate with your compatriots around New Earth and gather up some folks to be ready to go into the ICS?"

"Absolutely, David. I got it. I can't believe he is now a Bishop. Man, I can't believe that place. I'm so glad my mom left."

Chapter 9:
Two Hundred Thousand Square Kilometers

(AP) December 25, 2029

Tales of Chaos on New Earth, Christmas on Earth a Muted Celebration

Ankara, Turkey – President Westinghouse-Lewis assured the global public yesterday that although there were some problematic reports, officials on New Earth, as well as the Casitians there to assist the immigration have everything well in hand. She blamed much of the chaos on countries that chose not to send official representatives to New Earth two years ago during the first wave.

Around the world, Christmas was a muted celebration for the first year, as people are preparing to leave and looking at their future with uncertainty. Retailers in most countries say that Christmas sales were down 50-60% from last year, as consumers are more careful about what they acquire, given weight restrictions for cargo when emigrating.

Colony Ship, July 24, 2029

"Wow, what an amazing view. I didn't think I'd ever get to see Earth from orbit, but here it is. And it's the last time I'll ever see it. That feels strange, to know we'll never be back on Earth again."

Joanne nodded. Therese, Maria's wife, hadn't been at all part of the team during the Casitian Crisis. Joanne and Maria had been in orbit many times, but this is the first time for both of them in a long while. Joanne was sitting next to Maria and Therese on the colony ship headed for New Earth. She was feeling a mix of feelings. She had finally, through more than a year of recovery, come to terms with her losses, and was ready to find a new role and a new life on New Earth. She was happy to be able to be immigrating with her friends. They planned to settle in an area now called "New California" even though it wasn't in New America. It had started during the first settling of New Earth as a group of communities in the South Central Independent Zone.

Several new large communities had been built in New California after the first wave, including New Oakland, where they would live.

Maria and Theresa had several friends who were already living in New California, and just about all of their friends were going to move there at one point or another.

She didn't quite know what she was going to do with her life, once she got to New Earth. She wanted to do science again, and she'd heard about the large fish they had found in the big lakes of New Earth. They weren't mammals, but they might be interesting. There were any number of scientific topics she could start investigating. She was thinking that might be her first choice.

She also thought about writing. The story of the "Hiders" was an interesting one, and as a participant, she had become a minor celebrity when the whole thing came to a head. It might be a story people would want to read in the future. She knew that several of her Hider companions had chosen to wait it out until the end. One of them had even moved to a very remote part of Alaska, hoping to avoid detection. She expected she'd see him on New Earth in ten years.

Lakota Territory, New Earth, Month 2, Year 33

Wachiwi had been pleased with how Marianne had fulfilled her promise to his sisters and brothers of indigenous people all over the world. He was about to leave for the all-nations summit that was to occur near a new settlement of Washoe people, by the big lake in the south they named Lake Tahoe. Representatives of peoples from all over the world would be there to discuss mutual interest, discuss preparations for the waves of immigrants, hash over a few border disputes that still were simmering, and celebrate their freedom.

He remembered his last conversation with Marianne that was mostly an argument. She had wanted to build several hospitals in their region, which required infrastructure like rail lines. None of them wanted this. The purpose of asking for more land, and autonomy, was that they would live exactly as they had lived in the past, before the Wasi'chu ever came to their regions. No rail lines, no roads, and as little electricity and widenet as they could get away with. As it stood now, there were about five small settlements scattered about their territory which had buildings and electricity, which served as the administrative centers of the indigenous territories. Otherwise, everyone lived in small villages, with dwellings characteristic of their people, such as tipis and long houses. It did mean that news took a lot longer to reach everyone. They had recruited hundreds of runners to spread news when needed.

In the end, Marianne had relented, but not before she had explained to Wachiwi that she felt some level of responsibility for them and would find it hard to forgive herself if there were an epidemic, or some other sort of health care crisis. Wachiwi explained that he understood, but he also reminded her gently that it felt somewhat insulting that she felt responsible for them. She had taken that comment quite well.

The first ripple, as they were now being called, of the second wave had brought about 50,000 people, from all over the world to their territory. Some of them were still in the process of traveling to where they would eventually live. It was, from what Wachiwi had heard, a much quieter and calm landing than most on New Earth.

Eastern Europe, New Earth, Month 3, Year 33

Jasmine was on her way to a new settlement in the far southeastern part of the European region. She had been given a region of about 200,000 square kilometers to monitor. The southeastern part of the European region included such countries as Croatia, Albania, Serbia, Bulgaria, and others. Her region primarily consisted of parts of Croatia, Serbia, and Bosnia. Kosovo, which was a part of this region on Earth, had opted to be located in the far eastern part of New Aard. It bordered on parts of Europe and Asia, but wasn't in her region, and didn't share borders with its usual neighbors.

This region was a mess. The first ships that were part of the second wave deposited about a half million people here, with more on the way in a matter of months. None of the countries in her region had sent representatives in the first wave, so no buildings or settlements were built. The basic infrastructure of roads, rail lines, electricity, water, sewer and widenet were all built. In her region, there were a smattering of pre-fab buildings here and there. Otherwise, everyone was in tents, and extraordinarily unhappy.

This had been the perfect job for her. She was on her own most of the time, and she had no orders, save to do her best in covering the ground under her care as much and as often as possible. She was not the only means of monitoring this region, but she was the best - her on-the-ground reports were an important part of the process and couldn't really be replaced by AI monitors. She expected that she might manage to cover it all in about 2 years, and then she'd have to start all over again.

She was on her way to one of the most populated settlements. It was to eventually become Zagreb, the capital of Croatia. She hadn't had a chance to get here yet, and she wasn't looking forward to it. Marianne said that she'd gotten a very angry message from the representatives who had finally come with the second wave, and Jasmine knew that she'd be facing some angry government officials when she arrived.

But Jasmine had gotten to be very good at deflecting their anger. Pretty much the first thing out of her mouth was "what do you need right now?" If they were reasonable, which they weren't always, she could promise them that they'd get things in a few days or so.

She slowed down her vehicle as she approached the settlement's edge. There were tents along the road, several deep, and she could see a line forming where the food was being distributed. As she came closer to the center, she saw that about 20 pre-fab buildings had been set up, probably before this group arrived. She parked her car in front of the one likeliest to hold an official person.

As she got out, a group of men descended on her, and started speaking rapidly in a language she didn't understand. She put up her hands. "Anyone here speak English?"

One of the men stepped out. "Yes, I do."

"OK, so who are the official representatives here?"

The man who spoke English pointed to another man, who came forward. Ah, Jasmine thought. What fun. Translation was always inexact and had led to some unfortunate misunderstandings in the past. Jasmine started.

"We need to get some settlements built as soon as possible. I can send for one of the planners to come and work with you to figure out where things should be built."

The man who spoke English translated what Jasmine had said, and then translated the response. "Why wasn't there anything already built?" Ah, that particular anger. Some of them seemed to expect them to have telepathy, or something.

"Your country didn't send anyone in the first wave to help us plan. We did our best to create this infrastructure," she pointed to the road, "but the buildings needed your help and planning. Now that you are here, we can start building in earnest. Building a settlement that can house 50,000 or so takes about a week. Building a city, like Zagreb, should only take a month."

They went back and forth for a while, and it seemed that they finally got the picture. Jasmine promised a planner visit, as well as some more pre-fabs for temporary housing. They also needed some rudimentary medical equipment and supplies to start with, and she got that order in as well.

As she drove off, heading out to find a quiet spot without people to camp for the night, she felt some satisfaction in what she was doing. She still wanted to eventually move to Casiti, but it would be OK to be doing this for a while, first.

Casiti, 140 Nird, 786

Jal'end'a put down the tablet that had the Casitian translation of the Kinder story "Elfer." She knew the background. Marianne's niece had been married to a Kinder man, who had published a large number of his grandmother Dbor's stories – and got arrested and sent to the mines for it. The stories made their way back to New Earth when Marianne's niece was rescued, and she and Ngellin, a Kinder deserter had translated the whole set of stories into English. They had sent this story to Marianne, who had, with Ja'el's help, translated it to Casitian, then sent it along to Jal'end'a. Beatrice and Ngellin had wanted Casitians to read the story that a Kinder woman had written.

Tears were streaming down Jal'end'a's face. Even that one single Kinder woman could write work of this quality – and of this content, was somehow astonishing to Jal'end'a. And that astonishment brought to Jal'end'a's attention her assumptions about the Kinder. Even though she had been the one to chastise the Caraj for the sins of calling the Kinder accursed, she realized that somehow, deep inside herself, she still thought that.

A few things crossed her mind. First, she would publish the set of these stories when translated with an introduction from Beatrice, that would tell the story of Dbor, Pkygy's grandmother, as well as a preface from Jal'end'a. Somehow, that didn't seem enough. What if some Kinder were to come and live here? It seemed, well, preposterous on its face. But what Jal'end'a realized was that if all three branches of humanity lived on both open planets, perhaps there would be a chance, someday, of reconciliation with the Kinder on Kinder Home.

She began to compose a message to Ngellin.

Kinder Settlement, New Earth, Month 2, Year 34

"Love, you've been chewing on this for months, now."

"I know, Beatrice. But I'm not so happy with the fact that you are willing to go along with me no matter what I choose. It's too much like ..."

Beatrice was playing with their daughter, who was almost 3 years old. She was a quiet child, named after Tivyl. Everyone called her 'Tiv.' She stood up, picked Tiv up, and walked over to where Ngellin was sitting. She sat next to him and placed Tiv between them.

"Ngellin, we are not on Hilcyon. I know that you respect me. I know that you listen to what I want. I know that you love me in ways that few Kinder men love their wives. You cook most of the time for heaven's sake! The reason I am willing to go with you is because I want you to be able to make a decision that you feel is right for the Kinder in the long haul. If my moving with you to Casiti means that there is one tiny bit better of a chance of true human unity, then it is worth it for me. Besides, either New Earth or Casiti are both great places to raise our children."

Ngellin nodded. "I want to go, Beatrice."

Beatrice shook her head, and then looked up at Ngellin with a smile. "I've known that since the instant you read the message from Jal'end'a. You can be one infuriating man sometimes."

"There are about 450 others that wish to go, also. Many have families. I'll let Jal'end'a know. I think it's the right decision."

"I agree, Ngellin. The better that the Casitians understand the Kinder, and vice versa, the better the chance that when they come calling, which they will, we can work together."

New Columbia, New Earth, Month 2, Year 36

Kurt walked into the apartment not sure how exactly he was feeling. Kenneth looked like he was making dinner.

"Hey."

"Hi." Kenneth came out from the kitchen and kissed Kurt.

"Oh, my, Kurt. What happened?"

"Valorie is not running."

"What? Why?"

"She feels like she's done her job. She wants to retire and move to Casiti."

"That's becoming a trend."

"I know."

"You're going to run?"

"Are you kidding me? I like being Chief of Staff."

"Valorie wants you to run, doesn't she?"

"Yes, she does."

"Well, you certainly are known to a lot of people on both planets, now. I'd say most people would already put you as the front runner."

Kurt went to the couch and sat down heavily. Kenneth sat beside him.

"Babe, you would make a great President."

"Ah, don't say that!"

"I mean it. And, you fucking know it, too."

Kurt, sadly, did. If there was one big change he noticed in the pre- to post-Casitian landscape, it was that the leaders chosen were not the ones that really especially wanted to lead. He thought that was a great change. He didn't want to personify it, however.

He heard his phone beep. Marianne. He wondered what she wanted.

"Hi Marianne."

"Hey Kurt." Marianne's voice was a bit tinny. The widenet, which was now carrying more voice and data traffic than it was ever designed for, was getting a bit stressed.

"What's up, Marianne?"

"Valorie called me."

"She didn't."

"Yeah, she did."

"Fuck that."

"Language! So, you know what I'm going to say."

"You want me to run."

"Yes, I do. All of the other likely candidates are Terran, Kurt. And although I've corresponded with some of them, I trust none of them to have the best interest of New Earth, or humanity in mind."

"And you trust me."

"As do many people, Kurt. Your work over the past 12 years has been nothing short of remarkable."

Kurt sighed. How could he say no to that?

"OK. I'll run."

"If I were there, I'd give you a big kiss! Thanks!"

"And if I win, one of these days, I'm going to call this debt due, my friend."

Kurt could almost hear Marianne's smile. "And I'll be happy to pay up."

Ankara, Turkey, August 10, 2031

Diana looked over the latest emigration report. Two years had gone by since the start of the main emigration effort. In total 18 waves of emigrants had left Earth, to go to both New Earth and Casiti. That meant that the planet had about 1.4 billion less people on it.

It was being felt. There already had been massive economic changes, mostly negative, all over the world. Once it was clear that everyone was leaving, the market for many items, including all luxury items and cars and such had evaporated overnight. The good thing was that in their place, whole industries arose dedicated to things like light and sturdy furnishings that would fold and be easily packable, transportable items of all sorts, survival gear meant to work on New Earth, as well as things that would be useful once people moved.

This made the economic disruption more bearable. The other big problem had been agriculture. Farmers, agricultural companies and food distributors were hot to get off of Earth early, to get a head start on New Earth. But the government couldn't allow that - because then people on Earth would starve. So the government had to step in, and force many of these people to stay on Earth, and work to make sure the food production and distribution systems still provided for the people left.

"Madame President?" Her aide, Cecilia popped her head in.

"Come in, Cecilia. How goes it?"

"I have a bit of a sticky wicket for you."

"OK, let's hear this sticky wicket."

"I need to give you a bit of background. As you might or might not recall, we put out a call for rapeseed growers and rapeseed oil manufacturers, because we got the information that there were large swaths of area on New Earth that would be perfect for its cultivation. And we need it, primarily for biodiesel, but for other uses on New Earth."

"It's one of those little facts I filed away somewhere but forgot. OK, go ahead."

"Of course, all of those companies and growers jumped at the chance to get to New Earth early..."

Diana interrupted, "I think I know where this is heading."

"Yes. They are all gone. We don't have any growers or manufacturers left, but we have 6 years left on Earth. Our Agriculture Ministry has gotten screaming complaints from all over the world because of the lack of rapeseed and rapeseed oil."

"What is it used for here besides biodiesel?"

"Canola oil and animal feed, mostly."

"Substitutes?"

"Olive oil, corn oil, etc. I don't know what can replace it in animal feed, but we haven't gotten too many complaints about that. Most of the complaints have been from processed food manufacturers who are already stressed. The substitutes are more expensive."

"So what can we do? Is there anything we can do?"

"My suggestion is to give the processed food companies subsidies to be able to use the substitutes more cheaply. It won't make them happy, but it will be something."

"OK, work with Angus in Ag to figure that out. This printing money for subsidies seems dangerous, but we keep doing it, and it seems to ease things, so I'm trying not to worry about it too much. Actually, while you are at it, can you also check with Deirdre about economic impacts? Thanks for bringing this to my attention. We're going to face this over and over again, aren't we?"

Cecilia nodded her head. "Six more years, Madame President, only 6 more years."

New Columbia, New Earth, Month 4, Year 36

She sat in the front pew of her church in San Francisco, looking at the sun come through the stained-glass depiction of Julian of Norwich, the 14th century mystic. She loved that stained glass image. She sat in silence for a while, watching the candle flames dance on the altar.

She heard a soft chime and looked down at her widenet phone. She had a message from one of the diocesan staff here on New Earth, asking to see her. She sighed. She picked up the tiny remote control that was lying in her lap and pushed the 'end' button. The small drab room that she was really in and the single chair that she sat on returned.

She hadn't put in a requisition yet to have her church reconstructed, because she felt conflicted about where it should go. It was, for sure, one of the most beautiful modern church buildings in the world. She was sure she wouldn't be staying on New Earth for a lot longer. She felt that her time as a priest was coming close to an end, and she wanted to move to Casiti, to write, to do other things. She would be here another few years, getting the Episcopal Church settled in New America, and then she would be gone.

It sometimes surprised her that her church in New Columbia had more parishioners than her church in San Francisco. Having the first official Episcopal Church in New America was what made the difference. She knew that many of her parishioners hadn't been church goers when they were on Earth, but the wrenching nature of the change to New Earth was enough to get them in the door.

She walked back toward the diocese offices and observed the busy streets. New Columbia had become a very busy place. Tall buildings had been built for government and commercial uses. Every significant company from Earth now had a presence in New Columbia, in hopes of influencing the government.

She laughed internally at that one. The government of President Lira was impeccable, from everything Patricia had heard. In some ways, it was because she got a chance to start almost from scratch. The governments of the previous Presidents had been almost non-existent, and then the scandal of the kidnapped teenagers had scoured the government of everyone who had any connection to that scandal. President Lira got to bring in a totally new group, and they were honest, straightforward, and about as apolitical as it was possible for government people to be.

And now, she had heard that Kurt Wilson was running for President of the United States on New Earth. She was happy that things had turned around so much from what things had been and could turn out so differently than things at home.

Jul'when, Casiti, 130 Paqn 785

Chin had originally planned on moving to Rel'toro after the initial effort to prepare for the Jul'when immigrants, but she had gotten so absorbed in teaching people how to farm in the Casitian way that she lost track of her desire to go to Rel'toro. And she started to feel like Jul'when was her home. Now, winter was on its way, and she had spent the last month preparing for it. Including something which surprised her. She'd met a Casitian man, Rt'len in the course of her work, and they decided to spend the winter as companions. His home was back on Rel'toro, but they decided to spend the winter here, on Jul'when, in her dwelling, which suited them both. She wondered whether she would ever choose to move to Rel'toro.

One of the things she wanted to learn this winter was how to write Casitian language. Rt'len had promised to help. She was one of a relatively few Chinese who had chosen to immigrate here, and she wanted to start translating some Chinese literature into Casitian. She had learned that the Casitians were avid readers in general and had become avid readers of Earth literature. Translators could hardly keep up with the demand.

In her spare time, she'd been reading the books of the series of "Stories of Dbor" which had become famous on both worlds. The Casitian translations were not complete yet, so she had been reading many of the stories to her Casitian friends who knew some English.

She had kept contact with her family back in Beijing, all of whom immigrated to China on New Earth. She promised she'd visit sometime. She was happy here on Casiti, and even enjoyed the cold months. And she was looking forward to Rt'len's company.

Dlejon, New Earth, Month 3 Year 40

Ja'el said, "too bad you can't vote."

"Love, it's fine. I'm helping Kurt in as many ways as I can without breaking any rules."

"I know. I'm glad you think he'll win. He's quite a stunning young man."

"He is, isn't he? I talked with Leticia about him a while ago. She's known him for more than 30 years and has remarked on how much he's changed."

Ja'el and Marianne were sitting on their couch, looking at their respective tablets, working companionably. "Love, on another subject, I have a colloquialism that I need to work out."

"OK, shoot."

"Beatrice and Ngellin have this phrase in one of the stories 'watch your tongue.' I know it is an English colloquialism, and I pretty much have come to understand what it means. As you might imagine, there is not anything remotely like it in Casitian."

Marianne smiled. Of course not. She thought of a number of ways to say it in Casitian, but ... there just wasn't anything that quite fit. Then she wondered...

"Ja'el what do Casitian parents say to children when they begin to say inappropriate things?"

"Inappropriate things? What could children say that would be inappropriate?"

Marianne rolled her eyes. Sometimes, Casitians were a bit much.

"OK, so how about this. A kid, say a 1 year old, is running around the house and a stranger they have never seen comes by. Let's say the stranger is weird looking in some way, and the kid says something rude."

"Ah, I see what you are getting at. Well..."

"It needs to be short, not a long loving speech."

Ja'el laughed. "The closest thing I can come up with would be 'joe'lista foera kl'eroter, zas karen'a wilena. It's a bit specific to children, though."

"Not so bad. What about modifying zas to zasa and karen'a to karen'o?"

Ja'el nodded. "Yes! That will work. Thank you."

"It's a lot longer than 'watch your tongue, but ...'"

Ja'el smiled. "I have learned so much about how we are different in this translation process. I look forward to spending time with Beatrice and Ngellin to talk about this."

"Oh, right, I was supposed to book that shuttle, wasn't I?"

"Thanks, yes, you were."

"I'm on it."

New Columbia, New Earth, Month 3 Year 40

"85% of the precincts on Earth are now reporting, 100% of precincts on New Earth are reporting. MSNBC, ABC, Fox, Disney, and NETV have all now called the race for Kurt Wilson." A huge cheer went up from the room. Kurt was in a relatively small room, with close allies and friends, including Kenneth, Valorie, Mira, Leticia, Terrance, Suzanna and Geoffrey, even David and Marianne were here. It was looking a lot like he would be the new President, the first of the new United States on New Earth.

Marianne sat down next to him. "So, how does it feel?"

"Horrible."

Marianne put her arm around Kurt's shoulders. "I have to say, I'm sort of glad you said that."

Kurt laughed. "But I know it's good for the US, and good for New Earth. That part makes me happy. I have to admit to being a little surprised by the whole thing. I'm not so surprised that most US citizens living here voted for me. The shocker is that most US citizens living there voted for me too. I'm the youngest US President in history." He grinned.

"They saw in you someone who knew what life was like on New Earth and was prepared to make a new way. All the other candidates hadn't even moved here yet."

Kurt nodded. "I guess so. Anyway, my inauguration is in two months. Coming?"

"Wouldn't miss it for the world, dear. I hear the Supreme Court is moving on the next wave so that the Chief Justice can be in town to swear you in!"

Terrance, who would become Kurt's chief of staff, walked over. "Hey there. Time to address your public, my friend. The other candidates have conceded the race."

Kurt smiled. He found it so hard to believe that 32 short years ago, Kurt was the sullen teenager who bullied the boy who became the amazing man standing in front of him.

"Alright, let's get going."

He followed Terrance through the halls to the large ballroom where his victory celebration was being held. As he walked in, the cheers became deafening. He couldn't hear himself think. Luckily, he didn't have to think. The victory speech was already written. He walked up to the podium, and looked out at the crowd. It was quite a mix. A lot of young people like him who had grown up on New Earth, as well as many older folks who had recently arrived. He had been gratified by how many people worked on his campaign who were new arrivals.

He smiled and waved for a while, as did Kenneth, who stood beside him. He finally raised his hands, asking for quiet. The room quieted down. There was a large group of press in the back, with cameras and taking photographs. He wished that this could be live on Earth, but communications through the wormhole had about a 2 hour delay.

"My fellow Americans, both here, in New America, and at home on Earth, I thank you for giving me the chance to serve you at this momentous time...

Chapter 10:
Ten Percent

(AP) December 25, 2035

Two More Years to Go as Earth Empties Out. People Who Remain Celebrate in Small Ways.

Annapolis, MD (AP) -- There are fewer people on Earth than there are on New Earth this Christmas. Churches here are mostly empty, families split up, and few stores remain open. Jake Green, from Annapolis Maryland, explained that he had drawn the short straw, somehow, and didn't get a berth on a colony ship until toward the end.

"It's OK," he says. "it's giving me a chance to do some things I had wanted to do. And it also means that by the time I get to New America, I won't have to worry."

People who would not normally gather together are having parties and festivals, to conquer boredom, and have fun. One community spent three weeks gathering all of the Christmas lights they could find, and stringing them up all over town, creating a collaborative light display that was hard to match.

Kinder Settlement, New Earth, Month 1 Year 41

Beatrice handled the hardbound book with a wonderful cloth cover, and embossed title "Stories of Dbor: The Kinder Writings." It had finally been printed in an actual book, and somehow, seeing it like this made it feel more real.

It had been published in electronic form, and spread all over New Earth years ago, but for some reason, just over the past 5 years, it had become more and more popular. The Casitian translation was about to be published on Casiti – Ja'el had dedicated most of the last few years of her life to it. She had been giving readings all over New Earth over the past two years and had already been asked by a dozen people to give readings on Casiti to people who knew English.

She felt that Pkygy would have been happy for this day, and happy that his grandmother's writings were so loved by so many. Beatrice wished she could go back in time and bring his grandmother to this point. She imagined that her only regret would be that her home planet was still closed off.

Beatrice remembered that she had left copies of the stories behind with Krely and hoped that Krely had been able to pass them on. Perhaps they might eventually become as famous there as they were here.

She opened the book, and started to read, again, the story of Elfer.

Moon Station, May 27, 2038

David and Joel were sitting in a joining room on the Moon station, looking over the latest emigration and immigration reports from Earth and New Earth. David had come to Earth for a last visit. He'd spent time with Diana and Janie, visited with Joel and Laura, had spent time with Torf'ki doing sightseeing, as he'd promised years ago. They had visited a number of monuments and the like. It had been odd to go to some places that were near deserted. Yosemite didn't even have any park staff anymore – people were free to range about and go wherever they wanted. Few people were traveling anymore, even those who had a couple of years left on Earth.

David and Torf'ki were good friends now, but no longer companions. Torf'ki had taken another companion, a Terran man he'd met while doing construction work on New Earth. David was in between companions, although he and Heg'ellin were spending a lot of their free time together lately.

David looked back down at the emigration reports. It had mostly been smooth sailing. A few hiccups now and then, and that stubborn approximately 150 million people who refused to apply for emigration berths. They had begun to do what they were calling "extraction planning." He hated the phrase and hated what it would mean. But there really was no choice in the matter.

"David, these immigration reports are staggeringly bad."

"Staggeringly? C'mon man, give us a break."

"The reports of Cholera in the ICS are troubling. Millions of people either in tents or actually camping outside. I mean, I know it rains on New Earth, David."

"Joel, most of New Earth is doing fine. No one in any of the independent zones are even in pre-fabs, unless they chose very small, remote settlements. That's true of New America, and at least a hundred other country territories. The native and indigenous people's immigration has gone swimmingly. Of the 3 or so billion people now on New Earth, only about 400 million are in bad shape."

"That's more than 10%!"

"That's ONLY a bit over 10% Joel! Do you have ANY idea what it's been like on New Earth for the last few years? I'm amazed that 1/2 the people aren't in tents and that no one is starving!"

"OK, you're right. I apologize. We expected nightmares here on Earth, and things to go smoothly on New Earth. It seems the opposite has happened."

"Until extraction."

Joel sighed. "Yes, until extraction. But I'll be gone by then."

"What?"

"Laura and I have decided to move to Casiti, and we're leaving in about a year. Neither of us can stand the idea of watching the extraction process, so we're leaving before it begins. There are enough folks here to deal with it, anyway. We're not really needed."

"Casiti, eh? It's becoming a popular destination. Diana and Janie are planning to retire there."

"Yeah, we're actually going to be living in the same community on Rel'toro."

"I liked Casiti a lot, but I like how New Earth is shaping up. I think I'll stay. I've been invited by Marianne's niece Leticia to live in a small community up in the NCPIZ, and that seems like fun. There will be a lot of younger folks, but there are also a good group of people about our age settling there. It has an amazing view."

"Sounds nice. Is it too out of the way for your work?"

"What work? Dude, the minute this shit is done, I'm retiring."

Joel laughed.

"What are you laughing at?"

"Mark my words, David. No one is going to let you retire."

New Earth Casiti Transport, 60 Hevl 786

Beatrice looked out of the window to see the bulk of New Earth recede. Ngellin, Tivyl and she were on their way to Rel'toro, to a community that would include about 50 Kinder/New Earth families, as well as Casitians. She was looking forward to seeing Casiti and getting to know it better.

They would be arriving in late summer. Not the optimal time to immigrate to Casiti. She and Ngellin had a small garden on New Earth, which she tended with care. She was looking forward to doing that on Casiti. The idea of growing food in a greenhouse, which was also standard Casitian practice, was exciting to her too.

She turned to Ngellin and put her hand on his. He looked up at her and smiled.

"Well, we are certainly on our way, aren't we?"

"We are."

"Beatrice, I have been asked by Jal'end'a to collaborate with the Kinder to create a written history and, in a sense, encyclopedia of the Kinder. It feels like such a daunting task."

"Ngellin, collectively, I bet you all know so much. It will just take time to figure out how to put it together. Kler is a walking encyclopedia of Kinder Supreme Chiefs!"

Ngellin smiled. "Yes, that was a hobby of his, the history of Supreme Chiefs."

"I want to hear about Klor."

"Ah, Beatrice, that is going to be a tricky one."

"Why?"

"It's a very sensitive story. I get the impression that it's sensitive for the Casitians as well."

"Somehow, I get the feeling that the crux of the issues between Casitians and the Kinder are buried in that story. And from what I hear, you both feel betrayed by the other in that story."

Ngellin nodded.

"It has to be told, Ngellin."

"I agree, dear, I agree."

They chatted for a while about what their life might look like on Casiti. After a while, Ngellin drifted off into a nap, like Tivyl, and Beatrice was left with her own thoughts.

Illsenor Station, Month 1 Year 44

Marianne looked at the tablet with data. "So, you are saying that stubbornness is the only problem?"

David said, "yeah, honestly. The ICS who refuses to allow any Casitians on the ground. Countries that are constantly in our way when we are trying to give them what they asked for. About 25 countries who focused on roads and don't have enough fuel to get everyone around. Actually, that last group isn't such a big deal. They are all quite happy when the light rail systems get installed, so we're focusing a lot of resources on that."

"So, what can we do?"

David shook his head. "Not much, Marianne. I've been spending a lot of time going from place to place trying to work things out as much as possible. Well, of course, except for the ICS. The ICS..."

"We keep dropping supplies. Leticia has been doing amazing work with the medical teams. The infectious outbreaks seem to be in control. It seems like some of it is naturally easing as people leave."

"Since people can't vote with a ballot to throw the bums out, they are voting with their feet in droves. Joel said, by the way, that the number of people changing their immigration applications from the ICS to New America is growing."

"Is this creating a problem for New America?"

"No, Marianne, the government there is handling the overflow quite well. And some of the overflow is going to other places."

"Well, we've got less than 5 years left. I'll be glad when this is over."

"You and me both."

"David, I got an interesting missive from Jal'end'a. She wants me and a few other leaders, to come to Casiti to discuss the future."

"The future? Is there a future?" He smirked.

"Seriously, David. We do need to begin to figure out what the heck we're going to do once this is all said and done. Problem is, I can't see when any of us can possibly get away for a few weeks to spend on Casiti."

"I think we can do it. I'd say in about two years, we'll be pretty much smoothed out here."

"You think so?"

"I do."

Zagreb, New Earth, Month 1 Year 45

Jasmine was glad to be here. She drove her car into the small parking lot next to the New Earth Immigration Service building, pulled out her bags, and walked into the small, squat building. She walked up to the desk.

"Jasmine! How are you?"

Jasmine liked Marija and liked getting to see her. She would be sad not to see her again, at least not for a long while. "Doing fine Marija. Ready to throw in the towel. This region doesn't need me anymore."

"Going somewhere else to monitor? I hear there are some real nightmares further south."

"Nope. I'm leaving. I got the final approval to emigrate to Casiti. I'm going to be living in Rel'toro."

"Casiti? Wow, that sounds neat. I'm looking forward to visiting someday."

"You'll always be welcome to visit me. I'll send along my Casitian network ID once I get one. Anyway, the car is here, the last reports are filed, and I have a train to catch."

They hugged, and Jasmine picked up her bags and walked out of the building. As she walked down the sidewalk toward the train station, she remembered what Zagreb had looked like eleven years ago. Now, it looked like a real city. Some of the most prominent buildings, like the Cathedral and the Theatre, had been reconstructed. There were some very tall buildings, and lots of neat apartment complexes. One of the other buildings they had reconstructed was the Zagreb train station. As she walked across the street, before entering into the building, she looked up at the four columns in the central tall portion of the station, and the arched windows, and the statues on the top. It was spectacular, and she imagined it helped people to see a tangible piece of their history, even though it wasn't the real thing.

As the train pulled out of the station, and speeded its way west and north to Paris, where she'd grab her shuttle to the one of the regular New Earth/Casiti transports, she thought about what her life might be like on Casiti. She remembered, years ago, when Marianne had said that it wasn't all that she might be expecting. She wasn't sure that she cared. She just knew that she needed something different than anything on New Earth could provide.

Mecca, New Aard, New Earth, Month 4 Year 45

Olam was walking around the Kabaa. The Kabaa! He couldn't quite get his mind around the fact that the city of Mecca was here, on New Earth. It had taken a long time, and a lot of effort by many people to figure out what to do with Mecca. Islamic scholars here and back on Earth had argued back and forth for years about whether or not Mecca should stay on Earth or be rebuilt on New Earth. It fractured the Islamic community into two factions that Olam guessed would never be one again. Those that felt that Mecca should stay on Earth forever, and one of the central pillars be postponed for 1000 years, and those who felt that Allah willed that Mecca move with humans.

Once it was clear that the majority wanted Mecca moved, where it would go wasn't anywhere as difficult. It was placed pretty much in the center of New Aard. Olam didn't know what the faction who insisted that this was not the real Mecca would do when it was time for the Hajj.

This was, he knew, far from isolated. Christians were dealing with the issue of the Church of the Holy Sepulchre and Vatican City. Buddhists were dealing with Sarnath, Bodhgaya and Dharamsala, Hindus with the holy Ganges, which could not be replicated. And on and on. But it seemed that in places where the replicas were built, people were by and large taking them as if they were the real thing. Olam thought that perhaps most Muslims would be able to do the same with Mecca, eventually.

New Oakland, New California, New Earth, Month 4 Year 45

Joanne bent down to weed her garden, which was overgrown. The tomatoes were doing well. Her pepper plants were not doing so well. Apparently, there was a little native pest that just loved pepper plants. She hadn't had a chance yet to go get the compound that would kill the pest, so her plants were droopy, and there weren't any peppers yet.

The climate here was similar to the climate in Northern California, except wetter, so she was able to grow a lot of food she was familiar with. She was also trying out some Casitian crops, too.

"Hi there!"

She looked up to see Maria standing on the sidewalk next to her garden. She stood up and walked over. They hugged.

"It's good to see you, Maria. I feel like I don't see you very often."

"I've been busy, so busy. The PR business is booming."

Joanne smiled. "I can imagine."

"How are you these days?"

"I've been pretty busy myself. This is actually the first time I've been home in a month. I just got back from a field study of the *Gurlops oceanus*. It's an amazing creature. I also happily report that it has a brain the size of a pea. No chance of provisional status."

Maria laughed.

"I'm finishing a final draft of the paper for publication this week. It's good to be a scientist again."

"Have you been going to meetings these days?"

"When I'm here, yes. There's one downtown on thirdday that I'm especially fond of, and I try to get to the sixthday women's meeting uptown." Joanne felt good about where she was in life and didn't want to jeopardize it.

"Well, I came here to invite you to Thanksgiving dinner at our house."

"Wow, it's almost Thanksgiving, isn't it? I rarely look at my Earth calendar anymore - it's hard to keep the two in my mind."

"Yeah, me too, although I hear there is a movement to have New Earth adopt Earth's calendar."

"How could that be, with the longer days and shorter years?"

"Someone figured out how to do it, and adjust for the differences, etc."

"Well, that would be fine with me. Anyway, sure, I'm happy to come. We can finally get sweet potatoes and squash, and I've managed to scrounge some spices. I'll make my infamous dish."

"I love it. See you then. In the meantime, be well, my friend."

They hugged again, and Joanne went back to weeding her garden.

Chapter 11:
Twenty Years' Time

(AP) December 12, 2037

Last Colony Ships to Leave Earth in 10 days

Ankara, Turkey (AP) -- The last of the colony ships will leave Earth in 10 days. The ships will be filled with workers who have stayed behind to wrap things up, as well as the more than 80 million people who had to be extracted from their homes and hiding places all over Earth.

"It's a tragedy," said President Diane Westinghouse-Lewis. "I'm sorry that more people didn't take advantage of all of the resources available to them earlier. But we don't have a choice in the matter."

In the United States, National Guard troops have been scouring the cities and countrysides for people still remaining. All over the world, military troops have been put to the task of finding people. The President and her team are confident that all humans will be removed from Earth with the final Colony ships.

Moon Station, September 26, 2036

"You know, I never cleaned out that storage locker I had in Palo Alto."

"Storage locker?"

Joel laughed. "Yeah, when I lost my apartment in the middle of the Casitian Crisis, I took all of my stuff, and put it in a storage locker. When we left to go travel, I gave the proprietors a big chunk of money which would pay for 20 years' time, just in case, even though I expected to come back and live on Earth again. And, well, you know what has happened. So, I still have that storage locker full of stuff I haven't seen in 24 years."

"And I have a basement full of stuff at my sister's house. She left for New Earth last year, so who knows what state that stuff is in. I'm not sure I care."

"I gotta go down and open mine up. Somehow, I can't bear to leave not having looked through it, at least."

"OK, well, let's take a little trip, shall we?"

Palo Alto, Earth, September 28, 2036

The storage place in Palo Alto looked like it had been deserted for years. Most of the storage units looked like they had been forced open. Joel guessed that people had been looking for some sorts of valuables they could take with them when it was time to go. He distinctly remembered the locker number, because it happened to be the same number as his birth year, 1975. They walked down the row of the 1900s, and locker after locker had been forced open. Finally, they reached 1975. It was a mess. It clearly had been open for a long time. The furniture was moldy, everything was strewn about. Yellowed papers were everywhere. Joel opened some boxes, and everything had been destroyed by water.

"So much for that idea." Something caught his eye. In a deep recess was a trophy. He'd forgotten all about it. He'd been on the swim team in High School and had kept his trophies. The gold plastic was flaking off, and the plaque on the bottom had rusted so you could no longer see what it said. He threw it back.

"Somehow, it feels bad knowing this shit will rot here for 1000 years before anyone sees it again. Oh well. Nothing here to take. Are you still sure you want to see what's in your sister's basement?"

Laura nodded. "Even if it's in this shape, I want to know."

There were now five small-sized plastic shipping crates on the sidewalk next to the shuttle. Laura had been luckier. No one had bothered to break into Laura's sister's house, since it appeared to be completely empty. Most of her stuff in the basement was still in good shape, although there wasn't a lot she wanted to take with her. Joel was walking up the stairs with the sixth, and Laura was following.

"I guess this means we're ready to go, doesn't it?"

"Yup. We've got a berth on the last Casitian Colony ship to leave Earth. We're getting out right before extraction starts. Our work is done, Laura. And I'm ready for some relaxation."

New York, Earth, December 1, 2037

"Hello, this is Joh Appel, and I'm here with President Westinghouse-Lewis, who is on a tour of the world before we all have to leave. Madame President, why the tour?"

"Well, Joh, I know it seems strange, but it's almost like a captain going down with his ship. I want to make sure that this final month of arrangements for people leaving goes smoothly."

"Madame President, the vast majority of the people leaving on this last wave are leaving quite reluctantly."

"That could even be an understatement. I know. We've been extracting people all over the world, unfortunately. It's been an unpleasant task for the folks whose jobs it is to do it. We'd hoped that there wouldn't be as many as there have been. Part of the reason for this tour is to see how the extraction process has been for people and see if there are things we can do to help."

"On another subject, I hear you are moving to Casiti?"

Diana nodded. "Yes, Joh, my partner and I decided that it would be best for us to retire there, instead of New Earth. I'm sure we'll be visiting, though. Where are you headed?"

"New Earth. Our whole network is moving, and I'll be doing pretty much the same work there."

"Joh, do you mind if I ask you a question?"

"Not at all Madame President."

"Call me Diana, Joh. I'm only President for the next month, and, honestly, most people left on Earth don't care."

Joh smiled, inclined his head. "Diana."

"Why did you decide to stay so long?"

"I wanted to see what Earth looks like mostly empty of people. It's a curiosity thing, one the network was happy to indulge me in. We are filming a documentary starting next week, filming many abandoned areas of Earth and such."

"I'm looking forward to watching that on Casiti, Joh."

"Thank you."

Rel'toro, Casiti, 100 Gont 787

Beatrice was soaking in a large, deep tub. The lights were low, and there was very soothing music playing. If she weren't having labor pains, she might even be enjoying this.

"Mami, how are you?" Tivyl, her oldest, who was sixteen, eight, or two depending on which calendar one was paying attention to, was hovering.

"I'm OK, Tiv. I hurt sometimes."

Ngellin came into the room. "Tiv, it's time for bed."

"But Mami might have Pkygy when I'm asleep Da!"

"If she does, you can meet him in the morning sweet. Off you go."

Beatrice groaned. Her midwife, Lo'et, asked her how frequent the contractions were.

"About every two minutes."

"OK, we're getting there, very close now."

She was sitting on the couch, with Pkygy nursing at her breast. It was the easiest childbirth she'd had so far, after her two daughters, Tivyl and Marianne. It was late at night, and Ngellin was busy helping her doula clean up. She was glad she had named her son Pkygy. Ngellin had made the suggestion. When she found out it was a boy, she asked Ngellin for a good Kinder male name, maybe one of his relatives. He'd said, simply, 'Pkygy is a great Kinder name.' Beatrice agreed.

She was happy on Casiti, as was Ngellin. He, and many of his Kinder fellows, were busy working on the history and encyclopedia that Jal'end'a had requested. It was work he really liked. On the side, he was also learning Casitian. He hoped to translate into Kinder language some of the epic givs of the Casitians, like the one of Ul'tretor, one of the early Casitian leaders. From what she had heard, there was a lot of discussions of the Kinder in that giv. She didn't especially look forward to the moment when Ngellin read, uncensored, the Casitian opinions of the Kinder.

Rel'toro, Casiti, 102 Gont 787

"Oh my God, he is so cute!" Laura was holding Pkygy and rocking him in her arms. Ngellin had thrown her a bit of a surprise party, with Joel and Laura, Jal'end'a, and Kinder and Casitian friends. There was Casitian, Kinder and Earth food and drink, and everyone was having a great time.

Joel walked up to her, giving her a hug, and congratulating her. "Beatrice, I just finished reading the stories of Dbor. They are amazing. I know the writing was great, but you and Ngellin must have done an amazing translation job."

"Thanks, Joel. It was a lot of work, but worth it."

"So, what's next?"

"What's next? Raising three children. It's a lot of work, you know." Beatrice smiled.

"Are you going to follow the Casitian standards? Will Tivyl go to a youth community?"

"Yes, she will. But Pkygy will be my last. And I guess in about 3 years or so, I'll have to figure out what to do with my life. But I'm in no hurry."

Disney World, Orlando, Florida, Earth, December 15, 2037

The park had been closed for 5 years, enough time that its decomposition was evident. Joh walked through the gates to the castle in the Magic Kingdom, there were costumes scattered about and litter.

He was mapping out the places he wanted the crew to film. They were currently busy down on Main Street, USA. He didn't think this part of the park was going to be especially interesting. He walked back toward the crew when his walkie-talkie squawked.

"We found some people. We called the National Guard. They'll be here in a few minutes to extract."

"Can we film it?"

"Already ahead of you. Subjects have already signed waivers. They are kids. They are kind of happy they will be moderately infamous."

"Be there in five." He picked up his pace and started running.

Madrid, Spain, Earth, December 15, 2037

Roberto Martinez, a Sargento, and two of his Soldados were patrolling the outside perimeter of Valdemingómez, one of the worst slums in Madrid. They were searching for signals indicating people, or traces where people had recently been.

Things here were a mess. There was garbage in the streets, the buildings, poorly built to begin with, were crumbling. This area had gotten cleaned up a lot after the Casitian Crisis, but then when the evacuation became clear, it went downhill again.

"Over here." Roberto looked toward one of his Soldados.

"What do you have?"

"One individual. From the scanner signals, this person looks pretty sick."

"Call the medical corps."

New York, Earth, December 15, 2037

Greg hated this duty. As a soldier in the National Guard, he had been assisting people during the whole emigration process. Now, it was at its end, and his duty was to find all the stragglers. This was the last few days, and there were only a few people left.

He had a series of Casitian scanners and monitors that would find people within buildings and in basements and the like. Today, he was working in the South Bronx. He would find people, figure out how to get them out of wherever they were, and get them to a shuttle. It was nasty work, usually. The people left were belligerent, drunk or stoned, or sometimes mentally ill.

He heard a beep. Ah, three people in that brownstone there. He walked up the stairs and knocked on the door. "National Guard. Please open up." He waited. He heard shuffling, and then the door opened, and a small woman who he could swear was 100 years old answered.

"I'm not leaving."

"I'm sorry ma'am, but you have to."

"I'm not leaving, and neither is my husband or son."

Greg sighed. "Ma'am, don't make this harder on me than it already is. Please pack up some things. I'll help you, if you want. We need to leave."

"I told you already. I am not leaving." Greg, of course heard this all the time, especially from older people. He hated to do this, but it was his job, and they all had to leave. Reason never worked on these folks who were adamant.

He turned away and turned on his communicator. "Three people, at least two elderly, possibly all three, refusing to leave. I need extraction."

The scenario for people like this was simple. A group of National Guard, generally with medical staff, would move into the house, and physically remove them, and put them in a truck to go to the holding areas waiting for shuttles to the colony ships. A team of AI powered bots would go inside the house and with some educated guesses, pick out stuff from their dwelling and dump it into cargo containers to be shipped with them to New Earth.

He turned back. "Ma'am, some folks are coming to remove you and your stuff. Please make it as pleasant for them as possible."

She looked at him and said, "did you hear what I said?"

"Yes, ma'am, I did. Have a nice trip."

He walked down the steps, shaking his head. Extractions had been on whatever was left for television here for months, and people still somehow didn't believe it would be done to them.

Birmingham, Alabama, Earth, December 15, 2037

Diana's shuttle landed on the tarmac across from the large hanger that was currently serving as a holding area for people who would be leaving on the last 1000 ships to New Earth. She and her phalanx of security guards entered the hangar and saw the chaos.

There was a sea of cots, with people sitting on them, or roaming around. When some people saw her, they ran toward her. In a matter of half a minute, a sizable crowd had formed around her.

"Why can't we go home? When are we leaving?" People were tossing questions out at her. Why hadn't they been given any information?

"I'm sorry that you all are experiencing this. It is because you refused to apply for emigration. You cannot go home. The last colony ships are leaving within 15 days, and you will be on one of them. In the meantime, you'll have to stay here."

There were angry murmurs, but nothing else. She had some conversations with a few people, and then went in search for whoever was in charge. At the far end of the hangar, behind a large glass window was a man with his feet up on his desk, smoking a cigar, and watching what looked to be a game of some sort on the television. She knocked on the door.

He looked up, annoyed, and then recognized her and the cigar dropped out of his mouth. He got up quickly and opened the door.

"Madame President ... no one told me you were..."

"That was on purpose. Why haven't these people been given complete information?"

"Well, the Major said..."

"The Major?"

"Major Johnson, of the Alabama National Guard is in charge of this holding area. I'm just here making sure they all get fed and taken care of. He comes around every other day or so.

"And what did he say?"

"He said we didn't need to tell them nothing."

Diana sighed, and several curse words came to mind, but she did not vocalize them.

"Tell Major Johnson when you see him to call me, please? If he doesn't, I'll call on him, and he will be sorry."

"Yes, yes, I will, Madame President."

She turned and walked through the hangar, and out into the sun. Six down...

Casiti, 50 Paqn 787

Marianne and Jal'end'a were sitting in Jal'end'a's office, with cups of fuge.

Marianne said, "I have to say, I haven't had a cup of fuge this good since I left."

"Thanks for coming to visit Marianne. And I'm glad Ja'el came, it's always good to see her. We had a nice visit."

Marianne nodded. "I heard. Jal'end'a, I have to admit that it's hard to wrench ourselves from the present to look at the future, but I know it's necessary."

"How are things going right now?"

"Most of New Earth is fine, except for a few pockets of disaster. Most of those are being dealt with, thankfully. Earth, well, that's another story. We're in the last phase of the evacuation, what has been dubbed 'Extraction.'"

"Extraction?"

"Forcibly taking people from their homes and hiding places. We estimated that there were about 80 million people that would need extraction. We're about 15 days from the deadline, and we're still finding people. The good news is they won't close the wormhole before we finish, but we've been getting extreme pressure from the Krumptia. They are angry that we weren't done a year ago. They can't understand why some people won't leave."

"Well, they are all bureaucrats! What would they know?"

"Anyway, I think we'll be done, but it's going to be under the wire."

"The purpose of this trip is for us to start to think about how our two planets should work together and cooperate."

Marianne nodded. "Yes, I think that will be important going forward. I hate to focus on just our two planets."

"What do you mean?"

"Well, I know we cannot communicate with the Kinder, but we do have Kinder with us, on both planets, and we hope that someday, all three planets can be united."

"We don't only hope, Marianne, we expect. That's the only way we'll be allowed back into the Galactic Community."

"True. I just want to make sure that we leave space for the Kinder voice."

"Hmm. You know, I learned a lot from being on Earth, those years ago. We Casitians, work by consensus, and choose our Caraj members not to represent some faction or constituency, but by the nature of what we think they will contribute. But your global governmental bodies are not set up that way. They are set up to represent constituencies."

"Yes. You are thinking...?"

"I wonder if we should have a human council. One with representatives from Casitians, Terrans and Kinder - the three branches of humanity. The hope would be that eventually, Kinder from Kinder Home would sit to represent themselves. But now, it is the Kinder among us."

"Jal'end'a, that is brilliant. Thank you so much for that idea."

"And, of course, you would be the first head teacher."

"Whoa there. Slow down. Jal'end'a, I have been in public leadership one way or the other pretty much non-stop since Ja'el let drop that we weren't alone in the galaxy. That is a very long time now, getting on to 27 Earth years. I'm done. I'm retiring from all public work. There are lots of people who can take my place."

Jal'end'a nodded. "Yes, I can understand your desire to retire. I'm looking forward to that sometime soon myself, returning to my cloistered life."

"Now that we have this idea, how can we make it a reality?"

Independent Christian State, Month 3 Year 49

David sat looking at a tall, young, but balding man who was the new Bishop of the ICS. Bishop Kramer had died in his sleep a few weeks ago. David was here for a couple of reasons, neither of them pleasant. He had no idea what Bishop Trout was going to be like. He looked young enough to have grown up in the ICS.

"Mr. Lopez, what has prompted your visit here today?"

"Well, first, I thought it would be good to introduce myself to you, given your new role."

"That was unnecessary. I don't expect us to have much contact with the world leadership."

"I understand. The other reason is more critical."

"Go ahead."

"I received word that someone in the ICS tried to place an order for 2.5 million cubic feet of Tulip tree lumber."

"Yes, our construction efforts have used up the current supply. So?"

"Bishop Trout, each territory is required to use Tulip Trees sustainably. You cannot order that much lumber."

"What are you saying? You are going to deprive our people of housing?"

"Bishop Trout, the only thing depriving your people of housing is your stubborn insistence that no Casitians touch ICS ground."

"That is your perspective. Our perspective is that you are not willing to do anything without the devil's influence."

David realized that this was like the old Who song. "Meet the New Boss/Same as the Old Boss."

"In any event, you are not getting any more Tulip tree lumber. I know several vendors of Bamboo, who will be happy to fill orders for bamboo lumber, or better yet, help you start bamboo plantations."

"Do you have anything else to say?"

"I guess not." David rose, and put out his hand. Bishop Trout did not move.

"Goodbye, Bishop." David walked out, vowing never to return again.

Chapter 12:
Fifteen Around the Table

(AP) February 16, 2038

New Earth to Adopt Earth Calendar

New Orleans – The new all-World council, modeled after the United Nations, the global intergovernmental body in place before the global democracy existed, has passed a resolution that New Earth adopt the Earth calendar. Because New Earth days are 46 hours long, some modifications to the calendar system on New Earth were put in place, including adding an extra day or two per month, depending on the month. This would mean a synchronization of New Earth's calendar and Earth's calendar. It would also mean that January 1, 3038 would be the date that humans could hope to return to Earth.

Earth Orbit, December 27, 2037

Diana gazed at the Earth as the small Casiti-bound transport moved slowly among the large colony ships on their way to the wormhole. She remembered what Marianne had said about her last trip away from Earth, to Casiti – and wondered how different or similar the feeling was. She found it hard to believe that finally, all humans were gone from Earth. The years of chaos and strife were over, on Earth, at least. The Dolphins and other creatures of Earth finally had a place to call home without human interference.

She was on her way to Casiti. She didn't quite know what she thought of that. The five million or so people who had been allowed to emigrate to Casiti's main continent, Rel'toro, had been a very well screened bunch. She had requested to emigrate, with the idea that when things calmed down on New Earth, she might spend some time there as well. Marianne was, unsurprisingly, staying on New Earth, settling down finally and retiring from leadership. Ja'el was staying with her.

The mix on New Earth was staggering: Terrans from the first migration, Kinder army deserters who became citizens, Terrans from the second migration, and finally, a substantial contingent of Casitians who felt that a Casitian presence on New Earth would be helpful. Diana knew that the leaders of New Earth had their hands full.

"Penny for your thoughts." Janie put her hand on Diana's arm, gently.

"I don't know, you might have to give me several dollars, sweetheart."

Janie smiled knowingly. "Worried a bit about going to Casiti?"

"Yes, I am, that and just worried about humanity. But anyway, I don't quite know what to expect on Casiti. I remember Marianne didn't really like it that much."

"I'm looking forward to it. Not that I'm sure we should stay forever, but I think it's worth checking out, especially given the warm invitation we got from Jal'end'a.

"This is a new chapter in Human history, isn't it? One we could have never predicted."

"I do hope human beings get to go back to Earth someday."

Illsenor Station, December 31, 2037

"There's the signal coming back." Everyone was looking at the large viewscreen in the joining room. This scene was being played all over the two systems. Marianne imagined that the Kinder on Hilcyon didn't care, but they were going to send a small communications beacon through to Hilcyon with a repeated message and video from this moment. She wondered if they would destroy it before they bothered to find out what it was.

A ship was in front of the Casitian wormhole, and the New Earth wormhole. Each wormhole had the capacity to go in a multitude of directions - basically, to any other wormhole present in the galaxy. Today, they saw two Keeelo ships exit the wormholes, and then enter them, and they knew that once those ships entered, they would be locked out from the rest of the galaxy.

For some reason, the Krumptians wanted them to test the wormholes, to make sure that they were unable to go anywhere except between their three worlds. They sent ships between Casiti and New

Earth wormholes, and they were just getting back signals confirming that it was impossible to pass through to any other systems.

"Signal confirmed. We're locked out." There was dead silence in the room. Marianne bet there was dead silence everywhere on Casiti and New Earth.

"Send the Hilcyon beacon."

"Sent."

Marianne said, "we're done here."

It was done. Marianne knew that in the unlikely case that some humans had managed to stay on Earth, there might be a ship or two sent into the New Earth system in a few weeks, or months, but otherwise, there would be no traffic, no technology, no news, and no travel anywhere in the galaxy for any human being for 1000 years.

The room was still silent. Marianne spoke. "Everyone, we have gone through what I imagine is one of the hardest transitions any species in the galaxy has been asked to go through. And it was done with little violence on our part. I think we managed admirably, and in a way that, perhaps, presages a new era for humans. One that is harmonious and peaceful.

We still have a ton of work to do both on New Earth, and Casiti. But let's celebrate, today. Let's remember this day, every year, for 1000 years."

They filtered out of the joining room, and Marianne and a few others caught a shuttle to the surface. She was going to spend the rest of the day and evening with Ja'el.

New Orleans, New Earth, March 30, 2038

Marianne was happy to be sitting in the audience, rather than at the table. It was an historic moment. All three branches of humankind were now sitting around one council table. She was gratified of her role in creating the council, but glad she didn't need to sit on it.

There were five representatives from each of the three branches. Of course, the Kinder deserters were acting as a proxy for the Kinder of Hilcyon. That couldn't be helped. She knew that they, and every other Kinder representative that followed, would have as a goal to finally bring the Kinder from Hilcyon into the council. It was the council that would form the basis for whatever peace and cooperation that would be necessary in order to re-join the galactic community in 1000 years.

The five Casitians sitting at the table were mostly new to her. Casiti insisted on having their representatives chosen from those that lived on Casiti's main continent, Rel'toro. Marianne could understand the rationale for that. Terran representatives could be elected from Terrans living either on New Earth or Casiti. She was happy to see Leticia sitting at the table as one of the five. She was growing into a good leader.

She heard a little gurgle next to her and looked down to see little Pkygy in Beatrice's arms. Marianne's mother complained bitterly about Beatrice naming her first son Pkygy. "No one can pronounce it!" She smiled. She was happy for Beatrice's new life on Casiti with Ngellin and the small group of Kinder who moved with them to Rel'toro. And Beatrice was getting used to her newfound fame, both on Casiti and New Earth, as the publisher of the enormously popular series of Kinder stories. Beatrice was on New Earth to visit because Ngellin was one of the five Kinder representatives.

David had been chosen as the head teacher of the new council, which came as no surprise to anyone except him. He had been stalwart, dependable, and sane, especially during the chaos of the final waves, and given that he had experienced so much on all four planets, it made a lot of sense to Marianne that he be the first leader of this new council.

The Caraj was still in place for Casitians, and there was a global body in place for Terrans on New Earth – more like the old UN than the truly global government that was in place on Earth before the evacuation. Marianne knew that Diana felt that loss keenly – it had been such a momentous change on Earth for there to have been one global government, but losing it had been inevitable, for now. Marianne hoped that eventually, all humans on New Earth could re-form into a government that would work.

After mostly formalities, the first council meeting was over. David, Heg'ellin, Marianne and Ja'el had dinner at one of the new Cajun restaurants in New Orleans.

"I'm still kind of stunned that this council exists, Marianne. And I'm equally stunned that I'm supposed to run the thing."

"David, you'll do fine. You know that." Ja'el put a reassuring hand on David's shoulder

Marianne added, "besides, my friend, better you than me." They all laughed.

"I wish Joel, Laura, Diana and Janie were here."

Marianne said, "we'll have to plan a reunion, although I heard tell that Diana and Janie are thinking about coming to New Earth for Casitian winter."

"I don't blame them one bit."

Heg'ellin playfully responded, "oh, c'mon David, tell me you wouldn't want to spend a season in bed with me."

Marianne laughed. It was hard to imagine this day, after so much. After meeting Ja'el that fateful day 27 years ago, to being banished to New Earth, to the galactic edict, to this moment. This moment, both bitter, having all of the wormholes to the rest of the galaxy finally closed, but also sweet. She could see the beginnings of what might finally become a united, peaceful human race.

Capital, Hilcyon, Sdert 50 1170

Krely saw the last of them out and closed the door behind them. She realized that she had only a couple of hours to prepare dinner for Sadre. Sadre was a bit more demanding these days, now that he was a Second Chief.

As she set the breadmufs to rise, soaked the trell leaves, and took out the beef ribs to marinate, she pondered the meeting that had just ended. There were only eight of them, and they must tread so carefully. Eight women who were dedicating themselves and their lives to changing Kinder culture.

After the complete disaster of Ylen's Supreme Chiefdom, and the horrible repression that Supreme Chief Jurrl had imposed, there was no room for reform among chiefs. She understood that. Reform from above was never going to work again. But reform from below, that was possible.

Krely had no illusions. She would not live to see a new Kinder society. Krely and her group of women would keep meeting. They would keep teaching their children, and grandchildren that there were different options, different ways to be. And their children and grandchildren would teach their own children, and one day, the Kinder could rejoin the rest of humanity.

Sometimes Krely missed Btric. She was glad that it seemed that Btric had gotten to leave to go to her people after her husband had been killed. Btric had given Krely a set of books, with stories from her husband's gamma. Krely had been painstakingly copying the books in secret, and all the other seven of her group members had copies, hidden very carefully, and they were copying them too. Soon, many people would have these stories, stories that questioned old Kinder ways, and gave ideas of new ways.

###

ABOUT THE AUTHOR

Max has been a science fiction fan since he could read. He has written and published poetry, creative nonfiction, and technical writing. Max lives and works in Cazadero, CA, and Seattle, WA.

Connect with me online:

https://author.maxwellpearl.com

www.ingramcontent.com/pod-product-compliance
Lightning Source LLC
Chambersburg PA
CBHW030738030726
47497CB00001B/40